CHILDREN

OF

MARID

CHILDREN

OF

MARID

BOOK I

of

The LonTobyn Chronicle

DAVID B. COE

TOR®

A Tom Doherty Associates Book / New York

CHILDREN OF AMARID

Copyright © 1997 by David B. Coe

This book is printed on acid-free paper.

Edited by James Frenkel

A Tor Book
Published by Tom Doherty Associates, Inc.
175 Fifth Avenue
New York, NY 10010

Tor Books on the World Wide Web:
http://www.tor.com

Tor® is a registered trademark of Tom Doherty Associates, Inc.

Design by Lynn Newmark

Map by Ellisa H. Mitchell

Library of Congress Cataloging-in-Publication Data

Coe, David B.
    Children of Amarid / David B. Coe.—1st ed.
        p. cm.—(The LonTobyn chronicle ; bk. 1)
    "A Tom Doherty Associates book."
    ISBN 0-312-85906-6 (acid-free paper)
    I. Title. II. Series: Coe, David B. LonTobyn chronicle ; bk. 1.
PS3553.0343C49 1997
813'.54—dc21   96-52647
                                                         CIP

First Edition: May 1997

Printed in the United States of America

0 9 8 7 6 5 4 3 2 1

For Nancy,
who believed even when I did not.

Acknowledgments

I owe thanks to a great many people whose contributions to this book deserve more than a simple acknowledgment.

My dear friend Harold Roth agreed to serve as my agent, putting his substantial reputation on the line to sell what was, at the time, a very rough, partially completed manuscript. Harold's success in this endeavor is testimony to his talents as an agent rather than to mine as a writer.

I am deeply grateful to Tom Doherty for taking a chance on an author of unknown ability, and to James Frenkel, my editor at Tor Books, for recommending that he do so. Jim has a keen sense of what I am trying to do with my world and my characters. That his editing has improved this book goes without saying, but I am amazed by the magnitude of that improvement.

I am also indebted to: James Minz, Jim's editorial assistant; all the wonderful people at Tor who helped get this book into print; my friends Alan Goldberg and Chris Meeker, who read early drafts of the novel; and my siblings, Bill, Liz, and Jim, and my parents, the late Jacques Coe, Jr., and the late Sylvia W. Coe, who gave me their love and support even though they didn't always understand what I was doing with my life.

Finally, and most importantly, I must thank my wife, Nancy Berner. She not only watched me trade in a stable but dissatisfying career as a historian so that I could pursue my dream of writing fantasy, she urged me to do so. I am grateful not only for her insights and her astute criticisms of the manuscript, but also for her unwavering encouragement and love. Without her, this book would never have been written.

1

Gerek awoke with first light, rose, and dressed quietly. He kissed his wife, who stirred slightly before turning over and going back to sleep. Then he stepped noiselessly to the next room, where his son slept. Gerek smiled when he saw the boy, still asleep, sprawled ridiculously in his bed. Kori's small feet rested on the pillow and his head leaned against the wall. Gerek sat down on the bed by his son and shook the boy gently.

"Kori. Kori," he called softly. "I'm going to the island to pick some *shan* leaf. Do you want to come along? Or do you want to sleep some more?"

The boy turned over and yawned, his eyes still closed. "I want to go with you," he replied sleepily.

"All right," Gerek continued in the same hushed tone. "Then you have to get up now."

"All right," Kori answered, although his eyes remained closed.

His father laughed quietly.

A moment later, the boy opened his eyes and yawned again. His father helped him out of bed, dressed him, and led him by the hand out to the common room.

"Do you want something to eat now, or do you want to wait until we get back?" Gerek whispered.

The boy considered the question for a moment, his face, still puffy from sleep, wearing a thoughtful expression. "I think I'm hungry now," he said at last. His father held a finger to his lips indicating that he should speak quietly. "Can I have a piece of sweet bread?" Kori continued in a whisper.

Gerek nodded and stepped lightly into the pantry. He returned with two pieces of the soft bread, giving one to his son and biting into the other himself. When they finished eating, both man and boy donned heavy brown overshirts and silently left the house.

The early morning air felt cool and damp, and the briny scent of the nearby harbor lay heavy over the village. The sky was azure, and the first rays of sunlight cast elongated shadows in front of them as they crossed through the village and down to the shore. When they reached the waterfront they walked among the small, wooden boats that sat on the sandy beach until they reached the dugout Gerek had fashioned the previous spring. In the boat lay three wooden paddles, two of them full sized, and one of them, clearly intended for Kori, half the size of the others. Kori removed his paddle and one of the larger ones, struggling slightly with the latter, and his father pushed the dugout along the sand until it glided onto the glasslike surface of the harbor. There, he held it still, allowing Kori to climb in and move to the front. Then Gerek took his place at the stern and began to paddle away from the shore.

A fine mist, rising slowly from the water's surface, parted and swirled past the sides of the dugout as the small boat glided toward a large, wooded island half a mile from the shore. The island's trees were mottled with numerous shades of green, their leaves still young with the spring. Thin strands of steam curled over the wooded island like fingers on some ghostly hand. Beyond the island, in the distance, a thick fog lay like a blanket over the pale, green rise of the Lower Horn.

In the prow of the little boat, Kori paddled, smoothly shifting the oar from side to side the way his father had taught him. Gerek smiled and shook his head. *It's not possible,* he thought to himself, watching the boy, *that he can already be* five *years old. Where do the years go?*

"You're paddling well, Kori," he called. "We'll have you sitting back here and steering soon."

Kori turned to look at his father, a proud smile on his young, sun-lit face. Then the boy faced forward again and began to paddle with even more determination than before. Again, Gerek smiled.

When they reached the island, the man steered the boat around to a small beach at the south end, hopped out of the dugout, and pushed it up onto the shore. Kori climbed out of the boat and, together, he and his father moved into the forest.

A narrow, worn path, one the man and boy had taken before, wound among the maples, oaks, elms, and aspens, climbing steeply away from the beach before leveling off several hundred feet into the woods. Sunlight slanted through the trees, casting shafts of alternating light and shadow through the smokelike mist that permeated the forest. The drumming of a woodpecker echoed through the woods, and a thrush sang from a hidden perch.

Gerek and Kori began searching along the lush floor of the wood for the tiny, velvet-blue shan leaves for which they had come. One usually smelled shan before seeing it. It grew low to the ground, snaking inconspicuously among the leaf litter and other shrubs. But it had a distinctive sweet, cool fragrance that only hinted at its full flavor. Many in western Tobyn-Ser used the dried leaves as a seasoning, and some even chewed the leaves as they found them. In higher concentrations, steamed shan had medicinal value, and, in all forms, it was a popular and precious market item. Gerek planned to trade most of what they found this morning with an Abboriji trader, who had promised in return to deliver several yards of a fabric that Shayla had admired. They could never have afforded such material simply on what they earned from Gerek's fishing and Shayla's basketry. Gerek had told Shayla as much. But, with this shan . . . Gerek smiled to himself; he couldn't wait to see the expression on Shayla's face.

He and Kori moved slowly through the forest, filling their sacks with leaves, the boy covering the area to the right of the path, Gerek harvesting the leaves to the left. After nearly an hour, Gerek returned to the trail and called to his son.

"How are you doing, Kori?"

"Fine," the boy called back. A moment later he stood breathlessly in front of his father. "Look how much I got!" Kori opened his sack, which was nearly filled with blue leaves. Their aroma seemed to permeate the forest.

"That's great," Gerek said, "but let's leave a few for next time, all right?"

"All right. I'm hungry anyway."

"Again?" the man asked with mock amazement.

The boy nodded and laughed, and the two of them began to make their way back through the forest toward the boat. They had only taken a few steps, however, when Gerek heard something moving in the woods behind them. He turned and saw, through the branches and the mist, a distant figure approaching slowly. The stranger was tall and lean, and he moved among the trees with an easy grace. He wore a hooded cloak of deep forest green, and carried a long staff on top of which was mounted a glowing, crimson stone. And on his shoulder sat a great, dark bird.

Gerek grinned, feeling his pulse quicken as it always did when he saw one of Amarid's Children. It seemed funny in a way that, even now, even though he was a father with a five-year-old son, the sight of a mage could affect him so.

"What is it, Papa?"

It took Gerek a moment to respond. "It's a Child of Amarid," he said at last, still gazing at the approaching figure. He did not recognize the man, and he had never seen a hawk or owl as large or as dark as the one this mage carried.

"Is it Master Niall?" Kori asked excitedly. "I can't see him!"

Gerek picked up his son and pointed. "See? There he is, although I don't think it's Niall, not unless he's gotten a new bird."

"You mean it's another one?" Kori asked, his voice rising and his eyes growing wide. "Is this one a Hawk-Mage or an Owl-Mage?"

"Hawk-Mage or Owl-*Master*," Gerek corrected, and then, looking back at the mage, who was drawing closer, he shrugged. "I'm not sure," he told the boy, still unable to recognize the strange bird on the figure's shoulder. In truth, Gerek knew little about the hawks or owls to which the Children of Amarid bound themselves, and from which, it was said, they drew their powers and healing abilities. He knew Amarid's Hawk, as most did, and he could distinguish a hawk from an owl. But beyond that, he couldn't tell one bird from another. He did know, however, how unusual it was to see a mage other than the one who served this portion of the land. There were only a few dozen mages in all of Tobyn-Ser, most of them serving specific areas. Niall, who served the Lower Horn and the shore of South Shelter, visited Sern and the other coastal villages twice a year—more often if the people had need. He had been doing so for as long as Gerek remembered, first as a Hawk-Mage, and, in more recent years, as an Owl-Master. The mage had been a close friend of Shayla's father, and he had come to Gerek and Shayla's wedding. He was a familiar figure in Gerek's life, but still, every time Gerek saw the beautiful bird Niall carried, and the long green cloak that betokened the mage's membership in the Order, Gerek could not suppress the excitement bordering on giddiness that overcame him. And this was not Niall. Gerek could not remember the last time he had seen a mage other than the silver-haired Owl-Master; Kori, he knew, had never seen one.

"Greetings, Child of Amarid," Gerek called out formally. "We are honored by this meeting."

Gerek's salutation brought no response, and, he noticed, even as the figure came closer, the hood of the cloak continued to conceal the mage's face. Slowly, not understanding why it happened, Gerek felt his excitement begin to give way to something else.

Amarid's Children were, along with the Keepers of Arick's Temples, the most honored men and women in Tobyn-Ser. They roamed the land serving and protecting its people, healing them when they were ill or wounded, and guiding them in times of trouble. In the absence of a centralized government binding together the land's cities, towns, and villages, the Order, in an uneasy alliance with the Sons and Daughters of the Gods, functioned as Tobyn-Ser's leadership, guarding the people from outside threats and settling disputes among different communities.

They were as much a part of the land as the Seaside Mountains, which rose majestically from the coastline just to the east of Sern; they were nearly as important to Tobyn-Ser's people as Arick, Duclea, and the other gods. The feathers the mages left as tokens of their service were prizes to be cherished; indeed, even finding a feather in the woods or on a beach was considered to be good luck. Gifts from Amarid, they were called. As a child, Gerek had longed to join the Order himself, and Kori already spoke of it as well. Any man or woman who donned a forest-green cloak and bore a mage's staff, even a stranger, was a friend and a protector.

And yet now, confronted with this silent, hooded figure and the strange black bird, Gerek suddenly, inexplicably, felt vulnerable and afraid. Within him, everything he had learned as a child—everything he, in turn, had taught Kori—battled with an overpowering, instinctive urge to flee. Battled, and lost.

Still holding Kori in his arms, he turned and began to walk quickly down the path toward the safety of the boat.

"Can't we stay and talk to him?" Kori asked, gazing back over his father's shoulder, his words jarred with each of his father's steps.

Gerek didn't answer, concentrating instead on keeping his footing and avoiding the roots and rocks that cluttered the trail.

"I want to see his bird!" Kori said, his tone becoming more insistent and plaintive. "Why are we leaving!" Then Kori's tone changed utterly, and he whispered fearfully, "Papa, I think he's coming after us!"

Gerek whirled and saw the figure, its benign, leisurely bearing gone, striding purposefully and menacingly toward them. Still, Gerek could not discern the cloaked face, nor could he identify the strange bird. He began to run. Kori clung tightly to his neck and bounced in his arms. Twice they nearly fell, but both times Gerek righted himself and maintained his grip on his son. He knew without looking that the figure was pursuing them, gaining on them with each step. And then, just as they reached the descent to the beach, Kori screamed.

"His bird!"

Gerek stopped and swung around again, his breath coming in ragged gasps. The huge, black creature was already in flight, overtaking them with sickening speed. Gerek put Kori on the ground and picked up a short, heavy stick from beside the path.

"Kori! Run to the boat! Don't wait for me! Just paddle home as fast as you can!"

"But, Papa—"

"*Move!*" Gerek exploded.

He saw Kori begin to back away, the child's eyes locked on the approaching creature, the expression on his young face a mix of fascination and horror. And then Gerek was aware of nothing but himself and the great bird. He could now see that it was a hawk, but an enormous one, larger than any he'd seen before. Its feathers were unnaturally stiff and glossy. Its knifelike talons and sharply hooked beak seemed strange somehow, far more threatening than those of any other hawk he had encountered, although even they were not as alien as the bird's bright, glimmering eyes. These were golden in color, and, impossibly, horribly, they appeared to have no pupils.

As the creature reached him, Gerek leveled a ferocious blow at its head, but, at the last moment, with extraordinary agility, the bird wheeled off to the side. The force of his swing threw the man off balance momentarily, but he recovered quickly and spun around to face the hawk with the stick held in front of him.

The creature hovered before Gerek for a few moments. Then it suddenly rose up above him and dropped toward his head, its claws outstretched. Gerek dove to his left, rolled, and sprang to his feet just in time to raise the stick and block a swooping blow from the bird's fisted talon. The bird moved with incredible speed, swooping again while Gerek still recovered from the force of the last attack. Again Gerek dove away, this time rolling to the far side of a tree, where he was able to gain a moment's respite. He scrambled to his feet and, keeping his back to the tree and holding his stick before him, stepped around into the clearing. He expected an immediate assault from the creature, but the great bird was nowhere in sight. Instinctively Gerek looked up, guarding his head with the stick and his arms, but the hawk was not above him. He looked over to where Kori still stood and, as he did so, Kori screamed and pointed. From behind another tree, the hawk rushed at Gerek's head, its beak open and its talons poised to strike. Gerek, caught off guard by the attack and impeded by the tree he had tried to use as protection, wrenched himself desperately to the side and flung the stick toward the bird. The creature veered off to avoid it, but caught Gerek's left arm just below the elbow with one of its razor claws. Gerek gasped in pain and blood began to soak through his overshirt. He heard Kori start to sob. He tried to flex his hand, but the hawk's talon had sliced through his tendons, leaving him with little strength or control in his fingers. Keeping his injured arm close to his body, Gerek grabbed another fallen branch to use as a weapon and watched as the hawk glided back toward him again.

He readied himself for another attack, but the bird merely hovered above him, just barely out of reach, seeming to sense that Gerek was weakening and toying with him, feigning attacks and gliding from side to side. And with each passing moment, the sleeve of Gerek's overshirt grew heavier with blood. With his injured hand, he clawed repeatedly at the perspiration that stung his eyes, but Gerek could do nothing about the fatigue and pain. He was growing light-headed; he could barely stand, much less fight.

And then, as suddenly as it had begun, it ended. His strength failing, Gerek gathered himself for one last assault on his foe. Hoping to lure the great bird within striking distance, he lowered his good arm as if too tired to maintain his defensive posture. The hawk swooped in close to Gerek's head and the man swung his stick with all the force he could muster. It nearly worked. Maybe, if he had been able to use both arms . . .

Maybe. But he was hurt, and the creature was so quick, so unnaturally quick. Gerek missed. And the power of his swing threw him off balance, leaving his back exposed to the bird. He felt the creature's talons raking his shoulders and back, and he fell to the ground. He tried to stand again, but the hawk pounced on him and tore at his neck with its beak. He tried to scream to Kori, to implore the boy to run, but he could not tell if he made himself heard.

Kori had watched with helpless fury as his father fought the horrible bird. He began to cry when he saw the creature cut his father's arm, and he screamed with terror when Gerek fell to the ground with the angry red gashes across his back. For the second time that day, he heard his father tell him to run, and this time he did. With all the speed he could muster, he dashed down the path toward the beach, never once looking back, and unaware that he still clutched the small sack of shan leaves in his hand. Soon he could hear the water lapping on the beach, and, through the clearing at the end of the forest, he could see the little dugout. But just as he reached the bottom of the trail, he felt some-thing hit him heavily from behind and he pitched forward onto the hot, white sand of the beach. He looked up over his shoulder and saw a huge, black shape descending on him, blotting out the sun.

The cloaked figure had stood on the fringes of the clearing watching the battle in detached silence. The outcome, he knew, had never been in doubt, although he would grant that the man had fought courageously. He had, however, for-gotten all about the child. When the man screamed, and the boy started to run, he feared for a moment that the child might get away. But then he saw how his bird soared after the boy, and he smiled within the dark hood, chiding himself for ever doubting. He walked to the bloodied body of the man to be sure that he was dead. Again, he smiled at the efficiency of the creature, and he started down the trail toward the water.

He found the boy lying facedown on the beach, blood from the gash on his neck darkening the white sand. The figure held out his arm and the black bird glided to it and hopped delicately to his shoulder. Then he knelt beside the body of the boy and reached into his cloak. Pulling out a single black feather, he tucked it carefully into a tear in the back of the boy's shirt, where it was clearly visible but anchored against the wind. The figure started to rise, but then, almost as an afterthought, he reached into the sack that lay beside the boy, removed a small blue leaf, and put it in his mouth. Then he stood, and, with the black creature still on his shoulder, he walked casually back into the forest.

2

"Looks like spring's going to be late this year," Jaryd's mother remarked, pushing a lock of her grey-streaked hair back from her face and watching the rain drip off the roof just outside the kitchen window. "I can't remember the last time we had this much rain so late."

"One of the traders told me that everything's already in bloom south of here," her husband replied, spooning himself a second portion of hot cereal and returning to his seat. "It's just the Upper Horn and us that's still got winter."

Drina nodded and smoothed back her hair again. "Over a month since the Feast of Arick and it's still raining. We may have rain on Jaryd's birthday this year."

Jaryd smiled and shook his head. "You realize, of course, that you two have this exact same conversation every year." His parents looked at him in feigned disbelief. "It's true," he insisted, "and don't look at me like that. You've been saying the same thing since I was a kid; it always rains on my birthday. I've never seen two people learn so little over such a long period of time."

"Ah," his brother broke in, "the schoolmaster has spoken."

His father snorted with mock disdain, and his mother turned to her elder son. "Royden, you settle this: who's right, your brother or us?"

Royden rose from his place at the table and put his empty plate in a bucket of soapy water. And as he did, Jaryd remarked to himself, as he often had before, how much like their father Royden looked. While Jaryd was lean and wiry like his mother, with her straight brown hair and grey-blue eyes, Royden and Bernel had the same stocky, muscular build and the same reddish-blond hair—although their father had somewhat less of it, and what was left was flecked with grey. Both had wide-set brown eyes, and a broad, open smile that Royden now flashed at their mother. "I'm not getting involved in this," he told her.

"Wise man," said Bernel, grinning.

Royden put on an overshirt and cap and moved toward the door. "I'm heading over to the smithy, Papa. I need to finish up those wagon wheels for Hadrian. What should I start on after that?"

Bernel thought a moment. "I guess Jorrin's tools are next. But I'll be along soon, and I'll let you know for sure."

Royden nodded and looked over at Jaryd. "You teaching today, or will I see you at the shop?"

"I'm teaching this morning," Jaryd replied, "but I'll be in this afternoon to do some real work." With this last comment he looked sidelong at his father, who snorted again.

Royden laughed and opened the door.

"Where do you think you're going?" Drina growled.

Royden closed the door, gave a sheepish look to Jaryd and his father, and leaned over to kiss his mother on the cheek. "Sorry, Momma," he said opening the door again. "Bye, Momma."

The door closed and Jaryd rose from the table. "I should probably get going, too. Don't want to keep the kids waiting." He put his dish in the water bucket and then turned to Drina. "You know, Momma, I told Royden that I'd be at the shop, but if you need my help with the tilling, I can just as easily go to the field after school, can't I, Papa?"

Bernel nodded, but Drina declined the offer with a wave of her hand. "Thank you, Jaryd, but I'll be fine on my own. Besides," she added with a crooked grin, "there's just so much I can do right now with this unusual weather we're having."

Jaryd laughed and kissed his mother. Even with the silver in her hair, her face was still youthful, like Jaryd's, and her hands were hard and tanned from working the fields year-round. She rarely required any help with the farming, but Jaryd always offered. He stepped into the bedroom he shared with Royden and reemerged a minute later wearing his overshirt and cap and carrying a pile of worn books. "I'll see you both later," he called over his shoulder as he stepped out into the cool rain.

He walked toward the schoolhouse as quickly as he could, holding his books close to his body in a futile effort to keep them dry. And, as usual, the people he passed in the village center stopped and stared as he walked past.

They had started staring almost a year ago, when word of Jaryd's dreams first spread through the town. The first dream had come on a stormy night late in the previous winter. He dreamed of water—cold, turbulent water that swept over him and dragged him downward away from light and air into blackness. He had awakened gasping for breath and shivering. His brother, roused from his slumber on the other side of the dark room, asked him if he was all right, and Jaryd, thinking it only a bad dream, told Royden that he was fine, that he had just had a nightmare. The next day, however, a missing boy, the wood-crafter's son, was found drowned in the river that flowed past the town.

Jaryd tried to convince himself that this had been nothing but a disturbing coincidence, and he spoke to no one of his vision. But a month later, he had another nightmare, this one even more vivid and frightening than the first. He dreamed of a raging fire that spiraled wildly into a night sky, its searing heat scorching his hands and face and scalding his lungs when he tried to scream. This time, Jaryd awoke to find one of Royden's shirts burning and his brother frantically trying to stamp out the flames. Jaryd was soaked with perspiration; his breath was coming in ragged gasps, and his heart was pounding.

After extinguishing the blaze, Royden lit a candle and sat at the foot of Jaryd's bed. He was breathing hard, his dark eyes fixed on Jaryd, and his features pale and grim. He sat staring at his brother for a long time before he spoke.

"What in Arick's name is going on, Jaryd?" he finally asked in an urgent whisper. "First you have that nightmare last month that had you thrashing in your bed like a wild man, and now this. What's going on?"

Jaryd tried to calm himself. He was far more frightened than Royden looked. "Tell me what happened tonight," he demanded, his voice trembling.

"What do you mean, what happened tonight! You lit my shirt on f—"

"Tell me what happened! What did I say, what did I do?"

Something in Jaryd's tone stopped Royden and imposed on him the calm Jaryd had sought for himself.

"You were tossing a lot," Royden began slowly, "like you couldn't get comfortable. And then you started to talk—"

"What did I say?"

Royden shook his head. "I couldn't make it out. I heard the word 'fire,' but the rest of it was just babble. And then you cried out, just a sound, it wasn't a word. The next thing I know, my shirt's on fire." He paused, staring at Jaryd. "What's going on?" he asked again.

Jaryd took a deep breath. "That nightmare I had last month wasn't just a nightmare."

"I don't understand."

"I dreamed that I was drowning," Jaryd explained, his voice sounding thin and small to his own ears. "And the next day they found Arley."

"That's just a coincidence," Royden said, trying to sound convincing.

"Well," Jaryd continued, "I guess we'll find out. Tonight I dreamed of fire, and this dream felt even more real than the other one."

Royden remained silent for a moment. "What about my shirt?"

"I'm sorry about your shirt, Royden," Jaryd said with regret. "Momma can make you a new one."

"No." Royden shook his head and gave a small laugh. "That's not what I was asking. I meant, how did it catch on fire? You sound like you think you lit it."

"I did," Jaryd said with sudden certainty.

"How?"

"I don't know."

"Then how do you know that you did it?"

Jaryd shook his head. "I'm not sure of that either. I just know that I did. I also know that, at least for now, I don't want to tell anyone about this, not even Momma and Papa."

Royden didn't respond, and Jaryd held his breath. He didn't want to have to explain himself. He wasn't even sure that he could. He knew that his visions would frighten his mother, and he didn't want that. He wasn't really sure how his father would react, but Bernel had always been much closer to Royden and somehow Jaryd knew that this would only serve to make things worse. But his plea for Royden's silence was prompted by more than just these concerns. He was, at the moment, afraid of himself. He felt like a freak, a monster of some sort, and he had no explanation for what had happened. Until he did, he wanted his dreams to remain a secret. After several moments, Royden stood up. "Well, I guess if we want to avoid any questions we'll have to hide what's left of this shirt and air out the room."

Jaryd smiled with unfeigned relief. "Thanks, Royden."

"Don't thank me," Royden responded, his expression still bleak. "I'm not sure enough of why I'm going along with this to deserve your thanks."

His smile fading, Jaryd opened the window and then helped Royden clean up the charred remains of the shirt. They did not speak the rest of that night, nor did they mention it the next day. Royden did have to lie about the smell of smoke in their room, telling their parents over breakfast that he and Jaryd had fallen asleep with a candle burning, and that the candle had burned all the way down and singed a cloth. As their mother bustled around the kitchen and scolded the boys for their carelessness, Royden fixed Jaryd with an icy glare.

That evening matters turned far more serious. Jaryd had been on edge all day, constantly reliving his dream and wondering if this one, like the last, would prove prophetic. The answer came just after nightfall. As the brothers and their parents sat eating dinner, they heard alarm bells start to ring in the town square.

"Must be a fire," their father said, jumping to his feet. "We'd better get going."

Neither Royden nor Jaryd moved. They sat staring across the table at each other, both of them pale.

"Come on, boys!" their mother urged with impatience. Bernel had gathered their overshirts and now threw them to his sons as he opened the door. Royden and Jaryd followed their parents out into the night. In the distance, through the trees, they could see the flames. Above the village, the sky was heavy with a dark, billowing smoke that glowed balefully with the yellow-orange glare of the fire.

"Looks like a big one," Bernel observed somberly, running a hand through his thinning hair. "We'd better hurry." He and Drina ran toward the town square, leaving Royden and Jaryd by the house.

"You're going to have to tell them!" Royden's voice was tense and challenging. "We can't keep this a secret! Not now; not after this!"

"I'll tell them when I'm ready," Jaryd responded with equal intensity, "and when I know what it is I'm telling them about!"

Royden shook his head, the fear manifest on his open face. "Jaryd, this is serious, this is—"

"Royden!" Jaryd snarled, silencing his older brother. "I of all people know just how serious this is! You gave me your word that you'd keep quiet! I'm holding you to it!"

Royden held Jaryd's angry gaze a moment longer. Then he turned toward the town center and the fiery glow of the night sky. "I hope you know what you're doing," he said, his voice now drained of emotion, "for the sake of us all." Without another word, Royden started toward the fire, and Jaryd followed, still trembling with emotion, and gripped by an uncertainty that terrified him.

When Jaryd reached the center of town he found three shops engulfed in a fierce blaze, and most of the townsfolk forming a bucket brigade between the river and the fire. He joined the effort and, for much of the night, the people of Accalia fought the flames with grave determination. Several were so overcome by heat and smoke that they had to be carried back to their homes. But despite the villagers' struggle, all three of the shops, as well as a fourth, burned to the ground. And one man, Iram, the apothecary, died when part of his shop collapsed on him as he attempted to save his most valuable oils and medicines from the blaze.

For a while after the fire, Jaryd's dreams stopped. And, although the visions had frightened him, waiting for the next one proved far worse. He grew to dread sleep and fear dreams, but he hungered to know whence the two visions had come. Mostly, though, he wanted to understand what had happened so that he could explain it all to Royden and to their parents. Following their angry exchange the night of the fire, the two brothers had grown distant. For the first time in Jaryd's life he felt that he could not turn to Royden for guidance. His older brother had made his feelings all too clear; Jaryd would find no comfort there.

So he waited. Winter relinquished its icy grip, giving way to the rains, and still no more visions came. Then, soon after the rains ended, on a clear, moonlit night, Jaryd dreamed again. In a nightmare far more terrifying and real than either of the others, Jaryd saw the town assailed by mounted bandits with scarred, begrimed faces, wearing leather jerkins and brandishing huge, curved blades, lances, and clubs. They razed Accalia's homes and storefronts, and then began to murder the townsmen and rape and kill the townswomen. Jaryd watched as his father was decapitated by the sweeping blade of a scimitar. He saw Royden fall with a spear in his broad chest, blood streaming from the wound. He watched his mother, with several other women, being chased by two men on horseback. And he saw himself, standing transfixed, observing it all. Then, as he watched, the dream-Jaryd, his youthful face distorted with rage, opened his mouth in a desperate scream and raised a strange staff from which leaped a killing sapphire flame that enveloped and obliterated the men chasing his mother. The dream-Jaryd then threw his fire at the other bandits, destroying them utterly, and saving what remained of the village.

Once again, Jaryd awoke soaked in perspiration and gasping for breath. A candle cast its light across the room, and Royden sat beside him, his expression somber, his wide-set eyes betraying his concern.

Jaryd lay still for a moment, watching the light of the candle dance along the wall beside him, and allowing his breathing to slow to normal. Then he turned his head and smiled wanly at Royden. "Woke you again, eh?" he asked with an effort. "I'm sorry," he added when his brother nodded.

"You have another dream?"

This time it was Jaryd's turn to nod. He sat up and drank some water from a cup on his nightstand. "I'm ready to tell people now," he said, brushing a sweat-dampened lock of hair from his forehead. "I have to: there are bandits coming."

"Soon?" Royden asked, tension creeping into his voice.

"Soon. I think dusk. At least, that's what it looked like." Jaryd described his dream, although he left out what he had seen himself do. He needed to think about the implications of that part of his vision before he discussed it with anyone.

By the time Jaryd finished telling Royden about the dream, the first soft glimmer of dawn had begun to illuminate the bedroom window. Royden and Jaryd dressed and went to their parents' room, where they woke Bernel and Drina and told them of Jaryd's vision, and of those that had come before. The blacksmith and his wife listened in silence, and, even after the brothers had finished their story, their parents said nothing for a long time. Drina sat very still on the bed, staring down at her sun-darkened hands, and occasionally pushing her hair back from her face in a characteristic gesture. Bernel, who had moved to the window as Jaryd described the dreams, stood motionless, his face silhouetted against the early morning light, his expression unreadable.

"So, it has come at last, just as he said it would," Drina finally said in a small voice, more to her husband than to her sons.

"Just as who said it would?" Jaryd asked, looking from his mother to his father.

Bernel turned toward Drina, his broad frame blocking the light. "I don't wish to discuss this right now," he told her with finality.

"But, Papa—"

"Not now, Jaryd! There are more important things to deal with. We need to alert the rest of the town and prepare for the possibility that your vision is genuine."

"Bernel," Jaryd's mother replied, tears starting to flow down her cheeks, "we both know that this is a true seeing. We've known—"

"Enough, Drina!" Bernel snapped. He closed his eyes and took a deep breath before continuing in a softer tone. "We'll discuss this later, I promise. But this isn't the time."

Bernel and Drina exchanged a tense look, brown eyes locked on grey. After a few seconds Drina nodded, assaying a thin smile that looked more like a grimace.

While Royden and Drina spent the rest of the day at the house, boarding the windows and gathering what weapons they owned, Bernel and Jaryd went to the village to warn Accalia's leaders. With the help of Leuel, the Keeper of Arick's Temple in Accalia, they gathered together most of the town council, as well as the chief constable and his officers. At first, the village leaders seemed skeptical, but Bernel offered cryptic assurances that Jaryd's vision carried the weight of prophecy, and in the end, he managed to convince them to arm and organize the townspeople in preparation for the attack.

As he hurried back toward home with his father, Jaryd felt a battle waging within himself between the questions that he burned to ask and his desire to avoid angering his father, who, as usual, seemed reluctant to speak about what had happened. Finally, though, unable to contain his curiosity, he broached the topic as gently as he could.

"Papa," he began tentatively, "why were you and Momma so willing to believe me?"

"You're our son," Bernel replied simply. "If you tell us that you saw these things, we believe you."

Jaryd shook his head. "No, that's not what I meant. Why are you so sure that my visions are—what did Momma call them—true seeings?"

Bernel said nothing for a moment, and Jaryd wished that he had kept silent. He and his father rarely spoke unless they needed to; Jaryd couldn't remember the last time they had a conversation. On the rare occasions when Jaryd initiated a discussion, Bernel usually made him feel as if he had violated some unspoken agreement to maintain his distance. But this time his father surprised him. His answer, when it came, was mildly, even kindly spoken, although cautiously phrased. "Our family—my family—has a history of similar . . . abilities."

"Abilities?"

Bernel let out a slow breath. He seemed to regret answering the question at all, but he pressed on. "Prophetic dreams; the power to predict the future."

"Can you do it?" Jaryd asked with astonishment.

"No, I can't. But my mother could, and her mother before her. And others."

"Have you tried?"

Bernel smiled ruefully. "There was a time when I did, yes. I don't anymore, though. Either you have it or you don't."

Jaryd considered this for a moment. "Who did Momma mean when she said that *he* told you that this would happen?" he finally asked, chancing one last question.

One too many, it turned out. "Enough, Jaryd!" his father warned, the familiar severity returning to his voice. "As I said before, this is not the time to discuss these matters."

"Sorry, Papa."

For reply, Bernel put his arm around Jaryd's shoulder in a rare gesture of affection, and they walked the rest of the way home without speaking.

That evening, when the bandits attacked, they were confronted by an angry crowd of townspeople armed with torches, farm implements, forging tools, and kitchen knives. The outlaws were killers; they were well armed and they had the advantage of being on mounts. But the horde they faced that night fought for their homes and their families. The battle lasted less than one hour. The bandits did little damage and captured few goods before being driven off. When it was over, two of the invaders lay dead. Only seven of the townsfolk had been hurt.

In the wake of the attack, and the villagers' successful defense of their homes, Jaryd became a celebrity. All had heard of his dream and timely warning and recognized that the Sight he possessed marked him as different. And even now, a year later, as he tried to shield his books from the rain, he paid the price of that difference in the stares of his neighbors and old friends. Some in the town, giving in to ancient superstitions, came to fear him. Most, however, considered his Sight a gift and admired him for it. Even so, it set him apart. His friends treated him differently now, with respect and deference, to be sure, but not with kindness and certainly not with the humor and playfulness that they once had. What disturbed him even more was that things also changed between him and his mother and father.

Drina had always been overly protective of him—far more than she was with Royden—and she became more so after she learned of his dreams. She also seemed at times to be in awe of him, which left Jaryd feeling awkward and sad. And his father, despite their warm exchange the day of the attack, grew even more distant. It almost seemed to Jaryd that Bernel blamed him for the bandits' appearance. But that was not all. Although he told himself repeatedly that he was imagining things, Jaryd could not help but notice that his father envied his newly acquired fame.

Even his new job as a teacher at the school came as a result of his prophecy. Well, Jaryd thought to himself, smiling inwardly, that isn't entirely true. He had always been quick to learn, the quickest in all of his classes. But, at seventeen, he had become the youngest teacher in memory, and he was smart enough to know why they had chosen him. So it was in Jaryd's life since the dreams: he had respect and status, but he had almost no friends. Indeed, the only one who treated him normally—the only one who wasn't afraid of him, or jealous of him, or awed by him—was Royden. After Jaryd and Royden told Bernel, Drina, and the rest of the town of Jaryd's dreams, their relationship returned to normal. It seemed ironic in a way that at the same time Jaryd became isolated from the rest of Accalia, he regained the love and trust of his best friend. The two brothers spent nearly all of their free time together, and many in the town came to believe that both of them had the Sight and kept watch over the safety of Accalia.

Jaryd knew that people constantly spoke about him behind his back, and he hated it. Royden urged him to ignore the gossip and those who spread it, pointing out that there was little he could do to stop them. But Jaryd remained uncomfortable and often found himself straining to hear what the people he passed on the street were saying. It was in one of these passing conversations, soon after the battle with the bandits, that he first heard people speculate that he might be one of Amarid's Children. Just the mention of it made Jaryd's heart race with excitement. The Children of Amarid, with their spectacular birds and glimmering crystals, had served Tobyn-Ser for over a thousand years, protecting its borders and aiding its people. Jaryd had seen only two of the wandering mages in his lifetime. One, of course, was Hawk-Mage Radomil, who had served the northwest corner of Tobyn-Ser for over two decades, and who had become a fixture in the lives of every man, woman, and child in Accalia. The rotund, bald mage was unfailingly kind and generous, and Jaryd had grown to love him as he would a second father. He anticipated the mage's regular visits, and the sight of his graceful, pale hawk, with as much enthusiasm as he did the seasonal festivals of the gods.

And yet it was the memory of the other mage, the one Jaryd had met only once, that embodied the wonder and excitement that he associated with life as a member of the Order. The Hawk-Mage had visited many years before, when Jaryd was still just a child. Nonetheless, Jaryd remembered the encounter with a clarity that defied both his youth at the time and the intervening years. The mage was tall and slender, with hair the color of Bernel's and bright blue eyes. He wore the hooded, forest-green cloak of the Order, and carried a long, wooden staff with intricate carvings and a glowing, orange crystal mounted at the top. And on the mage's shoulder sat a magnificent grey falcon with dark, intelligent eyes. The mage, Jaryd recalled, had been friendly, with a warm smile, and he had spoken with Jaryd for a long time, although, surprisingly, Jaryd could recall nothing of their conversation. Jaryd also remembered that Drina and Bernel appeared to know the Hawk-Mage, and that his father and the mage argued before the cloaked man left. And he remembered that, from that day forward, he had wanted to wear one of the green cloaks signifying membership in the Order of Mages and Masters.

Recalling this, Jaryd was confronted by another memory, more vivid than the first, and as wondrous as it was daunting: his vision of himself, wielding a mage's staff and blasting the outlaws with blue fire. If his dreams did indeed foresee the future, then did it not follow that Jaryd would one day carry such a staff and master the Mage-Craft? The mere possibility overwhelmed him.

Yet, the possibility that he might someday join the Order, and the conversations he overheard to this effect, had begun recently to bear a darker side. Over the past few months, word had reached Accalia, through the news brought by traveling merchants, bards, and musicians, of renegade mages and corruption within the Order. Whisperings from farther south spoke of feathers left at the sites of devastating fires and crop destruction, and even on the mutilated bodies of men, women, and children, in a horrible perversion of the Order's tradition of leaving feathers as tokens to indicate a mage or master's gifts or service. Jaryd listened to these stories with a skeptical ear, but, as the tales persisted and the crimes attributed to the mages worsened, he grew increasingly despondent and fearful, not only for himself, but for all of Tobyn-Ser.

When he reached the school that rainy morning, drenched and carrying an armful of soggy books, most of his students had already arrived. Schoolmaster Fyrth had started him off with the youngest children, the four- and five-year-olds who were just beginning their schooling. And, as he stood in the antechamber and shook off his sodden overshirt, he could hear them shouting and laughing. He entered the classroom and, immediately, the children fell silent and hastened to their seats. One of the advantages of being feared, he thought to himself, not without humor.

He had already taught them their letters and numbers, and, the previous week, he had started teaching them Tobyn-Ser's history, focusing for much of the time on Amarid's discovery of the Mage-Craft and his establishment of the Order. Today's lesson began with the Abboriji invasions, and the Order's successful wars against the northern raiders. Jaryd told his class of Fordel, Decla, and Glenyse, the only three Eagle-Sages in the land's history, who on three separate occasions, over a span of two hundred and fifty years, led armies of both mages and brave men and women against the mercenaries of Abborij, driving them back across the strait and thwarting their efforts to conquer Tobyn-Ser. Three times the lands went to war, and three times the invaders were driven back, until, after the last, Eagle-Sage Glenyse and the leaders of Abborij forged a peace that had lasted for more than four hundred years. And, inwardly, as he told the tales, Jaryd smiled to see the wonder and awe with which his students listened. As a youngster, he, too, had been fascinated by stories of the old wars and the heroics of Amarid's Children. The morning flew by, and, at midday, he dismissed the students, smiling again at their shouts and laughter as they charged out of the classroom.

The rain had slowed to a fine mist when Jaryd emerged from the schoolhouse and started toward the smithy. Even from this distance, and through the rush of the river and the sound of water dripping from trees and roofs, Jaryd could make out the familiar alternating rhythm shaped by the ringing beat of his father's hammer and the heavier thud of Royden's sledge. He guessed that they were forging Jorrin's tools, and he quickened his pace, knowing that they would need him at the bellows. Jaryd looked forward to his time in the shop, especially after a few hours of teaching. He found the physical nature of ironwork a welcome change from his more sedentary job at the school. Often, he volunteered to do the arduous, less-skilled tasks in the shop, like tending the fire and manning the bellows, simply because he enjoyed the labor.

As he crossed through the village, however, moving toward the sound of Bernel and Royden's hammers, he noticed a crowd gathering in the town square, beside the meeting hall. Several of the people there were pointing down a path that led to the footbridge across the river. Stopping to cast his eye where their outstretched arms indicated, Jaryd saw a figure on the far bank approaching the bridge, and he felt his heart leap within his chest. The stranger wore a hooded cloak of green and carried a great bird.

Watching the mage walk slowly across the bridge, Jaryd knew that this could not be Radomil; this person was far too tall and slender. For an instant Jaryd wondered if the Order had sent a second mage to serve Leora's Forest and the Upper Horn, but then he saw that, like the mage he recalled from his childhood, this one carried a staff crowned with a gleaming orange stone. This mage's bird, however, differed from the one Jaryd remembered. Rather than a grey falcon, the approaching figure carried a brown owl with a pale, streaked belly, a round face, and bright yellow eyes. This, then, was an Owl-Master, more experienced and with higher authority within the Order than the Hawk-Mage Jaryd had met as a child. Jaryd had never seen an Owl-Master before.

As the mage stepped off the footbridge, the crowd grew quiet and tense. Others in Accalia had heard the stories of sinister forces within the Order. The mass parted, allowing the figure, still hooded and moving slowly, to pass through, but the people watched with obvious apprehension each movement the mage made. The figure paused in front of the meeting hall and deliberately surveyed the crowd and the surroundings. When his gaze fell upon Jaryd, the mage froze momentarily and then threw back his hood and began striding purposefully to where Jaryd stood. For his part, Jaryd remained motionless, too intimidated and amazed to do anything but watch the mage approach him. As the man drew closer, Jaryd recognized him as the same mage he had met as a child. The Owl-Master's reddish-blond hair was thinner now and peppered with grey. But his vivid blue eyes and warm smile were just as Jaryd remembered.

"You're Jaryd," the mage said, stopping in front of the young man and placing a hand on his shoulder. "I'd know you anywhere. You have your mother's eyes."

"Yes, Child of Amarid," Jaryd replied, remembering to use the formal title, although unable to control the flutter in his voice.

"Do you recall our first meeting?"

Jaryd nodded. "I remember you. But not this bird."

"No," the mage agreed, "not this bird. You would have met Skal, my falcon. This is Anla." The mage regarded Jaryd for a moment, the smile fading from his face. "Do you know who I am, Jaryd?"

Jaryd knew the mage's formal title, Owl-Master, although he did not know his name. But this didn't seem to be what the tall man was asking. Then Jaryd thought back to a conversation he had had with his father nearly a year before. "You and I are related, aren't we? On my father's side?"

The mage narrowed his bright eyes. "Did he tell you?"

Jaryd gave a small laugh. "No. He and I have never spoken of your visit. But he mentioned once that the Sight runs in his family. In your family," he added, correcting himself. "And you look alike."

"We should," the Owl-Master said with a grin. "My name is Baden. I am your uncle; Bernel is my brother."

Jaryd's expression must have been comical, because Baden began to laugh, although Jaryd thought he saw another emotion flicker in the mage's eyes before giving way to mirth.

"Well," the Owl-Master said, still chuckling, "I'd guess from the look on your face that you didn't know that you had an uncle Baden." He looked down at the ground. A smile lingered at the corners of his mouth, but when he spoke again a note of sadness had crept into his voice. "I suppose some things don't change. Even with the passage of all these years; even between brothers."

For a moment longer a cloud seemed to darken Baden's brow. And then it was gone, leaving the dazzling grin and the cheer in his voice. "But I've interrupted your day. You were headed somewhere?"

"Yes," Jaryd said, suddenly aware again of the hammering coming from his father's smithy, and acutely conscious of the crowd of people watching him speak with the Owl-Master. "I was going to the shop, to help Papa and Royden."

"I see." Baden took a deep breath and glanced around the town with uncertainty. Then he seemed to make a decision. "Well," he breathed, "if I may accompany you, I think it's time for a family reunion."

"Sure," Jaryd answered, shrugging awkwardly. They walked toward the shop. Jaryd could feel the townspeople's eyes boring into his back, and he wondered if Baden sensed their stares.

"I take it all in your family are well," the mage said casually.

"Yes, thank you."

"Good." They were silent for a few strides, and then Baden surprised him. "You get used to the stares after a while, Jaryd," he commented in the same relaxed tone. "With power, and a certain amount of status, come attention and scrutiny. In time, you grow accustomed to it. You have to."

Jaryd looked at the mage. After a moment, he nodded. "Do you and Papa like each other?" Jaryd asked after another brief silence. He winced immediately, knowing how stupid the question probably sounded.

But if Baden thought the question inappropriate, he showed no sign of it. "I suppose, at some level, we have a certain affection for one another," the Owl-Master began thoughtfully. "We were always very different; we never spent much time together, even as children. He and our father were very close, and I was much closer to our mother than to our father."

"Papa told me that your mother also had the Sight."

"Oh, yes, your grandmother had the Sight, and a good deal more. Lynwen was a powerful Owl-Master in her time."

Jaryd stopped, his expression incredulous. "Grandma Lynwen was in the Order?"

Baden smiled and nodded. "Yes, and so was Lyris, her mother, my grandmother."

Jaryd shook his head slowly and began to walk again as Baden continued. "Your father never showed any signs of having the Sight or any other manifestations of power, at least none that he mentioned. And, when I did, we . . . drifted apart."

Baden had not said it, but it hung palpably in his words. "Was Papa jealous?"

Baden looked at Jaryd for a long time, the expression on his lean face unreadable. Finally, the mage shrugged. "Perhaps."

They had reached the shop, but Jaryd hesitated on the threshold. "Why are you here?" he asked his uncle.

"That," Baden replied, his eyes gleaming mysteriously, "is a long tale. For now, let's just say that I'm here for your birthday."

"I don't understand."

"I know. But this is not the time to discuss it."

Jaryd grinned and pushed the hair out of his eyes. "I think you and Papa are more alike than you realize."

Baden paused, considering this. Then he started to nod, a slight smirk tugging at the corners of his mouth. "Perhaps," he said, "perhaps."

Without another word the Owl-Master stepped into the smithy. Jaryd followed.

As soon as they entered, the heat of the shop blasted them like a summer wind, the air heavy with the mingling smells of burned leather, hot metal, smoke, and perspiration. The smithy was dimly and strangely lit, illuminated at one end by the cool, cloud-dampened daylight coming in through the shop's entrance, and at the other by the hot, reddish glow of the hearth. Iron-forged tools and pieces of scrap metal lay in disheveled piles on the dirty stone floor. Bernel stood at the fire, his broad, muscular back to the door. He held a blackened pair of tongs in the flames as he shouted instructions to Royden, who was out of sight, manning the bellows behind the hearth. Removing the tongs from the fire and placing the white-hot piece of iron they held on the anvil, Bernel struck the piece several times with his hammer. Red sparks flew from the metal, some singeing his leather apron, others falling harmlessly to the floor. He thrust the metal into a trough of water that sat at the base of the hearth, sending a cloud of steam into the air, and then placed it back in the fire.

"I'll be with you in a minute," he called over his shoulder without turning around. "Jaryd, if that's you, Royden could use a hand with the bellows."

"Hello, Bernel," Baden said evenly, his words carrying over the noise of the bellows.

Bernel straightened at the sound of Baden's voice. Without turning around, he placed the metal back in the water, sending another burst of steam up into the rafters of the shop, and laid the tongs along the edge of the hearth. Only then did he turn to greet his brother, his face ruddy and glowing from the heat of the fire.

"Baden," he said, his voice flat. "I guess I should have expected you."

"Maybe. It's been a long time."

"You're looking well." Bernel glanced at the bird on the tall mage's shoulder. "And I suppose congratulations are in order, Owl-Master." Neither man had moved toward the other, and their voices carried little warmth, but Jaryd sensed no irony or hostility in his father's words.

Baden allowed himself a smile. "Thank you, it's been nearly six years now." The mage looked around the smithy and then nodded at Jaryd and toward Royden, who had emerged from behind the hearth. "It seems that you've done well for yourself, too. You and Drina."

"We've been fortunate, yes." The blacksmith and the mage stood in awkward silence for a moment. Then Royden cleared his throat purposefully. "Oh, that's right," Bernel said, sounding somewhat embarrassed. "Uh . . . I guess you've met Jaryd. This is Royden, our eldest. Royden, this . . . this is your uncle Baden."

Royden stepped forward and embraced Baden in formal greeting, his brown eyes wide, a child's smile on his lips. "I remember you," he said, stepping back, "from when Jaryd and I were young. I didn't know who you were then, but I've never forgotten your visit. It's not every day that a mage other than Radomil honors our village."

Baden bowed his head slightly. "Thank you. I, too, recall our meeting. Even as a boy, you were gracious and kind."

Again, a lull in the conversation left the four of them standing uncomfortably, looking from one to another. The only sounds in the room came from the shifting coals of the fire and from Baden's owl, which sat on the mage's shoulder preening itself. At last, Bernel turned to his two sons. "Baden and I have a good deal of catching up to do. Royden, do you think that you and Jaryd can finish the work for Jorrin?"

"Yes, we should be able to. There's not that much left to do."

"Good. Then your uncle Baden and I will see you both at dinner." Bernel removed his apron, put on his overshirt, and gestured for Baden to lead the way outside. The Owl-Master said nothing, but he smiled warmly at his nephews before stepping out of the shop.

When they had gone, Royden turned to Jaryd and posed the same question Jaryd had intended to ask. "Did you know?"

A small laugh escaped Jaryd. "Do you mean did I know that our uncle was a mage, or did I know that Papa even had a brother?"

Royden laughed in turn. "I guess both. I wonder why Papa never told us. Or Momma, for that matter."

"That's not all they kept from us."

"What do you mean?"

"Baden and I spoke on the way over here. Did you know that Grandma Lynwen was an Owl-Master, as was her mother?"

"He told you that?" Royden asked, his eyes widening again.

Jaryd nodded absently, but he was already thinking of something else. "You told Baden that you recalled his visit. What do you remember of it?"

Royden thought a moment. "I remember being excited at seeing a mage. I remember his bird seemed huge; it was the most beautiful thing I'd ever seen. And I remember Baden being friendly and talking to me for a long time."

"Do you remember what you talked about?" Jaryd asked with some urgency.

Royden narrowed his eyes. "No," he answered at last, shaking his head. "Everything else is clear, but I have no memory of what we talked about."

"Neither do I," Jaryd said pointedly. "My memories of his visit are almost exactly like yours. They're remarkably vivid, except for that conversation."

"What do you think it means?"

Jaryd shrugged, brushing back his hair with an impatient gesture. "I don't know."

They stood without speaking for a long while. "Did he tell you why he's here?" Royden finally asked, tying on his father's leather apron.

Jaryd gave another slight laugh. "Sort of. He told me he'd come for my birthday."

Royden raised his eyebrows. "Any idea what he meant?"

"None," Jaryd replied, shaking his head. "None at all."

Royden picked up the metal tongs and gestured absently at the shop. "Well, we're certainly not going to figure anything out in here. The sooner we finish Jorrin's tools, the sooner we'll see Baden and Papa again."

Jaryd nodded his agreement. "I'll work the bellows."

The work went slower than they had anticipated, and when they finally left the shop, hungry and tired, night had fallen. They arrived at their home to find Baden, Bernel, and Drina sitting around the dining table, and Baden's owl perched atop the cupboard, its eyes closed and its feathers slightly ruffled. Bernel and Baden sat grimly across the table from each other, staring at the table and saying nothing. Drina sat between them, her eyes red and damp with tears. Empty dishes sat on the table, and the familiar spicy aroma of their mother's beef stew permeated the house.

"You get everything finished?" Bernel asked, shifting slightly in his chair.

"Finally, yes," Royden responded, as he and Jaryd removed their overshirts and sat down at the table. "I'm still not as fast as you are."

Bernel nodded and tried unsuccessfully to grin. "Give yourself twenty-five years; you will be."

Drina rose from her seat. "We already ate," she said with false brightness, wiping her eyes with her apron, "but we saved plenty for both of you." She moved to the hearth and spooned the stew into two bowls, which she then placed in front of her sons before sitting back down.

Jaryd and Royden began to eat, and no one spoke until, after several spoon-fuls, Royden glanced around the table, his expression somber. "Is one of you going to tell us what's going on," he demanded, "or do we have to guess?"

Jaryd kept his eyes on his bowl of stew, fearing his father's response, but as anxious as his brother to understand what had passed between Baden and their parents. He knew that he could never have said such a thing, that his parents, particularly his father, would not have tolerated it. But Royden was different. Perhaps because he was the older son, perhaps because he and Bernel were so close, he could say almost anything without fear of reproof. This had been true since their childhood, and Royden had often used his leeway on Jaryd's behalf, as he had just now.

In this instance, however, Jaryd feared that Royden had gone too far. Bernel glared at his older son for several moments, saying nothing. But then, to Jaryd's great surprise, he actually smiled, though sadly, and he turned his dark eyes to the mage, who was watching him with interest. "Baden," he said with un-characteristic gentleness, "I believe this is your story to tell."

Baden held his brother's gaze for some time. At length, a smile spread across his lean face and he began to nod slowly. Jaryd could see that, since their reunion in the shop earlier in the day, possibly in the wordless exchange they had just shared, the mage and his father had reached some sort of understand-ing.

The Owl-Master looked at Royden and then at Jaryd. When he began to speak, it was in a voice deeper and richer than Jaryd remembered from the afternoon. "The magic I wield, that all of us in the Order wield, we call the Mage-Craft. But while this power becomes manifest with the binding of mage to bird, it dwells always within the woman or man. We don't know why some possess it and others do not. It was a gift of the Goddess Leora to the land, given, some have said, because she favored Tobyn over Lon and wished to leave her mark on the land he shaped. Like all of Leora's gifts, the Mage-Craft is random and unpredictable. But sometimes it is passed between generations. Jaryd will have told you, Royden, of what he learned today: your grandmother and her mother before her were, in their day, powerful Owl-Masters. When you both were young, I came here to see if I could discern the seeds of this power within either of you." He had been looking from one of his nephews to the other as he spoke, but now Baden fixed his gaze on Jaryd, and within the blue of the mage's eyes, Jaryd thought he saw the brief flicker of an orange flame. "I found what I sought in you, Jaryd. You carry more than just the Sight. You have the ability within you to be a mage of great strength and skill, just as Lyris and Lynwen were." Jaryd sensed a power coursing through the Owl-Master's words, and, though not sure how it was possible, he perceived the truth in what Baden had said. And with that perception came once more the memory of the vision in which he had seen himself throwing mage-fire at Accalia's attackers.

A strained silence settled over the room. To be broken, of course, by Roy-den. "So, I guess this means *I* still have to work in the smithy," he stated in a voice laden with irony. The humor, so unexpected after what had just been said, dissolved the tension and left them all laughing.

Then the moment passed, and Baden again looked soberly at Jaryd. "During my visit all those years ago, your parents and I agreed that we would wait to tell you any of this until you were older and could decide for yourself what to do with this power. Your eighteenth birthday is at hand, Jaryd. You are old enough now to be a Mage-Attend. It's time for you to choose what path you will follow."

Jaryd looked from Baden to his father and, finally, to his mother. All three watched him closely, although with different emotions playing across their features. The Owl-Master regarded him eagerly, with eyes that appeared to glitter like those of a hawk preparing to hunt. His father's look was grave and impenetrable, but his mother's youthful face, marked once more by tears, shone with pride and a gentle sadness. When Jaryd finally spoke, his voice sounded strange and thin after Baden's power-laden words. "What path I will follow," he repeated. "I'm not sure that I understand the choices well enough to make such a decision."

"Simply put," Baden explained, "your choice is between the life I have led, as a mage and a member of the Order, serving the land and its people, and the life you have known here in Accalia, as a teacher and a blacksmith's son."

"And as an object of curiosity," Royden broke in, his words edged with bitterness, "who has to endure the stares and gossip of small-minded people. It seems an easy choice to me, Jaryd. Go with Baden. You have power, a gift from the Goddess. You should use it."

Jaryd turned toward his brother, a sad smile on his face. "I hear you, Royden. But leaving you and Momma and Papa isn't as easy as that."

"Jaryd's right. This decision is not as simple as Royden or Baden have made it sound." All of them turned to Bernel, and Jaryd noted that while his father's voice carried neither the resonance nor the shadings of power that Baden's did, in this room he commanded the strict attention of all of them. "Tell me, Baden," Bernel demanded in a hard tone, his wide-set eyes fixed on his brother, "isn't it true that even should Jaryd choose to remain here, he may soon find himself bound to a hawk?"

Baden sighed deeply. "Yes, that is quite possible," he conceded. "But—"

"And when this binding comes," Bernel continued in a softer voice, his gaze shifting to Jaryd, "won't he need the guidance of those who have knowledge of Leora's Gift and the powers and burdens it carries?"

Jaryd felt his world shift abruptly with his father's words. He could see, in the raw sadness exposed in Bernel's eyes, the cost of the gift his father had just offered him. A gift, and an acknowledgment, Jaryd knew, that there had been no real choice; only a single path marked through the years by signs of a power that neither he nor his parents could control. Drina took Bernel's large hand in hers and held it to her lips. He gently brushed a tear from her face.

After what seemed a long time, Baden answered quietly, "Yes, he'll need such guidance as we can offer."

Without taking his eyes off his father and mother, and feeling awed by the swiftness with which his life was about to change, Jaryd offered the only response he could. "In that case, Baden," he said evenly, "I'll go with you."

"Splendid!" Baden exclaimed, a grin spreading across his features, his solemn bearing of a moment before utterly gone. "You'll need a day to pack and settle your affairs here," he began, as much to himself as to Jaryd and the others, "and the day after tomorrow is your birthday, and we can't have you leaving on your birthday. So we'll leave with daylight on the third day." The Owl-Master rose and moved toward the door that led to the bedrooms, his owl hopping down to his shoulder. "I'm going to retire for the evening," he said. "I suggest the rest of you do the same. We have much to do in the next two days."

"Baden, wait!" Jaryd called after the mage, jumping to his feet. "Where are we going?"

Baden stopped and turned to face his nephew, his bright blue eyes gleaming once more. "To Amarid, of course," the Owl-Master explained matter-of-factly, "for the Midsummer Gathering of the Order."

3

Jaryd's next two days in Accalia proved to be just as frenzied as Baden had predicted. Except for saying good-bye to his family, Jaryd had not expected that leaving the town would be difficult. But Accalia was, as Royden reminded him the night before he and the Owl-Master planned to depart, the only home he had ever known, and, on his birthday, he spent several hours bidding farewell to friends and acquaintances. Schoolmaster Fyrth seemed particularly sad to see Jaryd leave, not only because he liked Jaryd, but also because, as he told Jaryd, finding a replacement for him would be troublesome. Three of Jaryd's friends put in together to buy him a carry sack from one of the local peddlers, and—an even greater gift—they apologized for spending less time with him after his dream of the bandits.

Bernel and Royden spent much of Jaryd's birthday at the smithy, returning home that evening with an object, wrapped in cloth, that they presented to Jaryd just before dinner. Removing the wrapping, Jaryd found a dagger, in a brown leather sheath, with a hilt made of a glasslike black stone contoured to fit his hand. He pulled out the knife, revealing a finely honed blade of burnished silver. Unable to speak, Jaryd turned the dagger over repeatedly in his hands, gazing with wonder at every detail.

"I didn't know you could work silver," Baden commented quietly to Bernel. "At least not this skillfully."

Bernel grinned shyly. "Neither did I. Royden's been bothering me to try it for some time now." He shrugged. "This seemed as good a time as any. The sheath is from Jorrin," he continued, looking at Jaryd. "He sends his thanks for the work you did on his tools, and he wishes you well in your travels."

Drina, too, had a gift for him: a new overshirt, woolen and heavy enough for the cold he and Baden would encounter crossing the mountains. Remarkably, it was almost exactly the color of Baden's cloak. Her pale eyes were wide and damp when she gave it to Jaryd. "I bought the material long ago," she said, her voice trembling slightly. "I wasn't sure when I was going to give it to you, with spring coming, and all. I guess on some level I knew all along what path you'd choose." She gave a small laugh, although the expression in her eyes remained sad. "Maybe I have a bit of the Sight myself." After Jaryd opened the gifts, the five of them sat down for his birthday supper. Drina had made Jaryd's favorite meal, roasted fowl seasoned with shan leaf, as well as honeybread pudding.

Royden did not give Jaryd his gift until later that night, after their parents and Baden had gone to sleep. Jaryd had climbed into bed and was ready to extinguish his candle when Royden pulled a small bundle from the chest at the foot of his bed.

"Wait, Jaryd. I have something for you, too."

Jaryd sat up as Royden walked over to sit beside him.

"I couldn't think of anything to get you, at least nothing that seemed to suit the occasion. And then I remembered that you've always admired this." Royden handed him the bundle, which felt surprisingly light in Jaryd's hands. Jaryd unwrapped the gift, pulling away layer after layer of paper, until he reached a small box. Within the box lay a carved gold ring Royden had discovered in the crawl space under the smithy when they were children. The ring was heavily worn and dull, but the image of Arick carved into the flattened crown still showed clearly.

Jaryd looked from the ring to his brother. "Royden," he said, overwhelmed, "I can't take this. Thank you. This is an incredible gift. But I can't take it." He tried to hand it back to his brother, but Royden shook his head.

"Jaryd, please. I can't wear it while I'm working in the smithy anyway. And I'd really like you to take it." Jaryd started to say something, but Royden cut him off. "Look, if it makes you feel better, we'll call it an extended loan. But we've always referred to this as my good luck ring, and, right now, I think I'd like you to have it."

Jaryd relented and placed the ring on the little finger of his right hand. Then he embraced his brother fiercely. "By the gods, I'm going to miss you," he said through tears. Royden silently returned the embrace and then went back to his bed and put out his candle. Jaryd blew out the candle by his own bed as well, but he lay awake for a long time, staring out the window into the night and absently playing with the ring.

The brief farewells spoken the next morning, as the eastern sky was just beginning to brighten, belied the difficulty of the moment for Jaryd. His mother, holding him in a tight embrace by the door of the house, spoke to him, quietly and tearfully, of how proud he had made her and of how much she loved him. Royden, after the emotions of the night before, was jocular and playful as he offered advice on how Jaryd might use his new status as Mage-Attend to an Owl-Master as a ploy to attract young women. And his father, gruff and awkward as always, though not entirely able to mask his sorrow, grasped Jaryd's shoulder and told him how much they would miss him at the smithy. Then he led Jaryd a few steps away from the others.

"Don't let that power you have go to your head!" Bernel warned him with quiet intensity. "It changes people, you know. Don't let it change you."

"I won't, Papa," Jaryd assured him. "I promise."

Through the sadness and excitement, the fears and expectations, Jaryd tried to listen carefully to each thing they said to him, to remember every word. But only a few hours later, walking behind Baden through a fine, cool mist on a wooded path that curved and looped with the course of the surging Mountsea River, Jaryd could recall little of it. Indeed, of all the words spoken that morning, the ones Jaryd remembered most vividly had not even been directed at him. He had overheard his father speaking with quiet intensity to Baden, before those two had shared an awkward though seemingly heartfelt embrace of their own.

"It has never been easy between us, Baden," Bernel had said. "That's no secret. I still find it hard to forgive Mother and you for being away when Father died." Baden started to say something, but Bernel stopped him with a raised finger and a shake of his head. "It's not important anymore. We have our own lives now and it's time I stopped dwelling on what's past. Jaryd's path lies with you. I see that now." He hesitated, looking uncomfortable. "Take care of him, Baden. Please," Bernel had finally said, his brown eyes fixed earnestly on the tall mage's face. "For all that he is, and all that you say he will be, he is still our youngest. Keep him well, and may Arick guard you both."

Jaryd heard his father's words over and over within the rhythmic beat of his footsteps as he strode along the path. *For all that you say he will be . . .* In many ways, he still found it difficult to accept the future that Baden had predicted for him. He did not doubt that the mage would be right about these things. He remembered his own dreamed visions with frightening clarity, and he had perceived the truth in Baden's words when the Owl-Master had declared that he would be a powerful mage. But despite all that had happened over the past year, he still thought of himself as just Jaryd, son of Bernel and Drina, who would one day become a blacksmith or, perhaps, a teacher. On the day after his eighteenth birthday, walking with an Owl-Master to the Gathering of the Order of Mages and Masters, he felt younger than he had in many years.

He adjusted his carry sack slightly and, for the fifth or sixth time that day, inwardly thanked Rhys, Nelek, and Gissa for their gift. The sack, made from tough cloth and just enough leather to reinforce the bottom and the shoulder straps, was exceptionally lightweight and comfortable. It had ample room for all that Jaryd might have wished to bring. But, in the end, warned by Baden that their journey would be long and strenuous, and that the mage would offer neither help nor sympathy if he tried to carry too much, Jaryd packed far less than he had expected. He had a sleeping roll and a canvas tarp for shelter, a change of clothes, some dried meat and fruit, a skin for carrying water, a small cooking pot, a length of rope, a flint, and his dagger, which he wore on his belt.

While packing, Jaryd had realized that Baden carried no satchel at all. When he asked the mage about this, Baden explained that, between his powers, Anla's hunting prowess, and the hospitality of the towns and villages he visited during his travels, he needed to carry little. His cloak, like the cloaks of all members of the Order, offered protection from harsh or cold weather, but was light enough to be worn year-round. "And," the mage had added with gentle humor, "when you get a bit older, and a bit tougher, you'll find that you won't need a sleeping roll anymore." Baden did reveal that within the spacious folds of his cloak, he bore a few supplies: rope, a water skin, and a dagger of his own, with a worn hilt of polished aqua stone. And, of course, the Owl-Master carried Anla on one shoulder and, in the opposite hand, the long, carved wooden staff with its glowing crystal.

Jaryd and Baden walked in silence for much of the morning, stopping occasionally to drink from the cold waters of the Mountsea River or to snack on dried apples and pears. Water from the heavy mist gathered on the swollen buds and emerging flowers of the maples, ashes, and willows that grew beside the river, and fell to the path in large drops. Beside the trail, young, curled green heads of ferns and small, tender blue-velvet leaves of shan peeked out from beneath the leaf litter. Occasionally, squirrels dashed across the path in front of the travelers, and juncos, nuthatches, and titmice descended from higher branches to investigate or scold. And always, the gurgle and splash of the churning river drifted among the trees, a backdrop for the other forest sounds.

After what seemed like several hours, Baden turned off the path and onto a short, narrow spur that led down to the stony bank of the river. There, the mage sat down on a large rock that jutted out into the stream, removed his shoes, and dipped his feet into the torrent. Jaryd watched the Owl-Master's long frame tense with the initial shock of the cold, and then gradually relax as he wiggled his toes in the water. Baden sat with his eyes closed for several moments before taking a deep breath and looking up at Jaryd, a tired smile on his face.

"It's a bit of a jolt, but after a few seconds it feels very nice. I recommend it."

Jaryd gave him a skeptical look and then glanced down at the mage's hands, which still gripped the stone with white, rigid fingers. Baden followed his look and then gave a small laugh. "All right," he conceded, "maybe it takes more than a few seconds, but we've a long way to go today, and your feet will feel better if you soak them awhile."

Jaryd nodded. "Actually, my feet do hurt a bit," he said, removing his pack. "But you should have seen the look on your face when you first put them in."

Jaryd dropped his pack to the ground, experiencing a fleeting sensation of weightlessness as he shed the burden and felt the cool air reach his perspiration-soaked back. He pulled off his shoes and, sitting down on the rock next to Baden's, stuck his sore feet in the river. And immediately jerked them out of the frigid water, gasping.

"By the gods!"

Baden looked at him mildly. "And you laughed at the expression on *my* face?"

Jaryd said nothing, concentrating instead on easing his toes back into the stream. Baden pulled some dried meat from a pouch that he carried in his cloak and offered it to Jaryd. For a moment, they sat chewing on the tough, smoky meat and enjoying their rest. After a while, Jaryd glanced around him, noticing that the mage's owl was gone. "Did Anla go off to hunt?"

Baden nodded. "Yes. I hope she finds something." In response to Jaryd's puzzled look, the mage elaborated. "She's a bit out of her element here; her species by nature is better suited to open country."

"Where did you find her?"

"On the Northern Plain, near where the Dhaalismin enters Tobyn's Wood."

Jaryd stared into the river, shaking his head slightly, a smile on his lips. "I've never even seen the far side of the Seaside Range."

"Well, that's about to change, isn't it?"

Jaryd turned back to his uncle and grinned broadly. "I guess so. How long will it take us to reach Amarid?"

Baden took a few seconds to calculate before responding. "If we make good time, we should be there in about seven weeks, well in time for the start of the Gathering on Midsummer's Day."

"Seven weeks!"

"It's a long way from Accalia to Amarid's home—clear across Tobyn-Ser. I believe it's close to two hundred leagues. And that includes two mountain ranges."

Jaryd stared at the water again. The idea of walking such a distance daunted him. He liked Baden, and was anxious to see more of Tobyn-Ser, but this morning's walk had been silent and, at times, tedious. He didn't know how he would endure close to two months of this.

Baden seemed to read his thoughts. "It's not too late for you to go back to Accalia," the mage told him matter-of-factly. "But I was hoping to use this time to begin your training as a Mage-Attend: to teach you of the Mage-Craft, and of the history and traditions of the Order."

Jaryd sat for a long time, gazing at the river and absorbing what the Owl-Master had told him. At length, he shook his head. "I don't want to go back," he said quietly. "And I want to learn all that you can teach me about the Mage-Craft. I just . . ." He stopped, unsure of where the thought was going.

"You just didn't know that becoming a mage would involve so much work."

Jaryd looked sharply at Baden, stung by his words.

"I intended no injury, Jaryd," the mage reassured him in the same even tone. "Indeed, I harbored similar doubts when I began my apprenticeship. We all want to be Amarid, but we sometimes lose sight of the work he did so long ago on our behalf. I was raised by a mage, and yet, before my apprenticeship, I knew little about the hawks and owls with which I would one day bind. I did know a bit about the traditions and practices of the Order, probably more than you do right now. But that was merely a product of my upbringing, and, even with that advantage, my training was long and challenging. It was also, I assure you, quite rewarding. In many ways, the time spent as Mage-Attend is a reenactment of Amarid's labors and those of the other early mages. By serving as an apprentice, you honor them and the Order."

Jaryd felt his initial anger sluicing away, leaving him somewhat abashed by his awareness that Baden was right: he had expected this to be easy. He knew nothing of birds and was ignorant in the ways of the Order. He had, he re-alized, just expected to bind with a hawk and immediately know how to be a mage. He chided himself for his foolishness. He also sensed within himself a renewal of the excitement he had felt when he first understood that he might be one of Amarid's Children, tempered, to be sure, by a clearer appreciation of what this meant, but perhaps stronger for having returned despite this knowledge.

A few moments later, Anla returned clutching a brown and white mouse in her talons and, alighting on a nearby branch, she began to tear at it with her beak. And for a long time, the three of them—mage, bird, and apprentice—sat and listened to the river, enjoying their rest and a small bit of food.

Finally, as Anla cleaned her beak on the branch, Jaryd stood and looked at his uncle. "I'm ready to go on when you are."

Baden nodded. "Good."

Jaryd and the mage put on their shoes and, as Anla flew to Baden's arm and the mage picked up his staff, Jaryd shouldered his sack.

"When does my training begin?" Jaryd asked, as they walked back up to the path.

Baden stopped and turned, a mischievous smirk on his face. "I believe it already has."

Jaryd smiled ruefully. "That's not quite what I meant."

"I know." Baden laughed. "The answer to your question is 'anytime you want.' I wasn't sure this morning if you were ready, having just left your family. But we can start right now if you'd like."

Jaryd nodded. "I think I would."

Baden smiled again. "Very well," he said, turning and starting down the trail.

For the rest of that day, Baden began to teach Jaryd about life as a mage. He pointed out various shrubs and trees, telling Jaryd which could be eaten and which could heal, which wood was best for crafting, and which plants contained valuable oils and dangerous poisons. He taught Jaryd to recognize the reddish stem of hawksbalm, the roots of which mages used to heal the wounds or illnesses of their familiars, and the waxy, white berries of Parnesroot, which could be mashed for use in a healing poultice. And he told Jaryd about the hawks and owls that inhabited the northern portion of Tobyn-Ser, describing their appearances and habits. Jaryd absorbed as much as he could of what Baden told him, tasting, so as to imprint on his memory, those plants that Baden said were edible, and examining closely the others he pointed out. He found it much easier, however, to remember what Baden told him about the hawks and owls. He had always been moved by their grace and power, and he was enthralled with the notion that he would someday bind to one of them. Occasionally, Jaryd steered his lesson one way or another by asking questions, but for the most part Baden allowed the landscape and what they discovered along the way to guide their discussion.

That first night, after setting up camp and eating supper, Baden had Jaryd work on a mind exercise that, according to the Owl-Master, would help Jaryd communicate with his familiar when the time finally came for his first binding.

"There's nothing in your previous life that can prepare you for the connection you'll feel with your first hawk," the mage explained. "And there's nothing I can tell you that can do it justice." He paused, gently stroking Anla's chin. "Who is your closest friend, Jaryd?"

"Royden," Jaryd replied without hesitation.

Baden nodded. "Yes. I sensed the strength of your bond during our time in Accalia. I would never belittle what the two of you share, but believe me when I tell you that you'll be far closer to your familiar than you are to your brother. Your bird will become a presence in your mind. Your communication will be thought itself." Baden shook his head. "It's impossible to describe adequately. It's wondrous. And yet it also carries risks. In effect, you'll be allowing a wild creature to share your thoughts. You must learn to open your mind to the bird, while at the same time maintaining the clarity of your own consciousness. It's quite difficult at first, even a bit frightening. And, as I said, there's really no way to prepare you for it. Even these exercises are a poor substitute for the actual experience. But they can be helpful in giving you the mental discipline you'll need."

The mage paused again, placing another branch on the fire before fixing his gaze on Jaryd once more. "We'll begin simply: I want you to close your eyes and try to empty your mind of all thought."

Jaryd laughed. "That's easy. My students do it all the time."

"No, they don't," Baden corrected, his expression and tone serious. "Perhaps they daydream, perhaps their minds wander. But I'm talking about something quite different. I want you to empty your mind completely, to have no thoughts at all. It may sound simple, but I doubt very much that you'll be able to do it, at least at first."

Chagrined by the Owl-Master's tone, Jaryd nodded and then did as he had been told. Or at least tried. As Baden had warned, the exercise turned out to be far more difficult than he had expected. Trying for the first time in his life to think of nothing at all, Jaryd found himself confronted by an endless stream of stray thoughts. What were Royden and his parents doing right now? With what kind of hawk would he eventually bind? What would the Gathering be like? What would it be like to walk clear across Tobyn-Ser? Every noise—every snap of the fire, each call of a distant owl—seemed to reach him, to tug at his mind.

At length he opened his eyes again and stared at his uncle. "I can't do it," he admitted with a shake of his head.

Baden grinned. "You will eventually. It just takes time, and you've had a big day. You should get some sleep; we'll have plenty of time to work on this."

Again Jaryd nodded, and while Baden lay down next to the fire, Jaryd pulled out his sleeping roll and arranged it on the soft ground.

"Sleep well, Jaryd," Baden offered.

"Thank you, Baden. You, too."

But Jaryd lay awake for a long time as the questions and musings continued to flow through his head, as persistent as the river that rolled by their camp.

The next several days resembled the first. Baden's lessons marked their progress along the trail during the day, and Jaryd spent at least some time each evening learning to discipline his mind as Baden had taught him. Often, as they rested along the trail, or at night, as they ate supper, they exchanged stories about their family. Baden told Jaryd about growing up with Bernel or about Jaryd's grandparents, and Jaryd told Baden about his life with Bernel, Drina, and Royden. And occasionally, as the fire burned down before they retired for the night, Baden would start to sing some of the old ballads in his deep, mellifluous voice, urging Jaryd to join in. Mostly, because they were the songs Baden seemed to like best, they sang of the gods, their voices twining to tell the story of how Arick, the most powerful of the ancient gods, gave to his sons, Lon and Tobyn, a great expanse of land to which the two young gods were to give shape and life as they saw fit. They sang of Leora, the Goddess of Light, whose forest they were in, and whose beauty and capricious-ness fueled the bitter rivalry that soon divided the two brothers. And they sang of how this feud between Tobyn and Lon drove Arick, in his fury and frustra-tion, to cleave the world he had given them, and how this act so pained Duclea, their mother, that her crying filled the oceans and swelled the rivers that her sons had carved out of their now separate lands.

On the eighth day after their departure from Accalia, as the trail began to climb steeply away from Leora's Forest into the Seaside Mountains, the weather broke. The last of the spring rains drifting in from Arick's Sea passed over the mountains and on toward the Northern Plain. In their wake, the rains left a brilliant indigo sky and a warm spring sun that drew steam from the still-damp forests. But even as spring came to the Goddess's wood below, coaxing flowers and leaves from the branches of her trees, the path they followed led Baden and Jaryd farther into the cold mountains and the fresh snow left there by the retreating clouds. As the air thinned, their journey grew more difficult and their footing became increasingly treacherous, slowing their progress con-siderably. Despite the sunshine, the chilling mountain wind scythed through Jaryd's clothing. His new overshirt offered some relief, but only some, and he found himself eschewing rests along the trail in order to stay in motion and thus stay warm. At night, he huddled by the fire, pulling his clothes tight around him, and even going so far as to wrap himself in a canvas tarp. At the same time he silently cursed Baden, who wore his cloak hooded and closely bundled, but otherwise seemed unaffected by the cold.

Yet, even with the harsh conditions, Jaryd was continually awed by the raw power and spectacular beauty of the mountains. On days when their journey carried them up above the treeline, Jaryd gazed with childlike wonder at the seemingly infinite rows of jagged crests, shrouded in ice and snow, that ran toward the horizon in all directions. When they descended into the lush green valleys that wound among the peaks, he marveled at the vast groves of giant evergreens and the rolling mountain meadows newly covered with a dazzling palette of lupine, aster, paintbrush, and thistle. And, after nearly a fortnight in the Seaside Range, as he and Baden came within sight of the Northern Plain, Jaryd realized that he would miss the mountains after all.

They set up camp that last night in the mountains on a small outcropping that offered a clear westward view. Below them, the plain stretched out like a great sea of grass, dotted with islands of dark, low-growing trees, and carved into three huge sections by a forked, meandering river. The Dhaalismin, Jaryd thought to himself, looking down on the scene.

"We lost some time up here," Baden commented, moving to stand beside him. "I guess the snow slowed us down. But whatever the reason, we're going to have to make up some of the distance as we cross the plain and Tobyn's Wood."

Jaryd shrugged and allowed himself a grin. "I feel up to it. And, I must say, I'm looking forward to walking on level ground for a while."

Baden returned the smile. "How would you feel about a home-cooked meal and a night's sleep in a real bed?" he asked.

"Are you serious?"

"Quite. There's a small town at the base of this mountain—it's called Taima—and I know some people there who would gladly lodge us for the night."

"It sounds wonderful."

"It shortens our walk tomorrow more than I'd like," Baden continued, as much to himself as to Jaryd, "but perhaps it will rejuvenate us for the rest of our trip."

Jaryd nodded. "I'd welcome a night in a real bed."

They stood for a while longer, watching the shadows of the mountains fall gradually across the plain as the sun set behind them. At length, Baden suggested that they start dinner, and they set about preparing their meal.

Later that evening, as Baden toyed with the fire, Jaryd attempted once more to focus on his binding exercises, as Baden called them. Over the past few days he had grown increasingly adept at schooling his mind, until he could cease all thought for several minutes at a time. It was a strange sensation when it worked—a sort of waking sleep that he actually found quite relaxing. But on this night, perhaps because of their impending visit to Taima, Jaryd found himself preoccupied with the stories he had heard about renegade mages and trouble within the Order. It was not the first time on their journey that he had thought about these things, although, on the other occasions, he had been reluctant to broach the subject with Baden. On this night, though, it occurred to him that he had a right to ask; that in a sense this, too, was part of his training. He sat without speaking for some time, gathering his courage, until Baden finally noticed that Jaryd was watching him.

"Shouldn't you be practicing?" the mage inquired mildly, stirring the fire with a long stick.

The Mage-Attend shrugged. "I can't concentrate."

"Oh? What's on your mind?"

"Are the stories true, Baden?" Jaryd asked impulsively by way of reply.

For some time, the Owl-Master said nothing, as he continued to stir the embers. Then he sat back and regarded Jaryd soberly, his blue eyes reflecting the firelight. "I had wondered when this would come up," he said at length. He took a breath. "If you are asking if there have been unexplained attacks on villages, I'm afraid the answer is yes. If you are asking whether or not mages are responsible . . ." He hesitated, shrugging slightly. "That I can't tell you."

"Can't or won't?" Jaryd challenged.

The mage narrowed his eyes, and his lean features appeared to harden. His reply caught the Mage-Attend completely off guard. "Tell me, Jaryd," he demanded, "what do you know of Amarid?"

Jaryd considered the question for some time before answering. "Well," he began tentatively, "he was the first and greatest of the mages. He discovered the Mage-Craft. He founded the Order and created the set of laws that governs its members. He started many of the traditions of the Order, like wearing the green cloak and leaving a feather as a token to indicate gifts or service. And,"

Jaryd added with a smirk, hoping to ease the tension somewhat, "he lived an impossibly long distance from Accalia."

Baden nodded and offered a small laugh. "That's a good place to start." But then the mage's eyes narrowed again, and he pressed on in a more serious tone. "And what do you know of Theron?"

Jaryd shivered involuntarily. "Theron was a renegade mage who lived in Amarid's time," he replied in a guarded tone.

"What else?" Baden demanded, the firelight illuminating his face.

Jaryd took a deep breath. "He brought a curse down on the Order. Theron's Curse."

"And what is Theron's Curse?"

Baden's eyes were locked on Jaryd's, and Jaryd's mouth had gone dry. "I'm . . . I'm not totally sure," he stammered. "It has something to do with what happens to a mage who dies unbound."

Baden nodded. "Good."

"Why are you asking me these things?"

"Why did you ask me about the attacks?"

Jaryd hesitated. "Because if I'm going to be a mage, I should understand what's going on within the Order."

Baden smiled. "And that's why I'm asking you about Amarid and Theron. Every mage should know their story, and before I told it to you, I wanted to see how much you already knew." He looked into the fire. "Did you know that when they first met, they became close friends?"

"Amarid and Theron were friends?" Jaryd asked doubtfully.

Baden nodded. "It might also surprise you to find out that Theron was the first Owl-Master, and that many of their contemporaries believed that he, and not Amarid, was the first Hawk-Mage."

Jaryd sat silently, trying to digest what Baden had told him. In all the tales he had heard about Amarid and the establishment of the Order, beginning with those his mother had told him when he was a child, he had never heard these things. Amarid was a figure of almost mythic proportions in the history of Tobyn-Ser. He discovered the Mage-Craft; he committed the Order to serving the land. At least this is what Jaryd had learned; certainly, this was what he had taught his students just a few weeks ago. And Theron. Theron haunted the sleep of children throughout the land. He had tried to destroy the Order, and, failing that, he had cast a terrifying curse on all the mages who came after him. The idea that Amarid and Theron could be friends seemed as impossible to fathom as the notion that mages could be responsible for the recent attacks. Which, perhaps, was Baden's point.

"I tell you these things," the mage went on after a moment, "so that you might hear Amarid and Theron's tale with the knowledge that some of your preconceptions are wrong."

Jaryd started to say something, but Baden held up a hand to silence him. "I realize that you've been taught these things since childhood. I don't mean to find fault with you; I merely wish to remedy a previous distortion of the truth."

Baden paused briefly to place another piece of wood on the fire. Jaryd shifted his position slightly, and leaned back comfortably against a contoured stone.

"In many ways," Baden began, his voice taking on the deep, resonant tones Jaryd remembered from that evening in his parents' kitchen several weeks before, "the legend of Amarid and Theron is, except for the story of Lon and Tobyn, the most important tale in the history of Tobyn-Ser. Their friendship, and its lamentable deterioration, shaped the creation of the Order, and nearly caused its destruction. Indeed, it is a story as dramatic and tragic as any script that Cearbhall himself ever crafted for the stage.

"They met as little more than boys, in what's now called the Meeting Grove, two hundred leagues south and east of here. Early on, the grove was the site of the annual Gatherings, but after what came later, it was abandoned and forgotten by most. When Amarid and Theron met, both had already bound to their first hawks and had begun to master the use of their powers. For this, they had been exiled from their homes by people who feared sorcery as a wicked art. I should add here," Baden remarked to Jaryd, breaking the cadence of his story, "that Amarid eventually reconciled with his family and friends; Theron did not. In effect, he remained an exile for the rest of his life."

The Owl-Master paused, stirring the fire again. "Amarid and Theron sealed their friendship that first day, drawn together by loneliness and shared power, and by their curiosity as to whether there were others in Tobyn-Ser with similar abilities. From the start, both took it for granted that, from that time forward, they would travel together. Amarid, whose Sight was always the stronger of the two, described for Theron an island he had envisioned, where, Amarid believed, lay something of value and importance. From Amarid's description, Theron guessed that the island was Ceryllon and they agreed that this should be their first destination. They also agreed, given their similar experiences, that, for the time being, they would be unwise to reveal their powers to others.

"They reached Ceryllon during the following summer, after a long and adventure-filled journey. There, they found a cave, and within that cave they found the cerylls, which, they soon discovered, focused and heightened their powers, much the way a lens can be used to concentrate the heat of the sun. They also carried back with them the Summoning Stone, the largest and most powerful of all cerylls. Amarid later altered the stone, pouring his power into it much as a mage today might alter a piece of wood, thus infusing it with a magic that linked the stone to all cerylls throughout Tobyn-Ser." Baden paused again, shaking his head as if unable to comprehend what the First Mage had done. "I cannot begin to imagine the power such a feat would require. To alter a stone as large as my ceryll would be difficult enough, but something as vast as the Summoning Stone . . ." He left the thought unfinished, shaking his head once more and kneeling to place another log on the fire. Jaryd gazed at the orange, multifaceted crystal that glowed atop the Owl-Master's staff.

"How is the color of a mage's ceryll determined?" Jaryd asked.

Baden shrugged. "We don't really know. The crystals themselves are colorless before they are removed from the cave. Each mage brings to the stone a different color. In a sense, our link to the stone is as unique as our binding to our familiars. A mage can only be bound to one ceryll at a time, and no mage can channel his or her power through another's stone."

"Mine will be blue," Jaryd stated, remembering his vision from a year before as he gazed absently into the fire.

Baden looked at his nephew for a long time, and then nodded. "Yes. I've seen this as well. Amarid's was also blue."

They sat without speaking for a while before the mage continued with his tale. "Upon their return from Ceryllon, Amarid and Theron resumed their wanderings, but they agreed that the time had come to reveal their powers. When they reached towns and villages they sought out the sick and injured and healed them, they demonstrated their ability to ignite fires and shape wood, and, when they met with hostility and threats, they made it clear that they could also use their powers to defend themselves. At first, many feared them, but their healing talents, and their gentle persistence, allayed most of these apprehensions. In these endeavors, Amarid was somewhat more enthusiastic than Theron. Amarid believed, as do most of us today, that the Mage-Craft is a gift from Leora, one for which we give thanks through our service. For this reason, mages have never received material payment for their services. Theron, however, saw the craft not as a gift, but as a sign of his own superiority, something that set him above the land's people. As you might expect, he had quite a different vision of the craft's position in Tobyn-Ser. He came to believe that mages should lead the land and enjoy the privileges and riches that their powers might bring them. But Theron's views on this matter evolved slowly. In the early years, he cooperated with Amarid, and both of the young mages enjoyed the attention and gratitude they received for their deeds.

"Within a few years," Baden continued, "Amarid and Theron also began to encounter other hawk-bound mages. At first, while their numbers remained small, these other mages joined Amarid and Theron or journeyed in small groups to Ceryllon to find their crystals. But as their numbers grew, this became less practical, and Amarid and Theron told all the mages they encountered that they would gather each year at Midsummer in the Meeting Grove. This, in effect, marked the beginning of the Order.

"But around this time, Amarid and Theron's friendship began to sour. Amarid fell in love with another mage, a woman named Dacia, and awkwardly, and not without bitterness, he and Theron parted. Amarid and Dacia returned to the region near Riverhaven, Amarid's home, which was later renamed in his honor, and they served that part of Tobyn-Ser. Other mages settled into more confined areas as well, healing those in nearby towns and becoming parts of the local communities. Theron took longer to settle. And, embittered by what he saw as Amarid's casual dismissal of their friendship, he became twisted by anger and resentment. He attended the annual Gatherings, but as Amarid began to assume the role of leader of the Order, and to codify his vision of the mages as servers and protectors of the people and the land, Theron's contempt for this vision festered and grew. He declared that he had as much claim to the leadership of the Order as Amarid, and a sizable group of mages, particularly the younger ones, who were most taken with Theron's charm, agreed. He also found that he could manipulate the actions of the villagers and towns-folk he encountered, and he used this power to compel them into his service and to acquire wealth.

"Around this time, Theron's first familiar died, and Theron spent several months unbound. It was a terribly difficult time for him, as it is for all mages. His powers were diminished, and, as the first of his kind to lose a familiar, Theron had no idea whether he would ever bind again, or whether his powers would ever return. And for the first time in his life, he found himself truly alone. He had been exiled by his family long ago; his friendship with Amarid was in shambles; and now, he had lost his hawk, who had been a constant presence in his mind for years. Lonely and bitter, he disappeared into the Emerald Hills, and, for nearly a year, Amarid and the others heard nothing from him.

"No one saw him again until he arrived at the next Gathering carrying an owl on his shoulder. All in the Order, even Amarid, praised Theron for this achievement and named him the first Owl-Master in the Order. The following year, Amarid lost his hawk, and he too bound to an owl. For a short time, Amarid and Theron grew closer once more. But their continuing struggle for control of the Order, and their profoundly different visions of the Order's role in Tobyn-Ser, soon poisoned their friendship again.

"A few years after Amarid's second binding, Theron traveled back to his hometown of Rholde, where he fell in love with a beautiful woman. Though Theron had learned to compel people to serve him for brief periods, no mage or master could force someone to love him or her. The constant expenditure of power would exhaust both magician and bird. So, much as he tried to win the woman's heart, Theron could not make her love him. Indeed, she loved another man in the town. Not a man with power, or wealth, but just a simple shopkeeper. Theron raged with jealousy and grew to hate this man. He forced the man to do the most demeaning tasks for him, and he berated him and cursed him constantly.

"One day Theron came upon the man, and before he could force him to do anything, the man offered his service and expressed sorrow at the fact that his love for this woman had caused the Owl-Master such pain.

"No doubt, he meant well, but this was too much for Theron. Tormented as he was by the woman's preference for this man, he was infuriated by the man's sympathy and pity.

" 'I require nothing from a maggot like you,' he raged. 'Be gone!' And with the words, and in his fury, Theron, perhaps without intending to, forced his will on the man. Shortly after, before Theron understood what he had done, the man took his own life.

"Word of the incident swept through the town and it awakened old fears of the Mage-Craft and those who wielded it. Almost everyone in Rholde demanded vengeance, but feared the Owl-Master too much to try to exact it themselves. Instead, they sent word to Amarid and the rest of the Order, formally demanding that Theron be punished. And, as others in Tobyn-Ser learned of the incident, they, too, pressured the Order to take action.

"The discussion of Theron's fate dominated the next Gathering and marked the culmination of the long feud between Theron and Amarid. No member of the Order had ever been considered for punishment before, so the mages had no procedures in place to deal with such a discussion. All agreed, however, that Theron should be given an opportunity to defend himself and that Amarid, as the senior member of the Order, should present the case against Theron.

"Theron rose to speak, leaning heavily on his staff. It is said that, though he looked haggard and pale, and most agreed that he had aged considerably since the last Gathering, his resonant voice still commanded the attention of all who listened."

Baden rose, leaning on his long staff as he had described Theron doing. And, when next he spoke, it seemed to Jaryd that his voice had changed, growing still deeper, but with a hint of ire and madness that was not his own. He appeared to become an apparition, an embodiment of the long-dead Owl-Master.

"I deeply regret what transpired this spring in Rholde," Baden began quietly, speaking Theron's words, his eyes focused on the ground in front of him. "I meant the poor man no harm; I certainly didn't mean for him to kill himself." Pausing, he looked around the fire, and Jaryd could almost see the other mages who had gathered to hear Theron's plea. Then he continued, a note of defiance creeping into his voice. "But am I to be punished because some people in Rholde and other parts of Tobyn-Ser harbor old prejudices against our abilities? Am I to be punished because these fools demand it? We of this Order are special. We have mastered the Mage-Craft. We are not servants of the ignorant, nor are we bound by their weakness." The Owl-Master's voice grew stronger and his gestures increasingly animated as he spoke. "If I am to be punished because you, my fellow mages and masters, demand it, well, then, so be it. I will accept your judgment. But if you are acting because others tell you to act, then I must ask you: did we form this Order to govern ourselves or to be governed by others? This regrettable incident has taken a toll on us all; let us not compound this tragedy with poor judgment and ill-considered actions."

Baden straightened, and, when he spoke again, his voice was once more his own. "Theron had captivated his listeners, as much with his sonorous tone as with his words. But Amarid had yet to speak."

Again, Baden's demeanor changed. He stood straighter, leaning less on his staff. And when he continued, his voice was no longer that of Theron. Now he was Amarid, with a tone less vibrant but equally resolute, and laden with wisdom and power.

"Well spoken. Well spoken, indeed. You were always the more articulate one, weren't you, Theron?"

"Yes," Theron replied acidly, reappearing for just an instant in Baden's stance. "I suppose I was."

"More articulate," Amarid repeated. "And more reckless. You've really done it this time, Theron." The sarcasm was gone from Baden's voice—or was it Amarid's? Jaryd had become so engrossed in the tale that he could no longer tell. The Owl-Master sounded weary and despondent as he went on with Amarid's oration. "This is not an easy task for me."

"I'm sure," Theron snorted derisively.

"I don't expect you to understand, old friend," Amarid replied, and then he lifted his voice to include everyone there. "All of you in this circle know that Theron and I have had our differences. But we were close once and we built this Order together. That is not a small thing. He is arrogant and difficult, but he is my friend. What we are discussing today, however, is not just Theron's future, but the future of the Order and the Mage-Craft. Those of you who are older will remember what it is like to be an outcast because of your powers. We were all exiles once, banished from our homes because the people of this land feared us and our magic. Those of you who are younger do not remember this, because this Order has gained the trust of Tobyn-Ser by serving the people: by healing their wounds, by curing their illnesses, by mediating their disputes. I would not have us bound by their whims or hostage to their ignorance. But we must preserve their trust and ease their fears. We are of this land as much as they and, ultimately, we are subject to its common laws just as they are. Theron's crime—and yes, he has committed a crime—must be punished. To do less would disgrace this Order. To do less would make us outcasts again."

Once more, Baden adjusted his stance, becoming Theron again. "Well," the Owl-Master began, "who's the arrogant one now? Amarid is telling all of us how we shall act and what this Order shall be. *Serving the people,*" he repeated contemptuously. "Since when do the strong serve the weak? Since when do the wise minister to the foolish? I will not listen to these absurdities any longer."

"At that point," Baden related in his own voice, "Theron turned and began to leave the Meeting Grove. But Amarid stopped him, and, when other mages also demanded that he remain, including some of the younger ones, who had supported him in the past, Theron finally understood the depth of his troubles. If the younger mages were not with him, he had no chance.

"The Order debated bitterly well into the night. Amarid and the older mages and masters had always outnumbered Theron's supporters, and some in the latter group had become disillusioned with Theron in the wake of the incident at Rholde. Those who still supported the Owl-Master argued stubbornly for leniency, but in the end, Amarid and his followers prevailed.

"Called back before the gathered mages well past midnight, Theron listened defiantly as Amarid pronounced his sentence. Saying that he had disgraced the Order and violated its most basic principles, Amarid informed the Owl-Master that he would be executed at first light the following morning.

"Theron stood dumbfounded, unable to believe what he had heard. And then, unwilling to give his rival the satisfaction of carrying out the punishment, the Owl-Master did something that even Amarid could not have foreseen. Closing his eyes, and lifting his staff over his head, he cast the most powerful spell ever devised by a mage."

"From this night on," Baden cried out in Theron's voice, adopting the posture he had just described, his voice ringing off the peaks behind him, "those in this Order who perish unbound will never rest!"

Baden opened his eyes again. And as the echo of his words drifted into the night, silence settled over the campsite like fog over a shoreline. "With Theron's last word, a bolt of green light burst from his staff into the night sky. In the same instant, the great owl on Theron's shoulder leapt into flight with an unnatural shriek, and when she fell to earth, she was dead. Theron's ceryll lay in shards at the Owl-Master's feet, and the top of his staff was blackened and smoking. His last words to Amarid were these: 'Remember, old friend, you have done this, not I.'

"Theron was to be executed by burning the next morning, but when the other mages went to find him and bring him forth, he was already dead."

"So Theron cursed himself," Jaryd broke in, his voice sounding harsh and alien in the stillness shaped by Baden's tale.

"Yes. As with so many other things, Theron was the first of our Order to become one of the Unsettled."

"The Unsettled?"

"That is what we call those mages who die unbound. As a result of Theron's Curse, the spirits of the Unsettled return to the places of their first bindings, where they walk the night in eternal unrest." Baden absently stroked Anla's feathers as he spoke. "That is one of the reasons why the time between the death of a familiar and one's next binding is so difficult. Not only are our powers diminished, and," he added, glancing at the bird on his shoulder, "a creature we love lost. We also run the risk, should something happen to us, of falling under Theron's Curse."

"So Theron is still . . . alive?" Jaryd asked.

"No," Baden replied, but the catch in his tone sent a chill through Jaryd's body. "Theron died that night in the Meeting Grove hundreds of years ago," he explained. "But his spirit still lives, and can be seen between dusk and dawn in what's known now as Theron's Grove in the Shadow Forest in southern Tobyn-Ser."

"So, he's a ghost?"

"I suppose that could be another word for it," Baden agreed. "We prefer to call them spirits."

"But that's a matter of semantics," Jaryd persisted.

After a moment, Baden conceded the point. "Yes, it is."

Jaryd considered this for a time. "Does Theron's spirit have Theron's powers?" he asked at last.

Baden hesitated. "That's a complicated question. In truth, we know very little about the Unsettled. For a number of reasons, many of them quite apparent, we rarely seek them out. We don't really know if they have access to the Mage-Craft. But even if they do, Theron's spirit is a special case. Most of the Unsettled appear holding their staffs, or whatever else might have borne their cerylls, and with their first familiars. And, at night, and within the area in which they were first bound, yes, they may have power. Theron's ceryll, however, was shattered that last night of his life by the explosion of power that accompanied the spell he cast. He carries no crystal. So whatever powers he has are . . . untamed; wild, if you will. On the other hand, his powers in life were immense, far greater than those of any other unsettled mage. We just don't know the extent of his abilities." Baden started to say something else, but then he stopped himself and waited for Jaryd's next question.

Again Jaryd sat pondering all that he had learned. Finally, pushing the hair back from his forehead, he looked across the fire at the mage. "I'm sorry, Baden. I interrupted your tale."

Baden made a small gesture dismissing the apology. "There really isn't that much more to the story. When the Gathering ended, a small group of young mages who had supported Theron renounced their membership in the Order and left Tobyn-Ser. To this day, we don't know where they went or what became of them.

"As for the Order, probably the most important consequence of the entire affair was the formal acceptance of what we now call Amarid's Laws as the guiding principles for our use of the Mage-Craft." Baden's eyes narrowed. "Do you know of Amarid's Laws?"

"I know that they govern the Order," Jaryd said, smiling sheepishly, "but I couldn't tell you what they say."

Baden shook his head sadly. "Everyone should know them," he remarked quietly, "but that's not your fault." Then he raised his voice. "Hear them now, and remember: 'Mages shall guard and serve the land. They shall be the arbiters of disputes. They shall use their powers to give aid and comfort in times of need.'

" 'Mages shall never use their powers to extract service or payment from the powerless.'

" 'Mages shall never use their powers against one another. Disputes among mages shall be judged by the Order.'

" 'Mages shall never harm their familiars.' "

His words rang out into the stillness of the night with a power and clarity that reminded Jaryd of the sound of his father's hammer. As the last word echoed off the mountains and died away, a strange silence enveloped the camp once more. In the distance, an owl hooted, and Anla, suddenly alert on Baden's shoulder, uttered a rasping response.

When Baden spoke again, it was in a soft, tired voice. "We should sleep. Even stopping in Taima, we have a substantial distance to cover tomorrow."

Baden lay down beside the fire, and Jaryd did the same, not bothering this night to pull out his sleeping roll. The Owl-Master's breathing soon slipped into a slow, even rhythm, but Jaryd lay awake for a long time. He thought about Amarid and Theron; about spirits and what it meant to be condemned to eternal unrest; and about the depths of emotion that could drive two friends to do such things to each other and to the Order they had created. Gradually, the campfire died away, the flames dwindling until all that was left was a bed of glowing coals that settled noisily into the fire pit. In the darkness, Jaryd could make out the bright stars hanging overhead, and he lay awake for a while longer picking out the constellations he knew. Duclea, weeping on her knees for her sons, and for her husband's fury; Leora in her ceaseless dance; and Arick, lower in the sky and to the west, with his fist raised high over his head, poised to smite the land he had created for Tobyn and Lon.

When finally Jaryd drifted into a fitful, uneasy sleep, he dreamed of a mage. At first, in a corner of his mind that observed his dream, he thought that he was seeing himself as he would be someday. But the mage carried a ceryll of deep red and a dark bird with strange, bright eyes. As he watched, the mage moved toward him, extending a hand that carried a slender black object. All the while, the mage remained hooded, his or her face shrouded in shadow and unrecognizable. But as the figure drew near, Jaryd saw that the offered object was a black feather, and, when Jaryd took it in his hand, the feather flared brightly before turning to grey ash.

* * *

Jaryd awoke to find Baden shaking him gently, the mage's lean, somber face illuminated by the early morning light.

"A strange vision came to me last night," Baden told him. "I don't know what it meant, but I think we should get going."

Jaryd nodded slowly and tried to force himself awake. Baden offered him the last of the dried fruit and some water, both of which helped, and soon they had broken camp and started down the trail toward the town. They walked as quickly as their steep descent would allow. Baden, who seemed impatient to reach Taima, said little, and Jaryd spent much of his time on the trail reflecting again on the tale he had heard the night before. They stopped briefly at midday to refill their water skins at a small spring and to eat what was left of the dried meat before continuing down the mountain.

The heavy smell of charred wood and grain reached them just an hour or two later, and from a small clearing near the base of the mountain, they caught their first glimpse of Taima. An unnatural cloud of dark grey smoke hung balefully over the town, and the frames of several buildings stood blackened and smoldering in the town center.

"Fist of the God!" Baden hissed through clenched teeth, his pale eyes pained as he looked down on the ruined town. "We're too late!"

4

Standing in the mountains above Taima, seeing the anguish etched across Baden's face as the mage surveyed the charred structures below, Jaryd recalled a lesson from a morning early in their journey, one of the many Baden had offered since they left Accalia.

One spring, when Baden was five or six years old, he had gone to visit Owl-Master Lyris, his grandmother, at her home along the banks of the Little River. It had been a wet winter, and the river was running much higher than usual. Soon after Baden's arrival, the rains began, flooding the river and destroying a nearby village. When she went to survey the damage, Lyris took Baden with her, and, while they were there, Baden saw that his grandmother was crying. Having never seen her cry before, he grew frightened, and he asked her why she was sad. Lyris took his hand and placed it on the green cloak she wore. "When I put on this cloak," she told him, "I became the land. When it hurts, I hurt."

"It took me a long time to understand what she meant," Baden had explained that morning a few weeks ago. "In fact, I don't think I fully appreciated her words until I got my cloak. The Mage-Craft is a gift from the Goddess, and, in a sense, from the land itself. In return, we who are fortunate enough to master the Mage-Craft become the land's guardians. When the people are sick, we care for them. When the people fight each other, we bring them together. And when the land itself brings harm, it falls to us to ease the suffering. Just as my grandmother was pained by what she saw that day, I'm pained every time there is flood, or drought, or fire, or plague that I've been unable to prevent. I suppose it's the price I pay for wearing this cloak."

Now, feeling his own horror at what he saw below them on the plain, Jaryd began to understand what Baden had been trying to tell him. "Is this what you saw in your vision last night?" Jaryd asked, his voice subdued.

Without taking his eyes from the town, the mage nodded. "At least part of it."

Jaryd started to ask what else his uncle had seen, but thought better of it.

"They'll need our help," Baden said grimly. "We'd best get down there."

Baden and Jaryd walked the rest of the way to Taima in silence. The smell of smoke grew increasingly oppressive as they drew close to the town, and, as they emerged from the mountains onto the plain and into the town square, they saw a large crowd of people standing amid the darkened skeletons of their shops and inns. A large building in the middle of the town, probably the town hall, had also been burned, and off on its own, closer to the mountains, stood a single blackened structure from which smoke still drifted into the clear sky. From its narrow, pointed spires Jaryd guessed that this had been the God's temple. Smoke still rose from the buildings in the town square as well, and the blackened remnants of tools and goods that the people had tried to salvage from the blaze lay scattered in the street. Without breaking stride, Baden and Jaryd advanced toward the throng. But as several of the townspeople pointed them out to the others, Jaryd felt a sudden and inexplicable foreboding. "This could be difficult," Baden told him with quiet intensity. "Stay behind me and say nothing."

A hush fell over the crowd as the mage and Jaryd approached.

"We see that we have come in troubled times," Baden said, his voice pitched to carry. "Can we offer you our assistance?"

At first, none of the townspeople spoke. For what seemed to Jaryd an eternity, he and the mage stood facing a host of people wearing icy expressions and the stains and injuries from a night spent combating a fire. Then a man stepped forward. He was young, no more than a year or two older than Royden, Jaryd guessed. His clothes and face were smeared with soot and one arm bore an ugly, black wound. But most of all, Jaryd noted the man's eyes. They were deep brown and, once, Jaryd thought, they might have been kind. But now, beneath the impossible tangle of matted hair that fell across the man's forehead, they looked out at the Owl-Master with a terrifying mix of fear, grief, and hatred.

"Don't you think you've done enough already, Mage!" the man charged in a tone that matched the wild expression in his eyes. *Mage,* Jaryd thought to himself, not *Child of Amarid.*

"I'm afraid I don't understand," Baden responded, his voice placid.

"You lie!" the man retorted savagely.

Baden took a deep breath. "Perhaps we should start over," he offered in the same tone. "Your town has obviously suffered a terrible loss. We would like to help you."

"We don't want your help," the man said through clenched teeth, the fist on his uninjured arm opening and closing spasmodically. "We want you gone!"

Baden held the man's gaze until the other looked away. Then the mage surveyed the rest of the horde. Jaryd did the same, and, as he did, he noticed a stocky bald man wearing a long silver-grey robe that was stained and blackened now. The Keeper of Arick's Temple, Jaryd thought, seeing the man smirk at Baden's discomfort. We'll have no help from him.

"I'm sorry for what has happened to you," Baden began again, raising his voice so all could hear. "But we wish only to offer aid. Many of you are hurt. Will you not make us welcome and allow me to heal your wounds?"

A stony silence met the Owl-Master's question. To be broken at last by the strained, chilling laughter of the injured man.

"You're confused; you wish to know why we don't welcome you with our arms and hearts open. Is that what troubles you, *Child of Amarid?*" he said. And there was no hint of deference in his use of the formal title; only heavy sarcasm and the rage, bordering on lunacy, that Jaryd had heard in his voice a moment before. "Fine!" he spat. "I'll tell you. And then you can answer a question for me."

Baden held himself very still as the man turned to look at the fire-ravaged buildings. "You see what has happened to our town. Many of us lost our businesses, our livelihoods. But we are a strong people. We've had fires before and we've rebuilt. But look beyond these shops to the tall building there." Jaryd turned to look in the direction indicated by the man's outstretched arm. Behind the burned stores in the foreground stood the charred remains of a towering cylindrical structure. Within its frame lay a large, blackened mound from which smoke still poured.

The man turned back toward Baden. "Do you know what that is, Mage?"

"The silo," Baden responded softly.

"The silo," the man repeated, his voice rising. "And do you know what that is still burning inside what's left of our silo?" He didn't wait for a response. "Our grain. Our entire supply for the plantings that were to begin today. Without it, our animals will die. We'll have nothing to trade. Nothing to eat. Nothing to feed our children."

"You couldn't save it?" the Owl-Master asked. And from what he saw flare in the man's eyes, Jaryd knew that it had been the wrong question; that, indeed, it had brought them to the heart of the matter.

The man squeezed his eyes closed and, as he did, tears began to roll down his face. But when he opened them again and began to speak, an unnatural calm seemed to have come over him. "We tried, Mage. We tried. We have a well next to the silo that is off limits for everyday use. No one drinks from it. It exists solely to guard against a fire at the silo. But late last night, after we were all asleep, the fires began. And when we reached the well, the rope had been cut and the bucket allowed to fall to the bottom. We had no water with which to save the grain." The man had spoken with his eyes wide and unseeing, but now he glared at the Owl-Master. "Do you know what we found at the well, Mage?" The man pulled something from his shirt pocket and extended his hand to Baden. "This."

Jaryd gasped. In the man's hand lay a black feather, just like the one Jaryd had seen in his dream the night before.

The man had been so intent on Baden that he had barely registered Jaryd's presence. But now, hearing Jaryd's reaction, he turned toward the Mage-Attend, his dark eyes gleaming triumphantly.

"Well, Mage. Even if you won't deal with us honestly, at least your young friend seems to recognize this token."

Baden gave Jaryd a questioning look. "Jaryd?"

"I dreamed of it last night."

"What!" Baden hissed.

"I saw it in a dream last night. It was given to me by a mage, and when I took it in my hand, it burst into flame."

The Owl-Master turned to stand directly in front of his nephew, his eyes boring into Jaryd's. "Jaryd, this is very important: did you see the mage?"

Jaryd shook his head. "No. His face was shaded by his hood. I couldn't see anything."

"What about his bird?" Baden demanded.

"This is foolishness!" the man broke in viciously. "I have answered your questions, Mage!" he said, confronting Baden. "Now will you answer mine as we agreed?"

Baden nodded tersely.

"Good." A malevolent grin spread across the man's begrimed face. "My question is this: why shouldn't we kill you and your friend right now for what you've done to us?"

Jaryd felt the hairs on the back of his neck stand up as a murmur of assent ran through the crowd. Baden gathered himself for a reply to the man's challenge.

Before he could speak, however, a stern voice broke in. "Enough, Leyton! All of you, enough of this!"

Jaryd turned to see an older man striding quickly toward the throng. He had a tanned, healthy face and a lithe frame that belied the white shock of hair on his head. Like Leyton, this man bore stains and burns from the blaze he had battled the previous night.

"That's Cullen," Baden whispered to Jaryd. "We'll be staying with him and his wife, Gayna." After a moment the mage added, still in a whisper, "I hope."

Jaryd shot the mage a look, but Baden was already looking at his friend, listening to what he had to say.

"I know this mage," Cullen assured the townspeople, making his way through the crowd until he reached Jaryd and the Owl-Master. "This is Baden. He's been visiting our town, healing our sick and wounded, helping us through troubled times since before some of you were born. He would do us no harm. And," he continued, glaring at Leyton, "he deserves better than these accusations and threats."

"But Cullen," came another voice, "you've heard the talk. We all have."

"Yes," the older man admitted, "I have heard the talk. And I've tried my best not to believe it. The Children of Amarid are too much a part of the fabric of this land; I can't believe they'd do these things."

Leyton gestured at the charred buildings that surrounded them. "Even now? Even after this?"

"After this, I'm not sure what to think," Cullen conceded wearily. "If the stories are true, I fear for all of Tobyn-Ser. But," he persisted, his voice strong once more, his eyes flashing angrily, "I don't believe that Baden would have any part in the atrocities of renegade mages!"

"Then you're an even greater fool than I thought, old man!" Leyton replied, his tone low and dangerous. "This mage is the demon who destroyed our lives last night. And I intend to make him pay." As he spoke, Leyton pulled a large knife from a sheath on his belt and pointed it menacingly at Baden. Anla, alert on the mage's shoulder, puffed her feathers and hissed at the sight of the blade. Another murmur of agreement swept through the crowd, though, this time, Jaryd also heard dissenting voices. Slowly, surreptitiously, Jaryd placed his hand on the hilt of his dagger.

Baden regarded the knife with a composed expression. "Tell me, Leyton. Had I gone to the trouble of attacking Taima at night and guarding my identity, as you accuse me of doing, why would I return here in the light of day and risk being discovered?" The Owl-Master's voice betrayed no hint of fear.

But Leyton was ready for his question. "Maybe you're not through with us yet. Perhaps this is all a part of your plan. You might wish to gain our trust by healing our burns from the fire, only to betray us again. Or maybe you just wish to gloat over your success of last night. I'm a simple man, Child of Amarid. I don't claim to understand what drives a powerful mage to do these things."

Baden nodded. "I see. And if I am as powerful as you say," the mage went on, his tone suddenly cold and imperious, "what's to stop me from destroying you where you stand, before you can finish whatever it is you hope to do with that blade?"

For the first time, Jaryd saw a flicker of uncertainty in Leyton's eyes. The hand holding the knife fell to his side and, again, tears rolled down his face.

Once more, a voice called from the multitude. "But if you didn't come to destroy us, why are you here?"

"A fair question," Baden responded, speaking to all of them. "My companion and I are on our way to Amarid, for the Gathering of the Order. And I assure you that we of the Order will discover who has done these things and we will stop them. I also give you my word, sworn in Arick's name, that my friend and I had nothing to do with the burning of your town."

A stillness descended on the town center. For what seemed to Jaryd a very long time, no one moved or spoke. Then a woman stepped out of the crowd. She was supporting a man with an angry gash across his forehead, and she looked at Baden, a plea in her eyes. "Can you heal my husband?" she asked, her voice barely more than a whisper.

"Gladly," Baden answered, smiling kindly.

Throughout what remained of the afternoon, Baden healed the burns and gashes of the townspeople. Assisted by Jaryd and Cullen, who saw to the comfort of those who waited for the mage, Baden moved through the crowd tending to injuries, which mended and vanished beneath his touch. Many of those to whom he ministered looked warily at him and the owl on his shoulder. A few, Leyton among them, refused treatment entirely. But most accepted the Owl-Master's aid and, by the time Cullen led Baden and Jaryd back to his home on the outskirts of town, the first stars were beginning to emerge in a darkening sky of deep blue.

Cullen and Gayna's house stood within sight of the Dhaalismin River, a fair distance from the town square. Theirs was larger than most of the other homes in Taima, although, like the others, it was constructed of dried red clay and covered with a low-pitched thatch roof. Unlike the tall wooden homes of Accalia, it was built low to the ground, perhaps, Jaryd thought, to protect it from the strong winds that swept across the plain. Several wooden pens built along the side of the home housed cows, pigs, horses, and fowl, and, in a large, well-tended plot behind the house, young green shoots stuck out of the dark soil in neat rows. Led inside by Cullen, Jaryd saw that within, the house felt as homey and comfortable as it had looked from outside. The front door opened onto a common room, which was brightly lit by the hearth at the far end of the room, and by a number of lanterns mounted along the walls, whose light reflected off the polished wood floor. Near the fireplace and to one side stood two matching chairs made of a dark wood with swirling grain. On each sat a small, quilted pillow with a pattern matching that of a sofa that faced the chairs from the other side of the hearth. Between them, a low table, made from the same fine wood, supported a decanter of dark, red wine and two crystal glasses.

Through a doorway, to the left of the fireplace and chairs, Jaryd caught a glimpse of the kitchen, where shining copper pots hung on the wall. At the same time, the rich aroma of roasting meat reached him, and he realized with a pang in his stomach that he was famished.

"Is that you, Cullen?" came a melodic voice from the kitchen. A moment later a woman stepped into the room.

If he had not known that Cullen and Gayna were married, Jaryd might have thought them brother and sister. Like her husband, Gayna had snow-white hair, a warm, ruddy complexion, and dark blue eyes. But while he was slender and wiry, she was stocky and solid.

When she saw the Owl-Master, she put down the dish cloth she carried and walked toward him. "Baden," she said, smiling warmly and embracing him. "It's been too long."

The mage returned her smile. "It's good to see you, Gayna. I'm just sorry I didn't come in happier times."

Her grin faded. "I know." She looked toward Cullen. "Were you able to save any of the grain?"

Cullen shook his head and she frowned. "Well," she sighed, "we've got enough stored here to get most of the town's plantings in. I just hate to leave ourselves with such a small margin in case something like this happens again." She paused, staring sadly at her husband. Then, noticing Jaryd for the first time, her face brightened. "I don't mean to be so glum, especially not with guests." She extended a tanned, work-roughened hand to Jaryd. "I'm Gayna. Welcome."

Jaryd shook her hand, feeling her strong grip. "Jaryd. Nice to meet you."

"Jaryd is my Mage-Attend," Baden added, somewhat unnecessarily. "I'm taking him to the Gathering."

"Well, you just make sure that he treats you right, Jaryd," Gayna called over her shoulder as she stepped into the kitchen. She returned a few seconds later with two more wineglasses, which she placed on the table.

"Actually—you might be interested in this, too, Cullen—he's not only my Mage-Attend, he's also Bernel's son."

Cullen's eyes widened slightly and Gayna moved toward Jaryd and looked closely at his face. "Now that you say so," she said to Baden, "I definitely see a small resemblance. To you as well as to Bernel."

"You know my father?" Jaryd asked.

"Yes," Cullen answered. "We also knew your grandparents."

"When your father and I were young," Baden explained, "we sometimes traveled with our mother to the Gatherings. And we often stopped here. In fact, I introduced Gayna to Cullen."

Cullen laughed. "What he means is, he had a crush on Gayna and brought her to dinner at my parents' home. And I stole her from him."

"And what Cullen's not saying," Gayna commented, walking back toward the kitchen, "is that we were all about twelve at the time, and it took him four more years to get up the nerve to even ask me to take a walk with him."

Jaryd joined in their laughter as Cullen moved to the table by the hearth and poured four glasses of wine. When Gayna returned with a basket of bread and a wooden board on which sat three slabs of cheese, they each raised a glass.

"To old friends," Cullen said, and, looking toward Jaryd, he added, "and new ones. May Arick guard you both and guide your journey."

Baden inclined his head slightly, acknowledging the toast, and all of them sipped from their glasses.

"You're looking well, Baden," Gayna observed after a brief silence. She turned to look at the mage's owl, who had glided to the mantle above the hearth and now sat hunched and motionless, her eyes closed. "And Anla looks more beautiful every year." Gayna took a tentative step toward the bird and glanced back at Baden. "Will she let me stroke her head?"

Baden smiled and nodded. "I'm sure she will, but try scratching beneath her chin. She prefers that."

Gayna nodded and did as the Owl-Master had suggested. Anla opened her eyes briefly at the woman's first touch. But then the bird closed them again and stretched out her neck so that Gayna might caress her more easily.

"What of Trahn?" Cullen asked.

"The last I heard he was doing quite well," Baden replied. "But that was early in the winter, just after an attack near my home village."

With Baden's mention of the attack a shadow seemed to envelop the room, though the fire and lanterns remained bright. For some time the four of them said nothing.

"Forgive me," Baden offered at last. "I didn't mean to reopen that particular discussion. Please," he added, looking from Cullen to Gayna. "Tell me how you've been. I'd much rather speak of that."

For another moment the farmers said nothing. Then Gayna smiled warmly and motioned for them to sit, and Cullen began to describe for Baden the past year's events. Life on the plain seemed to Jaryd to consist mainly of storms and market prices for livestock, but Baden appeared genuinely interested. When Cullen finished, the Owl-Master launched into a lengthy narrative of happenings within the Order, much of which Jaryd did not understand. After a time, Cullen and Gayna asked Jaryd for news of his family, and he told them a bit about his life in Accalia, which, he realized as he spoke, already felt distant and unfamiliar. Soon, they moved to a small dining room on the far side of the kitchen, where, over supper and a second decanter of the rich wine, they continued their conversation.

It was not until they had finished their meal, and one last wave of laughter had crested and receded, that Baden's expression grew serious. He turned his gaze toward Cullen.

"So," the mage said, altering the mood in the room with the tone of his voice, "what do you make of what happened last night?"

Cullen, who had been raising his goblet to his lips, stopped and carefully placed the glass on the table. He shook his head slowly. "I'm not certain what to make of it. We've all heard the talk. I didn't want to believe it; I'm still not sure that I do. But I fear we're reaching the point at which the question of its truth becomes secondary." He stood up and moved to a window, gazing absently out at one of the stock pens and passing a hand over his creased brow. "You saw Leyton today. He believes that you razed the town square. And though it saddens me to say it, I don't think that he's alone. Regardless of who's responsible for last night's fire, or any of the other crimes attributed to so-called renegade mages, in the minds of many people, the Order can no longer be trusted."

Gayna looked at Baden. "Is it true that, in addition to the type of mischief we suffered, people have been murdered?"

Baden nodded.

"Arick help us," Gayna breathed.

"What about you?" Cullen asked, his blue eyes fixed on Baden. "You must have a theory as to who's doing this."

"Yes, I do," the mage replied cryptically, "but it's just that: a theory. No more."

Cullen regarded the Owl-Master intently, but he did not force the issue.

Jaryd listened to the conversation with increasing frustration, a question burning within him. He tried to remain calm, although the wine, rather than quieting him, had left him flushed and agitated. Finally, as Baden launched into a discussion of how elusive the renegades had been, and how they had managed to attack nearly every region of Tobyn-Ser, Jaryd leaped to his feet, nearly toppling the table.

"If you're so interested in who they are and where they've been," he sputtered, "why are we just sitting around? They were here just last night! Shouldn't we be following them?"

Baden regarded him with a mild, slightly amused countenance. "How would you suggest that we follow them?"

"I . . . I don't really know," Jaryd stammered.

"Ah," Baden nodded sagely. His features hardened. "Sit down, Jaryd," he said sternly. "Pour yourself another glass of wine and relax. By the time we arrived here this afternoon, whoever lit the fire had a head start on us of approximately half a day. He or she could have gone anywhere. Taima sits on the edge of a great plain. Would you have us go north in pursuit of them? South? The Dhaalismin lies only a few miles from here. They might have had a boat. Or perhaps they retreated into the mountains. Are you ready to search every valley within a day's walk of here? I could have sent Anla to search for them, but I chose to keep her with me so that I could heal those injured by the fire. Do you doubt that decision as well?" He paused to take a sip of wine. Jaryd, who had sat down at Baden's command, stared at the glass in front of him, his cheeks and ears burning. "So, tell me, Jaryd, what should I have done? Where would you have had me search?"

"I'm sorry, Baden," Jaryd replied, his voice barely more than a whisper. "I shouldn't have spoken to you that way."

"No," Baden agreed, his tone still severe. "You shouldn't have. I've been accused of many things in my life, but no one has ever mistaken me for a fool. If there had been a way to track this person—or these people, as the case may be—I would have done so."

Jaryd nodded. "I'm sorry," he repeated.

Baden took another sip from his glass. When he spoke again, his voice had softened somewhat. "I understand your frustration, Jaryd. All of us within the Order feel the same way. This has been going on for too long."

"When was the first feather found?" Cullen asked.

"Almost a year ago," Baden responded, but he suddenly seemed distracted. After a long pause, he began to shake his head. "I knew I had been forgetting something. I may be more of a fool than I care to admit." He turned to Jaryd. "Tell me about this dream you had last night," he demanded with some intensity.

Jaryd shrugged. "There's not a great deal to tell. I saw a mage, or at least someone wearing a mage's cloak. He walked toward me and handed me a black feather like the one Leyton had today. And when I grasped the feather by its shaft, it flared and turned to ash."

"Can you describe the mage?" Baden asked, his gaze still intent.

"No. As I told you this afternoon, I couldn't see his face."

Baden narrowed his eyes. "Yes, I remember. But each time you describe your vision, you use 'he' or 'his' to describe the person you saw. Is there something about the vision that made you think the mage was male?"

"Not really," Jaryd responded with some uncertainty.

"But possibly," the Owl-Master insisted.

"Yes."

Baden leaned closer to Jaryd. "I'd like to try something. I'd like to see if I can induce the return of your vision. It's perfectly safe; no harm will come to you. But it might improve your recollection a bit. May I?"

Jaryd hesitated, and then nodded. Baden smiled reassuringly and then, gently, he placed his middle three fingers on Jaryd's forehead. After a few seconds, the Mage-Attend's vision of the room melted into blackness to be replaced a moment later by a new setting.

Suddenly, Jaryd was no longer in Cullen and Gayna's home. Rather, he was back in the Seaside Mountains, watching once more as the strange mage advanced on him. Every detail seemed clearer this time. The mage's staff looked unnaturally smooth, and the stone at its top was the color of blood. The man's bird—and yes, it was definitely a man—was tremendous, larger even than Jaryd remembered, and black as the night sky. Its eyes were golden; not yellow, like Anla's, but actually golden. And they were alien in some way—indeed, the bird itself seemed peculiar, although Jaryd still could not put into words exactly what made it so. But the feather that the mage carried was just as Jaryd recalled; it was the same feather Leyton had showed Baden that afternoon. And once again, Jaryd watched as it burst into flame.

Then it was over, and Jaryd sat at the dining table once more. Baden had withdrawn his hand from Jaryd's brow, and Cullen and Gayna sat perfectly still, their expressions unreadable. Jaryd blinked his eyes as his vision cleared, and then he turned toward the Owl-Master. "I saw him again!" he said with some excitement. "He had on a green cloak, and he carried a staff just like—" He stopped, sobered by what he read in Baden's eyes. "It didn't help very much, did it?"

Baden tried to smile. "It helped a bit," he offered, but his tone said otherwise.

"But not as much as you had hoped."

"No," Baden admitted.

Jaryd sighed. "I'm sorry."

The four of them sat in silence for some time. "Why don't we return to the front room," Gayna finally said, "and I'll fix some tea before we go to sleep." The men agreed and rose from the table. When they reached the front room, however, they heard a voice calling from outside the house, and, looking toward the window, they saw through the translucent curtains the light of many torches. Baden held up a hand, silencing Jaryd, Cullen, and Gayna. And as they listened, they heard someone calling in a singsong voice, *"Owl-Master! Owl-Master!"*

The mage looked toward Cullen, a question in his blue eyes.

"Leyton, I'd guess," the grey-haired man said grimly. "And his friends."

Baden raised an eyebrow.

"Despite what you saw today, Baden, he's bright and persuasive, and he's popular with the younger townsfolk. Don't underestimate him or his influence."

The mage nodded slowly, seeming to consider what Cullen had said. He took a deep breath. "Well, I suppose I should see what he wants."

Baden lifted his arm for Anla, who flew to him from her perch near the hearth. Then the mage opened the door and stepped out into the night. Jaryd followed him onto the front steps, as did Cullen and Gayna. A small group of people, perhaps thirty, stood in front of the house, most of them men, nearly all of them holding torches or weapons. At the head of the pack stood Leyton, brandishing a cudgel in one hand and his knife in the other. He had not yet cleaned himself or changed his clothes, and the wound on his arm still looked untreated. When Leyton spoke, Jaryd realized with alarm that the man had been drinking.

"Owl-Master!" he said with mock courtesy, an invidious grin on his face. "So nice to see you again."

"What do you want, Leyton?" Baden demanded icily.

"Isn't it enough to just want to chat?" the man asked, his arms open in supplication. Then his voice dipped lower and grew more menacing. "We never had a chance to finish our conversation this afternoon."

The mage raised his eyebrows, feigning surprise. "Oh? I was under the impression that it had ended quite satisfactorily."

"Well, my friends and I disagree." All pretense of deference had vanished from Leyton's tone, leaving only the anger and malice that Jaryd remembered from earlier. "You see, we still don't believe your denials of responsibility for the fire. And we don't want you in our town any longer."

"So, you've come to make me leave?" The tone of Baden's voice as he asked the question was a match for Leyton's blade. "How do you plan to do that?"

Leyton's eyes flicked nervously to Jaryd, and then to Cullen and Gayna. "Maybe if you had no place to stay," he said, not quite as sure of himself as he had seemed a moment before, "if something were to happen to the home of your friends . . ." He trailed off, allowing the naked threat to hang in the air between them.

A low rumbling of dissent swept through the mob standing behind the man. "But, Leyton," a voice called out, "you told us that no harm would come to Gayna and Cullen."

"Only the mage, you said," another man added. "Only the mage." Others nodded in agreement.

Leyton whirled on his companions. "Fools!" he spat. "This mage burned our town and you want to spare the traitors who house him!" Jaryd saw vacillation in the eyes of Leyton's companions. "Cowards!" Leyton growled in frustration. "Idiots!" The man spun back to face Baden, his eyes raw with rage and loss.

"Go home, Leyton," the mage commanded. "It's late, and this is not a battle you can win."

"I'll fight you, Mage!" he shouted. "I'll fight you here and now!"

Baden shook his head. "But I won't fight you," he said evenly. "I swore an oath when first I donned this cloak that I would serve the people of Tobyn-Ser. I won't break that vow for you. But you shouldn't doubt—none of you should doubt," he added, raising his voice to reach Leyton's companions, "—that I will protect this house and these people with all my strength. Do any of you believe that you're a match for my power?"

He stared out at the crowd, and none of those present met his glance. He turned his eyes to Leyton, who looked up at him defiantly for but a moment, before looking down at the useless weapons he carried.

Many in the crowd began slowly to move away from the house and back toward the town center. Baden turned and motioned for his friends to reenter the house.

But in that moment, Leyton dropped his cudgel, and, in one startlingly swift motion, grabbed a torch from the hand of the closest man and flung it toward the thatch roof of Cullen and Gayna's home. Jaryd tried to cry out a warning. But before the words left his mouth, he was blinded by a brilliant flash of orange light. When he opened his eyes again, he saw the burning splinters of what had been the torch scattered on the ground well short of the house. Baden had barely moved. Leyton lay prone on the ground, where he had been thrown by the force of the mage's blast. He climbed to his feet slowly, regarding the Owl-Master with awe, and more than a little fear.

"Go home, Leyton," Baden repeated, and, oddly, a note of kindness had crept into his voice. "Go in peace. My friend and I will be leaving tomorrow. And whether or not you believe me, I give you my word that we will find out who attacked your home. They will not go unpunished."

Leyton eyed the mage silently for what seemed to Jaryd a very long time. At last, the man nodded, almost imperceptibly, and turned to walk back into town.

Baden and Jaryd watched him retreat into the darkness before following Gayna and Cullen into the house.

Once inside, Baden turned to his hosts. "I'm sorry if we've placed you and your home in jeopardy. That certainly wasn't my intention."

Cullen shook his head. "You've done nothing wrong, Baden. Gayna and I know you didn't set the fires. So all you've done is heal the wounds of our injured and put a bit of fear into some young men who probably needed it. Besides, I don't think we'll have any more trouble from Leyton. Our influence in this community is considerable; most harbor no ill will toward us. And Leyton will do nothing on his own."

"You're probably right," the mage agreed. "Nonetheless, Jaryd and I will be leaving at first light." He held up his hand to quiet his hosts' protests. "It's not just because of what happened tonight. Jaryd and I are a long way from Amarid and, after today's events, I'm more determined than ever to be there for the opening of the Gathering."

Baden and Cullen exchanged a long look, their expressions unreadable. At length, Cullen smiled and nodded. "You will at least allow us to give you food for your journey?"

The Owl-Master returned his friend's smile. "I was counting on it."

After a few more minutes of conversation, Gayna led the Owl-Master and Mage-Attend to a guest room in the rear portion of the house. Like the rest of Cullen and Gayna's home, the room was tidy and comfortable. There were two small beds, one on either side of the room, and a window between them that looked out onto the moonlit garden. Jaryd was exhausted. He wrapped himself in the warm blankets, enjoying the luxury of a real bed. He found, though, that his head was filled with thoughts of the day's events, and, for the second night in a row, he could not sleep. He lay silently in the darkness for a long time, wondering if Baden had fallen asleep. After some time, he heard a rustling of blankets across the room as the mage turned over, and he hazarded a question.

"Baden?"

"You should be sleeping," the mage said in a muffled voice.

"I can't sleep."

"So you thought you'd keep me up?"

Jaryd said nothing. At length, he heard Baden roll over again. "I'm having trouble sleeping, too. What's on your mind?"

Jaryd hesitated. "Who do you think attacked Taima?"

"You heard me tell Cullen that I didn't know."

"I heard you tell Cullen that you had a theory, but little more," Jaryd said, gaining confidence as he spoke. "I got the impression, though, that you have more than just a theory."

He heard the Owl-Master give a small laugh. "I see. And how is it that you've come to know me so well in so little time?"

"As I told you the day we met," Jaryd answered, smiling in the darkness, "you and my father are more similar than you might care to know."

"Ah, yes. I remember." After a long pause, Baden relented. "Yes, I've an idea of who attacked Taima and who has committed the other crimes attributed to the Order." He paused again, and, a moment later the candle sitting by the mage's bed jumped to life, revealing Baden sitting on the edge of the bed facing Jaryd, his features looking even leaner than usual in the flickering light. "I tried to figure out who, within the Order or outside of it, might wish to discredit the mages and masters of Tobyn-Ser," Baden explained, as if relieved to have someone with whom to share his musings. "I could think of a few within the Order who might be disgruntled. But none, I believe, would be bitter enough to do these things. And even if they were, there aren't enough of them to explain the number of attacks that have occurred across the land." As he spoke, Baden stared at the candle as if, Jaryd thought, he could see the key to this mystery within its dancing yellow flame. Jaryd kept utterly still, afraid that any movement might shatter the mood that had produced this rare moment of candor in his uncle.

"And then I thought of the one person," the mage continued, "the only person who would have both cause to subvert the Order, and the ability to do it." Baden looked suddenly toward Jaryd, pinning his Mage-Attend with the intensity of his gaze. "I haven't told anyone else of this, Jaryd, and, even when we reach the Gathering, I don't want you to repeat a word of this without my consent. Is that clear?"

Jaryd nodded, his heart racing with the excitement of the moment, and his elation at having been taken into the mage's confidence.

An instant later, however, when Baden spoke the name of the one he suspected, Jaryd's exhilaration evaporated, leaving a cold dread that settled like a stone in the pit of his stomach. Baden blew out his candle, and Jaryd lay huddled in his bed, staring wide-eyed into the darkness and wondering why he had asked the mage any questions in the first place.

Cullen woke them while it was still dark, opening the door to their room and allowing the light from a hallway lantern to spill across the floor. "It will be dawn soon," he told them. "We've fixed some breakfast for you when you're ready."

The mage and his apprentice rose and dressed quickly. Jaryd had slept poorly, but he was now as anxious as Baden to be moving again. When they entered the kitchen, they found Jaryd's pack filled with dried fruit, salted meat, cheese, dry breads, and two extra skins containing the dark wine they had enjoyed the previous night. Baden thanked Gayna and Cullen, and Jaryd did the same, after he secured from the mage a promise that they would take turns carrying the pack.

Jaryd and the Owl-Master ate a quick breakfast and said their farewells, setting off toward the Dhaalismin just as the sun appeared on the edge of the great Northern Plain. They reached the river by late morning and turned to follow it south toward the confluence of this, the main fork, and the north fork, which flowed out of the Seaside Mountains near the northern edge of Tobyn-Ser and snaked through the upper reaches of the plain. Coming to the junction of the two streams late the next day, they continued south, walking much of the way by moonlight, until they reached a stone footbridge that crossed the now-united waters of the Dhaalismin.

For the next several days they endured similarly long hikes, rising at dawn to recommence their journey and continuing by the bright, silver light of Duclea's moon well after the setting of the sun. As a result, they crossed the plain in relatively little time, entering Tobyn's Wood only a week after leaving Taima. They tried to maintain their pace as they moved through the wood, but found that the waning of the moon, the darkness shaped by the huge, densely growing trees, and the roughness of the forest path made night travel difficult. Still, the terrain being fairly level, they managed to cover a good amount of distance while there was light, and they emerged from the forest after less than a fortnight. During their journey across the plain and through Tobyn's Wood, they encountered few people and only a handful of large settlements. Those people they did meet regarded them warily, but with none of the manifest hostility they had found in Taima. At a small village on the eastern edge of the plain, Baden healed the broken leg of a farmer's plow horse, and he and Jaryd were rewarded with a night's lodging and a large pouch of dried meat. And, when they met a trader on the path through the wood, Jaryd, under the approving eye of the Owl-Master, exchanged his sleeping roll for some dried fruit, cheese, and dry breads. The merchant also offered several gold pieces for Royden's ring, but Jaryd politely refused.

Two of the villages they entered had no inns, and both times the villagers directed the travelers to the Temples of Arick. There, much to Jaryd's surprise, the Sons and Daughters of the Gods offered them food and shelter, and, equally surprising in Jaryd's mind, Baden accepted. In the days of Amarid, the Children of the Gods, those who devoted their lives to the worship of Arick, Duclea, Tobyn, and Leora, had viewed the creation of the Order with suspicion, seeing the mages and the council they formed as unwanted rivals for influence and status. And, though there had not been any overt conflict between the mages and the Keepers of Arick's Temples since the days of Theron's trial, the authority they shared in the land had been a recurring source of friction. When Jaryd asked Baden about this, after they had returned from a light dinner to their small room in the second of the sanctuaries, the Owl-Master merely shrugged.

"In large part, the tension between the Children of the Gods and the Order has flowed in one direction only," he explained. "The temples were here long before Amarid bound to Parne, and we mages have never seen ourselves as a replacement for Arick's servants. We accept their role in the land, and we have always hoped that they would come to accept ours. So whatever comfort they're willing to offer me as I travel through the land, I'm more than happy to accept."

Mostly, however, the Owl-Master and his Mage-Attend slept along the trail. With the food they received from Cullen and Gayna, the supplies they acquired along the way, and the game Anla killed for them, they had plenty to sustain themselves as they journeyed across Tobyn-Ser.

Jaryd felt himself growing stronger each day, and he found that, far from dreading the hikes, he came to look forward to them. On a number of occasions during these days, he also found himself laughing at the memory of the trepidation he had felt at the outset of their journey. It all seemed so long ago: those fears, his life in Accalia, the doubts about his decision to follow Baden. His misgivings had vanished long ago, leaving him with one essential truth: he was going to be a Hawk-Mage. Nothing else in the world seemed to matter as much as that.

The final leg of their journey carried them through the Parneshome Mountains. Once called the Northguard Range, the mountains had been renamed for Parne, Amarid's first hawk, who bound to the mage in a valley on the eastern slope of the range over a thousand years ago. As he and Baden began the ascent into the mountains, Jaryd grew quiet and contemplative, awed by the realization that he had entered Amarid's homeland. The ridges and valleys, he knew, had changed little since the time of the First Mage, and Jaryd made his way through the landscape wondering what Tobyn-Ser had been like before the Order and the Mage-Craft. Baden and Jaryd did not speak much during this final leg of their journey. The Owl-Master appeared preoccupied with concerns of his own, and both were content to walk in silence.

But several times during these final days of travel, as they rested along the trail during the day, or set up camp late in the afternoon, Jaryd would glance at Baden, only to find the mage watching him with a strange expression on his face, as if he were seeing Jaryd for the first time. In the waning light of their last day in the mountains, as they waited for Anla to return with the evening meal, Jaryd turned to Baden to ask a question, and saw the Owl-Master staring in his direction, but at something above and behind where he stood. Jaryd pivoted quickly in an attempt to catch a glimpse of what the mage was watching, but he found nothing. When he spun back around, Baden was looking at him again with the same appraising expression. Jaryd asked the mage what he had seen, but Baden deftly turned the conversation in another direction. A few weeks before, Jaryd might have pursued the matter. He had learned, though, that the mage seldom revealed what he wished to keep to himself and rarely withheld information without cause. Jaryd let it drop.

The following morning, as they prepared for the hike into Amarid, Jaryd felt himself growing giddy at the thought of what awaited them in the forest below. They were about to reach the home of the First Mage, where they would meet literally dozens of other mages and masters. Tomorrow, he would witness the commencement of the annual Gathering of the Order. As a child,

Jaryd had dreamt of such things, and on this morning, as Baden pulled out some fruit and breads for breakfast, Jaryd found that he was too excited to eat.

As he often did, Baden appeared to read his thoughts. "Jaryd," he began, in a serious tone that the Mage-Attend recognized, "there are a few things we need to discuss before we reach Amarid." The Owl-Master hesitated, as if unsure of how to proceed. "It may be because of who I am, of how I do things; or it may be because you are, in addition to everything else, my nephew, but our interaction is much less formal than that between most mages and their apprentices. Not that I feel you've acted inappropriately or been at all disrespectful," he amended hastily. "I'm just telling you that our relationship is a bit more . . . familiar than is expected. And so, once we reach Amarid, I'd like you to refer to me as Master Baden, and I expect you to address all the mages and masters you meet in the traditional manner."

Jaryd nodded. "Very well. Master Baden." The phrase felt awkward, and Jaryd knew it would take some getting used to.

"I also expect," the mage went on, biting into a dried pear and handing the pouch containing the fruit to Jaryd, "that you remember the conversation we had the night we stayed with Cullen and Gayna." Jaryd's mouth went dry. He remembered. Indeed, the memory of it had haunted his sleep for the past four weeks. "I want to reiterate," Baden was saying, "that I told you what I did in confidence. No one is to know who I suspect until I've had a chance to discuss the matter with some of my friends. Is that clear?"

Again, Jaryd nodded.

"Good." Baden smiled. "You must be very excited. To tell you the truth, I am as well. Even with the seriousness of what the Order faces right now, I find the Gatherings quite exhilarating. And there are several people down there who I'd like you to meet."

Jaryd said nothing. He handed the sack of fruit back to the mage without taking any, and Baden returned the pouch and some other items to Jaryd's pack. In a few minutes, they were on their way. Baden, walking in front, was unusually effusive. He pointed out landmarks along the way and spoke at length of some of the more eccentric mages Jaryd would soon meet.

Jaryd tried to act attentive, but the Owl-Master's mention of their conversation in Taima had shattered his earlier mood, replacing his excitement with a slow, creeping fear. He was going to the Gathering of the Order. But the Order was faced, Baden had told him that night, with a deadly foe; one more powerful than any mage alive, than any mage who had ever lived, save one. How does one defeat a legion of ghosts? Jaryd asked himself, as he had so many times over the past few weeks. How can we possibly defeat Theron and the Unsettled?

5

Long before they reached Amarid, they saw the great city from the mountain trail, a vast, gleaming expanse of white stone and slate-grey rooftops surrounded by the deep green of Hawksfind Wood and fringed on its southern extreme by the Larian River, which reflected the bright sunshine like a satin ribbon of emerald green. In the center of the metropolis, framed by five large thoroughfares that radiated from it toward the outer reaches of the town, and rising far above even the tallest of the white buildings, stood a huge oval structure, also made of white stone, but with a magnificent dome of pale-blue tile. Atop the dome stood a statue of a figure holding on its forearm a bird with its wings outstretched. The sculpture appeared to Jaryd to have been carved from glass, but it glistened with extraordinary brilliance in the sunlight and shimmered with a myriad of colors. Two smaller structures, both of them round with shimmering white spires, adjoined the oval building. Atop each of these towers stood a sculpture, also fashioned out of glass, of a bird.

"That is the Great Hall of Amarid," Baden explained in response to Jaryd's questions about the exquisite building. "The statue on top of the Gathering Chamber shows Amarid holding Parne, and the figures above the quarters of the Owl-Sage and her first represent Amarid's other two familiars, Beile and Wohl." Jaryd merely nodded in response, his eyes still riveted on the scene below. But when the mage added that all three had been carved from massive individual crystals brought back from Ceryllon, Jaryd swung his astonished gaze to Baden. The Owl-Master smiled in response. "I thought that might get your attention."

Jaryd shook his head in wonder and turned back toward Amarid. He had never imagined a city so large, and so beautiful. The lustrous white and austere grey of the buildings in the city created a visual effect that was, in its own way, as striking and powerful as even the most beautiful natural vistas Jaryd had seen during the journey across Tobyn-Ser. And the dazzling figure of Amarid on top of the Great Hall, to which Jaryd's eye was repeatedly drawn, seemed to hover above the city, offering a kind of protection or, perhaps, inspiration to all below.

Pulling his eyes once again from Amarid's statue, Jaryd noticed a small section of the city adjacent to the river that stood in stark contrast to the rest. Its buildings looked dark and run down, and its streets lacked any semblance of regularity.

"That is the old town commons," Baden explained, noticing the direction of Jaryd's gaze, "preserved just as it was in Amarid's day. And that," the mage went on, pointing to a patch of trees that stood incongruously amid the houses and businesses closest to the mountains, "is Amarid's home."

Jaryd looked at the mage once more. "You mean the house in which he grew up?" he asked.

Baden nodded, and again Jaryd shook his head. This was, indeed, the First Mage's city; already Jaryd could sense his presence in every nuance of its design. Even from above, he could see that no matter where one went in the great metropolis, there would be some reminder of the man for whom the city had been named.

They enjoyed the view for a few moments longer before beginning their descent from the mountains to Hawksfind Wood. With his first glimpse of the splendid city, the excitement that Jaryd had felt early that morning began to return. Thoughts of Theron faded from his mind, to be replaced by the anticipation of moving among mages, of actually witnessing a Gathering. He felt like a child on the eve of Tobyn's Feast.

"Baden?" he called impulsively to his uncle, as the two of them made their way around the glimmering, windswept waters of Dacia's Lake, named a thousand years ago for Amarid's wife.

"Yes?"

Jaryd hesitated momentarily, unsure of what he really wanted to say. "Thank you."

Baden stopped, turning to face the young mage. "What for?"

Jaryd shrugged, suddenly embarrassed. "I don't know. Everything, I guess. Taking me with you. Bringing me here." He shrugged again. "I don't know," he repeated.

A smile spread slowly across the Owl-Master's face, the kind, indulgent smile Jaryd remembered from so many years ago, when Baden had first visited Accalia. "You're welcome," he said simply. Then he turned once more and the two of them, Owl-Master and Mage-Attend, continued on toward the First Mage's city.

Early in the afternoon they reached the banks of the Larian River and crossed a worn wooden footbridge into what had been the town commons of Riverhaven, Amarid's home village. Like the bridge, the buildings in the old village were made from rough-hewn logs that were darkened and smoothed by a thousand years of rain, wind, and sun. Still, they looked solid and Jaryd was not at all surprised to see that the structures still housed shops and inns. Dozens of merchants and hundreds of other people crowded the dirt streets of the old commons, and, unlike the inhabitants of the villages they had visited during their journey, these people welcomed Baden with courtesy and enthusiasm. The traders offered the mage and his Mage-Attend breads, dried meats, and fresh fruit, and many people bowed to the Owl-Master or called out in formal greeting. Jaryd returned the nods and smiles directed toward him, stopping occasionally to accept a gift from a merchant. At one point, he noticed two young women, who watched him with smiling eyes and whispered to each other. Blushing, he looked away and hurried to catch up with Baden.

Jaryd found the Owl-Master speaking with Radomil, who served Accalia and the rest of Leora's Forest. Radomil stood nearly a foot shorter than the Owl-

Master, and, next to Baden's lean frame, the Hawk-Mage's round belly seemed to accentuate the height difference. His cleanly shaven head and thick brown goatee and mustache gave Radomil a severe look, but Jaryd knew better.

"Ah, here's Jaryd now," the Mage-Attend heard Baden say as he drew near.

"Greetings, Jaryd," Radomil said with a grin. "I'm glad to see that your uncle has finally brought you to a Gathering. Another year and I would have made you my Mage-Attend."

"That would have been my pleasure, Mage Radomil," Jaryd replied with sincerity.

The Hawk-Mage inclined his head slightly, acknowledging the comment. "I hope you enjoy the city and your first Gathering, Jaryd." He turned back to the Owl-Master. "Baden, it's good to see you again, even in these dark times. I hope we'll have the opportunity to catch up before the Gathering ends."

Baden smiled at the mage and placed a hand on his shoulder. "I hope so as well. Until tomorrow, Radomil."

"Until tomorrow," the Hawk-Mage returned. He nodded once to Jaryd, and then walked off toward a cluster of shops.

"He's a good man," Baden commented as he watched the mage move away. "Though few would admit it, many of us enter the Order hoping to attain influence or prestige. Almost everyone hopes to reach the level of Owl-Master, and I've seen several mages grow bitter when they fail to do so. But not Radomil. This is his third binding to a hawk, and he still serves the land with as much enthusiasm and care as he did after his first binding." He looked at Jaryd. "He wanted to bring you to last year's Gathering, to begin your training on an informal basis, but I told him of the bargain I had struck with your father."

Jaryd gazed after the Hawk-Mage. "He would have been a good teacher, too, I think."

Baden nodded.

"What part of Tobyn-Ser do you serve?" Jaryd asked, as they continued through the old commons. "I don't think you've ever told me."

"That's because I don't serve any particular area. There are two types of mages: we call them nesters and migrants. Nesters, like Radomil, serve a certain portion of the land. Migrants, like me and a few others, roam throughout Tobyn-Ser, offering our service where we find need."

Jaryd reflected on this for a moment. "Is that a choice you make yourself?"

"Yes," Baden answered, "and it's often a hard one."

Something in the Owl-Master's manner told Jaryd that his decision had been especially difficult. The Mage-Attend considered pursuing the issue, but then thought better of it.

"We'd best find lodging for the next few nights," the Owl-Master commented, changing the subject. "There's an innkeeper who usually sets aside a room for me, but he'll rent it to someone else if I keep him waiting for too long, and I don't usually need a room with two beds."

They quickened their pace somewhat and soon reached the limit of the older section of the city, stepping onto a wide cobblestone thoroughfare lined on both sides by homes and shops made of the immaculate white stone and grey slate roofing they had seen from the mountain trail. At the end of the avenue, just a few hundred yards away, loomed the lofty spires and huge dome of the Great Hall with their spectacular crystal statues. Jaryd halted, and stood staring at the structure for several moments, marveling once again at its splendor. Yet, standing in the shadow of the hall, Jaryd began to feel a strange sense of discomfort at what he saw—vague, nameless, but very real. He also noticed, as he examined the hall more closely, that the blue tiles of the dome were marked with small golden circles, each about the size of a large coin.

"What are those on the dome?" Jaryd asked.

"Ah!" Baden exclaimed. "Those just might be my favorite part of the Great Hall. They are small commemoratives that mark the acceptance into the Order of every mage ever to serve Tobyn-Ser. In the center of each one is the insignia of the Order, representing the three elements of the Mage-Craft—mage, bird, and ceryll—and along the outer edge is carved the mage's name and that of his or her first familiar."

"Do you have one up there?"

"Of course. As I said, there is one for every mage who has served Tobyn-Ser since the founding of the Order."

Jaryd shot the Owl-Master a sharp look. "Every member?" he asked pointedly.

Baden's expression sobered as he grasped the import of his Mage-Attend's question. "No," he conceded, "not every member. There is one missing."

And there it was again, the gnawing fear that seemed long ago to have settled in the back of Jaryd's mind—and Baden's too, Jaryd saw from the darkening of the Owl-Master's expression. Of course, Theron's name would not be included among those honored with the gold commemoratives. Not after his crime and his disgrace. Not after the curse. Standing in the magnificent city named for the First Mage, in the shadow of the crystal image crafted to honor his deeds, Jaryd began to sense the magnitude of the tragedy shaped by the two founders of the Mage-Craft. Together they harnessed and controlled the power; together they formed the Order. Yet, over the centuries, as one had been exalted, attaining near godlike status, the other, still haunting the land, the victim of a curse of his own making, had been reviled, his accomplishments ignored in Tobyn-Ser's history.

Jaryd turned to Baden, feeling an inexplicable anger rising in his chest. "Is there anywhere in this city, in this entire land," he demanded, unable to keep the exasperation from his tone, "where Theron is remembered and honored for what he did and what he was before the curse?"

Still looking at the statue of Amarid, his expression somber, Baden offered the only answer he could. "We in the Order remember, and we pass the story of Amarid and Theron on to those who follow, as I did to you."

"That's not really what I was asking," Jaryd retorted, his tone harsher than he had intended. He closed his eyes and took a deep breath. "I'm sorry," he added.

Baden looked at him and tried to smile. "It is a difficult tale, made more difficult by the difference between their fates." He indicated the dome and statue with his hand.

Jaryd merely nodded, but a voice from behind him put into words the thought in his head. "Perhaps that difference lies at the root of the danger we face today."

Baden and Jaryd turned around simultaneously to see who had spoken. Standing just behind them was a dark-skinned man with long black hair that fell to his shoulders, and vivid green eyes that almost matched the hue of his mage's cloak. He was of medium height and build, and he carried on his shoulder an exquisite hawk of deep brown, with warm, chestnut-colored wings and a white tail boldly marked with black.

"Trahn!" Baden exclaimed, grabbing the man in an embrace so fierce that both Anla and the Hawk-Mage's bird took to the air to avoid injury. Trahn returned the embrace, obviously as pleased as Baden by their reunion. At length, Baden stepped back, a broad grin lighting his thin face and bright blue eyes. "By the gods, it's good to see you. You're well, I trust?"

Trahn smiled and nodded. "Yes, thank you. You also are looking well, although every time I see you, you have less hair." As Baden laughed, Trahn turned toward Jaryd and bestowed upon him a dazzling smile. "You must be Jaryd. Baden has told me much about you. I'm Trahn."

"Mage Trahn, I am honored by this meeting," Jaryd said, bowing as Baden had taught him.

Trahn glanced at the Owl-Master. "My, but he's well trained." He turned back to Jaryd, still smiling. "I appreciate the effort," he said, "but formalities are wasted on me. Just call me Trahn."

Jaryd glanced at Baden uncertainly.

"I'm afraid we're confusing him," the Owl-Master commented ruefully. "Just this morning I warned him about addressing mages too informally, including me."

"I see," Trahn said, nodding sagely. "Well, far be it from me to undermine your uncle's authority. At least in private you can drop the decorum." He looked questioningly toward Baden, who nodded in approval. "I took the liberty of holding a room at the inn for the two of you," Trahn continued. "Maimun has raised his rates again, but he's still managed to fill every room. And you know how he feels about giving up cash to accommodate us."

Jaryd looked from one mage to the other. "I don't understand."

"Mages don't normally carry gold or silver," Trahn explained. "The leaders of the Order decided long ago that the temptation to use our powers to acquire wealth would be so great that members of the Order should be barred from using specie under any circumstance."

"The rest of the Order balked at making this legally binding," Baden added, "so, instead, they merely established it as a custom. Mages carry little or no coinage, and merchants and innkeepers accept our services and aid as recompense for their goods."

"Occasionally, though," Trahn broke in with a smile, "men like Maimun chafe at this . . . custom."

"He seemed pleased enough with it two years ago when we healed his cuts and mended his wooden tables after that brawl in his place," Baden growled. "One would think he'd be more grateful."

Trahn shrugged noncommittally, a slight smile still lingering on his lips. He glanced at Jaryd. "Baden doesn't care very much for Maimun," he informed the Mage-Attend in a confidential tone. "The innkeeper once beat him at ren-drah, taking what little money your uncle was carrying at the time."

"He did not beat me," Baden said angrily. "He cheated. Nobody could be that lucky. I just couldn't prove it."

Jaryd tried unsuccessfully to suppress a laugh, and Trahn was now grinning broadly. Baden blushed, and then he, too, began to laugh. "You're a bad influence on him, Trahn. As you noted before, I had him well trained."

"Not well enough, it would seem," the Hawk-Mage returned.

Baden shook his head slowly. "It's going to be a long Gathering. I can tell already."

"In that respect, I hope you're wrong," Trahn commented, his mood instantly turning serious.

Baden nodded in agreement, his expression growing grave as well. "We have much to discuss. But first, I should go to the hall and present Jaryd to Jessamyn."

"Shall we meet at the Aerie for supper?" Trahn asked.

"Yes, we'll see you there."

Trahn gripped Baden's shoulder. "I'm glad to see you," he said warmly. "And you, Jaryd," he added, smiling at the Mage-Attend. The dark man walked off toward the old town center, and Jaryd and Baden began moving toward the Great Hall.

"Who is Jessamyn?" Jaryd asked.

"Owl-Sage Jessamyn is the leader of the Order," Baden answered distractedly. "She's also an old and dear friend." The Owl-Master's face still wore a somber expression, but an instant later, he pulled himself out of his thoughts. "So, what do you think of Trahn?"

"I like him very much."

"He is as close a friend as I have in this land. I'd trust him with my life. And yours," Baden added after a moment, "which may say even more."

Jaryd said nothing, but he thought back to the words he had heard his father say to Baden just before he and the Owl-Master left Accalia so many weeks ago. *For all that he is, and all that you say he will be, he is still our youngest. . . .*

They walked in silence for a few strides, and then Jaryd observed, "The people here seem much less hostile than they did in Taima and the other towns we visited along the way."

"Yes," Baden agreed, "the people of Amarid still honor the Order. Indeed, many of the people you see journeyed here just to observe the Gathering. Actually," he went on, a now familiar note of concern creeping back into his voice, "this is the smallest number of people I've ever seen in Amarid at the time of a Gathering. The attacks are taking a toll."

They reached the entrance to the Great Hall, and, once more, Jaryd found himself awed by the majesty of the structure. Three long marble steps led to an arched portal that reached nearly to the bottom edge of the dome. Framing the opening, swung open to welcome those who sought entrance, stood two tremendous wooden doors, each over two inches thick. Both doors were inlaid with thousands of pieces of wood, each of which possessed a unique shade of brown, red, or grey. These inlays were arranged to portray dozens of different hawks and owls, every species, Jaryd knew instinctively, that could be found in Tobyn-Ser. At the edge of each door, halfway between top and bottom, appeared half of the Order's insignia, fashioned so as to make the image whole when the doors were closed.

"Spectacular, isn't it?" Baden commented, somewhat unnecessarily. "The inlays include samples from every variety of tree found in Tobyn-Ser. Follow me," he commanded, ascending the steps and entering the building.

Given the resplendent beauty of the outside of the Great Hall, Jaryd was surprised by the austere decor he found inside. In the center of the chamber, resting on a plain marble floor, sat an immense oval table made of dark wood. Large chairs made from the same wood surrounded the table, and two slightly more ornate chairs stood at the far end. A narrow strip of wood, ending in a horizontal bar obviously intended as a perch for a mage's familiar, curved up and away from the back of each chair. Milky-white translucent windows wound around the entire circumference, allowing a surprising amount of light into the chamber. But, like the floor, table, and chairs, the windows were plain. In fact, the only ornate aspect of the building's interior was a tableau painted on the domed roof depicting Amarid, looking somewhat frail and remarkably young, standing in a snowy clearing with his arm held aloft. Descending to his arm, with its wings spread and its mouth open as if crying out, was a robust, fierce-looking hawk with a pale grey belly and breast, and slate-grey wings and back.

"It's the scene from the statue," Jaryd remarked aloud, more to himself than to Baden.

"Yes," the Owl-Master affirmed. "Amarid's binding to Parne." They stood in silence for several moments, staring up at the painted scene. And Jaryd felt once again the vague uneasiness he had sensed on the street as he had gazed at the Great Hall, stronger now, but still undefinable. He tried to assign a name to the inchoate emotions stirred by the huge portrait of Amarid, but could not. When Baden told him to follow, adding, "There's something else I want to show you before you meet Jessamyn," Jaryd reluctantly tore his eyes from the image and followed the Owl-Master to the far end of the room.

There, between two austere wooden doors, one closed and the other slightly ajar, resting in a heavy wooden stand, sat an immense crystal, too massive for Jaryd to have encircled with his arms. It was irregularly shaped but flawlessly clear. Jaryd knew that it was a ceryll, but, unlike the others he had seen, this one appeared quiescent, giving off neither light nor color.

"The Summoning Stone," Baden said, his voice deepening, "altered by Amarid himself so that when it is awakened, it pulses with a rhythm that is conveyed to every other ceryll in Tobyn-Ser. This allows the Owl-Sage or her first to summon all other members of the Order to this chamber at times other than the Midsummer Gathering. In essence, the stone was a gift from Amarid, not only to the Order, but to all of Tobyn-Ser. With it, we can respond quickly to any crisis that threatens the land."

"Is it used often?" Jaryd asked.

"Thankfully no, only when there is great need. I believe the last time was when Feargus died, and the Owl-Masters were convened to choose a new sage." Baden smiled and gestured toward the door next to where they stood. "And now you can meet the person we chose."

The Owl-Master knocked on the door, and, at the sound of the welcoming call from within, swung the door open and led Jaryd inside. The Owl-Sage's quarters, like the Gathering Chamber, were modest compared with the external grandeur of the Great Hall. Spacious, round, and brightly lit by the same translucent windows found in the chamber, the room had an expansive marble fireplace, a polished wood floor partially covered by a multicolored woven rug, and, along the circular wall, three large tapestries, which, Jaryd guessed, depicted scenes from Amarid's life. One portion of the chamber, the sleeping quarters, Jaryd surmised again, was shielded from view by a curtain that matched the rug in pattern and color. Opposite this curtain, next to the hearth, sat a low table of light-grained wood and several ample, comfortable-looking chairs covered with pale blue and green material that picked up hues found in the wall hangings.

The two people seated in these chairs rose as Baden and Jaryd entered the room, and one of them, obviously Jessamyn, moved to greet them. The Owl-Sage was a diminutive, white-haired woman with delicate features and warm brown eyes. When she was young, Jaryd thought to himself, she must have been beautiful. Indeed, even with the deep lines etched in her tanned face, she still was. Jaryd noted with some surprise that, despite her position as leader of the Order, she wore a mage's cloak just like Baden's, unadorned by any emblem of authority. As she stood, a white owl, so big that it seemed to dwarf her, flew to the woman's shoulder and regarded her new visitors with bright yellow eyes.

"Baden!" she exclaimed in a clear voice, extending her hand as she stepped toward him.

"Sage Jessamyn," Baden returned, taking her hand and bending to touch his forehead to the back of it. Then he straightened and released her hand. "I am honored by your welcome."

"The honor is mine," she replied. "Your journey here was pleasant, I trust?"

Baden hesitated for just an instant. Two months ago, Jaryd might not even have caught it. But Jessamyn was who she was, and she and Baden had known each other for many years. The smile with which she had welcomed them faded and the soft lines of her face seemed to harden. "I would wait until tomorrow to hear these tidings, if that suits you," she said, holding his gaze. "This is a day for greetings and reunions."

Baden nodded. "I agree. I've brought someone I'd like to present to you. This is Jaryd, my Mage-Attend."

Jaryd stepped forward. "Sage Jessamyn, I am honored by this meeting," he offered formally. He even copied Baden's gesture when Jessamyn extended her hand.

The Owl-Sage's smile returned, and she spoke to Jaryd with a simplicity and directness that he found disarming. "Be welcome, Jaryd. I hope that you'll treasure your first Gathering. No other will be as special or as memorable for you."

The other person in the room had remained in the background, waiting quietly as Jessamyn greeted her guests. Now he stepped forward to meet Jaryd and welcome Baden. He was a tall man with pale grey eyes that looked out from beneath a thick shock of raven black hair peppered with silver. He had a handsome, weathered face, and he grinned broadly as he embraced Baden in greeting.

"You're looking well, Baden. It's good to see you again."

"And you, Sartol."

The tall mage turned to Jaryd, still grinning. "Jaryd, it's an honor to meet you. Welcome to Amarid."

"Thank you, Owl-Master. The honor is mine."

Sartol swung his gaze toward the Owl-Sage and bowed slightly. "Thank you for receiving me, Sage Jessamyn. I should be on my way."

Jessamyn smiled up at the man. "You're always welcome here, Sartol. I look forward to seeing you again tomorrow."

Sartol raised his arm and Jaryd saw a large, dark form drop to it from an unseen perch. The mage's owl was similar in size to Jessamyn's, but it was heavily barred with brown and grey, and had prominent tufts on its head above its large, impassive yellow eyes. With a nod and smile to Baden, Sartol departed, leaving Jaryd and his uncle alone with the Owl-Sage.

Baden glanced after the tall man as he left and then cast a knowing look toward Jessamyn. "A bit of pre-Gathering wheedling?" he asked.

Jessamyn shook her head in disapproval. "Now, Baden, that's not fair. He's a decent man. We shouldn't judge him just because he tries a bit too hard sometimes. It's understandable after all he went through."

"You're right, of course." He stepped forward and embraced the Owl-Sage and then stepped back slightly, leaving his hands on her shoulders. It appeared to Jaryd that the Owl-Master was nearly twice her size. "How are you, Jessamyn?" Baden inquired with a mix of kindness and concern.

"As well as can be expected in these times," she replied, with no hint of self-pity in her tone. "I fear there are dark days ahead, and I curse myself for being old and weak." She gestured toward the chairs by the hearth. "Please sit," she said. She picked up a small crystal bell that sat on the table and rang it once. A moment later a young woman, no older than fifteen or sixteen, entered the chamber. "More tea, please, Basya." The girl bowed and left the room.

"We don't think of you as old," Baden said with a smile, "we value your experience and wisdom."

Jessamyn arched an eyebrow. "Now who's doing the wheedling?" she remarked dryly, evoking a laugh from the Owl-Master. She shifted in her chair to face Jaryd. "If those are the types of compliments he's giving out today, I'll speak with you, Jaryd. Where do you come from?"

"Northwestern Tobyn-Ser, Sage Jessamyn. A village named Accalia, in Leora's Forest."

"Yes, I've heard of it. In fact," she went on, looking at Baden, "isn't that where—" She stopped herself, a smile spreading over her face, and then she turned back to Jaryd, her brown eyes dancing. "Of course. There's even a slight family resemblance. Not as much to you, Baden, as to Lynwen. Particularly around the eyes. Your family has a long and distinguished history in the Order, Jaryd. You should be very proud."

"Thank you, Sage Jessamyn," Jaryd said, even as he remarked to himself with irony that she probably knew more of that history than he did.

The young servant returned with a crystal platter that held three cups of tea and a small teapot, and, as they sipped the sweet herbal drink, Baden and Jessamyn exchanged news about themselves and various members of the Order. At length, they stopped speaking, sharing a silent look that appeared to communicate a great deal.

"It all seemed much easier when we were young," Jessamyn said at last, a smile on her lips but concern in her eyes. "Or am I just fooling myself?"

"It did seem easier," Baden agreed, a wan smile on his thin face, "but not because we were younger. The Order hasn't faced anything like this in a thousand years. You and I are just lucky enough to see it," he concluded, his tone thick with sarcasm. He glanced at Jaryd. "But we should take heart, Jessamyn. We don't face this challenge alone. There are young mages to fight beside us, and others, like Jaryd here, ready to take up the battle should we fail."

Baden rose, as if preparing to depart, and Jaryd did the same.

Jessamyn looked with kindness at the Mage-Attend. "I'm sorry to be such gloomy company, Jaryd. I hope that we'll have a chance to speak on other, happier occasions."

"I'd like that as well, Sage Jessamyn. I've enjoyed meeting you." Jaryd paused. Then, not sure why he did so, he added, "I would repeat what Master Baden said before: even though I'm not yet a member of the Order, I recognize the value of your wisdom. You don't seem old to me, and I'd gladly follow you into whatever battle may be coming." As soon as he finished speaking, he flushed at the realization of what he had said, and could not meet the Owl-Sage's warm gaze.

But Jessamyn stood and embraced him. "Bravely said," she whispered. "I see now why Baden has chosen you, and it's not just kinship." She released her embrace and turned to Baden. "I'm glad you're here, Baden. I can't imagine a Gathering without you."

"Did you really doubt that I'd come?" Baden asked softly.

"Not really. But I know that sometimes things come up." She reached out and squeezed Baden's hand. "I'm glad you're here," she repeated.

Baden and Jessamyn stood together for a moment longer, and then, almost reluctantly, it seemed, the sage let go of his hand. "Well," the Owl-Master sighed, "we should be on our way. Until tomorrow, Jessamyn."

"Until tomorrow. Farewell, Jaryd."

Baden and his nephew stepped out of the Owl-Sage's quarters and nearly collided with a stocky, muscular mage who had a close-cropped beard and long yellow hair that he wore tied back. He carried on his shoulder an impressive pale hawk with a rust-colored back and intelligent eyes. The mage scowled as he stopped short and almost said something. But, recognizing Baden, he controlled himself with a visible effort.

"Baden," he said gruffly, "pardon my haste. I'm anxious to see the Owl-

Sage." His dark eyes flicked once toward Jaryd and seemed to dismiss him.

"It's quite all right, Orris," Baden answered politely. "I'm pleased to see you again."

"As am I," Orris replied with a nod. He glanced a second time toward Jaryd with the same expression of indifference, and then turned to knock on Jessamyn's door.

Jaryd cast a questioning look toward Baden, who responded with a slight shrug before gesturing that they should leave. Once outside, Baden began to lead them deeper into the main section of the city. "What was that all about?" Jaryd asked as they walked along another of the bustling cobblestone avenues.

"You mean Orris?" Baden replied. He shrugged again. "I'm not certain. Orris is one of the leaders of a small faction of mages, mostly young men, who believe that the Order has grown complacent, that it lacks a guiding purpose. I believe that he sees me, and other older members of the Order, as impediments to change."

"Are you?"

Baden looked sharply at his Mage-Attend and, for a moment, Jaryd thought that he had angered the Owl-Master. But Baden's response when it came was reflective and mildly stated. "I can understand how some might see me in that light. It's funny, actually: as a young man I counted myself among the more radical mages. I saw every act of injustice in Tobyn-Ser as an affront against the Order and advocated a far greater role for its members in the governance of the land. But as I've grown older, I've come to see the wisdom in the path chosen for us by Amarid. We serve the land because our powers can be potent tools against hardship. But I don't believe that mastering the Mage-Craft qualifies us to rule Tobyn-Ser."

"So," Jaryd ventured, "Orris's position is similar to that offered by Theron."

Baden stopped and faced his nephew. "You must be very careful in how you use Theron's name, Jaryd," he insisted sternly, although without anger. "To compare a mage's words to those of Theron is to accuse that mage of violating Amarid's Laws."

"That's not how I meant it."

"I know, but you need to watch yourself, especially here."

Jaryd nodded, and they began to walk again.

"Still," Baden went on in a more subdued tone, "there is some truth in what you say. The issues that divided Theron and Amarid remain at the core of today's disagreements. The bitterness has subsided; our debate doesn't threaten to sunder the Order, as it did then. And I certainly don't believe that Orris and his allies share Theron's arrogance or wish to extract service from the people of the land. But the Order is still trying to define its role and position in Tobyn-Ser. As arbiters of disputes and protectors of the land, we walk a fine line between serving the land and leading it. Like many of the older mages, I prefer to err on one side of that line; Orris would prefer to walk on the other." Baden stopped again to scrutinize a small alley on the left side of the thoroughfare. "I think this is it," he said, following the passageway between two buildings.

With the late-afternoon sun beginning to slant across Amarid's rooftops, the alley was shaded and cool. It led them past two rows of buildings before opening onto a small stone courtyard edged with badly neglected gardening plots and littered with old fragments of broken glass. The air in the courtyard smelled of stale ale and urine, and at the far end of the atrium stood a begrimed building that might once have been white. A weather-stained piece of wood covered part of the front window, where a pane of glass should have been, and a faded sign hanging over the doorway read: "AERIE—Inn & Tavern." Baden approached the building, stopping before it to admire the sign with a grin on his face.

"I feel like I've come home," he commented wistfully.

"This is where we're staying?" Jaryd demanded incredulously.

"Yes," Baden said with enthusiasm. "Oh, I know that it looks a bit run-down—"

"A *bit* run-down!"

"Look," the Owl-Master retorted, his patience waning, "the rooms are clean and the food is the best in the city. So unless you care to sleep in the forest for another night, I'd suggest you give it a chance."

"Yes, Baden," Jaryd responded with resignation. After a reproachful look from the Owl-Master, he amended, "Master Baden."

Inside, the Aerie was not quite as seedy as it appeared from the courtyard. Not quite. The odor, at least, remained outside, replaced within the tavern by a blend of pipe smoke, the aroma of roasting meat, and the slightly musty smell of wine. The inn was dimly lit by the daylight filtering through its dirty windows, and by a number of candles suspended high above the dusty hardwood floor on a ponderous wooden chandelier. A few patrons, scattered throughout the room, sat at small round tables drinking ale or wine, but most of the chairs were empty. A long oaken bar stood at the far end of the tavern, and behind it stood a hulking man with curly brown hair, a thick, drooping mustache, and dark eyes set deep beneath his jutting brow. His sleeves were rolled up almost to his shoulder, revealing massive, hairy arms, and he wore a dark apron around his waist. Two serving women, both of them dressed in low-cut white blouses and long brown skirts, stood speaking in low tones with the barkeep, who dwarfed them both.

Noticing Jaryd and Baden standing near the door, the large man bellowed, "Owl-Master!" and stepped out from behind the bar to greet them.

"Hello, Maimun," Baden said with somewhat less enthusiasm than the tavern-keeper had shown.

"Master Baden!" Maimun gushed, undeterred by the Owl-Master's tone, "I am so very pleased to see you again. You're looking well. Mage Trahn was in earlier and, as I told him, I have your room all set aside for you. And who is this?" he went on, noticing Jaryd.

"That is Jaryd, my Mage-Attend."

"Pleased to make your acquaintance, Jaryd. Any friend of the Owl-Master's is welcome here." Maimun turned his attention back to Baden, placing a bear-sized arm across the Owl-Master's shoulders, leading him to a table by a corner window, and talking the entire time about the state of the tavern business, the excessive ale and wine taxes levied by the city elders, and the year-by-year degeneration of the quality of his clientele. "Excluding you and Mage Trahn, of course, Master Baden. Members of the Order are always welcome here."

"Of course we are, Maimun," Baden commented in the same bland tone.

The innkeeper hurried off to check on the progress of dinner, assuring them as he walked away that a serving woman would tend to them shortly. A few moments later, one of the barmaids to whom Maimun had been speaking, an attractive, petite woman who looked to be about Jaryd's age, came to their table bearing two tankards of a dark, sweet ale.

"Supper will be ready in another half-hour," she told them, eyeing Jaryd as she spoke. "Do you want some biscuits and butter in the meantime?"

"That would be fine," Baden said, suppressing a smirk. When the woman walked away, Baden gave Jaryd a look that made the Mage-Attend flush deeply. "Perhaps I won't need that second bed in the room after all," the Owl-Master commented. "Just remember that the opening procession begins an hour after sunrise."

His face still red, Jaryd tried to act disinterested. "She's not really my type," he said in an offhand way.

"Oh? You appear to be hers."

She returned carrying a basket of assorted breads, a plate of butter, and some silverware and cloth napkins. "I'll bring your supper when it's ready." She looked at Jaryd, who held her glance for an instant before averting his eyes toward the window. "If you need anything, just ask for Kayle."

"Thank you, Kayle," Baden called after her. He looked back toward Jaryd, another quip on his lips, but, at that moment, Trahn, carrying a tankard of ale and shouting something over his shoulder to Maimun, joined them at the table. He sat down shaking his head, a grin on his dark face.

"For someone who knows we carry no money," the Hawk-Mage observed wryly, "Maimun certainly spends an inordinate amount of time fawning over us."

Baden grunted in agreement.

"How was your visit with Jessamyn?" Trahn asked.

"Fine," Baden said simply. "Uneventful. We avoided any discussion of . . . recent events. She looked a bit tired, a bit worn."

"Well, she's been receiving a constant stream of visitors for two days now. I would imagine she's exhausted."

Baden nodded in agreement. "Actually, Sartol was there when we arrived, and we met Orris on his way in as we left. Jaryd was struck by Orris's congenial manner," the Owl-Master added, his tone laden with irony.

"He's the first rude mage I've met," Jaryd chimed in.

Trahn laughed. "I actually like him, although I can certainly see where he might come off as abrupt."

"That," Jaryd commented, "is an understatement."

"Perhaps," Trahn acknowledged, still laughing, "but I do believe that some of what he has to say about the Order merits notice. And he does have a significant following among the younger mages." Jaryd considered this for a moment as the three of them sipped their ale. Then Trahn inquired about their encounter with Sartol.

Baden shrugged. "There was very little to it. He was friendly."

"Oh, Sartol is always friendly," Trahn remarked, laughing again.

Jaryd looked at Baden. "You said something similar about Sartol to Jessa-myn."

Trahn's green eyes widened. "You did?"

"Yes," Baden admitted. "And she chastised me for it."

"What did you say?"

"I don't remember exactly. I guess I referred to him as a wheedler."

Trahn snorted, suppressing a laugh. "That sounds about right to me."

"Why?" Jaryd asked. "He seemed nice enough."

Baden gave Trahn a reproachful look before turning to Jaryd. "You're right," he began. "And so was Jessamyn this afternoon. Sartol is a decent man, and he's perfectly harmless. He just has a tendency to be a bit too studied in his politeness. He can be overly solicitous at times."

"You're being more generous than I would be," Trahn broke in. "I don't trust him. I just think he's currying favor with all of us so that, when the time comes, we'll make him Owl-Sage."

"Maybe," Baden countered, "but where's the harm in that?"

"I guess that's a good point," Trahn conceded. "I just don't like him very much."

"Jessamyn mentioned something about how it's understandable that Sartol is like this given what he went through," Jaryd reminded Baden. "What did she mean?"

"Soon after Sartol received his cloak," Baden explained, running a hand through his thinning hair, "he returned to his home in northern Tobyn-Ser. There, he began to extract payment from the people in return for his services, a violation of Amarid's Law. He was reprimanded by the Order and prohibited from wearing his cloak for a year. To his credit, he accepted the reprimand and his punishment, repaid all that he had taken, and continued to serve that same area, which seemed to me quite courageous. Since then he's become one of the most influential mages in the Order; many of us thought that he'd become Owl-Sage after Feargus died. But instead, the Owl-Masters chose Jessamyn, who was the senior member of the Order."

"Who did you vote for?" Jaryd asked.

Baden smiled enigmatically. "None of your business." After a brief silence, the Owl-Master continued his tale. "Though no one admitted that the vote for Jessamyn was intended as a rebuke to Sartol, there was an underlying sense at the time that the vote represented one final slap on the wrist. Most of us expect that Sartol will be the next Owl-Sage, but, in the meantime, Sartol isn't taking any chances."

"Did you know him when he was reprimanded?" Trahn asked.

Baden nodded. "Yes, although not very well. I had been attending the Gatherings for a number of years with my grandmother and mother, and I was in the early months of my apprenticeship with Lynwen. Sartol and I had met; I think we had even spoken briefly a few times. But that was all." He paused, staring blankly at the empty tankard he held in his large hands. "Sartol was proud in those days, to the point of arrogance. Yet even then, he had a charm that made him a leader among the youngest members of the Order."

Again, silence descended upon their table, broken this time by the arrival of dinner and a second round of the dark brew, called Amari Ale, that was served here in the First Mage's city. Baden had said that the Aerie served the finest food in Amarid, and Jaryd now learned just how fine that was. Dinner consisted of a rich, spicy stew, somewhat similar to his mother's, but made with fowl rather than beef and flavored with an aromatic herb that he did not recognize. It was, Jaryd had to admit to himself, as delicious a meal as he had ever tasted.

"What did you think of the Great Hall?" Trahn asked him as they ate.

Jaryd hesitated, recalling the uneasiness he had felt on the thoroughfare outside the hall, and again in the Gathering Chamber. "It's very beautiful," Jaryd said with uncertainty, "particularly the crystal statues."

Trahn narrowed his eyes. "But?"

"I'm not sure how to put it. I guess it made me feel . . . uncomfortable."

Trahn cast what seemed to be a look of satisfaction toward Baden before turning back to Jaryd. "Go on."

Jaryd shook his head. "As I said, I'm not certain that I can put it into words. It's just—well, Amarid was a man. Yes, he was the First Mage, but he was just a man. That hall has the feel of one of Arick's Temples, but on a much larger scale. It just seems . . . inappropriate."

Trahn turned again to Baden, smiling triumphantly. Baden shook his head thoughtfully. "Trahn has been telling me much the same thing for years now," he said. "I don't really see it that way, but I respect both of your opinions."

"I think what bothered me the most," Jaryd ventured, "relates to something we discussed earlier today. There's just far too much distance between this reverence for Amarid and the omission of Theron from all aspects of the Order's traditions, even from its monuments. Amarid is made into some kind of deity, while Theron's name is equated with a violation of Amarid's Law. It seems to me that there's a need for some balance."

Trahn and Baden exchanged a look. "This, too, Trahn has been telling me for some time," the Owl-Master said somberly.

Jaryd turned to Trahn, remembering something from their first encounter on the avenue. "You said this afternoon, when we first met, that the difference between Amarid's fate and Theron's might be causing the problems we're facing now. What did you mean?"

"You should know before you answer," Baden interrupted, his blue eyes fixed on the dark mage's face, "that Jaryd already has heard my theory on what's happening now in Tobyn-Ser."

Trahn raised an eyebrow. "Perhaps I should as well."

The Owl-Master's voice fell to a whisper and he glanced around to reassure himself that no one else could hear. "I believe that all these attacks are the work of Theron and the other unsettled mages. I'm not sure how; maybe they've found a way to alter the curse and allow their spirits to roam beyond the confines of their binding places. And I don't know whether the other Unsettled joined Theron willingly, or whether through power, or trickery, he coerced them. I have wondered why, but perhaps the two of you have hit upon the answer to that mystery. But I am convinced that Theron is behind this; I just don't see any other explanation."

For a moment, Trahn said nothing, his expression unreadable. Then he sighed deeply. "I have, reluctantly, reached a similar conclusion. I can think of no one else with both the contempt for the Order, and the power necessary to carry out so many attacks in so many different parts of the land." He looked at Jaryd, and the Mage-Attend could see the pain in his bright green eyes. "It saddens me deeply, not just for the lives lost and ruined, but also because I share your dismay at what's been done to the memory of Theron. We might have averted this sorrow by finding a place for Theron in the history of the Order."

"What can be done now?" Jaryd asked, trying unsuccessfully to keep his voice steady.

Neither mage responded, and their silence scared Jaryd more than anything either of them had said. Finally, Trahn spoke. "I believe we must go to Theron's Grove and attempt to prevail upon Theron to end his attacks."

"I agree," Baden stated, "but you understand what it is we're advocating."

"I do," Trahn replied.

Again the two mages shared a look, and, this time, Jaryd's blood froze at what he saw pass between them. "I don't," he blurted out. "I don't understand at all."

After a long pause, Trahn glanced at Baden, a smirk playing at the corners of his mouth. "This is yours to tell."

Baden held the Hawk-Mage's gaze for a moment longer before nodding and turning to Jaryd. "That last night in the Seaside Mountains," he began in a quiet voice, "when I told you the story of Theron and Amarid, I left out a few things. I said that Theron's spirit appears without a ceryll, but I base this only on what I know of his last living night. We don't really know what Theron's spirit looks like, because in the thousand years since his death, no one who has entered Theron's Grove has returned."

Jaryd's mouth went dry, and he felt as if Theron himself had reached out from the grave to place an icy finger on his heart. "How?" he managed to say in a voice that sounded more like a croak.

"Do you mean how did they die? That I don't know. As I told you that night, Theron's power was wild and vast. We know little about it. And, as you might expect, no one has dared enter the grove in hundreds of years. But soon after Theron's trial, the people of Rholde, Theron's home village, petitioned the Order to protect them from the Owl-Master's spirit, who had been terrorizing them continuously since his death. Amarid sent a party of mages to the grove, hoping that they would find some way to appease or subdue the spirit. Some of the villagers followed the mages to the grove and saw them enter. In the hours that followed, they heard wails of horror and despair and saw bright flashes of green light emanating from within the grove. But they never saw any of the mages again.

"Theron continued to torment Rholde, and again the villagers called upon the Order to protect them, but Amarid refused to risk the lives of any other mages. Some in Rholde demanded that the First Mage himself do battle with Theron. Amarid refused to do this as well. Soon the people of Rholde chose to abandon their village rather than endure any more of Theron's cruelty.

"In the years that followed, other mages did enter the grove, some hoping to make peace with Theron, others, perhaps, seeking glory. But none was ever heard from again. Eventually, all the people of Duclea's Wood, as the Shadow Forest was once known, abandoned their homes and villages, believing that Theron would never leave them alone. To this day, that part of the land remains deserted." Baden paused, sipping his ale thoughtfully. "So you see, Jaryd," he concluded after a moment, "confronting Theron carries tremendous risks."

"Then what's to be gained by trying to speak with him?" Jaryd asked, his composure beginning to return.

"This time, I think I'll defer to you," Baden remarked to Trahn. "It was, after all, your idea."

Trahn smiled and inclined his head in acceptance. "What's to be gained?" he repeated. "Much, if we can manage to survive the night. Theron may be using the attacks to get our attention, and, once he knows that we're listening, he may stop. Or he may want something that we can give him and thus appease him. It's also possible that we could learn something during our discussion with him that will allow us to neutralize the power of the Unsettled or control their actions. And, if by some chance Theron is not responsible, he may know who is. The Unsettled have wisdom and vision that goes well beyond ours. Again, provided that we get out of the grove alive."

The openness of Trahn's expression, the simplicity of his tone almost made it possible to forget that he was talking about confronting the unsettled spirit of Theron. Almost. And yet, in that moment, taken into their confidence as if he were already a mage, privy to their fears as well as their resolve, Jaryd felt that he would have followed Baden and Trahn anywhere in Tobyn-Ser. Even Theron's Grove. At the same time, another question came to him, one that frightened him deeply. Thrusting it away, he grinned and looked from one mage to the other. "So," he asked buoyantly, "when do we leave for the grove?"

Trahn gave a small laugh. "I'm not sure *we* will be going anywhere. I can't imagine the other mages including you in such a journey when you don't even have your cloak."

"They should," Baden asserted. "He's seen the mage who committed the attack on Taima."

"What!" Trahn exploded.

"The night before we reached Taima, Jaryd had a vision."

From the moment he had met Trahn, Jaryd had noticed that the Hawk-Mage treated him with respect, as if they were peers. It was one of the reasons Jaryd had come to like the dark mage so much, so quickly. But now Trahn regarded him with a look of awe and wonder in his green eyes that made Jaryd feel self-conscious. "Please," the Hawk-Mage requested in a soft voice, "tell me about this vision."

"There really isn't much to tell," Jaryd said awkwardly. "Baden tried to induce a return of my dream the next night, and even that didn't reveal much." He glanced at Baden, who nodded with encouragement. "I saw a man in a mage's cloak who carried a large, black bird and a staff with a glowing red stone. He had his hood drawn up over his head, so I couldn't see his face. But he handed me a black feather, and, when I took it in my hand, it burst into flame." Jaryd shrugged. "The next morning we found out that Taima had been burned, and whoever lit the fire left a black feather."

Trahn looked from Jaryd to Baden, his expression grim. "There has been a black feather left at the site of every one of the attacks."

"Jaryd," Baden said gently, "I may ask you to describe your vision again at some point during the Gathering."

Still feeling self-conscious, Jaryd recoiled from the idea. "But I thought Mage-Attends were prohibited from speaking during formal deliberations."

"Usually they are. But in this case, I'm sure Jessamyn will allow it. I simply want you to be prepared to describe your dream, exactly as you just did for Trahn. All right?"

Jaryd nodded reluctantly.

"Do you think Jessamyn would risk sending a delegation to Theron's Grove?" Trahn inquired of Baden.

"I hope so," the Owl-Master breathed. "In Arick's name, I hope so."

The three of them ordered another round of the rich ale, and two more after that one, and they continued talking well into the night. Their conversation soon shifted from the grave subject of Theron to more entertaining stories of past Gatherings and the adventures Baden and Trahn had shared. As the night wore on, and Jaryd felt the alcohol haze enveloping him like a warm blanket, the names and images conjured by his companions' tales began to blur and fade, leaving him with his own meandering thoughts. At one point, he scanned the tavern for Kayle and, with a small pang of regret, spotted her laughing quietly at another table, with another patron. He thought of Gissa, one of his closest friends in Accalia, and the only girl with whom he had made love. And he realized with an inward smile, he had been right: Kayle was not his type.

Baden and Jaryd did not stumble upstairs to their small, dark room until well past midnight. When he awoke the next morning to find the Owl-Master not only awake, but ready to assume his place in the opening procession of the Gathering, Jaryd could not even recall how he had managed to remove his own boots and climb into the bed in which he now lay. Only by the sheer force of the Owl-Master's will did Jaryd get out of bed, wash, and dress. Trahn met them in the courtyard outside the Aerie, and together the three of them started through the alleys and streets of Amarid toward the First Mage's home, where the procession was to begin. Jaryd's head spun dizzyingly as they hurried through the city, and when Baden asked if he wanted to stop for breakfast, Jaryd actually felt himself turn green. The sound of Baden and Trahn's laughter at the sight of this scythed painfully through Jaryd's head, and he swore at that moment that he would never drink Amari Ale again.

By the time they reached the First Mage's home, it appeared that most of the other mages had already assumed their positions in the procession. The column created by the cloaked mages stretched like a river of forest green along the side of the old house and into the scattered pines and cedars that surrounded it. As Jaryd and his companions walked by the older Owl-Masters and Hawk-Mages toward their positions, Baden and Trahn nodded and smiled at their colleagues, stopping occasionally to embrace old friends or exchange greetings. Jaryd remained silent, but looked with admiration at the myriad of different birds, mostly owls, that he was seeing for the first time. Some were so small that they were able to hide within the folds of a cloak or a hood, and at first, Jaryd had trouble spotting them. Others were larger than Anla, and one in particular, a tremendous grey, round-headed bird with closely spaced yellow eyes, dwarfed even the great owl Jaryd had seen yesterday on Sartol's shoulder. Most of the Hawk-Mages, he knew, were younger and farther back in the line. But he hoped that he would have an opportunity to see their birds up close as well.

Amarid's home, the house along which the line had formed, was, like the buildings in the old town commons, crudely constructed of logs and heavily worn by a thousand years of exposure to the elements. As Jaryd looked at it, he thought to himself that it could have been the home of any citizen of Tobyn-Ser, and he realized that this only served to heighten the power of this monument to the Order's founder. Despite the crystal statues and the grand murals, Amarid had been the son of common, hardworking people, a fact that, in happier times, had served to strengthen the bond between the Order and the rest of Tobyn-Ser.

Jaryd and Baden took their place in the line and, as Trahn left them to find his position, they stood waiting with the other mages for their march through the city to begin. The procession was arranged from front to rear by length of service within the Order. Of the nearly sixty mages currently in the Order, Baden ranked approximately twentieth in seniority, and he and Jaryd stood several places in back of Sartol, and two places ahead of Radomil. As his Mage-Attend, Baden had explained, Jaryd was allowed to join the Owl-Master at his place near the front of the procession. When he became a mage, however, Jaryd would walk at the end, with the other young mages. Looking back there now, Jaryd saw at the end of the line a woman who looked to be about his age. She had long, luxuriant dark hair and, despite her loose tunic and breeches, Jaryd could see that she was lithe and athletic.

"Who is that?" he uttered reflexively, having not intended to speak aloud.

Baden followed his glance. "At the end of the procession? That's Alayna, the newest member of the Order. I take it she is your type?" the mage ventured. Jaryd's face reddened in response. "She must be," Baden said with a smirk, answering his own question. "That's the first color other than green I've seen in your face today. She would be mine as well," he added without irony, "were I a few years younger. She's not only beautiful and intelligent, she also has vast potential as a mage; indeed, many believe that, someday, she'll lead the Order."

"How can you know that already?" Jaryd asked, still gazing in her direction.

"Well, we can't for certain. But even with the newest of mages, there are indications of such things. In Alayna's case, the most important evidence of her potential is her first binding. Do you recognize the bird on her shoulder?"

Jaryd had not noticed the majestic grey bird until Baden asked the question. "Amarid's Hawk."

"Yes. Binding to Amarid's Hawk usually portends exceptional power, particularly when it's the first binding."

Jaryd did not respond, but continued to look at Alayna. Then, suddenly, she met his gaze and their eyes locked. Jaryd felt his heart skip a beat, and he saw her eyes widen slightly as she stared back at him. It lasted but a moment; as abruptly as it had begun, she turned away, leaving Jaryd to wonder what had gone through her mind in that brief exchange. A few moments later, as the bells of the Great Hall began to toll in the distance, Jessamyn and a white-haired mage with a small, reddish owl took their places at the head of the procession, and the Order began its march toward the Gathering Chamber. But, for a long time, Jaryd said nothing, as his mind replayed again and again his silent encounter with Alayna.

After emerging from the forest surrounding Amarid's home, the procession circled the city block taken up by the house and woodland and then continued onto one of the main thoroughfares toward the Great Hall. Along the way, they passed thousands of people who waved to the mages and cheered. Pulled out of his musings by the sight, Jaryd soon joined Baden and the other mages in returning the waves and the smiles that accompanied them.

"A nicer reception than we received in Taima, wouldn't you say?" Baden said over the sounds of the crowd.

Jaryd nodded and then remembered a question he had thought to pose earlier. "Who is the older mage walking with Jessamyn?"

"That's Peredur, Jessamyn's first."

"I've heard you speak of the First of the Owl-Sage before, but it's never really been clear to me what he does."

Baden gave a small laugh. "It's a strange position," he commented. "Different firsts serve their sages in different ways. Some are advisors on matters of policy and leadership. Others spend much of their time taking care of the everyday needs of the sage, thus freeing him or her to lead the Order without those mundane concerns." The Owl-Master paused. "I guess I'd say that Peredur falls somewhere in between. He was never a particularly powerful mage, nor was he especially vocal during Gatherings. But he and Jessamyn received their cloaks at about the same time, and they've been friends since childhood. I've known him to offer advice on some matters, but for the most part he takes care of her and sees to it that she doesn't push herself too hard, which Jessamyn is inclined to do."

The procession reached the Great Hall and began to circle the structure as it had Amarid's home. The bells in the twin spires of the structure continued to peal loudly, the sound echoing through the streets and alleyways of the city.

"So, what happens after the procession ends?" Jaryd asked.

"We'll enter the Gathering Chamber, where we'll sit at the table you saw yesterday," Baden replied. "Jessamyn will welcome us and all those who have journeyed to Amarid, and she'll formally open the Gathering. This morning's session will be open to the public, and will tend to some ceremonial and procedural matters. It could last for several hours." Baden made a sour face. "That's the one part of the Gatherings that I hate. I really don't know how Jessamyn does it every year." He paused and shook his head before continuing. "In any case, the first closed session takes place this afternoon; that's when discussions of the attacks on Tobyn-Ser are likely to begin."

They walked for some time in silence. But just as they reached the entrance to the hall, Jaryd remembered the question that had come to him the night before as Baden, Trahn, and he sat in the Aerie. And, moved by an impulse he did not fully understand, Jaryd blurted out, "Baden, what if you and Trahn are wrong?"

The Owl-Master looked around him, but no one in the procession appeared to have heard Jaryd's question. "Wrong?" he repeated in a soft voice. "You mean about . . . about who we think is committing the attacks?"

"Yes," Jaryd said, also lowering his voice. "What if someone else is responsible?"

The Owl-Master took a deep breath and said nothing for what seemed a very long time. His answer, when it finally came, frightened Jaryd every bit as much as the thought of confronting Theron. "If we're wrong, then there's a conspiracy within the Order, and there are traitors in this procession."

6

Still reeling inwardly from the impact of Baden's words, Jaryd ascended the marble steps and crossed the threshold into the Gathering Chamber. Some of the older members of the Order, including Jessamyn and Peredur, had already moved to stand behind their seats at the far end of the enormous oval table, indicating to Jaryd that the strict ordering of the procession carried over to the seating arrangement within the hall. Indeed, Baden moved quickly to a chair on the right side of the table, and, next to it, Jaryd found a seat, obviously intended for him, which lacked the curving perch attached to the other chairs. Following Baden's example, Jaryd stood by his chair in silence, watching the other members of the Order file into the chamber and wishing that his head would stop spinning. When all the mages had taken their places around the table, observers from the crowd that had lined the thoroughfare began to enter the chamber and fill in the open area near the magnificent wooden doors. This took several minutes, during which the mages remained still and silent.

When, finally, all those who could be squeezed into the allotted space had entered the hall, the bells ceased tolling—a small blessing, given the pounding in Jaryd's head—and the silence of the mages spread to the observers. Slowly, Jessamyn raised her staff, with its glowing aqua ceryll, over her head.

"In the name of Amarid, First Mage and founder of this Order," she declared in a clear, ringing voice, "I bid you all welcome and proclaim this Gathering open!"

As if on cue, all the other mages at the table raised their cerylls. Light burst from each one, creating a virtual rainbow of color that converged on the Owl-Sage's ceryll, only to be channeled into a brilliant blaze of white light that burst from her stone. A thunderous cheer went up from the crowd at the far end of the chamber, and, when it subsided, Jessamyn said, in a quieter voice, but one that still carried, "Please be seated." With a rustling of cloth and feathers, the mages allowed their familiars to hop to the perches attached to their chairs, and then sat down.

"Peredur and I are so glad to see all of you here again," the Owl-Sage continued. "As always, many of you have traveled great distances to attend these deliberations and we all appreciate that effort. We gather this year in difficult times," she said, her voice growing stronger and more serious. "We face a challenge that none of us fully understands. The people in the back of this chamber, in the streets of this city, and in all the villages and towns of this land look to this Gathering for answers and protection. Let us resolve that when we leave this chamber two days hence, we will be united in support of a course of action and in our determination to see it through." Her words were met by a murmur of assent from those seated around the table, and several mages nodded their heads in agreement.

"Before we turn to such things, however," Jessamyn resumed, "there are a few matters to address. First, I believe that Owl-Master Sartol has something to say. Sartol?"

The tall mage stood and inclined his head toward Jessamyn. Out of the corner of his eye, Jaryd noticed that Alayna stood as well. "Thank you, Owl-Sage," Sartol said in a smooth voice. "Masters, Mages, I am honored to present to you, and to this Order, a new mage."

"Tell us of this new mage, Owl-Master Sartol," Jessamyn replied.

"She is Alayna of Brisalli," Sartol responded, indicating the young mage with his hand. "Daughter of Gareth and Idalia. She has been deemed worthy by Fylimar, and is doubly honored, for Fylimar is one of Amarid's Hawks."

The white-haired sage nodded and raised both her arms as she looked around the table. "Mages and Masters of the Order, Sartol has brought to us a new mage, Hawk-Mage Alayna. Shall we make her welcome?"

In answer, the rest of the mages stood again, as did Jaryd at Baden's prodding, and raised their staffs in salute.

Alayna stood at her place, with her hawk on her shoulder, and passed a hand awkwardly through her long hair. Her dark eyes flicked nervously around the table.

Jessamyn smiled at her. "Be welcomed, Alayna. You may be seated," she added, raising her voice so that all would hear her. As the rest of the Order sat back down, the Owl-Sage paused, letting Alayna's moment pass, before continuing in a more somber tone. "Sadly, two of our friends come to this Gathering unbound. Hawk-Mage Laresa recently lost Kortha, and Hawk-Mage Mered lost Elhir late in the winter. We extend to them our sympathies, as well as our wishes for auspicious and long-lasting bindings in the near future." Once again, a chorus of agreement went up from around the table, and Jaryd scanned the room for the two unbound mages. He barely noticed what Jessamyn said next. "We also welcome a newcomer to the Gathering, Owl-Master Baden's Mage-Attend, Jaryd."

Jaryd felt Baden's elbow poke him in the ribs. "Stand up!" the Owl-Master whispered fiercely. "They're all waiting for you to stand up!"

Realizing suddenly what was happening, Jaryd stood abruptly, nearly toppling his chair, and so startling Anla that she jumped into the air and circled the chamber once before returning to her perch. Jaryd felt his face turning deep red as the mages and several members of the audience began to laugh. Stealing a glance toward the far end of the table, he saw Alayna watching him with a slightly mocking grin on her face, and he sensed the color of his face deepening even further. As he sat back down, Baden leaned toward him. "Welcome to the Gathering," the Owl-Master said quietly.

His face still burning with embarrassment, and his head spinning with renewed intensity, Jaryd looked toward Jessamyn as if to will her to move the Gathering on to its next order of business and shift attention away from him. But when the sage's brown eyes met his gaze, she favored him with a smile so complete in its warmth and compassion that he instantly felt his chagrin starting to recede. Glancing around the table, he saw that most of the other mages had already turned their attention back to the Owl-Sage, although Trahn, still looking his way, grinned at him ruefully, and Sartol offered a wink of encouragement.

As Baden had predicted, Jessamyn began an extensive discussion of the history of the Gatherings, and the time-honored procedures that the Order would follow over the next few days. Jaryd saw Baden shift in his chair and prepare himself for a long morning of ritual and protocol. Jaryd began to do the same, but suddenly heard a now-familiar voice cut into the Owl-Sage's oration.

"Pardon my interruption, Owl-Sage," Trahn said, standing as Jessamyn's eyes blazed with anger. "I mean no dishonor to you or to the customs of the Gathering. But, as you yourself pointed out, we've come together in difficult times; we must address this crisis without delay."

Peredur, sitting just to Jessamyn's right, jumped to his feet, his long face distorted with rage. "Even if it means defiling the traditions of the Order and the memory of our First Mage?" he demanded.

One of the young mages stood, a woman with short, dark hair. "Yes, First of the Sage, even then," she asserted.

"Then we've already lost," said an older woman sitting directly across the table from Baden. Arguments began to break out along both sides of the table and spread noisily to the crowd of observers in the back of the chamber. Baden, looking around the hall in bewilderment, caught Trahn's eye and gave the Hawk-Mage a questioning look. Trahn took a deep breath and shook his head slowly, as if unable to comprehend how he had managed to spark such bedlam.

Then, an instant later came a single word that pierced through the clamor like a sword, and thrust all in the room into silence. "Enough!" the Owl-Sage commanded in a voice that seemed to come directly from the legendary figure painted on the chamber's ceiling. "Enough!" She seemed to grow in stature as she swept the room with an icy glare, and most at the table looked away rather than meet what they saw in her brown eyes. "What have we become that we should begin a Gathering like this? What is to become of us if we fail to respect our traditions and ceremonies and heritage? Perhaps what Sonel says is true: perhaps we have already lost this battle!"

For several moments, no one in the chamber spoke. At the far end of the room, the people of Tobyn-Ser waited breathlessly to see or hear what would come next. Jaryd wanted to look around the table again, to see the response of the other mages. But he remained utterly still, afraid that any movement at all would bring Jessamyn's wrath down on him. Sitting thus, with his eyes trained on the table, he sensed, rather than saw, Baden rise.

"I think you know that isn't true, Jessamyn," he said gently, "as does Sonel." Jaryd glanced across the table at the Owl-Master named Sonel in time to see her give Baden a small smile, and a look that conveyed much more. "This Order is more than merely the sum of its rituals and customs," Baden went on, his voice pitched now to carry throughout the chamber, his fingertips resting on the table. "We are servants of the land, and, right now, the land is in pain. Trahn and Ursel, and the others who feel that we need to begin immediately to heal this pain, should not be rebuked for their impatience." Some of the other Owl-Masters began to protest, but Baden raised a hand to quiet them. "Our rituals will still be here when we're ready for them. But, for now, I agree with Trahn: we must first address the dangers we face."

Remembering Baden's intolerance for the formalities of the Gathering, Jaryd concealed a smirk, although he said nothing. Baden sat back down, and all eyes in the room swung back to the Owl-Sage, who suddenly appeared old and very frail. Peredur still stood beside her, glaring in the direction of the younger mages, his lanky frame trembling with anger. She placed a hand on his shoulder and spoke to him softly. After a moment, the First of the Owl-Sage sat back down. "I suppose you're right, my friend," Jessamyn said to Baden wearily, in a voice utterly devoid of the steel with which she had silenced them all moments before. "I just wonder if I was meant to be sage in such times."

Baden said nothing, but for the second time that morning, he raised his staff over his head and let a bright orange flame leap from his ceryll. It was joined instantly by the colored mage-fire of every other member of the Order. Her eyes glistening, the Owl-Sage slowly, almost reluctantly raised her own staff, accepting their power and channeling it once again into a radiant white light. From the back of the chamber, building slowly at first, but swelling soon to a roar that threatened to topple the Great Hall itself, came cheers from the people of Tobyn-Ser who also loved Jessamyn and continued to place their faith in her.

"Lead us, Owl-Sage," Baden said. "We've chosen to follow you, and you've given us no cause to question the wisdom of that choice."

Jessamyn nodded. "I will lead you as I always have: by listening. I would hear counsel from any who wish to offer it, although first I would ask our guests to leave us so that we might discuss these matters in private."

A murmur of dissent rippled through the crowd, but most of the people in the back of the chamber began to make their way outside. Those who lingered were escorted to the doors by the blue-clad stewards of the Great Hall. As the observers exited, Jaryd leaned over to Baden and whispered, "Do you think that's wise?"

Baden looked at him blankly. "What do you mean?"

"Well, you said yourself that these attacks have eroded the people's confidence in the Order. Don't you think that by discussing the attacks behind closed doors we heighten their distrust?"

Baden weighed this for a moment. "An interesting point, although I'm not really sure what we can do. The Order has always held its formal deliberations in closed session. We can only challenge precedent so many times in a given day. And don't forget," he added with a grin, "within the next few moments, I'm going to request that my Mage-Attend be allowed to address the Gathering."

Jaryd swallowed nervously. He had not forgotten, and this was one challenge to tradition he could have done without.

The sound of the heavy wooden doors closing echoed through the chamber, announcing the recommencement of the Gathering's deliberations. "I would hear your counsel," Jessamyn repeated, surveying the faces arrayed around the table.

"Perhaps, Sage Jessamyn," Sartol suggested, "we should begin with a brief summary of what we know of these attacks. I'm certain that all of us know something of what's happened, but I for one would like to know more."

"A good suggestion, Sartol," Jessamyn agreed. "Peredur?"

The First of the Sage rose and nodded to Jessamyn. "Unfortunately," he began soberly, "there isn't much information available. We know of twenty-three attacks thus far. They've been attributed by the people of Tobyn-Ser to mages because a single black feather has been left at the sight of each incident; as of yet, no one has actually seen the person or people responsible. The first incident took place approximately fourteen months ago, the next almost six weeks later. They've been increasing in frequency ever since and have occurred in nearly every part of the land. They've ranged from minor mischief—crop destruction, vandalism—to more serious crimes such as arson and, as of this spring, murder." Jaryd could tell from the expressions on the faces of several of the mages that this last detail came as a shock. Whispered conversations spread through the Gathering.

"What was the most recent attack, First?" came a voice from the back end of the table.

"A devastating fire in the village of Taima on the Northern Plain," Peredur replied. "Although that was nearly four weeks ago; there may have been an incident since of which we have not yet heard."

Baden and Jaryd exchanged a look. Then the Owl-Master rose. "We were there at the time," he announced.

An uncomfortable silence fell over the room. "What did you say?" Orris demanded, leaning forward, his dark eyes narrowing.

"Jaryd and I arrived in Taima the morning after the fire," Baden explained. "We were on our way here from Jaryd's home village in Leora's Forest. I have friends in Taima, which is fortunate. Had I not, we might have been attacked ourselves. The people of Taima were quite suspicious of us. One might even say hostile."

Jaryd noticed that a number of mages glanced knowingly at their neighbors or raised a speculative eyebrow, and, with a surge of anger, he realized that they suspected Baden.

"Had they cause for this hostility?" Orris asked pointedly.

"Their town and their entire supply of grain had just been destroyed by a terrible fire," Baden responded evenly, "and their access to the water they needed to quell the flames had been cut off by those responsible. I understood their anger."

"That's not what I meant!" Orris said in a voice laden with innuendo.

"How dare you accuse Baden!" Jaryd shouted at the burly Hawk-Mage, knocking over his chair as he leapt to his feet.

"Jaryd!" Baden hissed.

"Mage-Attend Jaryd, please be seated!" Jessamyn commanded coldly. "As you are a newcomer to the Gathering, I will remind you that only members of the Order may speak during formal deliberations."

His face reddening once more, Jaryd nodded and sat down silently. Baden gave him a reproachful look, but then squeezed his shoulder. "Thank you," he whispered. "But I can handle Orris."

Before the Owl-Master could speak, however, Jessamyn turned her fury toward Orris. "Although Jaryd spoke out of turn, Orris, I must admit that I share his outrage! Your veiled accusations are most inappropriate!"

"With all due respect, Sage Jessamyn," Orris began in his usual gruff tone, standing as he spoke, "what was appropriate in the past may be naive and weak in our current situation." Words of protest rang out from the Owl-Masters seated near Jessamyn, but Orris went on, silencing them with a glare. "All the evidence we have indicates that there is a traitor to the Order and a murderer of innocent people in this room. Now is not the time for decorum."

"That may be true, Orris," Trahn conceded. "But Baden has done nothing to warrant our suspicions. Why, if he had destroyed Taima, would he admit to having been at the scene of the attack?"

Orris passed a hand over his rough beard. "A good question," he conceded reluctantly. "I may have jumped to a conclusion too quickly." He glanced at Baden and then sat down abruptly. The Owl-Master inclined his head slightly as if acknowledging an apology, but Orris's tone had left Jaryd doubting that this had been his intention.

"Baden, did you learn anything while you were in Taima?" asked one of the older masters.

"Not from the people there, no," Baden replied, shaking his head. "I healed many of them, and, as I did, I asked them about the attack. But no one saw or heard anything. At least no one from Taima." He glanced quickly at Jaryd, as if to prepare him. "But the night before, Jaryd had a vision of the attacker." After a moment of shocked silence, the entire room seemed to erupt with shouted questions and exclamations of astonishment. It was several minutes before Jessamyn succeeded in restoring calm. "With my assurance that he will not yell at any more mages," Baden said wryly, "I would ask that he be allowed to address this Gathering in order to describe his vision."

Jessamyn scanned the room. "Does anyone object?" Her question was met with utter stillness. "You may speak, Jaryd," she said simply.

And so, for the second time in as many days, with the most powerful men and women in Tobyn-Ser staring at him with expressions of eagerness and, he thought, even a bit of fear, Jaryd related his dream of the hooded mage.

When he finished, a voice from the far end of the table spoke his name. Even before he turned to face his questioner, he knew that it was Alayna. "This strange bird you saw in your dream—do you see it now, sitting in this room?"

Neither he nor Baden had thought of this, and he quickly stood to scrutinize every bird. The black creature was not in the room. "No," he conceded, facing Alayna. "It's not here."

"How about the ceryll?" came another voice. "Do you see a crystal that matches the color you saw?"

"No," Jaryd said again, discouragement creeping into his tone.

"Don't despair, Jaryd," Sartol offered, his handsome face stretching into a sympathetic smile. "Not all of our dreams can be taken so literally. You've had a powerful vision, and, before this episode is over, I'm certain that its meaning will be made clear."

"Well said, Sartol," Radomil agreed from his seat to Jaryd's left. "But for now, I'm afraid that we're right back where we began."

"Radomil is correct," Orris said loudly, rising from his seat. "We have no idea who is committing these attacks or why, and it's time we acknowledged that."

"What do you propose, Orris?" Baden asked, his calm tone a sharp contrast to the churning impatience so manifest in every movement of the Hawk-Mage.

Orris hesitated, his dark eyes scanning the room as if he was not completely comfortable with what he was about to say. "It is time to reestablish the psychic link."

Several of the older mages cried out in protest and the Gathering again fell into turmoil.

"I don't understand what's happening," Jaryd said to Baden above the din.

Baden nodded. "It's not a simple matter to explain. The psychic link is just what it sounds like: a constant telepathic web connecting all mages within the Order. It was first used during Amarid's time after Theron's death and the self-imposed exile of Theron's followers. Amarid feared that they would return, attempt to win control of the Order, and place the people of Tobyn-Ser in servitude. He believed that the link would allow the Order to maintain a watch along the shores of the land." Baden paused as Jessamyn attempted once more to reassert her control over the Gathering. When he began again, his voice had fallen to a whisper. "Orris seeks to use the link in a slightly different way, as a means of monitoring the activities of all members of the Order."

"Doesn't that make sense?" Jaryd asked quietly. "I mean, given the possibility that there is a traitor within the Order?"

Before Baden could respond, Jessamyn began to speak. "I must ask you all to please refrain from bickering amongst yourselves. This is a Gathering, and we do have certain rules of conduct." The diminutive sage encompassed the room with her piqued gaze as the last of the side conversations died out. "Now, Orris, you were saying?"

The Hawk-Mage cleared his throat. "I am calling for the reestablishment of the psychic link first created by Amarid."

A silver-haired Owl-Master shook his head. "Invoking Amarid's name to justify your recommendation is misleading, Orris, and you know it. Amarid's link was created to protect the land, not to allow mages to spy on each other."

"Using the link as you propose," another Owl-Master objected, "would be a direct violation of Amarid's Third Law."

Jaryd looked questioningly at Baden, who recited quietly, " 'Mages shall never use their powers against one another. . . .' "

"That's ridiculous, Odinan!" one of the younger mages argued. "The Third Law also states that the Order shall be the arbiter of all disputes among mages.

What Orris is advocating allows the entire Order to police itself. I believe that conforms to the spirit of the law."

"Besides," Orris added, appearing to gain confidence as he spoke, "given the severity of the recent incidents, the link would be protecting the land. And that purpose rests at the core of Amarid's Laws."

"You're talking about a tremendous expenditure of power that could be better used in other ways," countered the one named Odinan.

"Odinan is right," the silver-haired Owl-Master agreed. "That was the reason Amarid's link was eventually broken. That, and the fact that many thought Amarid had been wrong to create it in the first place. The mages at that time thought that the First Mage had been a bit paranoid about Theron's followers. I must say that I'm inclined to see this proposal in the same light. We have no proof that a member of this Order is responsible for the attacks."

"That's precisely why we need the link!" Orris stormed, crashing his fist down on the table.

"Mage Orris," Jessamyn began in a soothing tone, "is there another way by which we might achieve what you wish to accomplish with the link?"

With a visible effort Orris calmed himself. "Perhaps," he breathed, his stocky frame coiled dangerously. "If we could organize groups, maybe ten, each consisting of about six mages, we could then send each group to a different region of Tobyn-Ser. That way, each member of the Order would be accounted for, and, if someone outside of the Order was responsible, we would have mages in the vicinity of any subsequent attack who could investigate the incident much more quickly."

Again, a number of the older mages shook their heads. "You're talking about uprooting the lives of every person in this room," the one with silver hair complained.

"What we're talking about," Orris exploded, "is a threat to the lives of every person in this land! Far be it from me to inconvenience you, Niall, but I thought that this Order was created to protect Tobyn-Ser!"

The Owl-Master stood abruptly, his brown eyes blazing. "How dare you lecture me as if I was some fledgling mage! I've been a member of this Order since before you were old enough to walk!"

"Yes, you have," Orris said in a low voice, his beard bristling. "Perhaps that's your problem."

"Meaning what?" Niall growled.

"Meaning, Niall," Baden broke in, "that perhaps older mages like you and me have grown a bit too comfortable. We've let our guard down and now we seem unwilling to pay the price of our negligence." He turned to Orris. "Is that about right?"

The Hawk-Mage hesitated a moment and then nodded. "That's close enough."

Baden shot a glance toward Trahn, who nodded once. Then the lean Owl-Master continued, standing as he spoke. "I'm inclined to support Orris's proposal for the creation of these . . . patrols, as one might call them, with two provisos. First, some of the older members, whose wisdom and experience we value so highly, are, nonetheless, ill-suited to the rigors of this plan. They should be exempted." He paused, looking at Orris, who, with some reluctance, indicated his approval with a curt gesture. "Second, Trahn and I have a theory as to who might be responsible for these attacks and we would like to propose the creation of a small delegation to investigate."

"What is this theory?" Sonel asked, her green eyes meeting Baden's.

The Owl-Master took a deep breath, as if preparing himself for the furor he was about to create. "We believe that it may be the Unsettled, led by the spirit of Theron, who have done these things. We wish to journey to Theron's Grove to confront him."

Jaryd had expected commotion, shouted protests and denials, an eruption similar to those he had already witnessed several times during the course of the morning. But instead, Baden's words elicited an eerie silence that settled over the Gathering Chamber like thick smoke from a distant fire.

Finally, after what seemed an eternity, a voice cut through the stillness. "Why?" Sartol asked. "Why would the Unsettled be doing these things?"

It was Trahn who answered. "We don't know why, but the Unsettled could do nothing without, at least, Theron's cooperation. More likely, he is leading them, and I'm certain that no one in this room would deny that Theron has cause to resent the Children of Amarid and the influence they wield in this land. I know of no other people outside of this chamber who have the power to commit so many attacks over so vast an area."

"You're assuming, then, that they have found a way to overcome the constraints of the curse and move about the land," Odinan commented in his thin, raspy voice.

"Yes," Baden acknowledged.

"And you wish to send a delegation to the grove to face Theron? Why, if he can wander the land at will, would he still be in the grove?"

Baden smiled thinly. "A fair question. The truth is, we can't be sure that he will be. But it seems the best place to begin looking for him."

"Surely, Baden," Sartol began in an almost gentle voice, his pale eyes intent beneath the shock of thick, dark hair, "I need not remind you that no one has ever survived a journey to the grove."

"I've had some thoughts on that subject," Trahn declared. He flashed a smile at Baden, adding parenthetically, "Amari Ale has a way of firing the imagination." He turned toward Sartol, his expression growing more serious. "It seems to me, from what I've heard and read of past ventures to Theron's Grove, that, with the exception of the very first party sent by Amarid, all those who made the journey traveled singly or in pairs. Given Theron's power, it may be that a larger delegation would stand a better chance of surviving the encounter." He hesitated a moment before continuing. "I would also suggest that those who are chosen to meet with Theron enter the grove without their cerylls."

A cry of protest went up around the table, but Baden, still standing, began to smile and nod. "No, Trahn is correct," he said above the growing tumult. "Please, listen for a moment." The noise in the chamber subsided as the mages turned their attention to Baden. "Trahn is right," he said again. "Theron died without a ceryll—he destroyed his when he cast the curse. Without a ceryll he has no way to focus his power. We've always assumed that because his strength was so great, his spirit didn't need a ceryll to defend the grove from intruders.

But perhaps he channeled his power through the cerylls of those who entered his domain. Without our crystals, and in greater numbers, we might be safe."

"But if he has no way to channel his power," Orris demanded, "how could he commit the crimes that you ascribe to him?"

"I'm not saying that, without a ceryll, Theron has no access to the Mage-Craft. Even without a means for focusing it, his power may be enormous. And don't forget, he wouldn't be acting alone."

"Why would the Unsettled follow him?" Sonel asked.

"All of this is only a theory," Baden admitted, "but he was the first to be unsettled and it was his curse. Perhaps this was his intention all along: to avenge himself on the land by commanding an army of the Unsettled. They may follow him because they see him as their leader, or he may have forced them into his service."

"How the other Unsettled may have come to serve Theron seems unimportant to me," Sartol commented. "What I want to know, Baden, Trahn, is what you would say to Theron; what you would hope to accomplish with a journey to the grove."

"As I said," Baden explained, "Trahn and my belief that Theron and the Unsettled are behind the attacks is no more than speculation. But if we're right, then there's a certain inevitability to this. If Theron is determined to destroy the Order, eventually we'll have to face him, and any delegation sent to the grove should be prepared to do battle with the Owl-Master's spirit. If he merely wishes to get our attention, then again, we'll have to meet with him. And, as Trahn pointed out to Jaryd and me last night," he concluded, indicating the dark mage with a slight nod, "even if Theron is not responsible for the attacks, and provided we are able to speak with him and survive the night, he may have some information that will help us defeat those who are responsible. The advantage of what we're proposing is that it doesn't require us to wait for yet another attack. Hopefully, we can prevent a recurrence of what Jaryd and I witnessed in Taima."

"Who would you send, Baden?" Odinan asked.

Baden shrugged. "That's for this Gathering to decide, if it chooses to send such a delegation. I'd be willing to go, and I'm certain Trahn would as well." Glancing over at his friend, Baden seemed gratified to see the Hawk-Mage nod in agreement.

"As would I," Sartol announced, "and I would suggest, provided she approves, of course, that Alayna be included as well. She has studied the old texts describing the events leading to Theron's Curse and Amarid's Laws extensively. Her knowledge of Theron's life might prove valuable."

"I would go," Alayna said simply, her expression serious and her voice betraying no hint of fear.

"A delegation of such import would also have to include the Owl-Sage and myself," Peredur insisted.

Jessamyn nodded. "I quite agree."

"I would also recommend," Baden stated, "that Jaryd be a part of any company sent to the grove."

"What?" one mage exclaimed in disbelief. Another voice said incredulously, "The Attend? But he's unfledged!"

"Unfledged?" Jaryd repeated, turning to Baden with a look of confusion.

Baden, paying no attention to his Mage-Attend, was attempting to quiet the flurry of protest that had greeted his suggestion, but a voice on his other side answered Jaryd's question. " 'Unfledged' is a term we use to describe those who show signs of power, but have yet to experience their first binding," Radomil explained quietly. "I assure you that they mean no disrespect," the mage added with a smile.

Jaryd returned the smile. "Thank you, Mage Radomil."

"I know that including a Mage-Attend in such a mission is somewhat irregular," Baden acknowledged, having at least partially succeeded in restoring calm to the chamber, "but we can't ignore Jaryd's vision of the attacker at Taima. He obviously has a role to play in this crisis. We may need him before this journey is over."

"If there is to be a journey," Orris corrected belligerently. "I'm opposed to sending this delegation, as you call it. It would be a waste of time and an unwarranted risk. You yourself admit that you're not even certain Theron is involved. And now," he continued, a note of derision creeping into his voice, "you insist that this boy be included in your company? I don't see this as a serious alternative to my plan."

A number of the younger mages murmured in agreement, and Jaryd, enraged at being referred to as a "boy," started to his feet, a stinging retort on his tongue. Before he could say anything, however, Baden knocked him back into his chair with an inconspicuous but effective elbow to the belly.

"First of all, Orris," Baden countered, his tone growing intense, " 'this boy,' as you refer to him, will one day be more powerful than any mage in this room. I tell you this with certainty, because I've seen it." He paused, letting the impact of his words spread through the chamber. "Second, Trahn and I did not propose this journey as an alternative to your plan or anyone else's. You can still form your patrols and await the next attack. But, if we succeed, you'll be waiting for quite some time."

Baden and Orris stood glaring at each other in silence as other mages around the table picked up their argument and the chamber fell once more into disarray. And as the people around him argued the relative merits and shortcomings of forming patrols, of reestablishing the psychic link, and of sending a delegation to Theron's Grove, Jaryd turned again toward the far end of the table, where, as he knew he would, he found Alayna looking in his direction, the expression on her delicate features unreadable. They held each other's gaze for several moments before she finally averted her eyes.

Jessamyn soon reestablished order and declared a recess in the proceedings. At the same time, the Great Hall's attendants, in their shimmering blue robes, brought a light meal to the table. It consisted of cheese, dried fruits, and a light-colored wine, but, even though Jaryd had recovered somewhat from his drinking the night before, he chose not to eat. When the repast was done, debate resumed, and while the mages discussed their alternatives in a more reasoned tone, they showed little sign of approaching any consensus. It seemed to Jaryd that they repeated the same arguments over and over without actually listening to each other, and he eventually found himself losing interest in the proceedings. Baden and Trahn spent much of the afternoon defending their plan, but Orris and his followers remained convinced that sending a company to Theron's Grove would endanger their efforts to monitor the activities of all members of the Order. When the daylight shining through the chamber's translucent windows began at last to fade, the mages appeared no closer to an agreement than they had that morning.

The Owl-Sage reluctantly adjourned the Gathering until the following day, and formally invited all the mages to a celebration of Midsummer and the Feast of Duclea that night at the home of Amarid. In the excitement of the opening of the Gathering, Jaryd had forgotten that this night marked the feast, and, reminded by Jessamyn's invitation, he found his excitement, and his appetite, returning. He actually preferred the Autumn Feast of Leora and the Spring Feast of Arick, but all four of the seasonal celebrations were times of enchantment and gaiety in Tobyn-Ser. To experience the feast here in Amarid would only add to the wonder of the event.

But it was the memory of something else that moved Jaryd, as he and Baden stepped out of the Great Hall into the deeply slanting late-afternoon sunlight, to stop at the bottom of the marble steps and turn toward the Owl-Master. "Do you really think that I'll someday be the most powerful mage in the Order?" he asked, unable to contain a smile.

"What?" Baden responded absently as Trahn joined them.

"I asked you if you meant what you said during the proceedings: that I'll be the most powerful mage in the Order."

Without responding, Baden turned to Trahn. "That didn't go as well as I had hoped," he observed. "You're right about Orris: he has quite a following among the younger members."

"You're equally popular with the Owl-Masters," Trahn asserted, "but I don't think our cause will be helped by pitting one faction against the other. No matter what the Order chooses to do, we won't succeed if we're divided."

"I agree," Baden said grimly. He glanced back toward the Great Hall. "I think I'll have a word with Jessamyn; her support in all this will be crucial."

"You may have to wait a bit: Orris is already speaking with her, and she'll be departing for Amarid's home soon to prepare for the feast."

"The feast," Baden breathed, shaking his head. "I'd already forgotten about that."

"I hadn't," Jaryd said cheerfully. "I bet the celebration here is pretty spectacular. I can't wait."

For the first time since the adjournment of the Gathering, Baden seemed to take note of his nephew. He exchanged a look with Trahn and then took a deep breath. "Jaryd," he began tentatively, "I'm afraid we won't be attending the feast, or, more accurately, you won't be."

"What?" Jaryd exclaimed with dismay. "Why not?"

Baden glanced at Trahn again, apparently unsure of how to proceed. "Trahn and I have a great deal to do this evening in preparation for tomorrow's deliberations. We'll have little time to observe the feast, and we probably won't return to the Aerie at all." Baden flicked his pale eyes toward Trahn before continuing. "Without us there, Maimun won't allow you to stay in the room unless you pay. So I'm sorry to say that you'll have to sleep outside of town tonight."

"You mean in the forest?" Jaryd demanded, unwilling to believe what he was hearing.

"Yes."

"But I don't want to. I don't want to miss the feast, and I certainly don't want to sleep on the ground again."

"I don't recall offering you a choice," Baden countered impatiently. "Do you have the three gold pieces you'd need to stay at the inn?"

"No," Jaryd replied in a subdued tone.

"I thought not. Now you'd best get moving. It will be more difficult to find a suitable place to sleep after the sun sets."

"But, Baden, why can't I stay with you and Trahn?" Jaryd asked plaintively. "I can go one night without sleep, and I want to attend the f—"

"Jaryd!" Baden said sharply, his eyes flashing. "Enough! Since when does an Owl-Master explain himself to his Mage-Attend? It is sufficient that I require it of you!"

"Yes, Master Baden," Jaryd said quietly.

Without another word, Baden turned with a swirl of his cloak and ascended the steps back into the Great Hall. Trahn lingered for a moment and placed a sympathetic hand on Jaryd's shoulder. "I understand your disappointment, Jaryd," he offered in a gentle voice, "but I've never known Baden to deprive a friend of something without cause."

Jaryd nodded curtly and, with a quick glance at the Hawk-Mage and an unsuccessful attempt at a smile, he stomped off toward the old town commons and the footbridge back to the forest. As he made his way blindly through the mass of people wandering the streets, and past the crowded shops and markets, Jaryd seethed with an anger that overwhelmed his disappointment at missing the feast. He was, he decided, in the charge of a despot, who cared little about his feelings or his needs. Baden could have no justification for exiling him on this of all nights. Here he was, hundreds of miles from his family and friends, being forced to miss one of the Four Feasts. It was completely unfair. And, as he approached the first of the bridges that led across the Larian and into Hawksfind Wood, it suddenly occurred to him that he could turn back. He did not need to be with Baden to attend the feast; Jessamyn had invited everyone in the chamber. She would welcome him, as would Sartol and Radomil. They seemed to like him, and certainly they would understand his desire not to be alone on Duclea's Night. He halted at the edge of the bridge, and even started to walk back toward town. But then he stopped. Trahn was right, of course: Baden wouldn't have told him to go to the forest without a good reason. Moreover, defying Baden in this way would have ramifications far beyond tonight's feast. Sighing heavily, Jaryd turned for a second time and crossed the bridge into the forest. As he did, he felt his anger sluicing away, leaving him dejected and just a little bit lonely.

Absorbed in his self-pity, he did not notice the two strangers on the trail until one of them had grabbed him and locked an arm around his throat. Jaryd struggled to get free, but the man had a grip like a vise.

"What have we got here?" the other one asked, taking Jaryd's dagger from its sheath and holding it to Jaryd's throat. "It's a bit late to be alone in the woods, don't you think, Velk?"

The man holding Jaryd laughed and tightened his grip.

"You better leave me alone," Jaryd warned in a trembling voice, knowing as he did how ridiculous he sounded. "I'm a mage," he bluffed, "so you'd better let me go."

Both men laughed, and the one with Jaryd's dagger, a short, wiry man with a scruffy beard and small grey eyes, shook his head and grinned, revealing yellow, crooked teeth. "I don't think so," he countered in a voice low and dangerous. "I don't see no cloak or bird." He looked at Jaryd's hand. "But I do see a gold ring that I like very much." His expression hardened. "Take it off," he commanded coldly.

"But it was a gift from my brother," Jaryd pleaded, struggling again.

"I don't care if it came from Arick himself. Take it off!"

Reluctantly, with tears welling in his eyes, Jaryd tugged at the ring. It wouldn't budge.

The man glanced passed Jaryd's head to the one named Velk, and shrugged. "Hold him still," he instructed. And, grabbing Jaryd's hand, he moved the dagger to the base of Jaryd's little finger.

"No!" Jaryd wailed in desperation, and in that instant, unsure of why he did it, Jaryd closed his eyes and formed a vision of fire in his mind. A split second later, the man in front of him howled in pain. Opening his eyes again, Jaryd saw that the man's overshirt was engulfed in flames. Velk threw Jaryd to the ground and ran to his friend, flailing urgently at the fire. That was the last Jaryd saw of them. He grabbed his dagger and then sprinted into the forest, following the trail and running as fast as he could until the shouts of the bandits had faded entirely.

It was nearly dark when he finally stopped at a small tributary of the Larian. He decided abruptly that it would be a suitable place to spend the night. Certainly, the bandits would not come after him again. And, as he bent over, trying to catch his breath, it finally dawned on him that he had used the Mage-Craft to escape. Somehow, he had used the Mage-Craft. He thought suddenly of Royden's shirt burning in the room they had shared in Accalia, but he knew that this had been different. This time he had done it consciously. He didn't know how, but he had. A sudden wave of giddiness passed through him, and he quickly gathered several pieces of wood and made a small pile on which he could test his newfound power again. Closing his eyes in the gathering darkness, and drawing on the skills he had gained from the exercises Baden had taught him, he emptied his mind of all thoughts save for an image of fire. And as he did, he felt something flow through him, cold and swift, as if his blood had become a mountain stream. At the same time, he felt a presence in his mind, and, for a strange, disorienting instant, he saw an image of himself as he might appear to someone watching him. He seemed both close and far away, brighter and clearer than he should have been, given the lighting in the woods, but flat and slightly distorted. Then the feeling was gone, replaced by the smell of smoke filling his nostrils, and the soft crackling sound of burning wood. He opened his eyes to see the kindling blazing brightly on the ground in front of him. His anger at Baden a distant memory, his fear of the bandits gone, Jaryd stared with wonder at the fire he had shaped out of the twilight. "I'm a mage," he said out loud. And then he shouted it, for the entire forest to hear. "I'm a mage!"

He found another piece of wood and, closing his eyes again, tried to shape it as he had seen Baden do. Nothing happened. He tried it a second time, and, though the strange presence touched his mind again briefly, the appearance of the log did not change, and he started to feel dizzy. Placing the log on the ground a few feet from the fire, he closed his eyes once more and, for a third time that evening, tried to conjure a blaze. There was the presence again, and, once more, Jaryd felt something coursing through his body. A river it was, stronger than the stream he had felt a few moments before, but still cool and brisk. In a few seconds, the log burst into flames, although Jaryd's dizziness increased. "Well," Jaryd said to the night, grinning broadly, "it's a start."

He stared happily at the flames for a long time, trying to remember the sensations that had come with the use of his power. Finally, long after the last vestiges of light had vanished from the sky, he realized that he was hungry. He stood and searched the area around him for some of the edible plants and roots Baden had taught him to recognize so many weeks ago. When he had gathered enough for a meal, he carried them to the stream and cleaned them. Returning to the light of the fire, he ate his modest dinner and settled back comfortably onto the fragrant pine needles to try to sleep. I'm a mage, he thought again, smiling like a child.

7

Calbyr stood alone at the edge of the clearing, watching and waiting. His hood was thrown back, letting the light breeze ruffle his sand-colored hair, but his eyes were fixed on the impossible darkness of the forest to the east of the clearing. He could hear the others behind him, whispering softly in groups of two and three, and he had an urge to silence them. It would have taken a single word, perhaps even a silent glare. They were afraid of him, he knew. They'd do as he ordered. But there was no sense in it, really. They weren't making a lot of noise, and it wasn't their fault that the mage was late. Venting his frustration on his men might make him feel a bit better, but it wouldn't accomplish much.

He hated to be kept waiting. He prided himself on his own punctuality and the precision with which he carried out his plans. Lateness was a result of incompetence. And incompetence could get a person killed. That they were waiting for a mage made it even worse. That they were waiting here, in this forest, so close to the city and to the Children of Amarid, who had gathered there, made it nearly intolerable.

He knew that their proximity to the city was necessary. If they wanted to maintain the illusion that the mages were responsible for the attacks his gang had carried out, they had to strike quickly after the Gathering ended, and they had to do so within a believable distance of the city. But he preferred to keep moving, and it made him nervous having his entire band together for any length of time. It carried too many risks.

He glanced back over his shoulder and surveyed the clearing. If someone came across them now, Calbyr and his men would have little choice but to kill the unfortunate passerby. Chance encounters with the land's people were to be expected, but on an individual basis, not en masse. Not with fifteen of them together in this small clearing, all of them carrying the same bright crimson stones and the same huge ebony, golden-eyed birds. Even the most ignorant of Tobyn-Ser's citizens would know immediately that something was not right. And he or she would have to die. Not that Calbyr was averse to killing—that was, after all, why they had come. But he had made plans, and they had to be carried out carefully. A random killing at this particular time would do more harm than good.

Calbyr himself had insisted that all members of his gang carry red stones. At the time, he had believed that they would allow his men to recognize each other with greater ease, even from a distance. Perhaps they did. But they also made gatherings like this one far too dangerous. It had been the one significant flaw in their meticulous preparations.

He turned back toward the forest, his eyes straining to catch a glimpse of the mage's glowing stone in the blackness. Seeing nothing, he spat a curse under his breath. At times Calbyr wondered if the mage did this to him on purpose; neither he nor the Child of Amarid had made any effort to hide their mutual antagonism. Actually, their belligerence was convenient in a way, because it allowed Calbyr to conceal the other emotions that the mage brought out in him. He would never have admitted this to the others, but the Child of Amarid made him uncomfortable. In Lon-Ser, surrounded by the reassuring clarity of the Nal, immersed in the comfort of technology, he had been taught to distrust superstition and mysticism. Magic existed solely in the games of children, and dreams were no more than fanciful images that troubled his sleep at night. But here, in this strange land, dreams held glimpses of the future; at least that's what the mage had told him. And magic was real. He had seen it himself.

Calbyr did not fear many people. There was Cedrych, his Overlord back in Lon-Ser, he reflected, absently tracing a finger along the thin white scar that ran from his left temple to the corner of his mouth, and he had once been afraid of his father. And like everyone else in Bragor-Nal, he did his best to avoid the Sovereign's security forces. But that was all. From what he knew of the Order, he believed that the Children of Amarid were pompous and weak-willed, complacent and inept. This mage—*his* mage, he amended, smiling at the thought—was no exception. But by betraying the Order and joining forces with Calbyr and his men, the Child of Amarid had exhibited a ruthlessness that Calbyr respected. And Calbyr had seen the mage, with no more than the wave of a hand, do things that challenged everything Calbyr knew to be true. He wouldn't go as far as to say that he feared the mage. But the power that the man wielded, and the imposing bird that he carried, made Calbyr uneasy.

He still remembered, with a clarity that he found deeply unsettling, their first surprise encounter with the mage. Calbyr and his men had gathered in the foothills of the coastal mountains—the Seaside Range, they called them here—to discuss strategy for the commencement of their raids. Indeed, it had been a night much like this one: warm and clear, with a light wind that carried a scent like distant rain. They had, of course, learned much about the Children of Amarid. The spies that Cedrych had dispatched to Tobyn-Ser had brought them detailed descriptions of their appearance, their customs, and their history. How else could they have hoped to impersonate the mages and implicate them in the crimes they would commit? But none of them had ever actually seen a mage. Until that night.

Calbyr recalled that he had been struck by the irony of it, even as he had felt his heart leap into his throat: they had managed, up to that point, to avoid all encounters with natives of Tobyn-Ser. Only to be discovered, all of them together, by one of the mages. The Child of Amarid had seemed surprisingly undisturbed by the sight of them. He had paused at the edge of the clearing, surveying the scene with a slight smirk on his lips. If he was shocked to see them, with their identical stones and birds, he showed no sign of it.

Calbyr and his men—there had been sixteen of them then—had stood absolutely motionless. Their stunned expressions must have seemed comical to the mage. Or perhaps he had been too focused on their strange birds to notice. It had been hard to tell. And then Yarit—of course it would be Yarit—had panicked, thrusting out his weapon to fire at the mage. He never got the chance. So swift had been the Child of Amarid's response, and so bright had been the fire that exploded from his staff, that Calbyr did not realize what had happened until his man fell to the ground, his cloak, hair, and bird a whirlwind of flame. Calbyr had used a variety of hand weapons in his life, and he had been very impressed with the firepower of the thrower, disguised as a mage's staff, that he now carried. But none of them matched the force of what the mage had conjured up in that moment with, it had seemed, little more than a gesture.

The Child of Amarid had then bared his teeth in a fierce grin and turned to Calbyr, knowing somehow that he was the group's leader. "Tell them to drop their staffs or I'll kill all of them!" he had demanded in Tobynese. After a moment, Calbyr had nodded once and given the order in Bragory. His men had complied, though reluctantly, and never lowering his staff, the mage had proceeded to ask who they were and why they had come. Even as Calbyr replied to the questions, carefully measuring each word in the strange language so as to give enough information to satisfy his inquisitor without giving away too much, he had realized how lucky he and his men had been. It was clear from the mage's tone and manner that he was not about to kill them or have them imprisoned. He listened to Calbyr's responses with the air of a man appraising the qualities of a newly purchased weapon. And in those few minutes, in a forest clearing lit only by the blood-red stones of his men, and the bright yellow crystal of the mage, an alliance was forged. Uneasy, to be sure, made unnecessarily difficult by the rancor that quickly came to characterize Calbyr's interaction with the Child of Amarid, but born of a potent mutual need.

The alliance had served Calbyr well over the past year. There was no disputing that. But at times like these, when the mage kept him waiting, or addressed him with the arrogance and disdain that seemed to come to him so easily, Calbyr found his growing dependence on the man galling. Feeling uneasy around him was one thing, but to need him like this . . . Calbyr shook his head. When all this is done, he promised himself grimly, I'll kill him.

The thought calmed him, and, when at last he saw through the trees the soft yellow glow of the mage's ceryll, he noted with satisfaction that his nerves remained steady.

"He's coming," Calbyr announced.

Immediately, the other figures in the clearing ended their conversations and stood to face the approaching light. In another moment, the mage stood before Calbyr, the glow from his ceryll mingling with the red crystals of the others to light the clearing with a strange orange luminance. His bird seemed small and pale as it surveyed the clearing and hissed at the black creatures on the shoulders of Calbyr and his companions.

"Your bird seems frightened, Child of Amarid," Calbyr said, a note of mockery in his voice. "Do we make the two of you uncomfortable?"

"You mistake distaste for fear, Calbyr," the mage replied icily. "Errors like that can be dangerous." He allowed himself a smile and gently stroked the chin of his bird. "Besides, my familiar can't be faulted for being discriminating; she merely prefers the company of real birds."

"And what about you?" Calbyr asked in the same tone. "Do you prefer the company of real mages?"

Again, the mage smiled, although his eyes betrayed no hint of mirth. "I prefer to work alone."

They stood for some time in silence, glaring at each other, the space between them seemingly charged with their belligerence.

At length, Calbyr broke eye contact. "Well, what tidings do you bring us from your Gathering?"

"I bear good news," the mage replied smugly.

"Our work is having an effect?"

"Oh, yes. The Order is worried; today's session was as unruly a meeting as I've ever seen in the Great Hall. Mage accusing mage; Hawk-Mages and Owl-Masters at each other's throats. I must say I found it quite amusing."

"I'm glad you were entertained," Calbyr remarked dryly.

The mage held up a finger. "Ah, but I haven't even told you the best part," he said, a malevolent grin spreading across his features. "Thanks to Baden, we literally have them chasing ghosts."

"I don't follow."

"Baden believes that your attacks have been orchestrated by the unsettled spirit of Theron," the mage explained, barely containing his glee. "And I believe he's managed to convince quite a few of the others."

"Theron," Calbyr repeated to himself, as if trying to place the name.

"Of course, you don't understand," the mage commented impatiently. "I sometimes forget that you're not of Tobyn-Ser. Listen then, and learn." The mage briefly explained the history and meaning of Theron's Curse, and the plight of the Unsettled. "If Baden sways the rest of the Order to his view," he concluded, "they will undertake a journey to Theron's Grove to confront the Owl-Master's spirit."

"And this will buy us more time?" Calbyr asked, still not fully comprehending the mage's excitement.

The mage threw back his head and laughed. "Oh, it will buy us much more than time, Calbyr. No one has ever survived a journey into the grove. This is our opportunity to rid ourselves of Baden and the old hag who leads the Order."

Calbyr smiled venomously. "Ah, Child of Amarid, if your friends in the Order could only hear you now."

The mage's laughter ceased and his voice, when he spoke, was shockingly cold. "I have no friends in the Order."

The smile vanished from Calbyr's face. "How can you be certain that the journey to Theron's Grove will fail?" he demanded after a long pause. "How do you know that this Baden and the one you call the Hag will die?"

"I'll be part of any delegation that travels to the grove," the mage replied simply. "I'll make sure of it."

"Without dying yourself?" Calbyr asked, arching an eyebrow. "I thought you said that no one—"

"Leave this to me, Calbyr," the mage commanded in a tone that left no room for argument. "You just take care of your end of things."

Calbyr stared at the mage for a moment before nodding once. "We're ready to move to the second phase of our plan," he announced crisply. "Until now the feathers have been the only clue we have left as to the identity of the attackers. Beginning with our next strike, we'll leave witnesses, who will have seen our cloaks and birds and staffs. We'll also continue to escalate the level of violence. Soon, the Order will be disgraced and its standing in Tobyn-Ser will be completely undermined. You will rule the land as you desire, and we will have access to your resources as we desire."

"Limited access," the mage corrected pointedly, "and only to those resources for which we negotiate a price. You would do well to remember, Calbyr, that soon—very soon—I will be more powerful than all the mages in Tobyn-Ser combined. You and your friends will get your resources, but in a manner, and at a price, that I decide."

Calbyr smiled coldly. "Of course, Child of Amarid. I would not have it any other way."

"Good. I'm glad to hear you say so. I'd hate to have to remind you that I hold your life and that of your companions as a small thing in my hand; that I could reveal you and have you killed before you could say anything about my role in your little plot. In fact, that reminds me of something," the mage continued, addressing himself to all of those in the clearing. "Baden's new apprentice had a vision of one of you, which he described to the Gathering this morning, in stunning detail, I might add."

"What!" Calbyr exploded, as his companions looked at one another in alarm.

The mage laughed. "Calm yourself, Calbyr. Such visions are quite common among my kind. I'm surprised that this boy is the only one to have seen you." Calbyr glared at the mage, his expression unchanged despite these reassurances. "He merely described your cloak, staff, and bird," the mage went on. "He saw nothing that would tell him that you come from Lon-Ser. But, to be safe,

I would suggest that you maintain your facade at all times and that we keep our meetings short and to a minimum."

Calbyr nodded. "Do we have any more business to discuss?"

The mage considered the question and, at length, shook his head. "I don't believe so. Where will your next attack take place?"

"The town of Kaera, on the west fork of the Moriandral, within a fortnight."

"Why Kaera?"

Calbyr shrugged. "No reason, really. We just wanted a target that would be close enough to the site of your Gathering to be plausible."

"Very well," the mage said, turning to leave the clearing. "Do you still carry the ceryll I gave you, in case I need to contact you?" he asked over his shoulder.

"I do," Calbyr replied.

The mage nodded once, and without another word, he stepped out of the clearing.

Calbyr watched the glow of the mage's ceryll recede into the blackness of the forest, and, as he did, he felt a knot loosening in his stomach. *When all this is over,* he repeated to himself, *I'll kill him.*

He was walking quickly. Too quickly. He needed time to think, and, at this rate, he would be back in Amarid too soon. He stopped and tried to force himself to calm down. Calbyr did this to him: made him edgy, made him say things he didn't mean. He didn't know what it was about the strange man from Lon-Ser that disturbed him so. They were actually quite alike, the mage thought with a rueful smile. Perhaps that was the problem. They were too much alike. Given the malice, bordering on madness, that the mage saw in Calbyr's dark eyes, that scared him.

There could be no denying the fact that Calbyr and his company had proven themselves useful in the year since he first happened upon them in western Tobyn-Ser. No doubt he had been an equally valuable ally. They needed someone who understood the Order and its workings. And he needed someone on the outside who could help him destroy his rivals within the Order. Alliance or no, however, he did not trust the outlander, and he certainly didn't like him. He knew that the verbal parry and thrust in which they engaged each time they met was counterproductive, perhaps even dangerous. But he could not help himself. All his composure, all the self-control that he used to conceal his treachery when he attended Gatherings or met with other mages, seemed to disappear when he spoke with Calbyr.

Nonetheless, things did appear to be going well. The attacks carried out by Calbyr and the others were having the desired effect. People across the land had lost faith in the Order, and the Order was already showing signs of tearing itself apart. And then there was Baden. . . .

The mage smiled as he resumed his walk toward Amarid at a more normal pace.

"Baden, you have given me a gift beyond my wildest dreams," he said to the night.

For months he had wondered how he might rid himself of Baden and Jessamyn. The others were foolish and weak. They did not concern him. But these two . . . Jessamyn, he knew, elicited love and loyalty from the other mages, emotions that could unite and fortify the Order in the hands of a wise leader—and, he had to acknowledge, she did have a certain wisdom. Baden represented a danger of a different sort. Indeed, in another time and place, the mage thought, smiling at the irony, he might have liked Baden. Despite his pomposity, Baden had a sense of humor, he was intelligent and persuasive, and he was more powerful than most of them realized. The mage laughed; it seemed that he also had much in common with a second adversary.

What mattered now, however, was that Baden had handed him a means of eliminating his most dangerous opponents in the Order: Theron's Grove. He was honest enough with himself to admit that he found the idea of this journey daunting. Powerful as the mage was, he realized that he was no match for Theron's spirit. But his recognition of the opportunity with which he had been presented far outweighed his fear. And in thinking about this he remembered something else Baden had said during today's session in the Great Hall. Jaryd, Baden had predicted, *would one day be more powerful than any mage in the room.* Leave it to Baden to bluster on about his Attend's potential, the mage thought with more than a little contempt. Perhaps he had merely been boasting; perhaps he had exaggerated. But the mage could not take that chance, and Baden, by asking that the boy be allowed to accompany them to Theron's Grove, had provided him with a solution to this problem as well. If necessary, he would join Baden in the Owl-Master's effort to have the boy included in the delegation, even if he was unfledged. And Jaryd would die with the rest of them.

Even before he had fully awakened, as the sounds of the stream and the forest morning seeped into his sleep and gently tugged him toward consciousness, Jaryd sensed that he was being watched. He tried to rouse himself, hoping that the feeling would vanish like a dream. But as the singing of the birds and the sound of water dripping from the branches above grew clearer, so did the sensation. Thinking suddenly of the bandits, Jaryd opened his eyes with a start, and found himself covered with dew. The fire he had conjured the night before had died out. Rays of early sunlight filtered through the mist and trees, and small birds chattered noisily as they flitted in and out of sight among the fir boughs. Sitting up and turning his gaze in the direction of the stream, Jaryd froze. No more than ten feet from where he sat, perched on a low stump and staring intently in his direction with its head slightly cocked to the side, sat a large slate-grey hawk with a pale belly and fierce red eyes.

"Amarid's Hawk!" Jaryd breathed, not quite believing what he was seeing.

It was his last clear thought for some time, for in the next instant his mind was deluged with a bewildering stream of seemingly random thoughts and images, some wild and dizzying, others so alien that Jaryd could make nothing of them other than a vague emotion. At one point he saw the same image of himself that he had seen the night before as he lit the wood on fire, and then the vision seemed to waver and fade, and suddenly Jaryd saw himself as he appeared in that very moment, staring at himself, his features looking slightly odd and distorted. And as the images continued to pour into him he felt something else as well: a presence in his mind, similar to the one he had felt the previous night, but far, far stronger. It was as if something or someone was reaching to him, compelling him to share his thoughts. Without any conscious effort, acting on instinct, but drawing on the skills he had gained from Baden's exercises, Jaryd reached back.

Baden had warned him of the difficulties, even dangers, of sharing one's mind with a wild creature, but until that moment, Jaryd had not truly understood. The first images sent by the hawk had astounded him with their fluidity and swiftness. But with the connection that Jaryd and the creature established in that moment came a tidal wave of thought, memory, sensation, and emotion that threatened to obliterate Jaryd's sense of reality. Abruptly, he was flying, darting with bewildering speed among branches and tree trunks, changing direction with the flick of a wing or the twist of a tail. Then he was tearing hungrily into the still-warm carcass of a jay, both exhilarated and nauseated by the hot blood that flowed over his beak and claws. Flying again, he fisted his talon and dove at a large brown hawk, barely able to control the rage that filled him, driving him to pursue the other bird. Through it all, clinging to the last scrap of his sanity, Jaryd fought to resist the tide, to impose some hint of rational order upon the rush of chaotic thought. But there was too much to hold, too much to control. He felt himself becoming more bird than man; he felt as though he were drowning. He was flying again, stooping to hunt, tearing into another carcass, tasting the blood and flesh once more. And in some distant corner of his mind, with the last remaining sliver of his own identity, Jaryd felt his stomach heave. Overwhelmed by his connection to the bird, yet terrified that he might break it if he allowed himself to be sick, Jaryd fought the urge to retch, choking down the bile that rose in his throat.

And with that effort, with that last, desperate assertion of his own mind, he heard once more the words Baden had spoken to him in Leora's Forest their first night out from Accalia: "You must learn to open your mind to the bird, while at the same time maintaining the clarity of your own consciousness." And remembering his uncle's instructions, Jaryd stopped fighting. Instead he allowed himself to be carried by the current he had struggled against a moment before. And he was flying again, pouncing again, but it began to make sense. Accepting the images as the hawk sent them, rather than trying to force them to match his own conception of time and reality, he sensed a pattern emerging, one that he could follow. It came slowly at first, but with each moment, comprehension grew easier, and Jaryd felt the chaos subsiding as his own consciousness reasserted itself within his mind.

He found that he could see again with his own eyes. The hawk—Ishalla! The name somehow came to him. Ishalla remained in his mind, though he no longer felt quite so overwhelmed by her presence. *Her* presence. He knew somehow that Ishalla was female.

The flurry of images and thoughts continued to flow through his mind although they seemed to grow more familiar with each moment. He saw the Parneshome Mountains and Tobyn's Wood; the Northern Plain and Taima; and finally, most unexpectedly, he saw his home in far-off Accalia. His mother was there, and Bernel and Royden as well. So vivid was the image that Jaryd felt he could reach out and touch them. He had to suppress an urge to call out to them. The sight of them filled him with joy, and yet his heart grew sore with how much he missed them. Struggling to control his emotions, it took Jaryd several moments to realize that this image, like the others, came from Ishalla. Just as her thoughts and memories had become a part of his mind, she seemed to be telling him, his thoughts and memories had become part of hers. They had bound to each other. He really was a mage now.

Slowly, stiffly, he climbed to his feet. The bird still sat before him, as motionless as the crystal statues atop the Great Hall. The sun had climbed higher over the clearing and burned off the mist. Jaryd had no idea how much time had passed, but, given the angle of the sun, he knew that the morning was almost gone. Certainly the mages in Amarid had reassembled some time ago. Moving carefully, so as not to startle the hawk, Jaryd walked toward the great bird. As he drew closer to her, he was struck by her awesome, wild beauty, just as he had been when he first saw the painting of Amarid's familiar on the ceiling of the Great Hall. She was as large as any hawk he had seen at the Gathering the day before. Her back was bluish-grey, and her long grey tail was banded with broad black lines. Her breast and belly were pale and finely barred. And her head, with its black cap and cheeks and a white stripe over each red eye, gave her a look of intelligence and ferocity unlike any bird Jaryd had ever seen. Still staring at her, still moving slowly, Jaryd trembled as he approached her. He stopped just in front of Ishalla and held out his arm. Without hesitating, she hopped on to the offered perch.

Jaryd winced, feeling her powerful talons grip his arm, the sharp claws digging through his shirt sleeve and into his flesh. Still, despite the pain and his continued trembling, he managed to hold his arm fairly steady. Given her size, Ishalla felt surprisingly light.

Unable to take his eyes off his familiar, Jaryd grinned with unrestrained delight. If only his family could see him now, Jaryd thought. Even Bernel might have smiled at the sight of his son with such a magnificent bird on his arm. Jaryd couldn't wait to see the expression on Baden's face.

"I'm a mage," he said out loud, just as he had the night before. And then, as if to confirm it, Jaryd spoke her name. "Ishalla. I know that your name is Ishalla."

By way of reply, the hawk hopped up to his shoulder and began preening herself, seeming so comfortable that Jaryd actually laughed out loud. Her talons carved into his skin again and Jaryd felt a small trickle of blood on his shoulder, but somehow it didn't matter.

"We should get going," he told her. "With all the running I did last night, I have a feeling we're a good distance from Amarid."

An image entered his mind: flying swiftly among pines and spruce, striking at a smaller bird, wheeling back and swooping to find it on the ground, ripping at its flesh.

Yes, Jaryd sent back, the connection feeling both strange and thrilling, *I understand. Can we meet farther up the trail so that I can start back toward the city?*

Another image came, of the two of them doing just that. An instant later Ishalla leaped off his shoulder, her talons digging into him so suddenly that he gasped in pain.

Rubbing his wounded shoulder Jaryd watched her dart across the stream and into the trees. And, as he did, he felt their connection growing weaker. He began to miss her presence immediately, odd though it seemed to him, given how briefly they had been bound to each other. For just a second, he worried that she might not return to him. He shook his head, smiling at his foolishness, and then he started down the trail. After just a few steps, however, he paused, gazing back over his shoulder at his campsite. "The place of my first binding," he remarked to himself, thinking incongruously of Theron and the curse. He flinched slightly at the thought, and after another moment, he turned again and began to walk back toward the Great Hall. A short while later, Ishalla joined him, startling him as she alighted on his shoulder, her claws tearing his flesh once more.

"I'll have to get used to that," he said aloud. She merely began to preen. But, much to his relief, he again felt her presence in his mind. From what Baden had told him, he knew that, as time passed and his bond with Ishalla grew stronger, temporary physical separations would have less effect on the bond they had just forged. Right now, though, Jaryd had trouble imagining that their bond could grow any stronger. Already, her presence in his mind seemed to have become part of him. In a way, he found it a bit distracting; it was almost as if he were constantly catching a glimpse of something out of the corner of his eye. But he had realized during her brief absence that having access to her thoughts also gave him access to her perceptions. As he walked along the trail, Jaryd found that his awareness of his surroundings was far greater than it had ever been. He still saw things through his own eyes, but his peripheral vision seemed greater, his hearing sharper. He felt attuned to the forest, as if he had lived here all his life. And he made his way back to Amarid slower than he knew he should, savoring his journey through the wood.

When Jaryd reached the Great Hall he found the gathered mages just ending their midday meal. Naturally, because they were looking for him, Baden and Trahn spotted him first and practically jumped out of their chairs to greet him. Walking toward them, acutely aware of Ishalla's weight on his shoulder, Jaryd suddenly understood the magnitude of what Baden had done for him the night before.

"You knew, didn't you?" he asked his uncle as the mages reached him. "That's why you sent me out into the forest last night."

Baden nodded. He was grinning now, as was Trahn. "I spotted the hawk following us during the last few days of our journey across the mountains. I had a feeling she would find you if I gave her the chance."

"Thank you," Jaryd said earnestly. "I'm sorry I wasn't more cooperative."

Baden laughed and shrugged. "Think nothing of it."

Jaryd turned to Trahn. "You knew as well?"

The Hawk-Mage shook his head. "Not until this morning, when Baden explained it to me. But as I indicated to you yesterday, I know that Baden rarely acts out of caprice." Trahn glanced at Ishalla, who was looking around the chamber, cautiously eyeing the other birds. "She's beautiful, Jaryd," he said. "May Leora make your time together long and rewarding."

"What's her name?" Baden asked, admiring the bird.

"Ishalla."

"Ishalla," Baden repeated, unable to mask the pride in his voice. "I trust your binding went well; you both seem to have come through it all right."

Jaryd nodded. "We're fine. My shoulder's a bit sore," he said, drawing grins from the older mages, "but everything went well. Everything, that is, except for the bandits I ran into last night."

Baden's eyes widened. "Bandits!"

"They tried to take Royden's ring," Jaryd explained, "and when it wouldn't come off, they tried to take my finger as well. But I managed to escape by lighting one of them on fire. Later, I lit my campfire the same way."

Baden's expression turned serious. "So you bound to Ishalla last night."

"No, this morning."

"But you began to manifest signs of power last night?"

Jaryd nodded.

Again, Baden and Trahn exchanged a look, although this time their faces wore expressions of wonder.

"What does it mean?" Jaryd asked, a bit frightened by the looks he saw on their faces.

Baden looked at him appraisingly. "I don't know," he said candidly. "I've not heard of anything like this before." He glanced at Trahn, who shook his head as if to say that this was new to him as well. "But," Baden continued, turning back to Jaryd, "I don't think it's cause for alarm. If anything, it merely confirms my vision of the bright future that awaits you."

Jaryd smiled at that.

Baden placed a hand on his nephew's shoulder. "Welcome to the Order, Hawk-Mage Jaryd."

Trahn glanced at the far end of the chamber, where Jessamyn now stood. "Looks like we're about to start again," he observed. "I should get back to my seat." He looked at Jaryd once more, a broad smile on his dark features. "Congratulations, Jaryd. I look forward to hearing more about your binding."

Jaryd grinned in return and began to move toward Baden's spot at the council table. Baden stopped him, however, holding him back with the hand that still gripped his shoulder.

"Just stand here and follow my lead," the Owl-Master commanded under his breath, a smile playing at the corners of his mouth. Suddenly feeling extremely self-conscious, Jaryd mimicked Baden's attentive stance, and silently faced the rest of the mages.

For a minute or two, no one took note of them. Trahn walked casually to his seat, and quiet conversations continued around the table. But soon Jessamyn noticed them standing there, and a moment later Jaryd saw her register Ishalla's presence on his shoulder. Instantly, a bright smile softened the lines of her face. Others, also seeing the Owl-Sage's grin, followed the direction of her gaze to see Baden and the newest member of the Order standing near the great doorway. Gradually, amid murmurs of surprise and, Jaryd thought, admiration, awareness of his binding spread through the chamber. Alayna, sitting nearest to where Jaryd and Baden stood, was one of the last to notice the excitement. When she turned in her seat to face him, and saw that, like her, he carried one of Amarid's Hawks, she turned pale and quickly looked away.

"Owl-Sage," Jaryd heard Baden begin in a voice so clear and ringing that it actually startled him, "I present to you and to this Order a new mage."

"Tell us of this new mage, Owl-Master Baden," Jessamyn replied ritually, the smile lingering on her lips.

"He is Jaryd, of Accalia," Baden returned in the same resonant tone. "Son of Bernel and Drina, grandson of Lynwen, great-grandson of Lyris, both of whom graced this hall with their power. He has been deemed worthy by Ishalla, and is doubly honored, for she is one of Amarid's Hawks."

Jessamyn nodded and raised both her arms as she looked around the table. "Mages and Masters of the Order, Baden has brought to us a new mage, Hawk-Mage Jaryd. Shall we make him welcome?"

In answer, the rest of the mages stood and raised their staffs in salute. Jaryd watched Alayna as she did this, but she would not meet his gaze. In another moment, the tribute was over and Jaryd was surrounded by the other mages, who congratulated him and complimented him on his beautiful familiar. Even Orris patted him on the back awkwardly and offered his praise, although the Hawk-Mage's expression remained dour. Jessamyn approached him last and embraced him. "No one has ever had their first binding coincide with a Gathering, Jaryd," she said quietly. "You are indeed destined to do extraordinary things." She released him, smiled kindly, and made her way back to the far end of the table.

As the mages were offering their congratulations, servants of the Great Hall placed a new chair, complete with a perch for Ishalla, at the near end of the table, just next to Alayna. Overcome with excitement and just a touch of anxiety, Jaryd walked to his seat and communicated to Ishalla that she should jump to the perch. She did so immediately and, smiling, he sat down.

Alayna sat motionless beside him, staring straight ahead, as if oblivious to his presence. He looked at her sidelong for a moment and then leaned slightly toward her. "Did I miss anything this morning?" he asked.

"No," she said curtly, without so much as a glance in his direction. "We just sat here in silence, waiting for you to return."

"How nice of you," Jaryd shot back, "but I wouldn't have minded if you had spoken amongst yourselves."

She looked at him, her expression unreadable, and, a moment later, Jessamyn began to address the Gathering and Jaryd faced forward again.

After a few moments, Alayna leaned closer. "This morning's discussion went much like yesterday's," she whispered. "Lots of noise, but very little progress."

"Thanks," he returned. "That wasn't so hard, was it?"

She looked at him sharply and then she, too, turned back toward the Owl-Sage.

For some time, as Jessamyn spoke and the mages resumed their debate over how to respond to the unexplained attacks that had occurred throughout Tobyn-Ser, Jaryd sat, hearing nothing, lost in his own thoughts. At first, he brooded over his exchange with Alayna, wondering why she seemed so hostile and sifting through his memory of their interactions in search of anything he might have done or said to her to give offense. But soon, his chagrin gave way to the wondrous realization of where he was and what he had become. He looked around the table at which he sat, not quite believing that he actually belonged there. At one point, Jaryd found that Sartol was watching him, and, as if reading the thoughts running through Jaryd's mind, the handsome Owl-Master offered a wink and then a kind smile, which Jaryd returned.

The silent exchange pulled Jaryd out of his musings and he turned his attention back to the debate taking place around the table. Initially, it seemed that the mages were merely rehashing their discussion from yesterday, just as Alayna said they had done all morning. Orris and his allies continued to argue with the older members of the Order, who, Jaryd thought, sounded lazy and weak-willed in their resistance to nearly all suggestions of how to combat the attacks on Tobyn-Ser. Jaryd soon noticed, however, that Baden and Trahn appeared every bit as frustrated as Orris with the course of the debate. Given the better part of a day to ponder the dangers of Baden's plan to confront Theron, several of the older mages had backed away from the tentative support for the idea that they had expressed the day before. Instead, led by Odinan, the aged Owl-Master who had argued with Orris during the previous day's debate, they now proposed an alternative to both Baden's plan and Orris's call for organized patrols.

"What we recommend," Odinan explained in his thin, nasal voice, "is that a group of mages remain here in Amarid. As soon as there is a report of another attack, those mages, along with the sage and her first, will use the Summoning Stone to send a small group to the site of the incident to investigate. That way we can respond as quickly as Orris would like without uprooting the entire Order. If these mages find evidence to support Baden's theory," he continued, "then we can send a delegation to Theron's Grove."

"That's not a plan," Orris said contemptuously. "That's a veil for inaction and cowardice." The stocky mage rose, glaring at Odinan. "That's worse than doing nothing, because it pretends to be something more. It's mere complacency. It offers no way of determining if there's a traitor in this Order, and, by the time news of an attack reaches Amarid, any possible trail will be cold."

"I must say, Odinan," Baden broke in, standing to face the Owl-Master, "I'm forced to agree with Orris. This proposal would do very little to help us identify our enemies and even less to protect the people of Tobyn-Ser. It's also a waste of our resources; the Summoning Stone requires a tremendous amount of power to transport people. You would need a very large group of mages, or you would have to limit the number of investigators to one or two. Either way, this doesn't strike me as a credible alternative to Orris's plan or to my own."

"It is a measured response to a situation we don't yet fully understand," argued another Owl-Master—Jaryd thought that he remembered the man's name as Niall. "Until we know more, it would be folly to risk Theron's Grove or to disrupt the lives of every person in this room."

"What about the lives of the people living in Taima or any of the other towns that have been attacked?" asked one of the younger mages. "How do we explain to those people that we've done nothing because we choose not to inconvenience ourselves?"

"I am not saying that we should do nothing!" Odinan replied angrily. "My plan—"

But before he could finish, a sudden shattering of glass reverberated through the chamber, shocking everyone into silence. On the southern side of the building, halfway between Jaryd's seat at one end of the table and the Owl-Sage's chair at the far end, a large rock crashed through one of the Great Hall's translucent windows, scattering shards of white glass across the marble floor. From outside the window, on the street now plainly visible through the gaping hole in the glass, came shouts of "Murderers!" and "Traitors!" and then the sound of rapidly retreating footsteps. For a moment, all of the mages remained utterly still. And then pandemonium broke loose. Several mages leapt toward the hole in the window, attempting to catch a glimpse of whoever had thrown the rock. Orris and Trahn dashed outside and, seconds later, ran past the gap in the window. Others rushed to Ursel, the young Hawk-Mage by whom the rock landed, as she assured them that she was fine. Hawks and owls circled overhead, crying out in alarm.

"Is everyone all right? Is anyone hurt?" Jessamyn called out several times, trying to restore calm to the chamber.

Jaryd had jumped to his feet with the burst of activity that had followed the initial silence. But he remained by his chair, with Ishalla on his shoulder, surveying the scene before him and trying to slow his racing pulse. Alayna was standing as well, her lithe frame taut and her face pale. They looked at each other briefly and then, without a word passing between them, walked together to where Ursel and a few others had begun to clean up the broken glass.

Several minutes later, as the commotion in the Great Hall began to die down, Orris and Trahn returned, breathless and flushed. "There were only two of them. We tracked them to an inn a few blocks from here," Trahn announced to no one in particular. "The city constable saw us running and followed. The vandals will be dealt with."

"What of it?" came a severe but familiar voice from the middle of the hall.

Jaryd spun around to see Baden still standing by his seat, his lean face stony and white, except for a bright spot of red high on each cheek. The Owl-Master's bright eyes smoldered like the embers of a fire as he swept the room with an arresting glare.

"What of it?" he repeated, filling the sudden stillness. "Imprisoning them will do nothing. You might as well let them go."

"Let them go?" Peredur asked indignantly. "They have desecrated the Great Hall of Amarid." Several Owl-Masters shouted their agreement.

"This is not one of Arick's Temples," Baden countered hotly, glancing briefly at Trahn, "and Amarid was not a god. This hall has not been desecrated, it has been vandalized. We would do well to remember the difference."

Peredur, his face reddening, began to respond. But Jessamyn placed a calming hand on his arm and looked toward Baden. "What is your point, Baden?" she asked, and Jaryd heard controlled anger in her voice; Baden was treading on dangerous ground here.

But the Owl-Master did not back down. "That rock was a message. We've grown arrogant and complacent, and the people of this land no longer trust us to take care of them. Jailing those two would be a meaningless, spiteful act.

Meaningless, because there are thousands more where they came from who are just as resentful of this Order as they are. Spiteful, because we are but servants of the land and this is their building as much as ours. They broke some glass and wounded our pride, so let them recompense the city for the former. And let us see to the restoration of the latter."

"How?" Orris demanded. There was a challenge in his tone and in the way he stood, with his hands on his hips and his legs planted on the marble floor. "How are we to do this?"

"By taking action," Baden stated matter-of-factly. "By facing our enemies. The two who broke the window called us murderers and traitors. That's how many in Tobyn-Ser see us right now. I'm not a murderer and I'm not a traitor; and I would prefer to believe that the rest of you aren't either. But to prove that to the people of this land, we must find and stop those responsible for the attacks." Murmurs of agreement spread throughout the room, but Baden quieted them with a sweeping glance. "Odinan," he said, turning to face the wizened Owl-Master, "I sympathize with your concerns. But you, who have been a part of this Order for so many years, must see how desperate the situation has become. The Great Hall of Amarid has been marred by citizens of Tobyn-Ser. We must do something to show the people that we care." Baden held the gaze of the older mage for what seemed a very long time, until finally, with some resignation, Odinan nodded. Baden acknowledged the Owl-Master's acquiescence with a grateful smile, but it lingered only a moment before the hard glare returned. "Let me add this," he said, and his voice suddenly was a drawn blade. "If there is a murderer and a traitor in this hall right now, hear me: I will find you, and I will use all my power to destroy you."

A strange silence descended on the chamber as the other mages glanced at one another awkwardly, as if wondering whether the men and women around them had betrayed the Order. And in that instant, Jaryd knew that someone in the room had heard Baden's warning and accepted his challenge. There was indeed a traitor in the Great Hall.

And then, as quickly as it had come, the feeling disappeared, leaving Jaryd to wonder if it had been a true insight or merely a flash of paranoia.

"Sage Jessamyn," Trahn called out, shattering the tense quiet. "I propose a compromise."

"Let us hear it, Trahn," the Owl-Sage replied.

"I suggest that we form a delegation to journey to Theron's Grove. All those mages who are not included in the delegation may choose between joining one of Orris's patrols and remaining in Amarid as part of Odinan's group. That way, all mages would be accounted for, we could explore Baden's theory, and we would be able to keep at least a limited watch on the rest of Tobyn-Ser."

Again the Order grew silent as the mages considered Trahn's proposal. At length, Orris spoke. "It's less than I'd like," he said, his voice tinged once again with the familiar mix of impatience and anger, "but I'll accept it."

"Odinan?" Jessamyn asked.

"It is acceptable," the Owl-Master agreed.

"Baden?"

Baden looked at the Owl-Sage and smiled. The color had returned to his features. "At the risk of overwhelming my colleagues with enthusiasm," he said dryly, "I actually like this plan."

The other mages laughed.

"Then we should vote on it," Jessamyn suggested. "Those in favor of the proposal?" she asked. Most of the mages in the hall raised their hands, although some showed decidedly less enthusiasm than others. "This, then, is the course we shall follow," the sage announced. "Our next task is to select the delegation for . . . whatever happens in Theron's Grove. I believe that Peredur and I should make this journey, and, since Baden and Trahn first presented the idea, I'll assume that they still wish to go." She paused, and both Baden and Trahn nodded in agreement. "Sartol, you said yesterday that you would be willing to be a part of this delegation as well. Is that still the case?"

"It is, Sage Jessamyn," Sartol replied.

"Very well. And you, Alayna; Sartol expressed his belief that you would be a valuable addition to the group. Will you join us?"

"Yes, Sage Jessamyn," Alayna answered in a clear voice.

"Are there others who wish to accompany us?"

"Sage Jessamyn, if I may," Baden began. "I said yesterday that I thought Jaryd should be included in this mission, and my colleagues reminded me that he was, at the time, unfledged, and therefore an inappropriate choice for such a task. Today we welcomed Jaryd into the Order, and now I repeat what I said yesterday: Jaryd has a role to play in this, and I would like to include him in the delegation."

"Jaryd," Jessamyn said, turning her gaze in his direction, "do you wish to journey to Theron's Grove?"

"I do, Sage Jessamyn," Jaryd answered, hoping that his voice sounded as steady as Alayna's.

"Good," Jessamyn stated with a nod. "We seem to have our delegation, and we shall leave—"

"Sage Jessamyn," came a voice with which Jaryd was becoming all too familiar. "I wish to make this journey as well." All eyes in the room turned toward Orris.

"You, Orris?" Jessamyn said with astonishment. "I didn't think you approved of this mission."

"I don't," the stocky mage asserted, "and that's precisely why I wish to go. I believe that there should be at least one in your company representing those who oppose this plan. I volunteer to be that one."

For a minute, no one spoke. Then Jessamyn smiled. "I'd be pleased to have you with us," she said warmly.

That makes one of us, Jaryd thought to himself, glancing sidelong at the ill-mannered mage.

"As I began to say a moment ago," Jessamyn continued, "we have our delegation and we shall leave with first light the day after tomorrow. The rest of you should decide whether you wish to stay in Amarid, with Odinan's group, or join one of the patrols—Orris, who will organize your patrols if you are with us?"

"I will, Sage Jessamyn," offered Ursel.

"Fine. Thank you, Ursel. When you have made your choice," the Owl-Sage went on, addressing the entire Order, "please speak with Odinan or Ursel." She paused to ring the crystal bell that sat on the table beside her. "We have had an eventful and productive afternoon," she commented with a look of satisfaction. "Perhaps we should recess briefly to catch our collective breath."

As she spoke, several blue-garbed attendants entered the chamber carrying trays filled with fruits, cheeses, and breads, and crystal decanters containing a fragrant pale wine. Jaryd began moving back to his seat, but, glancing toward Baden, who had been joined by Trahn, he saw the Owl-Master call him over with a gesture.

As he reached them, Baden indicated the chair to his left. "Have a seat," the Owl-Master said cheerfully. "Radomil has joined some of his friends on the far side of the table, so his place is free."

Jaryd took Radomil's seat and Ishalla hopped from his shoulder to the perch on the chair.

"That actually went better than I feared it might," Trahn observed quietly, as one of the attendants placed a large platter of food, a carafe of wine, and three crystal glasses in front of them on the council table. "I never thought I'd see an attack on the Great Hall itself, much less be grateful for it, but I think that it helped galvanize the Order into action."

Baden nodded as he poured wine into the three glasses. "So did a rather timely and effective compromise, I might add."

The dark mage inclined his head, acknowledging the compliment, before sipping from his goblet.

Jaryd also sampled the wine, which was light, and tasted of honey, without being too sweet. He broke off a piece of bread, took some cheese, and then passed the platter to Baden. He was famished, he realized. He hadn't eaten since the night before. "Does either of you think it strange," he asked between mouthfuls, "that Orris should want to journey with us to Theron's Grove?"

Baden shrugged. "I suppose it is a bit curious, given his initial reaction to the idea. But Trahn knows him better than I," he added, glancing toward his friend.

Trahn gave a small smile. "I'm not certain how well any of us knows Orris," he conceded, "but no, I don't think it's that strange. Orris is a natural leader," he explained, looking now at Jaryd. "The mannerisms that you see as gruff and abrupt, others may perceive as resolute and forceful. And, as a leader, he's sometimes reluctant to trust to others things he feels competent to do himself. It seems logical to me that he'd want to join our delegation."

"To make certain that we don't mess things up, you mean," Baden commented with a smirk.

Trahn smiled. "Something like that, yes."

They paused to eat, chewing on the soft, sweet bread and the pungent, salty cheese.

"Mind if we join you?" came a voice from behind them.

The three of them turned to see Sartol, smiling broadly, and Alayna, looking decidedly less comfortable and steadfastly avoiding Jaryd's gaze.

After a moment's hesitation, Baden grinned and indicated a pair of nearby chairs with his hand. "Not at all, Sartol, Alayna. We'd welcome the company." He paused, casting a glance and a grin at Jaryd. "Do we all know each other?"

Jaryd stood to face Alayna, and, taking more than a little satisfaction in the discomfort he saw behind her fixed smile, extended a hand. "We haven't been introduced formally," he said. "I'm Jaryd."

"Alayna," she replied, shaking his hand awkwardly and quickly sitting down. Jaryd sat as well.

"Even in these trying times," Sartol observed to Baden and Trahn with a nod toward the younger mages, "I can't help but be reassured to see our two newest colleagues both have their first bindings to Amarid's Hawk."

"I hadn't thought of that," Trahn agreed. "I think this is the first time it's happened since I got my cloak."

"Come to think of it," Baden admitted, "I've never seen it either."

Jaryd noticed that Alayna had begun to blush. Sartol appeared to notice as well, because he immediately changed the subject.

"You did us all a service today, Trahn. That proposal you offered turned around what could have been a disastrous session. I was afraid that stone through the window would destroy any chance of our reaching a decision."

"Thank you, Sartol," the Hawk-Mage responded, seeming uncomfortable with the Owl-Master's praise, "but if I hadn't offered it, someone else would have. I think those vandals might actually have helped us."

Sartol considered this. "You may be right. Nonetheless, we all appreciate what you did."

Trahn raised his glass in acknowledgment before taking another sip of wine. Again the conversation ebbed as they all ate and drank a bit more.

"I hope that Alayna and I didn't interrupt a private conversation," Sartol said at length, concern written on his tanned features.

"Not at all," Baden assured him. "We were just discussing the make-up of the delegation to Theron's Grove, a topic to which you two have probably given some thought as well."

Sartol nodded, chewing on some bread. "An interesting group," he commented. "Orris surprised me."

"Us as well," Baden concurred.

"He must believe that he has something to gain by going," Sartol observed. He looked at Trahn. "Any idea what it might be?"

The muscles in Trahn's jaw clenched, and the look in his green eyes seemed to harden. "The same could be asked of any of us," he said pointedly. "We've all volunteered to enter a place that no one has ever survived. I'm sure we all have our motivations, wouldn't you say, Sartol?" Listening to the Hawk-Mage, Jaryd suddenly remembered, from their conversation two nights before, that Trahn neither liked nor trusted Sartol.

And in that instant, for the first time since he had met Sartol, Jaryd saw a slight crack in the Owl-Master's congenial facade. It didn't last long, perhaps only the span of a single heartbeat. But the anger that Jaryd saw flash in Sartol's pale eyes was palpable, and frightening. Glancing at Baden, and seeing the intensity of the look his uncle gave to Trahn, Jaryd realized that Baden had seen Sartol's ire as well.

"Where do you come from, Alayna?" Jaryd found himself asking in an attempt to change the subject and break the tension.

To her credit, Alayna flashed him a grateful smile and cheerfully launched into a lengthy description of her home village of Brisalli at the northern edge of Tobyn's Wood, near the shores of the Abborij Strait. Some of what she told him about the moist climate of her region and the dense woodlands surrounding her village reminded Jaryd of Accalia. But he remained acutely aware of the lingering animosity between the older mages with whom they sat, and he did not hear much of what she said. When Alayna finished, she asked the same question of Jaryd, but before he could answer, Sartol began to laugh.

"It seems that our young friends have already mastered the art of diplomacy," he commented, smiling at Trahn and Baden. "Perhaps we might learn something from them." He paused, turning to face Trahn. "I'm sorry, Trahn, if my question sounded inappropriate. I meant no harm, and I certainly didn't mean to imply that Orris had done anything wrong; I'm simply aware that you know Orris better than I, and I believe many of us who have spent less time with him were surprised by his request to join the delegation."

Trahn sat perfectly still for several seconds before he gave a small laugh as well. "I'm the one who should apologize, Sartol. I shouldn't have reacted the way I did. It's been a difficult Gathering—for all of us—and I didn't mean to take it out on you. The truth is," he concluded, "I have no idea why Orris made his request, but he probably feels that he has a role to play in the resolution of this crisis."

Sartol nodded. "I'm sure you're right, and I'll be glad to have him with us." The Owl-Master turned to Jaryd. "I didn't mean to interrupt you, Jaryd," he said in a congenial tone. "Please, tell us about your home."

Jaryd glanced at Alayna, who offered a smile seemingly free of irony. "Actually," he began, still holding Alayna's gaze, "given what Alayna said about Brisalli, I'd say that our two villages are rather similar." He turned to Sartol. "But let's be frank, Owl-Master: we have more important things to discuss than the climate in Accalia." Encompassing Trahn and Baden in his glance as well, he continued. "I'm honored to have been included in this delegation, but I'd like a better sense of what our journey, and our confrontation with Theron, are going to entail. What makes you think that we can survive an encounter with him when no one else has? How are we going to keep ourselves alive long enough to say to Theron whatever it is you intend to say?"

The older mages looked at one another. "I must say," Sartol admitted, gazing at Baden from beneath the shock of black and silver hair, "I've wondered about this as well; it's the question I tried to raise during yesterday's discussion."

"I remember," Baden commented wryly, "and I did my best to avoid a direct answer." He looked at Jaryd and then at Alayna. "Sartol and I got the two of you into this. Not that I doubt your willingness to go," he added quickly, as both of the young mages began to object, "but we did volunteer you. You deserve an answer, Jaryd, but I don't really have one. I don't know what to expect. We're going to be improvising under the most dangerous of conditions, and I'm counting on the collective wisdom and courage of the delegation to get us through."

Jaryd shrugged. "Fair enough," he said simply. His eyes flicked toward Alayna again. "Although I'll be glad to have someone with us who knows a bit about Theron's life." He looked at Baden again. "How long will the journey itself take?"

Baden hesitated, calculating the distance and time in his mind. "I expect that Jessamyn will secure horses for the delegation," he said at last, "in which case it should only take us a bit more than a fortnight."

"Horses?" Jaryd asked, unable to conceal his alarm. "We'll be riding?"

"It would be a very long walk, Jaryd," Baden replied with some amusement. "And there is some urgency to our mission."

"Is there a problem, Jaryd?" Trahn asked, suppressing a smirk. "Do you dislike horses?"

"No," Jaryd responded, suddenly feeling self-conscious. "Horses are fine." He hesitated. "The truth is," he admitted with resignation, "I've never done much riding, and I'm not very comfortable with large animals."

Baden shook his head. "Amazing," he remarked in a voice laden with irony. "We're going to Theron's Grove, and he's worried about his mount."

The others laughed, and, after a moment, Jaryd joined in.

"In all seriousness, Jaryd," Trahn offered at last, "you have nothing to fear from a horse. I've been riding since I was a boy and I'll be more than happy to teach you what you need to know."

Jaryd smiled gratefully at the Hawk-Mage and nodded. Just then, Jessamyn returned to her place at the head of the table and called the Order back into session. Trahn and Sartol moved quickly to the far side of the table, and Jaryd and Alayna walked together to their seats.

"That was an interesting exchange," Alayna commented quietly along the way.

"Trahn and Sartol?" Jaryd asked.

She nodded.

"Yes, it was," he agreed. He considered saying more, perhaps mentioning Trahn's comments about Sartol two nights before. But, remembering that Alayna had been Sartol's Mage-Attend, he thought better of it.

The rest of the afternoon proved to be far less eventful than the early part of the day had been. Jessamyn spent a good deal of time delegating responsibility for the preparations and gathering of provisions that would take place tomorrow. She also took care of many of the ceremonial functions that she had postponed the day before. Together, these things took up what remained of the afternoon, and, by the time the mages adjourned, the daylight filtering into the chamber had begun to fade. Jaryd felt listless and drained as Trahn, Baden, and he made their way back to the Aerie.

Alayna had joined Sartol and left the Great Hall almost immediately after Jessamyn ended the session, giving Jaryd little chance to say anything to her. And now, as he walked with his companions through the alleyways and streets, Jaryd found himself reflecting on his various interactions with the beautiful Hawk-Mage, and wondering whether she was thinking about him. At times she seemed so aloof, even hostile, that he felt she must despise him. But at other times, when he would glance at her, only to find her watching him, or when they would share a smile, Jaryd felt a bond and a kinship that belied the newness of their . . .

Of our what? Jaryd asked himself. They weren't friends, not yet. They certainly weren't in love. So what were they? Jaryd smiled inwardly and shook his head. We're nothing, he told himself. At least for now, we're nothing.

Trahn and Baden had been chatting as the three of them walked. But now, Trahn leaned forward slightly to look at Jaryd. "Our friend seems preoccupied," he commented to Baden.

"Ah, don't you see it, Trahn?" Baden asked with gravity. "Our friend is smitten."

"Smitten?" Trahn repeated. And then, his vivid eyes narrowed into a sly look. "Alayna?"

"Alayna," Baden responded knowingly.

"Don't you two have more important things to talk about?" Jaryd asked with exasperation.

"More important? Certainly," Baden remarked, grinning. "But nothing as entertaining."

Jaryd rolled his eyes and took a deep breath.

"She's very special, Jaryd," Trahn said, his tone kind. "I can see why you would find her attractive. And," he added, glancing at Baden, "I find it interesting that you both have bound to Amarid's Hawk. Perhaps there's meaning in that."

"So you think that she and I—you think that it could work out?" Jaryd asked with sudden excitement.

"I don't know," Baden replied, winking at Trahn. "Do you want me to go back and ask her?"

"Come on, Baden!" Jaryd pressed. "I'm serious."

Baden regarded his nephew for several moments saying nothing. Then he shrugged. "I suppose anything is possible," he said cautiously. "I really don't know much about Alayna. For all I know she's married or betrothed. But even if she's not, you should know that relationships among members of the Order can be difficult. That's why most mages marry outside the Order. Right, Trahn?"

Trahn smiled. They had reached the Aerie, but they lingered in the darkening courtyard outside the inn as they continued to speak.

"Are you married, Trahn?" Jaryd asked, looking intently at the Hawk-Mage.

"Yes. My wife's name is Siobhan. We've been married for nine years. We grew up together."

"Do you have children?"

Trahn nodded and smiled broadly, as if he could see them there before him. "Two daughters; Jaynell is seven years, Osyth is four."

Jaryd took a minute to absorb this before he turned to his uncle. "Have you ever been married, Baden?"

The Owl-Master gave a wry smile, although Jaryd thought that he saw a different emotion in the older man's blue eyes. "No," Baden said at length. "Although there was someone once who I believe was willing to spend her life with me, and I with her."

"So what happened?"

Again, the mage smiled. "It didn't work out," he replied cryptically.

As Baden spoke, Jaryd remembered something he had seen during yesterday's discussion. "Sonel?" he ventured.

Baden gave him a look of genuine surprise, and then the Owl-Master began to laugh. "You are quick, aren't you? We'll have to be on our toes with this one, Trahn," he said to the Hawk-Mage, without taking his eyes from Jaryd. "Yes, Sonel and I were once in love," he admitted quietly, "many years ago." He paused for a long time, and when finally he spoke again, the crispness had returned to his voice. "So you see, Jaryd, when I warn you of the . . . challenges inherent in carrying on a relationship within the Order, I speak from experience."

Jaryd nodded, his expression turning glum.

"I'm not telling you how to live your life," Baden continued in a more gentle tone. "I'm certainly not telling you to forget about Alayna. That's not my place. But you just met her, and you don't know any more about her than I do. I think you're getting ahead of yourself. Don't you?"

Again, Jaryd nodded. "I guess," he murmured. Without another word, the young mage opened the door to the Aerie and stepped inside. And ducked just in time to avoid being hit in the head by a hurled tankard that bounced off the frame of the door and clattered noisily to the floor. Jaryd barely had time to recover before he had to lurch to the side to avoid being crushed by two large men, locked in combat, who tumbled against the wall beside the door. As Jaryd struggled to regain his balance, Ishalla let out a sharp cry and dug her talons into his shoulder, tearing a gasp from his throat. After finally finding a safe place to stand, behind a broad wooden pillar several feet from the door, Jaryd saw that the rest of the tavern was as chaotic and dangerous as the doorway had been. Everywhere he looked, men and women wrestled and fought; tankards, goblets, and plates flew through the air; and tables and chairs, at least those not being used as weapons, lay overturned on the floor. In the center of the room stood Maimun, the enormous barkeep, who tried to restore calm to his inn, mostly by pummeling into unconsciousness those who were doing the fighting.

"Your first barroom brawl?" Jaryd heard someone ask him in a breathless voice that carried over the din of the fighting.

He turned to see the serving girl from their first night in Amarid—her name, he remembered, was Kayle—standing next to him, flushed and smiling, her light brown hair pulled back except for a few wisps that fell attractively over her forehead.

He nodded and gave a small laugh. "Do you have a lot of them here?"

She shrugged, absently surveying the chaos before them. "We have one every couple of weeks. Nobody ever gets hurt too badly. I think they're kind of fun, although I hate cleaning up after them."

They both ducked as another tankard whizzed by their heads.

"I didn't see you last night," she said, facing Jaryd again.

She really was quite pretty, Jaryd thought to himself as he tried to explain why he had slept in the forest the night before. She had sapphire-blue eyes and a few light freckles across the bridge of her nose. There was a delicate fragrance about her that reminded him of wildflowers and spring rain. And

Jaryd could not help but notice how the low neckline of her blouse revealed the beginning of the gentle curve of her breasts.

"So you spend one night in the forest and you come back with one of Amarid's Hawks," she said with a crooked grin, as she gently stroked Ishalla's chin. "Is it always that easy for young mages to find their first binding?"

"No, it's not," came Baden's voice from over Jaryd's shoulder. "Jaryd is rather special, Kayle," the mage added.

Jaryd blushed deep scarlet as Baden and Trahn joined the conversation.

"I hope you didn't start this fracas," Baden remarked to Jaryd, indicating the bar with a sweep of his hand, and winking at Kayle as he spoke.

"He's been very well behaved, Owl-Master," Kayle assured the mage in a sincere tone. "I'm keeping an eye on him."

"I'm certain that you are, Kayle," Baden replied in a tone laden with innuendo.

She laughed as the two older mages moved on to find a table in a safe corner of the bar.

"How did you know that this was one of Amarid's Hawks?" Jaryd asked her, his composure returning.

Her expression hardened. "You think that just because I work in a bar, I don't know anything about Amarid and the Mage-Craft?" she asked coldly.

Jaryd shook his head. I seem to have a knack for irritating beautiful women, he thought to himself with regret. "Not at all. It was an innocent question; I didn't mean to offend you," he assured her. "It's just that, before I met Baden, I never would have known Amarid's Hawk from a barn owl. I was merely wondering how you knew."

She looked at him skeptically for a moment before her familiar, slightly crooked smile returned. She shrugged again. "I don't know. I grew up in Amarid, and I used to watch the processions with my parents each year. I guess I eventually learned the names of the various birds I saw. And," she added with genuine admiration, "Amarid's Hawk was always the easiest to remember."

They stood in silence for a few seconds, holding each other's gaze. At length, glancing around the bar and noticing that the fight had played itself out, Kayle said quietly, "I should get back to work." Jaryd nodded as she went on. "You go join your friends, and I'll bring you some food and ale." She started toward the bar, glancing back at him once with a flirtatious smile.

Blushing slightly, Jaryd joined Baden and Trahn at their table. Both mages grinned as he sat down. "I thought she wasn't your type," Baden commented.

"And I thought you were interested in Alayna," Trahn chimed in.

"She's not," he told Baden, "and I am," he added, turning to Trahn. "But that doesn't mean I can't flirt a little, does it?" His friends laughed. "Besides," Jaryd went on, "given how indifferent Alayna seems half the time, it's nice to know that someone, at least, is interested in me."

At that moment, Kayle arrived carrying a tray with three tankards of ale and a large platter of roasted meat, breads, and some steamed roots that Jaryd did not recognize. She served them without speaking, although she smiled at Jaryd when she gave him his ale.

"Well," Baden commented after she was gone, "she certainly does seem interested." He winked at Trahn. "Maybe you should have her talk to Alayna for you."

Jaryd shook his head as Trahn began to laugh. "Can we change the subject, please?" the young mage requested a little desperately.

The three mages began to eat, and, as they enjoyed their meal and the dark ale, they reviewed the day's events. Soon their discussion shifted, and Trahn and Baden told Jaryd more of the history of the Order and of the mages they had known. As they moved to their second and then third tankards of ale, they began to exchange more personal stories about their homes, their past loves, and their families. Occasionally, they tore off pieces of the tender roasted meat and fed it to their familiars, but mostly they gorged themselves, until Jaryd wondered if he would ever be hungry again. It was a late night, as all nights in the Aerie seemed to be, and it was not until the three of them slowly climbed the stairs to their rooms that Jaryd remembered his vow not to drink any more of the city's rich, dark ale. It was, he knew, an oath he should have kept.

8

His room was dark, save for the constant yellow glow of his ceryll and its soft reflection in the large, impassive eyes of his bird. He lay alone in the bed, thinking back with satisfaction on the events of the day. All had gone well, better than he could ever have expected. Sometimes, he reflected, all the planning in the world—all the cunning, and the attention to detail, and the artifice—was no match for plain, dumb luck. The stone crashing through the window had startled him as much as it had everyone else in the Great Hall. He had been quick to recover, however, and quicker still to recognize the opportunity that this random act offered. He had considered saying something that would allow him to seize the opening he had been given, something to galvanize the Order into action. But he didn't have to. Baden, his most dangerous adversary, proved once again to be a valuable, albeit unwitting ally. It was Baden's challenge to the Order that had spurred the Gathering to send a delegation to Theron's Grove. A delegation, the mage amended, grinning in the shadows, of which I am now a member. Let the others go out on their patrols or huddle around the Summoning Stone. Once I am rid of Baden and the Hag, none of them will have the power or the will to stop me.

He closed his eyes in an attempt to get some sleep, but one memory from this day still troubled him. "If there is a murderer and a traitor in this hall right now," Baden had challenged, "hear me: I will find you, and I will use all my power to destroy you." It hadn't been the words themselves that had bothered him; he was confident that he would defeat Baden when the time came. But in the stillness that followed Baden's declaration, the mage had felt exposed somehow, as if someone in the Gathering Chamber had sensed his treachery. He did not know who it was; indeed, for all he knew, he might have imagined the whole thing. But the feeling at the time had been quite vivid, and, he had to admit, more than a bit unnerving. He shuddered at the memory.

"Not that any of them could stop me," he said aloud, as if to convince his familiar. "No one has any reason to believe that I've betrayed the Order. And by the time they realize it, it will be too late."

His bird cocked its head slightly, and then began to groom itself.

Again he closed his eyes, trying to calm his nerves. It was all going so well; he would be foolish to lose sleep over some fleeting sensation that had probably been conjured by his own overanxious imagination. The Gathering, he knew, made him nervous. It was a small matter to fool the idiots he supposedly served, and he had little trouble hiding his thoughts from one mage, or even a few. But spending day after day with the entire Order, having to watch everything he said, every action and every facial expression—it was nerve-wracking. He could not be faulted for knowing one brief moment of paranoia. It was only natural. Besides, tomorrow the Gathering would end, and the next morning the delegation would depart for Theron's Grove. It would be easier once they were on their way.

His fears slowly receding, he felt himself beginning to drift toward sleep. But his slumber, when it finally came, was troubled by dreams of a shadowy figure carrying a brilliant sapphire ceryll.

The next morning, when Baden, Trahn, and Jaryd reached the Gathering Chamber, preparations for the departure of the delegation and the commencement of the patrols had already begun. Jessamyn and Peredur sat at the head of the otherwise empty council table, assigning tasks to mages and the stewards of the Great Hall, and coordinating the gathering and packing of supplies. Glancing to his left as they approached the Owl-Sage, Jaryd noticed that the window shattered the day before had been patched temporarily with a square of pale wood, and the stone and shards of glass had been removed.

The sage and her first looked up as the three mages drew near. "Ah, Trahn!" Jessamyn said with relief. "We've been waiting for you. Would you be willing to find mounts for the eight members of the delegation? No one in the Order knows more about horses than you."

"Certainly, Sage Jessamyn," Trahn answered with his familiar broad grin. "I already have mine, and I know of a trader who always has fine animals and, more importantly, who owes me a favor."

"Good," the Owl-Sage said. "Tell your friend that he shall be compensated above and beyond the full value of the horses. Baden and Jaryd," she went on, turning her dark eyes in their direction, "Sartol and Alayna have gone to gather food for the journey. I'd like the two of you to assemble and pack some cooking gear and any other equipment you think we might need. I believe there is a great deal of old equipment in the attic of the back room; anything you can't find there, you're welcome to buy in the marketplace. When Sartol and Alayna return with the food, they can help you pack that as well."

"Very well, Owl-Sage," Baden said with a nod, and, as Trahn went off to find the horse trader, his chestnut hawk sitting upon his shoulder, Jaryd and Baden walked to the rear of the Great Hall.

"Cooking gear?" Jaryd asked in a whisper as they walked.

Baden grinned. "Jessamyn and Peredur have lived in the hall for many years," he explained quietly. "They've grown used to some of the comforts of life here. I think they're entitled, don't you?"

Jaryd nodded.

"Don't let that fool you, though," Baden warned. "They're both tougher than they look."

"I'm sure they are," Jaryd said with a smile. Something else Jessamyn had said had aroused his curiosity, however. "If mages carry little money, as you told me the other day," he ventured, "how can Jessamyn afford to pay for the horses and equipment?"

"Individuals carry no money," Baden told him, "but the Order itself has quite a reserve of gold and silver." They paused at the bottom of a narrow, spiraling stone staircase that led up to a small storage area. "In the earliest days of the Order, towns and cities often sent tribute as thanks for the services provided by mages," the Owl-Master explained. "Later, after the first of the Abboriji invasions several hundred years ago, the Order briefly assumed responsibility for the maintenance of a standing army, and it collected voluntary duties from some of the larger towns. The temples objected and the army was soon disbanded, but when the Order attempted to return the funds, many of the towns refused to take back what they had sent. Indeed, for some time, they continued to give, perhaps feeling that somehow they'd be safer if they did. Whatever the reason," Baden concluded, "over the years, the Order amassed a tremendous amount of wealth that it continues to draw upon today."

"Shouldn't we return what we haven't used?" Jaryd asked.

Baden smiled. "We do," he assured his nephew, "in our own way." The Owl-Master gestured for Jaryd to climb the steps to the attic, and Baden followed him up the winding stairway.

Jaryd was not sure what he had expected the loft of the Great Hall to look like, but he certainly had not expected it to resemble so closely the attic of his parents' home. Notwithstanding the fine marble floors and high ceiling of the hall's storage area, it was just like the crawl space above Jaryd's old bedroom, the one in which he and Royden had played as children. It was dark, illuminated by a single translucent window just above the staircase, and, like the attic in Accalia, it smelled of mold and dust. Throughout the space, strewn in jumbled piles, some reaching to the height of Jaryd's shoulders, lay an unimaginable variety of old paintings, furniture, trinkets, and tapestries.

"What is all this junk?" Jaryd asked in amazement, as the grey bird on his shoulder hopped to a nearby perch and began to preen.

"Junk!" Baden exclaimed. "I suggest you look more closely."

Stepping closer to one of the piles, and brushing away some of the dust, Jaryd realized that Baden was right. The workmanship on the pieces of furniture was incredibly intricate, and many of the curios, when polished even slightly, shone with the dazzling beauty of crystal and gold. Jaryd glanced back at the Owl-Master, wonder in his grey eyes, and a question on his lips.

"Gifts for the Order," Baden explained, "from every corner of Tobyn-Ser. This room contains some of the finest works the people of this land have ever produced. Woven rugs with strands of silver and gold, paintings by the greatest artists in our history, tables and chairs carved from the rarest of woods, silver work and gold work by smiths of incomparable talent." He shook his head, gazing sadly from pile to pile. "These things should be on display, and instead, they sit up here gathering cobwebs," he concluded.

"Why?" Jaryd asked, sifting through a mound of exquisite silk clothing.

Baden shrugged. "We've never taken the time to decide what to do with it." Jaryd shot him a look, and Baden added, "I know that isn't much of an excuse, but it's the truth. We've never even discussed it during a Gathering. At least not in my memory."

"So what?" Jaryd asked harshly. His tone carried more anger than he had intended, but he pressed on. "Where is it decreed that everything has to be approved by the entire Order? Sometimes someone just has to take the initiative and do something! By the gods!" he stormed, indicating the riches in the space with one hand, and brushing the hair from his forehead with the other. "Now I understand why Orris is so angry all the time!" He stopped, suddenly aware that he had been yelling at Baden. "I'm . . . I'm sorry, Baden," he stammered sheepishly. "I didn't mean to be disrespectful."

But to Jaryd's surprise, the Owl-Master was smiling at him. "It's all right," he said quietly, "we're peers now. And I'm glad of it. Perhaps, if others among the younger mages share your passion, there's still hope for us." The Owl-Master took a weary breath. Perhaps it was the dim light of the Great Hall attic, but it seemed to Jaryd that his uncle looked much older than he had just a few days before, when they had hiked down out of the Parneshome Mountains into Amarid. "I believe the cooking equipment is back here," Baden said, as much to himself as to Jaryd, as he stepped over a pile of paintings toward the far end of the storage space.

Jaryd glanced around the attic again. *The finest works the people of this land have ever produced.* He shook his head, and went to help his uncle, who was already rummaging through the equipment.

They spent what remained of the morning gathering and cleaning off the lightweight pots and pans, utensils, and plates that the delegation would need for their meals. They also found several coils of sturdy rope, a dozen sheets of light tarpaulin, and eight saddlebags, which they hoped would be enough to carry all of the food and equipment. At midday, one of the blue-robed stewards of the hall brought them a light meal and a carafe of the honey-flavored wine that had been served to the Order the day before. Baden and Jaryd paused from their work to eat and then spent another two hours looking through the old equipment for anything else the delegation might need. In the end, they took everything they had found during the morning, as well as three sturdy backpacks and several skins for carrying water.

They climbed down the narrow stairway and returned to the Gathering Chamber carrying as much of the equipment as they could manage. When Jessamyn saw them, she quickly dispatched two attendants to retrieve the rest of the gear.

"Sartol and Alayna returned with the food a short time ago," the Owl-Sage told Jaryd and Baden in a crisp tone. "They're in the kitchen sorting it and will need some help with the packing."

Jaryd started toward the kitchen, but Baden's voice stopped him. "Owl-Sage," the Owl-Master began, "I have . . . an errand to which I must attend, but Jaryd will be more than happy to help Sartol and Alayna."

Baden and the Owl-Sage exchanged a glance before Jessamyn nodded knowingly, a small smile tugging at her lips. "Of course, Baden, I had almost forgotten. Go and see to your errand. The three of them can manage the packing."

"Wait!" Jaryd blurted out as Baden turned to leave. "You're not going to leave me alone with—"

"Is there a problem, Jaryd?" Jessamyn asked, as Baden regarded him placidly.

"Uh . . . no," Jaryd replied hesitantly. He paused, and took a deep breath. "No, Owl-Sage," he said with resignation, "there's no problem."

"Good. They're waiting for you in the kitchen."

He looked once more at Baden, who was grinning. "Say hello to Alayna and Sartol for me," his uncle told him.

Jaryd gave the Owl-Master a sour look before turning away and walking into the kitchen. He found Alayna and Sartol standing before a long white marble counter on which they had spread out and sorted the tremendous amount of food they had purchased earlier in the day. Dried fruit, rounds of cheese, dry breads, cured meats, and flasks of wine sat in tidy groups on the stone surface. The saddlebags and other equipment that Jaryd and Baden pulled from the attic had already been carried into the kitchen and piled neatly on the floor beside the counter.

The two mages looked up as Jaryd entered the room. Alayna quickly turned her attention back to the packing, but Sartol rose and welcomed Jaryd expansively, telling him all about the food market they had visited and complimenting Jaryd and Baden on their thorough search through the old equipment. Given the awkwardness of his previous conversations with Alayna, Jaryd had feared that this would be a painfully long afternoon. So much needed to be done, however, that the young mages scarcely found time to speak to each other. They filled the saddlebags under Sartol's scrupulous supervision, and, while Alayna remained tight-lipped and businesslike, Jaryd answered Sartol's numerous questions about Accalia, his childhood, and his brief apprenticeship with Baden. In this way, the afternoon passed quite rapidly. Before he knew it, Jaryd had finished packing the last of the equipment.

He followed Sartol and Alayna back into the Gathering Chamber, where Baden and Trahn chatted casually with Jessamyn, Peredur, and several other mages. With a polite word of thanks to Sartol, who had begun to speak with an Owl-Master Jaryd did not know, and a brief glance at Alayna, who continued to avoid his gaze, Jaryd walked over to where Baden and Trahn stood. His friends made room for him in their circle, but they continued their conversation, which, he gathered, concerned a heated argument between two mages during a Gathering several years ago that had centered on a rather obscure point of protocol, but had developed into a bitter personal feud. Jaryd recognized few of the names he heard and he quickly lost interest.

He found himself glancing around the room. The light in the chamber had already begun to wane with the onset of evening, and, as the sky outside continued to darken, more and more mages entered the Great Hall. Soon, the attendants of the hall, in their flowing blue robes, emerged from the back room and began to light dozens of candles, which they placed in holders and distributed at evenly spaced intervals around the perimeter of the chamber. As he watched the lighting of the candles, Jaryd noticed Orris, standing alone in a far corner of the chamber, staring at the circle of mages of which Jaryd was a part. The burly mage quickly looked away when he realized that Jaryd had spotted him. But the expression that Jaryd had seen on Orris's face made him uncomfortable, and, Jaryd realized with some surprise, left him feeling sympathy for the disagreeable Hawk-Mage.

A moment later, Jessamyn stood up and rapped her staff on the marble floor. "It is time," she announced, in a voice that stopped every conversation in the chamber.

Jaryd looked at Baden in confusion. "For what?" he asked.

"The Procession of Light," the Owl-Master replied, his blue eyes appearing to dance in the flickering glow of the candles. "We will retrace the path of the opening procession to Amarid's home, where we'll feast and Jessamyn will lead the closing ceremonies." Jaryd thought that Baden wanted to say more, but instead, the mage moved to take his place in the procession. Jaryd started to follow, but then, suddenly conscious of Ishalla sitting on his shoulder, he stopped and tried to figure out where he was supposed to go.

Unlike the opening procession, which began as a simple column, this procession seemed to begin with the mages lining the perimeter of the hall, each man or woman positioned just in front of one of the candles. Spotting Alayna, who had already assumed her place in the circle, Jaryd walked to the vacant space to her right. As usual, she ignored him. But when one of the attendants came before the two of them and presented each with a woven basket, large and deep enough to hold a loaf of bread, she shot him a questioning look.

He shrugged in response. "I have no idea," he commented.

Alayna turned to the mage standing next to her, a tall young woman who carried a small, dark falcon on her shoulder and who, unlike Alayna and Jaryd, had already received her cloak and found her ceryll. "Neysa, do you know what these baskets are for?" Alayna asked.

The woman was already looking at them, and had registered their confusion. "Yes," she responded enigmatically, an indulgent smile on her lips. "You'll understand soon enough," she added kindly. "Carry them with you as we walk through the streets of the city, and savor what you're about to experience."

She turned to look at Jessamyn, as did Alayna and Jaryd, and, as if on cue, the Owl-Sage, her large, white owl perched on her shoulder, raised her staff, with its glowing aqua ceryll, and extinguished the candle beside her with a quick breath. Immediately, Peredur, standing beside her, raised his pearl-colored ceryll and blew out the candle next to which he stood. The next mage followed suit, and so on around the chamber as the yellow flicker of the candles gave way to the steady rainbow of light given off by the crystals of the Order. Jaryd watched Baden lift his radiant orange stone up above Anla's head, and, a few seconds later, he saw Trahn raise his staff, which was crowned with a rich, reddish-brown ceryll.

As the process neared its end, Jaryd became acutely aware of his lack of a ceryll, and he wondered what they expected him to do.

"This much I've seen," Alayna whispered, as if reading his thoughts. "Just blow out your candle when it's your turn."

He nodded once. "Thanks," he whispered back, and was gratified to see her glance at him briefly and smile.

Their turns came quickly, and when Jaryd extinguished his candle, the only light left in the chamber was that cast by the myriad ceryls held aloft by the mages. Without pause, Jessamyn began leading the Order out of the chamber and into the streets of Amarid. It took some time for the entire procession to work its way outside, but even before he reached the door, Jaryd could hear the cheers of the people greeting the mages as they emerged from the Great Hall. When finally he and Alayna stepped out into the night air, Jaryd saw that all the lanterns along the street encircling the Great Hall had been extinguished, and all the window shades in the buildings lining the street had been drawn, so that, aside from the half moon shining brightly overhead, the ceryls continued to provide the only light. Seemingly thousands of people lined the street, cheering the Order and, at least for the evening, obscuring the memory of yesterday's attack on the Great Hall. And as Alayna and he reached the bottom of the marble stairs and stepped onto the cobblestone street, people from the crowd began to approach them. The first to reach them was a small, light-haired girl, accompanied by her mother, who stepped in front of Alayna and dropped a small feather into the woven basket Alayna had been handed just a few moments before.

"Wear your cloak well, Daughter of Amarid," the girl said shyly, glancing back at her mother occasionally for reassurance, "and may Arick guard you."

Alayna started to thank the girl, but, before she could, another person, this one a handsome young man, placed another feather in her basket. "Wear your cloak well, Daughter of Amarid, and may Arick guard you," he repeated in a serious tone.

By this time, an elderly man had placed a feather in Jaryd's basket. "Wear your cloak well, Son of Amarid, and may Arick guard you," he said with a wink and a grin.

So it went for the entire journey around the Great Hall and through the streets of the city to Amarid's old home. All along the route, which was lined with crowds of people, the street lanterns had been turned off. Only the light of the ceryls guided them, and Jaryd thought that he had never seen anything as beautiful as the glowing, prismatic column that stretched out before him through the city thoroughfare. As the procession moved through the streets, literally hundreds of men, women, and children approached Jaryd and Alayna, dropped feathers in their baskets, and welcomed them to the Order with the ritualistic greeting. Some smiled, or even laughed, while others remained solemn. And by the time the Order reached the wooded grounds of the First Mage's home, both Jaryd's basket and Alayna's overflowed with feathers of various sizes and colors.

Beginning at the very fringes of the land set aside around Amarid's home, and continuing as the procession wound along the path that led to the house itself, Jaryd saw dozens and dozens of large round tables bathed in light cast by tree-mounted torches, and covered with flasks of wine and platters of meats, greens, fruits, breads, cheeses, and cakes.

"On this night," Neysa commented, looking over her shoulder at the two younger mages walking behind her, "the Order feeds all of Amarid. It's our way of saying thanks to them for hosting the Gathering."

Glancing behind him, Jaryd realized that the throng lining the procession's path had, in turn, followed the Order to the First Mage's home, and was now spreading out among the food-laden tables, singing songs, laughing, and reaching first for the wine carafes.

"All of Amarid?" Jaryd asked incredulously.

"All who choose to come," Neysa answered, surveying the scene with amusement.

Jaryd turned again to watch the people taking their seats, and, as he did, his thoughts went back to the conversation he had shared with Baden earlier that day. Perhaps this was part of what the Owl-Master meant when he said that the Order did pay back, in its own way, the wealth it had received from the people of Tobyn-Ser.

Neysa, Alayna, and Jaryd hurried to catch up with the rest of the mages, who had reached Amarid's house and begun to seat themselves around a large, horseshoe-shaped table. There did not seem to be any formal seating arrangement, although Jessamyn and Peredur sat at the top of the U, and Jaryd noticed that Trahn and Baden had saved him a place between them. Alayna moved quickly to sit beside Sartol; and, with a smile and a brief word of congratulations on Jaryd's recent binding, Neysa joined several of her friends, leaving Jaryd to make his way to where Baden and Trahn sat.

They were grinning as he reached them. "How did you enjoy your first Procession of Light?" Trahn asked.

Jaryd smiled broadly in reply, and held out his basket of feathers for his friends to see.

"I still have many of the feathers I was given when I first walked in the procession," Baden said, pulling out Jaryd's chair and gesturing for the young mage to sit down. "I leave one each time I perform some service for the people, but I still haven't come close to running out. I still save Anla's feathers," he added, stroking the brown owl's chin, "just in case I ever need more. But I don't think I'll ever get to them."

"What did you do with your baskets?" Jaryd asked them both.

Trahn chuckled. "The basket you give back."

Jaryd gave a small laugh. "Then how do I carry all these feathers?"

Baden looked at him with a puzzling grin. "How, indeed?" he responded mysteriously.

The blue-robed attendants of the Great Hall, aided by other stewards wearing red robes, who, Jaryd learned, cared for Amarid's home, brought platters of food to the mages' table. There was roasted fowl and mutton, cooked greens, and rich, spicy stews that surpassed in flavor anything Jaryd had ever tasted. There were several kinds of breads and cakes, a startling variety of fruits, and pungent cheeses that were complemented perfectly by the robust, dark wine that flowed so freely with the meal. And through it all there was music played by skilled musicians and sung by honey-voiced bards who described with appropriate humor or heartache Tobyn-Ser's greatest triumphs and most bitter tragedies. Helped by the wine, and the torchlight, and the swirling melodies, Jaryd could almost see Arick sundering the one land into Tobyn-Ser and Lon-Ser, and hear Duclea's cries of despair at her husband's wrath and their sons' disgrace. He imagined himself sharing Amarid's wonder at the First Mage's discovery of the Mage-Craft, and he found himself sobbing quietly to the strains of "Amarid's Lament," the song written so many centuries ago after the death of Dacia, Amarid's wife.

After what seemed to be hours of celebrating, the music abruptly ceased, and Jessamyn stood, white-haired and smiling, and silenced them all with a simple gesture. Whatever her own doubts of her ability to lead the Order, Jaryd thought to himself in that moment, there could be no doubt that the other mages believed wholly in her, and would have followed her anywhere, even into Theron's Grove, if she asked.

"This year has seen the passing of three of Amarid's Children," she said in a voice both commanding and forlorn. "Verene, who served the Upper Horn; Holik, who served the Emerald Hills; and Sawni, who served the Great Desert, and who once was mentor to Trahn."

Jaryd looked over at his friend and saw tears flowing down his dark cheeks.

"Let us be silent for a moment," the Owl-Sage went on, "as we ask Arick and Duclea to open their arms to our friends."

The silence in the grove surrounding Amarid's house was a palpable thing, shaped not only by the mages of the Order, but by the thousands who had followed them through the streets to this place and had somehow heard Jessamyn's entreaty.

A moment later, Jessamyn broke the silence with a voice suddenly filled with joy and excitement. "This year has also seen the first binding of two who wish to serve this land with the Mage-Craft. Alayna of Brisalli, and Jaryd of Accalia, would you please come and stand before me?"

Jaryd stood, as did Baden, who offered an encouraging smile and then led Jaryd to the spot indicated by the Owl-Sage. The young mage suddenly felt acutely conscious of Ishalla's talons gripping his shoulder, and of her presence in his mind. He was growing more and more accustomed to the link they shared. Indeed, he was already having trouble remembering what it had been like before their binding, before he had constant access to her perceptions. He knew that most people in Tobyn-Ser spent their entire lives with just their own thoughts, without this magical connection. It suddenly struck him as a very lonely way to live.

In another moment, he and Baden, and Alayna and Sartol, stepped into the space created by the U-shaped table and stopped in front of where Jessamyn now stood regarding them with a smile on her lips. Jaryd glanced briefly at Alayna, and found that she was already looking at him with a strange expression on her delicate, attractive features.

"Alayna and Jaryd," the Owl-Sage began, "Arick has favored you both with exceptional first bindings. Indeed, I must deviate somewhat from the normal course of this ceremony to acknowledge publicly what many of us have noted in private: this is the first time in any of our memories that we have welcomed to the Order two mages in the same year who have bound to Amarid's Hawk. I know not what that bodes," she added, glancing briefly at Baden and Sartol, "but I think it must be something splendid." She paused before recommencing the rite. "You both have been welcomed by the mages and masters of this Order. Now you both must choose. Will you vow to use the powers you possess in service to this land?"

"I will," Jaryd and Alayna responded simultaneously.

"Will you vow to honor the laws created by Amarid to govern this Order?"

"I will," the young mages intoned.

"Recite the laws with me now," Jessamyn commanded.

Jaryd had not tried consciously to remember Amarid's Laws since that night in the Seaside Mountains, so many weeks ago, when Baden had spoken them to the darkness. If someone had asked him earlier this day whether he could repeat them, Jaryd would probably have said no. But here, in front of Jessamyn, with the entire Order and most of the city of Amarid watching, with the First Mage himself seeming to hover at his shoulder, Jaryd found the words and gave them voice.

"I shall serve the people of the land," he declared in unison with Alayna. "I shall be the arbiter of disputes. I shall use my powers to give aid and comfort in times of need.

"I shall never use my powers to extract service or payment from the powerless.

"I shall never use my powers against another mage. Our disputes shall be judged by the Order.

"I shall never harm my familiar."

There was a brief silence, and then a cheer went up around the table, which was echoed and amplified by the multitude surrounding Amarid's home. The cheering went on and on, stretching to a roar and soaring upward into the night. Standing there listening to the crowd, Jaryd knew that the cheers were meant as much for the Order and Amarid as they were for Alayna and him, probably more. But he also heard in the voices a plea, intended, he thought, for the two young mages to make whole again, for the Order and for Tobyn-Ser, what had been defiled by the recent attacks. And hearing that plea, he silently vowed to do so.

As the cheers died away, Jessamyn gazed at Sartol and then at Baden. "They are ready," she said simply.

Jaryd felt a light hand on his shoulder and, turning toward Baden, he saw that the Owl-Master held a new hooded cloak of forest green. Like Baden's, its sleeves and hood were edged with a delicate, pale green trim, and its sash was intricately embroidered in black and gold. Jaryd was relieved to see that the arms and shoulders of the cloak were reinforced with strips of leather to afford him some protection from Ishalla's talons. He also noticed that the pockets within the cloak were ample enough to hold all the feathers he had been given during the Procession of Light.

Smiling so broadly that his cheeks began to ache, Jaryd turned his back to Baden and spread his arms, allowing his uncle to put the cloak on him. Alayna had also turned to allow Sartol to do the same, and the two of them stood facing each other, both grinning, while Ishalla and Fylimar leapt from their shoulders into the air. A moment later, after both of them had received their cloaks and had turned to face Jessamyn once more, the two slate-colored birds, seemingly identical, settled back on their shoulders.

"Congratulations," Jessamyn said with a smile as the cheers returned. And suddenly they were surrounded by the other mages, who offered handshakes and hugs and welcomed them to the Order. But before both of them were swept up in the whirl of people and festivity, Jaryd turned back to Alayna and gazed into her dark eyes. "Congratulations, Hawk-Mage Alayna," he whispered.

She offered a smile in reply. "And you, Hawk-Mage Jaryd."

The rest of the night seemed a kaleidoscope of song and dance and wine. The musicians returned, supplemented by several more players, who added energy and rhythm to the ballads sung earlier. Jaryd, not usually inclined to dance, found himself compelled by both the music and an invitation from Jessamyn to do so anyway. And before the night was over he danced with a number of townswomen and several of the female mages, including Alayna once, although only briefly, and only because that particular dance involved the frequent exchange of partners. Mostly he danced with Kayle, who found him as soon as his first dance with Jessamyn had ended and stayed close to him for much of the night.

Shortly after Alayna and Jaryd received their cloaks, Jessamyn announced that she was retiring for the evening, and that the delegation to Theron's Grove would be leaving from the Great Hall with first light, regardless of how late some of its members remained at the celebration. Nonetheless, the music and dancing continued well into the night. Jaryd, Baden, and Trahn did not leave Amarid's home until just before dawn, and still the celebration was showing no signs of winding down. They accompanied Alayna and Sartol back to their inn, which was not far from the Aerie, and waited while they retrieved their belongings from their rooms. From there, the five mages hurried to Maimun's establishment, where Jaryd, Baden, and Trahn quickly reclaimed their things. They then started back toward the Great Hall, but they ran into Kayle at the edge of the Aerie's courtyard.

"Hawk-Mage," she called to Jaryd in a sleepy voice, the familiar, crooked grin on her face. She walked up to him and kissed him lightly on the cheek. Her breath smelled of wine. "I was wondering where you'd gone." She looked at the other mages. "You leaving the city so soon?"

Jaryd glanced briefly at Alayna, and was somewhat gratified to see her eyeing the barmaid warily. He turned back to Kayle. "Yes," he told her quietly, "we're leaving." He smiled. "Try to stay out of trouble, all right?"

"I will. Where are you going?" she asked in the same lazy tone.

Jaryd hesitated.

"We're going to Theron's Grove," Baden told her matter-of-factly.

"Arick guard you," she said reflexively. The smile vanished from her face, along with much of the color in her cheeks. "Is he serious?" she asked Jaryd, her tone suddenly urgent.

Jaryd nodded. Yesterday, her response would have brought back all of his fears. But he had taken a vow this night; two actually: one that he had taken aloud, and another that he had taken in silence. He could ill afford to be frightened.

"Arick guard you," she repeated, trying to grapple with what Baden had told her. She looked at Jaryd for a long time, saying nothing. Somewhere in the distance, a bird began to sing.

"Jaryd, we should go," Baden said quietly.

Jaryd nodded again, but he held Kayle's gaze. At length, he smiled. "Be well, Kayle. I'll see you again. I offer you my word on that." He stepped forward and kissed her cheek, as she had done a moment before. And without another word, the mages began to walk away, leaving Kayle in the dingy courtyard. Jaryd looked back once, just before they turned into a wider alley, and saw Kayle's lone figure, seeming small now, and lonely, still staring after them. He paused, but only briefly, and then turned to begin his journey toward Theron's Grove.

9

The company departed for the grove with surprisingly little fanfare. Radomil and Sonel were there to see the mages off, and several of the blue-robed stewards of the Great Hall had come out to help saddle the horses and secure the saddlebags. But that was all. By the time Jaryd and his four companions arrived, Jessamyn and Peredur were bidding their attendants farewell. Orris had already mounted his steed and was looking as forbidding and impatient as usual. Baden, Alayna, and Sartol quickly went to their horses and began adjusting their saddles, leaving Jaryd to make peace with the animal Trahn had found for him.

The creature was bay and white, with a splash of black on its nose, and though Jaryd thought that it looked terribly large, he had to admit that it was somewhat smaller than the horses the dark mage had gotten for the rest of the company.

"He's a gelding," Trahn said, standing beside Jaryd and placing a reassuring hand on his shoulder. "He may not be quite as fast as the stallions I got for the others, but he'll be swift enough for this journey, and he's far less likely to throw you or bolt."

His friend's assurances did little to allay Jaryd's fears, but the animal stood absolutely motionless for several minutes as Jaryd tried repeatedly and awkwardly to fling himself into the saddle. And when finally he had succeeded in mounting the horse, Jaryd began to believe that perhaps he could get along with this wonderfully docile and infinitely patient beast.

A few moments later, the company rode away from the Great Hall, following a wide thoroughfare into the old town center and then taking one of the ancient wooden bridges across the Larian River and continuing into Hawksfind

Wood. For the first several miles, Trahn rode alongside Jaryd and tried to instruct him in the rudiments of horseback riding.

"Riding is really quite easy," Trahn explained, obviously trying to sound comforting. "Just try to move with the horse. Rather than bouncing in the saddle as your mount gallops, you should try to rise and fall in rhythm with the animal. It may take your body some time to get used to this," the mage added with a grin, "but it will save you a good deal of discomfort."

Jaryd agreed that the mechanics of it seemed simple enough, and he was pleased to find that the gelding responded with alacrity to his sometimes desperate efforts to steer and stop it. But he quickly realized that Trahn's help and the gentleness of his mount could not overcome his inexperience with horses and the fact that his body was not at all ready for the rigors of the journey. Within an hour of the mages' departure from Amarid, the muscles in Jaryd's thighs, buttocks, and back began to scream with fatigue and pain. Two hours later, when the company stopped for a brief rest and a bite to eat, Jaryd found that he could barely lift his leg high enough to dismount. Once on the ground, he certainly could not walk. And so he sat in the dirt, just next to the horse, and chewed on a piece of smoked meat, wondering why he had ever been anxious to join this delegation.

The mages rested twice more during the day before stopping for a fourth time to make camp beside an emerald-green lake in the high country of the Parneshome Mountains. Jaryd heard the others commenting on the magnificence of the view and the beauty of the glacial lake, but, still sitting on his horse as the animal chomped loudly on the alpine grass, he could not even bring himself to look. He was aware of nothing save the pain, which had spread from his legs and back to every muscle in his body, including many of which he had never before been aware. Even his connection with Ishalla seemed to grow distant and faint, obscured by his agony and his fatigue. When he finally dismounted, Jaryd merely collapsed on the ground near his mount. Unable to walk and too exhausted to eat, he lay motionless on his back, listening to his horse chew, and waiting for sleep to carry him away from his misery.

"If you can roll over onto your stomach, I might be able to soothe those muscles a bit," he heard someone say as he lay there.

Opening his eyes, he saw the Owl-Sage standing over him, her expression sympathetic, although tinged with amusement. Slowly, agonizingly, he turned himself over. Jessamyn knelt beside him and placed her hands on his back. Immediately, Jaryd felt her power seep into his body, warm and soothing like the summer sun.

"One's first ride can be very hard," she said with compassion. "Lack of experience often leads to a great deal of suffering at first, but it's bound to get better with time."

"I know," Jaryd managed to croak. "I just didn't expect it to be this bad."

"I was speaking to the horse," Jessamyn responded in a flat tone.

And it seemed that he still had it in him to laugh, although it hurt terribly to do so.

The sage continued to heal him for perhaps a half hour, her hands deft and sure as they moved slowly over his back and legs. The pain did not vanish, but it did subside until it was only a dull ache. When she was done, Jaryd found that he could walk again, though awkwardly, and that he was, in fact, ravenous. After eating, he crawled off to a spot near the fire and fell into a deep, dreamless sleep. He felt even better the following morning, but his recovery proved to be only temporary. After a light breakfast the company remounted. And with his horse's first jarring step, all Jaryd's discomfort began to return.

The agony of the second day's ride seemed, incredibly, to surpass that of the first. The mountain terrain remained brutally rough, and they rode longer than the day before. Again, Jessamyn healed his aching muscles in the evening, and again he recovered enough to eat and sleep, only to find that his pain returned with the commencement of the next day's ride. The pattern repeated itself for one more day as the company completed its trek through the mountains and descended into Tobyn's Wood. But midway through the fourth day of the journey, as the company rested in the cool shade of the vast forest, Jaryd noticed that the soreness had begun to abate. As they remounted and rode on, he also realized that his horsemanship had improved. He was being jolted less; he felt himself moving more in concert with the animal beneath him; and he sensed that his horse now labored less than it had, no doubt in response to his growing comfort and confidence. Perhaps sensing this, Trahn steered his mount closer to Jaryd and said with an impish grin, "See, I told you this was easy."

Baden fell in beside him as well. "You seem to be doing better," the Owl-Master ventured with a sympathetic smile.

"I am," Jaryd responded with genuine relief. "I feel as if I've come back from the dead."

"Good. You and Theron will have something to talk about," Trahn quipped.

The three of them laughed, and they continued to ride together for much of what was left of the day, exchanging stories and engaging in the easy banter that they had begun to develop during the Gathering. Jaryd was glad to be with them again and thankful that his aches had subsided enough to allow him to enjoy their companionship.

Riding with his friends a few strides ahead of the rest of the company, Jaryd began to take note of the terrain through which he was moving. During the first several days of riding, he had been able to enjoy little of the scenery offered by the Parneshome Range. He had been vaguely aware, through the miasma of pain and weariness, of the snowy peaks and majestic vistas around him, but most of what he saw failed to reach him. Now, however, as the delegation made its way through Tobyn's Wood, and Jaryd's discomfort diminished, he began to drink in the splendors, both striking and subtle, of the God's forest.

He and Baden had crossed the northern portion of Tobyn's Wood during their journey from Accalia to Amarid, but for some reason, the wood had not affected him then as it did now. To walk through Leora's Forest, the woodland Jaryd had come to know through his childhood and adolescence, was to experience a playful colloquy between light and shadow. The forest itself, with its myriad shades of green, its endless natural patchwork of clearings and copses, seemed as quixotic and spirited as the Goddess for which it had been named. Jaryd had assumed, he realized, that all of the land's forests would be like the Goddess's. But Tobyn's Wood was different. Its massive, towering oaks, maples, hickories, and elms crowded the path that the company followed, the trees' lofty branches meshing to form a thick, ponderous canopy that allowed little light to reach the wood's floor. Where Leora's Forest appeared to dance with the sunlight, Tobyn's Wood brooded stubbornly in its own shadows, powerful but moody, like the God who had created it. And yet, despite its heaviness, its melancholy, the forest pulsed with life. Hundreds upon hundreds of tiny rivulets bubbled ceaselessly through the wood, fed by rain and the snows of the Parneshome range, feeding larger streams that meandered to the south and west toward Fourfalls River and, eventually, the mighty Dhaalismin. Beside the brooks and rills grew ferns and jewelweed, hawksbalm, and the velvet-blue leaves of shan, all of them flourishing as if in defiance of the shade cast by the wood. The flutelike refrain of thrushes echoed among the hulking trunks of the trees, squirrels and chipmunks chattered noisily as they chased each other on the ground and through the branches, and an occasional fox slipped furtively through the undergrowth. That night, as the company ate and conversed around the bright evening fire, crickets and cicadas serenaded them, and owls called from nearby perches, making the mages' birds uneasy.

After finishing their supper, Baden and Trahn worked with Jaryd on developing the young mage's mastery of the Mage-Craft. They had him light fires, large and small, and they taught him to shape wood. They also requested that, for what remained of the journey, the other mages bring to Jaryd all their minor bruises and scrapes, so that he might practice the healing art. Without a ceryll, Jaryd found it difficult to focus his power sufficiently for some of the finer tasks, but even in the course of just that first night, he felt himself growing more confident and adept. He also felt his connection to Ishalla growing stronger once more, and he welcomed their renewed intimacy the way he would a home-cooked meal after days without food.

The next morning, as the mages ate their customary breakfast of dry breads, cheese, and dried fruits, Jessamyn expressed concern about the rapid depletion of their food supplies. The company agreed that they would stop at the first settlement they reached to buy or trade for additional provisions. It was not until late in the morning, however, that they finally came to a small village, nestled among the huge trees of the wood and fronted by a swift, narrow stream. They turned off the main path and approached the settlement, but they never reached the center of town. Coming to a small wooden bridge that offered the lone access to the village, the mages were confronted by a group of twenty or thirty townspeople, all of them armed. The mob did not attack the company, for how could they? Thirty men and women carrying axes, knives, and tools would have no chance against eight mages. They could not even mask the fear in their eyes as they faced the company. But none of the mages was blind to the resolve and—there was no other word for it—hatred that also burned in the townspeoples' grim features.

One burly man, somewhat older than the rest and carrying a heavy, double-bladed ax, stepped forward to the center of the bridge and addressed the company.

"If you're here to destroy us," he told them in a strong, even voice, "we'll fight you until every one of us is dead, even knowing that such a fight is futile." He paused, slowly surveying the delegation. "If you've come for some other purpose," he went on, his tone still strong but lower, "forgive us, but we would ask that you move on, and leave us alone."

No one in the company responded for what seemed an eternity, until Jessamyn, her voice tight with emotion, said simply, "We'll go." She then turned her horse without another word, and continued through the wood, trailed by the rest of the delegation.

The mages made good progress for the rest of the day, pausing only briefly to rest and eat, and to feed and water the horses. But after their encounter with the villagers, a shadow seemed to settle over them. No one spoke except when necessary, and none of them seemed to take note of the remarkable terrain through which they moved. For his part, Jaryd could only hear the words of the ax-wielding villager repeating themselves again and again in his mind. He had faced an angry mob at Taima, but this had been worse. At least the people of Taima had a reason for their anger. But, as far as Jaryd could tell, these people had suffered no attack at all. There was no evidence of fire or bloodshed. The townspeople had just refused to let the mages into their village. Talk of corruption within the Order was taking an even greater toll than Jaryd had feared.

Late that afternoon, the delegation came to the ancient Riversmeet Traverse, a tremendous moss-covered stone bridge constructed just below the point where the Sapphire and Fourfalls rivers united with the main stream of the Dhaalismin. Built thousands of years before Amarid and Theron discovered the Mage-Craft, the bridge spanned the broad, roiling current in a high arc whose grace and delicacy seemed to belie the immensity of the stones that made up the structure. Its only visible supports were four enormous pedestals, two at each end of the bridge, the weight of which held the other stones in place. These pedestals supported statues that, despite their weatherworn appearance, were clearly intended to depict Arick, Duclea, Leora, and Tobyn. Smaller stones, piled neatly to the height of Jaryd's thigh, lined both sides of the broad traverse to serve as a guardrail. It was an awe-inspiring sight, as impressive and imposing as anything Jaryd had ever seen. And yet, even this could not lift the dark mood that had gripped the mages since their confrontation with the townspeople.

The company stopped for the day just beyond the traverse, setting up their camp in the shadow of the ancient structure. Jessamyn and Peredur retired just after supper, and the rest of the mages sat around the fire saying nothing, all of them still brooding on the day's events. Surprisingly, it was Orris who finally broke the grave silence.

"We should have stayed and spoken with them," he said, his tone uncharacteristically subdued. "We shouldn't have just left."

"To what end?" Sartol asked. "They obviously were afraid of us. They wanted us to go."

Orris glared at the Owl-Master. "So we just let them continue to think the worst of us?" he demanded. "We need to start rebuilding our bond with Tobyn-Ser's people."

"You may be right, Orris," Baden commented, "but I'm not certain that this would have been the best time to start. I don't think they would have been open to any overture we made."

"We don't know that," Orris returned. "It might have worked."

"I agree with Orris," Jaryd chimed in, surprising himself, and Orris as well, judging from the expression on the burly mage's face. "There may never be a good time to start repairing the damage that's been done, but we have to try anyway."

"So you're saying that we should have forced our way into their village in order to make peace with them!" Alayna countered hotly, her dark eyes boring into Jaryd. "That's ridiculous!"

"I didn't say that!" Jaryd returned. "But we could have tried to reason with them. I just don't think that leaving was our best option."

"Well, maybe we should make you Owl-Sage instead of Jessamyn," Alayna fired back, "since you seem to think you know what's best for all of us!"

Wondering how this had become his fight, Jaryd glanced at Orris, who offered a sympathetic grin and a slight shrug of his broad shoulders. "I didn't say that either," Jaryd replied, turning back to Alayna. "All I did was disagree with you, Alayna. Adults do that sometimes. It's called a discussion. Perhaps someday, when you're a bit older, you'll be able to have one, too."

Even in the firelight, Jaryd could see Alayna's face turn deep red. She sat utterly motionless for another moment, glaring at him, before abruptly rising and stomping off into the night.

No one else spoke for some time, until Trahn finally looked at Jaryd across the fire. "She had no right to say those things, my friend, but don't you think that you were a bit hard on her?"

Jaryd nodded. "I suppose," he said quietly. "I just don't know why she treats me the way she does. I guess I decided that I'd had enough of it."

Trahn nodded, and over the next few minutes the rest of them drifted away from the fire, leaving Jaryd alone. He stayed there for a long time, listening to the ceaseless roar of the rivers, and wondering if he and Alayna would ever have a friendly conversation.

Throughout the following morning, the muted sound of raindrops hitting the leaves above filtered down to the riders. Water dripped on them from the branches and ran down the trunks of the trees. But by the time they stopped for lunch, the rain had ceased. Late in the day, as the company drew near the edge of the wood, the forest abruptly grew sparse, and deeply slanting rays from the sinking sun burst through sudden gaps in the canopy. Moments later, the company rode out of the shadows of Tobyn's Wood and into a place awash with light. To the west loomed the densely wooded Emerald Hills, shrouded in a ghostlike mist that seemed to emanate from the trees themselves. To the south, its tall grasses shimmering as they swayed in the light wind, sprawled Tobyn's Plain, reaching uninterrupted to the horizon.

The mages stopped for the night, retiring early and rising just before dawn the next morning to begin their ride across the plain. After a light breakfast, as Jaryd prepared to mount his gelding, Jessamyn approached him. As always, Peredur was by her side.

"Are you feeling more comfortable in the saddle, Jaryd?" the Owl-Sage asked him without preamble.

Jaryd grinned somewhat sheepishly and nodded. "Yes, Owl-Sage. Thank you."

She returned the smile. "I'm glad to hear it. I would like to increase our pace now that we're on the plain. We moved a bit slowly through the mountains and Tobyn's Wood, and I'd like to make up some of the time we lost. Do you feel up to it?"

Again he nodded. The sage gave him a quick smile, gently squeezed his arm, and then walked away.

A few minutes later, as the sun appeared on the eastern horizon, huge and orange, the mages began to ride. For the three days that followed they thundered southward across the plain with their birds flying above them. Late the second morning, they came within sight of the Moriandral, and for what remained of that day, and all through the next, they rode along the east bank of the slow-moving giant. Far to the west, storm clouds crept across the skyline like dark spiders, the rain beneath them dangling like long, delicate legs. Occasionally, a thin sliver of distant lightning flickered silently from cloud to ground. But the sky above the company stayed clear, and, in the afternoons, heat waves rose from the land, causing the horizon to waver and dance. They passed several towns as they rode, but, given their experience with the villagers in Tobyn's Wood, the mages chose to move on without stopping.

During their third day on the God's plain, Sartol, who had been riding with Alayna ahead of Jaryd, slowed his mount slightly, allowing Jaryd to catch up with him.

"Are you riding alone by choice, Jaryd," the Owl-Master asked, "or may I join you?"

"I'd be happy if you rode with me, Sartol," Jaryd replied. But he knew that his tone betrayed a different emotion. Alayna, rather than joining him as well, had spurred her mount forward to ride with Baden and Trahn. She had not spoken to Jaryd since their angry exchange by the Riversmeet Traverse. This of course was nothing new; she had avoided him throughout the journey, spending most of her time with Sartol, but leaving him whenever Jaryd and her mentor struck up a conversation. But puzzled and hurt as he had been by her silent indifference, Jaryd found her overt hostility far worse. They had been traveling together for days, yet the gulf between them seemed wider than ever.

He watched her for another moment, noting how skillfully and gracefully she rode. Then he realized that Sartol was talking to him. Despite Baden and Trahn's warnings about Sartol's unctuous nature, Jaryd liked the Owl-Master. He thought him highly intelligent and uncommonly thoughtful, and he appreciated the fact that, unlike the others, Sartol seemed willing, even eager, to discuss their mission to Theron's Grove.

"I find it very interesting," the dark-haired mage was commenting now, "that the Order has come full circle back to Theron."

"Full circle?" Jaryd asked, trying to make himself heard over the drumming of their horses' hooves. "I'm not sure that I follow your meaning."

"Consider the history of the Order and the Mage-Craft. Notwithstanding the legends bandied about by the people of Tobyn-Ser, we mages know that Theron, as much as Amarid, was responsible for the discovery of the Mage-Craft and the founding of this body. Obviously, he abused his powers, and, quite appropriately, he was punished. But with the curse, and his death, the mages of his time lost sight of his contributions to their heritage, an error that we perpetuate to this day. I suppose I just find it interesting that the path to our own salvation should run through the grove of the outcast."

Jaryd reflected on this for some time. "Do you think that he planned it this way?" he asked at length. "Do you think that's why he's doing all this, if he's the one responsible?"

"Good questions," Sartol responded, "and I'd be as interested to hear your thoughts on the matter as you would be to hear mine. But I'm intrigued: 'if he's the one responsible?' " the Owl-Master repeated. "Don't you share your uncle's certitude?"

"I don't know that Baden's all that certain," Jaryd confided. "I think it's more of a working theory than it is a conviction, although both he and Trahn believe that even if Theron isn't responsible, he might be able to tell us who is."

Sartol gazed forward at Baden and Trahn, who were talking quietly with Alayna. "That he may," the Owl-Master said at length, more to himself than to Jaryd, so that Jaryd strained to hear, "if he says anything at all."

Jaryd kept silent, choosing not to pursue that particular line of thought.

A moment later, Sartol seemed to become aware again of Jaryd's presence next to him. "It sounds as if your uncle has thought things through quite carefully," he declared. "If this mission succeeds, the Order, and all of Tobyn-Ser, will be indebted to him."

Baden glanced back at them, a wry grin playing at the corners of his mouth. "And if it fails?" he called over his shoulder.

"I'm sorry, Baden," Sartol said smoothly, "I didn't realize that you were listening."

Baden shook his head. "I hadn't been," he assured the Owl-Master. "I just happened to catch your last comment."

"Ah. Well, I meant it."

"You're too kind," Baden told him, again calling over his shoulder, "but you haven't answered my question."

"If it fails," Sartol remarked, without any hint of mirth, "I doubt that many will give much thought to you one way or another."

Baden nodded once, and the company rode on in silence. But Jaryd reflected on Baden and Sartol's exchange for a long time.

A few hours later, the company came within sight of the Southern Swamp, its hollowed, sun-bleached dead trees and isolated clumps of brown grasses signaling a marked shift in terrain from the level, fertile prairie of the plain. Even from a distance, they could smell it. The heavy, sickeningly sweet odor of stagnation and decay oozed from the place like blood from a wound. Jaryd feared that Jessamyn intended to cross the fen immediately, but instead the sage turned the company to the southwest and they rode a few leagues more, skirting the swamp's edge, before stopping for the night.

For the next two days they continued along the edge of the quagmire, intending to cross it at its narrowest point, which lay sixty leagues to the south. They stayed just barely within sight of it, but still they were close enough for its stench to reach them whenever the wind picked up. And with every hour that brought them closer to the crossing point, Jaryd grew increasingly apprehensive. Baden estimated that even at its narrowest, the fen was nearly twenty leagues wide. They would be in the swamp, breathing its foul air, for an entire day.

By the time the company reached the crossing point late the second afternoon, the other mages seemed to have grown as concerned as Jaryd. For the final hour of the day's ride, they settled into a strained silence that persisted for the rest of the evening. The company's mood was made even worse by the fact that Sartol seemed to have taken ill during the course of the day. To his credit, the Owl-Master never actually complained of feeling sick, but he ate nothing after breakfast, and when he retired for the night, he was burning with fever. Baden tried to reduce the fever, but to no avail.

The following morning the mages rose with first light, and Jessamyn, seeing that Sartol's condition had not improved, offered to delay the crossing for a day or two. Sartol declined, however, and the Owl-Sage, obviously anxious to reach Theron's Grove as soon as possible, took the Owl-Master at his word. They broke camp a short while later and drove their horses toward the fen. As they approached it, riding through the thin mist that still hung over the plain, Jaryd gagged on the foul odor and quailed at the prospect of what they were about to do. And immediately upon entering the swamp he realized that this day's ride would be the longest and hardest he had yet endured. The smell was unbearable and Jaryd knew that as the day progressed, it would get worse. But, as the sun climbed higher in the sky, he also realized that the rankness of the swamp was the least of their concerns.

The heat posed a much greater danger, particularly to Sartol, who now looked unnaturally flushed, his chiseled features glazed with perspiration. Jessamyn and Peredur, who were older than the rest, also appeared to be wilting alarmingly under the relentless force of the sun. But none of them was spared. Unlike the plain, where a steady breeze had kept them cool despite the lack of shade, the swamp seemed dead, utterly still, shrouded in an invisible fog, fetid and stifling. Riding might have helped, had they been able to move swiftly enough. But they were slowed by the thick, oozing mud and could find no relief from the intense heat.

Mosquitoes, gnats, wasps, hornets, and biting flies of every imaginable color, size, and shape buzzed continuously around Jaryd and his companions, driving all of them, and their horses, to distraction. Jaryd had not seen this many insects in his entire life, much less in a single day. Late in the morning Jessamyn signaled for a rest stop, to eat a light lunch and feed and water the horses. Immediately the company was beset by a swarming cloud of bugs so ferocious that they hurried to care for the horses and remounted as quickly as they could, without feeding themselves. They rode on without pause, snacking on whatever they could reach without dismounting, and hoping that the horses would endure what remained of the crossing. Early in the afternoon, with the heat growing increasingly unbearable, Jaryd sat bundled and hooded in his cloak for protection. Still, he found that his face and hands were covered with red welts. By late afternoon, after riding for hours without rest, the muscles in his legs and back burned with a pain he had not experienced since the earliest days of the journey.

The mages reached the end of the swamp as the sun went down behind them, but they continued to ride for several more miles, until the foul smell had faded to a bad memory, and they had come to the edge of the Shadow Forest. When he finally saw Jessamyn raise her hand for the company to stop, Jaryd slid painfully off his mount and lay down on the ground, grateful beyond words to be done with the day's ordeal. His relief was short-lived, however. Sartol's condition had worsened. The Owl-Master's cloak was soaked with sweat, and he tottered precariously in his saddle. Orris immediately started a fire, and Baden and Alayna rushed to Sartol's side, helped him off his horse, and, with Trahn, led the exhausted, feverish Owl-Master to a place beside the crackling flames. As he had the night before, Baden tried to relieve Sartol's fever, but the mage's ailment still defied Baden's healing powers. Orris and Jessamyn also failed in their attempts to ease the Owl-Master's discomfort. Eventually, with Alayna beside him, applying a cold compress to his forehead, Sartol drifted into a fitful sleep. Reluctantly, the rest of the mages began to eat.

After a few minutes, Jaryd piled some food in a clean bowl and took it to Alayna. He placed it on the ground beside her, but before he could leave, she stopped him.

"You don't have to go," she told him and, then, hesitantly she added, "Actually, I'd . . . I'd like the company."

Surprised by her invitation, Jaryd stood for a moment, before finally sitting down. He glanced at Sartol. "How is he?"

Alayna shrugged, concern etched across her brow. "He's sleeping," she said simply. "I suppose that's good."

Jaryd nodded, and they sat there awkwardly, without speaking. Lightning from a distant storm fanned out across the western sky, and a bird cried from the Shadow Forest, causing Ishalla and Fylimar to stare curiously into the blackness of the wood.

After some time, Alayna gave a small laugh and shook her head. "We're not very good at this, are we?"

"Well, I'm not the one who runs away every time we might have to say something to one another!" Jaryd shot back with more heat than he had intended.

The expression in Alayna's dark eyes hardened and she opened her mouth. But then she seemed to stop herself and she glanced down at Sartol. It was almost dark, and his damp features shone with the light of his ceryll, which Alayna had placed beside him. "I guess I haven't been very nice to you," she said at length. "I'm sorry." She looked at Jaryd again. "But you've been pretty mean yourself! You had no right to say those things to me the other night! Calling me immature! I've been a mage longer than you have!"

"You're right," Jaryd replied, raising his hands in a placating gesture. "I shouldn't have said what I did, and I apologize. But I'm confused. I've been racking my brain trying to figure out what I did to offend you."

Alayna smiled ruefully and shook her head. "You didn't do anything, at least nothing you could control."

Jaryd cocked his head. "Nothing I could control? I don't understand."

"I know," Alayna said. She took a deep breath. "Look, let's just start over, all right? Pretend none of this ever happened. Can we do that?"

Jaryd grinned and nodded. "Yes. We can do that."

She returned his smile. "Good."

They held each other's gaze for another moment, before Jaryd glanced over at the rest of the company. "If you want to get some sleep," he offered, turning back to Alayna, "we can set up shifts to watch over Sartol. I'm sure everyone would be willing to help, and I'll take the first one."

"Thanks, but I don't think that's necessary." She looked at the sleeping mage. "He seems to be all right. I'll just sleep over here. If he needs me, Huvan will wake me," she added, indicating Sartol's large owl, which was perched a few feet away, its bright yellow eyes wide and watchful, its ear tufts raised expressively.

"All right," Jaryd said quietly, as he climbed to his feet. "Sleep well." He took a few steps toward the firelight and then turned back toward her. "And thanks."

She smiled, and Jaryd went off to find a place to sleep, happier than he had been in many days.

"Cailin!" she heard her mother call, in a voice that sounded small and far away. "Cailin! It's almost time for dinner!"

The little girl smiled as she continued to play in the muddy sand along the riverbank. Almost time for dinner, her mother had said. That meant that she still had a few more minutes playtime before her father took his turn at calling her. When Papa called, then she'd start back to the house. Papa got angry sometimes if she didn't come home when he called.

She stood to admire her work, brushing her dark hair away from her face with a dirty hand. Then, belatedly aware of the sand on her fingers, she wiped both hands down the front of her plain, beige dress.

The castle she was building by the river was nearly finished, and she didn't want to leave it quite yet. Sometimes when she built castles and left them overnight, the older boys from her school would come by and destroy them. She wasn't sure why they did it, but by now she just expected it. And this castle was so good that she wanted to stay with it for a little while longer before she went home. It had high, thick walls with walkways on top of them, and a rounded tower at each corner from which guards could see in all directions. In the center of the courtyard sat the main keep of the castle, which was very large and had windows that looked out over the walls toward the slow waters of the Moriandral. Atop the keep, she could see multicolored flags that fluttered in the wind, and behind it, lit by the late-afternoon sun, the beautiful gardens of the princess who lived there.

Cailin found a few more of the river-polished stones that she had been using for the windows and carefully pushed them into the sandy facade of the keep. She had found soft green grasses and some tiny yellow flowers for the garden, and she had taken leaves from a nearby tree and torn them into flags for the castle's roof. But she was most proud of the deep moat she had dug around the edge of the castle. Using a sharp stick, she had made a canal leading from a still pool along the side of the river to the moat, and had managed in this way to fill the trench with water.

She put the last of her stone windows in place and stood to appraise the finished structure. This was, she decided, the best castle she had ever built.

"Cailin!" her father called. "Come on, now, it's dinnertime!"

Taking one last look at her creation, the child scrambled up the riverbank to the tall grasses of Tobyn's Plain and began running toward the cluster of wooden houses that sat at the base of the dark, forested hills in front of her. She counted to herself as she ran, "One one-thousand, two one-thousand, three one-thousand," timing herself as she raced home. Once she had made it in less than one hundred and ten; she wanted to try to do it again.

But about halfway there—she had counted to fifty-three—she caught a glimpse of something blue in the grass and stopped to look. Balanced between two blades of the tall grass as if it were hovering was a feather. It was almost as long as Cailin's entire hand, and it was entirely blue on one side of the pale shaft, and mottled blue and black on the other. Feathers, she knew, brought good luck—gifts from Amarid, her father called them—and while no one had actually told her so, she figured this meant that she could make a wish when she found one.

Taking the feather in her hand, she closed her eyes, making the same wish she always made. "I wish I was older," she said aloud. She was seven now, which was pretty old, but she wanted to be fourteen, like Zanna, the girl next door, who sometimes watched her when Cailin's mother and father were working. Then the boys might not destroy her castles, and, like Zanna, she'd be allowed to go to the town on the far side of the river. Cailin wasn't really sure what was there, but she had lived in Kaera all her life. The idea of leaving the town on her own, even just to cross the river, seemed exotic and exciting.

"Cailin!" came her father's voice again, and this time he sounded angry.

She gazed toward the house. He was standing on the porch outside the back door with his hands on his hips and his dark, curly hair blowing slightly in the soft breeze. Holding tightly to the shaft of the feather—if she lost the feather, she had decided long ago, her wish wouldn't come true—she started running again. She didn't bother to count.

"Get inside," her father said, holding open the door and letting her scoot under his outstretched arm. "Your dinner's getting cold." His tone was still firm, but he was grinning as she went past him into the house.

"Where were you?" her mother asked with a smile from her seat at the table. Her mother was the prettiest woman Cailin had ever seen. Her hair was the same color as Cailin's, but it was even longer, and her eyes, like Cailin's, were pale blue.

"I found a feather," Cailin answered breathlessly, holding up the token for her parents to see. "A gift from Amarid. I had to make a wish. You and Daddy told me they're good luck."

Her mother stopped smiling and looked at her father with a serious expression. Cailin thought that she almost appeared frightened. The little girl turned to her father, whose face also had turned grim.

"Aren't they good luck?" Cailin asked, suddenly uncertain.

Her father hesitated before nodding. "Yes," he replied, glancing briefly at her mother. "They're good luck." He bent over to kiss the top of Cailin's head. "Why don't you go and wash those dirty hands."

Relieved, Cailin turned toward her mother, who smiled at her again, although the expression in her eyes didn't change. "Yes, Papa," Cailin said, cheered by the knowledge that her wish would come true. She raced outside to the trough by the side of the house and quickly washed the sand off her hands. Gazing to the west, beyond the river, she saw the sun, huge and orange, just beginning to dip down below the horizon. She wondered if her castle was still all right.

Hurrying back inside, she took her place at the dinner table and sat with her hands folded on her lap as her father offered thanks to Arick for their meal. When he finished, and they all began to eat the blackened fish and steamed greens that her mother had prepared, Cailin told her parents all about the castle she had made by the river. They smiled as she spoke, occasionally asking her questions about the princess who lived in the castle, though Cailin was much more interested in telling them about the castle itself.

"Papa, are there princesses in Tobyn-Ser?" Cailin asked, when she had run out of things to tell them about her castle.

"No," her father answered, shaking his head. "But there is a queen in Abborij and I believe she has two daughters. Both of them are princesses."

"Why aren't there any princesses here?"

Her father glanced across the table at her mother. "Well," he began slowly, "we have no royalty in Tobyn-Ser because we don't need any. Each town governs itself, and all of the towns get along with each other."

"If they didn't get along, would there be a war?"

"Cailin!" her mother broke in with a small laugh. "What strange questions."

"They have wars in Abborij," Cailin said defensively. "Teacher told us so."

"That's true," her father told her, although his hazel eyes were fixed on her mother again. "But when there are disagreements between villages or towns in Tobyn-Ser, they're mediated."

"What's 'mediated'?" Cailin asked, having trouble pronouncing the word.

"That's when someone who isn't involved with an argument helps those who are involved settle the matter," her mother explained.

"So who 'mediates'?"

For some time her parents said nothing, staring across the table at each other. At length, Cailin's father turned back toward her and took a deep breath. "The Children of Amarid help us resolve our disputes," he said in a low voice. "At least they used to."

"Why did they stop?" Cailin asked, looking from her father to her mother.

"It's not that they stopped, dear," her mother began hesitantly. She fell silent, and looked to Cailin's father without finishing the thought.

"Cailin," her father said in a soothing tone, "I know that we told you that the Children of Amarid were our friends, that they protected us and took care of us." He glanced across the table again before continuing. "But sometimes, friends let us down, and then they're not really our friends anymore."

Suddenly, Cailin felt afraid. "The Children of Amarid aren't our friends anymore?"

Her father shook his head. "No," he said simply.

As long as she could remember, her parents had told her about the powerful mages who carried beautiful birds on their shoulders, and wandered through Tobyn-Ser, helping and protecting its people. She often had dreams of hawks and owls, and she desperately wanted to become a mage when she grew up. And now, abruptly, the Children of Amarid weren't their friends anymore.

"Not even Master Holik?" she asked.

Her father took a deep breath. "Master Holik died during the winter, Cailin. Remember when we told you that?"

She had forgotten. But she now remembered how sad she had felt. Even her mother had cried. Holik had been a nice man. He had let her stroke the chin of his small, long-legged owl. Now he was dead, and the Children of Amarid were not going to take care of them anymore. Cailin felt like crying, although she did her best not to. "Then who's going to protect us?"

"Your mother and I will protect you," her father assured her, "and so will Davon and the others at Arick's Temple, and Constable Rugnar and his men. You see, we still have friends here in Kaera and we have friends in the other towns nearby, too. We'll all protect each other."

Cailin nodded once, although she still was frightened. She felt tears welling up in her eyes and she looked down so her parents wouldn't see. The blue feather she had found sat on the table by her plate. "Does that mean that gifts from Amarid aren't good luck anymore?" she asked in a choked voice.

Her father gently reached out and cupped the side of her face in his hand, making her meet his gaze. "Amarid was still the greatest man who ever lived in Tobyn-Ser," he told her, wiping a tear from her cheek. "And gifts from Amarid are still good luck."

Cailin wanted to ask how, if Amarid's Children were no longer their friends, his gifts could still be good luck, but instead, she just nodded again and put the feather in her pocket. She looked at her mother, who also had tears on her face.

"It's hard for all of us," her mother explained, trying to smile as she wiped away her own tears with a napkin. After another long silence, both of her parents rose, as if on cue, to begin clearing the dirty plates from the table.

"It's getting to be your bedtime, Cailin," her mother said over her shoulder as she carried the dishes out to the trough. "Put on your sleeping gown and we'll be in to say good night."

Cailin knew that she should have done as her mother said, but she was still scared, and so she followed her mother and father out into the night. It was dark. The moon had not yet risen, and a high, thin haze obscured all but the brightest stars. Her parents did not seem to notice that she had joined them, and they cleaned the dishes in silence. But when they were done, her father walked to where Cailin was standing and lifted her into his arms.

"What we told you scared you a little bit, didn't it?" he asked softly.

"A little bit," Cailin admitted, nodding.

"We didn't mean to frighten you," her father assured her, as her mother joined them and kissed Cailin on the forehead. "But you're getting to be a big girl now, and being a big girl sometimes means hearing things that aren't very happy. Do you understand?"

"Yes," Cailin replied, smiling slightly. She liked it when her parents treated her as if she were older.

"Good," her mother said, responding to Cailin's grin with one of her own. "Now, let's get you to bed."

Cailin looked at her mother and then her father with a mischievous glint in her eye. "But if I'm a big girl now, don't I get to stay up later?" she asked.

Her parents glanced at each other and started to laugh. "If you wash your face, and get into your sleeping gown very quickly," her mother told her, "maybe your father will tell you a story before you go to sleep."

Cailin squealed with delight as her father put her down. She ran to the door of the house, but, as she reached it, all three of them heard cries of alarm from the center of the village. Cailin spun to face her parents, all of her fears returning in a rush.

"Edrice, take Cailin inside and close the door!" her father said crisply.

Her mother nodded once, her pale eyes wide with fright. She scooped Cailin into her arms and carried her inside. Once in the house, Cailin's mother put her down and bolted the door behind them. Cailin ran to the front window, which faced the village square. Her father was now in front of the house, where he was speaking with Zanna's father, who held an ax in one hand and a torch in the other. He looked pale and angry in the firelight. Cailin watched as the older man pointed toward the Emerald Hills, which loomed in the darkness beyond the village. And, turning her gaze in the direction he indicated, as her father did the same outside, Cailin saw two glowing red lights slowly descending the slope of the hills toward Kaera.

"What is it?" she asked her mother, who had locked the front door and joined her by the window.

"Arick save us," Edrice breathed a moment later, as if she hadn't heard Cailin's question.

"Mama?" Cailin pleaded, terror seeping into her voice.

Her father knocked once on the front door. Her mother unbolted it and let him in.

"It's probably nothing," he said without preamble, walking to the back door. "We don't know for certain that the stories are true. But we're not going to take any chances." He unbolted the door and stepped outside. A few seconds later he returned carrying an ax from the woodpile. He locked the door again.

"What is it!" Cailin repeated, her voice rising to a wail, and tears beginning to pour from her eyes once more.

"Cailin!" her father snapped. He closed his eyes and took a deep breath. Cailin was sobbing now. "Cailin," he began again in a more gentle tone, "just stay here with your mother and everything will be fine. I'll be back soon."

"Why won't you tell me what it is?" Cailin asked between sobs.

"Everything will be fine," her father repeated as he kissed her cheek and embraced Edrice. He opened the front door again and started to leave.

And in that instant, Cailin knew. "It's Amarid's Children, isn't it?" she said flatly. "They've come to get us."

Her father stopped in the doorway and stared at her mother. Neither of them spoke, but the expression on her father's tanned face told Cailin that she was right.

"Keep the door locked," her father said at length, his voice bleak. He stepped out of the doorway and Edrice bolted the door behind him. Cailin and her mother moved back to the window to watch as her father made his way toward the town center. Soon Cailin lost track of him amid the confusion of men and torches that had gathered to confront the mages. Instinctively, almost against her will, Cailin shifted her gaze back up to the two moving points of red light.

They had nearly reached the base of the hills. They looked closer now, brighter. Cailin stared at them, unable to look away, transfixed and horrified by their unrelenting advance.

"Would you look at that!" Cailin heard her mother exclaim, as much to herself as to Cailin, and in a voice tinged with pride.

Tearing her eyes from the red lights, Cailin saw Zanna's mother and several of the other townswomen emerging from their homes carrying metal rakes, pitchforks, cleavers, and other tools that might help them fight off the mages. The women gathered in the road a few hundred feet in front of Cailin's home and began to follow their husbands and brothers toward the town center. Cailin looked at her mother and saw a grim smile spread across her face. The fear Cailin had seen in her mother's eyes just a few minutes before had vanished, replaced by a look that seemed like anger, but not quite. Silently, Edrice went out the back door, and returned a moment later carrying a hoe.

"Stay here, Cailin," she said in a commanding tone, "and bolt the door after I leave."

Edrice ran to join the other women, and Cailin watched their progress from the doorway. "We'll all protect each other," her parents had assured her just a few minutes earlier. And now they were doing just that. Maybe they didn't need the Children of Amarid after all. Her mother and father and the rest of the men and women of the town would drive the mages away. They would keep Kaera safe.

"I want to watch," Cailin said to the night. And ignoring her mother's last command, the little girl began running down the road toward the village.

Immediately, she heard her name called sharply from the house next door to hers. Whirling around, she saw Zanna standing in the doorway. "Cailin!" the older girl repeated, louder now, "Where do you think you're going?"

"I'm going to watch them fight the mages," Cailin responded.

"Didn't your mama and papa tell you to stay here?" Zanna asked in a tone that told Cailin she already knew the answer.

Cailin hesitated and then, without answering, she spun and started running toward town again.

"Cailin!" she heard Zanna call. "Cailin!"

Over her shoulder, Cailin saw Zanna running after her, and gaining on her quickly. She tried to run faster, but, just as she reached the outskirts of the village square, she felt Zanna grab the back of her dress and pull her roughly to a halt.

"Cailin, are you crazy!" the older girl shouted, gasping for breath.

"Let me go!" Cailin cried, struggling to break free. "I want to find Mama and Papa!"

"No! You have to go back home! I'll take—"

The two of them abruptly stopped scuffling as they heard a loud cry of alarm go up 'from the far side of town. Then, suddenly, horribly, a bolt of blood-red light arced across the night sky above the storefronts, hissing and writhing like a serpent, and crashed with an explosion of flame into the shrine at which the townspeople paid homage to Arick and the other gods. A moment later another arc, and then immediately a third carved through the night, smashing through glass and wood as fire began to consume Kaera's markets and smithies. And a cry went up once more from the townspeople who had marched out to meet the mages, but even Cailin knew that this sound was not born of anger or defiance. This was a cry of terror and searing pain; a cry of death.

As the two girls stood together, now clutching each other for comfort and safety, the sky above the village seemed to come alive with flames, and screams, and the killing bursts of red light. At one point they saw a great dark, winged creature swoop above the buildings, stopping as if suspended above the fires before dropping again, its wings outstretched with an unearthly grace. They saw it again briefly, a few moments later, or maybe it was a different one; they couldn't tell. But they knew that the creature, or creatures, did not look like any bird they had ever seen before.

The first wave of heat reached them from the fires, and with it came the smell of burning wood and flesh. Men and women who had left their homes so bravely at the sight of the distant red lights just a short while ago now began to stream back toward the girls, their faces distorted hideously by their screams and their eyes wide with panic. One figure whose clothes and hair were ablaze—it wasn't clear whether it was a man or a woman—staggered forward along with the crowd before falling to the ground, its mouth stretched open in a silent, agonized wail. And behind, walking with an assurance and calm that seemed to mock the dread-filled horde they sent fleeing before them, came two men, each clad in a long, hooded green cloak. They carried staffs topped with glowing red stones from which poured the devastating crimson flames that claimed building after building, and person after person. And with them came the great birds, black as the night had once been, except for their bright eyes, which appeared to glimmer with fire and blood as they swooped down again and again, raking the necks and backs of the retreating townspeople with razorlike talons.

Staring at the oncoming mass, unable to pull her eyes away from the destruction of Kaera, Cailin saw her mother and father running toward her, panic-stricken like the others. Her father, still carrying his ax, was bleeding from a gash at his temple.

"Mama!" Cailin cried out. "Papa!" She took a step toward them as she saw them register her presence.

"Cailin!" her father called to her. "Run!"

They had almost reached her—her father had even started to bend over so that he might sweep her into his arms as they ran past—when one of the great, terrible birds dove down upon them like a falcon plummeting toward its prey.

Cailin heard her father howl with pain as one of the bird's claws slashed across his neck, sending him sprawling to the ground.

"No!" Cailin's mother shrieked, dropping to her knees beside him. "Dunstan! No!"

Cailin screamed out for her mother, but had no time to do anything else. One of the mages, now only a few steps from where her mother knelt in a growing pool of her father's blood, leveled his staff at her mother and, it seemed to Cailin, pressed his thumb into the side of the shaft, just below the stone mounted at its top. A crackling bolt of red fire leapt from the stone to her mother, blasting her to the ground, and enveloping her in flames before she could cry out. Again Cailin screamed, and this time the mage looked directly at her. He had his hood drawn over his head, but in the hot, orange light cast by the inferno that had been Kaera, she could see that he was bearded, with a crooked nose and dark, deep-set eyes. He smiled slightly as he regarded her. Then he casually raised his staff and moved his thumb again.

Cailin felt the heat of the red pulse as it rushed just past her head and hammered into Zanna, throwing the older girl backward and to the dirt as if she were a rag doll. Cailin tried to look back at her friend, even though she felt certain that Zanna was already dead, but the mage, his smile deepening now, held her gaze. She wanted desperately to run, or better yet, to retrieve her father's ax and kill this man. But instead, she felt her head begin to spin, and her stomach rising in her throat. The last thing she saw, as she fell to the ground and felt consciousness slipping away, was the mage walking toward her and then past her as if she weren't even there.

When Cailin came to, the fires were still burning. She still smelled the smoke and the charred flesh. But aside from the snapping of the flames, she could hear nothing. No cries; no voices of any kind. As she tried to focus her sight, she felt herself raised roughly into a sitting position. The blurry figure squatting before her was dressed in green, and a large, black shape loomed on his shoulder. And as her sight returned, she realized that it was the bearded mage. She struggled to get away.

"Not so fast, little girl," the man said, grinning ghoulishly. He had a strange accent, one that Cailin hadn't heard before.

She started to scream, but he put a callused hand over her mouth. "No scream," he commanded, and then he grinned again. "No one to hear, anyway."

So everyone is dead, Cailin thought, starting to cry.

"Listen to me," the mage told her, removing his hand from her mouth and bringing his face very close to hers. "Listen closely: people will come; they will find you. And they will ask you who did this. When they ask, you tell them that it was the Children of Amarid. You tell them that we no longer serve Tobyn-Ser. From now on Tobyn-Ser serves us. You understand?"

Cailin kept on crying, and she said nothing.

"Do you understand!" he repeated loudly, shaking her by the shoulders.

Cailin nodded.

The man smiled. "Good." He pulled a feather from his cloak and handed

it to her. It was black and very long. Seeing it made her think of the blue
feather that she still carried in her pocket, and of the wish she had made. Now
she wished she were dead. "When the people come," he told her, "give this
to them as well."

Then the man looked up at something over her head and behind her, and
he nodded once. A moment later, Cailin felt an explosion of pain in the back
of her skull, and she fell back into darkness.

10

By skirting the western edge of the swamp and crossing it to the south
of where they first encountered it, the company had taken a calculated
risk, minimizing their time in the swamp, but increasing the distance they
would have to cover in the Shadow Forest. The next morning, they began to
pay the price of that choice. Once, the lush forest in the southeastern corner
of Tobyn-Ser had been known as Duclea's Wood. Graced by the Goddess of
Water with an abundance of spring-fed brooks and sparkling cascades, bisected
by the Moriandral, and surrounded on three sides by ocean and gulf, the wood
had been one of the glories of the land. It had been a center of trade and,
with its rich variety of hardwoods, the home of the most renowned wood
carvers in Tobyn-Ser. But that had been before Theron bound to his first hawk
in a grove just outside the town of Rholde and left his home, a young exile
newly versed in what came to be known as the Mage-Craft, but what the people
of his day called black magic.

All that had changed a thousand years ago. With Theron's Curse, and the
return to Theron's Grove of the Owl-Master's unsettled spirit, Duclea's Wood
became a place of fear and evil. Within five years of Theron's death, the people
of Rholde, whom the unsettled mage tormented mercilessly, had abandoned
their homes. Within one hundred years, the entire forest, indeed all the land
below the Southern Swamp, had been forsaken. Theron's Grove became the
most dreaded place in Tobyn-Ser, its name synonymous with death, and Duclea's Wood became the Shadow Forest. It held neither the awesome power
of Tobyn's Wood, nor the dazzling beauty of Leora's Forest. But the Shadow
Forest had a wildness that those others lacked. It had lain undisturbed for
hundreds of years, shaped only by the passage of time and the changing sea-
sons. And now, in the bright sunlight of this warm, summer day, it resisted
the company's advance, as stubborn and indomitable as an ocean storm tide.

Nothing in the forest could match the virulence of what they had just experienced in the swamp. But the wood presented obstacles and frustrations of
its own. Their progress was maddeningly slow, hindered by the writhing tangle
of brambles and vines that wound among the trunks of the trees, and the false
paths through dense thickets that lured the company into the forest's shadows
and then vanished without warning, like candles extinguished by a sudden
breeze. The trees grew so thickly in some places that the mages were forced

to ride single file. Even in the more open stretches, gnarled roots and the impenetrable undergrowth made it impossible for them to ride at a full gallop. Jaryd had hoped to ride through the forest with Alayna, but it was all he could do merely to navigate his mount through the forest. He was so focused on riding that he was only dimly aware of Ishalla gliding overhead. For her part, Alayna was occupied with Sartol, who, though looking and feeling better than he had in the swamp, was still weak and uncertain on his horse.

The company rode until the sky that peeked through the branches overhead had darkened to a deep indigo and they could no longer make their way through the wood. Even so, they had covered just barely more than half the distance to Theron's Grove, far less than they had hoped. They sat around the fire that night, aggravated by their lack of progress, girding themselves for one last day of travel. For the first time in several nights, Sartol joined them, his weathered face looking gaunt and pale in the shifting light of the fire. His appetite had returned, and long after the rest of them had finished eating the fowl killed for them by several of the hawks, the Owl-Master continued to supplement his meal with cheese, bread, and dried meat. As he ate, Jessamyn began speaking to the company about their coming encounter with Theron.

"With luck, we will arrive at Theron's Grove late tomorrow afternoon," she explained, her brown eyes focused on the fire, as the white owl on her shoulder encompassed the company with a slow turn of its head. "If we do, I want to waste no time before entering the grove. Hence, I'd like to work out our strategy this evening, so that tomorrow, upon our arrival, we can make whatever preparations are necessary with a minimum of delay." She looked at Baden, who sat opposite her on the far side of the fire, his face looking even leaner than usual in the shifting light. "Baden, we're here largely because of you. I would ask that you speak for the Order tomorrow night."

"I'd be honored, Sage Jessamyn," the Owl-Master said soberly.

"Do you have advice for those of us who will accompany you into the grove?" the Owl-Sage asked.

Baden hesitated for a moment before responding. "It will come as no surprise to any of you that I've never done this before," he commented, a wry smile springing to his face and then vanishing just as quickly. "But Trahn and I have spoken of this at some length, and we have some thoughts on the matter." He stood and began pacing slowly in front of the fire, his lanky frame taut, his gestures angled and tense. "From what we know of the Unsettled, from what they have told us of themselves, it seems that they can't lie to us; they can merely choose to withhold information. Thus, our questions should be as specific as possible; the more pointed our questions, the more informative his answers will be."

"Provided that he chooses to speak with us at all," Orris interjected.

Baden nodded. "We have no guarantee of that," he concurred.

"Can we compel him to talk?" Jaryd asked his uncle.

"No," Baden answered, shaking his head. "At least, I don't think so." He glanced at Trahn, who also shook his head. "As Trahn has mentioned in the past," Baden went on, "we should also keep in mind that the Unsettled have knowledge that goes far beyond their realm. Even if Theron isn't responsible for the attacks on Tobyn-Ser, he may be able to help us find out who is."

Alayna looked at Baden, as if she wished to be recognized.

"Alayna," the Owl-Master invited, "do you have something to add?"

"I do," she said. She took a breath, glancing around the circle of mages. "Everything we know of Theron's life tells us that he had a keen and subtle mind. He may toy with us, giving us hints and clues in his phrasing or choice of words. We must listen closely to everything he says. We should also avoid sounding obsequious. He didn't respond well to that when he was alive, and he probably won't now, either. And we should be as honest with him as we can be—given how brilliant he was, he'll be hard to fool. I wouldn't want to be anywhere near the grove if he catches us in a lie. Finally, I'd suggest that we avoid any mention of Amarid's name when we address Theron. If we greet him formally, we should do so 'on behalf of the Order and the people of Tobyn-Ser,' not 'in the name of Amarid, founder of the Order.' We should refer to Amarid's Laws as 'the laws that govern the Order,' or something like that. If we want him to speak with us, we can't go to him as emissaries of the First Mage."

The others nodded in agreement. "Sound advice," Baden observed. The Owl-Master took a deep breath. "That brings us, I'm afraid, to the darker realities of this mission. As soon as we enter the grove, we'll alert Theron to our presence. From that time on, we'll be at grave risk. Trahn observed during the Gathering that Theron has no ceryll of his own, and that, without access to ours, any power he has might be limited. Obviously, we don't know if this is the case, but it makes sense in theory, and I'd recommend that all of us leave our cerylls before going to meet with him. Still, even if we take that precaution, Theron remains a very dangerous adversary. At the first sign of real trouble we must leave the grove. As we know from the history of this forest, his power extends beyond that small group of trees, but most likely he's strongest there. We'll have a better chance of withstanding his assault outside of the grove."

"Arick grant that it doesn't come to that," Peredur muttered quietly.

"I hope that he hears you, old friend," Jessamyn said, getting to her feet. "But as Owl-Sage, and leader of this mission, I must prepare for all contingencies." She glanced at Baden. "Thank you, Owl-Master, for your wise counsel." It was a dismissal of a sort, a reassertion of her control over this discussion. Taking it as such, Baden nodded once and sat down. "Thank you all for your strength and your good sense," the Owl-Sage continued. "We will have need of all that you have to offer before this is over. But not all in the same capacity. It seems to me that some in this company should wait outside the grove when the others go in, just in case our meeting with Theron . . . goes awry. Someone should be left to take news of our failure back to the Great Hall."

Jaryd felt the rest of the company take a collective breath. All of them, he realized, had come a long way to confront the unsettled Owl-Master. None wished to be excluded.

"Alayna, Jaryd," Jessamyn went on, looking from one of the young mages to the other, "I'm certain that I speak for all the rest of us when I say that I wish I could leave the two of you behind. Not because I've found either of you lacking. On the contrary: I see much promise in both of you, and I want to guard that for the future of this land. But Alayna, we need your knowledge of Theron. And Jaryd, as Baden has argued before, the vision you had outside of Taima started you down this path a long time ago. Arick has deemed that you have a role to play in this, and I'll not presume to deny his will."

If someone had told him six months ago that he would be pleased by the news that he was to enter Theron's Grove within a day, Jaryd would have thought that person a lunatic. But as he listened to Jessamyn, he felt a tremendous sense of relief. Glancing at Alayna, he saw the same emotion register on her features. She looked back at him, and they shared a brief smile.

The Owl-Sage looked down at the first, sitting beside her. "Peredur, my friend, I had also hoped to leave you out of this delegation, but leaders cannot always protect those whom they love the most." She raised her voice. "Baden, as I said, will speak for the Order. Peredur and I will be there as well. I have decided, therefore, that Orris, Sartol, and Trahn will stay behind."

Orris and Sartol began to protest, but the Owl-Sage silenced them with a gesture. Trahn, characteristically, said nothing, but Jaryd could see the muscles of the dark mage's jaw working as he stared into the fire.

"I know that all three of you wish to accompany us into the grove," she told them in a soothing tone. "And please believe me when I tell you that none of us questions your courage or your devotion to the Order and to this land. But Sartol, you have been ill, and you are still weakened, too much so for what we may face in the grove."

"I've recovered, Owl-Sage," the Owl-Master countered. "My fever is gone. You'll need me."

Jessamyn smiled at him, a kind smile. "You are getting better, Sartol. I see it, and I'm glad of it. But one doesn't recover fully from a fever such as yours overnight."

"But by tomorrow—" Sartol began.

"I have decided, Sartol," Jessamyn told him, effectively ending their discussion. She turned to Trahn and Orris. "The two of you have the trust and support of the younger mages. You'll be needed should the rest of us be lost."

"We'll be needed in the grove even more!" Orris argued, his beard bristling. "We're stronger than the young ones; we should go in their place. The boy has a vision and suddenly—"

"That's enough, Orris!" Jessamyn broke in angrily, her tone commanding. She glanced around at the others, her eyes glowing like embers. "My mind is set!" she told them in a hard voice. "I'd suggest that you all get some sleep."

Without saying more, Jessamyn stepped out of the firelight and walked off to find a place to lie down. Peredur followed her, leaving the rest of the company to sit in awkward silence, the Owl-Sage's words still ringing in their ears.

At length, Baden stirred and took a deep breath. "I suppose we should go to sleep, as she said."

Orris shot to his feet, glaring at Baden, a single, rigid finger leveled at the Owl-Master accusingly. He started to say something, but then checked himself, and stomped out of the circle.

Trahn watched the Hawk-Mage go before he, too, stood to face Baden, a sad smile on his lips. The two of them held each other's glance for some time before Trahn gripped his friend's arm and then walked off into the night.

Baden looked over at Sartol. "It wasn't my decision," he said softly, as if seeking absolution.

"I know," Sartol told him, trying to smile, but grimacing instead. "None of us blames you, Baden. We're just disappointed, and men like Orris need a target at which to lash out in times like these. Don't worry about it."

Sartol rose, and slowly, the two Owl-Masters went off in search of sleep.

"I suppose I should be mad at Orris," Jaryd said to Alayna, who was looking at him in the dying firelight, "given what he said about the two of us not belonging in the delegation. But I think that I would have felt the same way had I been in his position."

Alayna nodded, but she remained silent. When finally she spoke, she surprised him. "We wasted a lot of time that would have been better spent getting to know each other," she said, running a hand through her dark hair in a gesture Jaryd had come to know quite well, "and it's possible that neither of us will make it out of Theron's Grove alive. But if you'd be willing, I'd like to ride with you tomorrow."

Jaryd felt his heart skip a beat. It was funny, he thought, that after all he had been through, such a simple gesture from this woman could affect him so. "I'd like that," he told her. "But you should realize that if by some chance we do survive, we run the risk of becoming friends."

She laughed. "I guess that's a chance we'll have to take."

"I guess it is," Jaryd responded with a smile.

They both withdrew to find places to rest, and, for the second night in a row, Jaryd fell asleep thinking of Alayna.

He lay on a bed of leaves and pine needles, listening to the sounds of the forest night, and grinning in the darkness. "None of us questions your courage or your devotion to the Order and to this land," the Hag had said. And in his mind he had replied, *Yes, and for that, you will die.* Things were going very well. Oh, there were a few minor complications with which he would have to deal eventually, but nothing of consequence; nothing that he couldn't handle.

In all important respects, his plan was falling into place just as he had foreseen. One detail remained; only one. But it was the key to everything else, and it would require that he improvise, that he wait for an opportunity to present itself, recognize that opportunity, and seize it. It was the part of his scheme with which he was least comfortable, this need to allow events to show him the way. He preferred leaving nothing to chance, but that did not seem to be an option. It didn't matter, though. In less than a day, they would be at Theron's Grove; nothing was going to stop him now. He did some quick calculations in his head: if all had gone according to Calbyr's timetable, the attack on Kaera would have taken place within the last two nights. By now, word had begun to spread throughout Tobyn-Ser of the newest atrocities committed by the Order. His smile deepened. Things were going very well.

All of them knew that they would be at the grove by nightfall. Yet, this day began no differently than the rest, with the company rising with the dawn, eating a light breakfast, and riding out just as the sun appeared in the eastern sky. As they had agreed the night before, Jaryd and Alayna rode together throughout the day, sharing stories of their homes, their childhoods, and their families. They also described for each other their experiences as Mage-Attends, as well as their bindings, which, as it turned out, had been quite similar. Late in the morning, they rested beside the Moriandral, which the company's path had rejoined and begun to follow less than an hour after breaking camp. As he sat with Alayna, Jaryd noticed that she had a staff, complete with ceryll, tied to her saddle and saddlebag.

"Sartol gave it to me just after the cloaking ceremony that last night of the Gathering," she explained when Jaryd asked her about it.

"Congratulations," Jaryd replied, as he admired the finely carved wood of the staff and the glowing purple stone with which it was crowned. "It's very beautiful."

Alayna gazed wistfully at the stone. "It is. I'll never forget the moment he gave it to me. The stone had no color or light of its own until he placed the staff in my hands. And as soon as he did, the light just burst from it." She shook her head at the memory. "I'll never forget it," she repeated.

"So why don't you carry it?" Jaryd asked gently.

She shrugged, a shyness in her eyes. "I don't know." She paused. "I guess I feel like I still have so much to learn that I don't deserve to carry it yet." She shrugged again.

"You were chosen by the Owl-Sage herself to confront the spirit of one of the two most powerful men ever to walk this land," Jaryd told her. "I think you've earned the right to carry that staff."

She regarded him for a moment, smiling slightly. "Maybe you're right," she conceded. "Maybe I will start carrying it."

"Good," Jaryd replied. "Just don't carry it into the grove."

Alayna laughed. "I'll try to remember that."

A few minutes later, the company remounted and rode on. Jaryd and Alayna remained together through the afternoon, but, as they drew closer to the grove, their conversation, like those of their companions, tapered off. Their progress this day came even slower than it had the day before. The air grew hotter, and the company began to hear the muted sound of thunder rolling in the distance.

Late in the day, well after the sun started its long descent into the west, the forest suddenly gave way to more open terrain, and they came within sight of the ruins of Rholde, looming on the other side of the river. And beyond its crumbled buildings, beyond the open grasses and scattered trees of the land surrounding what once had been Theron's home, stood the grove. It looked no different from the Shadow Forest, which began again on its far side. It consisted of the same giant oaks and maples; it appeared just as dense and overgrown. But the power and malevolence that emanated from the place were unmistakable. Even Jaryd could sense it, though he was new to the ways of power, and inexperienced in the recognition of such things. Looking at the grove, he felt an instinctive, primal fear, as though his body was trying to flee, despite his mind's insistence that he stay. His horse had grown restive, and Ishalla cried plaintively, her grip on his shoulder tightening until he could feel her talons through the padding of his cloak. Alayna's bird called out in response, and Alayna and Jaryd exchanged a brief, anxious glance. Riding in single file, the company coaxed their nervous mounts across an ancient stone bridge that, though badly neglected, looked sufficiently sturdy. Once on the other side, the mages dismounted and set up camp much as they had each previous evening for the past two weeks. It almost seemed, Jaryd thought to himself, as he and the others had a light, early supper, that they all were trying to pretend that this camp and this night were just like the rest.

The horses knew better, however, and it soon became clear that the animals would not calm down until they were moved farther from the grove. While the rest of the company, at Jessamyn's suggestion, took some time to rest and at least attempt to relax, Baden and Trahn led the creatures back down to the river, where the sound of the rushing water might calm them. A short while after Jessamyn had gone to a different portion of the riverbank with Peredur to follow her own advice, Jaryd spotted the Owl-Sage making her way back toward the open area where he was standing in the gathering darkness with Alayna and Sartol. At one point, Orris stopped her and spoke to her briefly. She nodded once, and the Hawk-Mage walked off, alone, toward the ruins of the old city. Jaryd noticed that the wind had picked up. Thunder rumbled again in the background, closer than before.

"There's a storm coming," the white-haired sage observed as she approached them. "I need for one or two of you to cover the food and gear with tarpaulins, and for someone else to find wood for the torches that we'll be carrying into the grove tonight."

"Torches, Owl-Sage?" Jaryd asked.

"Without our cerylls, we'll need some light, won't we, Jaryd?" Jessamyn responded wryly.

"Of course," he replied, feeling a bit stupid.

"If Jaryd and Alayna would be so kind as to cover the supplies," Sartol offered, "I'll take care of the torches." He winked at the two young mages and flashed a knowing smile before starting toward a cluster of trees that stood between the camp and Theron's Grove. Alayna blushed slightly.

"That was nice of him," Jaryd commented with a smile, as he and Alayna hurried to where the supplies lay exposed.

She nodded, her face reddening again.

The wind continued to build, and the air grew colder.

Opportunities presented themselves in the strangest ways, Sartol thought to himself as he walked away from the camp. Two nights ago, as he lay by the fire weathering the illness that he had induced in himself, attempting to keep his ailment grave enough to resist Baden's healing power without making it so grave that he could not control it, he had listened with growing resentment to Alayna's conversation with Jaryd. He knew they had stayed up together last night, and he had watched as they talked and laughed throughout today's ride. After all that he had done for her over the past two and a half years, after all that he had taught her, she had never looked at him the way he saw her look at Jaryd today. It was galling; it made the thought of killing both of them, particularly Baden's presumptuous pup, that much more enticing. Not that he had any choice in the matter. The hawks that sat on the shoulders of the young mages and the promise of power they embodied had sealed Alayna and Jaryd's fate long ago. How fitting, then, that their little flirtation should have provided him with such an ideal opening to complete the most important part of his scheme.

The torches, of course; it was perfect. He should have known all along. He felt almost as stupid as Jaryd had sounded asking the Hag why they needed them. It should have been obvious to him from the moment Trahn first suggested that the delegation leave their cerylls outside the grove. The torches. He shook his head at his own blindness. Actually, Sartol had little doubt that Theron would kill the delegation without any help from him, but he thought it prudent to make certain. He stopped in front of the small copse where he hoped to find some torch-sized branches. Gazing beyond it toward Theron's Grove, just a few hundred yards away, he shuddered involuntarily. It was no small thing that Baden, the Hag, and the rest of them were preparing to do, he admitted to himself grudgingly. He wasn't sure that he would have considered actually entering the grove under any circumstances.

He shook his head again, as if with the motion he could fling these thoughts out of his brain. He had work to do. Stepping into the small thicket, he soon found several branches roughly the length and thickness of his arm. Spreading them on the ground in front of him, the Owl-Master chose one that looked slightly larger than the others. He knelt, and placing a hand over this larger stick, closed his eyes while simultaneously reaching out with his mind to the great owl that sat on his shoulder. Immediately, he felt the power surging through him as if it was an ocean tide, huge and unstoppable. If only they knew how strong I am, he thought with a smile, his eyes still closed. They had reprimanded him once, humiliating him for the sake of the fools he "served," and they had passed him over in favor of Jessamyn when Feargus died. But soon, very soon, they would quail at the power he wielded.

It took but a few moments. When he opened his eyes again, and removed his hand, there was a large cavity in what would be the shaft of the torch. He then reached into his cloak, and pulled out a loose ceryll, clear as glass, and just slightly smaller than the hollow he had created in the wood.

"A gift for you, Theron," he said quietly, a malicious smile spreading across his face. "Use it well."

He placed the ceryll within the branch, put his hand over the hole again, and, closing his eyes, reestablished his connection with Huvan. Almost immediately, he could feel the wood starting to close over the cavity beneath his hand.

And just then, he heard footsteps behind him.

"Sartol," Jessamyn said, "I realized after you went off that we had better have two or three extras, just in case—"

She stopped. He knew why: he hadn't turned around yet, hadn't acknowledged her presence there. He knew that he should, that she would grow suspicious, but he needed just a few more seconds. . . .

"Sartol." Her tone had grown more insistent. "What are you doing?" she demanded.

He listened as she moved closer, and, when she had almost reached him, he whirled around and staggered to his feet, his eyes wide with fear. "Who's there!" he gasped. He let relief creep into his voice. "Owl-Sage. It's only you, thank goodness."

"Sartol? Are you all right?" she asked, regarding him warily, but with concern.

He smiled inwardly.

"I think so," he replied, taking a deep breath. "I heard footsteps; I didn't know who . . . I must have blacked out. The last thing I remember I was looking for branches to use as torches." He wiped a hand across his brow. "I guess I'm weaker from that fever than I thought."

"So it would seem," she agreed, looking at him closely. "You do look a bit flushed." She glanced around the thicket. "Well, why don't I help you," she offered, moving past him, "and then we can get you back to the camp."

He tried to shield the branches he had gathered from her sight, but it was too late. He stood very still, waiting, knowing what would happen, and what he would have to do. Another flash of lightning lit the sky, and a loud thunderclap followed closely.

"It looks as if you found a few that will—"

He heard the sudden, sharp intake of breath as she spotted the altered torch, and he turned slowly to face her. Her expression looked almost comical: shock and fear chased each other across her wrinkled features as she looked back and forth between the Owl-Master and the branch with its half-concealed ceryll.

"Are you mad!" she breathed.

He felt surprisingly calm, relieved in a way to have the burden of his deception lifted, if only for these few seconds. And it pleased him that the Hag would know as she died that he had killed her. It was important, though, that he do this carefully; if the others saw mage-fire, they might recognize its color as his.

She took a step back, and he grinned, baring his teeth.

"I'm afraid, Owl-Sage," he said as he advanced on her, "that I can't allow you to leave."

She raised her staff to ward him off, and opened her mouth to scream.

Baden shook his head at the intensifying wind. Glancing up at the sky, he saw a large cloud drift in over the ruins of Rholde, blotting out the emerging stars one by one. He and Trahn had almost succeeded in calming the horses. Almost. The animals had grown less agitated with each step they had taken away from the grove and toward the churning waters of the Moriandral. By the time the two mages tied them to a cluster of trees by the base of the old bridge, the horses had relaxed considerably. Then the storm started up, with its bright flashes of lightning, and reverberating thunder, causing the animals to renew their nervous whinnying. Baden didn't think that they seemed overly excited, and he would have been satisfied to leave the creatures where they were. But Trahn had different ideas.

"These horses have carried you and your food nearly four hundred leagues," he reminded Baden pointedly, "and you're going to leave them here, unsheltered in this storm? I think you're getting grumpy in your old age, Baden," the dark mage concluded with a smirk.

"I'm not grumpy," Baden countered in a tone that belied his words. "You Southlanders are just too soft; next thing you know you'll want to give the animals sleeping rolls."

They untied the horses as they spoke and led them to the ruins of the old city, where they found what looked to have been at one time a farmhouse. What remained of the structure offered shelter from the wind and at least some relief from the rain that would surely follow, and the animals immediately began to chomp on the thick grass that grew through cracks in the decayed floor. It was, Baden had to acknowledge, a much better place for the company's mounts to pass the night.

As the two mages emerged from the ruined building, they spotted an amber light approaching them from what once had been Rholde's village square.

"Orris?" Baden asked quietly, guessing from the color of the ceryll's light.

"Yes," Trahn said with certainty. "I wonder what he's doing out here."

They waited in silence as the churlish mage marched to where they stood, and halted right in front of them. He glared from one to the other, his face pale, his entire frame trembling with emotion.

"I've just been in contact with Ursel," he told them in a raw voice. "She used the merging."

The Stone-Merging, Baden thought to himself with alarm. The *Ceryll-Var*, Amarid had called it, using the ancient tongue. *Something must have happened.* Mergings demanded more of mage and familiar than any other magic of the Mage-Craft. The difficulty lay not just in the establishment and maintenance of the mind-link, although that was draining enough. First, Ursel would have had to seek out Orris's ceryll with her mind and project her ceryll-hue into it, thus indicating to Orris whose mind he should seek in return. Baden tried to avoid mergings in all but the most extreme emergencies. He braced himself for what was coming.

"There's been yet another attack," Orris declared, his harsh, cold voice an accusation in the deepening night. "Two nights ago, the town of Kaera on the northern edge of Tobyn's Plain."

Kaera, Baden repeated to himself. He had been there once, as a younger man, as a Hawk-Mage; they had passed within twenty leagues of it only a few days ago.

"Ursel couldn't get enough people for the patrols to cover all of the plain," Orris was saying, as his dark eyes bored into Baden's. "Thanks to you and Odinan, there weren't enough people. And thanks to all of the Owl-Masters, we didn't establish the psychic link. This attack is on your head, Baden."

"Orris!" Trahn snapped. "That's enough! Baden isn't to blame for this!"

"Not alone, at any rate!" Orris countered, directing his fury at the Hawk-Mage. "Your compromise put us in this position as well!"

There was more, Baden thought, as he listened to Trahn and Orris trade accusations; *Ursel resorting to the merging, the anger and pain in Orris's eyes—there had to be more.*

"Orris!" he cut in savagely, shocking the Hawk-Mages into silence. "What happened to Kaera?"

Orris took a deep breath. "It was destroyed," he answered in a flat tone, "burned to the ground. Everyone who lived there is dead except for one little girl."

Baden felt like he had been kicked in the stomach. The entire town destroyed; every person except . . . "What happened to the girl?" he managed to ask in a strangled voice. He thought he might be sick.

Orris shook his head. "The people from the next town over said that they found her unconscious. She'd been struck in the head."

"Was she just lucky?" Baden asked, and regretted the choice of words as soon as they left his mouth.

Fortunately, Orris appeared to understand his meaning, or perhaps he didn't notice. "It's more likely that she was intended as a messenger," he replied. "They found a black feather tucked into her clothing."

"Has she told them anything?"

Orris shook his head. "She only came to a few hours ago, and she hasn't said a word. Ursel did mention, though," he added, the bitterness creeping back into his words, "that she seemed terrified of the mages who went to speak with her."

"I'm sorry, Orris," Baden found himself saying. "I'm truly sorry."

"*Sorry!*" Orris mimicked, his voice rising. "You're sorry? Tell that to the little girl. Tell that to every person in Tobyn-Ser who can't sleep tonight because they're waiting for renegade mages to attack their homes. We've betrayed them. I don't care that we were two hundred leagues away when Kaera burned: we betrayed them." He glowered at Baden and then at Trahn. He was breathing heavily now, and the veins on his temples stood out boldly in the light cast by the three mages' cerylls. "I hold the two of you responsible," Orris went on, "along with Jessamyn and Odinan, for what happened to Kaera. If we had established the psychic link and put every member of the Order into the patrols as I suggested, we could have prevented that attack; we could have saved those lives. I'm going to see Jessamyn right now, and I'm going to demand that we return to Kaera immediately to help Ursel search for whoever did this."

With that, he spun away and stormed off toward the camp, leaving Baden and Trahn to absorb the news he had borne. They stood without speaking, watching the light from his crystal grow dimmer, until finally it disappeared. And still they said nothing. As soon as Orris had mentioned the little girl, a vision of her face had blossomed in Baden's mind, like a flower or a flame, gaining clarity with each passing second. He tried now, desperately and in vain, to thrust it away. Soon, perhaps within the next hour, he would confront Theron's spirit. He could not enter the grove with the little girl's face, with Cailin's face—somehow he knew her name—intruding on his thoughts. He felt old and frightened, a far cry from the image of power and purpose that he had hoped to project to the First Owl-Master.

"You shouldn't have apologized to him, Baden!" Trahn said at length, his voice thick with anger. "He had no right to say what he did!"

Baden shrugged wearily. "It's not important," he murmured.

After a moment, Trahn nodded. "You're right," he conceded in a more subdued tone. He paused, and when he spoke again, there were tears in his eyes. "I keep seeing the little girl."

"Cailin," Baden said bleakly. "Her name's Cailin. I see her, too."

"She looks to be the same age as my Jaynell."

Baden could think of nothing to say in response. Perhaps sensing this, Trahn changed the subject. "What will Jessamyn do?" he asked. "Will she take us back to Kaera?"

"I don't know," the Owl-Master responded. "I can't imagine that she'd leave here without first entering the grove, but believe me when I tell you that she'll take this even harder than we have."

Lightning blazed overhead, and, a few seconds later, the ground shook with the answering thunder. They started making their way back toward the camp.

"Do you still think that Theron is behind the attacks?" Trahn asked, after they had walked a small distance.

Baden opened his mouth to reply. But in that moment, a voice cried out from the far side of the camp and then was abruptly, unnervingly silenced.

The mages stopped and stared at each other.

"Jessamyn!" Baden exclaimed, and they both began running in the direction from which the cry had come. They were far away, though. So far away.

"I'm definitely scared," Jaryd commented as he and Alayna rummaged through the gear, searching for the tarpaulins, "but I'm calmer than I had expected to be."

Alayna nodded. "Me, too. It's as if I've been preparing—here they are," she said, holding up the folded cloths, "—as if I've been preparing for this night my entire life. I don't really know how to explain it."

They unfolded the sheets of canvas and began placing them over the gear and food.

"I almost think that it would be harder to wait for the delegation outside the grove," Jaryd observed. "I don't envy the others at all."

"Did Trahn say anything to you about it?"

Jaryd shook his head. "No, nothing. But," he added, "that doesn't mean much, really. Trahn isn't one to express his feelings that freely. Why, did Sartol say anything to you?"

She shrugged. "Just that he wished he hadn't gotten sick when he did. He tried not to seem too disappointed, but I think he was holding something back."

"How about Orris?"

"You mean did he say something to me?"

"Yes."

Alayna laughed. "Of course not; I don't think that Orris talks to anybody."

Jaryd laughed also. "I'm relieved: I thought it was just me he didn't like."

"No," Alayna told him, her mirth subsiding, "but he does seem particularly hostile toward you."

"I've noticed that," Jaryd agreed, "although I have no idea why he should be."

"He doesn't seem to like Baden very much. Maybe it's just because you're Baden's nephew," Alayna suggested.

"Maybe."

They worked without speaking for a short while, tucking the corners of the tarpaulins under some of the equipment to keep them secure against the wind, and carefully arranging each piece so that it overlapped the last. At one point Jaryd paused to look over at Ishalla and Fylimar, who sat together on an old stump, so much alike that they reminded him of bookends.

"May I ask you something?" Jaryd chanced, turning back to Alayna.

She did not meet his glance, but a smile played at the corners of her mouth. "I'm not sure," she answered shyly. "I think I know what you want to ask, and I'm not certain that I want to discuss it right now."

"We may never get another chance, Alayna."

She looked at him then, her smile slowly fading as his eyes held hers. At length, she nodded.

"The other night, when you asked me to sit with you—"

"When I was taking care of Sartol?" she broke in.

"Yes."

"I thought so," she commented, smiling again. "Go on," she added.

"When I asked you what I had done to offend you," Jaryd continued, "you said that I hadn't done anything, and then you amended that; I think you said, 'At least nothing you could control.' What did you mean?"

They had stopped working, although they had yet to tie down the coverings. Alayna stood gazing at him, and Jaryd thought back to the first time he had ever seen her, on the wooded grounds of Amarid's home, as the mages of the Order had lined up for the opening procession of the Gathering. There was a storm coming; even now Jaryd could hear thunder. And yet, the air around them seemed suddenly to have grown still. Jaryd felt his heart hammering in his chest.

"You scare me, Jaryd," she said in a tight voice. "You scare me more than any man I've known."

"Scare you?" Jaryd said with bewilderment. "Why?"

"Do you remember the first time our eyes met?" she asked.

"Yes," he answered in a gentle voice, "very well."

She smiled. "So do I. But that wasn't the first time I'd seen you."

"I don't follow."

She took a deep breath. "I had visions of you long before the Gathering," she told him.

Jaryd didn't respond for some time; he wasn't sure how to respond. What she had told him should have come as a shock, but, he realized, he had expected something like this.

He looked at her and found that she was watching him closely. "What kind of visions?" he finally asked her.

She flushed slightly. "I'm not sure that I can describe them," she replied. "I'm still not certain what they meant."

"Did you recognize me right away?" he asked.

"At the Gathering, you mean?"

He nodded.

"I was pretty sure," she replied, "but I wasn't positive until you showed up the second day with your hawk. Then I knew."

Jaryd nodded again. Their interaction finally made sense to him. He understood why she had treated him so strangely. He, of all people, appreciated the power of unexpected visions. "So what do we do now?" he asked. "Was there anything in your visions that would keep us from being friends?"

Alayna hesitated, but only for an instant. "No," she said, smiling at him. "Nothing at all."

He smiled in return. "I'm glad." He stepped across the pile of supplies to where Alayna stood, and took her hands in his. "Look," he began, gazing into her eyes—green and brown they were, like a forest. "I don't even know if we're going to live through the night. But if we do . . ." He stopped, unsure of how he wanted to finish the thought.

She smiled at him radiantly and, stepping forward, kissed him gently on the cheek. "If we do," she repeated softly.

He moved to kiss her on the lips, but, out of the corner of his eye, he spotted Jessamyn coming toward them. Quickly, the young mages pulled away from each other and returned to their task, using several lengths of rope to tie the tarpaulins in place. Glancing up from their work a short while later, Jaryd noticed that the Owl-Sage had changed directions, and was now making her way toward the cluster of trees near Theron's Grove to which Sartol had gone to find the torches.

"That would have been embarrassing," Jaryd remarked with a wry grin.

Alayna shrugged. "I don't know," she said, returning his smile. "Jessamyn would understand. She'd probably think it was very sweet."

"Great," Jaryd returned with sarcasm. Then something occurred to him. "How would Sartol react?" he asked.

"Fine, I think. He did volunteer to get the torches so that we could be together," she reminded him.

"True. I just wondered because the two of you spend so much time together."

"You and Baden spend a lot of time together," she said pointedly. "Is there something I should know?"

Jaryd felt himself blushing. "Point taken," he surrendered as Alayna giggled.

"What about the blonde?" she asked a moment later, her tone more serious.

"The blonde?"

"The one who kissed you the morning we left Amarid," Alayna reminded him. "How many blondes are there in your life?"

Jaryd nodded with recognition. "You mean Kayle." He smiled. "Are you jealous?"

"Don't play games, Jaryd," she insisted. "Not with this."

"I'm sorry," he told her. "Kayle's just a friend. I promise."

"She seemed like more than a friend that morning."

"I know how it seemed," he replied, trying to sound reassuring. "But we're just friends."

She stared at him, her eyes locked on his, as if she was trying to gauge whether he was telling the truth. After several moments, she nodded, and they continued to work in silence.

Just as they finished securing the tarpaulins, they heard footsteps and, turning toward the sound, they saw Peredur approaching them.

"Have either of you seen Jessamyn?" he asked without preamble.

"Yes, First," Jaryd told him, "we saw her just a few minutes ago. She was going up to that thicket," he added, pointing toward the small copse, "in the direction Sartol went."

"Thank you," Peredur responded absently, already moving off in the direction Jaryd had indicated. "She tells us all to get some rest," he muttered as he walked away, "but she gets none herself."

"He really takes care of her, doesn't he?" Alayna observed as she watched the First of the Sage make his way toward the thicket.

"To the extent that anyone can," Jaryd agreed with a small laugh. "I don't think she'd be very easy to take care of."

Lightning illuminated the terrain, making it seem, for a split second, as if daylight had returned. They braced themselves, waiting for the thunder. It came sooner than Jaryd expected, crashing loudly, and causing the ground beneath them to vibrate.

"So, are we done here?" Alayna said, looking down at the protected supplies.

"I think so," Jaryd answered. "That should hold. Why don't we go find the shelter that Jessamyn set up and see if we can stay dry, too."

Alayna continued to stare at the tarpaulins, the look in her eyes rueful. "Actually," she said sheepishly, "now that we're finished, I'm kind of hungry."

Jaryd laughed, and pulled a small sack of dried meat from the folds of his cloak. "Luckily for you, I had a little foresight."

She looked at him coyly. "Well, aren't you just—"

She never finished the thought. From the cluster of trees to which Sartol and then Jessamyn had gone came a cry for help that ended with frightening abruptness.

"That sounded like Jessamyn!" Alayna declared.

Jaryd nodded once, and the two of them took off toward the thicket with their hawks gliding overhead.

She was surprisingly strong, given her age, and he had expected her to attack him, not simply to cloak herself protectively in her own power. For these reasons alone, she managed to cry out before he could silence her. But silence her he did. It took only a moment for his mastery of the Mage-Craft to overpower her warding, and then, with a quick gesture, no more than the tightening of his fingers into a fist, he stopped her breathing. It gratified him to see the terror in her eyes, to see written across the Owl-Sage's distorted features her shock at the ease with which he was killing her. Surely, he thought—and perhaps it crossed her mind as well in these last few seconds of her life—no mage has known such power since Amarid and Theron themselves walked the land.

He had worked so hard for so many years making himself this strong, stretching the limits of his endurance and that of his bird, honing his skills with the Mage-Craft until he could kill with little more than a gesture. He remembered one night in particular, when he had stood by the shores of a small, secluded lake near his home in the northern reaches of Tobyn's Wood, pouring his mage-fire into the water for as long as he and Huvan could bear.

He had lost all sense of time and place, conscious only of the tide of power moving within him. But when finally he collapsed in an exhausted heap, he had found the water of the lake bubbling and steaming like a pot of broth on a fire, bringing hundreds upon hundreds of dead fish to the lake's surface. He had lain there for hours, too spent to move. But the following night, he did it again.

And now, finally, his labors were paying off. Too late, the white owl leapt off Jessamyn's shoulder and tried to attack him, but Huvan, the more powerful of the two birds, managed to drive the creature off. A moment later the Owl-Sage dropped to her knees, her eyes beginning to bulge from her skull, her rigid hands, white knuckled, still clutching her staff. She stared up at him, imploring him to spare her.

He smiled grimly. "I'm sorry, Jessamyn," he said to her, "that you had to learn in this way how powerful I've grown. You see, don't you, that they should never have made you Owl-Sage? That I was the one who deserved it? It's unfair, really, that you should have to pay for their error, but, if it's any consolation, you won't be the only one. Others will pay as well. If I'm this strong now," he added, "imagine how my power will flow when I've linked myself to the Summoning Stone."

Still staring at him with wide, wild eyes, the Owl-Sage toppled over onto her side and writhed pitifully on the ground. It wasn't as amusing to watch now, and he looked away as she died. Doing so, he beheld the pearly light of Peredur's ceryll as the First of the Sage entered the thicket. He had known, as soon as Jessamyn screamed, that the others would be coming. But he had not expected any of them this soon. There was nothing he could do, except kill Peredur as well.

"Jessamyn?" he heard the old man call out, his voice quavering with alarm. Then the Owl-Master spotted him and hurried forward. "Sartol, have you seen—?" Peredur froze, paralyzed by the sight of Jessamyn's body sprawled on the ground before him.

Without giving the old fool time to raise an alarm, Sartol closed his eyes for an instant to convey a single thought to Huvan, who had just settled back onto his shoulder. Immediately, the great owl hurled itself at Peredur's head. The mage flinched, and, in that moment, Huvan altered her course sharply and seized the first's small owl in her outstretched talons. She alighted on a nearby branch, severed the head of the smaller bird with a quick, wrenching motion of her powerful feet, and began to tear hungrily into the body of her prey.

"It would seem, Peredur, that you're about to join the ranks of the Unsettled," Sartol remarked in a mocking tone. "I had hoped that Jessamyn would join you, but, alas, her bird escaped."

The first tried to shout something to the others, but this time Sartol was ready. Closing his hand into a fist again, he cut off the old man's breathing. He then fisted his other hand and, bringing the two together, made a twisting motion not unlike the one Huvan had used to kill Peredur's owl. The first's head snapped to the side unnaturally, breaking his neck, and he collapsed in a contorted heap next to his beloved.

Even as the first fell to the ground, however, Sartol could already hear others running toward the cluster of trees. Alayna, and Baden's brat, he guessed. He shook his head, glancing briefly around the thicket. Events were spiraling beyond his control at an alarming rate; he could not go on killing every member of the company this way. Or could I? he wondered. Standing alone, no mage in the entire Order could defeat him. He could kill off the delegation, inflict a few ugly but harmless injuries on himself, and blame their murders on Theron, claiming to have escaped death himself only by sheerest good fortune. Jaryd and Alayna together posed no threat: she had only begun to develop her powers, and the boy did not yet even have a ceryll. Baden and Trahn represented the only real danger, because they always traveled together, and he felt fairly certain that he could handle them. Now, if by some chance Orris ended up with them . . . well, that was a scenario that Sartol did not even wish to consider.

The young mages had almost reached him; he could see the purple light of the ceryll he had given to Alayna. He had to decide. Looking around him again, he realized that he had little choice in the matter. Huvan still tore at the carcass of Peredur's familiar; the altered torch lay on the ground next to the bodies of the Owl-Sage and her first. He had been careless. He had ruined what appeared to be a perfect plan, and so had brought himself to this moment. He would have to kill the young mages; he might have to kill all of them. But with a bit of luck, it wouldn't come to that. Once again, he would have to look for an opportunity.

Jaryd and Alayna burst through the trees and halted a few feet from where he stood. He watched the horror register on their features as they surveyed the scene before them. It began to rain in large, pelting drops.

"Sartol, what happened?" Alayna asked breathlessly, unable to tear her eyes from the bodies of Jessamyn and Peredur.

Poor Alayna, he thought to himself with amusement, you'll be dead before you realize how I've betrayed you.

"You killed them, didn't you?" Jaryd challenged in a strong voice, his pale eyes narrowing. There was courage here, Sartol admitted, though there was nothing to back it up.

"Jaryd!" Alayna snapped. "How could you even think that!"

"Look!" Jaryd countered, pointing up at Huvan and the blood-soaked body of Peredur's bird. "That's the first's owl she's killed, isn't it, Sartol?"

Alayna stared at the bird in disbelief. "Sartol?" she said, almost sobbing as she spoke his name.

"Do you have any idea, Jaryd, how much it will please me to kill you?" he asked, squeezing his fingers into a fist, and grinning with satisfaction as he watched the boy clutch suddenly at his throat, a panicked expression on his youthful, rain-drenched face.

Alayna whirled around as Sartol spoke to Jaryd, and, seeing what was happening, screamed out the boy's name. Purple mage-fire exploded from her staff and hissed toward Sartol's head.

To be blocked, almost effortlessly, by Sartol's ceryll, which seemed to absorb the energy from her staff.

But in that instant, when he had to guard himself from Alayna's blow, Sartol relinquished his hold on Jaryd. Gasping for breath, the young Hawk-Mage dove to the ground and picked up one of the torches—indeed, the altered torch—to use as a weapon. And for the first time that night, Sartol felt a surge of fear. Any other mage in the company could have picked up that same piece of wood, with the dormant ceryll half-concealed within it, and nothing would have happened. But, unlike the others, Jaryd had yet to be linked with a stone. As soon as he placed his hand on the torch, the ceryll came to life, emitting a brilliant sapphire light through the narrow gap in the wood. Incredibly, without seeming to hesitate—probably without even knowing how he did it, Sartol thought with detachment—Jaryd sent his own mage-fire at the Owl-Master. Again, Sartol blocked it with ease, but he now found himself doing battle with two mages, both of them carrying cerylls. And, despite all his preparation, he was starting to tire. He had to find a way to end this, soon, before he had to fight Orris, Baden, and Trahn as well.

"Huvan!" he shouted. Immediately, his owl swooped from her perch to attack Alayna's familiar. Ishalla flew to Fylimar's defense, and the three birds, the two identical hawks and the heavier, stronger owl, climbed through the rain to do battle above the trees. Sartol grinned. "Now let's see how the two of you do with your birds fighting for their lives," he said, moving to block their path back toward the camp. "I still have command of my abilities," he assured them. "Do you?"

Alayna and Jaryd glanced at each other for a moment and then leveled their staffs at him. Sartol prepared himself to block their fire. But at the last moment, Jaryd yelled for Alayna to run and, grabbing her hand, led her toward the back side of the thicket. Cursing his own stupidity, Sartol gave chase, crashing through branches and brush only a few strides behind them. But when they reached the open terrain beyond the cluster of trees, Jaryd and Alayna began to pull away, and Sartol roared with frustration and fury. He had been fortunate thus far; he had not had to risk giving himself away to those who remained by using his mage-fire. Now, it seemed, his luck had run out. The young mages would reach the Shadow Forest before he could catch them, and, once they did, they would be very difficult to find. Reluctantly, he stopped running and leveled his staff at them.

But then he stopped, a smile spreading across his features. Jaryd and Alayna were not headed toward the Shadow Forest, he realized. They were running straight into Theron's Grove. He lowered his staff and started after them again. If he could force them into the grove—

He did not know why he happened to glance to his side at that particular moment. A movement perhaps, or a small sound that drew his attention away from his quarry for an instant. Whatever the reason, the gesture saved his life. Seeing the mage-fire streak toward him from Orris's ceryll, Sartol had just enough time to hurl his own blast back at the Hawk-Mage with a desperate, twisting thrust of his staff. The two salvos, one amber, the other yellow, collided just a few feet away from him with an explosion that knocked Sartol to the ground.

"You're a traitor and a murderer, Sartol!" Orris called to him. "Surrender or I swear in Arick's name that I'll kill you!"

Sartol climbed stiffly to his feet and took a long breath. He was growing dangerously fatigued, and, as Huvan glided back to his shoulder, he sensed that she was weakening as well. He could still take care of Orris—and he would enjoy doing so—but he knew that he could not risk another encounter after this one.

"I won't surrender, Orris," he shouted above the sounds of the storm, gathering himself, "so you'll have to kill me. But I promise you: you'll die trying."

He glanced over his shoulder in time to see Alayna and Jaryd disappear into Theron's Grove, and then, a grin tugging at the corners of his mouth, he turned to do battle with Orris.

11

It began to rain just as Baden and Trahn reached the camp. Grape-sized drops of water pounded noisily on the tarpaulins that covered the food and supplies, and the rich, sweet smell of the storm settled heavily over the grassy clearing. They had heard only the one, truncated cry; nothing more. And now, as they surveyed the deserted camp, utterly still save for the rain and wind, Baden tried with little success to keep his growing apprehension in check. He had been reasonably certain that the voice they heard calling out in the night had been Jessamyn's. No doubt, the others had heard her as well, and had hurried to find her. But where?

"Baden, look," Trahn said with some urgency, pointing in the direction of Theron's Grove. "There's light coming from those trees."

Baden saw it as well: a faint glimmer issuing from a small group of trees just in front of the grove. The colors were dim and hard to read, although it seemed obvious that they came from more than one ceryll. Then, even as they stood there staring at the thicket, another voice—Alayna's voice—screamed out Jaryd's name, and purple light blazed brilliantly from among the trees. A few seconds later, a second beam of color burst from the copse, this one deep blue. Baden recognized the hue immediately, although he could not explain its presence here. Somehow, he and Trahn were already racing toward the thicket, painfully aware of the time that had passed since Jessamyn's cry, and of the distance they had to cover before they could respond to Alayna's.

"Did you see that?" Trahn shouted over the storm, his words jarred as they ran.

"Yes," Baden yelled back as he tried to grapple with the implications of that flash of blue.

"None of us has a blue ceryll," Trahn commented, and there was fear in his voice. "Were we followed?"

"No," Baden answered. "That was Jaryd."

"Jaryd! He has a ceryll?"

"Not that I knew of," Baden conceded. "I have no idea where that ceryll could have come from, but I've had visions of Jaryd as a mage. I'm certain that's his color."

"What, in Arick's name, does it mean?" Trahn asked.

Baden shook his head. "I wish I knew."

The two mages sprinted on toward the thicket, but, before they could reach it, they heard shouts coming from the far side of the trees and saw mage-fire illuminating the night like lightning.

They stopped, both of them breathing hard, as their familiars settled to their shoulders.

Trahn stared intently at the flashing sky. "Those are Orris's and Sartol's colors," he said.

"Yes," Baden agreed, "but are they fighting each other, or someone else?"

"I don't see any other mage-fire," Trahn remarked grimly. "I'd guess that they're fighting each other."

"As would I. So what should we do?"

Trahn looked at the Owl-Master, his dark features glistening with rain and the glow of his ceryll. "I'm not certain that we can do anything. We don't know why they're fighting, and we can't intervene without tipping the balance one way or the other. I'm afraid we just have to wait and see who prevails before we can do anything."

Baden cursed under his breath. "First Jessamyn screams, and then Alayna. Now Orris and Sartol are trying to kill each other, and we can't do a thing about it." He shook his head in frustration. "We can at least go and be witnesses to what happens," he said after a moment.

Trahn nodded, and they ran on.

As they reached the cluster of trees, an unearthly wail rose suddenly from the Shadow Forest and then died away. The mages slowed, moving quietly around the perimeter of the copse until they came within sight of Theron's Grove. There, in the clearing just in front of the grove, Baden and Trahn saw a lone figure carrying a pale yellow ceryll and walking slowly and unsteadily in their direction. The figure paused briefly as a large owl glided out of the darkness to land delicately on his shoulder. Then Sartol continued toward them. As the Owl-Master drew closer, Baden could see that he had a blackened, oozing burn on his leg and a jagged gash on his forehead. Dark, thickening blood stained his owl's talons.

"Baden!" he called with concern as he approached the two mages. "Trahn! Have you seen Alayna and Jaryd?"

"No," Trahn replied warily, "why?"

"I was afraid of that," Sartol said without answering Trahn's question. "Arick guard them."

"What's happened, Sartol?" Baden demanded sharply.

The injured Owl-Master's features looked pale beneath his wet black and silver hair, and his trembling hands clutched his staff tightly. "We've been betrayed," he stated in a quavering voice.

"What happened to Jaryd and Alayna?" Baden persisted. "Where's Jessamyn?"

"Jessamyn is dead, as is Peredur. Orris killed them. And I'm afraid that Alayna and Jaryd have inadvertently entered Theron's Grove."

"What!" Baden hissed.

Trahn exhaled through his teeth, shaking his head slowly in denial. "Orris did this?" he asked.

"Yes," Sartol responded heavily.

"Where is he now?"

"He got away from me," Sartol said with bitterness, his grey eyes downcast. "I tried to subdue him, or kill him if I could, but he was too strong—much stronger than he should have been," the Owl-Master added, looking up at Baden again. "I don't understand how he could be so powerful, but that must be how he killed the Owl-Sage and the first."

"What about Jaryd and Alayna?" Baden demanded again, biting off each word.

Sartol shrugged and made a helpless gesture with his hands. "They must have surprised Orris when he was . . ." The Owl-Master faltered. He swallowed hard and closed his eyes to compose himself. "When he was killing Jessamyn and Peredur," he continued a moment later. "I was hurrying toward that cluster of trees because I heard Jessamyn call out. Alayna screamed and I saw mage-fire. When I got there the sage and the first were dead, so I went on. Orris was chasing the young ones. I tried to stop him, eventually I did, but not before Alayna and Jaryd ran into the grove." He looked from Baden to Trahn, his expression dismal and frightened. "Alayna was still carrying the ceryll I gave her."

"We have to find them!" Baden cried, starting toward the grove.

Sartol held out a hand to stop him, shaking his head. "We can't take that risk. Theron will kill us all."

Baden spun past Sartol and began running toward the dark mass of trees that loomed malevolently only a short distance away.

Sartol called after him several times, but it was Trahn's voice, cutting through the night, that finally made him slow to a halt. "Baden! Sartol's right!" the Hawk-Mage shouted. "Theron has Alayna's ceryll. If he wants to use it to kill them, nothing we could do or say would save their lives. We'd just be killing ourselves."

Baden turned to face them. "But we have to do something," he said, almost pleading with them.

"Not this," Trahn asserted. "This is folly. With a ceryll Theron is just too strong. Their fates lie in his hands, and Arick's. There's nothing we can do."

"We have to consider Orris," Sartol added. "If Theron kills us, and Orris has betrayed the Order in some way, who will know the truth? Who will oppose him?"

Baden spun back toward the grove. "Jaryd!" he shouted. "Alayna!" No reply. He had not really expected one. In his heart he knew that Sartol and Trahn were right. He closed his eyes, feeling light-headed. Again, as he had when he learned from Orris of the latest attack, he thought he might be sick. It was all too much for one night: first the destruction of Kaera, and now all this. Jessamyn and Peredur dead; Jaryd and Alayna in Theron's Grove, carrying a ceryll. It was too much. He was very tired. Walking back toward Trahn and Sartol with the rain running down his face, he longed to go to sleep, to wake in the morning and find the company still camped in the Shadow Forest, still a day's ride from Theron's Grove.

"I don't believe that Orris has betrayed the Order," Trahn was arguing as Baden returned to where the two mages stood. "Orris wouldn't do such a thing." The dark mage's fists were clenched at his side, and he was eyeing Sartol with obvious skepticism.

"Orris and I had our differences," Sartol said, addressing Trahn, "but I would never have thought him capable of this, either."

"Could you have been mistaken, Sartol?" the Hawk-Mage asked in a hard voice.

"No," Sartol answered flatly. "He tried to kill me."

Trahn, Baden knew, had never liked Sartol, never trusted him. Now that mistrust, which had seethed dangerously just below the surface since the beginning of this year's Gathering, had begun to seep into the Hawk-Mage's tone and words. Even now, exhausted and aggrieved, Baden could feel himself shouldering old burdens once more. He wanted to weep for Jessamyn, to dash into Theron's Grove and search for Jaryd. But here he was, trying to keep the peace between Trahn, his closest friend in the world, and Sartol, the Owl-Master who, it suddenly seemed, would lead the Order through its most harrowing time in a thousand years.

"Keep in mind, Trahn," Baden heard himself saying, "that when Orris left us, he was going to confront Jessamyn. And he was very upset."

"Upset about what?" Sartol asked quickly.

"There's been another attack," Baden told him, "worse than the others."

"Much worse," Trahn added, his tone harsh. "Orris told us that he was going to speak with the Owl-Sage and demand that we leave at once to help Ursel search for those responsible."

"That may be why he killed her," Sartol offered. "Perhaps she refused to leave without first going into the grove and Orris killed her out of anger and frustration."

"I don't think so," Baden countered, suddenly feeling himself emerging from the torpor that had enveloped him a minute before. "If that was the case, why would he kill Peredur? Why would he try to kill Jaryd and Alayna? Why would he try to kill you? If he killed her out of anger, what would he have to gain by attacking the rest of you?"

"We witnessed his crime," Sartol observed. "Maybe he was trying to protect himself from punishment."

"No," Baden said, shaking his head. "There must be more to it than that." He paused, his mind abruptly shifting to address another mystery from this horribly strange night. "Sartol, as you rushed into that cluster of trees, after you heard Alayna scream, did you see a flash of blue mage-fire?"

"Blue?" the Owl-Master repeated, considering the question. "No, not that I noticed," he replied at length, "but I don't remember there being a blue ceryll in the company."

"You're right; there wasn't one. But Trahn and I saw blue mage-fire just after we saw Alayna's purple." Baden gazed over his shoulder into the darkness of the thicket. "I want to take a look at the place where . . . I want to see where all this happened." He turned back to Sartol. "But if you'd like, I'll heal those wounds first."

Sartol nodded, and sat down on the wet grass. Baden knelt beside him, placing his hand gently over the burn on the Owl-Master's leg as Trahn went to work on the cut over Sartol's eye. Within a few minutes, they had mended the injuries, although the discoloration on Sartol's leg remained, and would linger, Baden knew, for several days.

"Thank you," Sartol said, climbing stiffly to his feet. "Thank you, both," he amended, encompassing Trahn in his gaze.

Baden nodded. "You're welcome." He took a deep breath. "Now, can you show us where you found Jessamyn and Peredur?"

Wordlessly, Sartol stepped past Baden and Trahn and led them into the cluster of trees. Rain still tapped on the leaves and branches, and lightning continued to flicker in the night sky, but the thunder sounded more distant now, and the wind had begun to abate. Pushing their way through a web of branches and brush, the three mages soon reached the center of the thicket, where the russet light created by their cerylls revealed the bodies of the Owl-Sage and her first. Jessamyn's eyes stared sightlessly into the darkness, and Peredur's head and neck jutted from his torso at an impossible angle. Jessamyn's white owl sat on her arm, regarding the mages and their birds with suspicion. As they drew closer, the bird hissed menacingly, although she refused to leave the Owl-Sage. Sartol's owl raised its wings and ruffled its feathers, assuming a threatening posture.

"What are we searching for, Baden?" Trahn asked in a subdued voice.

Mastering his emotions and his shock at the scene before him, Baden tried, as best he could, to sound strong and composed. "Given what we've seen tonight," he told his friend, "and what Sartol has told us, I have two questions. I believe they're linked, and I believe that their answers will tell us why Orris killed the Owl-Sage and the first, and why he tried to kill Alayna and Jaryd." Trahn nodded for him to continue; Sartol had moved closer so that he might hear as well. "First, what was Jessamyn doing here, amongst these trees and so far from the camp? And second, where did Jaryd get a ceryll?"

"Jaryd?" Sartol asked, his eyes narrowing. "What makes you think that Jaryd had a ceryll?"

"The blue mage-fire that we saw came from Jaryd."

"You know this?"

Baden nodded. "Long ago, I had a vision of Jaryd as he would appear after he came into his power. The ceryll he wielded in that vision glowed with the same blue fire that Trahn and I saw tonight."

Without another word, Baden began to search the thicket for clues that might help him explain Orris's actions. Trahn and Sartol did the same. As he passed by Jessamyn's body, Baden paused and, bending carefully so as not to startle the white owl, he reached down and closed the Owl-Sage's eyes with his hand. The owl hissed at him again, but she did not fly.

"Baden!" Sartol called from just a few feet away. "I think I found the answer to your first question."

Baden stepped hurriedly to where the Owl-Master rested on one knee. Trahn had stopped moving and had turned his attention to Sartol, but he did not come nearer.

"Look at these," Sartol said, indicating several thick pieces of wood laid out side by side on the ground.

Baden nodded slowly. "Torches. Of course. We'd need them if we were going to enter the grove without our cerylls." He shook his head, a rueful smile playing at the corners of his mouth. "It was just like Jessamyn to get them herself, rather than sending someone else."

Sartol smiled at the remark. "Yes," he agreed, "I suppose it was." He stood, as did Baden. "But what could Jessamyn preparing torches have to do with Jaryd finding a ceryll?" he asked.

Baden ran a hand through his wet hair and sighed. "I don't know," he replied finally. "I just don't know."

"I'm not sure that we have the luxury of taking a lot of time to figure that out right now," Trahn commented, approaching the two Owl-Masters. "If Sartol is right about Orris—and," he conceded grudgingly, glancing at the Owl-Master, "that does seem possible—we need to return to Amarid before Orris does, and warn the others. The Owl-Masters also need to select a new sage; the Order shouldn't be without one for very long."

"But if Orris is intent on killing Alayna and Jaryd," Baden countered, "shouldn't we remain here to protect them when they emerge from the grove?"

Trahn placed a hand on Baden's shoulder. "They may already be dead, Baden."

"But they may not be," the Owl-Master returned pointedly.

"Maybe we should split up," Sartol suggested, looking from one man to the other.

Baden nodded. "Good idea. I'll stay here."

Trahn shook his head. "You have to go back; you know you do. As an Owl-Master, you have to be there to choose the new Owl-Sage. I'll wait here, and I swear to you in Arick's name," he pledged, "that I'll guard them from Orris and from any other danger, or I'll die in the attempt." Trahn held his friend's gaze until Baden acquiesced with a reluctant nod. Then he turned toward Sartol. "I expect that the masters will make you the new sage. Congratulations," he offered without irony.

Sartol inclined his head slightly. "Thank you, Trahn. I'd be lying if I said that I'd never wished to be sage. But I'd gladly have postponed this distinction for many years in return for Jessamyn's life."

"We know that, Sartol," Baden responded kindly, "but Trahn's right. As Owl-Masters, you and I are obliged to act in the interests of the Order and of Tobyn-Ser, even if this exacts a toll on us personally. I believe that Trahn is also correct in predicting that the masters will select you as the new sage; I know that I'll support you. I don't envy you, though—this is a difficult time to assume leadership of the Order."

Sartol smiled briefly. "For that reason," he said with meaning, his pale eyes fixed on Baden, "I'll have to choose a capable first. I'd like you to consider the position, Baden."

The offer caught Baden off guard. After a brief pause, he nodded once, but he said nothing.

"Baden and I will leave with first light," Sartol declared, taking control of their discussion. "We'll take two of the horses and we'll bear the staffs of

Jessamyn and Peredur. Trahn, as soon as you learn what's happened to Jaryd and Alayna, use the Stone-Merging to contact us and let us know."

"Of course," Trahn assured them, gazing at Baden.

"In the meantime," Sartol continued, his tone growing more solemn, "we should build a pyre for the Owl-Sage and her first."

The three mages began gathering wood for the funeral rites, and they spent much of what remained of the night placing the timber in two large piles set side by side on the open ground by the camp. Just before dawn, as the first hint of light touched the eastern sky, Baden and Trahn returned to the cluster of trees to retrieve the bodies of Jessamyn and Peredur, and bear them to the pyres. Jessamyn's owl still sat vigilantly on the dead woman's arm, but she flew to a low branch when Baden stooped to lift the Owl-Sage, and she followed as Trahn and Baden left the thicket.

"Guard yourself on this journey, Baden," Trahn warned quietly, as they carried the sage and the first back toward the camp. "I know that you and Orris were at odds much of the time, but I still find Sartol's story hard to accept. If he is lying, then he's a traitor to the Order, and your life will be in danger."

"I hear you," Baden replied. "I'll watch my back. But you do the same. If Sartol is telling the truth, then you may have to face Orris by yourself."

Trahn smiled, although his green eyes gleamed fiercely. "If Orris did kill Jessamyn and Peredur, then he'd best keep his distance."

Baden grinned. "I'm going to miss you, my friend. Arick guard you."

"And you," the Hawk-Mage returned.

They reached the pyres, where Sartol waited for them, and without speaking they lifted Jessamyn and Peredur onto the mounds of wood.

Then standing shoulder to shoulder a short distance from the pyres, the three mages lowered their staffs and prepared to ignite the timber.

"With wood and fire, gifts from Tobyn and Leora, we release the spirits of Jessamyn, Daughter of Amarid, and Peredur, Son of Amarid," Sartol intoned. "Open your arms to them, Arick and Duclea, and grant them rest."

With the last word of Sartol's invocation, fire leapt from the cerylls of the three mages—yellow from Sartol, sienna from Trahn, orange from Baden— and enveloped the branches at the bottom of each mound. Despite the rain, which had slowed to a drizzle, the wood began to crackle, and the flames climbed slowly through the pyres to claim the bodies of the Owl-Sage and the first.

Baden faced a long journey, potentially a dangerous one, and he knew that as tired and grief-stricken as he was, he would need to remain watchful as he rode north with Sartol. Still, he allowed himself to weep silently for Jessamyn. She deserved that much, and he could not have done otherwise.

"Farewell, friend," he whispered, watching the flames reach toward the lightening sky. "Arick and Duclea grant you rest."

At that moment, as if on cue, the sage's white owl flashed overhead, pausing briefly to hover high over Jessamyn's pyre, and then continuing on northward, back toward its home in the cool reaches of northern Tobyn-Ser.

* * *

He didn't give a thought to where they were running; it didn't seem to matter. Sartol had blocked Alayna's burst of power and then his own without effort. And that had been with Ishalla and Fylimar right there on their shoulders. For all Jaryd knew, Alayna might have been perfectly capable of fighting off Sartol with Fylimar battling the Owl-Master's bird. But he had no idea how he had created that first blast of blue flame, much less how he was supposed to summon up another one without Ishalla's help. So he had grabbed Alayna's hand and fled, blindly, through the tangle of branches and undergrowth, and then across the grass, and finally into the protective darkness of the forest. Even as he ran, even as he had to drag Alayna with him because she could not accept that her mentor had just tried to kill them, he braced himself, expecting at any instant to be struck down by a killing explosion of mage-fire from Sartol's ceryll. Then he heard shouting, saw bursts of yellow and amber light reflected by the rain-soaked leaves of the trees in front of them, and, without pausing to see what had happened, he and Alayna plunged into the woods. Still he led her forward, not yet convinced that they had escaped danger. It was only when the flashes of light no longer reached them, and the shouting had faded, that Jaryd and Alayna finally slowed to a walk and began to wonder where they were.

It did not take them long to figure it out. Once they stopped moving, and their racing pulses and ragged breathing eased back toward normal, the realization came swiftly. The dark power that they had perceived when the company first regarded Theron's Grove from the safety of the ruins was magnified a thousand times here in its heart. Malice pulsed from the ground and the trees, pounding mercilessly at their senses; even the rain dripping from the leaves above seemed to burn as it fell on their faces and hands. Alayna's ceryll continued to glow with its vivid purple hue, and the blue light from the ceryll within the tree limb that Jaryd carried still shone through the gap in the wood. But both stones appeared muted here, as if stifled by the darkness of the grove.

"You know where we are, don't you?" Alayna whispered.

Jaryd nodded. "We're in the grove." His voice sounded loud and strange in the repressive silence of the forest.

"Good thing you told me to start carrying this staff," she quipped.

Jaryd laughed in spite of himself. In this darkest of all places, where no mortal man or woman had ventured in hundreds of years, Jaryd laughed, and Alayna with him. And in that moment, a realization hit him, and he thought, I could fall in love with this woman.

Their laughter passed quickly, however; Jaryd forced himself to turn away from that last thought. He and Alayna were in Theron's Grove, and for all they knew, Sartol was waiting for them just beyond the trees, ready to kill them if they managed, somehow, to escape from the unsettled spirit of the First Owl-Master.

"We have to leave this place," Alayna declared in a tense voice. "Now."

"I know. But not the way we came in. Sartol's there."

Alayna made a small gesture of impatience or denial; it was hard to tell which. "I still can't believe it," she murmured. "He tried to kill you."

"He would have if you hadn't thrown your mage-fire at him," Jaryd told her. "You saved my life."

"Why would he do that?" she went on, as if she hadn't heard him. "I don't get it."

Jaryd gripped her shoulder. "Alayna, listen to me. We have to get out of here. We can figure out Sartol later, but right now, we have to find a way out of here."

She took a breath, then nodded. Jaryd glanced around them, trying to get his bearings in the impenetrable darkness. They had come in from the west, and while he had not kept track of their progress through the forest as closely as he should have, he felt reasonably confident that they had continued in the same general direction. He had no idea where Sartol had gone, but the Owl-Master was only one man; he could not keep watch on the entire perimeter of the grove. If they circled back to the south, they would emerge from the woods closer to the camp, and to whatever help the others could offer.

"I think we want to go this way," Jaryd said, pointing to the south, he hoped. "But if you have another idea, I'd be happy to hear it."

Alayna shook her head. "I'm completely turned around. I'll follow you."

A sudden flapping of wings brought a shuddering gasp from Alayna and sent a cold wave of panic through Jaryd's entire body. An instant later, when Ishalla alighted on his shoulder, he nearly screamed in fear.

"I think that's the first time since I bound to Ishalla that I actually forgot about her," Jaryd commented, stroking his hawk's chin

"Under the circumstances, I'm sure she'll forgive you," Alayna replied shakily. "Is she all right?"

"I think so. How about Fylimar?"

"She seems to be fine."

Jaryd took her hand. "Good, then let's—"

"Jaryd, look," Alayna said in a voice that chilled his blood.

He knew what had come before he turned. He heard it in her tone; saw it in the shrinking fear that twisted her delicate features as she stared over his shoulder, her eyes wide and her cheeks abruptly colorless. The grove appeared brighter than it had a moment before. He knew what that meant as well. Pivoting slowly, Jaryd saw a diffuse emerald-green light moving toward them through the trees, shimmering like moonbeams on a windswept lake, and clinging like rain to the branches and leaves so that they themselves seemed to glow. Had he not been standing in Theron's Grove, Jaryd would have thought this display as beautiful as the shifting curtains of light that graced the autumn sky each year on the night of Leora's Feast.

But the Night of Light was more than two months away. Staring with wonder and horror at the approaching radiance, Jaryd discerned a figure walking at its center, its aspect vague at first, but gaining substance with each step until Jaryd found that he could make out certain details. The figure had a long, full beard and thick, shoulder-length hair that would have been grey if not for his green luminescence. Deep lines creased his face, but though his countenance made him appear aged, he carried himself like a young man, straight-backed and alert. On his shoulder, as spectral and radiant as he, sat a large falcon with a dark head and back, and markings on its face that made it look mustached. And in his hand, the man carried a long, wooden staff, at the top of which, where there should have been a ceryll, the wood had been splintered and charred.

"Should we run?" Jaryd breathed, never taking his eyes off the ghostly figure in front of them.

"Do you really think we'd make it?" Alayna whispered in reply.

He shook his head.

"Neither do I," she agreed, "but if we run, I'm sure he'll kill us. We might as well stay and try to talk to him."

Jaryd took a deep breath and nodded.

The specter drew closer, and, as he did, Jaryd saw his eyes. They were hard and bright as cerylls, a far cry from the soft green glow that surrounded him, and they carried within them a hatred and bitterness that had raged for a thousand years. Seeing those eyes, feeling themselves encompassed by the baleful gaze, Jaryd and Alayna quailed.

And then it was that they first heard the voice of Theron's unsettled spirit. "Can you offer one reason," the Owl-Master asked, his words rolling like thunder through the grove, "why I should not kill you both?"

Ishalla and Fylimar squawked nervously and raised their slate-colored wings, although neither bird tried to fly. Immobilized by Theron's piercing glare, his body trembling violently, Jaryd somehow mustered the courage to speak. "I'm Jaryd," he said in a faltering voice. "This is Alayna."

"I know who you are," the spirit rumbled impatiently. "I know who all of you are: the dead ones, the traitor, all of you. And I know why you have come. None of that concerns me. Tell me why I should not kill you; that, I would find amusing."

"We've done nothing to give offense," Alayna told him, sounding small and frightened.

"Your presence offends me!" Theron roared. "For a thousand years, I have tolerated no encroachments on my solitude, and I certainly have suffered no fools or pretentious children. Others who came went mad before they died. That could be your fate as well. Now I will ask one last time: why should I spare your lives!"

"If you know of the dead ones and the traitor," Jaryd answered quickly, "then you also know that we're not here by choice; that we only entered the grove to save our lives."

The Owl-Master's eyes narrowed, and a grin flashed across his face. "How ironic," he remarked maliciously. "Besides," he continued, his tone now guileful, "your group traveled a great distance to be here. Surely you would have entered this grove eventually, even without the traitor at your backs."

I'm playing a very dangerous game, Jaryd thought to himself, with a spirit that has walked this land for a thousand years. I must be crazy.

"Yes, we would have," Alayna joined in, "but only to seek your counsel, and only as part of a delegation that would have included the Owl-Sage and the First of the Order."

"This, I take it, is meant to impress me," Theron said with disdain. "It does not. Nor does it deceive me: you came to accuse me of crimes against the land, and to keep me from doing further damage. By persuasion, if you could; by force, if necessary. Isn't that so?" The spirit's tone was contemptuous, but something in his manner told Jaryd that he and Alayna had forestalled their deaths, at least for the time being.

"Yes, it is," Jaryd confirmed, "that's precisely why we came." Clearly, there would be no deceiving the Owl-Master; but, perhaps, if they spoke to him candidly . . .

"Fools!" Theron spat. "If I have chosen to take my vengeance, finally, after all these centuries, do you really believe that a handful of mortal mages could stop me?" He indicated the illuminated grove with a gesture. "Look around you. I am power itself, as are all the Unsettled. We are all walking incarnations of the Mage-Craft." He leveled a rigid finger at the mages. "Don't you see!" he thundered, causing the ground beneath them to shake. "You are nothing against me, *Children of Amarid!*" A bolt of green fire flew from his hand, passing between Jaryd and Alayna and crashing loudly into a tree behind them. Jaryd stood appalled, unable to respond, and half expecting to die in the next moment. But instead, the Owl-Master went on. "I was every bit as responsible for the discovery of the Mage-Craft and the founding of the Order as he was. And they send children to speak with me, children carrying Amarid's Hawk." He lanced Alayna with his glare. "That is what they call them now, is it not?" he asked.

"Yes, it is," Alayna replied frankly.

"And, no doubt, the two of you are regarded as being quite special because you are bound to them; that is probably why they included you in this delegation. Tell me this," Theron continued, motioning petulantly at the bird on his shoulder, "others have bound to birds like Jevlar, haven't they?" He did not wait for an answer. "Of course they have. But these birds are not known as Theron's Hawk, are they?"

"You're remembered for your curse, Owl-Master," Jaryd told him, amazed, as he heard himself speak, by his own presumption, "and for the torment you inflicted on the people of Rholde. Yours is the most feared name in Tobyn-Ser. Isn't that what you wanted?"

"*Silence!*" Theron roared, his eyes blazing. For a second time, Jaryd wondered if he was about to be killed. But then the Owl-Master began to chuckle, softly at first, and then building until he threw back his head to laugh at the sky. His bright emerald eyes, though, remained hard and without mirth. "Yes," the spirit said at length, laughing no more but grinning sardonically. "That is what I wanted." His grin faded and he looked from Jaryd to Alayna. "But you suspect that I have grown tired of merely being feared, that, perhaps, I am no longer satisfied with fright alone. For that reason, you believe I have committed these attacks that concern you so. Am I right?"

Jaryd and Alayna exchanged a glance. "For that reason," Jaryd said, "or maybe to get our attention."

"Ah, of course," Theron remarked with heavy irony, "because I value your consideration so."

"Did you have another reason?" Alayna asked. "One we might not have contemplated?"

Theron regarded her for some time, saying nothing. Then he swung his glowing eyes back to Jaryd. "Tell me, Hawk-Mage," he demanded, his tone suddenly low and elusive, "why is there a ceryll in that tree limb you bear? That does not look like any mage's staff I have ever seen."

Jaryd stared at the piece of wood, with the gleaming sapphire ceryll half concealed within it. He had not given the ceryll much thought; there hadn't been time. But now, as he pondered Theron's question, fragmented images from this terrifying night began to fall into place. Sartol killed Jessamyn and Peredur. Why? What was he up to? What was he doing? Jessamyn had asked him to gather torches. No! Jaryd realized with a start. She approached the three of us about covering the supplies and finding torches. Sartol volunteered to do the latter!

"Sartol put the ceryll in this branch!" he said excitedly, meeting Theron's gaze. He turned to Alayna. "This was supposed to be a torch, and he put a ceryll in it!"

Alayna began to nod as she followed his line of thought. "That must be why he killed Jessamyn," she suggested. "She went to find him and caught him as he was altering the torch. That's also why we can still see the ceryll: he never got the chance to finish."

"But where would he get a ceryll?" Jaryd asked. "Don't mages have only one?"

"They're supposed to have only one," Alayna corrected. "But mages get their stones from the Ceryll Cavern on Ceryllon. There's nothing to stop them from taking as many as they want; it's just considered a point of honor. At least, that's how Sartol explained it to me," she added, grimacing at the irony.

"Why would the traitor place a stone in that branch?" Theron boomed irritably, commanding their attention once more.

Jaryd faced the spirit again. "Our delegation had planned to leave our cerylls outside the grove. We believed that, without access to a ceryll, you'd be unable to harm us. So Sartol must have wanted you to kill us."

"And why would he have wanted that?"

"Any number of reasons," Alayna replied. "With Jessamyn dead, he'd be the leading candidate to replace her as Owl-Sage. He'd get Jessamyn out of the way, and you'd be blamed for it." She stopped, and regarded the Owl-Master for what seemed a long time. She ran her fingers through her long, rain-soaked hair, pulling it back from her face. Her brow was furrowed in concentration. "That's your whole point, isn't it?" she asked finally. "You're being blamed for these attacks, just as Sartol planned to blame you for our deaths."

"And if you killed the delegation," Jaryd added, "the rest of the Order would have seen it as confirmation of your responsibility for the attacks."

"Very good," Theron snorted derisively. "You have managed to establish my innocence. And all I had to do was lead you to that conclusion as if you were oxen, with rings in your noses. The Owl-Sage and her first come all this way, and it is the babes who solve the mystery."

"Would it have worked?" Jaryd asked the Owl-Master, ignoring the taunts. "Given what we planned to say to you, given the membership of the delegation, would you have used that ceryll to kill us?"

"Possibly," Theron answered, a cold smile on his lips. "I still might."

Jaryd hesitated, but only for an instant. "I don't think so," he ventured.

He was taking a tremendous chance, he knew, but he had thought about Theron a great deal since Baden first told him the story of the Owl-Master's curse. "You created the Order," he went on, "you and Amarid, and you don't want to see it destroyed any more than we do. You certainly don't want to be held responsible for its destruction. I don't think you would have killed the delegation, and I don't think you're going to kill us. We're the only ones who can help you stop Sartol."

"You should not place too much faith in my affection for the Order!" Theron said sharply. "As for Sartol, I understand him."

"You mean because he once took payment for his service to the land?" Alayna asked.

For the first time, the Owl-Master looked surprised. "I knew nothing of this," he admitted. "I was referring to his contempt for the weakness and lassitude of today's mages." He glanced at Jaryd. "Even if I still take pride in the creation of the Order, as you suggest, I no longer see in it much that I respect. It does not deserve to survive this crisis."

"You say that you understand Sartol," Jaryd challenged, "but you referred to him earlier as 'the traitor.' Surely, if you cared nothing for the Order, you wouldn't characterize his actions as a betrayal."

Theron stared at him for some time, tugging gently at his long beard. "You remind me of Amarid," he said at length, his tone wintry, "and not just because of your hawk and that blue ceryll."

"Nonetheless," Jaryd returned, his confidence growing.

"What is your point?" Theron demanded testily.

"Simply that you care about the Order, and the Order needs your help."

"I told you a moment ago," Theron maintained, "I feel no allegiance to the Order, and I feel absolutely no obligation to save you and your fellow mages! Yes, I wished to be feared, once!" he went on, his voice rising. "But I never thought that I would be ignored, that my place in the history of this Order would be dismissed as it has! I deserved better than that!" He paused, gathering himself. When he spoke again, his tone was more controlled. "I was the first to bind to an owl, you know. I may even have been the first to bind to any creature. We never figured that out for certain."

We, Jaryd thought. Theron and Amarid. It was hard to remember sometimes that their friendship lay beneath all that followed. There seemed to be so many dimensions to this tragedy. "We found the Summoning Stone together," Theron said quietly. "We created the Order together, and then, without warning, he had no more use for me." The spirit paused, seeming suddenly to remember that Jaryd and Alayna were there. "Well," he continued a moment later, his tone growing cold again, "soon the Order will be destroyed, and the rest of you can join me in my obscurity and superfluousness."

"Or you can help us," Alayna offered, "and reclaim your legacy."

The spirit made no reply, but Jaryd saw a flicker of doubt in his shining green eyes.

"What is this crisis, as you called it?" Alayna coaxed gently. "Why are you so sure that the Order will be destroyed?"

"Are there others like the two of you?" Theron asked, ignoring Alayna's prodding. "Young and bold and clever?"

"Yes," Jaryd replied, "there are others. There are many in the Order, particularly among the Hawk-Mages, who have grown impatient with the inaction of the older masters. We aren't all weak and lazy."

"And not all of us have forgotten your place in our history," Alayna broke in. "We haven't been as diligent in educating the rest of Tobyn-Ser as we should have been, but we haven't forgotten."

"Well, now it is too late," the Owl-Master commented.

Jaryd shook his head. "It doesn't have to be."

"You misunderstand," Theron responded. "It is not too late because of anything I might do or not do. The attacks on Tobyn-Ser have discredited the Order, made it an object of fear. For the mages to embrace my memory now would be imprudent. The people of this land would see it as proof of the Order's corruption." Theron's tone betrayed no emotion, but the longing in his eyes bespoke a pain so old, and so deep, that Jaryd could find no words with which to reassure, no arguments with which to counter the truths that lay at the core of what the Owl-Master had said. He had faced the spirit's ire, and endured his contempt. But Jaryd could find no reply to Theron's grief.

"It seems," Alayna remarked, gazing at Theron, "that we share a common enemy after all."

The luminous spirit stood motionless, considering this as his eyes held Alayna's. "That may prove to be the case," Theron conceded at length. "But I am not yet ready to embrace the Order as an ally in this."

"From what you've told us tonight," Jaryd said, again taking a chance, "I'm not sure that we can wait for you to make up your mind."

Too much of a chance, it seemed. "I will not be compelled by guilt in this matter!" the Owl-Master answered indignantly, his eyes blazing once more. "You would do well to remember to whom you speak!"

Jaryd gave a small laugh as he indicated the brightly lit grove with a gesture, much as Theron had done a short while ago. "I'm unlikely to forget, Owl-Master." Then, his tone hardening, Jaryd went on. "But with your help or without it, Alayna and I must try to keep Sartol from destroying the Order. So if you plan to kill us, do it now. Or else, let us go. Either way, we've already wasted too much time here."

Jaryd heard Alayna take a deep breath beside him, but, otherwise, she remained perfectly still. Theron glowered at him, his face rigid, one hand absently stroking his thick beard and the other wrapped tightly around the shaft of the scarred staff. Then the Owl-Master's expression changed, and the hint of a smile touched his lips. "You are bold, Hawk-Mage," the spirit rumbled, "I will grant you that. But I wonder how much of that bravado will remain after you have spent a night in Theron's Grove."

And saying this, Theron raised his arm and swung it forward, as if hurling a stone. Again a ball of green fire flew from his fingers, this time crashing into the ground between Jaryd and Alayna with an explosion that shook the earth and knocked Jaryd to the forest floor. Ishalla leaped into the air with a shriek and started circling overhead. Jaryd heard Alayna cry out his name and he scrambled to his feet, but already the young mages were separated by a wall of flame that climbed into the night, making the raindrops that still fell on the grove sizzle.

"Let us see how you endure a night as my guests!" Theron said, laughing in the thunderous voice.

Jaryd quickly scanned the grove, looking for the Owl-Master's spirit, but Theron was nowhere to be seen.

"Jaryd!" Alayna called again. Her voice sounded distant already.

"Alayna!" he replied. "Stay where you are! I'll try to reach you!" She didn't respond. Jaryd wondered if she had even heard him. He raised his arm for Ishalla, allowing her to settle back onto his shoulder. Then he tried to edge closer to the flames to see if he could catch a glimpse of Alayna, but the heat was too intense. Moreover, the flames were spreading, driving him away from her. Indeed, Jaryd realized in that moment, that was the fire's intent. This was no random blaze responding to changes in the wind or terrain. These flames seemed to act with purpose, like a pack of wolves stalking prey: they knew exactly where they wanted him to go. Jaryd gave ground grudgingly, refusing to flee, but he was fighting a losing battle. He felt himself being herded to some unknown destination; he could do nothing to resist.

The flames continued to creep forward for what felt like a long time, leaping from tree trunk to tree trunk, sweeping over the low brush that covered the floor of the grove, and all the time forcing Jaryd to retreat. There was no smoke, but Jaryd could feel the heat on his face and chest as he backed away. Occasionally he cried out for Alayna, but he sensed that she was out of earshot. He had no idea where he was; he had lost all sense of direction. Eventually the rain stopped, but the fire kept pushing him, until finally he reached a small hollow that was more open than the rest of the grove had been. There the flames halted their advance and spread along the perimeter of the hollow until Jaryd was completely encircled.

Jaryd's frustration and anger had mounted as the flames drove him farther and farther from Alayna, but now, standing in the hollow, waiting for whatever it was that Theron had in store for him, he felt those feelings giving way to a cold sense of dread. "Let us see how you endure a night as my guests," the Owl-Master had said. Jaryd shuddered.

"Jaryd," came a thin voice from behind him, catapulting his heart into his throat.

Jaryd spun around and gasped at what he saw. "No!" he breathed.

A small boy stood before him. His hair was long and straight like Jaryd's and he had a round face with a small upturned nose. His eyes, however, were utterly black, and a pale green luminescence clung to him like the smell of death. Ishalla let out a frightened cry.

"Do you remember me?" the boy asked, his voice sounding distant and small.

Jaryd nodded. His mouth had gone dry and his entire body trembled. Of course he remembered. This was the little boy who disappeared just before Jaryd had his first vision two winters ago. And the day after Jaryd dreamed of drowning in cold, turbulent waters, they found the boy's body floating in the Mountsea River. "You're Arley," Jaryd managed to say.

The boy smiled ghoulishly. "You do remember! Maybe you also remember my friend."

A second figure stepped into the clearing, appearing to materialize out of the flames. He was tall and thin, with a bald head and a bushy mustache. Like Arley, he glowed with a soft emerald light, except for his eyes, which were as black as night. Iram, Jaryd thought, surprising himself with his composure and clarity. Yes, he would be here too. It makes sense. Iram had been Accalia's apothecary until the fire that Jaryd foresaw with his second vision destroyed Iram's shop and claimed his life.

"Yes," Jaryd whispered, looking at the boy again. "I remember him, too."

"It's not enough to remember!" Iram said harshly, his voice, like Arley's, seeming to come from a great distance. "You owe us more than that!"

"Owe you more?" Jaryd repeated. He shivered as if from a sudden chill, and he felt his stomach tightening. "I don't understand."

"Iram's mad because you didn't save us," Arley explained, the horrible black eyes gazing at Jaryd. "You saw, but you didn't do anything."

Jaryd shook his head, his vision clouded now by tears. "Saw? You mean the dreams?"

Arley took a step forward, his head cocked slightly to the side. He looked so young, so innocent. But his eyes . . . "You saw what was going to happen to us, and you still let it happen."

Again Jaryd shook his head, unable to speak.

"You let us die!" Iram accused in a voice like a cutting wind. "You had the power to protect us and you let us die!"

"That's not true!" Jaryd insisted.

"Look at us!" Iram raged, his arms open wide. "Do you deny that we are dead? Do you deny having visions of what killed us?"

The young mage dropped to his knees, his arms limp by his side. Tears streamed down his face. He couldn't look at the ghosts. "I didn't know what the dreams meant," he pleaded. "I didn't understand until after the fire."

"And so we died," Iram pressed.

Jaryd took a long breath and met the apothecary's black gaze. "Yes."

Iram looked like he might say more, but then he stopped himself. At the same time, Jaryd saw two more figures step into the hollow. He rose, turning to face them. And again he gasped at what he saw.

"Sage Jessamyn!" he cried. "First Peredur!" He took a step toward them and then stopped. The sage and her first were suffused with green light, but while Jessamyn's eyes were as black as those of the other two ghosts, Peredur's eyes shone with a pearl-colored luminescence that matched the color of his ceryll. Both mages carried their staffs, and Jessamyn's great white owl still sat on her shoulder. Peredur, however, was accompanied by a small hawk that Jaryd did not recognize.

"I died unbound," the first explained in a far-off voice, as Jaryd stared at the bird. "Because of you, I am one of the Unsettled now."

Jaryd staggered backward as if he had been struck. "Because of me!"

"The sage gave you a choice," Peredur reminded him sternly, "you and the other one. And the two of you let the renegade see to the torches. We would be alive but for that choice."

"But how could I know?" Jaryd implored, feeling his tears flow once more. "I trusted Sartol! We all did! What was I supposed to do?"

"We do not always understand the consequences of our choices when we

186 DAVID B. COE

make them," Jessamyn told him. "But that does not make us any less responsible."

"But I didn't mean for any of this to happen!"

"You allowed the renegade to alter the torch." Peredur's tone offered no hope of forgiveness. "Jessamyn found him doing this and he killed her. Then he killed me. Had you gone to gather the torches, leaving the renegade and the other young one to cover the supplies, we would be alive."

"I didn't know," Jaryd said meekly.

"And your ignorance killed us!" the first railed. "In the end it may destroy Tobyn-Ser!"

Jaryd closed his eyes and shook his head. "No!" he shouted. "No!" He turned away from the ghosts, his body racked by sobbing. "No," he said again, softly this time, his face buried in his hands.

He remained like that for a long time, unwilling to face them again, until finally, he began to wonder if they were still there. And then he heard his name spoken again, in a different voice, although one with the same unearthly quality as the others.

Straightening, and wiping the tears from his face, he looked to see who had called him. Arley and Iram were gone, as were the sage and her first. Two women stood before him, or rather the ghosts of two women. They carried staffs and owls and wore mages' cloaks. One was tall, with short hair and lean, angular features. The other was shorter and stouter, with wide-set eyes and a round face. Yet, despite the differences in their appearance, they struck Jaryd as being somewhat alike. And though he did not recognize them, they seemed surprisingly familiar.

"Do you know who we are, Jaryd?" the tall one asked.

It was almost exactly the question Baden had asked him in Accalia early this past spring. "I think so, yes," he replied, his heart racing. "You're Lyris and Lynwen, my great-grandmother and grandmother."

The smaller woman nodded. "Yes. Very good."

"But I don't know which of you is which."

"I am Lyris," the smaller one said.

Jaryd swallowed. "Have I done something else wrong? Is that why you've come?"

Lynwen shook her head. "No. We've come to show you a way out."

"What!"

By way of an answer, the women turned their gazes toward the far end of the hollow. As they did, the flames there died down, creating an opening in the circle of fire. Jaryd looked back at the ghosts, uncertain of what they expected him to do.

"This way," Lyris told him, gesturing toward the opening with a glowing green hand.

Jaryd gazed at her for another moment, still unsure. Then he looked at his grandmother, who nodded encouragingly.

"All right," he murmured, as he began to walk toward the open end of the hollow. The ghosts followed, as did the remaining flames.

They walked for several minutes through a dense section of the grove and then down a steep bank. Jaryd heard the sound of rushing water, and a few moments later they came to a small, swift creek.

"Follow this downstream and you will come to the Moriandral just a short distance above the ruins of Rholde," Lynwen instructed. "From there you can find your way back to your friends."

Jaryd peered in the direction she had indicated, but the forest was too dense to see beyond the first bend in the stream. He turned back to his grandmother. "What about Alayna?"

The two ghosts looked at each other. "This is your only way out," Lyris told him, her black eyes fixed on his face.

"That's not what I asked."

"You entered Theron's Grove, and there is a price for doing such a thing. But both of you need not perish. This is your only way out," she said again, "and there is not much time."

Jaryd shook his head and crossed his arms over his chest. "No."

"Don't be foolish, child!" Lynwen snapped. "We're giving you a chance to escape!"

"You're telling me to exchange Alayna's life for my own!" Jaryd fired back. "I won't do it!" He looked from one of the ghosts to the other. "Would you really want me to? Is that what you'd expect from Bernel's son?"

Both women looked away. "If you refuse, there's nothing more that we can do for you," Lyris said quietly. "You'll be at his mercy again."

Jaryd nodded grimly. "Then so be it. I have to find Alayna."

Immediately his grandmother and great-grandmother began to fade. The fires burned down as well. "Be well, child!" Lynwen called to him, her voice growing fainter and fainter. "Arick guard you!"

"Remember us!" Lyris called, the words barely more than a whisper.

A moment later, Jaryd was alone in the dark. The only light came from the sapphire ceryll contained within the branch that he carried, and it still seemed muted by the power of the grove. Ishalla let out a small cry. Jaryd stroked her chin reassuringly. *It's all right,* he sent. *We'll find them.* He took a steadying breath, and then he started back toward the center of Theron's Grove in search of Alayna.

She had no idea where she was, and she didn't understand why the flames that now ringed her had driven her to this spot. But staring at the ghostly green figure standing before her, and sending soothing thoughts to Fylimar on her shoulder, Alayna understood that none of that mattered anymore. The little girl hadn't spoken; she didn't have to. Alayna knew who she was, though they had never met, at least not that Alayna could remember. The child looked so much like Alayna's mother—indeed, she looked so much like Alayna herself— that there could be no mistaking her. This was Danise, Alayna's older sister, who had taken ill and died at the age of four when Alayna was but an infant. She was beautiful, even with the terrifying black eyes that gazed up at Alayna's face.

Her parents had told her very little about Danise; from what she had heard

188 DAVID B. COE

and seen, they had told Faren, Alayna's younger sister, even less. But throughout Alayna's life, Danise had been a fifth presence in their home, hovering over all that the family did and said. As a child, Alayna had lain awake at night, wondering what it would be like to have an older sister and having imaginary conversations with Danise. And now, somehow, her sister stood before her. Looking at the little girl, Alayna could not keep herself from weeping. She was trembling uncontrollably, and when she tried to speak, she found that she could not.

"You know me," the ghost said coldly, in a voice that seemed to come from far away.

Alayna nodded.

"What do you have to say to me?"

"I—I'm not sure what you mean," Alayna stammered through her tears, her voice sounding loud and awkward. "I've often wished that I could meet you."

Danise gave a high, mirthless laugh. "Have you?"

"Yes!" Alayna assured her, taken aback.

"Strange," the little girl sneered, "it seems to me you've spent your whole life trying to make Mommy and Daddy forget that I'd ever been born!"

Alayna shook her head violently. "That's not true!"

"Isn't it!" the child fired back. "You've tried so hard to please them, to make them proud, all because you were afraid that they loved me more! You thought that if you could make them happy enough, they'd forget all about me!"

"No!" Alayna cried. She couldn't stop herself from sobbing. "It's not true!" she said again. But her denial sounded hollow, even to her own ears. There was more truth in the ghost's words than she wanted to admit.

Even as a small child, barely older than the girl who stood before her, Alayna had been aware of how much her mother missed her first daughter. And Alayna had spent much of her life attempting to ease her mother's pain the only way she knew how: by being the best at everything she did.

"I never wanted them to forget you," she finally told the child, wiping the tears from her eyes though they continued to flow freely. "That's not what I was trying to do."

"You just wanted to make them love you the most!"

"I wanted to make them happy!" Alayna shouted at the girl.

Danise took a step back.

She may be a ghost, Alayna reminded herself, trying to ease her frustration, but she's also a little girl. "They sounded so sad every time they talked about you," she began again in a quieter voice, "that I wanted to make them think about something else. Sometimes at night, after I'd go to bed, I'd hear Mom crying, and I knew she was crying for you. I just wanted her to be happy."

Black lines appeared on the girl's face. It took several moments before Alayna realized that Danise was crying, too. "So you were trying to take my place."

"No, Danise," Alayna said, shaking her head again. "I could never have taken your place. Nobody could. That's why Mom was so sad all the time. But you were gone, and Faren and I needed Mom and Dad to concentrate on us. Was that so bad?"

The ghost hesitated. "I don't know," she admitted. "I guess——" She stopped suddenly, her black eyes growing wide. "Someone's coming!" she whispered.

Immediately the glowing green image started to grow dim.

"Danise, no!" Alayna called to her. "Please don't leave!"

"Good-bye, Alayna!" her sister called, her voice already so distant that it sounded like little more than a warm summer breeze rustling the trees.

In another moment, Danise was gone. The fires had died out as well, leaving Alayna and Fylimar with only Alayna's purple ceryll by which to see. The Hawk-Mage peered through the trees, wondering who had come, and wishing that the light from her crystal could penetrate the stifling darkness of the grove.

She expected to see Jaryd's blue stone approaching, or, perhaps, the emerald glow of the Owl-Master's spirit. What she saw instead froze her blood. It was a yellow ceryll. Fylimar let out a cry of alarm and leaped off Alayna's shoulder. Alayna turned to flee as well, but before she could take more than a step or two, an all-too-familiar voice stopped her.

"Please don't run, my dear!" Sartol called. "I'd hate to have to kill you!"

Steeling herself and trying to ease the pounding of her heart, Alayna turned back to face her mentor. "I'm not sure I believe that," she said as he drew near. "You seemed all too willing to kill me just a short time ago."

He shook his head. "Not you, my dear. The boy, perhaps. But not you. In fact, as I remember our little encounter, you were the one who tried to kill me."

"You were killing Jaryd!" she shot back. "What was I supposed to do?"

"But that's precisely my point: my business was with the boy, not you." The tall mage took another step forward. "How could I ever harm you?"

"Don't come any closer!" she warned. Fylimar, who had returned to Alayna's shoulder, gave a low hiss.

Sartol laughed. "Or what? You'll kill me? I don't think so. Even if you could bring yourself to try, which I doubt, you're simply not strong enough."

"Then I'll die in the attempt!" she told him, pleased to hear how steady her voice remained.

"I'd rather it didn't come to that," he said, smiling disarmingly. "But you should know that regardless of what happens here, I am going to rule Tobyn-Ser. And there's nothing you can do to stop me. My hope is, my hope has always been, that you and I can rule it together. But one way or another, this land will be mine."

"I don't believe you!" she answered. "Baden and the others will stop you!"

"Baden and the others are dead. Only you and Jaryd remain. Don't you see, my dear: my success is ensured. If you refuse me I'll kill you as I did the others and blame Theron for all your deaths. Then I'll return to Amarid and assume control of the Order. No one will ever know what really happened."

Alayna was crying again. *Baden and the others are dead.* The man she had trusted more than any other in the world was a murderer and a traitor. And there was nothing she could do to stop him.

"Please don't cry, Alayna," he said gently. "There was nothing you could do to save them. But you can save yourself. I love you; I always have. And I want you to be my first. I want us to rule the Order together. If only you knew how strong I am, and how much stronger I can become! You can as well! I'll teach you, just as I taught you how to be a mage!"

"Why are you doing this?" she sobbed. "Why did you kill Jessamyn and Peredur?"

"Jessamyn and Peredur were in my way!" Sartol snapped. "They were weak, and they were making the Order weak! Under me the Mage-Craft will grow more powerful than it's ever been!"

Alayna straightened. "No! I won't allow it!"

"That's not for you to decide," Sartol replied, his voice low and cold. "Either you can join me and live, or you can refuse me and die. Those are your only choices."

Alayna leveled her staff at the Owl-Master. "Then I'll die!"

Sartol raised his staff as well. "I'm warning you, my dear. Don't be deceived by my affection for you. I will kill you if I must."

"You're going to have to, Sartol! Because if you don't, I'll spend every day of my life trying to stop you!"

"Don't be a fool, Alayna! I'm offering you your life and a chance to wield more power than you ever dreamed possible!"

Alayna grinned darkly. "I'm happy with the power I have."

"This is your last chance!" Sartol growled, baring his teeth.

Alayna braced herself for Sartol's blast of mage-fire, knowing that she could not stand against him. In that instant, however, she heard a voice call her name.

"Jaryd!" she cried back. And then, "Run, Jaryd! It's Sartol! R—" She stopped. Suddenly there was no need to yell. She stood alone in the forest. Sartol was gone, if he had ever been there at all. A few seconds later, Jaryd reached her and enfolded her in his arms.

"What was it you were calling to me?" he asked her after a short time, still holding her.

"It was nothing," she whispered, as unwilling as he to end their embrace.

Finally he released her, stepping back and gazing intently into her eyes. "Are you all right?"

She nodded. "I am now. How did you find me?"

"I saw the light." He glanced around them. "At least I thought I did."

She gave a wan smile. "There was more light here a short while ago."

"The fire?" he asked.

"That burned out a while ago," she said. "This was Sartol."

"What!"

"Or an image of him. I don't know anymore."

"What did he say?" the young mage asked, an expression of amazement on his youthful face.

Alayna shrugged. "He said he intends to rule the Order, and he wants me by his side as his first."

"Do you think he meant it?"

"I don't know," she answered candidly. "As I said, I'm not even sure that it was him. He vanished into thin air as soon as I heard your voice."

Jaryd nodded. "That fits."

Alayna narrowed her eyes. "What do you mean?"

"Just that things in this grove aren't as they appear," Jaryd replied. "Like that fire: it looked and felt real, but it didn't do any damage to the trees or brush."

"That's reassuring in a way," Alayna murmured.

"Why?" Jaryd asked, looking at her closely. "What else did you see?"

Alayna shook her head, taking a shuddering breath. "I'd rather not talk about it," she told him as gently as she could. "Someday, perhaps, but not now."

He nodded and took a long breath of his own. "I understand."

She gazed at him. Even in the dim light cast by their cerylls she could see the pained look in his pale eyes. "I believe you," she whispered. She kissed his cheek softly and gathered him in her arms once again.

"So what do we do now?" Jaryd asked wearily.

"I don't think there's much more we can do tonight," she told him. "We should try to get some rest."

Jaryd nodded his agreement. "You're probably right. But what if Theron isn't done with us yet?"

"I'm sure he'll wake us," Alayna said with a smile.

Jaryd laughed.

The two young mages searched the area around them for a place to sleep and soon found a particularly dense cluster of trees beneath which the ground was still dry.

"This looks good to me," Jaryd commented, stretching out on the dry leaves.

Presented now with a place where she might sleep, Alayna felt weariness wrap itself around her like a blanket. She lay down beside him. "I can't believe it," she said, already feeling herself slipping into a deep slumber. "We've survived a night in Theron's Grove."

"So it would seem," Jaryd responded sleepily. "Let's just hope that we survive leaving it."

12

Midway through the morning, the rain stopped entirely, and the sun burst dazzlingly through the thinning clouds. The grass and leaves, still wet from the storm, sparkled in the sunlight, and steam rose slowly from the ruins of Rholde. Baden and Sartol had been gone for several hours. Even now, they were riding north toward Amarid, while Trahn, hoping against hope that Jaryd and Alayna would emerge from Theron's Grove alive and unharmed, sat on the ground by the camp, watching the light grey smoke drift from what remained of the funeral pyres. For much of the morning, almost since the Owl-Masters had left, he had gone over the events of the previous night in his head,

trying to come to terms with the rather strong likelihood that Orris had betrayed the Order.

He could not honestly say that he considered Orris a friend, at least not in
the way that Baden was a friend, or Jaryd. Thinking of the young Hawk-Mage,
he scanned the edge of the grove again, looking for some sign that Jaryd and
Alayna were alive. He saw nothing, and, sighing deeply, he returned to his
musings. Even if Orris was not a friend, however, he was an ally; someone who
shared Trahn's vision of the Order and its proper standing in Tobyn-Ser, someone whose opinion Trahn respected. More than that, Orris had established
himself as the leader and the conscience of the younger mages. His abrasive
manner, which many of the Owl-Masters mistook for disrespect, Trahn appreciated as an outgrowth of the Hawk-Mage's passion. Certainly, Orris had a
temper—Trahn could almost accept the idea that he might kill Jessamyn in a
moment of fury. Almost. But Baden had been correct the night before when
he suggested that Peredur's murder, and the attempts on Jaryd, Alayna, and
Sartol, indicated that a deeper, more sinister purpose lay behind the killing of
the Owl-Sage. Baden had not actually said it, but Trahn had inferred from his
words that the Owl-Master suspected a plot against the Order that related in
some way to the recent attacks on Tobyn-Ser. This, Trahn could not accept,
at least not as far as Orris was concerned. Yes, Orris was caustic, rude, even
temperamental. But not devious. Which brought Trahn back to Sartol. That
one, he did not trust. He never had, and he saw no reason to start now. Were
it not for Trahn's absolute belief in Orris's integrity, which he knew Baden did
not share, Sartol's story would have seemed completely plausible. But what
proof did Sartol offer? Jessamyn and Peredur's bodies? Sartol could have killed
them himself. Jaryd and Alayna's disappearance? Again, the Owl-Master could
have been responsible. His own injuries? Orris could have inflicted them while
trying to save Jaryd and Alayna, just as easily as he could have trying to kill
them. Looked at from just a slightly different perspective, the evidence could
be construed to implicate Sartol instead of Orris.

"That, I would believe," Trahn said aloud, turning to face his brown hawk,
who sat motionless on an ancient stump a few feet away. The bird blinked at
him indifferently.

Trahn climbed to his feet and held out his arm. Reivlad flew to him instantly,
and the Hawk-Mage started toward the trees where Jessamyn and Peredur were
murdered. He had time; he would not be leaving until he found Jaryd and
Alayna, or at least learned something of their fates. This seemed as good an
opportunity as he would have to reexamine the site of the killings. Possibly,
because of the darkness, they had overlooked something last night, or maybe
Sartol had concealed something. In either case, the daylight could help.

Reaching the center of the thicket, Trahn stopped and tried to reconstruct
in his mind the horrifying scene they had encountered the night before. Just
in front of him, he saw the branches that Jessamyn had intended to use as
torches, still arranged in a tidy row. Her body had been lying just about where
he now stood, and Peredur had died a few feet to the left. . . .

Glancing in that direction, Trahn froze. Several feet away, at the base of a
tall pine, he spotted a small mass of feathers, wet and disheveled, and matted
with blood. Stepping quickly to where it lay, and stooping to inspect it more

closely, Trahn recognized it as the body of Peredur's familiar, headless and mutilated, but identifiable still. He searched the area with his eyes, and there, a few feet farther into the tangle of trees and brush, he discerned the owl's bloodied head. He felt his pulse quicken, although he could not say why. In and of itself, the discovery of Peredur's familiar signified nothing. Both Sartol's owl and Orris's hawk were powerful and swift enough to kill a bird of this size, even if it was an owl. But could Orris's hawk have torn the head off of this owl? Of that, Trahn was less certain. Sartol's great owl, on the other hand, would have had little trouble doing so. He stood again, his thoughts going back to the night before, when Baden and he first saw Sartol. The Owl-Master had been wounded, with a cut on his forehead and a burn on his leg. But while his owl seemed uninjured, its talons had been covered with blood. Trahn had assumed at the time that the blood had come from Orris's bird, but if he had been wrong, if Sartol's familiar killed Peredur's owl, that would lend a great deal of weight to the case against Sartol.

Another memory: an eerie wail emanating from the Shadow Forest just before Baden and he found Sartol, and only a few moments before they watched Sartol's bird glide back to the Owl-Master's shoulder. With a quick last glance around the thicket, Trahn moved through the undergrowth and back into the sunlight. He then made his way to the edge of the Shadow Forest, to the approximate area from which that strange wail had originated. Again, he did not have to search for very long. Along the fringe of the dense wood, within just a few yards of the grassy clearing, he found the body of Orris's pale, rust-colored hawk. It had a single red stain on its breast, where Sartol's owl had punctured its heart with a sharp, powerful claw, and, like Peredur's owl, it had been decapitated. Trahn sighed. Sartol's owl had killed this bird; there was no way to know whether the blood on its talons had come from Peredur's owl as well. The talons of Orris's bird bore no blood, but, given the rain that had continued to fall throughout the night and the first several hours of the morning, that told him nothing. Still, he felt his anxiety increase with each new discovery. Peredur's owl and Orris's hawk had been killed in very similar ways, each by a bird powerful enough literally to rip off its head. Obviously, Sartol's owl had killed Orris's familiar; had it also killed Peredur's?

Yet another memory from the night before flashed through Trahn's mind. When Baden, Sartol, and he entered the thicket, Jessamyn's owl had hissed at them. But what if she had been hissing not at the mages, but at Sartol's bird? If Orris had attacked Jessamyn, her owl would have tried to protect her, and, again, Trahn wondered if Orris's hawk could have prevailed in a fight with the white owl. He did not doubt for an instant that Sartol's powerful bird could have.

He shook his head grimly. He had found little that might prove Sartol's guilt or Orris's innocence; certainly not enough. He had only his knowledge of the birds, his suspicions of Sartol, and his stubborn faith in Orris's loyalty on which to rely. Still, he could not rid himself of the feeling that Baden's life was in danger. For an instant, as he started back toward the camp, he considered using the Stone-Merging to contact Baden and warn him, but he knew how his friend would react. "You have no proof," Baden would say. "You're allowing your emotions to cloud your judgment." And perhaps he would be right in saying so. Besides, Trahn thought to himself with resignation, if Sartol had betrayed the Order, contacting Baden would place the Owl-Master's life in danger. His friend had ridden north fully aware of the risk. For now, at least, Trahn would have to accept the fact that he could do nothing but watch for the young mages, and accept as well that Baden could take care of himself, even against Sartol.

Trahn looked over his shoulder, once again scanning the edge of Theron's Grove for some sign of the two young mages, and, as he did, he heard the horses start to whinny nervously in the distance. Immediately, he began racing toward the ancient farmhouse where he and Baden had taken the animals the night before, and where the six mounts that remained were still tied. Bears, wolves, and panthers inhabited this part of the land, and all of them possessed sufficient strength to kill a tethered horse. The nearer he drew to the old town, the more the intensity of the neighing increased, and he cursed himself for demanding that the company shelter the horses so far from the camp. Then, just before he reached the ruins, matters turned worse; far, far worse. The clamoring of the horses, which had been alarming enough, abruptly began to fade, and he heard their hooves drumming away to the west. With a cold, sick feeling in his stomach, he hurried on to the ruined farmhouse. But by the time he reached it, the animals were gone. Only the trampled grass and a few scattered hoof prints indicated that they had ever been there at all.

Jaryd awoke with a start late in the morning and immediately reached for Ishalla with his mind. She was perched beside Fylimar on a low branch just a few feet away, silent but watchful. Feeling her presence, he instantly felt more at ease. The sky had cleared, and sunlight filtered warmly through the leaves and past the gnarled, winding tree limbs of the grove. Turning his head, Jaryd found Alayna lying beside him, a slight smile touching her lips as she watched him. Her long, dark hair, tousled and still slightly damp from the rain, tumbled across her shoulders, and her dark eyes, rich brown like the earth, and flecked with green, glittered in the daylight.

"Good morning," she said softly.

He raised himself up on one elbow. "Good morning."

"Did you know that you talk in your sleep?" she asked.

Jaryd felt himself turn red, and Alayna began to laugh. "Actually, I did know that," he admitted.

She raised an eyebrow.

"My brother has told me," he explained. "We shared a room." He hesitated. "Why? What did I say?"

"Don't worry," she assured him. "I couldn't make out a word of it. It wasn't really talking as much as it was a kind of low mumble, like this." She made a noise imitating what he had done. Jaryd groaned with embarrassment and she laughed again.

"So, how long is it going to take before the entire Order hears about this?"

She looked at him with a hurt expression. "That's not fair," she said. "I wouldn't tell the entire Order." She paused, trying to suppress a smirk. "I'll just tell Baden and Trahn, and let them do the rest."

Jaryd nodded and laughed. "That would be a much more efficient use of your time," he agreed.

Their eyes met and locked as their laughter slowly died away, and Jaryd leaned forward to kiss her gently on the lips.

The soft smile lit her face again. "What was that for?"

Jaryd shrugged. "For being able to laugh, and to make me laugh, even when everything around us is falling to pieces."

"Ah. My grandmother taught me that," she told him, picking up a leaf and playing with it absently. "She always said that as long as you have your sense of humor, you can cope with anything."

"That sounds like good advice," Jaryd observed quietly.

Alayna nodded. "It ought to be," she said, "it kept her alive for almost ninety years." She sat up. "Of course," she went on, her tone growing more serious, "Gram never had to deal with unsettled spirits and renegade mages."

"Lucky her," Jaryd commented, climbing stiffly to his feet. Alayna held out a hand, and he pulled her up as well. He turned to look at the two birds and, with no more than a thought, called Ishalla to him. Effortlessly, the grey hawk sailed to his outstretched arm.

"Can you tell them apart?" Alayna asked him, as Fylimar flew to her with the same easy grace.

"Yes. Ishalla is slightly smaller, and her back and wings are just a bit darker. But," he added, "I have to look very closely to be sure. Can you?"

"Usually," she replied. "I see small differences in their faces, but I have to look pretty closely, too."

Jaryd gazed at Ishalla's head, with its dark cap, light eyebrows, and fierce red eyes. Then he looked at Fylimar. Whatever differences Alayna perceived were too subtle for him to notice. "I'll take your word for it," he remarked at last.

Jaryd's stomach made a sudden, loud gurgling noise. He felt his face redden.

"Hungry?" Alayna asked with a giggle.

"Famished."

Alayna nodded. "Me, too."

She closed her eyes for a moment and, almost immediately, Fylimar leapt from her arm in search of food. Jaryd conveyed a similar thought to Ishalla, who flew off in the same direction. As the hawks hunted, the mages gathered wood for a small fire and set aside two long, sturdy branches to use as spits for the game brought to them by their familiars.

"Have you given some thought to what we should do after we've eaten?" Jaryd asked as they worked.

"Some. But I haven't come up with anything too brilliant. You?"

Jaryd shook his head and pushed the hair back from his forehead in a gesture his mother would have recognized. "No. We don't know if Sartol is still out there; we don't even know who survived the night. And I'd like another chance to speak with Theron. I still think he can help us."

"I'm sure he can," Alayna replied. "The question is, will he?"

Jaryd shrugged and took a deep breath. "I think we should try, although if we had a way to find out what's going on outside the grove, it would make deciding on our next move a lot easier."

"We do," Alayna said brightly. "Haven't you ever flown with your hawk?"
Jaryd gave her a skeptical look.

"I'm serious," she insisted. "I'll show you after we eat."

He started to respond, but was interrupted by the sound of laboring wing beats, as Ishalla returned carrying a hare. A few seconds later, Fylimar reappeared as well, bearing a quail. Accepting their meals from the birds, the two mages sent their familiars off again so that the creatures might feed themselves. Then they sat down by the fire and began to prepare their food, skinning the hare and quail before impaling them on the two skewers.

"I didn't have the chance to tell you this last night," Jaryd said a bit later as he watched his meal cooking over the flames, "but I'm sorry about Sartol. Never mind what he tried to do to me; I know how close you are, and how much you admire him."

Alayna leaned forward and turned the branch that held her meal. "Thanks," she said, sitting back, a sad smile flitting across her features. "I feel really stupid; I should have seen through his facade. But he was always so kind to me—" She stopped and shrugged. "I should have known."

"How could you know, Alayna? There are people in the Order who have known him far longer than you have, and they didn't see it. And that includes Baden, Jessamyn, and Peredur. He fooled them, and he fooled me. You shouldn't blame yourself because he fooled you, too."

Alayna nodded, but she would not meet his gaze, and they finished roasting their meals without speaking. The hawks returned a few minutes later, Ishalla with a jay and Fylimar with a robin, and, as the mages ate, so did their familiars.

By the time they all finished eating, Alayna's spirits seemed to have lifted. She picked up her staff and handed Jaryd the torch that contained his ceryll. "Come on," she urged, taking his free hand. "I want to teach you how to fly."

As it turned out, what Alayna called "flying," Baden had referred to as "using the Hawk-Sight." In essence, Alayna explained, it merely demanded that he reach with his mind beyond his normal connection with Ishalla until her perceptions superseded his own. Then he would simply convey to her that he wished her to fly.

Easy as it sounded, it turned out to be a bit disorienting at first; indeed, Jaryd nearly fell to the ground with dizziness when Ishalla first rose into the air and began to circle. But he quickly grew accustomed to the turns and undulations of her flight, and he soon understood why Alayna called this flying. He felt as though he himself were riding the wind currents and gliding above the treetops, and he laughed aloud when Ishalla and Fylimar circled overhead and he was able to see Alayna and himself as they appeared from above.

After enjoying the sensation for a few moments, Jaryd saw, through Ishalla's eyes, that Fylimar had flown toward the campsite. Responding immediately to Jaryd's thought, Ishalla followed the other bird. In just a few seconds, they cleared the grove. Jaryd found himself looking down upon the grassy clearing in which the company had set up their camp the night before. He saw the cluster of trees where the young mages had encountered Sartol, and he recognized the tarpaulin-covered pile of food and equipment that Alayna and he had worked on. It appeared, from the careless way in which the tarpaulin now lay, that someone had gone through the supplies since then. Not far to the west and south, the Moriandral, its waters muddied and frothy, roiled under the stone bridge and past the ruins of the old city. Nearer to the camp, two large, blackened mounds of timber still smoldered beneath the midday sun.

But other than that, Jaryd saw nothing that would tell him who survived the night. He saw no people; he didn't even see the horses. He felt his stomach tightening.

After circling over the clearing several times, Fylimar wheeled back toward the grove. Again Ishalla followed. A moment later Jaryd heard Alayna speak his name and he broke the connection with his familiar. Opening his eyes, Jaryd nearly fell to the ground again. Alayna grabbed his arm to support him.

"Are you all right?" she asked, looking at him closely.

He gave a small laugh. "I will be in a minute. I like flying, but landing is still a bit rough."

Alayna laughed briefly, but her expression quickly grew somber. "I didn't see anyone," she said, sounding alarmed, "not even the horses."

"Neither did I," Jaryd agreed.

Alayna ran a hand through her hair. "What were those things that were burning?"

"Pyres, I think," Jaryd told her. "For Jessamyn and Peredur." After a moment he added, "I hope they were for them."

Alayna made no reply. For several moments they said nothing.

Finally, Jaryd took a long breath and made a helpless gesture with his hands. "This is almost worse than finding Sartol there alone," he commented, unable to keep the frustration out of his voice. "At least if we had seen Sartol, we'd know to stay here. But this—this tells us nothing."

"Actually," Alayna returned, "that's not entirely true. The pyres tell us that someone other than Sartol survived the night; he'd have no reason to bother with funeral rites if he was alone. And the supplies are still there, so everyone can't be gone."

"Maybe they started back toward Amarid and left the supplies for us, figuring that we'd need them if we survived the grove."

"I hadn't thought of that," she admitted. "That's a possibility."

"Or maybe Sartol hid the horses, left the supplies, and built the pyres to confuse us and lure us out of the grove," Jaryd suggested. "Is he clever enough to do that?"

"Absolutely," Alayna replied in a flat tone.

"So, in other words," Jaryd concluded, "we can't risk going out there yet."

"No, I guess we can't," she said with resignation. "I guess we'll have to try our luck with Theron after all."

Unsure of what else to do, the young mages passed the rest of the day on the banks of a small azure lake tucked away in a corner of the grove and fed by a small waterfall. Alayna had spotted it—or, rather, Fylimar had—as the birds circled, before they surveyed the campsite, and she had insisted that they go there.

"After fifteen days of riding," she said pointedly, "I would think you'd want a chance to bathe."

After a brief but refreshing swim in the cool waters, the young mages spent much of what remained of the day reflecting on their confrontation with Theron the previous night. Both of them were convinced that the Owl-Master knew who had committed the attacks on Tobyn-Ser, but, having experienced for themselves the spirit's bitter hatred of the Order, they could think of no way to enlist his aid. Nonetheless, Jaryd felt strongly that they should try to speak with the Owl-Master again.

"We need to find out what he knows," he insisted, as they sat by the lake in the late-afternoon sun.

"I know we do," Alayna conceded, "but we may be the only ones alive who know that Sartol betrayed the Order. We have to warn the Order. If Theron kills us, there might not be anyone left to stop Sartol."

"If Theron wanted to kill us, he would have done it last night," Jaryd countered, hoping that he sounded convincing.

In the end, Alayna relented. In return, Jaryd promised that even if they got no more information from the spirit tonight, they would leave the grove first thing in the morning and start back toward Amarid.

Just before dusk, they took some time to search for berries and roots with which to supplement the dried meat that Jaryd still carried in the folds of his robe. But as the sky darkened, and their encounter with the Owl-Master drew nearer, Jaryd found that he was not terribly hungry. For whatever reason, Theron had spared their lives the night before, but this did little to ease his fears. Baden had said that no one had ever returned from the grove alive. And they were still in the grove. Alayna seemed nervous as well, and, in the end, they ate very little before returning to the water's edge to await Theron's arrival.

Even by the lake, where the ancient trees of the grove could not fully obscure the sky, darkness came quickly. As the pale blues and yellows of twilight gave way to darker shades of purple and indigo and, finally, to black, stars began to emerge. Jaryd tried to calm his nerves by picking out the familiar constellations. To the west, he could see Arick, with his arms raised, one extended to give form to the land he offered to his children, the other poised to smite it. Almost directly overhead, Jaryd saw Duclea kneeling before her husband, her arms also open, but in supplication and grief. Much lower in the sky, just barely above the tops of the trees, stood the twins, Lon and Tobyn, with their backs to one another and their arms folded defiantly. And between them, forever spiraling in her graceful dance, and beginning now to rise slowly in the sky in order to assume her place of ascendance for the autumn equinox, Jaryd saw Leora, whose stars always gleamed brightest over Accalia and the forest that bore her name.

As Jaryd and Alayna sat silently by the lake, staring at these glowing denizens of the night sky, another light, pale at first, but gradually growing brighter, appeared at their backs. Aware, suddenly, of his heart hammering in his chest, and thankful that he had not eaten very much, Jaryd scrambled to his feet. Alayna was next to him, standing as well, and, sharing a quick glance, and what Jaryd hoped would be a reassuring smile, they turned to face for a second time the emerald luminescence of the unsettled Owl-Master.

"You are still here, I see," Theron commented sourly as he reached them, "though the traitor has left."

Jaryd and Alayna looked at each other.

"We . . . we didn't know that he was gone, Owl-Master," Alayna stammered.

"Apparently," the spirit rumbled. "And are the birds on your shoulders merely ornaments, or do you know how to communicate with them?"

Jaryd felt his pulse racing. "We looked," he said, the words sounding like a plea. "We didn't see anything."

Theron's expression hardened. "That is not my problem!" he countered harshly. "And it does not excuse your continued intrusion on my solitude! I would have thought that one night in this grove would be enough for you! But apparently I was too easy on you!"

"We are sorry, Owl-Master," Alayna offered. "Truly, we did not know that Sartol was gone."

"And if you had," Theron demanded, narrowing his eyes, "would you have left?"

Alayna hesitated. "We still have questions, Owl-Master. We need your help."

"When did your ignorance become my concern?"

Alayna glanced at Jaryd and shrugged slightly, as if unsure of how to proceed. Jaryd didn't know what to do, either. He felt his frustration mounting. And in that moment it occurred to him that, during their previous encounter with Theron, the spirit had not reacted well to their servility. Indeed, the only progress they had made with the Owl-Master—and admittedly, they had not made much—came when Jaryd and Alayna asserted themselves. Ignoring the pounding of his heart and the knot in his stomach, Jaryd took a deep breath and accepted the challenge he heard in Theron's tone, knowing as he did that, if he was wrong, the spirit would probably kill them both. "The stakes haven't changed since last night, Owl-Master," he said, meeting the spirit's bright, angry glare, "nor has our need for haste. If the rest of our company is gone, as you say, then we'll leave with first light. But you issued a challenge to us last night. I believe you said, 'Let us see how you endure a night as my guests.' We've met that challenge, Owl-Master. We survived. We've earned your consideration."

Theron's eyes flashed angrily, and Jaryd feared that he had miscalculated badly. "Impudent child!" the spirit raged. "You dare speak to me in this manner? I should strike you down where you stand!"

"Then do!" Alayna returned, seeming to understand Jaryd's tactic. "But stop playing games with us!"

The Owl-Master glared at them, his glowing features as hard and cold as a ceryll. And then, slowly he began to nod. "You have courage," he admitted grudgingly. "I saw it in each of you last night, and I see it again now. Perhaps there is some shred of hope for your Order after all." He paused, as if considering something. "Twice now you have invited me to kill you," he said at last. "I will not make you do it a third time. Ask what you will, Hawk-Mages. But know this: I will not simply give you the information you need. You must earn it. I will answer your questions as I see fit, and I will steer you in the right direction. But, ultimately, you must figure this out for yourselves."

Jaryd let out a slow breath, and he saw Alayna pass a rigid, white hand through her hair. Then she glanced at him, a question in her dark eyes. After a moment, Jaryd nodded. "Very well," Alayna said, turning back to Theron. "We'll be grateful for any help you can offer."

Theron gestured for the young mages to sit on the trunk of a fallen tree that lay on the ground not far from where they stood. He walked with them over to the tree, but, rather than sitting, he began to pace in front of them. He suddenly seemed agitated; his movements had grown tense and sharp. Jaryd and Alayna exchanged another look, both of them unsure of how Theron expected them to proceed. It was the Owl-Master, however, who broke the silence. "You must understand," he began, "that this is an adversary unlike any the Order has ever faced."

"More dangerous, you mean?" Alayna asked.

Theron nodded. "Yes, but not just that. Different." He sounded relieved in a way to be speaking, but he could not quite mask the tension in his voice. It occurred to Jaryd that perhaps the Owl-Master had wanted to help them all along. "You cannot defeat this enemy through conventional means. The Order will have to adapt. It will have to change."

Alayna stared at him, her eyes wide. "How?"

Theron halted his pacing and grinned. "You will have to work harder than that," he told her.

Alayna smiled and fell silent, and Jaryd tried a different tack. "What's Sartol up to? What's his role in all of this?"

Theron resumed his walking. "Be wary of that one," he warned. "He is very strong, stronger than any mage since Phelan. But do not focus on Sartol exclusively. He is but one piece of the puzzle, and, even if you can defeat him, greater perils will remain."

Stronger than any mage since Phelan, Jaryd repeated to himself. Phelan, the Wolf-Master; the only member of the Order ever to bind to a creature other than a hawk or owl. Phelan's power and his heroics during the third and final war with Abborij were legendary. Now Theron had compared Sartol's strength with his. No wonder Jessamyn and Peredur had been unable to withstand Sartol's assault.

Alayna, apparently, had been thinking along similar lines. "But if Sartol is so powerful," she said, a note of desperation creeping into her voice, "how could anyone else in Tobyn-Ser represent more of a threat?"

Again the Owl-Master stopped, and this time, he gazed so intently at Alayna that she averted her eyes and brushed back her hair self-consciously. "Your question reveals more than I could possibly tell you about the shortsightedness of the Order," he declared with fervor. "Look beyond your shores. Once, when I was your age, the Order could afford to limit its vision to this land. But the world has changed, even if Tobyn-Ser has not. You ignore these changes at your own risk."

Somehow, Jaryd was standing. "Do you mean," he demanded, "that the attacks on Tobyn-Ser have been committed by outlanders?"

Theron regarded him for a long time. Then he nodded once.

His mind reeling, Jaryd took several steps away from the tree trunk on which he had been sitting and stared across the lake. Ripples from the waterfall rolled gently across the surface, making the starlight reflected on the water dance and glitter. Outlanders, Jaryd thought to himself, shaking his head in disbelief. This had never occurred to him; as far as he knew, it had never occurred to any of them. Theron was absolutely right about that. He wanted to ask the Owl-Master where they were from: Abborij? Lon-Ser? Maybe someplace of which Jaryd knew nothing, not even a name. But he was sure that Theron would not give that information, at least not yet. He turned back to the Owl-Master. "Why would they do this?" he asked. "What do they want from us?"

The spirit shook his head. "I am not fully certain. And even if I was, I think this is something you must discover for yourselves. I will tell you this, though: their tactics reveal their weakness; foil their plan and you may save yourselves."

Jaryd looked at Alayna, whose ashen face told him that she, too, had been shocked by Theron's revelations. She shrugged slightly, and he faced Theron again. "We don't understand," he said. "What do their tactics tell us?"

"You will have to give that some thought," the Owl-Master replied enigmatically.

The three of them fell silent. Jaryd thought it ironic in a way. He had so many questions, and yet, now that Theron was willing to speak with them, he couldn't think of any.

"You said the others who came with us were gone," Alayna ventured after several moments. "Did they go back to Am—? Did they go back to the Great Hall?"

"I never said all were gone," Theron replied. "Just the traitor. One still remains."

"Who?" Alayna asked with concern.

"I don't know his name. He is dark-skinned, with a brown bird."

"Trahn!" Jaryd said with recognition. "He's a friend," he added, explaining to Theron.

"How do we know that?" Alayna demanded.

Jaryd shrugged, turning to face her. "We're talking about Trahn. Of course, he's a friend. Baden's known him for years."

"A few days ago, I would probably have given you similar assurances about Sartol," she argued. "We just can't be certain anymore, Jaryd."

"Sure we can." He looked to Theron for help. "I'm right, aren't I? We can trust Trahn."

The Owl-Master made an ambivalent gesture with his hands. "I cannot read what is in men's hearts," he explained. "I know of the traitor because I have seen him do . . . certain things. But I know nothing of this man. For what it is worth, I have not seen him take any actions that could be construed as a betrayal." He turned to Alayna. "I would also say this: do not let the duplicity of one person color all your friendships. The two of you cannot win this fight alone; eventually, you will have to trust others."

After a pause, Alayna gave a small nod. She then turned to Jaryd, who had been watching her closely. "All right," she breathed, "we'll find him in the morning. But we should be careful, just in case."

"That makes sense," Jaryd agreed.

Alayna faced the Owl-Master again. "Have you seen mages other than Sartol doing . . . whatever things you saw him do?"

"No," Theron replied, shaking his head. "He is the only traitor I have seen."

"Then maybe, Owl-Master," Jaryd said, "you can help explain a vision I had several weeks ago, just before one of the attacks." He stared at the blue ceryll shining from within the stick he carried, as if he might catch a glimpse once more of the mage he had seen in his dream so many weeks ago. "I saw a man," Jaryd recounted. "I thought at the time that he was a mage, although now I'm not as certain. I couldn't see his face, but he wore a mage's cloak. He carried a staff with a blood-red ceryll, and a huge black hawk sat on his shoulder. In my vision, he handed me a single black feather that burst into flames when I touched it."

"Do you remember anything else?" Theron asked, his bright eyes narrowed and intent. "Perhaps something about the bird's eyes?"

Jaryd looked sharply at the spirit. "You've seen him, too, haven't you?"

The Owl-Master did not respond. "What about the hawk's eyes?" he pressed.

"I remember them being strange, unlike the eyes of any bird I'd seen before. But I can't describe them. They were just different." He looked searchingly at Theron. "Owl-Master, have you seen this man, too?"

"Yes," Theron admitted, "a number of times. And," he added, after a brief hesitation, "I have seen more than one of them at once."

"How many?" Alayna demanded.

"Mostly, I have seen them in pairs or groups of three. But, on one or two occasions, I have had visions of as many as sixteen."

"Sixteen!" Jaryd exploded.

Theron nodded. "One of them has died, I know, but the others still roam the land."

"Died how?"

"That, I did not see."

"What do you know about the birds' eyes?" Alayna demanded. "What were you trying to get Jaryd to recognize?"

Again, the Owl-Master faltered. "In truth, I do not know. I have seen what your friend has seen, and I have noticed the alien appearance of the creatures' eyes, as he did. But I do not know what it means."

"You have an idea," she insisted.

"An idea, yes. But I am not prepared to tell you what it is," the spirit told her with finality.

She held Theron's gaze for a moment longer. Then she looked away. Again, no one spoke for some time. The sound of the cascade tumbling ceaselessly into the water drifted across the lake, and a light wind stirred the trees.

"I must do this my way," Theron said at last, breaking the stillness in a voice that offered no hint of concession, no room for compromise, "for reasons I have given you already, and for others I choose not to share. No doubt, you deem me capricious in all of this. If so, that is too bad. These are the terms under which I have agreed to assist you. If you find them unsatisfactory, you are free to leave."

Alayna shook her head. "We agreed to your terms, Owl-Master. Forgive me if I gave offense."

Theron shook his head. "You did not offend me," he told her matter-of-factly.

Another brief silence ensued, this one broken by Jaryd. "The man I envisioned," he said with sudden intensity, facing the Owl-Master, "and those you've seen; are they the outlanders?"

"Yes."

"And you said that their tactics revealed their weaknesses, right?" Jaryd continued in the same tone.

"I did," Theron returned, a fierce grin of recognition spreading across his features.

Jaryd turned to Alayna. "They're masquerading as mages while they commit the attacks so that they can get people to distrust the Order," he stated. "So that must mean that they can't fight us directly."

"Do they have magic?" Alayna asked Theron.

"Not as you know it," the Owl-Master told her cryptically.

Alayna frowned. "Is whatever they have as strong as the Mage-Craft?"

Theron paused, considering this. "A difficult question," he remarked finally. "In some ways, it is, and in others, it is not." He smiled as her frown deepened. "Your friend is right, though: they cannot defeat the Mage-Craft directly. That should tell you something."

"Is the destruction of the Order their ultimate goal, or just a means to another end?" Jaryd asked.

"Do not overestimate the importance of the Order," the Owl-Master told him coldly. "It is a figurehead, nothing more."

"Then are they trying to destroy the Mage-Craft?"

Theron shook his head in exasperation. "Think, Hawk-Mage! You should be able to answer that yourself!"

"If they were trying to destroy the Mage-Craft, Sartol wouldn't be helping them," Alayna said with conviction. "They must have offered him dominion over Tobyn-Ser to get him to cooperate. Which means that they can't rid themselves of the Mage-Craft, they can only try to control who wields it."

Jaryd nodded and then looked at the Owl-Master speculatively. "Can you see things beyond Tobyn-Ser's borders?" he asked.

"Not in the way you mean," Theron replied. "I cannot see events or people's actions as I can here in this land, but I see vague images—shadows, if you will—that give me some sense of what other lands are like." He shook his head. "I have never understood why this should be so, why I should be able to see even that much. I have always believed that the Mage-Craft flows from the land, but, if that were the case, my vision would end at the edge of Tobyn-Ser." He stopped, lost in thought, his cold, bright eyes focused on the ground before him. After a moment, he looked at Jaryd. "Why?"

The Hawk-Mage gave a small shrug. "I thought maybe, if you could see what went on in other lands, it might help us figure out where these people are from, and what they want."

"In time, you will find other ways to learn those things," Theron assured him. "You need not learn everything at once. You have already gleaned a great deal that will be of use to you."

Once again, silence descended upon them. Jaryd could not think of any more questions. Theron was right: the young mages had learned a tremendous amount. All that remained was for them to convince the Owl-Master to ally himself with their cause. Faced now with this task, however, Jaryd found himself unsure of how to proceed. Theron had made it clear from the outset that he would not be coerced or cajoled into helping the Order directly, and Jaryd had little confidence in their ability to sway him from that position. More than that, though, Jaryd realized that he did not wish to try. Recalling the grief that he had seen briefly in the Owl-Master's glowing eyes the night before, Jaryd knew that he could offer no compelling reason why Theron should assist them. The Owl-Master owed nothing to Tobyn-Ser that a thousand years of ostracism had not already exacted. It was enough that history had consigned him to infamy, forgetting all the good that he had done before. It was enough that he had been sentenced to an eternity of unrest by his own curse. Jaryd turned to Alayna, who was already looking at him. Gazing into her eyes, he understood that she harbored similar doubts. They both turned back to Theron, intending to thank him for his assistance, and then to leave.

But the Owl-Master surprised them. "I have answered a great many questions," he told them, "and now I have some of my own." He hesitated. "I can see a great deal of what goes on in this land," he explained a bit awkwardly, "but I know little of what it is like to live in today's world. I would be . . . interested in what you can tell me."

The young mages grinned, exchanging a brief glance. "We'd be happy to tell you anything you'd like to know, Owl-Master," Alayna replied.

And so they sat beside the starlit lake, bathed in the soft, green glow that emanated from the unsettled spirit, and they responded to Theron's questions with stories of their homes and their families and their upbringings. For several hours the three of them talked, until the waning moon appeared, large and orange, over the trees to the east. Seeing its light, reckoning the passage of time that it signified, Theron looked at his companions with an expression that Jaryd thought conveyed just a touch of regret.

"It grows late," Theron said quietly. "You will be anxious to leave with the coming of daylight, and you have a long ride ahead of you."

Jaryd and Alayna rose. "We wouldn't have traded this evening for mere rest, Owl-Master," Alayna remarked. "We've enjoyed our time with you."

"I am . . . pleased to hear that," the spirit returned, his eyes avoiding theirs. "You may sleep here, or I can lead you back to where you slept last night," he offered, changing the subject. "It is your choice."

"We'll stay here," Jaryd said.

"Very well." The spirit turned to leave, but then stopped, and faced the mages once more. "You may have need of me again," he told them. "I will leave something to help you contact me, should the need arise. You will find it in the morning."

"Thank you, Owl-Master," Jaryd answered, "for all your assistance. Be well."

Theron nodded, and began to walk away. "Farewell, Hawk-Mages," he called over his shoulder. "Arick guard you both."

Jaryd and Alayna watched the gentle radiance of the Owl-Master recede into the forest. Only when the emerald light had vanished completely did they lie down to sleep on the grass by the lake. Jaryd soon heard Alayna's breathing settle into a slow, regular rhythm, but he remained awake for a long time, looking at the stars, and listening to the music of the waterfall.

They awoke with first light, and, sitting up, gazed with astonishment at the token Theron had left for them. In the grass at Jaryd's feet lay the Owl-Master's staff, its top charred and splintered, and its shaft carved exquisitely with runes from *Mi-rel,* the ancient language.

"How is that possible?" Alayna whispered, her voice tinged with wonder.

Jaryd shook his head as he picked up the staff and examined it. It felt unusually light, but otherwise it seemed like any other wooden staff, although he marveled that this should be so. "I don't know," he breathed at last. "He said that he was power itself, a walking incarnation of the Mage-Craft. And it was his curse." He shook his head again, still gazing at the staff. "I don't know," he repeated.

A few moments later the mages rose and, after briefly diving into the lake, they called to their hawks and started toward the western edge of the grove. The walk took them close to an hour, and, by the time they emerged from the trees, sunlight was warming the grassy clearing.

Almost as soon as they stepped into the open, they heard Trahn's voice calling to them. Looking toward the camp, they saw the Hawk-Mage hurrying in their direction, a relieved grin spreading across his dark features.

"Jaryd! Alayna!" he cried out happily. "By the gods, it's good to see you!"

"Stop right there, Trahn!" Alayna warned in a hard voice, as the mage drew closer.

His smile faded, and he halted.

"We're sorry, Trahn," Jaryd said soberly. "After the other night, we just don't know who we can trust."

Trahn nodded. "I understand. Why don't you tell me what happened."

"Where are the others?" Alayna demanded. "Where are the horses?"

Trahn's eyes narrowed. "The horses disappeared for a while yesterday. I spent several hours recapturing them. One of them is still missing. Do you know something about that?"

Alayna shook her head. "No," she conceded. "But we sent up the hawks to look over the camp, and we saw neither the horses nor you. Where are the others?" she repeated.

"Jessamyn and Peredur are dead, but I assume that you knew that already." Jaryd and Alayna nodded, and he went on. "I haven't seen Orris, but his bird is dead. I think he may have been the one who let the horses go." He hesitated. "Baden and Sartol are already riding back to Amarid."

Alayna closed her eyes. "Arick save us," she whispered.

Jaryd spat a curse before glaring at Trahn. "We have to go after them," he insisted. "Sartol is a traitor. He killed Jessamyn and Peredur, and he tried to kill us."

Trahn took a deep breath. "I feared this," he said miserably, shaking his head. "I started to figure it out after they left, although I didn't know for certain until now. Sartol told us that Orris killed them, that he had intervened before Orris could do the same to you," he explained apologetically. "Baden and I weren't sure what to think, but Sartol was injured." He closed his eyes and swallowed. "He was very convincing."

"How long ago did they leave?" Jaryd asked urgently, knowing as he did so what Trahn would say.

"Yesterday. First thing in the morning." The dark mage looked at Alayna. "I understand your mistrust," he said, "and I can offer no firm proof of my loyalty to the Order. But I swear to you in Arick's name, I mean you and Jaryd no harm."

Alayna's expression remained grim. "I'd like to believe you," she told him. "Forgive my suspicion, but recent events have left me reluctant to trust anyone." She hesitated. "I'll try, though." She turned to Jaryd. "We'd better get going. They have a substantial head start on us."

"You're right," Jaryd replied crisply. He turned back to Trahn. The Hawk-Mage was staring with awe at the marred staff he carried. "It's Theron's," he said, somewhat needlessly. "We'll tell you about it along the way."

Still gazing at the staff, Trahn nodded. "I would like that," he commented, his voice barely more than a whisper.

The three mages rushed back to the camp, where they hastily packed the food and supplies before saddling the remaining horses. Then they mounted, and, with a last glance back toward Theron's Grove, they rode into the Shadow Forest, as Sartol and Baden had done more than a day earlier.

13

For nearly three days, the Owl-Masters rode at a punishing pace, pushing themselves and their mounts to the brink of exhaustion. Rising at dawn the first day, pausing to rest and eat as infrequently as they could, and continuing to ride well past nightfall with their cerylls blazing brightly to light their way, they managed to cross through the Shadow Forest in half the time it had taken the delegation to do so. It helped, of course, that they were only two, and that they had negotiated the wood once before.

Unfortunately, these factors did nothing to mitigate the slowness of the Southern Swamp, which they entered the following morning. They did get through the fen in one day, but they found once again that its maddening terrain made swift travel impossible. When they finally reached Tobyn's Plain that evening, shortly after dusk, they were too fatigued to go on, and they settled in for what remained of the night.

During this, their first day on the plain, however, they had more than compensated for their slow passage through the swamp. Already, they had covered over thirty leagues, and the western sky still glowed with the fiery brilliance of the setting sun. Even their birds had been hard pressed to keep up with them. At this rate, the return trip to Amarid would take little more than half the time consumed by the delegation's journey to Theron's Grove.

And Sartol would have Baden to thank. Since their departure from the grove, the lean mage had driven them toward Amarid with a grim single-mindedness. As a result, they had made excellent time, which ultimately worked to Sartol's advantage. Provided, of course, that they didn't kill themselves before they reached the Great Hall. Sartol's back and legs ached with fatigue, and his mount was lathered. Spurring his horse forward to draw even with Baden, Sartol caught the mage's attention by raising his staff.

"We should rest a moment, Baden," he called over the pounding of their horses' hooves, hoping that he didn't sound too desperate.

After a moment, Baden nodded.

They slowed to a halt and dismounted. Immediately, the horses began to chomp on the prairie grass, taking from it what moisture it had to offer. Baden drank some water and ate a few pieces of dried fruit before walking several feet ahead and staring northward across the darkening plain. Anla and Huvan flew off in search of food.

"We probably can't reach the river tonight," the Owl-Master finally said over his shoulder, his pale eyes illuminated by the dying sun, his thinning red and grey hair stirred slightly by the breeze, "but we can go a bit farther. I'd like to cover another six or seven leagues, if possible."

"Fine," Sartol agreed. "I'll be ready to go on in a few minutes."

Baden nodded again, and faced north once more.

That had been the extent of their conversations since leaving Theron's Grove: When do we leave? When should we rest? How far will we go today? Normally, Sartol would not have minded, but Baden had been so quiet, so withdrawn that Sartol had grown uneasy. It was fine if Baden's reticence grew out of his grief for Jessamyn and Jaryd. That, he could understand; perhaps he could even turn it to his advantage. But if Baden's silence arose from suspicion of Sartol, that was another matter. Unfortunately, there was little that Sartol could do. He could force a dialogue, but that might seem far more peculiar than merely accepting the silence. Besides, he had his own problems to ponder.

His plans for the delegation had fallen apart in rather dramatic fashion, although, with one significant exception, he had been quite fortunate in how matters had turned out. Jessamyn and Peredur had been ridiculously easy to kill; and, no doubt, Theron had taken care of Jaryd and Alayna for him—every day that passed without word from Trahn made that more clear. He could still count on the Owl-Masters to select him as the new sage; nothing had changed that. And, while he had originally hoped to rid himself of Baden in Theron's Grove, the Owl-Master was again proving himself a most valuable, albeit unknowing ally. If Baden could be persuaded to become his first, the Owl-Master's prestige, particularly his links to some of the younger members of the Order, would buy Sartol enough time to implement the second stage of his scheme. By the time Baden or anyone else suspected a thing, he would be more powerful than any of them; indeed, more powerful than all of them combined. After that, any opposition, even Baden's, would be irrelevant.

More important, however, Sartol hoped that Baden's backing would help him deal with the single largest problem he faced in the aftermath of that night by Theron's Grove: Orris had managed to escape before Sartol could kill him. It seemed ironic, in a way, that with all the lies he had told Baden and Trahn when they found him, it should be the truths that now troubled him the most. Orris was alive, and he had been stronger than Sartol had anticipated. Not so strong that Sartol could not handle him, but a good deal stronger than the sage and the first had been. Strong enough to surprise him.

Of course, it hadn't helped that Sartol was already fatigued from killing the ancient ones and battling Jaryd and Alayna. Orris had been unable to injure him—yes, the Hawk-Mage's bird succeeded in cutting his forehead, but Sartol had been forced to give himself that burn on his leg, if only to make Orris appear more powerful, and more threatening, than he really was. But Orris had been strong enough to stave off Sartol's attack and flee. Huvan had slaughtered his accursed hawk, but Orris was still alive, the only living soul who knew that Sartol had betrayed the Order.

That's where Baden came in. Baden and Orris had never gotten along—any fool could see that—and so Baden had been more than willing to believe Sartol's story. Beyond that, Baden, it appeared, had succeeded in convincing Trahn to believe it as well, which was no small feat. Sartol was aware of how Trahn felt about him. When the time came, he would enjoy killing the dark mage almost as much as he had relished killing Peredur and the Hag. But he was getting ahead of himself. What mattered for now was that, if Orris returned to Amarid and accused him of treason and murder, Baden would support Sartol's version of what happened by the grove. Orris would not be able to convince anyone of his own innocence, not with Baden against him.

The larger danger lay in the possibility that Orris and Trahn might find each other. If Orris swayed Trahn to his side, Trahn might be able to convert Baden. In that case, Sartol would have to have all three of them executed as traitors to the Order and Tobyn-Ser, a far more complicated proposition. He would need to move quickly to implement the next phase of his plan. Nothing mattered as much as that. But first, he had to be sure that Baden believed his story.

The lean mage turned to look at him. "Ready?" he asked.

Sartol stretched his back. "Do I have a choice?"

"Not really," Baden replied, grinning and shaking his head.

"Then I'm ready."

The Owl-Master gave a small laugh.

A smile, Sartol thought to himself. That's a start.

They remounted and began again to gallop northward, skirting the western edge of the swamp much as the company had done a few days earlier. Anla and Huvan soared into view from the east and flapped overhead, keeping pace with the mounts.

As the last vestiges of daylight vanished, the two mages again drew on their powers to light the plain with the cerylls they carried. Bright stars emerged in the sky above, and, in the distance, to the northwest, candles burned in the windows of a small cluster of homes. Still, they rode without speaking, thundering across the plain for several more hours, until at last Baden signaled with a raised hand for Sartol to stop.

As he painfully climbed out of his saddle, Sartol noted with satisfaction that Baden's movements were as stiff and awkward as his own. He thought about saying something about how much progress they had made, but, once more, he resisted the urge to pry conversation out of the Owl-Master. Instead, he pulled the cheese, dry breads, and dried meats from his saddlebag, sat down on an exposed rock, and began to eat. Baden sat on the ground opposite him, and Sartol tossed him the pouch containing the meat. Wordlessly, Baden removed a strip and began to chew on it, his eyes staring without focus at the grass at his feet.

"Can you pass me the water?" Sartol asked a few minutes later, indicating the leather bag that Baden had carried over with him from the horses.

Baden leaned forward and handed it to him, before sitting back and taking another bite of his food.

Sartol raged inwardly at the lean mage's silence. This was like traveling with a rock or a log. He no longer cared how it might seem; he had to find out if Baden suspected him.

"How are you holding up, Baden?" he chanced. "You've hardly said a word since we left the grove."

Baden gave a wan smile. "I know. I'm sorry. I don't mean to be such terrible company." He paused. "I'm worried about Jaryd, just as you must be about Alayna. And I still can't believe that Jessamyn is gone; she's been a part of my life for as long as I can remember."

Sartol nodded. "I know you were very close. I can't get my mind off Alayna. We were friends for only a short time compared with how long you knew Jessamyn, but I'm going to miss her terribly." And just once before I killed her, he thought to himself, I would have liked to feel her young body beneath me.

Baden looked at him gravely. "So, you've given up on the possibility that she and Jaryd survived the grove."

It took him by surprise. "Well, yes. I . . . I guess I have. You haven't?"

Baden shook his head. "I realize it's probably foolish of me, but I can't help thinking that they'll find a way out."

Arick forbid! Sartol said to himself with an inward shudder. "I certainly hope you're right, but I'm not optimistic."

Baden paused, taking another mouthful of food. A moment later, he continued. Sartol thought it funny in a way: suddenly, Baden seemed to be in a mood to talk. "Quite apart from everything that happened," the Owl-Master was saying, "I regret leaving before we could confront Theron. More than a fortnight has passed since the Gathering, and we've accomplished absolutely nothing."

Sartol smiled to himself, sensing an opportunity to strengthen his hold on Baden's support. "That's not entirely true," he countered. "We've unmasked a traitor within the Order. Surely, that has some value."

Baden gave a small nod. "I suppose you're right. But even so, we never even got the chance to interrogate Orris. The point is, we still don't know who's responsible for these attacks, or what their ultimate purpose might be, beyond just destroying the people's trust in the Order."

"Do you still believe that Theron and the Unsettled are involved?"

"I'm not certain anymore," Baden replied. "Orris's treachery must be connected in some way with the attacks—that may be why, at the end of the

Gathering, when Jessamyn decided to create this delegation, he suddenly seemed so anxious to join it. But I can't imagine why the Unsettled would need the help of a mage in carrying out their plan."

Sartol pretended to consider this. "Well," he said at length, "if not the Unsettled, then who?"

Baden shrugged helplessly. "I have no idea. I guess that's why I feel that we've accomplished so little. At least before, I had a theory; it may have been wrong, but it provided a starting point. Now, I don't even have that." Sartol said nothing, and Baden went on. "For the past day or so I've been going over the attacks in my mind, trying to discern some pattern, either in their timing or their locations."

"An interesting idea. Have you come up with anything?"

"Not yet," Baden answered, staring absently at the ground again. "The locations, at least, seem pretty random. There have been minor incidents in almost every part of Tobyn-Ser: both the Upper and Lower Horns have been hit; there have been several attacks in Tobyn's Wood, two in Leora's Forest, even one in the Great Desert. This spring there were the murders at Sern— on the island in South Shelter—and then, more recently, the attacks on the Northern Plain and Tobyn's Plain."

Sartol started to respond, but at the same time, Baden looked up at him as if he planned to say more. Both of them stopped, and Sartol gave a small, awkward laugh. "I didn't mean to cut you off," he apologized.

"Not at all," Baden remarked a little strangely. "What were you going to say?"

"Just that I saw your point: there's no obvious pattern there. With the incidents at Taima and Kaera, it appears that no portion of the land has been spared."

Baden nodded, his pale eyes fixed on Sartol's face. "Right," he agreed absently, as if preoccupied with other thoughts.

There was something in the Owl-Master's manner that abruptly made Sartol feel uncomfortable. "What about the timing?" Sartol asked, hoping to keep the conversation moving.

"Excuse me?"

"The timing of the attacks. Do you see any patterns there?"

"Oh, um . . . no. Nothing there, either," Baden said falteringly. His thin face had turned pale.

"Is something wrong, Baden?" Sartol didn't bother to conceal his concern. "You don't look well."

Baden smiled stiffly. "I'm fine," he assured Sartol. "I'm just . . . worn out, and, again, I apologize for being so distracted. I think that all the riding, combined with what happened at the grove, has left me a bit scattered. I can reflect on the past attacks all I want, but if I'm overtired, I'm not going to learn anything new, am I?"

"No, of course not," Sartol agreed. "We should sleep. We have another long day ahead of us."

"Indeed, we do," Baden said, lying back on the grass. "Thank you for drawing me out of my shell, Sartol. I found our talk very helpful."

"Good," Sartol replied, finding a place where he, too, could lie down. "I'm glad you were willing to share your thoughts with me. Good night."

"Good night."

Sartol closed his eyes, but he did not let himself sleep. Instead, he directed his attention to Baden's breathing. Something had troubled the Owl-Master. Maybe, as he claimed, it was merely fatigue and the difficulty of the past few days, in which case he would probably fall asleep quickly. But Sartol feared that it might be more, that perhaps Baden had remembered a detail from the night by the grove that would in some way implicate him, or that he had gleaned something from tonight's discussion. So Sartol lay in the grass and listened. He did not have to wait long. Within just a few minutes, the rise and fall of Baden's chest slowed and deepened into the regular rhythm of a peaceful sleep. And Sartol, knowing a moment of overwhelming relief, grinned in the dark. He would have to maintain his composure, he thought, chastising himself for growing so alarmed with no cause, and he would have to stop looking for crises where they did not exist. Baden's weakness lay in his honesty, in his lack of deviousness, and in his inability to recognize such qualities in others. The Owl-Master believed him, that was obvious; and as long as Sartol watched him closely, he had nothing to fear. He suddenly felt giddy: in a matter of days, with Baden's support, he would become Owl-Sage. After that, Tobyn-Ser was his.

Stretched out on the grass, feigning sleep, Baden struggled to control the cold panic that had gripped him only a few minutes before. His mind was reeling with the possible implications of his conversation with Sartol. It was such a small matter, and yet it loomed so very large.

Trahn had warned him repeatedly about Sartol's deceptive nature, but though Baden had listened, he had not really taken those warnings to heart. Sartol's version of what happened by Theron's Grove had seemed entirely plausible, and Baden had found no reason to doubt that Orris had betrayed the Order and the land. Until tonight.

Just now, Baden had mentioned the attack on Tobyn's Plain, and then, remembering that Sartol could not have known of the most recent incident at Kaera, he had started to explain. But there had been no need: somehow, Sartol already had heard of that attack. Baden thought back to the company's one, chaotic night by Theron's Grove, trying to reconstruct the events. As Trahn and he had finished sheltering the horses, Orris had confronted them with his news of the razing of Kaera. Then Orris had stalked off to find Jessamyn. The sage's scream came just moments later. By Sartol's own account, he did not come across Orris until the Hawk-Mage was chasing Jaryd and Alayna; and certainly Sartol and Orris did not discuss the incident while they were trying to destroy each other. When they found Sartol, Baden and Trahn informed him that an attack had taken place, but as far as Baden could remember, they never told him where. Baden knew that he had not mentioned the attack again until tonight. Sartol could have learned of it from Trahn, but when? The two mages did not spend any time alone together before Baden and Sartol departed the following morning. If Trahn had said something about it, Baden would have heard. And if Sartol had learned of the incident on his own, during their journey to the grove, he would have told everyone. News of such importance had to be shared.

There was, though, one other possibility: perhaps Sartol had prior knowledge of the attack, because Sartol had betrayed the Order to whoever had committed it. *Trahn, my friend, you may have been right all along,* Baden thought with alarm and regret. Then another sorrow, deeper, more frightening: Orris, whose guilt Baden had already accepted, was probably dead, murdered, quite possibly, by the true renegade, who expected to be chosen as Owl-Sage in less than a fortnight.

Baden considered his options, finding none that were terribly attractive. He knew that Sartol was very strong. Indeed, if Sartol had murdered the sage and the first and defeated Orris, all in the span of a few moments, the Owl-Master would probably be too powerful for Baden as well. And in a test of physical strength against the tall, athletic mage, Baden would find himself equally overmatched. Any attempt on his part to stop the Owl-Master from reaching Amarid would probably result in his own death. Besides, he could offer no solid proof of Sartol's guilt. There was a chance, however remote, that Orris or Trahn had told Sartol of the incident at Kaera. And despite his hopes to the contrary, Baden had to recognize the probability that all those who witnessed the murders, including not just Orris but also Jaryd and Alayna, had died three nights ago. If the young mages had entered Theron's Grove, they just might have survived. But, he realized with anguish, it had been Sartol who told them of Jaryd and Alayna's flight into the grove. If the Owl-Master had betrayed the Order and murdered the others, he would have had no compunction about slaying the young ones as well, and lying about their fates. In all probability, Jaryd and Alayna were dead.

The recognition of that likelihood paralyzed Baden with sorrow. It made him think of Bernel and Drina, and how the loss of their younger son would devastate them. It flooded his mind with visions of the young mage. He could see Jaryd as a small child that first time he had visited Bernel in Accalia, when he had first sensed the boy's potential. He recalled, with an image so vivid it took his breath away, his reunion with Jaryd on a rainy day this past spring, and the look of wonder in the young man's pale eyes as they stared at Baden from beneath the thick swoop of light brown hair, when the Owl-Master told him that he would someday become a powerful mage. Even then, Baden had not fully grasped the extent to which that prediction would prove prophetic. Yes, he knew the boy would be strong, but not so strong, and not so quickly. He had not known that Jaryd would be chosen by Amarid's Hawk until he spotted Ishalla following them through the Parneshome Range. Only then had he begun to fathom just how deep the boy's potential ran. And now, Jaryd was probably gone, in large part because Baden had insisted that he be included in the delegation.

Baden tried to close his mind to such thoughts. He could not blame himself, and he could not let himself be debilitated by mourning. Instead, he needed to focus on how to deal with his suspicions of Sartol. Unfortunately, given that he had no evidence with which to back up his claims against the Owl-

Master, he could only wait and watch, and hope that either the others had survived the night or that Sartol would make a second, more incriminating error. Neither seemed very likely. His despair deepening, Baden tried, with little success, to make himself sleep.

He could see the glow of their cerylls in the distance, two tiny, moving points of light, one yellow, the other orange, shining amid the blackness of the plain. He judged that they could be no more than a half-mile in front of him, and, in spite of the painful burns on his shoulder and side, Orris grinned. He had not thought that he would catch up with them so quickly. They had started north only a few hours ahead of him, but, with his injuries, he had feared that he might not have the stamina to exceed or even match their pace. And, with Pordath dead, he had been unable to increase the light from his ceryll enough to see clearly at night. The Shadow Forest had slowed him, and he had been forced to cross through much of the Southern Swamp in the dark of night, something he hoped never to do again. But he had grown up on Tobyn's Plain; he had ridden this terrain throughout his childhood and well into his adult years. Except, perhaps, for Trahn, no member of the Order could keep up with him here. Even without brightening his ceryll, he was able to make up ground on his quarry well past sunset. Besides, the two Owl-Masters in front of him had betrayed the Order and plotted to assassinate Jessamyn. He would have pursued them even if he had been blind.

The lights ahead of him suddenly stopped moving and grew dimmer, and Orris could tell from the way the glowing cerylls suddenly arced downward that Baden and Sartol had dismounted. Immediately, he stopped riding as well, unwilling to risk that they might hear his horse's hooves drumming on the sun-baked prairie soil. At some point, before they reached Amarid, he would find an opportunity to creep closer to them. For now, though, he would be patient.

The Owl-Masters appeared to be settling in for the night, which suited Orris just fine. He pulled some dried fruit from his saddlebag, and, lying down on the tall, cool grass of the plain, tried to relax his sore muscles, and to ignore the throbbing of his wounds. And with the effort, of course, came once again the grief and the loss. For nine years he had been bound to his hawk. She had been his first binding, and he missed her presence in his mind the way he would miss a newly severed limb. Every time he reached for the connection and realized that she was not there—every time he strained to see in the dark, or grew conscious of his burns, and tried to draw upon his powers, only to find himself powerless—he felt the pain of losing her as if for the first time. He had not experienced loneliness for nearly a decade. But here, alone on the plain, hurt and unbound, he felt more isolated than he ever had before. While he could not blame Sartol's owl for Pordath's death, for no familiar could refuse her mage's command, Orris could not help but hope that one day Sartol would feel as he did now; that before Orris killed him, the Owl-Master would know this aching loss.

He would not destroy Sartol's bird himself, though, not even out of revenge. It was not a thing he could bring himself to do. On the other hand, he would have no trouble killing the Owl-Master—both Owl-Masters, he amended; surely Baden had earned his death as completely as Sartol had earned his.

Baden's treachery had surprised him. True, he and the lanky mage had never gotten along, but Orris had respected him, at least more than he had Sartol and the other Owl-Masters. Baden seemed different from them: more trustworthy than Sartol, and more concerned with the people of Tobyn-Ser than Odinan, Niall, and the rest of the older mages. Moreover, Trahn liked him, which, in Orris's view, indicated that he must have possessed more than a few redeeming qualities. But either Trahn had been duped or he, too, had betrayed the Order. Orris had chosen to believe the former.

When he had come across the bodies of Jessamyn and Peredur, and then confronted Sartol as the Owl-Master chased the young ones into Theron's Grove, Orris had guessed that Sartol alone had deceived them all. The Owl-Master had been unthinkably strong; Orris had never imagined that a mage could wield that much power. He had hoped to destroy Sartol, or subdue him, but he soon realized that he would do well merely to escape with his life, and to rescue Jaryd and Alayna. In the end, he could not even do that much. He saved himself, barely, but lost Pordath. He had not been able to do anything for the young mages. So he had started back toward the camp, hoping to find Baden and Trahn in order to enlist their help. And he had been shocked to see the three of them together, apparently plotting their next move. He could not hear what they said, but he watched them, hiding in the dark, and soon learned that at least one of them—Trahn, he assumed—was not a part of the conspiracy.

Clearly, the Owl-Masters built funeral pyres to keep up appearances for Trahn, a theory confirmed the next morning when they rode off, leaving Trahn by Theron's Grove. Obviously, Orris could not be entirely certain of all this. It remained possible that Sartol and Trahn had conspired together, or that Sartol had worked alone. Orris could not be sure. So, later that day, rather than trying to slit Trahn's throat, or attempting to join forces with the Hawk-Mage, Orris stole a horse and set the others free. That, at least, had given him time to escape from the camp and begin his pursuit of the Owl-Masters.

The more he thought about it, though—the more he considered Baden's prominent role in setting up this delegation, and Sartol's actions by the grove— the more certain Orris grew that the two of them had worked together to undermine the Order's standing with the people, murder Jessamyn and Peredur, and establish themselves as the rulers of Tobyn-Ser. It was funny in a way: it was important to him that Trahn not be involved. He liked the dark mage; along with Ursel, and a couple of the other younger mages, Trahn came as close as anyone in the Order to being Orris's friend. Orris found himself regretting that he had cut the horses loose rather than approaching Trahn. It would have been helpful to have access to the Mage-Craft, and, he conceded to himself, he would have welcomed the other man's company. He shook his head. There it was again: that hollow, disjointed feeling that had haunted him since Pordath's death. He had to find a way to move past it, or at least to control it until he had killed Sartol and Baden. Then he would mourn her.

He could not say when he had decided to kill them. In truth, calling it a "decision" seemed inaccurate. They had slaughtered Jessamyn and Peredur; for all intents and purposes, they had murdered Jaryd and Alayna as well. Indeed, even if they did not commit the attacks themselves, they were also responsible for the murders at Sern and every death in Kaera. Clearly, the Owl-Masters deserved to die. More than that, though, they had to be stopped. Their flight toward Amarid proved beyond a doubt that they planned to install one of them, probably Sartol, as Owl-Sage. Orris could not allow this to happen.

Killing them would be difficult, though, especially now, possessing, as he did, little more than a residue of his powers. Instinctively, his hand moved to the hilt of his dagger, which he carried, sheathed and hidden, within the folds of his robe. He grinned again, darkly. He still could wield a blade, and he had learned to stalk and kill game in these grasses. The Owl-Masters' powers would do them little good when the blood from Baden's throat stained the soil, and Orris's blade buried itself hilt-deep in Sartol's skull. He would have to be doubly careful, however. If somehow he failed, and they killed him while he was unbound, he would join the ranks of the Unsettled.

"Arick's fist upon you, Theron!" he said to the night. "You and your evil curse!"

Theron's Curse. He had never really given it much thought; it had never seemed that important. Obviously, Pordath would have died eventually, but he saw no reason to worry about the curse while she was alive. And, on some level, he had assumed that his new binding would come quickly, that this time of weakness and uncertainty would last but a few weeks, perhaps a month or two. It had never occurred to him that he would lose his familiar in a battle, or that he would face this much danger without her. Yet, at a time when he needed his strength and his courage more than ever, he found himself not only deprived of his powers, but also stripped of his will. He knew that he had to keep Baden and Sartol from reaching the Great Hall, but, for the first time in his adult life, he felt afraid. Death had never daunted him; eternal unrest did.

He closed his eyes and took a deep breath. "May the God smite you, Theron," he said through clenched teeth.

He had heard much talk recently among members of the Order, young and old, about how Theron's legacy had been ignored and denigrated for too long. The Owl-Master had been as responsible as Amarid for the harnessing of the Mage-Craft and the founding of the Order, these mages argued. He deserved recognition, he deserved to be remembered for more than just his curse. It was not a sentiment Orris shared, particularly now. Any honor that Theron might have earned, he had forfeited when he condemned unbound mages to this kind of dread, and when he sentenced those who died to wander the land ceaselessly. Even before his curse, the First Owl-Master had seen the Mage-Craft as a path to power and wealth, while Amarid had viewed it as an opportunity to serve the land. Orris knew that some mages considered his own advocacy of a greater role for the Order in governing Tobyn-Ser as a turn toward Theron's philosophy, but he disagreed vehemently. Leadership, he believed, represented one form of service, and, right now, Tobyn-Ser desperately needed leadership. Amarid, Orris believed, would have approved. As for Theron, his approach bred the type of arrogance and corruption embodied in the two Owl-Masters who now threatened to gain control of the Order.

Orris sat up and glanced northward. Had Baden and Sartol departed, he would have heard their horses galloping, or at least felt it through the ground. He had not, and he could see a faint glimmer of light in the distance, where their cerylls lay in the grass. He assumed that they had gone to sleep, and that it was safe for him to do so as well. One of these nights, as the Owl-Masters slept, he would steal up to their camp and kill them, or die in the attempt. But tonight, exhausted and still recovering from his battle with Sartol, he needed rest.

Sitting down heavily on a large, sunlit rock along the riverbank, Glyn dropped his walking stick, with its glowing red stone, and commanded the huge black bird to hop from his shoulder to the ground. Then, gingerly, he removed his leather shoes and inspected the latest damage they had done to his feet. Seeing the raw, bloody blisters, he let loose with an impressive string of profanity.

"Calbyr says we're supposed to speak Tobynese," Kedar told him, struggling slightly with the alien language. "Someone might hear us, he says. So if you're going to swear, don't do it in Bragory."

"Tobynese curses don't make me feel any better," Glyn answered irritably in his native tongue. "They're boring. Besides," he went on, gesturing with both hands, "we're by the river; there's nobody within five quads of here. Who's going to hear me?"

Kedar shrugged. "I don't know," he replied in Tobyn-Ser's language. "Sartol said that the sorcerers can see us. Maybe they hear us, too."

"The sorcerers don't scare me," Glyn grumbled in Tobynese. He stared at his feet, and swore again. "Look at my heel, Kedar. It's torn to bits."

"I don't want to look at your stinking feet. Mine hurt enough without you reminding me of it. Now put on your shoes and let's get going."

Glyn shook his head and hobbled closer to the water. "Not until I soak my feet. You should do it, too."

"I don't want to," Kedar said, his voice tinged with annoyance. "I want to get moving. We were supposed to be there last night. Now the sun goes down in two hours, and we've still got four or five quads to go. At least, that's what I think," he added, looking around. "It's harder to estimate distances here than it is at home. There's too much grass and not enough buildings. It might even be farther."

"All right, all right. I'll be ready in a minute." Glyn sat down and put his feet in the cold water, wincing at the sharp stinging of his wounds.

"*Now*, Glyn!" Kedar insisted.

Glyn looked back at his massive, light-haired companion. Kedar looked a bit absurd in the green hooded robe. He was a killer—Glyn had seen him tear a man's arm off in a fight—and here he was looking like an Oracle with a big bird. It almost made Glyn laugh. He tried to imagine himself in the same getup, with his short beard, and the bent nose that he got, in the same fight, as it happened, from a man who was now dead. He probably looked pretty silly as well. But not as bad as Kedar, he decided. He couldn't look as bad as Kedar.

"Come on, Glyn!" Kedar barked. "Calbyr wanted this thing done already. Do you want to explain to him why we fouled up his plans?"

"I'm not afraid of Calbyr," Glyn said. But he stood and carefully made his way back to his shoes.

Kedar threw back his large head and laughed, his small eyes closing until they were mere slits. "No, of course you're not afraid of Calbyr. And Nal-rats aren't fond of sewers."

Glyn glared at his friend, saying nothing.

"Oh, don't get sore, Glyn," Kedar said gruffly. "I didn't mean anything by it. We're all afraid of him. I know I am, and I'm twice his size."

Glyn remained silent, but, after a moment, he nodded and gave a half-hearted smile. Kedar was right: everyone was afraid of Calbyr, even back in Lon-Ser. And, to be honest, every one of them who had come with Calbyr to Tobyn-Ser also feared the sorcerer Sartol, especially after what he did to Yarit the first day they encountered him. He shuddered involuntarily at the thought, and concentrated on putting his shoes back on without aggravating his tender feet. The cold water had helped, but only a little. He doubted that he would make it all the way to the next town. What was it called again? Watertown? That didn't sound right.

"Hey, Kedar. What's the name of the place we're going to, anyway?"

Kedar rolled his eyes. "I told you already, twice: it's Watersbend."

"Watersbend," Glyn repeated, "right." He looked at the big man again. "And there's no need to get grouchy about it. These names make no sense to me. Watersbend, Kaera, Woodsrest, the Moriandral. I can't keep them straight."

Kedar shook his head. "Are you ready yet?" he asked impatiently.

Glyn stood and tested his weary feet. "As ready as I'm likely to be." He retrieved his walking stick and called to the large, black bird. Immediately, it flew to him, its glittering, golden eyes catching the sunlight. "Let's go," he said to Kedar, "but you should prepare yourself: you might have to carry me before the day's over."

Kedar snorted skeptically. "Not bloody likely."

They climbed up the steep bank away from the water and back onto the plain. Then they continued southward, following the course of the river along its eastern shore. Within minutes, the throbbing pain in Glyn's feet returned, and he walked behind Kedar muttering Bragory curses under his breath. He hated Tobyn-Ser, with its strange language, its tedious food, and its simple-minded people. And he had become bored with this job; he was exhausted from the endless walking, sick to death of sleeping on the ground, and tired of looking at this useless wilderness. He felt ridiculous wearing the stupid green cloak and he was ready to throw these horrible, stiff shoes into the river. Most of all, though, he had grown weary of taking orders from Calbyr. Yes, he was afraid of the man, with his wild, dark eyes, the evil-looking white scar, and his lithe frame, which Glyn had seen kill so many times he had lost count. But just because he feared him, that didn't mean that he couldn't hate him as well.

At that moment, Glyn would have given everything he had in the world, which, admittedly, was not much, to be back in Bragor-Nal, sitting comfortably in his favorite bar, waiting for another job to come along. Calbyr wasn't the only Nal-Lord around, after all. Glyn had done all right before he met the man; he could do all right without him. Jobs in the Nal had never demanded this much work, or offered so little comfort. Here, even the weapons were odd. He found the long stick with its glowing red stone unwieldy. He missed the compact efficiency of his normal hand weapon. He felt safer with it: more secure, better able to protect himself. *I bet Yarit could have saved himself if he had been carrying a normal thrower*, he thought, deepening his own uneasiness. Still, he had to concede, this weapon carried more firepower than anything he had ever used at home. It had done quite a job on Kaera. He grinned at the memory.

In truth, he didn't hate everything about this job, and things hadn't been going so great in Lon-Ser before he left. Calbyr might be insane, but, if they succeeded, and if their payment amounted to even half of what he had promised them, Glyn would never have to work again. On the other hand, Calbyr had promised all of them a painful death if they failed. Later, in private, Glyn and Kedar had joked about it, wondering which Calbyr wanted more: the money or an excuse to kill them. The point was, however, none of them had any intention of failing. Calbyr had been able to choose his team from all the break-laws in Bragor-Nal—gangmen and independents. This crew wasn't likely to fail, not with the promise of unimaginable wealth spurring them on. When it came right down to it, Glyn was not about to give up his share of the spoils for a bit more comfort. It didn't really matter how miserable he was. He grinned, although without amusement: no doubt, Calbyr had counted on just that attitude in making his plans. Well, if he had, that was fine. As long as Glyn received his fair payment, he would allow Calbyr his small victories.

By far the best part about the job was the magnificent bird Glyn carried on his shoulder. He had grown quite fond of it during the training and work that had consumed much of the last two years. Watching its graceful flight and seeing the intelligence in its sparkling eyes, he found it easy to forget that the creature was actually synthetic. Real or not, though, the bird was just about the most proficient killer he had ever seen. Glyn respected that a great deal.

All along, Calbyr had remained noticeably tight-lipped about the identity of their sponsors. No doubt Cedrych was behind this, but, on his own, the Overlord didn't have the resources to come up with sixteen of these birds. This should have meant that the Sovereign was involved, too, but Calbyr had gone out of his way to avoid the Sovereign's security squads. Glyn knew from personal experience that avoiding the squads was always a good idea, particularly when trying to get any so-called "advanced goods" out of the Nal. But if the Sovereign knew about this operation it wouldn't have mattered to Calbyr as much as it had seemed to. Not that Glyn had ever really understood the Sovereign's paranoia about such things. From what he knew of Oerella-Nal, it seemed that the Matriarchy was uninterested in weapons technology. And nobody in Stib-Nal had brains enough to use any of it. Certainly the Sovereign couldn't be worried about anyone in Abborij or Tobyn-Ser attacking the Nal. But given the zeal with which the squads did their job, there could be no doubt that the Sovereign was concerned about someone.

Glyn shook his head and turned his thoughts back to the bird he carried on his shoulder. Whoever Calbyr's superiors were, they had spared no expense when it came to these creatures. The mechanical hawks moved like live birds, responded to commands like trained pets, killed like mercenaries, and even anticipated the tactics of their enemies. The technology required to create these creatures went beyond anything Glyn had ever encountered. He would have liked to keep his bird; he almost would have been willing to give up some of his payment for it. Almost.

In addition to the bird, the work itself wasn't all that bad either. Actually, aside from the walking, and the bad food, Glyn liked what he was doing. For all his adult years, going back even to his early teens, when he fancied himself an adult, Glyn had known that he possessed but one true talent. It was not just that he had a certain amount of skill as a killer. He knew of many who left Bragor-Nal to fight as mercenaries in the Abborij; wars, never to return. They, too, had known how to kill. But Glyn had a knack for bringing death to others while minimizing the risks to himself, either of reprisal or capture. He had learned to end human life in a variety of ways, both subtle and conspicuous—for the murder of one, made manifest in the proper way, could convey a message to hundreds—but always discreetly. Most likely, it was his care and his caution that had drawn Calbyr's attention in the first place. That was what set Glyn apart. At first, Glyn had been skeptical about this job. He preferred to work in Bragor-Nal; he knew the rules there, and he had valuable connections. He had never spent any time outside of Lon-Ser, and he had little interest in exploring the rest of the world. But Calbyr had assured him that his skills would be put to good use here, that the challenge would lie not just in killing, but in leaving enough evidence to implicate someone else. And finally, with the job at Kaera, Calbyr had been right.

For their first year in Tobyn-Ser, Calbyr had them doing petty stuff: vandalism, theft, arson. It was important that they follow a natural progression, Calbyr had said. This job could not be rushed. Glyn had quickly grown bored with it, though. Any kid could have done this work; Calbyr didn't need him. But, with Kaera, everything had changed.

"From now on, hold nothing back," Calbyr had told them at their last meeting. "Destroy everything, kill everyone; just leave yourselves one witness."

That was more like it; that was what they had been brought here to do. The attack on Kaera had been fun, and it had gone very well. They encountered few surprises; no one escaped. The throwers functioned perfectly, and the birds were nothing short of magnificent. Still, for tonight's job at Watersbend, Glyn would have to remember to tell Kedar to keep his stone covered until they got close to the town. Glyn did not relish the idea of facing another angry mob armed with clubs and farm tools. That seemed an unnecessary risk. He would also tell the big man that he was free to select their witness again. Calbyr had left it to each group to choose its own witnesses, and Glyn had left that to Kedar. Glyn didn't care one way or another, and he didn't really see the point. It wasn't as though that little girl in Kaera had survived to live out such a great existence. They had killed her family and burned her home; sparing her life didn't seem to be such a big favor. But Kedar had a thing about murdering kids, and Glyn would respect it, even if he didn't understand it.

They walked for two hours, their shadows stretching across the prairie as the sun swung slowly toward the western horizon. The pain in Glyn's feet grew worse and worse until, finally, out of desperation, he removed his shoes and, resisting the temptation to fling them into the Moriandral, hid them in the large pocket inside his cloak. As it turned out, Glyn found walking barefoot substantially less painful than wearing the blasted shoes, and their pace quickened. They came within sight of Watersbend just before twilight, and, after pausing briefly to cover their stones, continued on toward the town until they were about a half-quad away from the first houses. Then they stopped, eating a small meal as they waited for the sky to turn entirely dark.

As Glyn sat in the grass, watching the stars appear overhead, he felt the familiar tranquillity embrace him like an old lover. It was always this way before he did a job: he grew calm, everything and everyone seemed to move a little slower, and he saw the world with a clarity that he lacked at other times. He had never asked Kedar if it was the same for him; he found it difficult to speak at these moments, and, the rest of the time, he never felt like discussing it. But he wondered. Before a job, the big man kept to himself as much as Glyn did; it was one of the reasons Glyn liked working with him so much.

Finally, when the last rays of daylight had vanished from the western sky, Glyn glanced at Kedar and nodded once. They stood and, unsheathing their stones, began to advance on Watersbend. As they drew close to the first house, Glyn noted with satisfaction that the people inside it seemed completely unaware of their approach. He moved his thumb to the small button along the shaft of his weapon and, once again, gave Kedar a curt nod. Depressing the button, Glyn felt power surge through the shaft of the thrower, saw red fire spurt from the stone, heard it crash with a staggering detonation into the building in front of him. He heard a second explosion as Kedar's weapon blasted through the walls of a neighboring house. The family inside of his target began to scream. A man ran out of the house carrying an ax, and Glyn felt his mechanical bird jump off his shoulder to attack. He heard shouting from nearby homes and saw people gathering in the distance, some of them with torches. He knew then that they would face a mob after all; knew that it wouldn't matter, that the people of Watersbend didn't have a chance.

After that, Glyn lost track of time for a while. Kedar and he moved through the first cluster of houses with deadly, systematic precision, pouring their red flame in all directions, and sending their lethal black birds after all those who tried to escape. These were farmhouses mostly, not as far apart as the homes in Kaera, but far enough for their proper destruction to require a good deal of time. It took Glyn and Kedar half an hour to reach the center of town, but, once they did, their progress quickened. The mob had gathered there to make its stand, and, as a result, the birds could cut down more of them in less time. Glyn and Kedar turned their fire on the storefronts that surrounded them, as the flying creatures rose and fell again and again, their razor talons wet with blood.

Amid the chaos and the flames and the screaming, Glyn remained in his deadly, trancelike state. Only Kedar's sudden cry of alarm alerted him to the two points of light—one of them orange, and the other yellow—that were approaching rapidly from the southwest. And, by then, it was too late.

*   *   *

The fourth day of their journey resembled, in almost every respect, the previous three. Baden, riding slightly ahead of Sartol, set a swift pace and rested just often enough to keep the horses watered and fresh. As he had for the last three days, the Owl-Master rode in virtual silence, speaking only when absolutely necessary, and even then keeping his statements and questions brief. But, whereas during those first few days, Sartol had found Baden's reticence frustrating and, perhaps, a bit worrisome, he now found it downright disturbing. The relief he had felt last night, as he listened to Baden drift off to sleep, had evaporated under the day's hot sun, leaving a residue of self-doubt that Sartol thought he had already vanquished. By the time he had fallen asleep the night before, Sartol had convinced himself not only that Baden still believed his version of what happened by the grove, but also that he had managed to draw Baden out of his laconic shell. He now feared that he had been mistaken on both counts. Nothing in Baden's expression or bearing appeared to have changed, but the silence he shaped had taken on a new, more frightening quality. He no longer seemed a man too absorbed in his own thoughts to speak. Instead, Sartol sensed that Baden had himself tightly under control, as if afraid that he might say the wrong thing.

Driving his mount northward, with the Moriandral on one side and the sun descending toward Tobyn's Plain on the other, Sartol found himself compelled to consider the possibility that he would have to kill Baden after all. Just as the Owl-Master's support would have been invaluable, Baden's opposition or, even worse, his accusations of treason would probably be enough to keep him from becoming Owl-Sage. Sartol had two choices. He could wait until they arrived in Amarid and, if Baden declared himself in opposition to Sartol's appointment, publicly trade accusations of treason with the Owl-Master. In an open battle of that sort, however, Sartol knew that his chances of prevailing were no better than even. Or, he could rid himself of Baden on the plain, justify it as self-defense, and accuse the dead Owl-Master of collaborating with the traitor Orris. He might get away with that. Presented correctly, Baden's staunch advocacy of the journey to Theron's Grove, and Orris's last-minute request to be included in the delegation, could be made to appear rather suspicious. Trahn would oppose him, but, given the Hawk-Mage's close friendship with Baden, Sartol could argue convincingly that he, too, had been part of the conspiracy. He would have, he realized with some reassurance, the staffs of Jessamyn and Peredur, which remained the only physical evidence of what had transpired by Theron's Grove. He felt his thoughts coalesce into resolve. He had made his decision; he might even have nodded reflexively as he did. Not that it mattered. Baden remained in front of him, all his energy and attention focused to the north, on Amarid. Sartol allowed himself a small smile. The course he had chosen carried tremendous risks, but he felt better for having made his choice. He would have to do it soon: tonight, perhaps; tomorrow night at the latest. After that they would enter Tobyn's Wood, and, for logistical reasons, he did not wish to chance a battle with Baden in the forest.

His mind set, Sartol found the rest of the ride much easier to endure. They paused briefly at sundown, allowing the horses to drink from the river, and enjoying a light meal themselves. Then they remounted and went on, initially by the dying light of day, and then by mage-light. About an hour after their rest, they espied a large cluster of lights far to the north, and on the far side of the river. Baden slowed his horse so that Sartol could pull abreast of him.

"I believe that's Watersbend," Baden said, his voice carrying over the wind and the hoof beats. "We can stop there for the night."

"You mean in the town?" Sartol asked with some alarm.

Baden shook his head. "No. Not after our encounter with the villagers in Tobyn's Wood. We can stay on this side of the river, but I thought it would be a good stopping point. If you'd like, though, we can keep going."

It was Sartol's turn to shake his head. "I'm ready to stop. That's as good a place as any."

Baden nodded and spurred his mount forward again, leaving Sartol to rue his misfortune. He could not risk attacking Baden with mage-fire this close to a town; there would be too many witnesses. He could claim that Baden had tried to attack Watersbend, but no one in the Order would believe that Baden had made such an attempt while traveling with Sartol. And Sartol could not kill Baden the way he had Jessamyn and Peredur; Baden was far too powerful for that. Baden's death would have to wait until tomorrow night. He watched the Owl-Master as they galloped along the river's edge, wondering if this had been coincidence, or if Baden was clever enough to sense Sartol's intent and thwart him in this way. *I may have underestimated him,* Sartol told himself, his anxiety increasing. *He may have a devious streak after all.* It wouldn't matter, though. Baden would never reach Amarid alive.

A few moments later, Baden slowed again. "We've covered a lot of distance today," he said amicably. "I hope we can maintain this speed when we reach the wood."

"I'm sure the forest will slow us a bit," Sartol offered in a tone that betrayed no hint of his thoughts, "but I expect to be in Amarid within a week."

"I hope you're right."

Baden grinned awkwardly and then started to say something else. He never got the chance. Suddenly, the sky over Watersbend erupted with crimson light, and a few seconds later bright yellow and orange flames began to send a dark cloud of smoke over the town. Over and over the strange, red flashes illuminated the night sky, and, as they did, the glow of the fires intensified.

Baden jerked back on his horse's reins, abruptly stopping the animal. Sartol did the same.

"What in Arick's name is that!" Baden breathed, his eyes fixed on the glowing sky. Then, before Sartol could answer, the Owl-Master's eyes widened in alarm. "It's them," he cried, "they're attacking Watersbend." Immediately, without waiting for Sartol, he kicked his horse into motion and began thundering toward the town.

Sartol took a deep breath and drove his horse forward as well, trying to keep up with Baden. He had seen the dread etched across Baden's angular features, and he guessed that he wore a similar expression. Which was fortunate, because while his concern, no doubt, ran as deep as Baden's, it flowed from a different source. He cared little for the people of Watersbend; their lives were of little consequence, given what was at stake. What had frightened him was his immediate recognition of that initial flash of red light, and his knowledge of whom they would find when they reached the town.

Distances on the plain often could be deceptive, particularly at night. Watersbend had seemed close, but another half-hour passed before they came within sight of the stone bridge that crossed the river and led to the town commons. By then, the entire village appeared to be engulfed in flames, and explosions, coinciding with the bursts of crimson light, echoed repeatedly off the riverbank. Shrieks of pain and horror reached them now, drifting across the river with the smoke, and the smells of burning wood and charred bodies. Racing toward the town, Sartol had time to determine what he had to do.

Unfortunately, Baden's mount proved significantly faster than his own. Baden reached the bridge and started across well before Sartol. There was little Sartol could do about that. He could hope that this would give the attackers an opportunity to kill Baden, but he knew better. And so, he urged his horse on, covering the last bit of ground as quickly as he could, and preparing himself for the coming encounter with Calbyr's men.

14

The sights and sounds of the attack—the bright, angry flames and the dark smoke that poured from them; the incessant flashes of red light; the reverberating explosions and, as he drew closer, the wails of despair and anguish—hammered mercilessly at Baden's consciousness, upbraiding him again and again for his own impotence. People were dying at the hands of mages, or men posing as mages. They were dying for the Order, because the Order had been reluctant, or unable, to stop the killing. The thought of it appalled him, made him nauseous; and it drove him toward Watersbend with a fury that bordered on desperation. He realized that he was risking his horse's life by driving the animal so hard. He could feel the creature laboring as they approached the stone bridge, but he could not bring himself to slow down. He also perceived that he had pulled ahead of Sartol, that he would reach the town before the other Owl-Master. And he knew that this mattered, knew that he needed to remember why it should be important. But, hearing the cries for help, seeing the flames and smoke, he could focus on nothing else.

Baden steered his mount onto the bridge, noting as he did that the attackers had only begun their assault on the village square, and that the farmhouses in the southern half of the village had not yet been burned. He also realized that, with his approach, the flashes of red light had abruptly ceased. Grimly, the Owl-Master took his staff in hand, reached with his mind for Anla, who flew just above him, and readied himself for battle. Coming off the bridge, he turned sharply left and rode into the town's market area. He saw a crowd of villagers fleeing in his direction, many of them bleeding from wounds, others suffering from burns. But he could find no sign of their pursuers. Checking his horse, Baden scanned the storefronts and the hordes of people. Nothing.

"Where are they?" he yelled to one of the townspeople.

The man looked up at him and shied away, refusing to break his stride.

"I want to help you!" Baden shouted. "Where are they?"

"Behind us!" came the reply, over the man's shoulder as he continued to run.

"I know that," Baden said, more to himself than to the villager. He only realized later that the man's refusal to assist him had saved his life.

Turning back toward the northern side of the town, shaking his head in frustration, Baden saw the two crackling bolts of red fire already hurtling in his direction. He just barely had time to react, and still, he almost died. He managed to shield himself by throwing up a shimmering orange curtain of power that blocked, with a bone-rattling concussion, the one blast that had been intended for him. The other, however, crashed unimpeded into the right shoulder of his mount, bringing a nightmarish shriek from the animal, and knocking the creature off its feet. Thrown free of the horse, feeling himself cartwheel helplessly through the air, Baden could do nothing to cushion his fall. He landed heavily on his shoulder and side, rolled a short distance on the hard, dusty road, and then lay still, dazed and aching, trying to remember how to breathe.

At the sound of Anla's urgent cries, Baden struggled to raise himself painfully on his one good arm. Gazing over the smoking, prone body of his horse, he froze. The Owl-Master had never doubted that Jaryd had related accurately his vision of the mage at Taima. By the same token, however, he had also never thought to take the young mage's description of what he saw so literally. But here, tonight, he beheld Jaryd's vision for himself, doubled, actually, though that seemed impossible.

Advancing toward him, cautiously, came two men, both of them dressed in green hooded robes that resembled his own, and both of them carrying staffs with crimson cerylls. And in front of them, flying toward him with a swiftness that belied their huge size, Baden saw two black birds with eyes of gold, whose talons shone with blood. Scrambling to recover his staff, which had landed a few feet away, Baden thrust his ceryll out before him and propelled a stream of seething orange fire toward the closest of the hawks. It wheeled to the side, evading the mage-fire. This, however, Baden had expected. Already, a second orange blast was on its way, this one too sudden for the creature to dodge. It caught the bird full in the chest. Baden heard one of the mages cry out in dismay as the power of the blow sent the bird spiraling backward to land in a heap of flame and smoke and dust at the feet of its now powerless mage.

Keeping low to the ground, so as to shield himself from the other mage's fire, Baden then spotted the second hawk. It had attacked Anla, and was, even now, driving the brown owl toward the ground. Anla was by no means a small bird, and, like all owls, she was a skilled flier and hunter. But Baden knew, as soon as he saw her struggling with the black creature, that she was hopelessly overmatched. The other bird appeared to be three times her size, and just as agile. And, with the two birds darting and swooping so close together, Baden could not try to kill the hawk with his mage-fire without risking Anla's life as well. Instead, he closed his eyes and reached for his owl, projecting into her mind an image of what he wanted her to do. Without pause, she broke away from the larger bird and retreated directly over Baden's head. The larger bird followed, and Baden readied himself to kill it. But rather than simply flying over the Owl-Master, the black creature, seeming to anticipate the trap, soared in low over the dead horse, and slashed at Baden's head with its claws. There was little pain, really, but Baden could feel the blood flowering from the wound and flowing over his brow into his eyes. Clawing at the blood to keep his vision clear, Baden twisted onto his back in time to see the bird pivot sharply and dive back toward him, its outstretched talons reaching for his throat. With an effort that tore a gasp from his chest, Baden sent another burst of orange fire from his ceryll straight into the air, catching the bird as it descended upon him, and knocking it in a fiery somersault back into the sky and then to the ground beside him.

The Owl-Master allowed himself a deep breath and a moment of rest on the ground. It was over. He climbed tenderly to his feet and leaned heavily on his staff. Then he raised his arm for Anla and started walking toward the mages, watching his owl descend as he did. That brief glance toward his bird nearly killed him.

Hesitating only for an instant, the two strange men, dispossessed of their familiars, and thus stripped of their powers, at least according to the natural laws that had governed the Mage-Craft for a thousand years, lowered their staffs and threw two torrents of red fire toward Baden, who found himself utterly unprepared. Fighting through his astonishment, compelling himself to respond to a deadly attack from two men who should have been no threat at all, Baden managed with another wrenching exertion to shield himself from their assault, staggering and falling to one knee with the force of the hot, crimson blasts. Stunned by the attack, hardly able to respond, Baden blocked a second volley, bracing himself this time for the impact. He prepared to strike back, hoping to debilitate his adversaries somehow without killing them. But, as he did, he heard a horse approaching rapidly. Sartol, he thought.

He considered shouting a warning to the Owl-Master, but suddenly, there seemed to be no need. Seeing Sartol ride up to Baden, watching him dismount, the two strange mages appeared to waver. They looked at each other for a second. The larger one spoke, and then the other one turned toward Sartol and pulled back his hood, revealing a dark beard, misshapen nose, and deep-set eyes that appeared to widen with recognition as he gazed at the Owl-Master. He took a step forward, looking as if he might say something. Then he stopped, his eyes widening again, but in a different way. Baden looked up at Sartol in time to see the Owl-Master level his staff at the two men.

"*No!*" Baden cried out, flinging himself against Sartol's legs, trying to throw the mage off balance. But he was fatigued and hurt, and he was still on his knees from the force of the strangers' blasts. Sartol knocked him onto his back with a hard knee to the chest, and then turned back toward the two men. Baden tried to scramble to his feet, but, before he could, yellow mage-fire shot from Sartol's staff, forking at the last instant to hammer the two men to the ground, and consuming them in a whirlwind of flame that killed them instantly.

A cheer went up from the men and women of Watersbend and, in a moment, Baden and Sartol were surrounded by townspeople thanking them for their assistance and begging the Owl-Masters to heal their wounds.

Ignoring the crowd and the blood running down his face, Baden grabbed Sartol's arm and forced the Owl-Master to face him. *"What in Arick's name is the matter with you!"* he shouted, silencing the townspeople, who looked with confusion from one Owl-Master to the other. *"You killed them!"*

"Yes," Sartol responded coldly, yanking his arm out of Baden's grasp. "Despite your best efforts to stop me. You would have preferred that I wait for them to kill us?"

"That didn't seem to be their intention!" Baden said pointedly. "Not after you arrived!"

Sartol narrowed his grey eyes. "I don't know what you mean by that, Baden. All I know is that you tried to keep me from protecting these people. I succeeded despite your efforts, and now you're acting as though I killed your best friends." He indicated the crowd with his hand. "No one else here disapproves of what I did. Perhaps you can tell me why you do."

"Because now we can't question them!" Baden answered, driving each word into the Owl-Master. "We had two of the men who had committed these attacks right in our hands! They could have told us who sent them; they could have told us why they were doing this! But instead, you killed them, and we still know nothing!"

"So you wanted me to chat with them," Sartol stated in a maddeningly placid voice. Several people in the crowd snickered.

Baden tried to control his temper. "Of course not. I would have liked you to injure them in some way that would leave them harmless, but alive. That was what I intended to do."

"Come now, Baden!" Sartol snapped. "Have done with this farce! You tried to save their lives and I still managed to kill them! So now you're trying to put your actions in the best possible light! Well, it won't work! The rest of you saw!" the Owl-Master went on, raising his voice so all in the crowd could hear. "He tried to stop me from killing your attackers!"

Most of the people in the crowd nodded, and many shouted angrily for Baden's death.

Sartol bared his teeth in a triumphant grin. "He is a traitor to the land!" he went on, indicating Baden with his hand. "He must be arrested and returned to Amarid! There he will be tried by the Order and punished for his crimes!"

Baden suddenly felt himself being seized from behind. Anla hissed in alarm and then leapt into the air. *Fly, Anla!* Baden sent to her, fearing that Sartol might try to kill her. *Fly! We will find each other again!* He and Sartol both watched her disappear into the night sky, and then Sartol turned back to Baden and grabbed his staff.

"Don't worry," the dark-haired mage told the townspeople, a dark grin still stretched across his features as he tied Baden's staff to his horse's saddle. "Without his staff and his bird he cannot harm you."

"This isn't going to work, Sartol," Baden said with quiet intensity. "These people may believe you, but the rest of the Order won't."

"Don't be ridiculous, Baden," Sartol returned smugly, his voice lowered. "Of course they will. I've got a town full of witnesses. I saved these people's lives, and they will repay me by helping to convict you of treason."

"Should we take him to the jail, Owl-Master?" asked one of the men who had taken hold of Baden.

Sartol smiled broadly at this confirmation of what he had said. "Yes," he replied, still eyeing Baden. "And keep a close watch on him. He's quite clever."

"Can you heal our injuries, Owl-Master?" came another voice from the crowd. "Can you help us search for survivors?"

"Of course," Sartol told them, his gaze never leaving Baden's face. "I'm here to serve you."

The townspeople started to lead Sartol toward the northern end of town, while Baden's captors pulled him in the opposite direction.

"What will you do when the next attack occurs, Sartol?" Baden called. "You can't kill all of them! Eventually the truth will come out!"

"All of whom, Baden?" Sartol returned. "The renegades who have committed these crimes against Tobyn-Ser are dead. There are their bodies," he added, pointing to the charred corpses that still smoldered in the street.

"You want us to believe that two men were responsible for all of the attacks?" Baden countered. "Impossible. There have to be more, perhaps a great many more."

The villagers had been listening, warily watching the two mages. Presented now with this possibility, they whispered anxiously among themselves.

"Take him away!" Sartol commanded harshly. "He's trying to confuse and frighten you, to distract you from the fact that he's a traitor! Don't let him! Yes, these men committed many crimes all through the land, but those incidents took place over a long period of time. Perhaps they had horses that enabled them to cover great distances swiftly. It doesn't matter: however they did it, they're dead now. After an ordeal of this sort, it's hard for us to accept an ending, no matter how satisfying or pleasing it might be. But it is over. The mages are dead." Even to Baden's own ears, Sartol sounded reasonable. More reasonable, Baden knew, than he did. Baden also guessed that, with drying blood covering his face from the wound on his forehead, he probably appeared to the crowd as a bit of a madman. "Take him away," Sartol repeated, "and let us see to your loved ones."

Baden felt himself being pulled toward the jail again, and he tried the one thing that remained. "They weren't mages!" he shouted, bringing another murmur from the townspeople, and forcing Sartol to face him again.

"What do you mean?" Sartol demanded impatiently. "Of course they were mages. Renegades, perhaps, but look at their cloaks, and their birds—"

"Yes, I know. And their cerylls. But this much, at least, the people of Watersbend can confirm for us." Baden surveyed the crowd, and raised his voice to reach all those who stood in the town center. "You saw the battle," he declared. "You know that I'm right. Even after I killed their birds, they still retained their powers."

After a pause, several people nodded. "It's true," one woman said. And another agreed, "Yes, I saw that, also."

Baden looked at Sartol. "Whatever power these men had did not arise from the Mage-Craft!"

Sartol regarded him silently, considering this. "You may be right," he admitted after some time, his voice cold. "But regardless of what power they drew upon, they attacked these people, and you tried to protect them." The handsome Owl-Master paused, allowing the impact of his words to reach those who stood with him. And Baden saw the expressions in their faces harden. "Take him to your jail," Sartol commanded again, turning away and beginning to walk toward the smoldering wreckage of what once had been farmhouses. "I've heard enough of his deceptions and diversions."

Once more, Baden felt the three men who held him pulling him toward the jail. And this time he knew that there would be no stopping them.

The prison was not far from where the strangers lay dead in the street. It looked plain and solid, very much like the prisons in other towns. It was constructed of dried sod and clay, and the narrow windows along the side of the building were covered with cast-iron gratings. Inside, the jail was as austere as it had appeared from the street. It had a front room, with a simple table and several chairs, and, in the rear of the building, separated from the entrance by a thick wall and iron door, stood eight cells, four on each side of a narrow corridor. A bedraggled young man, who smelled of alcohol and vomit, slept in the first cell on the right; the rest stood empty, their iron doors ajar. The men locked Baden in the cell across from the drunk and returned to the front room, where they remained, talking quietly to one another. Occasionally, they would come back to check on him, their expressions apprehensive and watchful, but, for the most part, they left him alone. Baden could hear them speaking, though, and he gathered from their conversation that the constable and his deputies had been killed by the strangers, and it had fallen to these three to guard him until Sartol came for him in the morning.

His cell was small but surprisingly clean, and Baden lay down on the hard pallet and began to review in his mind the sequence of events that had followed Sartol's arrival in the village square. He was certain that the stranger who had pushed back his hood recognized Sartol, and had intended to say something to the Owl-Master. Which could only mean that Sartol had betrayed the Order. But Baden had suspected as much since his strange conversation with Sartol the night before. The question on which he found himself dwelling was far more unsettling: who were the men Sartol had killed, and from what source did they draw their power? Obviously, given their ability to fight him with fire even after he had destroyed their birds, they had not been mages. But, that being the case, Baden could not even begin to fathom who they might be, or whence they had come.

He pondered the question for a long time, turning it over and over in his mind, until eventually he must have fallen asleep. For the next thing he knew, a great commotion in the front room of the jailhouse had awakened him, and a familiar, though utterly unexpected voice was threatening the lives of his guards.

* * *

Fatigued from so many days of riding, and still pained by his injuries, he had slept later than he intended, and had awakened only because he heard the hoof beats of Baden and Sartol's horses reverberating through the ground as they started northward. The sun was already up, a huge orange ball sitting on the eastern horizon, and Orris had to wait for several minutes, until the Owl-Masters had ridden out of sight, before he could risk remounting and riding after them. As it was, he had been fortunate that they had not seen his horse standing in the grass near where he slept. Once he started riding, he maintained enough of a gap between himself and the Owl-Masters to be confident they could not see him; anytime they came within view, he slowed his mount, allowing them to pull farther ahead. And, an hour after climbing back into the saddle, when he reached the rippling waters of the Moriandral, he took the added precaution of crossing to the eastern side of the river and using its constant rumble to mask the sound of his galloping mount.

Throughout the morning and afternoon, and into the dark of evening, he followed them, resting when they rested, and pursuing at a safe distance as they rode. It had been easier on this day than it had been for the past few. As soon as he was awake and moving, his wounds became less of a problem. He could feel himself healing; time seemed to be doing what he had been unable to do for himself. As for the other pain, the one he felt each time he thought of Pordath . . . well, that would take a bit more time.

He had been satisfied to ride in their wake, to stay back for now, and wait until they entered Tobyn's Wood before attempting to ambush them. But then he had seen the explosions of red light over the distant town, had grasped almost immediately what they signified, and, keeping his glowing ceryll covered, had driven his horse forward with a rage and frustration that nearly caused him to overtake Sartol. Only the speed with which the Owl-Masters rode toward the fires and smoke, and, in particular, the genuine urgency with which Baden seemed to be spurring his mount, kept Orris from abandoning his strategy altogether and riding openly into the village. In truth, although he found this difficult to accept, he was not at all certain that he could have caught up to Baden even if he had tried. So he decided to keep his presence a secret for a while longer and watch what Baden did before sacrificing the one advantage he still had. He also had to admit to himself that, without his powers, he would have had little chance of stopping the attack on his own.

He reached the eastern fringe of the village square just in time to see Baden kill the two huge, black birds. He nearly hollered a warning to the Owl-Master when he saw, incredibly, that the two mages, or whoever they were, still retained their powers. And he watched with astonishment and then profound interest as Sartol rode into town, killed the strangers, and then had Baden arrested as a traitor. Had he not known of Sartol's treachery, he might have believed that Baden had been trying to protect the attackers, just as the townspeople apparently did.

But Orris had seen the one stranger pull back his hood upon recognizing Sartol, and it had seemed to him that the man intended to address the Owl-Master. Orris had been enraged when Sartol killed the men without first trying to subdue and interrogate them; so, too, it seemed, had Baden.

In that moment, it occurred to Orris that he might have been too quick to assume that Baden had conspired with Sartol in all of this. While he had bitter, personal knowledge of Sartol's treachery, he had no evidence at all of Baden's. Yes, he and Baden had often clashed in the past, and the Owl-Master had pushed very hard for this ill-fated journey to Theron's Grove. But, if he were to be fair, he would have to acknowledge that those things, taken individually or even weighed together, said nothing about Baden's loyalty to the land. On the other hand, Trahn's unwavering trust of the Owl-Master said a great deal. And so, too, did Orris's own memory of Baden's words to the Order just after a vandal's stone had crashed through a window of the Great Hall: "If there is a murderer and a traitor in this hall right now, hear me: I will find you, and I will use all my power to destroy you." Orris considered himself a powerful mage, or at least he had before Pordath's death, and he rarely allowed himself to feel intimidated. That day in the Great Hall, however, he had been daunted by what he saw blaze in Baden's lean face as the Owl-Master issued his challenge. Since leaving the grove, he had dismissed Baden's statement as posturing, for how else could he reconcile it with his belief that Baden had betrayed the Order? But on this night, crouched in the shadows between two shops, watching as Baden battled for his life against the strange mages and their enormous, ebony familiars, and then witnessing the Owl-Master's confrontation with Sartol, Orris found himself questioning his own judgment. It was a strange, unfamiliar sensation for him, this self-doubt and irresolution. But, since he had become unbound, he had been surprised repeatedly by the complexities of his own emotions.

Which, perhaps, explained the other sentiment with which he grappled as he continued to observe Baden and Sartol. Since the Gathering, he had begrudged Jaryd and Alayna their places in the delegation to Theron's Grove. They were barely fledged; they did not yet have full mastery of their abilities. However powerful they might someday prove to be, whatever the significance of their bindings to Amarid's Hawk, they did not belong on this mission. Or so he had told himself. He had even called them "the young ones," and referred to Jaryd as "the boy," he recalled, suddenly abashed by his own arrogance. Yet, tonight he had come face to face with the power of that "boy's" Sight. The strangers he had seen matched almost exactly the description Jaryd once offered of the mage he had envisioned at Taima. It was not as though Orris had never had a vision. He was a Hawk-Mage, and the Sight was a part of the Mage-Craft. But while he had seen things, and divined future events from them, he had never in all his days had a vision that he could take so literally, certainly not in a matter of such monumental importance. Thinking of this, he grieved for the loss of the two young mages, not just because their powers and insights would be needed in this battle, and not simply in response to the tragedy that their deaths represented. He mourned for them because he wished to apologize, to acknowledge that he had been wrong about them.

He shook his head. Again, he was not used to harboring such sentiments. He had once been told by an older mage that the times between bindings, while difficult and frightening, could also be periods of valuable self-exploration and growth. He had been young at the time, newly bound to his first familiar, and not inclined to pay much attention to such insights. Now, though, re-membering the conversation, he grinned again at his own vanity. The mage, whose name he had forgotten, had, of course, been absolutely correct. And, finally, Orris was listening.

On the main street of the village square, Sartol led the villagers toward the devastated remains of their homes, and three men dragged Baden toward the town jail, leaving the remains of the strangers and their birds unattended. Wait-ing until the mages and the crowd were no longer in sight, Orris crept to the spot where the dead men lay in the road, and uncovered his ceryll so that he might use its light to examine the blackened bodies. Little remained of their clothes or features.

But, when he next moved to the bird that had been catapulted back toward its masters by Baden's mage-fire, Orris halted, astounded and disturbed by what he saw.

What he had taken for a hawk had not been a bird after all. Indeed, it was unlike any creature or thing Orris had ever seen. Its feathers, or what had been made to look like feathers, were composed of a strange substance that appeared to have turned to liquid when exposed to the heat of Baden's mage-fire, and then to have hardened again, into a grotesquely deformed shape. In some ways, the material seemed to have the properties of iron or gold. But its light weight and its suppleness strongly suggested that it was not a metal, at least not one that could be found in Tobyn-Ser. Inside the creature, where there should have been blood, bones, and organs, there were instead strange metallic threads, chips and globules of glass, and more of the same substance of which the feathers were constructed. The talons and beak had been shaped out of metal, but a variety with which Orris was unfamiliar. It was exceptionally thin, but strong and razor sharp.

Most remarkable of all, however, were the creature's eyes. Obviously, given the way in which this strange bird had maneuvered and attacked, it could see. Yet, its eyes did not appear to be real. Both of them had been knocked out of their sockets by Baden's blast, or perhaps by the force of the bird's landing. Peering through one of the gaps into the bird's head, Orris could see the same collection of metal strands, glass, and the strange material that had comprised the rest of its body. And examining the eye itself, one of which he found on the ground a few feet away, Orris realized that it consisted of a flat disk of gold embedded in a curved piece of glass.

The Hawk-Mage walked quickly to where the second creature lay, knowing before he reached it what he would find, but wanting to be sure just the same. Like its twin, this "bird" had never been alive at all. In spite of its hawklike flight, and its anticipation of the tactic with which Baden and his owl had tried to lure it into danger, in spite of its obvious ability to see and hear and think just as Pordath had been able to do, the creature was no more than a tool. It was a blacksmith's bellows or a farmer's plow; it had been constructed by humans for their use.

But not by any people in this land. Orris knew that. The degree of me-chanical sophistication represented by this bird surpassed by far the capacities of anyone in Tobyn-Ser. Indeed, the distance between these birds and Tobyn-

Ser's most advanced tools was so vast, so overwhelming that Orris could barely grasp it. Deeply frightened, he scanned the dusty road for anything else that might offer some insight into the identity of the attackers.

Noticing their staffs, Orris stepped over to the nearest one and picked it up. From a distance, it had appeared to be made of wood and crystal, like his own staff and ceryll. But, picking it up and looking more closely, Orris saw that, once again, appearances had deceived him. The shaft had been fashioned to resemble wood, but, like the birds' feathers, it had melted in places with the heat of the fire that consumed its owner. It felt odd: overly light and poorly balanced. The red stone did appear to be a genuine crystal, but by now Orris had grown skeptical. A small square, located on the shaft just below the stone, drew his attention. Glancing around to be certain that no one could see him, he aimed the crystal toward the ground, placed his thumb over the square, and pressed it. Instantly, a beam of red fire surged into the road, creating a small cloud of dark smoke and causing the staff to vibrate slightly and to recoil upward.

Orris quickly returned the staff to where he had found it, fighting as he did to keep his fears in check. These men, or whoever had sent them, had crafted animate beings that imitated natural ones, and had constructed weapons that equaled the strength of mage-fire. An enemy with such abilities posed a grave threat to Tobyn-Ser; even the Order could no longer guarantee the land's safety.

Gazing at the staff, and then at the remains of the birds, Orris wrestled with the implications of what he beheld. And doing so, he thought back to a conversation he had early in the spring with a friend of his, Crob, an Abboriji trader who came regularly to the ports of Surfsfury Harbor, along the eastern edge of Tobyn's Plain. As he always did, Orris had teased the merchant about his land's constant, petty wars, wondering aloud why the people of Abborij could not be more like the peaceful denizens of Tobyn-Ser. Normally, Crob suffered these gibes with good humor. But, on this occasion, he had responded with anger.

"Our affairs are no concern of yours, Mage!" Crob had snapped. "Abborij has no need of meddling strangers! Our wars are our own business!"

Taken aback by his friend's response, Orris had held up his hands in a placating gesture. "I meant no offense, Crob," he assured the fair-haired man. "It was just a joke."

Crob had continued to glare at him for another minute, before breaking eye contact and giving a small nod. "I know that, Orris. I'm sorry."

"Is Abborij having problems with outlanders?"

"Some, yes." Crob hesitated, as if unsure of whether he should confide in the Hawk-Mage. "For many years," he explained at last, "the potentates have hired mercenaries to fight their wars, rather than risking the young men of Abborij." He smiled ruefully. "No doubt, given our fondness for combat, the practice has kept the population of our land from becoming entirely female. It has also, up until now, meant that the lesser lords, those with smaller coffers, had little chance to expand their territories."

"But something has changed this?"

Crob nodded again. "Yes. Recently, we've seen a large influx of mercenaries from Lon-Ser. By itself, this isn't surprising: Lon-Ser has always been a good place from which to recruit warriors. But the Lon-Ser authorities had always maintained a strict watch on the outflow of weapons and other advanced goods from that land. They were somewhat paranoid about it. Now, though, their vigilance has slackened, and Abborij has been overrun by men with terrible weapons. It used to be mercenaries killing mercenaries. Now it's mercenaries killing families and destroying towns."

"What kind of weapons?" Orris had asked, his apprehension increasing by the minute.

"Strange ones. Things I've never seen before. Things that throw fire; objects that fit in the palm of your hand and do more damage than a battering ram." Crob shook his head. "I fear for Abborij. I wonder if maybe we should try to hire mages to protect us."

Crob had tried to laugh, as if he had meant the last comment as a joke. But the look in his eyes had made it clear to Orris that the trader found nothing funny in the situation. And now, looking down on the remains of this bizarre and deadly bird that had found its way to a small town along the Moriandral, Orris began to fathom what Crob must have felt that day. Outlanders with staggeringly destructive weapons had come to Tobyn-Ser. They had destroyed its towns and murdered its people. And, like Crob's people, Orris found himself powerless to stop them.

The Hawk-Mage turned and wandered back to the other end of the street, where the first of the shattered birds lay. As he walked, he considered his next move. He had little choice, really. If Pordath had lived, he might have had more options. But given that he could wield only a small remnant of his usual powers, and given what he had witnessed on this night, he knew that he needed to act, that the time for waiting and observing had passed. Despite the dangers inherent in what he was considering, he saw no viable alternatives.

Reaching the first bird, Orris stooped and moved his ceryll close to the ground. He spotted the one eye that he had examined almost immediately, but at first he couldn't find the other. Then it caught the amber light from his crystal, sparkling in the dust of the road. Orris picked it up, holding it between his thumb and forefinger, and marveling that the false eye of this menacing creature could possess such simple beauty. Knowing that he was taking a tremendous risk, but also believing that the eye would prove helpful at some point, Orris placed it in a small pocket within his robe. With both of the eyes having been knocked free, he hoped that Sartol's suspicions would not be aroused by his inability to find one of them.

On that thought, he gazed toward the northern end of the town, just in time to see Sartol walking back toward the town center, alone now, except for his horse and the large owl perched on his shoulder. Concealing his ceryll once more, Orris swiftly retreated to his hiding place between the storefronts. Then he watched as the Owl-Master examined the bodies and the debris that lay in the street, just as he himself had done minutes before. Orris soon realized, however, that Sartol's inspection of the scene was not at all like his had been. For when the Owl-Master came to the huge, ebony birds, he merely picked them up and carried them to his horse, without so much as a second glance. It seemed impossible to Orris that Sartol could look at them and not notice that they had no blood or feathers, that they were, in fact, not real. Certainly he could not have handled them without noticing. But the Owl-Master betrayed no hint of surprise at their appearance. Which could only mean that he had known what they were all along.

I would strike you down where you stand if I had the power to do so, Orris said inwardly, gritting his teeth against the impulse to charge at the Owl-Master anyway.

Sartol had pulled two blankets from his saddlebag, and he now wrapped one of them around the carcasses of the two creatures and tied the bundle to his horse's saddle. He then retrieved the strangers' staffs and did the same with them. Watching him, Orris realized, with a rush of insight that left him feeling sick to his stomach, that the Owl-Master intended to destroy both birds and both staffs. It made sense, really. Had Orris been in his position, he would have done the same. He had killed the strangers and branded Baden a traitor. By destroying the birds and weapons, he eliminated the last bit of evidence that could undermine whatever lies he intended to tell the Order.

Orris heard someone call to Sartol from the north end of town and he watched as the Owl-Master turned calmly to face the returning villagers. *He is smooth,* Orris thought, *I'll give him that.* Sartol and the townspeople spoke briefly, and then all of them moved off to the south. Orris followed.

The town's inn, it seemed, had not been damaged in the attack, and the villagers now offered Sartol a place to sleep for the night. Sartol appeared to accept, and Orris hurried around to the back of the inn to watch the windows and see if he could tell which room Sartol occupied. Soon, a lantern illuminated the window in an upstairs room. Several minutes later, the window was opened, and the room's lamp dimmed sufficiently to reveal the faint yellow glow of a ceryll. Satisfied that Sartol had retired for the night, Orris crept back to the main street of the town and watched the last of the villagers leave the village square. Only then did he make his way, silently and in the shadows, to Watersbend's jail.

He would have preferred to win Baden's release without having to face any of the town's residents, but, under the circumstances, that didn't seem possible. So instead, he took the most direct approach and simply walked into the jailhouse. The three men who had escorted the Owl-Master from the town center sat in the front room, two of them speaking quietly to each other. The third had fallen asleep.

When Orris entered the building, the two who were awake rose abruptly from their chairs and backed away. One of them shook the sleeping man awake.

"Who are you?" the biggest of the three asked, his voice unsteady, his pale eyes betraying his fear. "What do you want?"

"Owl-Master Sartol sent me for the traitor," Orris replied, attempting to sound disarming. "I don't mean you any harm."

The three men looked at one another, their expressions uncertain. "He said they wouldn't be leaving till tomorrow," the big man finally said.

Orris forced a smile. "Yes, I know. But there's been a change of plans. We're leaving tonight."

The one who had been sleeping, a wiry man with dark eyes and unruly dark hair, looked Orris up and down. "I don't remember you from before," he commented suspiciously.

"Neither do I," the big man agreed. "We're going to have to check with the Owl-Master before we let you take the traitor."

He took a step forward, as if he intended to go find Sartol.

"Don't move," Orris commanded, pointing his staff at the three guards and using what little power he had at his disposal to make his amber ceryll brighten menacingly. "I didn't want to have to do it this way," he told them, "but one way or another, I'm leaving here with the prisoner. You can die trying to stop me, or you can cooperate and tell your friends about it in the morning. It's your choice."

The men stood motionless, staring at Orris's ceryll, and the Hawk-Mage knew from what he saw in their faces that his bluff had worked. "Give me the keys," he ordered. Still they did not move. "*Now!*" he exploded, shocking them into action.

The third man, the one who hadn't spoken, pulled the keys from his trouser pocket and handed them to the Hawk-Mage. Orris nodded once and motioned the three of them into the rear of the building.

Baden was in the first cell, standing by its door. He had a dark gash on his forehead, and his face was still covered with dried blood. "I think I'm very glad to see you," the Owl-Master said as Orris directed the men into the next cell and closed its door. "Should I be?"

The Hawk-Mage looked at him briefly. "I'm not sure yet," he responded honestly. "But I'd rather discuss that elsewhere." He turned back to the three guards. "Which key opens his cell?"

The men regarded him sullenly and said nothing.

He leveled his staff at them once more. "Which key!" he stormed. And seeing the men flinch at his tone and at the threatening glow of his ceryll, Orris berated himself for what he was doing. In all probability, these men had lost their homes and livelihoods during the strangers' attack. Perhaps they had lost wives and children as well. And here he was bullying them, threatening their lives as far as they knew, all for the sake of a man whom they believed had betrayed their village. He could not even say for certain that he understood what he was doing. For all he knew, Baden was a traitor who had been betrayed himself this night by his fellow conspirator. "Just tell me which key, and we'll be gone," he said, softening his tone somewhat.

"The large one with the square head," the wiry man finally told him, sounding beaten and forlorn.

Finding the key, Orris quickly opened the door to Baden's cell and ushered the Owl-Master into the narrow corridor. Before they could leave, however, the big guard called out to them from the adjacent cell. "Why are you doing this?" he asked. "Why Watersbend?"

Orris would have preferred to leave without answering, but Baden turned to the man, his face looking gaunt in the dim light of the jail. "I can't tell you why your village was chosen to suffer," he told the men in a kind voice. "Only the gods and the two men lying dead in the street know the answer to that. But I can tell you this: I'm not a traitor, and neither is my friend here. We vowed long ago to serve Tobyn-Ser, and regardless of what you may think, that's what we're doing still. Have faith in the Order; it remains your friend and the land's best hope."

The men stared back at them, and Orris couldn't tell if they believed Baden. But he knew that he and the lean mage couldn't afford to linger and find out. "Come on, Baden," he said, grabbing the Owl-Master's arm and compelling him to follow.

They hurried out into the street and around to the side of the building, where Orris's horse stood waiting for them. From there, leading the animal by its reins, they made their way stealthily out of the town and back into the tall grasses of Tobyn's Plain. Only when they were a safe distance from the nearest of the farmhouses did Orris allow them to stop.

"Thank you," Baden said quietly. "Sartol told the townspeople that he was going to take me back to the Great Hall, but I have a feeling that I wouldn't have survived the trip."

Orris stared at the Owl-Master for some time, offering no response. "Let me be honest with you, Baden," he began at last, his tone icy. "I got you out of that jail because I know Sartol's a traitor, and I know that I can't stop him alone. That doesn't make us friends; it doesn't even mean that I trust you. It just means that I wasn't sure what else to do."

Baden's features hardened and he nodded slowly. "I see. So what am I supposed to do, Orris? Prove to you that I'm loyal to the Order? Give you some irrefutable evidence of my innocence? Well, I can't. I don't have any. But you should know that, up until last night, I was convinced that you were the traitor, and that you had killed Jessamyn and Peredur, perhaps Jaryd and Alayna as well. That's what Sartol told us, and I believed him."

"But now you know that Sartol is a liar," Orris replied calmly. "You know that I betrayed no one."

Baden regarded him for some time, his expression unreadable. "I don't know anything anymore," he finally said with unexpected candor. "I'm going by hunch and instinct right now, and I find it very disconcerting."

"But you told the men in the jail that I wasn't a traitor," Orris replied. "Why would you say that if you weren't certain?"

Baden shrugged. "Because I want to believe it, and because, like you, I can't beat Sartol alone."

"So neither of us trusts the other, but we both need help fighting Sartol." Orris shook his head and allowed himself a small laugh. "That's not much of a basis for a trusting relationship."

Baden's expression remained grim. "No, it's not, but perhaps if you told me what happened by the grove the night Jessamyn and Peredur died—"

"Would you believe me?"

Again the Owl-Master shrugged. "I might. Try me; I can't see that we have anything to lose."

"Fair enough," Orris returned. "I'll tell you what happened that night, but in return, I'd like an explanation of your actions as well."

Baden nodded. "Of course."

Orris remained silent for several moments, trying to re-create in his mind the events of that harrowing night. "After I left you and Trahn," he began at last, "I went looking for Jessamyn. I had just reached the camp when I heard her scream. I ran toward the thicket where the sound had originated, and, as I reached it, I heard Alayna cry out, and saw a burst of purple light——"

"Did you also see blue mage-fire?" Baden interrupted.

Orris considered this. "Yes," he said at last, the memory coming as a revelation. "I hadn't given it much thought at the time, but, just after the purple, there was blue." He paused, staring at Baden. "No one in our company had a blue ceryll. Where did that come from?"

"Never mind," Baden replied softly. "Go on with your story."

But the Owl-Master could not conceal the grief laid bare by Orris's question. At another time, Orris might have used that pain as a tool or a cudgel, but he had sorrows of his own that could just as easily be exploited, and this particular grief was one which he shared with Baden. "The blue light came from Jaryd, didn't it?" he persisted.

Baden faltered, then nodded. "Please, go on."

Orris had an impulse to tell Baden how sorry he was about Jaryd and Alayna's disappearance, about how he had belatedly come to recognize their value to the delegation and the Order. But his relationship with the Owl-Master had never permitted that level of honesty. Instead, he continued with his account of their night by the grove. "After I heard Alayna's scream and saw mage-fire, I began to make my way into the thicket. But then I heard branches rustling and breaking, and I realized that whoever was in there was escaping through the far side. So I ran back into the clearing and circled around the trees. That's when I saw Sartol chasing Jaryd and Alayna toward Theron's Grove. I attacked him, and got him to break off his pursuit, but the young mages just kept running."

"So you saw them go into the grove?" Baden asked, apparently heartened by this news.

"Yes." Orris looked at him strangely. "This pleases you?"

"I know it sounds odd," Baden answered. "When Sartol told me the same thing, I was horrified. But as my doubts about him have grown, I've started wondering if he lied about that to cover up the fact that he killed them."

Orris shook his head. "I don't know if they survived their encounter with Theron," he offered, "but I assure you, they did escape Sartol."

"And so did you."

Orris looked sharply at the Owl-Master, but Baden's expression and tone carried no hint of accusation. "Yes," he replied simply. "Barely. He blocked my fire with little trouble, and he nearly overwhelmed me with his power. He's remarkably strong, Baden. I never knew that a mage could be so strong."

"He said the same thing about you."

"What else did he say?"

Baden paused, but only briefly. "He gave us the same basic story that you just told, except in his version, you were chasing Jaryd and Alayna. He managed to stop you, but you were far stronger than he had imagined you could be. You almost killed him before escaping, he said. And he had a cut over his eye and a burn on his leg to show for it."

"The cut over his eye came from Pordath," Orris explained, "but I have no idea how he came by the wound on his leg. Certainly it didn't come from me. He may have done it to himself."

"Possibly. It appeared quite convincing at the time. Although," Baden added, glancing at Orris's shoulder and side, "his injuries looked no more impressive than yours. Why haven't you—" The Owl-Master stopped, his features suddenly contorted with pained realization. "Oh, Orris," he breathed, "I'm truly sorry. I should have noticed earlier." He hesitated. "Did Sartol kill her?"

"His owl," Orris responded with difficulty. He suddenly felt self-conscious, as if all his defenses had been stripped away. He could not meet Baden's gaze.

"When Anla returns to me, will you allow me to heal your burns?" Baden asked with sympathy.

"Perhaps," Orris said gruffly. "They're healing on their own. And we have other things to discuss."

Baden started to object, but, instead, he let the matter drop. "Very well. You had questions for me, I believe."

"I do," Orris confirmed. "I saw you and Trahn speaking with Sartol after I fought him, and it looked to me as if the three of you had conspired in this matter. Then you went to the trouble of building the pyres for the sage and the first before leaving Trahn alone by the grove—"

"And you concluded that Sartol and I had plotted together, and had performed the funeral rites for Trahn's benefit."

"Something like that, yes. I assumed that the two of you rode north to take control of the Order; Sartol is in line to become Owl-Sage."

"I know," Baden remarked. "He's offered to make me his first, which, no doubt, would have confirmed your suspicions."

"Have you accepted?"

"I haven't responded one way or another."

"With you as his first, Sartol would have little to fear from me," the Hawk-Mage observed. "You have credibility with all factions within the Order; by accepting, you would, in effect, protect Sartol from any charges of treason, or even murder."

"You think that's why he offered me the position?"

"In all likelihood. Not that you wouldn't make a fine first," Orris amended wryly.

Baden grimaced. "It's hardly a position I covet."

"Either sage or nothing, eh?"

Baden gave a small laugh. "I assure you, I'm quite satisfied with my life as it is now. I'm not interested in accumulating power."

"That may be another reason why Sartol wants you as his first. A more ambitious mage might pose a greater threat."

"Possibly," Baden commented. "But I think there may be more to Sartol's plan than just controlling the Order."

"What do you mean?"

The Owl-Master hesitated, drawing a smile from Orris. "Ah, yes," the Hawk-Mage said knowingly. "We still don't trust each other, do we? That does complicate things a bit."

The two of them fell silent, each absorbed in his own thoughts. At length, Baden stirred. "This impasse we've reached can't be broken without a leap of faith. I've been growing increasingly leery of Sartol's story for the past day or so, and he did something tonight that I found very disturbing."

"Killing the strangers, you mean."

Baden looked at him sharply. "You saw that?"

Orris nodded. "It looked to me as if the one man was about to speak to Sartol. He clearly recognized him."

"I agree. We could have learned a great deal from those men, which may be precisely why Sartol killed them when he did." Baden's eyes narrowed. "If you saw Sartol kill the strangers, you also must have noticed that the men retained their powers even after I killed their birds."

"I did," Orris replied grimly.

"And what did you think?"

Orris took a deep breath. "That's a more complicated question than you know, Baden. I had a chance, after you were taken to the jail, to examine their weapons and the bodies of their birds." He paused, unsure of how to proceed.

"And?" Baden urged.

"None of it was real: not the staffs or the cerylls, and not the birds either."

"I don't understand."

Orris shook his head. "Neither do I. And I'm not sure how to describe for you what I saw." He stopped, tugging impatiently at his beard. Baden was staring at him, his sharp features looking pallid and drawn. "Your mage-fire did a good deal of damage to them, and yet there was no blood on them. They had no feathers or bones. They were constructed of a strange material that I've never seen before: flexible and lightweight, like canvas, but much stronger. Their talons and beaks were metal. Even their eyes were fake." He reached into his cloak and pulled out the golden disk he had found on the street. "Look at this," he added, dropping the disk onto Baden's outstretched palm.

The Owl-Master gazed with amazement at the golden eye, picking it up with his thumb and forefinger to look at it more closely. "This is its eye?" he asked, his voice barely more than a whisper.

"Yes. I believe it was knocked loose when the creature fell onto the street."

"No wonder Jaryd couldn't describe the eyes of the bird he saw in his vision," the Owl-Master breathed, still gazing at the disk. "What he saw would have seemed completely illogical." He shook his head, as if emerging from a daydream, and then handed the eye back to Orris. "You say their cerylls were unnatural as well?"

"Yes," Orris confirmed. "The staffs were made of the same material as the birds, and there was a device on them, a small square that, when pressed, caused fire to shoot from the stone."

Baden nodded slowly. "That would explain why I couldn't render them powerless by destroying their birds." He stared at the ground for a long time before finally turning his gaze back toward Orris. "But how could all this be possible?" he demanded, fear creeping into his voice. "Who could create the things you describe?"

"No one in Tobyn-Ser," Orris replied with certainty.

"Outlanders?" Baden asked incredulously.

"That's the only possibility."

"Outlanders," the Owl-Master repeated, as if the word itself were alien. He took a long, slow breath. "I would almost have preferred renegades," he said, more to himself than to the Hawk-Mage. Then he looked at Orris again. "Have you any sense of where they were from?"

"I have an idea," Orris confided. "No more than that." He told Baden of his recent conversation with Crob. "It seems too much of a coincidence to ignore," he concluded.

"Lon-Ser," Baden whispered. "These are dark tidings, Orris." He paused again, passing a hand over his brow and gazing blankly at the town. Then, abruptly, he looked back at Orris. "Do you have any other evidence of what you've told me, aside from the bird's eye?"

"No," Orris told him. "I was afraid to take any more. I thought it might make Sartol suspicious."

"So the weapons and birds are still lying in the street?"

"No. Sartol wrapped them in blankets and tied them to his saddle. I think he plans to destroy them."

Baden began striding back toward Watersbend. "We need more proof of what you've told me! We need at least one of those birds!"

Orris caught up with the Owl-Master and grabbed his arm. "We can't, Baden! He'll notice! He'll figure out that I'm here and that you've escaped!"

"But that eye isn't going to be enough to convince the others!"

"It convinced you!"

"Yes," Baden conceded, "but only because I saw the outlanders use their weapons after I killed their birds. Sartol has witnesses who will swear that I tried to save those men. We need something just as convincing."

Orris could think of no reply. Baden was right.

Suddenly, the Owl-Master looked up into the night sky. "Anla!" he said aloud. And the next moment Baden's round-headed owl glided out of the darkness and alighted on the lean mage's shoulder. Baden stroked the bird's chin for a moment and then looked at Orris, his pale eyes intent. "Are you coming with me?"

"All right," Orris agreed reluctantly, "we'll take one of the birds. But does this make us allies?"

The Owl-Master looked at Orris for some time. Then he nodded. "I guess it does." He ran a hand through his thinning orange and silver hair. "I know that our interaction has never been easy, Orris. You think me overly complacent, and I see you as rash and impudent. But we can't allow those feelings to obscure the more important issues. Tobyn-Ser is in grave danger, and you were right when you said during the Gathering that the Order has grown weak and passive. If we expect the rest of the Order to act as one, you and I will have to put aside our differences. We share a common link, you and I: our friendship with Trahn. He trusts you, he respects you, and, even when Sartol accused you of treason, he maintained his faith in you. Along with Jaryd, there is no person in this land who means more to me than he does, and if he thinks so highly of you, there must be a reason." He glanced back toward the devastated town.

"Sartol has got to be stopped, and I think that it falls to you and me to stop him."

Orris grinned savagely. "That would give me more pleasure than you could know." Then his expression sobered. "Even when I felt certain that you and Sartol had conspired together," he went on, "your friendship with Trahn gave me pause. I respect him a great deal. I'm glad to know of his regard for me and his faith in my loyalty, even in the face of Sartol's lies. And, if you'll join me in fighting the traitor, I'll gladly accept that I was wrong about you."

Baden nodded and gave a relieved smile. But in that moment, they both heard a sudden cry of alarm go up from the town.

"I don't like the sound of that!" Baden said, crouching down in the grass.

"Someone must have found the guards," Orris ventured, also ducking, and concealing his ceryll. "It won't be long before they start looking for us."

"Fist of the God!" Baden spat. "We need one of those birds!" He shook his head. "How could they have found them so quickly? Who would have gone to the jail?"

And in that moment, as if in answer to his question, the mages heard the drumming of hoof beats on the prairie. Peering up over the tall grass and looking to the north, past the charred remains of Watersbend's farmhouses, they saw a pale yellow ceryll retreating rapidly into the night.

"Sartol!" Orris said, somewhat unnecessarily. "I didn't think he was planning to leave until morning."

But Baden nodded. "Of course," he said, "I should have known. He couldn't risk letting me live through the night," he explained, turning to Orris. "I might have convinced the guards that he was lying, or maybe he knew that I'd escape somehow. He had to kill me tonight." The Owl-Master paused and grinned. "You saved my life. Thank you." He looked northward again, his expression turning somber. "Sartol has everything: the strangers' birds and weapons, the staffs of the sage and first, and a town full of witnesses who think I'm a traitor." He gave a small, mirthless laugh. "He even has my ceryll."

"What now, Baden?" Orris asked quietly, his eyes still fixed on Sartol's yellow light.

"I'm not sure," the Owl-Master managed in a raw voice. "We don't have many options." Baden didn't elaborate, but he didn't have to. Orris understood. One of them had lost his familiar and the other his staff. Even if they chose to pursue Sartol they could do nothing to stop him.

"Maybe he overlooked something," Orris said, looking back toward the town center. "Maybe we can find some other bit of evidence."

"Maybe," Baden agreed. "But as you said a minute ago, they're going to be looking for us."

As if on cue, the mages heard voices coming from the town, and looking in that direction, they saw a mob of villagers moving in their direction. They were carrying torches and weapons.

Both of them crouched lower, and Orris glanced nervously at his horse. It wouldn't be long before the villagers noticed the animal standing there.

"Now what?" Orris whispered.

"I don't know!" Baden hissed in return. "Why do you keep on asking me?"

"Fine!" Orris shot back. "I'll decide!" He paused for several moments, considering their options. They didn't have many. "Maybe now would be a good time to circle back into town and search the street again," he finally suggested.

Baden shook his head. "How do we know there aren't more of them searching the town?"

Orris rolled his eyes. "That's why I keep on asking you!"

Baden actually laughed. "You're right," he whispered. "We'll circle back to the village."

Keeping low, and leading the horse carefully through the grass, the two mages made their way back to the town, giving the searchers a wide berth as they did.

They found the streets of the town deserted, which, Orris realized belatedly, should have come as no surprise. Watersbend had lost a great number of its people this night. The search party he and Baden had seen probably represented most of the town's surviving adults.

Orris brightened his ceryll slightly, just enough to allow him to scrutinize the blood-stained dirt of the street on his hands and knees. Without his ceryll, Baden was forced to use Anla's eyes, and he stood in the middle of the street, his eyes closed, as his owl scanned the area.

They found nothing near the bodies of the outlanders, and they moved quickly to where Baden's dead horse lay. Again, Orris saw nothing unusual. But just as he was ready to give up, he spotted something small and dark lying in the road. It was almost completely covered with dust, but Orris knew immediately what he had found: a small scrap of the strange black material from which the birds had been made. A corner of it had melted, but, otherwise, it was smooth and intact.

He called to Baden, raising his voice as much as he dared. The Owl-Master was at his side instantly, bending down to look at what Orris held.

"What is it?" Baden asked, picking it up out of Orris's hand and examining it in the amber light of the Hawk-Mage's ceryll.

"This is what the birds were made of," Orris told him. "In effect, this is one of their feathers. Feel how light and flexible it is."

The Owl-Master nodded, his eyes wide in the dim light of the ceryll. He examined it for some time, turning it over in his hands, and trying to bend and stretch it.

"It's not much," Orris admitted. "But with the eye, it might be enough."

"Maybe," Baden replied, sounding less confident than Orris would have liked. "We should keep looking."

Orris nodded and Baden placed the black shard in a pocket within the folds of his cloak. Then they resumed their search of the street. Unfortunately, however, they turned up nothing else that might help them.

"At least we found something," Orris commented, as Baden pulled the shard from his cloak to inspect it once more.

Baden shook his head. "I'm afraid it won't be enough. I've never seen anything like this, Orris," he admitted, holding up the strange scrap of material. "I won't deny that. And I don't question your account of what you saw. But we need to convince the Order, and that won't be easy. Not with

Sartol offering witnesses of my alleged betrayal. We want them to look at that golden eye, and this scrap of . . . of something, and see creatures that can think, see, and fly like hawks. That's an awful lot to ask."

"Perhaps," Orris conceded. "But we don't have much choice, do we?" He took a breath, his eyes boring into Baden's. He was losing patience with the Owl-Master, and he struggled to keep his anger in check. "I violated Amarid's Law for you, Baden. I threatened those men and locked them in a prison cell so that I could break you out of jail." Baden started to say something, but Orris held up a hand to stop him. "It was my choice, I know," he went on, "but I've cast my lot with you now. As an Owl-Master, you'll speak for us at our trial, and if you don't believe that we can convince them, we've already lost. So you have ten days, Baden—maybe a week, if we can find a second horse and get back to Amarid faster—to make peace with what we've got and to think of some way to make it convincing. You owe me that."

Baden glared at him, his pale eyes flashing angrily. But he said nothing for a long time, and he appeared to consider Orris's words. In the end, he merely nodded.

"We should go," Orris said, his voice less strident than it had been a moment before. "The villagers will probably be returning soon, and Sartol's got quite a head start on us."

Again Baden nodded, and with one last glance around them, the mages left the town center. They assumed that they would be safer on the far side of the river, but, just after crossing the stone bridge, they spotted the torches of the search party. The villagers were also on the west side of the river, searching the prairie. But they were far enough to the north that they did not appear to see the mages. Orris concealed his ceryll, and he and Baden, crouching low in the grass, continued westward, intending to circle around the mob before starting back toward Amarid.

They had gone only a short distance, though, when Orris, glancing back toward the town to check their progress, saw something so unexpected, and so glorious, that he nearly cried out with joy. On the other side of the river, three riders were approaching Watersbend from the south, all of them carrying cerylls, which glowed with familiar shades of russet, purple, and sapphire.

15

It had been a gamble. All three of them knew from the start that it would be. But for Alayna, still wary of Trahn despite Jaryd's assurances and the comforting manner of the dark mage, it had been an especially difficult risk to accept. Trahn only knew of Theron's Path from legend and rumor; he admitted this himself. No one had traveled to the Shadow Forest in hundreds of years, and no traders had visited the ports of Tobyn-Ser's southeastern extreme in nearly as long. Only Theron could have confirmed for them what they needed to know, and they could not spend another night in the grove.

Alayna had argued vehemently against taking the ocean route, but, in the end, compelled by Jaryd's fervor, and by her own recognition that it offered their only true chance of catching up to Baden and Sartol, she had acquiesced. Her misgivings, however, had lingered.

They had ridden due east through the Shadow Forest for only a few hours when they spotted the first gulls circling high overhead, and noticed the subtle scent of brine in the cooling air. Still, the dark tangle of the forest kept their progress slow. They emerged from the trees into the tall, coastal grasses late that first morning, and rode for yet another hour before reaching the pale sands and rough blue waters of Duclea's Ocean. In the distance, well past land's end, the dark clouds of the storm that had struck during the company's one night by Theron's Grove floated serenely just above the horizon. Closer to shore, seabirds wheeled and dove over the pounding breakers, squawking noisily and fighting among themselves for food. Stones and shells and tree limbs, worn smooth by the sand and the waves, littered the beach, and dried kelp stained the sand in a jagged line parallel to the surf that stretched in both directions as far as the eye could see.

For Alayna, who had grown up within a mile of the Abborij Strait, the sounds, sights, and smells of the coast brought back a flood of memories. She could see her mother and father pulling shellfish from the waters near her home, and she could hear her sister's giggles as the two of them played in the sand, or jumped waves together, hand in hand. And with these images from her childhood came a pang of homesickness that startled her with its intensity. She had left Brisalli to begin her apprenticeship with Sartol two winters ago and, since then, had not once felt nostalgic for her home. To be sure, she missed Faren and her parents, but, until this day, when she saw for the first time the southern shores of Tobyn-Ser, that had been the extent of it. Standing beside her horse, with Fylimar on her shoulder and her eyes focused on the distant clouds, she had shaken her head. At any other time, it might have been funny. But, at that point, in a part of the land that no human had seen in centuries, and with Sartol and Baden at least a day's ride ahead of them, she had known that she could not afford the luxury of these emotions. She quelled the recollections with a ruthlessness that she had not known she possessed. Later, she told herself, turning away from the ocean and stroking Fylimar's chin. I'll think about them later, when this is over.

They had rested there for but a few moments before remounting and driving their horses north along the hard, moist sand just beyond the reach of the tide. They had two extra horses with them, the stallions ridden to the grove by Jessamyn and Peredur, and so they changed mounts every few hours to keep the animals fresh. Even Jaryd, who had ridden only the gelding throughout the journey to the grove, bravely consented to ride the swifter, larger mounts in order to maintain their pace. For what remained of the day, they followed the meandering contours of the coastline, riding along the edge of the sea, and periodically crossing shallow rivulets where fresh runoff from the Shadow Forest completed its journey to the ocean. It was a beautiful ride, more lovely even than the two days the company had spent crossing the Parneshome Range just after leaving Amarid. But they had been unable to enjoy it, focused as they all were on finding Theron's Path.

Legends spoke of a narrow strip of beach running between Duclea's Ocean and the edge of the Southern Swamp. According to the old tales, this had been the route that young Theron had taken northward, in exile and bitterness, after being banished from Rholde. If it existed, the path would allow the three riders to reach Tobyn's Plain in less time, and with less difficulty than the route leading through the Shadow Forest and the swamp. In effect, Trahn had speculated, it could allow them to make up a half day's ride on Baden and Sartol, perhaps even more. Even if the stories were true, however, they had no guarantee that the path had survived the passage of so many hundreds of years. It could have been washed away gradually, by changes in tidal patterns, or it might have been destroyed by the violent storms that struck Tobyn-Ser's eastern shore each autumn. If any one of these possibilities turned out to be the case, they would have to cross the swamp at its widest point. Then, all hope of overtaking the Owl-Masters before they reached Amarid would be lost.

They pushed themselves and their mounts, desperate to reach the path before nightfall made finding it impossible. But as the day progressed, as their shadows and those of the trees to the west grew longer, slicing across the beach until they reached the foaming water, Alayna realized—all three of them realized—that their ignorance of this terrain ran even deeper than they had thought. By Trahn's calculations, they should have reached the swamp—and the path that would enable them to pass around it—by late afternoon. And yet, they continued to ride well past nightfall, guided by mage-light, their horses' hoof beats muffled by the sand and swallowed by the constant thunder and retreat of the waves. It was not until the waning moon appeared in the sky over the ocean, dusky and red, and little more than a crescent, that Alayna finally caught the foul odor of the swamp mingling with the salt-smell of the sea. At the same time, Trahn, riding ahead of the younger mages, raised his staff, signaling them to stop.

"Do you smell that?" he called over the pounding of the surf, and then, not waiting for a response, he added, "We've reached the swamp. We can rest here for what's left of the night. Tomorrow we'll see if the path has survived the last thousand years."

They swung off their mounts and led the animals to another of the freshwater streams that carved through the sand to the ocean. Then they gathered driftwood and built a fire, huddling close around it and wrapping themselves in their cloaks to guard against the cold, damp ocean air. They nibbled on some dry breads and cheese as they stared at the flames, but all three of them were too exhausted to eat more than a light snack.

At one point, Jaryd turned and stared into the night, as though straining to see the path in spite of the darkness and the mist that had begun to float in off the water. "How far ahead of us do you think they are?" he asked, his voice sounding small amid the sounds of the sea, and his brown hair stirring softly in the wind.

Trahn looked at the young mage for some time before answering. "It's hard to say," he conceded at last. "They left a full day before we did, and the turnings of the coastline have made our journey longer than I had anticipated. They will have had some delays as well, however; don't forget that. Crossing the forest and the swamp will have slowed them a bit. If we can find the path, and reach Tobyn's Plain tomorrow, I still believe we'll be able to catch them."

Jaryd nodded, but his gaze lingered on the northern sky. "Do you think that Baden is all right?"

The Hawk-Mage smiled. "Yes," he said without hesitation, "I'm sure that Baden is fine. I learned long ago that worrying about Baden is a waste of time, both because he can take care of himself, and because he's too stubborn to control."

Jaryd gave a small laugh, and glanced at his friend. "You should meet his brother," the young mage commented wryly. "They're quite similar, much more so than either one would care to admit."

"And are you like them as well?" Alayna asked teasingly.

Jaryd turned his body back to the fire and rubbed his hands together. "I'm more like my mother," he replied with a grin. "I'm not as overtly headstrong as Baden and my father, but I manage to get what I want anyway."

"That's even worse," Trahn commented, winking at Alayna.

She smiled, finding it increasingly difficult to distrust the dark mage. Jaryd smiled as well, but, almost immediately, his grin vanished, leaving a troubled expression on his boyish features.

"Sartol is very strong," he said to Trahn, echoing a conversation they had already had a number of times since leaving Theron's Grove.

Trahn placed a reassuring hand on Jaryd's shoulder. "I know. You've told me. And, frankly, the way you described your encounter with him left me somewhat frightened as well. But there isn't much that we can do about it right now. Besides," he added, trying unsuccessfully to smile, "Baden is powerful, too—perhaps he can't defeat Sartol, but certainly he's strong enough to escape from him if he has to."

Jaryd nodded. He had heard these assurances before, earlier in the day, twice as they rode and once as they rested on the sand. But Alayna understood his need to hear them again, and so, too, it seemed, did Trahn. The dark mage appeared more than willing to repeat himself on this matter, and Alayna once again felt her doubts and suspicions of the Hawk-Mage slowly fading. But while she relinquished them gladly, the obstinacy with which a remnant of this distrust persisted bothered her. She had always had a capacity for trust, even as a child. Where Faren was shy and withdrawn, Alayna had been outgoing and quick to make friends. She had never had a suspicious nature. But abruptly, in the wake of Sartol's betrayal, she had found herself questioning Trahn's loyalty, though he had done nothing to warrant her doubts. What bothered her most was not simply that she had been wary of the Hawk-Mage—actually, given all that had happened, that was excusable—but rather that it was becoming increasingly clear to her just how wrong she had been about him. She considered herself a good judge of people, and yet, Sartol had fooled her utterly. Had she not witnessed his attempt on Jaryd's life, had she not seen the malice in his eyes as he advanced on the two of them in the thicket by Theron's Grove, she would never have believed that the man she considered her closest friend could be a murderer and a traitor. She knew him too well, or so she thought. She had been a fool. And now she had been mistaken about Trahn as well. Where is my judgment? she had asked herself on more than one occasion throughout this day. Where are my instincts?

Worst of all, at times it made her hesitant about Jaryd as well. If Sartol had deceived her so easily, if she could fail to recognize the decency of Trahn's motives, could she also be wrong about her burgeoning relationship with Jaryd? It was not that she doubted his motives—even in her current state of mind, she could see that the young mage was incapable of duplicity. But she wondered if she had placed too much faith in what they shared, if she had been too quick in allowing herself to care about him as much as she did. She felt uneasy, as if she were a child again, venturing out too far on tree limbs that could not bear her weight.

She sensed her mood darkening—another product of recent events, it seemed, was the return of the deep mood swings she remembered from her early adolescence. When Jaryd and Trahn rose to gather more driftwood for the fire, she joined them, but she said nothing, and she would not meet either of their gazes. And during what remained of their meal, as Jaryd and Trahn talked about Theron, she continued to hold herself apart.

The older Hawk-Mage had what seemed an infinite number of questions regarding the unsettled Owl-Master's statements and appearance. Most of all, though, Trahn was fascinated with the staff that Theron had left for them, and he asked repeatedly to be allowed to see and handle it. Jaryd gladly indulged the Hawk-Mage's curiosity, enthralled to be carrying such a token. Alayna shared their excitement, but on this night, not even Theron's staff could shake her from her black mood. Fylimar flew to her shoulder from a nearby piece of driftwood and stretched out her neck for Alayna to caress. Smiling briefly in spite of herself, the young mage obligingly stroked the feathers on her bird's chin. But Fylimar's attempt to cheer her did little good. All Alayna could think about was Sartol, and the ease with which he had deceived her. She knew, as Jaryd had reminded her now on a number of occasions, that the Owl-Master had fooled all of them. But, considering how much time she had spent with Sartol over the last two and a half years, she, more than anyone else in Tobyn-Ser, should have known. And there was the other sign she had gotten, the one that should have told her of Sartol's treachery, the one of which Jaryd knew nothing. Oh yes, she should have known. At least this is what she told herself as she stared at the fire, and maintained her self-imposed exile, as if by punishing herself she might make things all right.

After a time, Trahn moved off a short distance and lay down to sleep. Again a kind gesture from the Hawk-Mage—leaving Jaryd and Alayna to enjoy both the fire and their privacy. He deserved better than her cold silence. So, too, did Jaryd, who moved closer to her now, sitting on the sand beside her and staring, as she did, into the flames.

He remained still for a long time, and when at length he spoke, his words surprised her. Jaryd's instincts, it seemed, were perfectly intact. "I can help you with the pain you must be feeling," he offered gently. "If you and I are what I think we are, that's the least I can do." He hesitated, but only for an instant. "But you're going to have to overcome the self-pity and self-doubt on your own. I can tell you that I respect your judgment, that I see your wisdom;

I can tell you that I'm starting to fall in love with you. But in the end, all that means very little if you can't respect yourself."

It was not that he had said the wrong thing. She realized this later that night, long after she had driven him away, as she lay in the dark listening to the ocean and trying to stop the steady flow of her tears. Indeed, just the opposite was true. He had hit too close to the mark, had divined her thoughts all too well. And, of course, there was the other thing, the words that had made her pulse leap just when she needed desperately to feel that she had control over her emotions. It was not his fault at all. Nonetheless, her response, when it finally came, had been meant to wound.

"Regardless of what you think you know about me," she asserted coldly, "the only thing I've come to question is whether I've been too quick to trust people about whom I really know very little. Including you. Especially you."

He stared at her for but a moment before standing and saying in an even tone, "I'm sorry you feel that way; I had thought we'd moved beyond that." Then he walked off into the darkness to sleep, leaving her alone with the fire, her melancholy, and her self-doubt.

She slept fitfully that night, waking with the silvery light that came before dawn, to grey skies and a cold, penetrating fog. Trahn was already up, sitting with his back to her and gazing pensively to the north, his long, black hair untied and falling loosely around his shoulders.

"If the path isn't there," the Hawk-Mage whispered, not looking back at her, but aware, somehow, that she had awakened, "there will be nothing at all that we can do."

She did not know what to say. She felt disoriented, emotionally drained from her exchange with Jaryd the night before. She still felt the hurt of what Sartol had done, and, while she had finally begun to trust Trahn, she knew him only slightly, having spent little time with him prior to this journey. Glancing at Jaryd, who slept still, lying in the sand a few yards away—not nearly as far from her as it had seemed last night—she offered the only reassurance she could. "Jaryd hasn't doubted for an instant that we'll find a coastal route as you promised," she said quietly.

Trahn turned at that, a smile on his lips, and said in a gentle tone, "I hope someday to have such trust from you as well. If you and he are to be together, you and I will have to be friends."

Alayna looked away, turning her eyes back to Jaryd, whose face appeared at this moment so young and untroubled. *If you and he are to be together . . .* There was nothing she wanted more than that. Until last night, in spite of everything else that had happened since the company's departure from Amarid, Alayna had felt a contentment and excitement that she had never known before, all of it due to the young Hawk-Mage and the feelings they shared. But, looking at the young mage now, hearing again and again in her mind the words with which she had purposely hurt him, she feared that she had destroyed their life together before it had begun. She felt ill, she wanted to cry, and, once again, she did not know what to say to Trahn.

Instead of responding to his comment, she rose quickly, and, mumbling something about needing to wake herself with a bath, ran to one of the fresh-water streams and followed it back into the woods for a short distance. There, she undressed and plunged into the clear, frigid water, scrubbing furiously at her scalp and skin, as if she could wash away the memory of what she had done.

After a few minutes in the bracing cold, she stepped out of the water and stood shivering in the fog. It had not been, she thought ruefully, the smartest thing she had ever done. She had no change of clothes, no cloth with which to dry off. And so, with her teeth chattering, and her lips, no doubt, turning as blue as Jaryd's ceryll, she waited for the air to dry her skin. She had not dried off entirely when she finally dressed. Nonetheless, though still cold, she realized that her bath had improved her mood somewhat. It certainly had woken her up. Returning to the camp, with Fylimar gliding overhead, she saw that Jaryd was up, and that he and Trahn had rekindled the fire. Seeing her approach, Jaryd brought her a cup of some steaming liquid.

He handed it to her wordlessly, and then they started back toward the fire. Alayna wrapped both of her hands around the cup, feeling the warmth flow into her fingers and palms. From the sweet, cool fragrance of the steam that caressed her cheeks, she knew, before Jaryd told her, what the vessel contained.

"Shan tea," he said quietly, his grey eyes meeting hers for only an instant before looking away. He gave a wan smile. "Trahn's been holding out on us; seems he has a full pouch of the stuff."

"Thank you for bringing it to me."

He nodded, gazing at her again for just a moment. Then he moved away.

She sat down beside the fire and stared out at the ocean. Even without looking at him, she was aware of Jaryd's every move as he and Trahn prepared breakfast and then readied the horses for the day's ride.

The three of them ate quickly and then broke camp. All of them seemed impatient to be moving again, and anxious to see if the path existed. Almost as soon as they began riding, the odor of the swamp grew stronger, but, while the forest ahead of them and to the west appeared to be thinning, the fog made it impossible to determine precisely where the trees ended and the quagmire began. Only when the first ripples of the foul mud appeared through the pale sand several yards ahead of them did they realize that they had reached the fen. There was no sign of Theron's Path.

They stopped, and Trahn dismounted, walking until the sand beneath his feet began to give way to the dark ooze. Bending, he picked up a fist-sized stone and tossed it into the mud. It struck with a sickening splat and sank several inches into the mire.

"The horses can't cross this," he observed in a flat voice, still facing away from Jaryd and Alayna. "And the path doesn't appear to exist anymore." He turned around and held out his hands in supplication. "Forgive me; I was wrong."

Alayna felt a cold clenching in her stomach. As her trust of the Hawk-Mage had grown, so, too, had her belief that they would find Theron's Path, until she had shed almost all her skepticism of the old tales. Faced now with swamp and ocean, and nothing between the two, she felt her mood of the night before descending upon her once again. Unable to meet Trahn's sorrowful gaze, and unwilling just then to look at Jaryd, she swung her eyes toward the ocean. And doing so, she saw the tide curling in upon itself strangely several yards beyond land's end. She smiled, entertaining another memory from her childhood, and then she swung her horse around to face her companions.

"You may not have been wrong after all, Trahn," she declared, pointing to the churning waters. "Look there."

Both men stared in the direction she indicated, but, from their expressions, she could see that neither of them understood.

"I don't know what I'm looking at," Jaryd admitted. "I can see that the tide—" He stopped and looked at Alayna, comprehension lighting his face as though the sun had suddenly melted away the mist. "It's shallower there!" he cried with excitement.

Alayna nodded. "My father calls them sandbars," she explained to Trahn, who still appeared confused. "The path still exists—perhaps at a lower tide it still looks just as it did when Theron crossed it—but, right now, it's partially submerged."

Trahn began to grin as he looked with wonder at the roiling water. "So it is still here," he breathed. He turned to Alayna. "I would never have seen this," he said. "Without you here to point this out, I would have been forced to brave the swamp. Thank you."

"You would have figured it out in the sunlight," she assured him. "The water would look much lighter over the path."

"Nonetheless," the dark mage commented, smiling broadly now.

Alayna glanced at Jaryd, who was also beaming at her from beneath the mist-dampened hair that clung to his brow. "Well done, Hawk-Mage," he said.

She was embarrassed, and just a little bit unnerved, by how much his smile and his praise meant to her. She grinned—she could hardly help it—and met his gaze steadily. "Thank you." She guided her horse closer to his. "Does this mean we're friends again?" she asked quietly.

"I never stopped being your friend, Alayna. And my feelings haven't changed overnight. But," he went on, his voice soft but earnest, "I can't do this alone."

Her eyes held his for a while longer as her grin slowly faded. Finally, she nodded. "I'll try," she promised him. "Believe it or not, I have been trying."

She had expected him to laugh at that, or to challenge it. Instead, he just nodded. "I know you have."

Trahn had drifted off a short distance to let them speak, but now he drew nearer again. "I know that I don't have to remind either of you, but we do have need of haste. And I have no idea how to navigate a sandbar."

Alayna smiled. "Then follow me," she told him, spurring her mount into the waves. Almost immediately the water reached up to her horse's shoulder and darkened Alayna's cloak to her thigh. But, though she sensed her mount growing nervous with these initial steps, she soon guided the animal onto the strip of sand. It was surprisingly firm, and, once they were on it, the water barely reached the animal's shins. Turning to look behind her, Alayna saw Jaryd and then Trahn follow her onto the sandbar, and the three of them began to gallop past the swamp. To anyone watching from the shore, Alayna knew, they would have appeared to be riding on the surface of the ocean. But there was no one on the shore, and there had not been anyone for hundreds of years.

Their journey along the path went smoothly, although, once again, the distance proved much greater than they had anticipated. The three mages rode in silence, accompanied only by the rhythm of the surf, and the sound of their horses' feet splashing noisily in the shallow water, or, in those portions where the ocean tides had not covered the path, drumming on the damp sand. They switched mounts regularly, but, with barely enough fresh water for themselves and the animals, they had to keep their pace relatively slow. Early in the afternoon, when the sun began to burn off the cloud cover and mist, warming the day considerably and adding to the horses' fatigue, they were forced to slow their gait even more. While Trahn had tried over the last two days to ease Jaryd's concerns about Baden, the dark mage was obviously frustrated and discouraged by their slow progress. He rode in front, his green eyes fixed on the northern horizon, as if he might will Tobyn's Plain to appear and end their ride on Theron's Path. Jaryd chafed at their slow pace as well, riding at the rear and staring blindly at the sea, his concern for Baden manifest in his tanned face.

Riding between the two of them, Alayna concentrated on the movement of her horse, trying to forget about Baden and Sartol, and the attacks on Tobyn-Ser, just for a short while. But it soon became clear to her that such comfort was beyond her reach. Indeed, as she gazed absently at the shifting waters of the ocean, she found that she could not chase the image of Sartol's face from her mind. She summoned a vision of her family and of Brisalli, but he was there, charming her with compliments, and predicting that she would someday join the Order. She tried to think about Jaryd and her relationship with him, but all she could see was the young mage's face twisted with fear and pain as Sartol tried to kill him.

Everywhere she turned, Sartol appeared with his ingratiating smile and his disarming air, until she could no longer fight it. Jaryd was right: until she conquered her doubts and demons, she wouldn't be able to get past them. And so, riding on Theron's Path in the heat and the glare, she stopped running, and turned her mind's eye to face the Owl-Master.

The day before, as the three of them had ridden along the beach, she and Jaryd listening to Trahn as he told the story of Theron's Path, Alayna had found herself reflecting on how thoroughly her perception of Theron and his curse had changed in the past few days. The people of Tobyn-Ser viewed the Owl-Master as a monster. She herself had until just a few nights ago. But she understood him better now. He had been a man, no more and no less. He had power, to be sure, but, in the end, he had been done in by his human failings: arrogance, pride, envy. And she wondered if the land would ever forgive him. This thought, naturally, had brought her to Sartol, and the pain of his betrayal, which was still a raw wound on her heart. She had wondered if she would eventually come to accept that his treachery had likewise been a product of his humanity; if she would someday find it within herself to forgive him as well. Were not ambition and greed as much a part of the human condition as those faults she now found herself able to forgive in Theron? Now, though, as she embraced her anger and her resentment at his duplicity; as she allowed her hatred for what he had become and what he had done to consume her, she realized that forgiving him was not the issue—had never been the issue.

As Jaryd had seen, and had tried to tell her, she needed to forgive herself. And recognizing this, she laughed, inwardly, at her own sense of self-importance. Sartol had not simply betrayed her, or even the Order. He had betrayed the entire land—from what Theron had revealed to them, his actions had aided an enemy who threatened to destroy all of Tobyn-Ser. The enormity of what he had done, of what he was trying to do, staggered her. And it made her recent inner turmoil seem selfish and vain. She could not say that the recognition of this lightened her mood, or even that it lessened the hurt she still felt from Sartol's deception. But it did strengthen her resolve, and it made the rest of their ride along Theron's Path somewhat easier for her.

The sun had disappeared below the western horizon, and the sky had begun to darken when finally the mages reached the end of the path and steered their weary horses onto the dry sand that bordered Tobyn's Plain. Trahn had spotted the prairie grass nearly an hour before, praising Arick and Tobyn for their kindness and allowing himself his first smile since the sun had emerged earlier in the day. Jaryd, too, had emerged from his dolor, and had started to calculate out loud how much distance they had covered, and how much time they might have gained on the Owl-Masters. For her part, Alayna remained silent. But she allowed herself a grin and, glancing back at Jaryd, was pleased to see him gazing at her, a gentle smile tugging at the corners of his mouth.

They camped on the beach again that night, leaving the horses to rest in a large patch of grass. And, while the animals drank long and deep from another of the small streams that flowed into the sea, they showed no other ill-effects from their harrowing day. The mages lingered by the stream as well, fully slaking their day-long thirst and refilling their water skins before making preparations for dinner. Their supplies of dried foods nearly depleted, the three mages sent their familiars to hunt for them. Still, while Alayna savored the meal that Fylimar brought to her, she knew that they would soon have little choice but to visit a town or village to replenish their store of fruits, cheeses, and dry breads. It made her nervous; she did not relish the idea of facing another angry mob.

Once again, Trahn retired early, leaving Jaryd and Alayna to enjoy in private the fire and the cadence of the waves. For some time, they did not speak. Alayna watched the stars brightening in the night sky, and Jaryd played with the fire. At length, however, the young mages found themselves gazing at each other across the dancing flames.

"I'm sorry about last night," Alayna finally told him in a hushed voice. "You were right to say what you did. I thought about it today while we were riding, and I started to understand what you were telling me. I shouldn't have reacted the way I did."

"You don't have to be sorry," Jaryd replied.

"Yes, I do," Alayna insisted. "But I still think I should have known about Sartol."

"Alayna—"

"No," she said, stopping him with a shake of her head. "Listen to what I have to say." She paused, gathering herself. "I should have known because in one of the visions I had of you, you were fighting Sartol."

"What!" Jaryd breathed.

She nodded.

For several moments, Jaryd said nothing. Alayna felt herself growing frightened. Perhaps now he would think she was to blame.

But as he had so many times before, Jaryd surprised her. "A vision like that could have meant a number of things," he told her at last. "There was no reason for you to take it literally. In fact, for all you knew at the time, I might have been the traitor. I still don't think you should be blaming yourself. As I said before: Sartol fooled all of us."

"But nobody else knows him as well as I do."

"I don't think anybody really knows him, Alayna. Besides, he did more for you than he did for anyone else in Tobyn-Ser: he taught you the ways of the Order, he helped you master the Mage-Craft, he gave you your cloak and your ceryll. Of all of us, you had the least reason to suspect him."

"Do you really mean that?" she asked, wanting desperately to believe him.

He nodded. "Yes, I do."

She stared at the fire, considering what Jaryd had said. "Thank you," she murmured. "That helps."

By way of reply, Jaryd placed another piece of driftwood on the fire and moved over next to where Alayna sat. He took her hand and gazed into her eyes. "I also meant what I said last night," he told her quietly, "about falling in love with you."

She smiled; she couldn't help but smile. "Good," she whispered. "I'd hate to be doing this alone."

He started to say something else, but she placed a finger over his lips, and kissed him.

She had, of course, kissed other men in her life. One of them, briefly, before she left Brisalli, had been her lover. But only now, feeling Jaryd's lips on hers, feeling his warm hands on her neck and cheek, did she understand that she had never loved before. It differed from what she had expected. It was not that there was no passion. Quite the contrary: she had no illusions as to where this kiss would have led them had Trahn not been sleeping only a few yards away. But there was so much more. She felt that there was a tide within her, moving with the power of the moon and the ocean and the Goddess, who had bound them together, rising, cresting within her heart until she thought that she must weep, or laugh, or both. She felt her world shifting, remaking itself; holding on to all she was and all she had known, but creating a space within these things for this man she was holding in her arms, so that he might share it with her, bringing to it all that he was and all that he had known. And in that instant, in the eternity of that kiss, Alayna knew, with a joy that she found frightening even as it encompassed her, that her life would never again be as it had been.

Wrapped in Jaryd's embrace, her head resting on his chest, Alayna fell asleep listening to the sound of his heartbeat through his cloak. She slept better than she had in weeks, waking only once, when he stirred, to turn her head, as in a dream, and find his lips waiting for hers. She remembered the kiss, but nothing else, and she knew that, somehow, it had carried them both back across the threshold between awareness and slumber. When next she opened her eyes, the sun was emerging from Duclea's Ocean, casting a rich, golden light over the sand and the prairie grasses that swayed delicately beyond the beach. They rose quickly, ate a light breakfast, and were soon riding again. The horses seemed well rested and fully recovered from their day on Theron's Path. And Alayna realized, almost as soon as they started riding on Tobyn's Plain, how much even the firmest sand of the beach had slowed their progress and increased the burden on their mounts. Drumming across the prairie, the wind whistling in her ears and the tall grasses whipping at her feet and legs, she could sense the animal beneath her moving with a joy and abandon that it had lacked the past two days, as though it had been newly released from some form of captivity.

All through the day they rode, speeding across the level terrain as the sun turned its slow arc over the vast ocean of swaying grass that ran away from them in all directions. By mid-afternoon they had come within sight of the Moriandral, which cut a wide, meandering path through the landscape, and they began to angle slightly to the west, so that they might follow its path and camp that night along its banks. They paused to rest and switch horses periodically, but never for very long. Having reached the plain, and having allowed themselves to believe that they now had a chance to intercept the Owl-Masters before they reached Amarid, the three mages found themselves unwilling to tarry. More than that, all of them suddenly seemed to have more endurance, as if they had willed themselves to grow stronger. They ate a substantial meal late in the day, finishing off the last of their food. Tomorrow, they promised each other, they would find a village in which to trade for additional supplies. Until then, the river and their familiars would provide for them.

Night fell, and still they rode, lighting the prairie with their cerylls: russet, purple, and sapphire. Though she had ridden since she was but a girl, and felt comfortable with horses, Alayna had not yet grown accustomed to riding after dark, by mage-light. Hence, she had her eyes fixed on the ground just in front of her when Trahn abruptly raised his ceryll and tugged his mount to a halt.

"Did you see that!" he asked excitedly, as he scanned the night sky.

"I saw nothing," Jaryd admitted. "I'm just trying not to kill myself with a fall."

Trahn turned and looked at Alayna, a question in his clear, green eyes.

She shook her head with regret. "I was watching the ground as well. I'm sorry. What was it that you saw?"

"A flicker of light," the Hawk-Mage said, facing forward again. "In truth, it could easily have been lightning from a storm or—"

This time Alayna did see it, as did Jaryd, judging from his sharply taken breath.

"There!" Trahn exclaimed, stabbing a rigid finger northward. "Surely, you saw it that time!"

Alayna nodded.

"Yes," Jaryd confirmed, as he stared at the sky, "but I didn't see any storm clouds today."

"Nor did I," Trahn agreed. He paused, turning once again to look at Jaryd. "That could be mage-fire."

Jaryd met the dark mage's gaze. "Baden?"

Alayna had not taken her eyes off the northern sky, and now, as she continued to observe the strange flashes of light, she also noticed that the horizon was brightening with an ominous orange glow. "Look!" she commanded, her voice tinged with alarm.

"Trahn, is there a town or village in that direction?" Jaryd asked with intensity, as he looked at the fiery light.

"Several," the mage replied soberly, "on both sides of the river. The largest of them is Watersbend. You believe that's where they are?"

"If you mean Baden and Sartol, I'm not certain. But somebody's there— and I think the town might be under attack."

Trahn shot Jaryd a look, and then all three mages spurred their mounts forward.

They had rested not too long before, and, in the crisp night air, they were able to maintain a swift pace. Still, the mages had been more than ten leagues to the south of the flames when they first saw them, and, as the flashes of light continued, Alayna cursed the distance with a vehemence that would have shocked her mother. Perhaps a half-hour after they beheld the first volleys of light, Alayna saw the sky before them illuminated again, with flashes that seemed brighter than the others, although that could have been a product of the distance they had already covered, rather than a quality of the light.

"That was mage-fire!" Trahn shouted over the thundering of the horses, and the rush of the wind. "It had to be!"

The horizon seemed to flicker a few more times, and then the bursts of light ceased entirely, leaving only the consistent, sinister gleam of what Alayna knew now had to be fires—a great many of them, she thought despairingly. They galloped on without pause, driving their horses mercilessly for nearly two hours more before spotting the smoldering buildings and battered homes. As they drew closer to the besieged town, Alayna could make out the contours of the huge, dark cloud of smoke gathering in the sky above it. And even as the glow of the flames gradually diminished, the billowing shadow continued to expand.

By the time the three mages reached Watersbend, most of the fires had burned themselves out, leaving large mounds of embers that glimmered angrily in the darkness. The streets were empty and silent, and the windows of those houses that remained standing showed no light. The mages dismounted and walked slowly up the central street of the village, inspecting the damage and looking for some clues that might tell them who had been responsible for the destruction, and who had prevented the attackers from razing the rest of the town. The first thing they found froze Alayna's blood, and left all of them shaken and speechless. In the middle of the roadway, its chest and shoulders blackened and bloody, lay Baden's horse. Its saddle and saddlebag had been removed; none of Baden's belongings could be seen on or near the animal.

But with its chestnut body and black mane, and the crescent-shaped patch of white on its nose, there was no mistaking it. It was the Owl-Master's mount.

"What do you think it means?" Jaryd asked at length, his voice thick.

Trahn shook his head, unable to look the young mage in the face. "Truly, Jaryd, I don't know."

"It means nothing," Alayna declared with conviction. "At least for now, it means absolutely nothing." She looked at Jaryd intently, holding his gaze until, at last, he nodded weakly in agreement.

They moved on, coming a few moments later to two bodies, charred beyond recognition, that had been left untended in the street. Squatting down to view them with more care, Trahn exhaled through his teeth.

"Do you think it's Baden and Sartol?" Jaryd asked, looking over the mage's shoulder at the grisly sight.

Trahn shrugged. "It's hard to say. For all we know, they could be the only two victims of the attack, left here by the townspeople until tomorrow. But," he added quickly, assessing the devastation that surrounded them, "that seems unlikely. I'm more inclined to think that these two either attacked the town or intervened to save it."

Alayna shuddered as she looked down on the corpses. "I'd much prefer to believe the former," she said.

"As would I," Trahn concurred.

The dark mage stood and again they continued along the street. As they moved northward, the level of destruction increased dramatically. Smithies and storefronts lay in blackened, splintered ruins, and blood stained the dirt on which the mages walked. But, other than Baden's horse and the two bodies, any victims of the attack had been removed from this part of the village. Soon, the wrecked storefronts of the village square gave way to demolished homes, burned fields of crops, and slaughtered farm animals. And, finally, most horribly, the mages came to an open field at the northern fringe of the village, where they found the dead human victims of the night's violence. Obviously, they had been carried there by the surviving townspeople, who had arranged the bodies with what could only be described as loving care, in column after column after column. There were literally hundreds of them, adults and children, lying beneath the stars, mutilated and burned, some of them missing limbs, many as unrecognizable as the two in the village square, and all of them beyond help. Absorbing the appalling scene, unable to avert her eyes, Alayna felt her stomach heave. Dropping to her knees, her body racked with convulsions, she retched uncontrollably until her stomach was empty. Jaryd had spun away from the nightmarish scene, and was weeping, but Trahn merely stared at the carnage, his dark face as rigid and cold as obsidian.

"Come," he said finally as he turned away, his taut, controlled voice more terrible even than the bleak expression on his face. "We can do nothing here."

Jaryd helped Alayna to her feet and gathered her in an embrace that felt both tender and fierce, as if he sought from it the strength he would need to wreak his revenge on those who had done this. Then he took her hand and they followed Trahn back toward the center of the village. Before they reached the last of the still-smoldering farmhouses, however, they spotted a large group of men and women, many of them carrying torches, and all of them carrying axes, pitchforks, and other makeshift weapons. These people appeared to have seen the mages as well, for the mob now moved toward Alayna and her companions.

"Are you the ones the Owl-Master mentioned?" a bald, bearded man asked as the crowd reached them. "Have you come for the traitor?"

Alayna felt her heart jump and she glanced quickly at Jaryd. The young mage was staring at the man, his face looking pale in the torchlight.

"We weren't sent by anyone," Trahn replied at last. "But we probably know the Owl-Master of whom you speak. What's his name?"

The man furrowed his brow and looked at a woman who stood beside him, a question in his eyes. She shook her head. "I don't know," the man said, facing Trahn once more. "He killed the men who attacked our town, and," he added, indicating a long, dark mark on his forearm, "he healed our injuries. But he never told us his name."

"I am Mage Trahn," the dark mage offered. "With me are Mage Alayna and Mage Jaryd."

"I am Wenfor, leader of Watersbend's town council."

"We are honored, Wenfor," Trahn returned, his voice sounding tight, though he smiled at the man. "We've been looking for an Owl-Master, and we believe he may have come this way. Perhaps you can describe for us the man who healed you."

Wenfor nodded. "That I can do. He was tall and powerfully built, with dark hair and a kind face."

The image that flashed in Alayna's mind as the man described the Owl-Master triggered a thousand memories, all of them shaded with the now-familiar sting of friendship betrayed. "Sartol," she said, although she realized only when the man looked at her that she had spoken the name aloud.

"So you do know him," Wenfor observed, smiling at them.

"Was there another Owl-Master with him?" Jaryd asked, ignoring the man's comment. "Also tall, though leaner, with orange and silver hair?"

The man narrowed his eyes warily. "You know him, too, do you?" he replied.

"You've seen this man?" Trahn asked quickly.

"Sure. He's the traitor. We're looking for him now, him and his friend."

"What friend?" Trahn demanded, his tone growing increasingly urgent.

"He was a mage, too," came another voice. A lean man, with dark eyes and wild dark hair, stepped forward out of the crowd. "He was stocky and muscular. His hair was long and yellow, and he had a beard."

Orris, Alayna said to herself. He survived his encounter with Sartol. Arick be praised.

Trahn turned back to Wenfor. "You believe this man to be a traitor as well?"

"We know he is," the man replied. "He helped the tall man escape from our jail."

Trahn let out a slow breath. "When did all this happen?"

"Just tonight, in the last hour or so," Wenfor told him. "When your friend—Sartol, was it?—when he learned of the traitor's escape, he told us that he needed to hurry back to the Great Hall and alert the rest of the Order. But he told us that he would send mages back to retrieve the traitor and to escort the witnesses to Amarid. We assumed that we'd have to wait for these mages to come, but when I saw you, I thought that maybe—"

"Of course," Trahn interrupted. "We understand. But tell me: what witnesses?"

"All of us!" Wenfor replied, opening his arms wide. "Though I expect only a few of us will be needed for the traitor's trial."

Jaryd shook his head, as if unable to believe what he had heard. "You saw Baden . . . You saw him do something?"

"We saw him betray the land," Wenfor said coldly. "The Owl-Master raised his staff to kill our attackers, and the traitor tried to stop him. Fortunately, the Owl-Master was too strong for this Baden, and he killed the renegades anyway."

Jaryd started to say something else, but Trahn stopped him, placing a hand on his shoulder. "So now you're searching for the traitor and his friend?" the dark mage asked evenly.

"Yes," Wenfor answered, eyeing Jaryd, his manner a bit more reserved than it had been a few moments before. "The Owl-Master said that it would be safe. The traitor has no staff; the Owl-Master took it when we first arrested him. And the Owl-Master told us that the Hawk-Mage's bird is dead."

Trahn glanced at Jaryd and Alayna, his expression grim. "What else did he tell you?" he demanded, turning back to Wenfor.

Wenfor straightened and looked at the three mages defiantly. "He told us to find the renegades and return them to the jail," he replied. "And, failing that, he said to kill them."

16

Seeing the deep blue of Jaryd's ceryll as the three mages rode into Watersbend, Baden knew a moment of elation and relief that he would not have believed possible just a short time before. For days, the merest thought of his nephew had carried with it the ache of losing him. He had tried to believe that Jaryd and Alayna had managed somehow to elude Sartol and survive the grove, but with each day that passed with no word from Trahn, a little bit of his hope had died. And now, feeling tears of joy roll down his cheeks, he realized that, at some point in the last day or two, he had given up.

"Come on," Orris urged, a rare smile brightening his features. "We have to find a way to get their attention."

Maintaining a safe distance between themselves and the villagers, who also appeared to have seen the riders, and who were now hurrying toward the stone bridge, Baden and Orris crept back to the river. They then moved northward, marking their friends' progress through the devastated town. They watched as the townspeople approached the three mages, and for a moment Baden feared that the mob would assume that they were traitors as well. That did not seem to be the case, however, and, after some time, the villagers doubled back toward the town center, leaving Jaryd, Alayna, and Trahn alone.

When he felt certain that the search party was far enough away, Baden closed his eyes and conveyed a single thought to Anla. Instantly, the owl leapt from his shoulder and glided across the river to where the mages stood. Trahn saw her first, stabbing a finger into the air to point her out to his companions, as the owl wheeled above them and started back toward Baden.

"Let them see your ceryll," the Owl-Master told Orris, his gaze still focused on the three mages.

Orris uncovered the crystal, brightened its glow, and raised it over his head for just a moment. Long enough, it seemed. Again Trahn pointed, this time right at them. Immediately, the three mages swung themselves back onto their mounts and rode to a narrow footbridge that crossed the river at the north end of the town. Moments later they were on the plain, thundering toward Baden and Orris.

Jaryd reached them first, throwing himself off his horse almost before the animal stopped moving, and enfolding Baden in an embrace so fervent that the Owl-Master actually gasped for breath. Baden and his nephew held each other for a long time, neither of them speaking. Baden heard Alayna and Trahn ride up and greet Orris, but, for the moment at least, he didn't care.

At length, Baden stepped back and regarded Jaryd wordlessly, grinning, he knew, like an idiot, and heedless of the bright tears welling in his eyes. "By the gods," he whispered at last, his voice rough, "this is a gift beyond my wildest hopes." He glanced at Alayna, who favored him with a dazzling smile and walked forward to clasp him to her. She released him a moment later, but Baden continued to hold her hand, and he took Jaryd's as well, as if by feeling their fingers on his, he might convince himself that this was not a dream. "I feared you were lost," he explained needlessly, "that Theron . . ." He shook his head, overwhelmed by his emotions. "I thought I'd lost you."

Jaryd was smiling broadly. He looked older than Baden remembered, although it had been only a few days; he looked taller, more poised. This is not the same boy I led away from Accalia all those weeks ago, Baden thought to himself, noting as well the magnificent hawk poised on the young mage's shoulder. Bernel and Drina should see him now. Again, the Owl-Master shook his head.

"We were worried about you, too," Jaryd told him. "At least I was," he amended, glancing sheepishly back at Trahn, who, typically, had said nothing, allowing Baden and Jaryd to savor their reunion.

Letting go of Jaryd and Alayna, Baden approached his friend, and they, too, embraced. "Thank you, Trahn, for bringing them back to me," the Owl-Master said after a moment.

Trahn stepped back and grinned. "I did nothing," he admitted. "They dealt with Theron on their own, and without Alayna I'd still be braving the swamp." He paused. "I'm glad to see that you're well, Baden." He looked at the burly mage. "And you, too, Orris. Despite my reassurances to Jaryd, I was concerned. Perhaps with good reason," he added, frowning at the cut on Baden's brow. "Can I heal that for you?"

Baden smiled. "Later, perhaps."

"You know that it was Sartol?" Jaryd asked, looking at the Owl-Master. "That he killed the sage and the first, and chased us into the grove?"

"Orris told me as much," Baden replied, "and I was starting to believe him." He hesitated, gazing at Alayna. "I can only begin to guess what you're feeling," he added in a more gentle tone. "I'm very sorry."

She offered a thin smile, but he could see in her dark eyes that the wound was still fresh. "Thank you," she murmured. She looked sidelong at Jaryd, and, as she did, her smile deepened, and Baden saw something else in her eyes; something that made him smile to himself. "Fortunately," she went on, "I haven't had to deal with it alone."

Baden glanced at Jaryd, seeing, even in the dim, strange light of their cerylls, that his nephew's face had flushed deeply. A teasing comment leapt to his tongue, but he kept it to himself.

The young mages turned to Orris, who had kept himself apart from the others, watching the reunion in silence. Jaryd, a soft smile touching his lips, took a step forward and placed a hand on Orris's broad shoulder. "You saved our lives, Orris. I'm certain of it. If you hadn't challenged Sartol when you did, he would have killed us before we reached the grove. Please accept my thanks, and know that I'm deeply sorry about your hawk."

"That's kind of you," Orris replied awkwardly, his voice subdued. "I'm glad to know that I helped. I feared that I was too late, that I had cost you your lives."

"No," Alayna told him. "Jaryd's right. You saved us. You gave us a chance to get away. If you've been reproaching yourself for what happened that night, there's been no reason." She stepped forward in turn, and kissed the Hawk-Mage on his cheek.

"Thank you," Orris muttered, his features reddening. He cleared his throat, as Baden and Trahn chuckled at his discomfort. After regaining his composure somewhat, Orris turned to Trahn. "I see that you recovered the horses."

Trahn grinned. "Yes, eventually. But it took me much of the day."

"I'm sorry," Orris said with a shrug. "It seemed a necessary precaution." Trahn nodded, and Orris turned to the young mages again. "I would very much like to hear how you escaped from Theron, and what, if anything, you learned from him. Baden and I have tidings to share as well. But I don't think this is the time or place."

"I agree," Baden said crisply. He looked at Trahn. "How did you leave things with the villagers?"

"We're helping them search for the traitor and his friend," the dark mage replied with an ironic grin. "But I fear we'll have little success."

Baden smiled. "Good. Go back into town and tell them you found nothing. Try to get a room at the inn for the night; you all look as though you could use some rest."

"What about you?" Jaryd asked.

"Orris and I shouldn't be within sight of the town when the sun comes up. We'll follow the river north two or three leagues and then find a place to sleep. You can catch up with us in the morning. You should see if you can get some supplies from the townspeople," he continued. "Make it clear that you're allied with Sartol. Even with the devastation they suffered, they should give you something." Trahn looked at Baden sharply, a question in his vivid green eyes. Baden nodded grimly. "I know: I'd rather not take anything from them either, not after what they've been through. Under normal circumstances I wouldn't. But I don't want to risk a confrontation with another village, especially if word spreads of what Orris and I did here tonight."

"Can we give you one of the extra horses?" Alayna asked.

Baden considered this for a moment and then nodded. "I don't think the townspeople will notice. And we'll make better time with two mounts."

He and Orris bade the others good night, and the three Hawk-Mages returned to the town, although not before Jaryd and Baden shared a second embrace. Baden and Orris then started northward along the banks of the river, moving on foot for the first mile or so, and then mounting and riding a few leagues more before stopping for the night.

Jaryd, Alayna, and Trahn caught up with them midway through the following morning. As Baden had anticipated, the townspeople had been more than willing to give the mages what food and wine they could spare, and the company now had at least some provisions for their journey back to Amarid. Jaryd and Trahn both seemed anxious to keep moving, but Baden assured them that, at this point, they had little need for haste.

"Sartol is going to get to Amarid first," he told them calmly. "There's nothing we can do about that. And I'm not sure that it matters."

"Do you have any idea what he plans to do once he gets there?" Trahn asked.

"I expect the first thing he'll do is accuse Orris and me of treason and murder," Baden answered. "After that I'm not sure."

"He can't really think he'll get away with that," Jaryd countered. "Nobody would believe him."

Baden grinned. "I'd believe him, given the evidence he has. Don't forget, Jaryd, he thinks that you and Alayna are dead, killed by Theron. As far as he knows, Orris is the only living person who saw what he did by the grove. And Sartol has three witnesses who saw Orris break me out of jail."

"But you both have friends within the Order," Alayna pointed out. "Do you think he can convince them?"

"It's possible," Orris told her. "Conspiracies have a way of frightening people, and all of us have antagonized our share of mages at one time or another. We have as many enemies as we have friends."

"I'm afraid Orris is right," Baden confirmed. "These attacks, coupled with the defacement of the Great Hall, have scared a lot of people. And Sartol can be very convincing; he's deceived all of us for many years." Alayna averted her eyes, and Baden felt a pang of sympathy for her. She blames herself, he realized. She thinks she should have known.

He considered saying something, but, even as he did, he saw Jaryd move to her side and whisper briefly in her ear; saw her smile and nod in response. They are building something there, he thought, something special. Again, the idea of it made him smile to himself. Despite the warnings he had offered to Jaryd at the Gathering, despite his own painful experience with Sonel, he could not help but be pleased for them, and moved by the happiness so manifest in

Jaryd's bearing. And seeing the two grey hawks that they carried, so much alike that they appeared to be mirror images of each other, Baden found himself wondering whether the lessons he had drawn from his own unsuccessful relationship would have any relevance for them. It almost seemed to him in that moment that the gods had marked them, one for the other, and he felt his joy for them colored by another sentiment, one he had not expected at all—one he had not felt in a very long time. He was envious. He nearly laughed aloud at the realization.

"I understand that we don't need to hurry back to Amarid," Orris commented, pulling Baden from his musings, "but I'd like to put some more distance between us and Watersbend."

"That seems wise," Trahn agreed. "The two of you made some enemies there last night. I'd be interested in hearing your side of what happened."

Baden grinned at his friend. "I'm sure you would." Briefly, he described for Trahn, Jaryd, and Alayna the previous night's events, although for now he said nothing about the alien birds, or the peculiar weapons carried by the attackers. That could wait.

"I observed all of this from a distance," Orris added after Baden finished his tale. "I still wasn't certain that I could trust Baden. And, with Pordath . . . gone, I would have been of little use to him in his battle." The Hawk-Mage's discomfort was evident in both his expression and the sudden constriction of his voice, but he pressed on. "I agree with Baden," he concluded. "The stranger recognized Sartol, and was about to speak to him when he died." Orris started to say more, but then he stopped himself, glancing at Baden.

"Didn't the townspeople see that, too?" Jaryd asked, showing no sign that he had noticed the look that Orris and the Owl-Master had shared.

"They might have," Baden told him, "but even if they did, it wouldn't have meant anything to them. Sartol killed the men who were destroying their village. He protected his secret, and made himself a hero. He also managed to make it seem that I was protecting the strangers."

"You make it sound like he planned it all so well," Alayna said. "It seems to me that he just made the best of an impossible situation. He may have silenced his allies, but he raised your suspicions, and Orris's."

"But you forget," Baden returned, a rueful smirk on his lips, "Orris and I are traitors; at least that's what he'll claim. Our suspicions are of no concern to Sartol. No, the only thing that diminishes the shrewdness of his actions is the fact that you and Jaryd survived the grove. Otherwise, his plan would have been perfect. Frighteningly so."

The others considered this for some time, but no one responded.

At length, Trahn stirred. "There's more to this tale, isn't there?" he asked, looking at Baden and then Orris.

Baden nodded. "Yes, there is. But I think it best that we save it for this evening. You and Orris are right: we should get moving."

They were riding again within a few minutes, the firm soil and open terrain allowing them to set a swift but sustainable pace. Baden's companions were in high spirits, obviously pleased to be together again, and for some time all five of them rode together. Soon, however, Alayna and Jaryd moved ahead of the others and Baden found himself riding alone, reflecting on a strange and disturbing dream that had come to him the night before.

Naturally, Baden had the Sight, and he had learned to recognize prophetic dreams when he had them. This, he had been relieved to know, had not been one. But it had begun with an image that Baden knew to be real, because Anla had conveyed it to him. It was her perspective of Watersbend as she flew across the Moriandral to draw the attention of Trahn, Jaryd, and Alayna. Beyond where the mages stood, past the blackened ruins of farmhouses and the smoldering remains of decimated crops, Baden saw, through Anla's eyes, row after row of the town's dead. At first, in his dream, the bodies just lay there beneath the starlit sky. But then Baden saw a figure moving among them, and he knew instantly that it was Sartol. The Owl-Master walked slowly from corpse to corpse, healing gashes and burns with a touch, making whole again bodies that had lost arms and legs, and restoring life to all of them, so that each time he moved to the next victim, the previous one rose and followed him.

At that point, Baden had awakened, his pulse racing and his cloak soaked with perspiration. Exhausted as he was from his harrowing night, the lean mage had managed, after some time, to fall asleep again. But this morning, when Jaryd and the others arrived, their saddlebags filled with the supplies given to them by Watersbend's people, the image of Sartol healing the dead had returned. In spite of the devastation of its homes and shops, in spite of the lives it had lost, Watersbend was the first town whose trust and support the Order had reclaimed from the suspicion sown by the attacks on Tobyn-Ser. And they had Sartol to thank. The Owl-Master had betrayed Tobyn-Ser to the outlanders; in a very real sense, he was as responsible for the deaths and devastation as the two men he had killed. But kill them he had, betraying them in turn, and saving what was left of Watersbend. And then he had healed the survivors, mending injuries that, in a way, he himself had caused, and the people had thanked him for it, their faith in the Order restored just a bit.

Riding on the plain in the bright midday sun, Baden found the bitterness of that irony too much to bear. Willing himself to shift his thoughts elsewhere, the Owl-Master glanced ahead and saw Jaryd and Alayna riding together, her long hair trailing behind her in the wind, and Jaryd's slender frame, more muscular than Baden remembered, appearing relaxed and comfortable on his mount. They said little, but occasionally they pointed out to each other distant villages, or hawks circling high overhead. Since his reunion with the young mages the night before, Baden had not seen them stray far from each other, and once more, the emotions this stirred within him were conflicted. He would never begrudge Jaryd and Alayna their happiness. Indeed, he reflected, given the future he had foreseen for Jaryd, and the one presaged by Alayna's first binding, their marriage might one day provide the Order with the most stable, powerful leadership it had known since Phelan.

But seeing them together also forced Baden to confront the painful and, he had to admit, questionable choices he had made in his own life. He had not been completely honest with Jaryd about his love affair with Sonel. Yes, it had ended badly, in part because of the difficulties inherent in a romance between two mages. But Sonel had been ready to commit herself to him. There had even been an opening for a mage in the southern part of Tobyn's Wood, where she served. Baden, however, had been unwilling to take that step. He was a migrant, he had told her and anyone else who would listen, he was not a nester; settling down would have gone against his nature. He realized a few years later how great a mistake he had made, but by then Sonel had married. After some time, they became friends again, but the shadow of what had happened between them continued to darken their friendship, even after her husband died.

He had been wrong to present his experience with Sonel as an example Jaryd should heed in his dealings with Alayna. For while he saw many of Sonel's qualities in the beautiful Hawk-Mage, he and Jaryd were quite different. Thinking this, Baden looked again at his nephew, noting the ways in which the young mage had changed since leaving Accalia. He was still quick to smile, and he still carried the warmth and the passion that Baden remembered. But the Owl-Master perceived in him now an awareness of the people around him, a sensitivity that he had lacked before. Regarding him as he rode, Baden recalled the afternoon when Jaryd first met Orris, in the corridor outside Jessamyn's chambers in the Great Hall. The boy had taken an instant and effortless dislike to the Hawk-Mage, a feeling that had been magnified during the Gathering by Orris's gruff manner. So Baden had watched with interest last night when Jaryd approached Orris and thanked him for saving his life and Alayna's, and the Owl-Master had been gratified to hear the warmth and compassion with which Jaryd expressed his sorrow for the loss of Orris's hawk. Baden had also sensed a change in Orris. Perhaps Jaryd had perceived this as well. As unlikely as it would have seemed just a few weeks ago, Baden saw the potential for a meaningful friendship between the two mages.

Gazing still at Jaryd and Alayna, listening to the easy laughter coming from Orris and Trahn, who were riding a few yards behind him, the Owl-Master wondered if it was possible for all that had happened since they set out for Theron's Grove—the murders of Jessamyn and Peredur, Sartol's betrayal, Pordath's death, the attack on Watersbend—to have strengthened them, to have brought them closer. Could it lift the lethargy that had covered the Order like a musty blanket for all these years, or was that too much to ask? He turned the question over in his mind for much of what remained of the day. He was too wise and too sensible to believe that these transformations alone would defeat Sartol and the Order's enemies, but the riddle itself provided a refuge from the darker thoughts that had haunted him throughout the day's ride. It was a distraction he welcomed.

They halted at dusk, setting up camp on a small rise in the middle of the prairie. Surrounded by the tall, wind-swept grasses, far from the Moriandral, which curved away to the west just above Watersbend, and just barely within sight of the Emerald Hills, which rose gently from the plain on the northwest skyline, the mages arranged themselves around a small fire and enjoyed the food and wine given to them that morning by the villagers. They ate slowly, at a pace that matched the comfortable speed at which they had ridden this day. Tomorrow, they would push themselves harder, but this had been a day, and now an evening, of relative, much needed rest.

As the last remnants of daylight faded, and stars began to brighten the night sky, their conversation turned finally to Jaryd and Alayna's encounter with

Theron. Together, the young mages recounted all that they had seen and heard, one picking up the narrative where the other left off, and each supplementing what the other said with forgotten details. They described for the other mages the soft, green radiance of the unsettled Owl-Master and his falcon, and the bright, angry glare of his emerald eyes. They told of being forced to spend the night in the grove, although both of them said little about what they encountered during their separate ordeals. Most important, and in the greatest detail, Jaryd and Alayna shared with the others the information that the ancient Owl-Master had finally offered during their second encounter. And Jaryd displayed the remarkable token that Theron had left for them.

Holding Theron's staff in his hands, examining the aged wood in the glow of the fire and mage-light, Baden marveled that such a thing could come to pass. How could this token exist in both the realm of the Unsettled and the world of the living? "You said he referred to himself as an incarnation of the Mage-Craft?" he asked, absently running a hand along the staff.

"Yes," Jaryd replied, "in fact, he described all the Unsettled that way. At one point he said, 'I am power itself,' or something along those lines."

"Do you know what he meant?"

Jaryd grinned and shook his head. "Our discussion wasn't going that well at the time. It didn't seem prudent to press the issue." He glanced at Alayna, who gave a small laugh.

"I'm more interested in what he told you about Sartol and the attacks," Orris broke in, smoothing his beard with a brawny hand. "He warned you about Sartol's strength?"

This time Alayna answered. "He told us that Sartol was dangerous, that he was more powerful than any mage since Phelan."

Baden looked up at that. He had gone for weeks without thinking about Phelan, and now, for the second time this day, the legendary Wolf-Master had entered his thoughts. He wondered if this meant something.

"But he also made it clear," Alayna continued, "that Sartol represented just a part of the threat we face, and that he wasn't even the most menacing of our enemies." She paused, as if reaching for a memory. " 'Even if you can defeat him,' " she quoted after a moment, " 'greater perils will remain.' "

Orris looked from Alayna to Jaryd. "The outlanders?"

Alayna nodded. "That was how I took it."

"Me, too," Jaryd confirmed.

" 'Their tactics reveal their weakness,' " Baden murmured, repeating what Theron had told the young mages.

Jaryd met his uncle's gaze, his lean face looking serious in the firelight. "That's what he told us. We guessed that since they were trying to undermine the authority of the Order rather than fighting us directly, their weakness lay in their inability to defeat the Mage-Craft."

"Did Theron confirm that?"

"To a degree," Alayna told him. "But when I asked him if they had power, he implied that they did, although not a power that we would necessarily recognize."

Baden glanced at Orris, and found that the Hawk-Mage was already staring at him. Jaryd must have seen this as well. "When Alayna and I told Trahn of

Theron's belief that outlanders had committed these attacks," the young mage said pointedly to Baden and Orris, "he was shocked. But it didn't seem to surprise either of you. Why? How did you know already?"

"We didn't know," Orris told him quietly. "We merely suspected. You verified it for us with your story."

"I told you about my battle with the men who attacked Watersbend," Baden explained. "But I neglected to mention what Orris found afterwards, when he examined their weapons and the birds they carried." And so it fell now to Orris to offer a tale of his own. At Baden's request, the Hawk-Mage also repeated his conversation with the Abboriji trader. Then, finally, in a voice tinged with regret and fear, Baden revealed that Sartol had carried off nearly every bit of the evidence Orris had found.

"You think he'll destroy it," Trahn ventured.

"I would," Baden said matter-of-factly, "were I in his position."

Alayna caught Orris's eye. "You say he took almost all. You still have some proof of what you saw?"

Orris looked at Baden, who nodded once, drawing a smile from the Hawk-Mage. Reaching into his cloak, Orris pulled out a small, glimmering circle of glass and precious metal. "Behold!" he whispered, holding it forth in the palm of his hand.

Not surprisingly, Jaryd was the first to perceive what he held. "The eye!" he said with excitement, turning quickly toward Baden. "That's the eye of the bird that I saw in my vision!"

The Owl-Master smiled. "And a powerful vision it was, Jaryd. More accurate than I ever would have believed possible. The cloak, the bird, even the ceryll and its color; all were just as you described them, except that there were two of them."

"Actually," Alayna commented, "according to Theron there are fifteen of them."

Orris's eyes widened. *"What!"*

Jaryd nodded. "It's true; I had forgotten. I asked Theron about my vision, and he told us that he had seen these mages as well. Mostly, they travel in pairs or singly. But, on one or two occasions, he saw sixteen of them. He said one of them had died since then, although he didn't know how."

Trahn exhaled through his teeth.

"At least now we know what we're dealing with," Baden observed. "There are thirteen more of them roaming Tobyn-Ser, all of them capable of doing to a village what was done to Watersbend last night."

"You believe they're from Lon-Ser, Orris?" Jaryd asked.

"Yes," the mage answered. "Given what Crob told me, it seems to make sense. They're definitely not from Abborij; I don't see where else they could be from."

Baden nodded gravely. "I'm inclined to agree."

Alayna ran her fingers through her dark hair in a nervous gesture. "We know so little about Lon-Ser," she commented, giving voice to something Baden had been thinking as well.

"We know more now than we did yesterday," Orris countered, his brown eyes appearing almost black in the firelight. "They have knowledge that allows them to create weapons that can replicate nature. It's a skill that goes far beyond anything we possess here in Tobyn-Ser." He looked around the fire, addressing the other mages as well. "We've believed for many years that Lon-Ser's artisans were the most skilled in the world—all the goods that came to us from Lon-Ser, by way of our trade with Abborij, seemed perfectly crafted. The precision of their workmanship almost defied explanation." He paused, his eyes now focused on the blaze in front of him. "But if they can replicate nature, it stands to reason that they can replicate craftsmanship as well. I would guess that whoever or whatever created the outlanders' birds and weapons has also been used to create their exported goods. It would explain a great deal."

"There's a word for such abilities in the ancient language," Trahn said in a hushed voice. "*Melorsiad*. It means, literally, 'false knowledge of life.' "

"Crob referred to it as *mechanization*," Orris added. "The use of tools to create other tools, which in turn create other tools. And when I was looking at the outlanders' birds, that was the first thing that I thought of. They were nothing more than tools. Advanced, yes, and designed to fool us into thinking that they were real. But, if you strip away the artifice, they're little more than a glorified hammer or plow."

"*Mechanization*," Jaryd repeated, the word coming awkwardly to his tongue. "I think I prefer *melorsiad*."

Orris grinned. "As do I. But, you see," he went on, turning to Alayna, "we do know something about them."

"We know that they have abilities that we can just barely comprehend," Alayna said a little desperately. "That doesn't make me feel much better."

"That's not all," Orris persisted. "We also know that they don't have magic as we know it, and that they need something from us urgently enough to resort to this elaborate plot."

Alayna stared at the fire, her frown like a dark gash across her face. "I suppose that's something," she said bleakly, "but it seems very little when compared with what they appear to know about us."

Once again, she was giving voice to Baden's thoughts. "Alayna is right," he said in a voice that was nearly lost within the sound of the wind moving across the prairie. "They know of the Order, of how we dress, of the objects and creatures that we carry. They planned their last three attacks so that a mage attending the Gathering would still have had an opportunity to commit them. They even knew enough to leave feathers."

"Surely, Sartol could have helped them with those details," Orris suggested.

"That's possible," Baden agreed. "Still, they knew enough about Tobyn-Ser to focus their efforts on destroying the Order's reputation and undermining its standing in the land. Even that would require far more knowledge of our land than we have of theirs." He looked at Orris. "I've come to the belated conclusion that you may have been right all along. The time has come for the Order to reestablish the psychic link. Tobyn-Ser has been invaded for the first time in four hundred years. And we let it happen."

The burly mage gazed back at him, his expression unreadable in the strange light of their circle. After some time, he nodded.

Jaryd poked at the fire with the branch he still carried, the one containing his vivid sapphire ceryll. "What if the others won't agree?" He glanced up at his uncle from beneath the thick shock of hair that fell over his forehead. "Naturally, I believe what you and Orris have told us, but what if the others don't? From what I saw at the Gathering, it takes a good deal to spur the Order to action. And that single glass eye may not convince some of the more intransigent masters. Do you have anything else?"

Baden reached into his cloak and pulled out the black fragment that they found when they returned to the town center. "We found this," he said, passing it to Jaryd. "It's a piece of the material of which the birds' feathers are made." He watched the shard make its way around the circle.

"It's unlike anything I've ever seen," Trahn conceded, "but I still agree with Jaryd's assessment of our position. I, too, have no doubt that what you've told us is accurate. But others may find it difficult to look at the glass disk and this dark scrap, and see replicated birds and flame-throwing weapons. That's an awfully long distance to travel on faith."

Baden gave a small, mirthless laugh and glanced at Orris. "I know. I'm counting on Jaryd and Alayna's presence, and the staff that they carry, to bridge that gap. If we can convince the Order of Sartol's guilt, and get them to listen to what Theron had to say, these fragments may be enough to do the rest." He shrugged, a gesture of resignation. "They'd better be; they're all we have."

Baden gazed up at the stars. Leora was dancing in the northern sky. He felt weary, as much from the evening's discussion as from his battle the night before and the many days of riding. "We should sleep," he commented. "Even though we've conceded that Sartol will reach Amarid before we do, we don't want to give him too much time to flood the Great Hall with his lies."

The others rose slowly, all of them obviously as fatigued as the Owl-Master. Baden, Trahn, and Orris arrayed themselves around the fire, while Jaryd and Alayna moved off several yards, seeking a bit more privacy. Despite his exhaustion, however, Baden found that the thoughts churning in his head kept him from falling asleep. He fought it for some time, but, realizing eventually that this was a losing battle, he turned over onto his back and stared into the night.

Sartol had probably reached Tobyn's Wood by now, he mused. He would reach Amarid within five days. What would he do then? The Owl-Master wielded tremendous power and possessed a keen intellect. But, in many ways, he represented the least of their worries. Even given his strength and his guile, he was but one man. If Baden and his friends could convince the Order of his treachery, they would be able to defeat him.

Sartol's allies, however, were another matter. "This is an adversary unlike any the Order has ever faced," Theron had told the young mages. "The Order will have to adapt. It will have to change." *Or it will perish*, Baden added, completing the thought. Jaryd and Alayna had not indicated that the unsettled Owl-Master concluded his warning in that way. But there could be no mistaking the implication. And Baden knew that, without the Order, Tobyn-Ser could not defend itself against the outlanders. That, of course, was the point. That was the purpose behind the attacks, the cause of the mischief that had become vandalism, that had, in time, turned to murder. Those who planned the attacks, whoever they were, possessed enough knowledge of Tobyn-Ser to recognize that they would have to vanquish the Order. So they had seen to it that the Order would have little or no support from the people of Tobyn-Ser.

Clearly, that was the strategy of these Lon-Ser "mages," and it was disturbingly clever. But what was their purpose? The Abboriji invasions had been simple, straightforward. They were territorial wars, nothing more, and certainly nothing less. As far as any of them knew, this newest threat might have been prompted by the same drive to expand. But Baden believed that there was more to it than that. The cunning and ruthlessness of this invasion—or, more accurately, of this infiltration—bespoke a darker, more sinister purpose. The Owl-Master had no notion of what it might be, only a strong, albeit vague sense that much more than Tobyn-Ser's territorial integrity was at stake. This war, if war it was, he understood somehow would be fought for the land's very existence.

He also realized that if the Order was to prevail, it would have to turn to younger leadership. Odinan and Niall and the other older masters had shown themselves to be too resistant to change. Under their leadership, the Order would fail, and Tobyn-Ser would be lost. Even Jessamyn would have been ill-suited to lead the Order into this conflict. It pained him to admit this to himself, but he knew it to be true. This was what Theron had been trying to say. And this was what Baden would have to make clear to the Owl-Masters when it came time to choose Jessamyn's successor.

He took a deep breath. It was late. The fire had burned down, and the other mages had long since fallen asleep. Leora's endless dance had carried her higher into the night, and Lon and Tobyn now stood below her, one facing west, the other looking to the east.

17

Standing on a stony crag in the Parneshome Mountains, with the sun warming his back and a cool breeze ruffling his hair, Jaryd looked down upon the dazzling cityscape of Amarid. The last time he had seen the precise white and grey of the First Mage's home from a similar vantage point, as he and Baden concluded their long journey from Accalia to the great city, he had been a Mage-Attend, far from his home and family, awed by the notion of observing his first Gathering and moving among the most powerful men and women in Tobyn-Ser. Less than a month had passed since then, but it might as well have been a lifetime. He was a Hawk-Mage now, he mused, feeling Ishalla's presence in his mind. And not just any Hawk-Mage; he was bound to one of Amarid's Hawks and he bore the staff given to him in Theron's Grove by the unsettled spirit of the land's first Owl-Master. The mages with whom he traveled, whose mere presence once would have intimidated him and filled him with wonder, had become his closest friends. In a month's time he had even overcome his fear of horses, Jaryd realized with a smile, as the animal standing beside him nuzzled his shoulder. He stroked its nose absently.

A vision entered his mind, and for an instant he saw himself sleeping by a small stream. He recognized the scene: it was the place of his binding. *Yes,* he sent to Ishalla, from whom the image had come. *You're home again.* Immediately, this image disappeared and another entered his mind. A large owl was flying toward him, its powerful talons outstretched, its beak opened in a menacing scream. Sartol's bird. He felt his mood growing grim. There was one more thing that marked this journey into Amarid as different from the last one: this time, he planned to unmask a traitor, or to die in the attempt. *Fear not,* he sent to his hawk. *We will face them together.*

"Am I intruding?" came a soft, familiar voice from behind him.

"No," he answered, turning and holding out a hand to Alayna, who took it and stepped forward to stand beside him as he turned again to face the city.

"Is something wrong?" she asked.

"I think Ishalla is frightened," he told her. "And I'm not used to sensing fear from her."

She did not respond, and for a long time they stood wordlessly, his hand in hers, both of them staring at the buildings that gleamed below them in the sunlight. At length he began to wonder if she had even heard his last remark. But, when finally she spoke, he knew not only that his words had reached her, but that they had carried her mind in the same direction that Ishalla's image had taken his.

"He'll be ready," she murmured without taking her dark eyes from the city. "I know that Baden has thought things through very carefully, and that he's taking every precaution. But Sartol will be ready."

Jaryd glanced at her. "What do you think we should do?"

She shrugged. She suddenly appeared very young and more than a bit frightened. He could only guess how difficult these last several days had been for her, or how much harder these next few would be. "He's stronger than we are, Alayna," he told her. "He's cunning and deceitful, and he got to the Great Hall first, which means that he may have already swayed some of the others to his side. But we have to face him; it's the only way to save Tobyn-Ser. You heard what Theron said: if we can't defeat Sartol, we have no chance of stopping the outlanders."

"So we go down there, even if it means our death." She offered it as a statement, but the expression on her delicate, tanned features was unreadable.

Jaryd smiled. "We do, but it won't." He raised her hand to his lips and kissed it gently. "I just found you; I'm not going to let anything or anyone take you away from me. Not even Sartol."

She nodded and tried to smile. But the fearful look in her eyes remained.

Jaryd heard footsteps behind them. "May I join you?" Baden called.

"Of course, Baden," Alayna answered, though her eyes never left Jaryd's face. "We were just . . . talking."

A moment later Jaryd turned toward the Owl-Master. "Are we ready to get moving again?"

"Soon," Baden told him, "but there's something I want to discuss with you first." He stepped past the young mages to the edge of the bluff and looked out across the city as they had done a minute before. The wind stirred his thinning hair, and his always lean frame seemed almost frail under the ample cloak he wore. "As soon as we venture down into Hawksfind Wood," he remarked, "we're probably going to meet up with other mages returning to the Great Hall. Sartol saw to that a couple of days ago."

Jaryd glanced down at the ceryll he carried, seeing that its light still pulsed with the same, unwavering rhythm that had taken hold of it two nights earlier, as the company rode through Tobyn's Wood. Alayna's crystal flashed as well, as, he knew, did Trahn's, Orris's, and that of every other mage in Tobyn-Ser. They were all tuned to the Summoning Stone, which had been awakened to convene another Gathering. By custom, Baden had explained, this was appropriate. As an Owl-Master and the bearer of both Jessamyn's staff and the news of her death, Sartol had not just the right but the obligation to call for a Gathering of the Owl-Masters to select her successor. But rather than showing the intermittent flickering of a call intended only for the Owl-Masters, their cerylls were pulsating with the steady beat of a general summons. The entire Order had been called to Amarid for a second Gathering, no doubt so that Sartol could formally accuse Baden and Orris of treason.

"You both have assured me that Theron knew of no other traitors within the Order," Baden went on, "but still, I'd prefer to err on the side of caution. Sartol may have allies that Theron hasn't seen." The Owl-Master turned away from the view of Amarid to face them once more. The dark rings under his pale blue eyes made his features appear even more gaunt than usual, and his voice sounded tight. "Once we reach the wood, your lives will be in danger—if Sartol learns somehow that you're still alive, he'll do everything in his power to kill you. So, as soon as we're out of the mountains, I want to take the two of you to an isolated clearing that I know of just a few miles outside of the city. You can wait there for word of what we need for you to do."

Jaryd could feel Alayna's grip on his hand tightening as Baden spoke, and as soon as the Owl-Master finished, she shook her head emphatically. "Once you're in Amarid, Sartol will charge all three of you with murder and treason and have you placed under house arrest," she said harshly. "That is, if he doesn't find an excuse to just kill you. And you want us to sit idly in some clearing waiting for your instructions?" She shook her head again. "I mean no disrespect Owl-Master, but that's foolish."

Surprisingly, Baden grinned, as he looked from one of the young mages to the other. "You two were made for each other," he said. "Those words could easily have come from Jaryd." He held up a finger as his smile faded. "First of all, whatever else Sartol might do, he won't kill us. That would be too transparent; he'd be destroying himself. Second," he continued, raising another finger, "I fully expect to be charged and arrested as you predict. But remember, both of you, Trahn, Orris, and I have many friends within the Order. No matter how convincing Sartol may be, at least a few of them will maintain their faith in our innocence and will help us. I assure you, you won't have to wait long for our messenger."

Alayna still bristled defiantly next to him, but Jaryd nodded his agreement. "Do you know yet what you're going to do?" he asked.

The familiar smirk spread across the Owl-Master's features once more. "There won't be much that I can do," he observed. "As Alayna has said, we'll be arrested as soon as we enter the city. But as mages accused, we three will still have one choice that we alone can make: we can call for an immediate trial, or we can demand that our trial wait until the entire Order has returned."

"So that's what your messenger will tell us, which of those you've chosen."

Baden nodded. "We have a right to face Sartol when he accuses us," he explained, "and I'm hoping that we'll be able to tell at that time whether we'd be better off waiting or forcing Sartol's hand. But regardless of what we choose, your role in this remains the same. You must slip unseen into the city and make your way to our trial with Theron's staff and the two pieces of the outlanders' birds that we still have. I'm hoping that those pieces of evidence, and your description of what happened by the grove, will be enough to convince the Order of our innocence and Sartol's guilt." He turned to Alayna, who had listened in silence as he laid out his scheme, such as it was. "I understand your reluctance to accept this approach, Alayna," he told her with unexpected compassion. "As difficult as this encounter will be for all of us, it will be hardest for you by far. If you have another suggestion, I would gladly hear it. But I'm convinced that this plan offers our best chance of beating him."

Alayna held herself utterly still for another moment. Then she sighed, and closed her eyes. "I have no alternatives to offer, Baden, and I do see the logic in what you have in mind." She opened her eyes and looked at the Owl-Master. "I'm sorry for what I said before."

"You mean about my plan being foolish?" Baden asked, his eyes dancing.

Alayna laughed. "Yes, that."

"Well, don't apologize just yet," he told her. "It may prove to be as good a description as any for what we're about to do." He winked at them, as if he were about to deal out a hand of ren-drah. Then he motioned for the young mages to start back toward the mountain path. "Trahn! Orris!" he called out as he followed them. "Let's get going. It's time we dropped in on Sartol."

The trail plunged precipitously out of the mountains, seeming to Jaryd even steeper than the route he and Baden had taken into the great city from the west, before the Midsummer Gathering. As comfortable as he had grown with riding over the past several weeks, Jaryd found the descent harrowing. Twice, he nearly pitched forward over the head of his horse and onto the rocky path, and by the time the slope began to level off his cloak was damp with sweat, and his hands had cramped painfully from gripping the reins so tightly. Fortunately, the company encountered no one as they negotiated the mountainside. But almost immediately upon entering Hawksfind Wood, as they rode by the crystal-blue waters of Dacia's Lake, they heard voices approaching on a converging trail. Quickly, and as silently as they could manage, Jaryd and Alayna ducked into a nearby cluster of trees, while the others dismounted, pulled out some food, and pretended to be resting. Watching from within the shadows, Jaryd saw four Hawk-Mages ride into view. He recognized one of them as Radomil, but he could not recall the names of the others. They stopped briefly to greet Orris, Trahn, and Baden, but they did not dismount, and they soon moved on.

"That was close," Baden breathed, after the foursome was out of earshot.

"I would think that we can trust Radomil," Jaryd commented as he and Alayna emerged from the trees.

Orris, standing with his legs planted, and his burly arms crossed in front of his chest, nodded his agreement. "I know Mered fairly well. I trust him also."

"Both of you are probably right," Baden conceded. "I consider Radomil a good friend, and I have great respect for Mered. No doubt the other two are good people as well. But given the position we're in, we can't afford to assume anything. It's not merely a matter of whether these mages are trustworthy, although certainly that's part of it. We also have to be sure that they will believe in us, and keep faith with us, even after they've heard Sartol's accusations. We're going to be asking a great deal of whomever we take into our confidence, so we'd better be sure."

"Do you have someone in mind?" Trahn asked.

The Owl-Master hesitated. "I do," he replied. Jaryd thought that he might say more, but instead, he pressed his lips together and rubbed his fingers across his mouth in an oddly nervous gesture. "I do," he repeated after a moment.

Alayna ran her fingers through her dark hair. "This isn't the best place for us to stand around," she said.

Baden chuckled. "Probably not, no. I'll take the two of you to the clearing I mentioned." He glanced at Trahn. "You and Orris go on toward Amarid, slowly," he instructed. "I'll cut back to the trail a few miles ahead and wait for you there."

Trahn nodded, his green eyes bright with a mix of ferocity and anticipation that Jaryd had noticed on previous occasions. Not for the first time, Jaryd found himself thankful that the Hawk-Mage was on their side. The dark mage turned to face Alayna, and then Jaryd. "Arick guard you both," he said, "for our sake, and that of Tobyn-Ser."

"And you," Alayna returned.

Jaryd met his friend's gaze and smiled. "Take care of yourself, Trahn," he told the Hawk-Mage, hoping that the tone of his voice conveyed everything that his words could not.

Orris swung himself onto his mount in a swift, compact motion. "I look forward to seeing the two of you again," he said jauntily. "Try not to be late for our trial."

Jaryd nodded and grinned. "We'll do our best."

Without another word, the two Hawk-Mages, one dark and the other fair, both with their long hair tied back, wheeled their mounts and started along the trail toward Amarid. Jaryd watched them ride until they disappeared among the trees.

"Come," Baden commanded, steering his horse onto a narrow passage through the woods that Jaryd had not noticed before. "It's not far, but I'd like to rejoin Trahn and Orris before they meet up with anyone else. The fewer questions we raise, the better off we'll be."

Surveying the main trail and the surrounding forest one last time to be sure that they were not seen, Jaryd followed Baden onto the path, and Alayna fell in behind him. As the Owl-Master had promised, they did not have to go far, although the woods were dense and the terrain rough. They reached the place Baden had described in a quarter hour. Surrounded by thick groves of fir and spruce, and angled slightly with the gentle slope of a small knoll, the clearing was covered with thick, soft grasses and strewn with wildflowers of every conceivable color. The loud droning of a thousand bumblebees filled the air, hummingbirds darted among the blossoms, and two large deer, startled by the mages' arrival, bolted into the woods with a loud snort and the snapping of dried branches.

"You'll be safe here," Baden murmured, his eyes drinking in the tableau. "Only one other person knows of this place."

Jaryd read much in what he saw working on the Owl-Master's countenance, and he guessed who that other person might be, though he kept silent.

Alayna had climbed down off her mount and was gazing with unconcealed delight at the flowers and birds. At length, she looked up at Baden. "What an incredible place."

The Owl-Master managed a smile. "I'm glad you like it." He paused, clearing his throat, as if unsure of how to proceed. "I should be going," he began awkwardly, before faltering again. "I won't lie to you," he continued after a moment. "Our lives may well depend on your ability to get to our trial with the evidence you carry. But your first responsibility should be to each other. Protect yourselves; you're the land's best hope. If it comes down to a choice between stopping Sartol and the outlanders or saving us . . ." He stopped. And then a smile lit his face. "Listen to me. The two of you survived Theron's Grove; you don't need my advice on how to deal with Sartol."

"We'll be all right, Baden," Jaryd assured his uncle, "and we'll be there for your trial."

"Good," the Owl-Master responded. "Then I don't have to bother with a lengthy good-bye." He turned his horse and began trotting toward a far corner of the clearing, where, Jaryd guessed, another wooded path led toward the great city. He stopped, however, before he reached the trees, swinging his mount around a second time. "Arick guard you both," he called, his expression far more sober than it had been only seconds before.

By way of reply, Jaryd raised the altered branch that still held his ceryll and made it blaze momentarily in tribute. "And you," he cried in return.

Alayna came and stood beside the young mage, raising a hand in farewell.

Long after Baden had vanished into the forest, they remained in that spot, facing the dark woodland, their thoughts traveling with the others toward the city and all that awaited them there.

"I think that waiting for Baden's message will be the hardest part of this," Jaryd remarked. "I'd rather be with them, getting arrested myself—"

"Than here, alone with me?"

"That's not what I—" He stopped when he saw that she was smiling. "You know what I meant."

"Yes, I do," she told him, her smile fading. "I feel the same way, but Baden did convince me that this was the best chance we had." She glanced at the stick he carried in his hand. "Maybe we should use this time to help you hone your skills with the Mage-Craft. We could move your ceryll from that silly stick to Theron's staff, and that way you'd get some practice with wood-shaping."

"Theron's staff is as much yours as it is mine," he insisted. "He gave it to both of us. It's not fair for me to take it as my staff."

"I don't mind," she told him. "Besides, I already have a staff. Even if it was given to me by Sartol, it's mine, and I'll keep it." She smiled sadly. "I guess in a sense, Sartol gave both of us our cerylls."

And suddenly she was crying, the tears flowing freely down her cheeks. Jaryd gathered her in his arms and held her to his chest, feeling her entire body shake with her sobbing. She had denied herself this release for so long, he knew. Beginning with their encounter with Theron, and continuing through their furious ride northward in pursuit of Baden and Sartol, there had been no time for her to mourn the loss of her mentor.

Even now, he sensed that she was crying not only out of grief, but also out of fear. Yes, they had faced Theron and seen the horrors of Watersbend. But there was so much yet to be done, and all of it seemed to depend upon them. And, of course, there was still Sartol to be dealt with. So Jaryd held her, stroking her long dark hair and whispering to her soothingly. After a time, her sobs subsided. Jaryd eased his hold on her.

"No," she said softly, still clinging to him. "Don't stop holding me. Please."

She looked up at him, her dark eyes wide and her cheeks still damp with tears. Lacing her fingers through his hair, she slowly pulled his lips down to hers to kiss him long and deep. Jaryd returned the kiss, gathering her in his arms once more and feeling her body strain toward his. In that moment, their sorrows and fears seemed to vanish, leaving only the love and desire that rushed through them like an autumn wind, swirling through the limbs of one of Leora's trees and carrying them to the cool, fragrant grass as if they were the Goddess's golden leaves set free by the gale. And for just a while, as the warm sun caressed their skin and lit the flowers that surrounded them, they allowed their passion to carry them far from the world of outlanders and traitors and trials, until the only things that seemed real were the two of them and the soft ground on which they lay and the rhythm they shaped together in the sunlight and the light wind.

A person could get used to almost anything, it sometimes seemed. He could adjust to the strange daily patterns of travel, in which one might ride all day, until the movement of the horse became a sort of waking dream, and function in a more normal sense after dark, when the movement ceased. He could have his perceptions of the people around him, even the mythic figures of his childhood, altered so completely that it felt as though the world itself would have to change to accommodate his new outlook. He could even lose a friend, or a creature to whom he had been closer than he had to any human companion, and, eventually, he would adapt, and come to embrace the grief and the loss as but another part of life's lesson.

Orris did not consider himself an especially adaptable person, but neither did he see himself as overly rigid. He had grown used to the endless riding of the past several weeks. He had come to trust Baden, to admire Jaryd and Alayna; he would even concede, having listened to the young mages' description of their encounter with Theron, that the unsettled Owl-Master might not be the figure of pure evil that Orris had always assumed him to be. And, slowly, the Hawk-Mage had begun to accept that Pordath was gone, and that eventually, perhaps soon, he would bind to another bird. But on this day, Orris learned the limits of his tolerance: he could not abide being called a traitor.

Orris and Trahn did not meet anyone prior to their reunion with Baden on the main trail into Amarid. Soon after, however, as the three of them drew closer to the city, they began to see increasing numbers of mages returning from the patrols that Orris himself had advocated and Ursel had organized. Fortunately, none of the men and women they greeted along the path appeared to have any notion of why the Order had been called back to Amarid, and Orris, Trahn, and Baden made their way to the southern bank of the Larian River unmolested. At that point, though, things started to go very badly.

For the past several days, Baden had spoken casually, almost cavalierly of their impending arrest, until Orris had gotten used to the idea of it. Or so Orris had thought. Nothing, though, could prepare him for the humiliation of what awaited them on the central bridge leading across the Larian into Amarid's old town commons. As Baden had predicted, speaking in hushed tones during the final few miles of their ride, Sartol had not come, but he had seen to it that their arrest would be as public an event as possible. The traitorous mage had sent Niall to act in his stead, and the older Owl-Master stood in the middle of the bridge, his maroon ceryll held out before him and his pale owl hunched and indifferent on his shoulder. The chief constable of the city was there as well, waiting on the far side of the bridge with several of his officers and three of the largest, most imposing Great Hall attendants that Orris had ever seen. Behind them, in the streets of the old section of the city, a huge crowd had gathered, including not just residents of Amarid, but also a number of mages, many of whom Orris recognized. Immediately, Orris felt himself shrink from the open spectacle he knew was coming.

As the Hawk-Mage and his companions dismounted and stepped onto the bridge, Niall pounded the base of his staff on the thick wooden plank on which he stood. He did it only once, but that was sufficient to quiet the crowd and draw the gaze of every pair of eyes in the marketplace. Facing the Owl-Master, who looked taller and younger than he remembered, Orris could not help but recall the angry words he and Niall had exchanged during the Gathering just a few weeks before. He wondered with passing interest if the other man was thinking of this as well. An instant later, such idle thoughts vanished.

"In the name of Amarid, First Mage and founder of the Order," Niall proclaimed in a voice that carried clearly over the rush of the river, "and on behalf of Owl-Master Sartol, who serves Tobyn-Ser as interim Owl-Sage, I hereby command you to relinquish your staves and surrender yourselves to my authority."

"For what cause?" Baden inquired formally, speaking for the other two as was proper, given his status as Owl-Master.

Orris steeled himself.

"To answer charges that the three of you did conspire against the people of Tobyn-Ser in planning and carrying out recent attacks on the land, including the murders of two people at Sern, the razing of Taima, and the wholesale destruction and mass murders at Kaera and Watersbend. That the three of you did plan and carry out the murders of Owl-Sage Jessamyn, First of the Sage

Peredur, Hawk-Mage Alayna, and Hawk-Mage Jaryd. And that the three of you did conspire in the attempted murder of Owl-Master Sartol."

The mob erupted with a babble of excited conversation and exclamations of amazement. Several people shouted for the immediate execution of the three traitors, and others demanded that they be stripped of their cerylls and familiars, and handed over to the people for swift, appropriate justice. With a detachment that he knew was little more than a defense against the deeper emotions he was fighting, Orris noted that the huge, blue-robed attendants from the Great Hall might end up, before the day was through, serving as their bodyguards rather than their captors.

Niall, his dark eyes betraying a hint of apprehension from beneath his thick silver hair, struck his staff on the bridge several times in an effort to silence the increasingly unruly throng, but the clamor continued unabated. Orris glanced at Baden, and saw the Owl-Master staring avidly into the crowd. Incredibly, he was grinning. Following the line of his gaze, Orris saw why. Amid the angry faces of the men and women, in a small cluster of mages, stood Radomil, looking back at Baden. The Hawk-Mage had surreptitiously placed his right hand over his heart, his four fingers straightened and pressed together, and his thumb folded beneath his palm. The sign of fealty under the gods. Even after the accusations, before he had even heard their response, the Hawk-Mage had pledged his aid to their cause. Jaryd had been right: Radomil was to be trusted. In spite of everything, Orris permitted himself a slight smile.

Some time later, after he finally succeeded in bringing order to the thousands of onlookers, Niall fixed Baden with a stolid glare, as if to tell the Owl-Master that he was now waiting for Baden's reply to the catalog of accusations and his earlier demand that the three mages give themselves up.

Slowly, but with his shoulders straight, the shadow of a smile touching his lips, Baden strode forward to stand before Niall. "We will hand over our staves and place ourselves in your custody as you request, Owl-Master Niall," he said, his voice ringing out boldly over the city. "But hear me!" he went on, cutting off a second wave of whisperings that had begun to spread through the crowd. He seemed suddenly to have grown in stature, as he encompassed the gathered multitude with a confident gaze. "All who witness our peaceful compliance should know that it in no way signals an admission of our guilt. We hand over our cerylls because we respect the laws that govern the Order and this land, and because we are certain that a fair trial will exonerate us. We know who committed the crimes of which we have been accused, and, before this process is concluded, those responsible will be punished." Baden fell silent, but he continued to stare out at the crowd, as if his single gaze could hold all of theirs at once. After a moment, he motioned for Trahn and Orris to step forward and hand their staffs to Niall. No sound at all came from the assembled mass.

Orris knew, of course, that he had done nothing wrong. Nonetheless, as he moved toward Niall and relinquished his staff, he could feel every pair of eyes in the old town commons burning into his skin like glowing irons, branding him with words like *renegade* and *butcher*. There were mages in the crowd, men and women who had been and would continue to be his colleagues. And he wanted to scream at them all, to proclaim his innocence, to tell them who had really done these horrible things. But he remained silent—he wasn't sure how he managed it, the urge to cry out was so strong—and he kept his eyes riveted on Niall's face as the Owl-Master took his staff. The older man refused to meet his look.

It was over quickly enough—a small grace—and the three mages took a step back as Niall held up the staffs for the people to see. Orris had expected a cheer, or some other acknowledgment of their capitulation, but all he heard was a low ripple of voices commenting on what had transpired, and the impassive murmuring of the river. Two of the constable's officers came forward and led the mages' horses away, promising to care for them.

"Well, Niall," Baden said quietly, as the Owl-Master turned once again to face them, "why don't you lead us to the Great Hall. He'll be expecting us."

The silver-haired mage opened his mouth to reply. But then he closed it again and, without a word, turned and began striding toward the magnificent domed building where Sartol awaited them.

The sea of people parted peacefully for the mages as they moved through it. Many of the men and women stared at the accused with hostile expressions, but others seemed less certain of their guilt. In truth, though, Orris paid little heed to the crowd. He was more concerned with the mages who had watched as the drama played itself out on the bridge. To his relief, most of them had walked on ahead so that they might already be in the Gathering Chamber when Baden, Trahn, and he arrived for the formal issuing of charges. Eventually, he knew, he would have to face them. But he did not feel ready for that quite yet.

"That went pretty much as I had expected," Baden commented as they walked. "Sartol may be confident, but he still seems intent on stirring up public sentiment against us. He must be harboring some doubts."

"Quiet!" commanded one of the burly attendants.

Baden halted and glared at him. "We are free men who have been convicted of nothing, my friend," he said, his voice low and menacing. "You would do well to remember it." He moved closer to the brute, looking like a schoolboy next to him. "You might also keep in mind that, even without my staff, my bird and I are capable of turning you into a torch with no more than a wave of my hand."

The attendant flinched slightly and nodded. "Y-yes, Owl-Master," he stammered. "I'm sorry."

An instant later, Baden pivoted and began walking again. "Have you noticed," he asked blandly, "that the attendants seem to be getting bigger?"

Orris and Trahn burst out laughing, earning a sullen glance from the aggrieved steward, and a scornful look from Niall.

They came to the Great Hall several minutes later and, with little fanfare, continued up the broad marble stairs and through the great doorway. Even under the circumstances, Orris found himself moved by the sight of the hall as he and the others walked toward it on the main thoroughfare, and then around it to the arched wooden entrance. As always, the sparkling crystal statue of the First Mage and Parne; the enormous blue-tiled roof with its constellation of golden medallions, including, somewhere on the other side, his own—his and Pordath's; and the intricate inlaid images on the massive oak doors made him think back to his initial journey to Amarid, and the first time he saw the meeting place of Hawk-Mages and Owl-Masters.

Orris's memory of that first visit to the great city and its splendid hall grew even more distinct as he followed Niall into the Gathering Chamber and glanced upward, as he always did upon entering the structure, to see the portrait of Amarid at the moment of his binding to Parne. A moment later, however, Niall motioned for the three accused mages to stop, and Orris, reluctantly, let go of his recollections and focused on his immediate problems. Most of the mages had yet to return from their patrols; nearly two thirds of the chairs gathered around the oval table stood empty. The vast majority of those present were Owl-Masters, who had remained in Amarid with Odinan and Niall; there were only a handful of Hawk-Mages in the room. This, too, Baden had anticipated, although he had been far less concerned about it than Orris. As one of the younger mages, indeed, a leader among them, who had been more than willing to challenge the conventional wisdom of the Order, Orris feared that some of the older masters, like Niall and Odinan, would delight in seeing him condemned as a traitor. He recognized, however, that this was not reason enough to opt for a later trial. Indeed, if the preponderance of Owl-Masters did end up dictating their strategy, it would mean that he and his allies had learned nothing of Sartol's scheme. That was not an attractive proposition.

Thrusting his anxieties to the back of his mind, Orris glanced around the Gathering Chamber, searching for anything that might give him some insight into Sartol's intentions. He wasn't certain what he was looking for; perhaps a change in the appearance of the Great Hall, or even a change in Sartol himself. He hoped that he would recognize it when he saw it, or that, if he didn't, Baden or Trahn would.

At the far end of the huge, oval table that sat in the middle of the room, Jessamyn and Peredur's staffs lay across the arms of their chairs, and closer to where Orris stood, two empty baskets rested in Alayna and Jaryd's seats, no doubt the same ones the young mages had used at the Midsummer Gathering to carry the feathers they received during the Procession of Light. Proper displays of mourning for the four mages lost—or presumed lost—during the journey to Theron's Grove, Orris noted with an odd sense of detachment. Sartol was leaving nothing to chance. Orris also noticed, with somewhat less insouciance, that his chair, along with Trahn's and Baden's, had been moved from its place at the table and now stood, with the other two, just in front of where Niall had halted. The three chairs had been placed in a neat row, facing the table and the rest of the mages.

Wordlessly, Niall gestured for Orris, Baden, and Trahn to take their places. When they had complied with his tacit command, the silver-haired Owl-Master looked at Odinan, who sat at his place just to the right of the sage's chair, and nodded once. Returning the gesture, the aged Owl-Master, with his diminutive, large-headed owl clinging to his shoulder, rose stiffly and rapped his staff once on the marble floor. The sharp sound reverberated off the walls and the domed ceiling, bringing the other mages in the room to their feet. A moment later, Orris heard a door open at the far end of the chamber.

Looking in that direction, he saw Sartol emerge from the sage's quarters and make his way to the table. Tall and straight-backed, the Owl-Master moved with a grace and refinement that made everyone else in the hall seem ungainly. He had schooled his tanned, chiseled features so that they revealed nothing of his mood or his plans, and his eyes swept the chamber with a commanding assurance. The great owl sitting on his shoulder—the owl that had killed Pordath—also surveyed the room with its heavy-lidded yellow eyes, looking as impressive and composed as the man who carried it. Even as he glared at Sartol, cursing the bird that had rendered him unbound and hungering for the Owl-Master's death, even as he noted the fatigue etched in the man's features, Orris could not help but be daunted by the air of strength that the mage and his familiar projected. For that one instant, Orris was, once more, the young Mage-Attend, experiencing Amarid for the first time. And a thought flashed through his mind, incongruous and somewhat frightening: this is what an Owl-Sage should look like.

Orris perceived all of this in a single, dizzying moment. Then he was himself again, standing with Baden and Trahn, watching the traitor remove Jessamyn's staff from the chair so that he might take her place at the table. But even during that moment of disorientation, he had also seen one other thing, terrifying in its implications, that made it absolutely plain to him what he and his companions would have to do.

The rest of the mages sat back down, and Odinan began to enumerate the charges leveled against Orris and his two companions, his shrill, nasal voice echoing off the domed ceiling of the Gathering Chamber. Orris, however, could not stop thinking about what he had seen. He could not tell if Trahn had observed it as well, but he knew that Baden had. The Owl-Master had given that much away with a sharp breath and a slight widening of his eyes. Orris had found that reassuring, since he had already begun to wonder if he had imagined what he had seen. It had been so brief, a scintilla of a second. But Baden's reaction told him that it was real, that he had seen the pale yellow glow of Sartol's ceryll answered, for no more than the time it might take to draw a single spark from a flint, in the vast crystal expanse of the Summoning Stone.

Quickly, Orris scanned the faces of the other mages in the chamber to see if they had noticed it as well. Most, however, had been facing the table, rather than the stone and the approaching Owl-Master. Most. But not all.

Orris had known Radomil for nearly nine years, since the Gathering at which Orris received his cloak. The older Hawk-Mage had struck him as being nice enough: unfailingly courteous, but rather inconsequential. Radomil usually said little during Gatherings, and there seemed to be no clear pattern to his voting on important issues. And, of course, he was still a Hawk-Mage after his third binding, something, Orris had told himself on several occasions—he smiled inwardly at the memory of his youthful arrogance—that would never happen to him.

As with so much else, though, Orris's perception of the bald, goateed Hawk-Mage had changed, in part as a result of Pordath's death. At this point, Orris would have been happy with any familiar at all—hawk or owl—and he knew that he would never again belittle another mage's binding. But much more to the point, Radomil possessed courage and strength, in far greater amounts than Orris had ever acknowledged. He had shown that at the old bridge a short while ago, with an inconspicuous gesture, an offering of faith for which Orris was profoundly grateful. And now, sitting near the middle of the table, beside the empty place where Baden's seat should have been, Radomil was staring intently at Orris, his dark eyes knowing and expectant. Clearly, he had noticed the Summoning Stone's response to Sartol's ceryll, and he had marked Orris's recognition of it as well. Carefully, almost imperceptibly, his eyes holding Radomil's, Orris nodded, confirming what the portly mage appeared already to have known: they were allies in the fight against Sartol.

Odinan concluded his listing of the accusations against them, and Niall, still standing near their chairs, motioned for the three mages to be seated.

"You have heard the charges," Sartol intoned from the Owl-Sage's chair, his voice resonant and disconcertingly calm. "How would you proceed?"

"May we have a moment to consult amongst ourselves?" Baden asked mildly.

Sartol nodded. "You may."

Orris and Trahn leaned closer to Baden, who sat between them. They were aware that, with the hall relatively empty, even their whispers would echo and carry, but they could do little about that.

"You saw?" Orris inquired softly, looking at Baden and hoping that the question would reveal little to the other mages in the room.

"I did."

"Our choice seems clear."

"I agree." Baden offered a rueful grin. "It appears that you'll have to convince the Owl-Masters after all."

Orris shrugged, smirking in return. "I suppose so."

"I didn't see anything," Trahn commented, "but I take it we're opting for an immediate trial?" The dark man asked the question plainly, implying no reservation as to their judgment, but merely seeking confirmation of what he believed they had decided. The trust conveyed by his tone, on a matter of such monumental importance, left Orris humbled, and grateful beyond words for the Hawk-Mage's friendship. He saw the same emotions flash briefly across Baden's face.

"I think we'd better," the Owl-Master replied. "I'll explain later. But if you prefer—"

Trahn shook his head, cutting Baden off. "I never liked the idea of waiting," he said. "Let us unmask the traitor and be done with it."

Baden allowed himself another smile and gripped his friend's shoulder. Then he turned back toward Sartol. "As is our right under the rules that govern this Order," he announced in a ringing tone, "we demand an immediate trial, to begin tomorrow morning."

A murmur of surprise from the other mages greeted Baden's words, and Orris thought he saw fear and doubt chase themselves briefly across Sartol's features. But then the Owl-Master's mouth stretched into a grin, although there was no trace of mirth in the rest of his face, and, once more, Orris found himself questioning what he thought he had seen.

"My witnesses have not yet arrived from Watersbend," Sartol replied solicitously. "I would like to wait until they arrive."

Baden shook his head. "That won't be necessary, Sartol. You may present their testimony for them. I trust you to do so accurately. We shall begin tomorrow morning."

Sartol's smile faded. "Very well," he answered, and there could be no mistaking the animosity suddenly laid bare in his tone. "Tomorrow morning." He stood abruptly, his glare never leaving Baden's face. "Take them to the nearest inn and place them under guard. The bells will be rung at mid-morning to convene their trial."

He spun away from the table with a rustle of cloth and strode swiftly back toward the Owl-Sage's chambers.

Niall moved in front of Baden. "Come along," he said severely, gesturing with his staff. "I'll take you to your rooms."

The three of them rose, and Baden and Trahn followed the older man back out into the street. Orris lingered, however, watching Sartol retreat to the back of the hall. And, again, just as the traitor swept past the Summoning Stone, the massive crystal appeared to flicker with a pale yellow light.

18

"All of life's paths are circular," a popular saying went, "and the gods delight in making us dizzy." The inn to which Niall led them, it turned out, was the same establishment to which Orris and Trahn had chased the vandals who shattered the Great Hall's window during the recent Gathering.

"There's an omen in this," Trahn commented to Orris as they entered the building, the lightness of his tone not quite concealing his concern. "But I don't know how to read it."

The accused mages, and four other members of the Order who had been chosen to guard them, followed Niall up a narrow flight of stairs to the second floor of the tavern. There, in the dark hallway, unlit save for his wine-colored ceryll and the glowing crystals of the guards, Niall indicated the three rooms that had been set aside for the alleged traitors.

"You'll each take one of these rooms," Niall began. "In the morn—"

Baden placed a hand on the older man's shoulder, stopping him. "Thank you, Niall," he said crisply. "For now the three of us will meet in my room. We have much to discuss. Please arrange to have some food brought to us, and inform the mages you'll be posting here in the hallway that we're to be allowed visitors."

Niall hesitated, his brown eyes uncertain beneath the shock of silver hair.

"We haven't been convicted of anything, Niall," Baden went on in a gentler tone. "According to the laws of the Order, we're still free men. We surrendered to you as a gesture of our good intent, and we'll not break faith with you now. But, in return, we expect to be treated appropriately."

Niall regarded them for some time, the muscles in his jaw knotting with tension. At length he nodded. "Very well," he said. "Don't make me regret this."

Baden gave a small smile, and the three of them stepped into the middle room, closing the door behind them.

After the dinginess of the hallway, the sunlit room seemed bright, almost cheerful, albeit a bit spare. A small bed with a quilted cover sat along the right-hand wall with its headboard in the far corner. Next to it, by the single window, which had been left open to allow a light breeze to stir the thin white curtains, stood a small wooden night table with an oil lamp on it. There was a plain chair in the other corner and an overly large bureau against the unadorned wall opposite the bed. A beige-colored oval rug, stained in two places, lay in the middle of the wooden floor. Baden claimed the bed, reclining on it with his back against the wall. Trahn dragged the chair out into the middle of the room, and Orris sat on the windowsill, where he could enjoy the breeze and the warmth of the sun.

"You saw something," Trahn commented as he lowered himself into the chair, his green eyes swinging from Orris to Baden. "Tell me."

Baden took a measured breath and passed a hand through his thin red and grey hair. His angular features looked wan and fatigued. "Obviously, I can't speak for Orris," he began, "though I assume he marked it as well, but as Sartol emerged from the sage's quarters, I saw the color of his ceryll echoed briefly in the Summoning Stone."

"What?" Trahn whirled toward Orris. "You saw this, too?"

"I did."

"And you're both certain that it wasn't merely a reflection, a visual illusion that made the light appear to come from the stone?"

Orris shook his head. "This was no illusion; it happened a second time, when Sartol left the table and went back into the chamber."

Baden looked at Orris keenly before turning back to Trahn. "That, I didn't see," he admitted, "but I'm certain, too. What I saw was real."

Trahn exhaled through his teeth, making a characteristic hissing noise. "Arick guard us all," he whispered reflexively. "If he can link himself to the Summoning Stone, with the power he already possesses, not even the combined strength of the entire Order will be able to stop him."

"I know," Baden acknowledged. "That's why we had to demand an immediate trial. Obviously he's begun to alter the stone, but he hasn't mastered it yet and, we can hope, he won't be able to complete the process overnight."

"But even now, we don't know how far his control over the stone goes," Trahn pointed out, "and, with the trial set for tomorrow, he'll only need to defeat one third of the Order. I don't question the wisdom of the choice you made," the Hawk-Mage added quickly, "I just fear that we may already be too late."

Baden shrugged. "We have to proceed on the assumption that we're not, and concentrate on the more immediate task of swaying those mages who are present to our side."

"Radomil is with us already," Orris declared.

"That, I did see," Trahn confirmed. "He offered the sign of fealty at the bridge."

"He also caught my eye after the first flicker of light from the Summoning Stone. He understands what Sartol is doing."

Baden fixed Orris with an appraising eye. "I missed that as well. I think I'm glad to have you as an ally, Orris."

The Hawk-Mage felt himself flush slightly, and, before he could help it, he was grinning. "It took you this long to decide that?" he chided.

The Owl-Master chuckled. "Actually, no," he replied with meaning. "Just to say it."

"I've always liked Radomil," Trahn commented, "but I don't know him very well. Do you think we can trust him to carry a message to . . ." he paused, glancing suspiciously at the door, ". . . to the others?"

"I'm certain that we can," Baden answered. "But I don't think he's the best choice for that job."

Orris had come to trust Baden's judgment on such things. Nonetheless, this surprised him. "Why not?" he asked.

"Radomil was out on a patrol," the Owl-Master explained. "Sartol might try to raise doubts about his loyalty to the Order as well."

Orris shook his head. "It would never work. Even Sartol doesn't have that much nerve."

"You're probably right, but I don't want to take any chances at all. We'll be placing whomever we select for this task in grave physical danger; we can hardly help it. But we can try to minimize their risk. We need an Owl-Master who remained here for the entire time we were gone, so that if Sartol accuses this person of complicity in the attacks and the murders, the other Owl-Masters will be less inclined to believe it."

"I'm sure there are a few among those who stayed in Amarid whom we can trust," Trahn observed. "But do any of them trust us enough to help?"

Before Baden could respond, they all heard a soft knock at the door.

Grinning, the Owl-Master swung himself off the bed and reached for the door handle. "I believe," he said buoyantly, "that the answer to your question has just arrived."

It had been years, Niall thought, a great many years, since he had felt this good. For the first time in what had been a very long while, people within the Order were treating him as a man of consequence. He had respect and responsibility; he had a role to play in the momentous events currently unfolding in the Great Hall, events that would shape the future of the Mage-Craft. He had not been able to say that about himself for the better part of a decade. A *decade*. Sitting at a table in the darkest corner of the Crystal Inn—named for its proximity to the two small statues that adorned the round towers of the Great Hall, rather than for any sparkling quality of its interior design—Niall shook his head slowly, marveling at the swiftness of time's inexorable passage. Twelve years had gone by since his binding to Nollstra, twelve years since he became an Owl-Master. And it had been ten years since Vardis's death. Vardis, whose hazel eyes and black curls had lured him to her like a moth to a candle during his first visit to the Lower Horn, the region he would later serve as Hawk-Mage and Owl-Master; whose humor and love had warmed his days and fired his nights for more than half a lifetime. She had been so proud when she first saw Nollstra on his shoulder that she had cried.

He still remembered that night with a clarity that made it stand out above all the rest. How they had lain together in the afterglow of their passion, Vardis tracing patterns on his chest with her fingertips, her eyes large and luminous with candlelight and ceryll-glow, the playfulness of her smile unable to conceal entirely her pride in him.

"Owl-Master Niall," she had whispered, not for the first time that evening. "Perhaps someday you'll be Sage Niall."

He had laughed, gently. "You are a vain, power-hungry woman," he had teased. "You wish only to have a big home in a great city on the other side of the land, where men and women will come to you and kneel in obeisance."

"I care nothing for big cities," she protested with mock petulance. "I'm very happy on the Lower Horn. And, as for the rest, well, I feel it's the least I deserve. I would think it a small matter, now that you've become a man of stature, for you to have them bring the Great Hall to me."

"I'll see what I can do," he had said, laughing. And then, kissing her, he had added in a different tone, "I would move the moon and the stars for you if I could."

She had rolled onto her back then, pulling him over with her. "You already do," she had murmured, as they commenced their candlelit dance once more.

Niall recoiled from the memory then, as he always did at that point. Because, it sometimes seemed, that had been the last night of happiness they shared. In reality, there were a few more, but not many. Three months later, she started to complain of the dull ache in her stomach, and, not long after that, she began to spit up blood. The fear of losing her had gripped him then, as a harsh winter takes hold of the land, chilling him to his very core and forcing him to close in upon himself until the two of them and her sickness were the only things in his world. It was too soon, he had pleaded with the gods; they could not take her so soon. Would that they had not listened so well.

For nearly two years, he watched her waste away, taking care of her as best he could. The local healers were powerless against the illness, and his own magic could not reach the disease that raged within her. He could ease her pain for a time, but that was all. Gradually it took her, bit by bit: her joy, her beauty, her spirit, and, finally, mercifully at the end, her life. That had been ten years ago. A decade.

He had continued to attend the Gatherings while she was ill, and he saw to the needs of the people he served. She had insisted on that much. But, in the aftermath of losing her, his ambition, the dreams she had nurtured within him, evaporated. He immersed himself in the needs of the people, seeking refuge from his grief in the one thing he had left. But his passion had died with Vardis. He became a spectator, watching as his fellow mages positioned themselves for advancement or worked to shape the Order's priorities, but actually doing very little himself. Even his connection with Nollstra seemed to grow distant and weak.

It was so unlike who he had once been, and yet it felt so natural, so alluringly comfortable. As a younger man, newly bound to his first hawk, he had watched the aging of his father, a powerful Owl-Master in his own right, with impatience and a thinly veiled contempt. He had vowed to Vardis, and to himself, that he would not wither away as Padwyn had done; that he would never be satisfied merely to go through the motions. The Order was too important to the land to tolerate such complacency. And, when his father died, Niall had refused to offer a eulogy before the funeral rites. Later, too much later, he had come to regret that decision, just as he had come to understand the waning of his father's drive, which had begun, he realized in the depths of his own mourning, with his mother's death.

Eventually, after a few years, Niall had shaken off his depression and had grown more active in the deliberations of the Order. By then, however, others had made names for themselves and emerged as leaders of the various factions that vied for preeminence within the Great Hall. Niall understood that he did not wield the influence that these others did, and he knew that he would never be Owl-Sage. When Feargus died, his name was not even mentioned as a possible replacement. Unlike most of the other Owl-Masters, Niall supported Sartol over Jessamyn, although, of course, Sartol could not have known that.

All of which contributed to the surprise—and, Niall had to admit, gratitude—that he felt, just two days ago, when Sartol, who had a day before returned to Amarid with the shocking news of Jessamyn's murder and the conspiracy within the Order, took Niall into his confidence and requested his aid in combating the renegades.

Notwithstanding his past disagreements with Sartol and his awareness of the Owl-Master's indiscretions during his first year as a mage, Niall had always liked and respected him. Niall thought him wise, courageous; he admired the mettle Sartol had shown by continuing to serve the people of northern Tobyn-Ser even after receiving a reprimand for exacting payment for his services. And Sartol had been kind to him in the wake of Vardis's death, offering encouragement as he began to emerge from the despondency that had gripped him in the years that followed. Like most of the other Owl-Masters to whom he had spoken, Niall had long expected that Sartol would succeed Jessamyn as leader of the Order. As the bearer of Jessamyn's staff, he seemed to Niall the logical choice to serve as interim Owl-Sage. Hearing from Sartol of Baden's betrayal at Watersbend and of Orris's successful effort to free the renegade Owl-Master from the jail there had convinced Niall of this even more. The other masters agreed, and formally chose Sartol as their provisional leader the evening of his return to Amarid.

Late the next day, Sartol asked Niall to join him in the sage's quarters. The Order had entered a time of crisis, Sartol told him, and it needed a person of discretion, someone sensible and experienced, yet forceful enough to take action should the need arise.

"Conspiracies such as this one are dangerous things," the Owl-Master had said, as the two of them sat across from each other, the deep yellow of the late-afternoon sun coloring the light in the room. "They can leave some people incapacitated with fear, while they make others see betrayal everywhere. I need someone who can be cautious without slipping into paranoia, someone who can maintain his composure without being overly docile. And," he had added, "I need a person I can trust, a person who is above pettiness and rapacity." The dark-haired mage had risen then, walking to the dormant hearth and toying absently with a bauble that he found on the mantel. "There is too much ambition in this hall, Niall. We both know it. When I look around the table in that chamber I see ambition and weariness, and very little in between. I trust Odinan, and some of the others, but I don't see in them the energy or the will necessary to confront the Order's enemies. I need someone who possesses a unique blend of qualities: honor, poise, vitality, maturity, strength. In short, Niall," he had concluded, incredible though it seemed, "I need you."

Driven to his feet by what he had just heard, Niall found that there was nothing to say except, simply, "I'm with you, Sartol."

The Owl-Master had turned at that, a broad smile stretching across his handsome, tanned face. Stepping forward, he gripped Niall's shoulder and then led him to the door, telling him that they would speak again the following morning, at which time Sartol would tell him in more detail what he needed Niall to do.

Striding across the marble floor of the Gathering Chamber after that meeting, past the oval table and beneath the image of young Amarid binding to his magnificent grey bird, Niall could not help but grin. The Order was in danger, he knew; all of Tobyn-Ser was in danger. But the smile came anyway. It was not just that he was flattered, that he felt important again in a way that he had not for years, although certainly those elements were there. But rising above his excitement and his pride, he felt resolve and purpose coalescing within him, rousing a passion to which he had not known he still had access. He had never loved anyone or anything as much as he had loved Vardis. But second to her had come the Order and the Mage-Craft. The one he had lost long ago, he could not bring her back. The others, though, were still a part of his life. Threatened, besieged, but still a part. And they needed him.

The next morning, he learned the nature of that need. The summons came early. The blue-clad attendant of the Great Hall, a large man whom Niall did not recognize, knocked on his door and informed him that Sartol wished to speak with him as soon as possible. Dressing quickly, and pausing on the ground floor of the inn at which he stayed only briefly enough to grab a piece of sweet bread and a cup of shan tea, Niall hurried through the narrow alleys of Amarid until he reached the hall. He found Sartol in the sage's quarters, pacing nervously in front of the hearth. The Owl-Master looked tired, as if he had not slept at all the previous night.

He turned at the sound of Niall's knock, smiling briefly. "Niall! Please, come in," he said, waving the older man into the chamber. "I appreciate you coming on such short notice." He motioned toward one of the chairs, indicating that Niall should sit. Sartol continued to pace, however, his mouth set grimly and his pale eyes looking troubled. "I expect Baden and Orris to arrive this evening. Tomorrow at the latest. And there are things I'll need you to do when they get here." There was no flattery in his tone as there had been the night before; no attempt to charm or curry favor. Only the hard reality of what the Order faced in the next few days. Niall appreciated Sartol's directness, his lack of pretense. They were comrades in a battle for the very survival of the Mage-Craft and Tobyn-Ser. The land needed them to take action. This was no time for niceties.

"I'd like for you to watch for them, and to meet them at the city boundary," Sartol continued. "They'll be coming from the south; I expect them to cross the Larian at one of the old bridges." The Owl-Master stopped pacing directly in front of Niall. "I want you to accept their surrender on my behalf."

Niall looked up sharply. "But that falls under the purview of the sage, or, in this case, the interim sage."

Sartol resumed his pacing. Even now, tense as he was, striding back and forth across the polished wooden floor, Niall noted the economy and elegance of his motions. "I know," the tall man responded. "But I assure you, Baden will stop at nothing to save himself and his allies. He assaulted me at Waters-bend, and then he, of all people, insinuated that I had betrayed the Order, all of this in front of the villagers. He'll do the same if he sees me at the river. The attacks on Tobyn-Ser have already done great damage to the people's confidence in this Order. The public spectacle of Baden and me trading accusations would only make matters worse. Do you understand? Nothing would be served by my presence there, and much could be lost."

Niall nodded. It made a great deal of sense. "I'll go," he said, "but perhaps I should have the constable with me."

"A good idea. You can also take two or three of the hall's attendants if you'd like. You should have Orris's ceryll confiscated and then you should take them to an inn and place them in separate rooms until their trial begins. Have mages posted outside their rooms as guards."

"Do you expect them to resist?"

Sartol shrugged. "I don't know what they'll do, so we should prepare for all contingencies."

The dark-haired Owl-Master paced for another moment or two. Then he stopped for a second time and took a slow breath, as if preparing himself. "There is a second thing I must ask of you," he began, "something even more irregular, perhaps even distasteful." He dropped himself into the chair next to Niall's. "If you prefer not to do this, I'll understand. But I owe it to myself to ask you first, before I turn to anyone else." Sartol hesitated, wetting his lips before he went on. "As I said yesterday, Niall, conspiracies are dangerous. We must be wary of our own tendency toward paranoia. But, by the same token, we can't deny the facts: Baden and Orris have worked together to betray the Order and endanger this land. And, for all we know, their plot may reach deeper than just the two of them. They may be working with others about whom we know nothing at all. If they are, we must learn the identities of these other traitors."

"You want me to keep a watch on them, to see if I can figure out who else is involved."

Sartol hesitated, his grey eyes locked on Niall's. After a moment he nodded. "That's what I want. As I told you," he added without pause, "if you feel uncomfortable doing this I'll understand."

Niall did feel uneasy at the thought of it, but he also recognized the logic of what Sartol was asking. And that logic outweighed his personal discomfort.

"How do you want me to do this?" he asked, and he was moved by the relief that flashed across the other man's countenance.

Sartol smiled, placing a hand on Niall's shoulder for a second before replying. "It should be very simple. From a distance, from a place where you won't be noticed, just watch for anyone who goes to visit them. I don't expect there to be many—perhaps there will be none at all. But if someone should come, I want you to follow them. Find out if they try, in turn, to contact others. We must find out how far the conspiracy reaches."

"And then what?"

"To a certain degree, that's up to you," Sartol told him. "I don't want you to take any unnecessary risks—I'd feel terrible if something happened to you." He paused, holding Niall's gaze. "But if you find yourself in a situation in which you can deal with the traitors without endangering your own life, I leave it to your discretion to act. I'll back you up in whatever you do."

Niall could feel the color draining from his face. He was not certain how to respond, or what to think of the wide latitude Sartol had just given him. He was not even sure that it was Sartol's to give. Again, however, he saw the reasoning behind what the Owl-Master had proposed. What good was it to find other conspirators if one was unwilling to do anything about them?

Sartol appeared to read the doubt in his expression. "I've disturbed you, Niall," he said with genuine concern. "Forgive me. I didn't mean to overstep the authority with which you and the other Owl-Masters have entrusted me." He rose and began to pace again. "It's just that these are dark times, and I want to keep Baden and Orris, and whomever else they've enlisted in their cause, from destroying the Mage-Craft and all that you and I have devoted our lives to protecting."

Niall shook his head. "It's all right," he told the Owl-Master. "This is no time for squeamishness. Exigency creates its own rules." He knew as the words left his mouth that it was true that, under the circumstances, he could do what Sartol had requested. "If I find that there are others involved, I'll subdue them somehow, and I'll have them arrested along with Baden and Orris."

Again, Sartol grinned, his relief and gratitude manifest on his features. "Thank you, Niall," he said, as if letting out a long-held breath. "We may not know what they have in mind, or whom they've turned to their purposes, but at least now we'll be ready for them." The Owl-Master rose, and Niall had the sense that he was expected to do the same, that their meeting had ended. "Make whatever preparations you feel are required," Sartol told him, leading him toward the door. "Tell anyone who asks that you are acting at my behest."

Niall nodded and turned to go.

"Niall," Sartol called, stopping him. "There is one other matter I would like to at least mention before you leave."

The older man turned back to face him once more and waited.

"The circumstances are not what I would have chosen, but it seems likely that I'll soon be named Owl-Sage."

"It seems that way to me as well," Niall agreed. "The Order and Tobyn-Ser will benefit from your leadership."

"You're too kind." Sartol paused, absently stroking the chin of his regal owl. "I've been giving some thought to my selection of a first." Again, he faltered. "There's no graceful way to do this, except to say it: I want you to consider the position, Niall. The same qualities that convinced me to ask for your help in these matters would make you a fine First of the Sage."

Niall was speechless; it was so unexpected, so far beyond the aspirations he had allowed himself in recent years that he could think of no words with which to respond.

Sartol's smile broadened. "You'll want some time to ponder this, and I want you to give it serious thought. We can discuss it again in a few days."

"Of course," Niall managed. And then, "Thank you, Sartol. Thank you very much."

The Owl-Master had nodded, and Niall had walked out of his quarters, past the chairs of the sage and the first, which stood at the head of the Gathering Chamber's large, oval table, and out into the light of another clear, summer morning. All he could think of was how pleased Vardis would have been.

That was yesterday. Despite the preparations Niall made for the rest of that morning and throughout much of the afternoon, the traitors did not arrive before nightfall. Indeed, not until late morning on this day did the first word of their approach reach Amarid. And, it seemed, Baden and Orris were not alone. Trahn had joined them, and the three of them were but a few miles from the southern bank of the Larian. Niall hurried to the Great Hall, where he conveyed this news to Sartol.

The Owl-Master had appeared saddened by the information, but not surprised. "I would like to believe that Trahn is not involved," he remarked, his voice subdued, "that Baden and Orris have concealed their treachery from him." He looked up at Niall. "Perhaps we should act on that assumption, and arrest only the two of them."

"If Trahn is innocent," Niall countered, "the trial will establish that. But we'd be foolish to risk permitting him to wander freely through the city. You asked me to watch for possible accomplices: Trahn seems the most obvious. He and Baden are quite close, so much so that I find it hard to accept that Baden could conceal anything from him. I believe Trahn should be arrested with Baden and Orris."

Sartol considered this, passing a hand over his brow. At length he acquiesced with a reluctant nod. "If you feel that it's necessary, I'll accept your judgment. But I regret deeply that it's come to this."

Sitting in the Crystal Inn several hours later, Niall reflected on that exchange with a combination of sympathy for Sartol's despair and astonishment at his own implacability. It was not like him to be so firm, so unrelenting. Or, rather, it was not like who he had become. The old Niall, the man who had been married to Vardis, would have understood. It was not that he disliked Trahn, or that he did not share Sartol's hope that the Hawk-Mage would be found innocent. In truth, he was not only fond of Trahn, but also of Baden. The possibility that they might have betrayed the Order disturbed him greatly. He even hoped that Orris, with whom he had never seen eye to eye, would turn out to be blameless in all that had happened over the past several months.

But—and this was the point that Vardis would have failed to grasp even as the man he had been explained it to her again and again—his personal feelings had no bearing on what he had to do. Just as it would have been improper to let his difficult interaction with Orris influence his treatment of the Hawk-Mage, so, too, would he have been wrong to treat Trahn or Baden differently simply because he liked them. The three mages were being held in the rooms just above where Niall now sat because a member of the Order, indeed the man whom the Owl-Masters would, in all likelihood, choose to lead the Order, claimed to have discovered a conspiracy, and had presented plausible evidence to support his allegations. He even had witnesses. Niall could hope, in private, that all three men would be exonerated, but that did not relieve him of his responsibilities.

Which, of course, explained why he was sitting there in the first place, alone and inconspicuous in a dark corner of the tavern. "I don't expect there to be many," Sartol had said. "Perhaps there will be none at all." Niall thought otherwise. He couldn't say why, really. It was instinct, nothing more, the type of intuition that he had forgotten he possessed, that he had, in fact, lost a decade ago, only to have it return so abruptly, along with his resolve and his self-respect, in the few days since the unexpected summons to Sartol's quarters. He felt certain that someone would come to see the accused. Someone Niall knew. Soon. And that this person would lead him to others who also sympathized with the three men he had arrested. He expected this to happen; he was waiting for it, as he might anticipate a favorite scene from one of Cearbhall's classic dramas. All he had to do was remain patient.

As it happened, he didn't even need to do that much. Just a few minutes after he seated himself at the ale-stained table, he saw a figure in a mage's cloak enter the inn and move quickly to the stairs. With the hood of the cloak thrown over the mage's head, Niall could not make out any features. But he saw a leaf-green ceryll, and a darkly streaked owl about the size of his own, and he realized, with some surprise, who had come. The Owl-Master visited with the accused mages only briefly, descending the stairs several moments later and slipping outside into the late-afternoon light. Quietly, casually, Niall rose from his table and made his way to the door. He stepped into the sunlight, giving his eyes a minute to adjust before scanning the narrow street for the hooded figure. He saw no one, and he felt a cold panic begin to rise in his heart. Quelling it ruthlessly, he stopped and listened. Even a mage could not vanish into the city without a trace. He waited, holding his breath . . .

. . . and heard the echo of quick footsteps retreating through an alley to his right. Moving quietly to the mouth of the passageway, he caught a glimpse of the green ceryll and the owl. He sighed deeply with relief, feeling his pulse slow to normal, and he allowed himself a brief smile. Then Niall plunged into the shade of the alley to follow the Owl-Master toward the others who had conspired against the Order.

For those few hours lying with Alayna in the redolent grass, feeling the warmth of the sun on his skin, it seemed to Jaryd that time stood still. He and Alayna had lost themselves and their burdens in each other and, later, in the idyllic beauty of the clearing. Just before dusk, the deer that had bolted into the woods when Baden first led the young mages into the open space returned to resume grazing. A pair of hawks glided effortlessly over the knoll, hunting for the evening's meal and drawing the avid attention of Ishalla and Fylimar.

"This was what I saw in the other vision I had of you," Alayna confided as they lay together watching the hawks.

"What do you mean?"

"This," she said, blushing slightly. "Us, together in this meadow."

He grinned and kissed her gently on the lips. "That must have been quite a vision."

She giggled, returning the kiss. "It was."

A few moments later the sun disappeared behind the trees, and the air in the clearing began to grow colder. Reluctantly the young mages slipped back into their clothing and built a small fire. And with the cold air and the darkening of the sky came as well a renewed concern for Baden, Trahn, and Orris. The Owl-Master had given them no timetable for the events he planned to set in motion; he had not indicated when they should expect his messenger to arrive. And, given the way the afternoon had unfolded, the early arrival of whomever Baden sent would have been a cause for much embarrassment for Jaryd and Alayna. Nonetheless, as the two young mages sat in silence by the fire, roasting a pair of quail killed for them by their familiars, Jaryd felt himself growing edgy. He jumped every time he heard the snap of a twig under a deer hoof, or the call of an owl from the nearby forest, and, though they had not eaten for hours, and the bird he was roasting smelled wonderful, he found that he was not very hungry.

Sitting beside him, Alayna shifted slightly and gazed at him. "It may not be until tomorrow," she offered quietly, "and if they opt for a trial before the entire Order, we may have to wait for several days. You're going to have to find a way to relax."

"Am I that obvious?"

She shrugged slightly by way of reply.

Jaryd smirked ruefully. "I'm sorry. It's probably pretty annoying, isn't it?"

Again, the same shrug, although this time Alayna could not entirely keep a grin from her face. "Let's just say that, at this point, I'm hoping for an immediate trial."

He gave a small laugh. "All right, I'll work on it." He paused, turning the spit that held his dinner over the fire. "I feel like we ought to be preparing somehow," he remarked a short while later. "It feels strange to just be sitting here while Baden and the others are about to go on trial."

"What do you think we should be doing?"

Jaryd shook his head. "That's just it: I have no idea. There isn't much that we can do. But it still doesn't seem right." He turned to face her, an idea forming in his head.

"Tell me about Sartol," he urged, "about what we can expect him to do or not do."

She regarded him for a moment before passing a hand through her long hair in a familiar gesture. "I don't know him as well as I thought I did," she observed.

Jaryd heard pain in her voice. This wound would take a long time to heal.

"Perhaps not," he returned, "but you know him better than most of us do, certainly better than I do. Anything will help, Alayna." This last came out as more of a plea than he had intended, but it seemed to reach her.

At length, she nodded. "As I told you this morning," she began thoughtfully, "he'll be ready for whatever Baden does. He's a cautious man, a careful planner."

"Do you think he planned to kill Jessamyn and Peredur?"

"No. That was too sloppy and too dangerous. Something went wrong; he was improvising."

Jaryd shook his head. "And he might still get away with it."

"He's also clever," Alayna said grimly. "But the point I was making before is this: he won't just be counting on the trial going his way and the Owl-Masters selecting him to lead the Order. That's not how he works. There would be too much risk in doing it that way, too much uncertainty." Her face looked rigid and white in the glow of the fire, and her eyes, locked on Jaryd's, had grown wide with the doubt and apprehension that always seemed to come now when she spoke about Sartol. "He'll have planned for every eventuality," she went on. "He'll have taken into account every conceivable outcome of both the trial and the voting for the next sage. If he can help it, he won't allow himself to be surprised."

"I guess that's where we come in," Jaryd commented casually, hoping that his smile and tone conveyed more confidence than he actually felt.

She turned her gaze toward the fire, her expression unchanged. "Maybe," she breathed. "But I can't help thinking that he'll be prepared for us, too."

He could find no words with which to allay her fears; indeed, he felt his own returning with renewed strength. They both fell into a pensive silence, sitting in front of the low fire, absorbed in their thoughts as they waited for their dinners to cook. And they still had not spoken when, several minutes later, they first heard the footfalls coming toward them through the woods.

"That wasn't a deer," Jaryd whispered, instantly attentive as he reached for his ceryll and called Ishalla to his shoulder.

Alayna stood, her staff ready beside her. "No, it wasn't. I think it came from over there," she said, pointing to their right, "from the same direction Baden took when he left us."

"The messenger?"

"Or an enemy."

As if on cue, they both concealed their cerylls within their cloaks. Jaryd took a steadying breath. Then he stood and, with Alayna beside him, moved to the edge of the clearing near where the sound had originated. A few seconds later, they heard it again, closer this time, and, simultaneously, they spied a soft, green light radiating through the trees. For a wildly disorienting moment, Jaryd thought that Theron had come. But he quickly realized that this green was different—it was not the cold, baleful emerald hue that emanated from the unsettled Owl-Master. This looked warmer, more alive, as if it flowed from the grass or from the leaves of the maples and alders that grew in Tobyn's Wood.

"Do you recognize the color?" Alayna asked him.

"No. You?"

She shook her head.

Jaryd hesitated before taking another deep breath and whispering, "Forgive me if this turns out to be the wrong thing to do." Then he uncovered his ceryll and, thrusting it forward toward the forest, made it blaze brilliantly. "Stop and declare yourself," he commanded, striving to sound as menacing as possible, and lamenting the youthful timbre of his voice.

The footsteps halted. "I am a friend," came the reply. It was a woman's voice, clear and strong, though cautiously low. "I was instructed to tell you that 'Like you, I am allied with Theron,' although I don't understand it, and I don't even like saying it."

Jaryd allowed himself to relax, and muted the light of his ceryll. "I understand why you might feel that way," he answered, "but I would ask you to trust that the meaning of what you've said will be made clear to you soon enough. In the meantime, be welcome, Sonel."

"You know me!" she called, and even at a distance, Jaryd could hear the surprise in her tone.

"I know who you are, and I had a feeling that Baden would send you."

"And do I know you?"

Jaryd opened his mouth to respond, but, before he could speak, he felt Alayna touch his arm. Glancing at the young mage, he saw her shake her head in warning. It seemed unlikely that someone else might be listening or that the Owl-Master had been followed. But Alayna was right: he could not risk shouting their names through the forest. He signaled his understanding with a quick nod, and then turned back toward Sonel. "Come forward into the clearing," he instructed, "and you can see for yourself."

The sound of Sonel's footsteps commenced again, the soft crinkle of fir needles and the occasional crack of a twig under her foot floating gently into the open area in which Jaryd and Alayna stood. At the same time, the verdant glow of her ceryll grew steadily brighter, marking her progress through the trees. Soon, she emerged from the dense rows of evergreens into the clearing.

She was taller than Jaryd remembered—almost as tall as he—and younger looking as well. She wore her light brown hair tied back, and her green eyes seemed to capture and amplify the color of her ceryll. Her owl, similar in coloring and size to Baden's Anla, sat watchfully on her shoulder, its earlike tufts standing erect above the round, yellow eyes.

As she stepped into the open air, the Owl-Master raised her staff, brightening the mage-glow from her crystal in order to view more clearly the two figures waiting for her. And, seeing them, she gasped in disbelief and took a step backward.

"But we were told you had died!" she blurted out. "Both of you. That you were killed by Theron—" She faltered, staring at them wordlessly. Then, as comprehension chased the shock and confusion from her face, she began to smile. "Of course: Baden's shibboleth. 'Allied with Theron,' indeed!"

"There's more to it than even that," Jaryd told her, "but for now, that much will suffice."

"I'll take your word for it," she replied. "And I hope that you both will accept my apology for my initial reaction to seeing you alive. This is a gift beyond words, and unlooked for. Welcome back."

Jaryd smiled. "Thank you. Tell me though: how was Baden able to convince you that Sartol's accusations were false without revealing that we were alive?"

Sonel smiled enigmatically. "Baden wouldn't have to do very much to convince me of such a thing. I never believed the charges. And when he told me that he had friends outside the city who could prove his innocence, that was enough. Now you can answer a question for me: why do you wait here? Surely, you wouldn't face the charges with Baden and the others."

"No, probably not. But Baden fears for our lives."

"Why?"

Jaryd hesitated, and it was Alayna who answered. "Because we know that Sartol killed Jessamyn and Peredur; he was the one who chased us into Theron's Grove."

"Arick guard us!" Sonel whispered. "I wish I could say that I'm surprised, but after this day, I fear nothing will ever surprise me again." She looked at Alayna with sympathy. "This must be particularly difficult for you. I'm very sorry."

"That's kind of you," the young mage said with difficulty, awkwardly running a hand through her dark hair. "But we have greater concerns than my feelings."

Sonel looked like she might say more, but instead she simply nodded. "You're right. There's much to discuss," she commented after a pause, her tone crisp. "Perhaps we should sit."

Jaryd motioned toward the small fire in the middle of the clearing, and the three mages moved to arrange themselves around it.

"Baden, Trahn, and Orris have demanded an immediate trial," Sonel began a few moments later. "It will commence tomorrow morning. Baden recommended that you rise with first light and make your way to the southern bank of the Larian. From there you'll be able to hear bells ring, calling the gathered mages together. Wait for about a quarter of an hour and then come to the Great Hall. He also said that you should remember to bring the evidence."

"Good thing he reminded us," Jaryd remarked with sarcasm, allowing himself a small laugh.

Sonel grinned. "He does tend to supervise, doesn't he?"

"Do you know what made them opt for the immediate trial?" Alayna cut in.

The Owl-Master's expression immediately turned grim. "Yes." She took a steadying breath, and then: "Sartol is attempting to link himself to the Summoning Stone. He's already succeeded in altering it slightly. They don't want to risk giving him the opportunity to do more."

Alayna had begun to nod as Sonel spoke. "That fits," she commented flatly. "That sounds like something Sartol would do. May the gods protect us."

"What do you mean when you say he's 'altering it'?" Jaryd asked.

"Baden and Orris both saw the stone flicker with Sartol's ceryll-hue."

Jaryd shook his head in confusion. "I don't understand. If he already has a ceryll, how can he link to another one?"

"A good question," Sonel told him. "I'm not certain that I understand either. According to the natural laws that have always governed the Mage-

Craft, he shouldn't be able to do this. But apparently he has. He must be enormously strong. He would need to be in order to project his magic into a second, ordinary crystal, let alone the Summoning Stone."

"And he'll be that much more powerful once he's mastered it," Alayna added. "I hope tomorrow isn't too late."

"It mustn't be," Sonel said heatedly, her green eyes flashing in the firelight. "It won't be. We aren't alone in this fight. There are several others who support Baden, and there will be more still when the mages see the two of you and hear what you have to say. Sartol won't be allowed to gain control of the Order, not while I'm alive and capable of fighting him."

Alayna stared at the Owl-Master, her expression desolate despite Sonel's pledge. "But how do you defeat a mage who wields that much power?"

"By forming alliances. By working with others who believe in the same things you do. By resisting him at every turn, and even, if necessary, by turning the people of Tobyn-Ser against him." Sonel smiled fiercely, her features taking on a look of determination and fortitude that reminded Jaryd, oddly, of Trahn. Or, perhaps not so oddly. Like Trahn, Sonel was someone Baden loved, a person with whom the Owl-Master had trusted his life, and those of Jaryd and Alayna. "I don't care how strong he is," she concluded, "if Sartol believes that he can subdue us without a battle, he's a fool."

Buoyed by Sonel's forceful words, Jaryd turned to gauge Alayna's reaction. But, even as he did, even as he felt his chest expanding with courage and hope, he heard Ishalla and Sonel's owl hiss in belated warning, and he knew that any foolishness that Sonel might attribute to Sartol was nothing compared with their own. And when he heard the man's voice, one he thought he recognized, call out from the edge of the clearing, he feared that he might be ill.

"Bravely said, Sonel," the man called, "though I never would have figured you for a traitor. I will be very interested to hear more about these others of whom you speak, as, I'm certain, will Sartol. Right now, however, I will be satisfied with the names of your two companions."

Jaryd turned to see who had spoken—all three of them did. But all they saw was a maroon ceryll that flared dazzlingly, like a wine-stained sun, illuminating all the clearing as if it were midday, and shining most brightly, Jaryd understood with anguished clarity, on his face and Alayna's.

19

He had slept poorly, waiting for Sonel to return from the clearing with confirmation that Jaryd and Alayna had received his message. She would have been traveling on foot rather than horseback—all of them had agreed that she would attract less attention that way—and she had cautioned Baden that she might not return to Amarid until late. In which case she was to bring him word of her conversation with the young mages this morning, at first light. She knew him well, and there had been humor and gentle chiding in her strong voice and green eyes as she told him not to worry if she did not show up until daybreak.

"You know that I will," he had replied, "and not just about Jaryd and Alayna."

She raised an eyebrow, reading in the nuances of his voice all that he had hoped to convey. "Maybe I'll try to come back tonight after all," she had said with a coy grin, drawing smirks from Trahn and Orris.

At the time, he had smiled as well. But as the night progressed and she did not return, his anxiety grew. Finally, he drifted into an uneasy slumber, haunted by images of Sartol and the men who had attacked Watersbend.

When he woke, looking immediately toward the window and seeing the soft, pink light of dawn already filtering through the thin curtains, he felt panic rush into his heart, cold and relentless, like a winter wind. She should be here by now, he thought. She should have come back last night. He flung back the covers, pulled on his trousers, and hurried to the door without bothering to put on a shirt or his cloak. Rushing out into the corridor, he was confronted immediately by a blue-robed attendant whom he did not recognize. The man was almost as large as the brute Baden had threatened the day before.

"Yes, Owl-Master?" he inquired courteously. Niall had, at least, conveyed to the guards that the accused mages were to be treated with respect.

"I was expecting a visitor," Baden explained, unable to keep the urgency from his voice. "Did someone come while I slept?"

The big man shook his head. "No one, Owl-Master. Not since the inn-keeper brought your supper. Shall I convey a message for you?"

"No. Thank you, though."

Another door opened, and Trahn, fully dressed, with his long, dark hair still wet from washing, stepped into the hallway. A moment later, Baden heard Orris's door open as well, and the Hawk-Mage stuck his head out, his face looking puffy with sleep. Like Baden, the barrel-chested mage wore no shirt, and he ran a hand through the tangle of yellow hair that fell down around his shoulders.

"What is it, Baden?" Trahn asked with concern.

"Have either of you heard anything from Sonel?"

The dark mage shook his head.

"Orris?" Baden asked, turning to the other man.

"No," the Hawk-Mage answered, stepping out farther into the passageway. "But didn't she say that she might not get back here until morning?"

"She said daybreak," the Owl-Master corrected, "and I had expected her earlier than that."

Trahn exhaled through his teeth. "You think something's happened?"

"I'm not certain what I think." Baden looked at the attendant. "Bring our breakfasts to Hawk-Mage Trahn's room," he commanded, and then, turning back to Trahn, he added, "Orris and I will get cleaned up and dressed. We'll join you in a few minutes."

Baden stepped back into his room and, moving to the basin of water that had been placed in the room last night, he began to wash. But his thoughts remained focused on Sonel.

Try as he might to convince himself that she was fine, that all three of them were fine, he kept coming back to the one hard truth that continued to feed his fears: Sonel was never late. Indeed, she was obsessively punctual—she had been for all the years he had known her. It was one of the few things about her that had always annoyed him, particularly since he tended to be far less conscientious than she. If all had gone according to plan, she would have returned by now.

He explained as much to Trahn and Orris a short while later, as they all picked absently at the platter of grapes, cheeses, and breads brought to them by the innkeeper.

"In spite of everything," the Owl-Master observed, looking from one mage to the other, "we still know very little about what Sartol has in mind, and what resources he can draw upon. He may have followers within the Order who prevented Sonel from ever reaching the clearing. Or maybe they followed her and learned that the others are still alive."

"Or maybe," Orris insisted, "notwithstanding Niall's promise to treat us properly, Sartol's guards aren't letting any visitors into the tavern."

"That seems more likely to me as well, Baden," Trahn agreed, his tone sympathetic. "I know you're worried, but I'm not sure you need to be."

"He's got the Summoning Stone," Orris went on. "He probably figures that he doesn't need anything or anyone else."

Baden shrugged slightly. "You may be right. But given what I've seen so far, I can't help feeling that he'll be more careful than that. He's been planning this for a long time. He's not going to get sloppy now. I don't mind telling you both that I'm scared. Very scared."

Orris and Trahn said nothing—what could they say?—and the three of them sat in silence for the better part of an hour, eating occasionally, but otherwise consumed by their own thoughts. The day brightened, and the breeze that ruffled the window curtains grew warmer, but still they heard nothing from Sonel. Some time later, the bells of the Great Hall began to ring, startlingly loud. Baden had forgotten how close they were to the domed structure. The trial would be starting shortly, and Baden wondered if the young mages recognized the tolling of the bells as their signal. *Where in Arick's name is Sonel!*

Watching his two companions rise, their expressions somber, he wished that he could offer some encouragement, that he could say anything that might lighten the mood in the room. Less than a day before, Baden had felt confident; he had even allowed himself the luxury of flaunting that confidence during their confrontation with Sartol, knowing how it would affect the Owl-Master. But he felt certain now that something had happened to keep Sonel from returning. He could only hope that Jaryd and Alayna had survived the night. If they hadn't, Baden, Trahn, and Orris were doomed, and Tobyn-Ser with them.

An emphatic knock on the door caused Baden to jump, just as the bells had done a few moments before. He had to calm his nerves somehow. It wouldn't do for Sartol to see him like this.

Trahn crossed to the door and pulled it open. Niall stood in the hallway, his face looking uncharacteristically pale beneath the thick, silver hair.

"It's time," he said heavily, stepping slightly to the side, and motioning for the accused mages to go before him. He did not look any of them in the eye.

Baden followed Orris and Trahn out of the room, feeling the older man fall in behind him. The attendants were gone, but Niall's grim silence was like a fifth presence in the dark corridor, looming menacingly at Baden's shoulder. They made their way past the closed doors on each side of the hall, descended the steps to the ground floor of the inn, and pushed through the tavern door. Stepping into the daylight, Baden saw that thousands of Amarid's people—a crowd even larger than the one that had gathered the day before—had lined the thoroughfare leading from the inn to the Great Hall. Ahead of him, Orris glanced back, as if seeking reassurance, his dark eyes wide and fearful. The public humiliation that all of them had endured yesterday had been especially difficult for Orris, Baden knew, and today would not be any easier. Anxious to ease his friend's discomfort, to give him anything else on which to fix his attention, Baden turned to Niall, intending to ask him how many mages had reached Amarid since their meeting with Sartol the afternoon before. But something in the Owl-Master's bearing stopped him; Niall seemed in that moment unapproachable, as though he wouldn't have heard the question even if Baden had asked it. Without a word, Baden faced forward again in time to see Trahn whisper to Orris. Whatever he said appeared to hearten the burly mage and bring a semblance of calm back to his expression.

This crowd displayed less hostility toward the accused mages than the mob had the day before. A few people shouted obscenities and threats as they watched the trio walk by, but, for the most part, Baden sensed more curiosity than he did belligerence.

He remained troubled, however, by Niall's remote manner. The self-righteousness with which the older man had treated them yesterday seemed to Baden much more in keeping with what he knew about Niall. The Owl-Master was a highly moral man. Baden had often disagreed with him during Gathering debates, but he believed Niall to be honorable, and he had grieved with him when Vardis died. He refused to believe that the Owl-Master had joined Sartol in betraying Tobyn-Ser—such treachery was not in the older man's nature. No doubt, Sartol had secured his cooperation by presenting Baden and the others to him as dangerous enemies of the Order and the land. But Niall's behavior this morning had been odd, disturbingly so. And in that instant, with a dizzying flash of insight that terrified him with its clarity and the weight of truth it carried, Baden knew that Niall's dark mood and Sonel's failure to return were connected.

Again, panic gripped him, like an icy hand wrapping its fingers around his heart. He spun around to face Niall, the abruptness of his motion pulling the Owl-Master from his strange reverie.

"What did you do to her?" Baden whispered fiercely. "Where's Sonel!"

Niall gazed at him without speaking, his eyes regaining their normal focus, and his mien disconcertingly placid. "I don't know what you're talking about," he finally replied in a mild tone. "Please keep moving, Baden. Everyone is waiting for you."

"I'm not going anywhere until you tell me the truth!"

Orris and Trahn had halted, and they now moved closer to where the Owl-Masters stood facing each other.

"What's going on, Baden?" Orris demanded, eyeing Niall suspiciously.

"Niall is responsible for whatever happened to Sonel."

Trahn glanced appraisingly at the older mage. "How do you know?"

"I know." Baden grabbed Niall's cloak in his fist, drawing a rasping hiss from the mage's pale owl. "What have you done with Sonel?" he persisted, enunciating every syllable.

Niall's dark eyes continued to hold Baden's with that maddening serenity for another few seconds. Then he placed his hand firmly over Baden's, and disengaged himself from the Owl-Master's grip. "She's fine," he told them all, an admission in the words. "I'm not certain where she is right now, but, when I saw her last, she was unharmed."

Baden wanted desperately to ask about Jaryd and Alayna as well. But Niall had given no indication that he knew the young mages were still alive, and Baden could not risk giving them away. "If she's not," he threatened instead, somewhat fatuously, "I'll hold you responsible."

"So you've been watching us," Orris stated flatly, the burning look in his eyes an accusation. "You've been spying for Sartol."

It was this of all things that broke Niall's composure. "I won't be judged by you!" he said hotly. "And I need not explain myself to anyone! I'll answer to the gods when they feel I'm ready, and until that time I'll conduct myself as I see fit!" He swept the three of them with an imperious glare. "Right now, though," he went on, his voice lower, but no less indignant, "the three of you are to be tried for treason."

Without another word, he spun away from them, striding purposefully toward the Great Hall, and compelling the three accused mages to follow by the sheer force of his will, like dried leaves swept forward in the wake of a galloping mount.

Minutes later they ascended the marble steps and passed through the giant oaken doorway. The Gathering Chamber looked much as it had the day before. The three chairs that Baden, Trahn, and Orris usually occupied still stood in a row at the near end of the chamber, facing the rest of the Order, and leaving three empty spaces around the large table. Several more mages had arrived last night and early this morning, most of them Hawk-Mages who had been on Ursel's patrol. Indeed, Ursel, herself, hale and tanned, her short brown hair streaked with blond from days spent riding in the sun, was among those who had returned. Still, fewer than half the chairs arrayed around the table were full, and a majority of those present were Owl-Masters. Scanning the room, Baden noted with growing apprehension that Sonel had not yet arrived.

"By the gods!" Orris whispered with alarming intensity.

Immediately, Baden swung his eyes to the Summoning Stone, although he knew before he did what he would see. Yellow light. It was so faint that he would never have noticed had he not been looking for it. To an unsuspecting observer, it could have been no more than a trick of the eye, an illusion created by sunlight and the translucent windows of the Great Hall. But Baden had seen the flicker of light the day before; this was no mirage, no false vision.

"He won't be able to conceal this much longer," Baden said under his breath, seeing Orris nod unobtrusively in agreement. "He must be close to mastering it."

"Stand before your chairs!" Niall commanded, in a tone that silenced them.

The three accused mages did as they were told, and, as he had the previous afternoon, Niall signaled to Odinan with a curt nod that all was ready for Sartol. Odinan climbed awkwardly to his feet, self-consciously smoothing the wisps of white hair that stuck out haphazardly from his head. The rest of the Order also stood, and the aged Owl-Master struck his staff on the hard floor, sending echoes through the chamber, and quelling the whispered conversations that, an instant before, had filled the room.

A moment passed. Then another. All remained still within the vast chamber, until finally, a door opened at the far end of the hall, and Sartol swept into the room.

It had been another long night. Too long, Sartol judged, as he paced in front of the hearth in the Owl-Sage's chambers, cradling a cup of shan tea in his hands. Yet, not nearly long enough. He felt drained, overly tired considering what awaited him on this day. Twice he'd sent back the cup he held, complaining to the Great Hall's attendants that the tea they made was not strong enough. And, though they'd steeped this last batch for a full half-hour, it still had not eased his fatigue. The Owl-Master considered ringing the crystal bell once more, but then thought better of it. There were limits to what the herb could do, and he needed sleep, not stronger tea. Besides, it wouldn't do to let anyone know just how exhausted he was, even the inscrutable blue-robed stewards. He could not afford to appear weak; and he did not wish to invite speculation as to what he might be doing with his nights when he should have been resting.

He had planned to sleep for at least part of last night, just as he had for the previous two. But on all three occasions, he had become so engrossed in his effort to link himself to the Summoning Stone that he lost track of time. The first two nights, it had not bothered him; at least, not much. Last night, however—or, rather, this morning—he had been genuinely dismayed to see the first rays of sunlight streaming through the translucent windows of the Gathering Chamber. Reluctant to cease his labors, angry with himself for failing to keep track of the time, he had retreated hastily into his quarters only moments before the first of the attendants arrived and began to ready the hall for the impending trial.

A short while later, Jessamyn's servant—he seemed to remember her name being Basya—knocked on the door and entered, raising an eyebrow with more surprise than she had any right to show when she saw that Sartol was already up and dressed.

"Shall I bring your breakfast, Owl-Master Sartol?" she asked, all solicitude and courtesy.

"Just tea," he had replied, unable to keep the annoyance entirely from his voice.

She nodded and withdrew, leaving Sartol to curse his own stupidity and the too-swift passage of the night. It had been too early at that point to convene the Order for Baden's trial. He needed to hear from Niall first, anyway. And, of course, it was too late to sleep. So the Owl-Master had to compose himself by reflecting on the progress he had made with the stone. Unfortunately, throughout the hour that followed, his apprehensions regarding the trial had intruded continually on his thoughts.

Once again, as he had several times over the past week, Sartol forced himself to stop pacing, thrusting himself into a chair as small drops of the shan tea splashed from the cup onto his cloak. He had done far too much pacing recently—it was a bad habit, one that betrayed his anxiety dangerously. He found it more than a bit bothersome that he should be worrying so much now, on the very brink of his triumph.

Baden did this to him, he knew. Even under guard, stripped of his ceryll and denounced publicly as a traitor, the Owl-Master made him feel edgy. If only Baden hadn't seemed so damned sure of himself the day before, in the wake of his arrest. Orris had looked pale, despite his defiance, and had clearly been humiliated by the day's events, just as he should have been. Trahn, as always, had remained disturbingly unreadable. But Baden . . . Yes, he looked tired, but no more so than Sartol did himself. The Owl-Master hadn't appeared frightened, but Sartol had not expected that he would; like anyone accustomed to power and leadership, Baden could school his features to conceal his emotions. What Sartol found alarming, though, was that he *had* read feelings in the Owl-Master's face, just not ones he had anticipated. Baden had actually smiled at him as he demanded an immediate trial. *He had smiled.* And, for just a moment, although certainly long enough for Baden to see, Sartol had lost his composure. How could he help it? He was only human. And the man had smiled. Charged with treason and murder, facing a trial in which he could present no meaningful evidence of his own innocence, no doubt aware that Sartol had taken and destroyed every single item left in Watersbend by Calbyr's men, Baden had shown no signs of tension whatsoever. Sartol found it disconcerting; appalling, really.

A few minutes later, reflecting on the incident in the Owl-Sage's quarters, Sartol had assured himself that Baden's gesture had been bravado and nothing more. But it had been terribly convincing, so much so, in fact, that Sartol had begun to wonder whether Baden might have some evidence after all. Why else would they opt for an immediate trial? As younger members of the Order, Orris and Trahn had much to gain by waiting until all the mages had returned to Amarid, and still they chose to go ahead with the process right away. A part of him wondered why, what they thought they had to gain by rushing things. Grudgingly, he acknowledged the possibility that Baden had noticed the yellow flickering of the Summoning Stone, and had deduced that Sartol was attempting to link himself to the vast crystal. But there was nothing Sartol could do about that now, and, in another few days, it would no longer be a concern. The confidence manifest in the three mages' choice, however, did worry him. Apparently, they believed in their ability to convince the Order of their innocence. Why else would they take this path? He had to discover what they planned to do.

Which was where Niall came in. Serving as interim sage had many advantages, not the least of which was that it provided him with nearly unlimited access to the stone. But it did confine him to the Great Hall, and it demanded a certain decorum. He could not keep an eye on Baden and the others without drawing unwanted attention to himself, and he was not about to undo years of planning with carelessness and indiscretion. Instead, he turned to the silver-haired Owl-Master.

Sartol's cultivation of Niall's trust and friendship had begun several years ago, before Feargus's death and the election of Jessamyn as Owl-Sage, and several years after the Order had humiliated Sartol with its reprimand. The kernel of his plan had already formed by then, and he had started to nurture it, holding it close and quiet within his heart, but giving it room to take root and grow. Though he knew nothing yet of Calbyr and the outlanders, he had already recognized that he would need to develop a rapport with the other Owl-Masters; that, whatever form his plan ultimately took, their support would be crucial if he was to gain control of the Order.

It had been quite a while since Niall's wife had died, leaving him desolate and indifferent. Where once Sartol had seen a potential rival, he now saw a man devoid of ambition and purpose, unwilling or unable to take an active role in the Order's deliberations. Eventually, he knew that he would reach out to Niall, just as he had already to Odinan, Baden, and several of the others. But the older man's support did not seem crucial to his success anymore. Certainly, by that time, Niall did not represent any sort of threat.

But then Niall surprised him, all of them, in fact, by giving an impassioned speech during the final day of that summer's Gathering, after having observed the first two days of deliberation in near total silence. Sartol no longer recalled what issue it had been that roused Niall from his grief-induced torpor, although he knew that it had been a matter of little consequence, a procedural question, if he remembered correctly—this had contributed to the surprise they all felt at Niall's outburst. Sartol did recall, however, that Niall's comments had come immediately after his own, and that the Owl-Master had objected strenuously to almost everything Sartol said. Afterward, as the mages lined up for the Procession of Light, which would mark the closing of the Gathering, Niall approached Sartol, looking sheepish.

"Sartol, I'd like to apologize for the tone of my remarks earlier today," he had offered, his voice tinged with remorse. "I meant no disrespect; I certainly didn't mean to offend you."

Sartol had grinned, placing a hand on the older man's shoulder. "You didn't, Niall," he replied. "Frankly, it was nice to see in you the passion that I remember from . . . from before. I've missed that."

Niall had looked away then, his expression almost shy, and the ghost of a smile touching his lips. The look in his eyes had been pained, though, and, for just an instant, Sartol thought that he might cry. "I've missed it as well," he said at length.

"Then I hope that we'll see more of it."

"As do I, Sartol. Thank you." There had been so much gratitude in the Owl-Master's voice, and such warmth in his face at that moment, that Sartol knew he had won over an ally of tremendous value. This was not just a master who might someday support him in a contest for Owl-Sage. This, potentially, was someone whom he could trust with a favor, an errand of importance that might require a degree of circumspection.

An errand like this one. At subsequent Gatherings, Sartol developed his friendship with Niall, feeding it with compliments and confidences. He also observed Niall's hunger for a return to the inner circle of power. Many mages cared little for influence, but Niall had possessed it once. Desire for it was in his nature, and now he wanted it back. Sartol could see it in the way he hovered at the fringes of conversations among the more powerful mages; in the look of resignation with which he cast his vote for the new Owl-Sage after Feargus died; in the renewed vigor with which he participated in debates around the council table. Sartol doubted that any of the others noticed it; indeed, he had a feeling that Niall himself was but dimly aware of his own yearning. But Sartol watched the need grow within the Owl-Master, understanding how it felt, and how he might use it to steer Niall to his purposes. For, at root, Niall and he were quite similar. The only difference being that once Sartol had power, he would never let it slip away.

So he was not at all surprised by the ease with which he enlisted Niall's aid in keeping watch on Baden and the others. It was not just that he had spent several years securing the older man's loyalty. He was offering Niall a second taste of leadership, another chance to wield influence within the Order, to move in that circle from which he had fallen a decade ago. The Owl-Master could not refuse him.

Sartol had not taken into account, however, Niall's overly developed sense of morality. The Owl-Master had obviously been reluctant to spy on Baden, and he had blanched visibly when Sartol left to his judgment how to handle any of Baden's allies that he might encounter. In the aftermath of that discussion, Sartol had feared that he might have to entrust to one of the gargantuan thugs whom he had recruited as Great Hall attendants the task of rooting out those who sympathized with the accused mages. He did not relish the idea, for it carried great risks, but he could not allow Niall's priggishness to subvert his entire scheme. Fortunately, Trahn's unexpected arrival on the scene gave Sartol a chance to test Niall's resolve. Sartol never had any intention of allowing the dark mage to roam freely about the streets of Amarid. He was not a fool. But he needed to see how Niall would treat the situation, and the Owl-Master had responded splendidly. It had taken all of Sartol's will to maintain his grave demeanor when Niall declared his intention to arrest Trahn as well. Sartol had wanted to laugh aloud.

Experiencing once again the satisfaction he had felt in that moment, Sartol tried to make himself relax. Whatever advantage Baden thought he might have, Niall would learn of it, and so, too, would Sartol. In fact, the older mage would be arriving shortly to report on what he had seen and learned the night before. There would be no surprises on this day, at least not for Sartol. Others who entered the Great Hall, though, might be surprised, even shocked, if they took the time to examine closely the Summoning Stone. This was the other reason why Sartol should have had no trouble soothing his frayed nerves. Even if something did go wrong today—if, for instance, too many mages noticed the subtle but unmistakable yellow hue that now, in the wake of last night's work, emanated from the stone—he felt reasonably certain that he could subdue all of the mages in the chamber. Against the entire Order, he would not stand a chance, at least not yet. Against the number who had been there yesterday, however, and the few more who had probably trickled into the city last night and this morning, he could prevail. In a way, he almost hoped the others would give him an excuse to try.

He had prepared for this for so long. For a time he had even wondered if it was possible. As far as he knew, no mage had ever bound to two cerylls before. But then his alliance with Calbyr had forced him to try. He needed some way to communicate with the outlander. So he poured his power into one of the extra cerylls that he had taken from Ceryllon, much as he had poured his power into the wooded lake in Tobyn's Wood. And soon, this second ceryll glowed as brightly as his first. But he didn't stop there. Using his immense power, he then altered the second stone, tuning it to his first, as Amarid had tuned the Summoning Stone to all cerylls, so that he could contact Calbyr when he needed to.

After that, he knew that the Summoning Stone would be his. Yes, it was immense, but so was his power. It was just a matter of time and access, both of which he finally had. The night before, he had felt the power surge through his body like an ocean tide as he slowly, inexorably exerted his control over the giant crystal, turning it into a lens for the strength that he channeled from Huvan. And doing so, Sartol had experienced an exhilaration unlike any he had ever known before. He was so strong, so very strong. And he would grow stronger yet, until, just a few days from now, he would be the mightiest mage ever to have lived.

Already, he longed to use that power, to show the others just how far he had taken the Mage-Craft. They had chosen Jessamyn over him; they had reprimanded him for violating one of Amarid's Laws. But soon, very soon, they would realize that he had become more than Amarid, whom they exalted; more than Theron, whom they feared; more than they could ever be themselves, even if they combined their power and challenged him as one. They would not be able to stop him, and Tobyn-Ser would be his. Even Calbyr and his men, and the lethal creatures they carried on their shoulders, would fall before him. So very, very soon.

Sartol shook his head, resisting the temptation to stand and resume his pacing. He didn't really understand it. Even after all the planning, even given Niall's unwitting complicity and his own mastery of the Summoning Stone, why did he still find it so hard to calm himself?

He propelled himself out of the chair, striding impatiently to the folding oak desk that stood near the hearth.

"It's the waiting," he said aloud, as if by making himself hear the words, he might settle his nerves.

Perched on the mantel, Huvan opened her yellow eyes and turned to gaze at him dispassionately.

Sartol began to pace again. *It's the waiting,* he silently told himself again. *As soon as the trial begins, I'll feel better.* He took a deep breath, wishing Niall would get there already.

It was just a few minutes later when he heard the quiet knock at the door, although it seemed an eternity.

"Come in!" Sartol called, in a tone more intense than he had intended. *Carefully,* he cautioned himself as the older mage opened the door. "Come in, Niall," he said again, more gently this time, and with a smile. "You have news?"

The Owl-Master looked pale, shaken. Obviously, he had learned something. Sartol fought to slow his pulse.

Niall lowered himself into one of the chairs. He sat still for a minute, collecting himself, and then looked up at the Owl-Master. "You were right," he began, "this conspiracy goes far beyond just the three accused. Yesterday, late in the afternoon, Sonel visited their room, briefly, and then headed out into Hawksfind Wood. I followed her to a clearing, where she met with two other mages, and I hid among the trees so that I might eavesdrop on their conversation. They spoke of defying the will of the Order, of keeping you from becoming Owl-Sage; they even vowed to turn the people of Tobyn-Ser against us, if necessary."

Sartol sat down beside Niall, his eyes widening with unfeigned astonishment. This was more than he had expected, more than he had dared hope. Regardless of what evidence Baden might possess, Sartol now had another witness, this one an Owl-Master, who would confirm the existence of a conspiracy against the Order. Only an extreme exertion of self-control enabled him to suppress the fit of laughter that had begun to rise within him, like the cresting of a rain-fed river.

"You say it was Sonel?" he managed, trying to sound grave.

"Sonel, yes," Niall replied dismally, obviously pained by what he had seen and heard. "Along with two others."

"Did you recognize them as well?"

Niall shook his head, refusing to meet the Owl-Master's gaze. There was something else, something he wasn't saying. Sartol could read it in his eyes, in the pallor of his features, and in the nervousness with which he rubbed and twisted his trembling hands together. "I failed you, Sartol," Niall admitted after some time, "and I've done a terrible thing."

It couldn't possibly matter, so glorious were these tidings. "Tell me," Sartol said gently, placing a hand on the older man's arm. "It's all right, I'm sure. Just tell me."

Niall took a steadying breath. "After I listened for a while, growing angrier and angrier, I finally decided that it was time to . . . to do something. So, I stepped forward into the clearing, raised my ceryll-light, and demanded that they surrender themselves. Sonel froze—I think she was so startled by my appearance that she didn't know what else to do. But the other two . . ." Niall faltered, closing his eyes for a moment and allowing himself another long breath. "The other two ran. I yelled for them to stop, but they wouldn't. I yelled again—I was so angry . . . Before I knew what had happened I had flung a bolt of mage-fire at them. It all happened so fast; it was just instinct." He swallowed. "They're dead, Sartol. I killed them both. I hadn't intended to, but I did. And I was so upset at what I had done that I allowed Sonel to get away. I tried to chase her, but I lost her in the woods." He stopped, looking now directly at the Owl-Master. "I've let you down. I'm . . . I'm terribly sorry."

Let me down? Sartol wanted to say, again fighting the urge to laugh. *Let me down? You have done more than I ever dreamed you would. You have denied Baden two of his allies. You have given me further evidence of a conspiracy and the name of another accomplice. You have, in short, delivered the Order into my hands, Niall.* Instead, though, he picked up the crystal bell and rang it once. Immediately, Basya appeared at the door. "Bring Owl-Master Niall some water, please," he instructed. The girl nodded before hurrying off, and Sartol moved his chair closer to Niall's so he could place a sympathetic arm around the mage's shoulder. "I know that you will be punishing yourself for what you've done," he offered quietly. "I probably would do the same. But these mages betrayed the Order; for all we know, they had a hand in the attacks on Taima and Kaera and the other villages. No one will blame you for what's happened. Such a thing goes against your nature, I know; it will be a source of pain for you. But I'm grateful for the sacrifices you've made to protect Tobyn-Ser, and it is I who should be sorry for putting you in this position."

A single knock on the door stopped him, and Basya entered the room with a tall, crystal glass filled with ice water. "Thank you, Basya," Sartol said, as she handed the glass to Niall. She offered a small bow, and slipped silently out of the chamber.

Niall sipped at his water, and the two of them sat without speaking for a long while. Finally, somewhat abruptly, the older man stood, setting the half-empty glass on a low table in the middle of the room. "I should go," he said, his voice rough. "The trial will be beginning soon, and I've taken too much of your time already."

Sartol rose as well. "Not at all. But we should get things started. You will be all right?"

The mage nodded, trying without success to smile.

Sartol led him to the door, pausing at the threshold to grip Niall's shoulder. "I'll see you in the Gathering Chamber shortly, my friend. Thank you for all you've done. All the people of this land are indebted to you."

Niall gazed at him for a moment, his expression unreadable. Then, wordlessly, he turned and walked across the marble floor of the hall toward the massive portal at the far end.

Sartol closed the door to his quarters and allowed himself a broad grin. Niall had proven himself more valuable than he had ever imagined possible. Perhaps, he would keep his promise to make the Owl-Master his first, at least until he had complete control over the Summoning Stone. Why not make the old man happy?

But first, he would rid himself of Baden. He glanced over at his owl, which still sat languidly above the hearth. "Yes," Sartol told her, as if confirming something she had said. "It's time we rung the bells."

Again he picked up the crystal bell and shook it gently, and, again, Basya appeared at his door within a few seconds.

"It is time to begin the trial," he told her. "Have the bell-keep call the mages to order."

The attendant withdrew, and, shortly after, Sartol heard the heavy tolling of the bells begin. It would take a while, he knew, for the mages to arrive, and he sat down by the hearth to wait. The urge to pace had passed, replaced by a giddy thrill of anticipation. At last, it had come: the culmination of all his planning. This was not a time for impatience or disquiet; this was an occasion to be savored.

Soon, he began to hear voices in the Gathering Chamber, as masters and mages took their places around the dark wooden table. He rose, adjusting his cloak and running a hand through his thick, dark hair. The noise outside his quarters continued to swell, and then it took on a different tone, indicating to Sartol that Niall had arrived with the accused. It would not be long now. He closed his eyes, took several slow breaths. He had gone over what he would say again and again, until it had become a sort of litany, repeating itself constantly in his brain. It was very convincing; he almost believed it himself.

Odinan's staff rapped resoundingly on the chamber floor, silencing the other mages. Still, Sartol did not move. Eyes closed, he listened to his heartbeat. The delay would make his entrance that much more effective. Finally, slowly, he opened his eyes and raised his arm for Huvan. And then, feeling her alight on his wrist and hop up to his shoulder, he stepped to the door, flung it open, and strode purposefully into the chamber.

Immediately, every pair of eyes in the room swung in his direction. *Let them look upon us,* he sent to his familiar as he took the sage's chair, *let them see those who will rule this Order before the day is out.*

Watching Sartol arrive, Niall moved away from the accused mages to take his place at the table. Odinan was still on his feet, stooped and leaning heavily on his staff, and now he began to speak, formally convening the trial in his thin, wavering voice. "We heard yesterday the charges of treason and murder brought against Baden, Trahn, and Orris. Today, in accordance with Amarid's Fourth Law, the Order sits in judgment on the verity of those charges. According to the procedures established by Terrall, the second Owl-Sage to lead this Order, Sartol, who made these accusations, will present testimony first. He will be followed by Baden, who will speak for the accused. Sartol?"

"Thank you, Odinan," Sartol said with a grateful smile, standing as the ancient Owl-Master sank back into his chair. He looked out across the room, his expression turning somber. "I stand before you today, faced with the most painful task I have ever known. I do not wish these men ill, nor do I care to relive in testimony the disturbing events which have led us all to this day. But neither can I remain silent, given what I have seen. Crimes have been committed against the Order and Tobyn-Ser. Four of our comrades have been taken from us, among them our wise and brave leader, and a young woman whom I considered my closest friend. And across this land, many, many others have suffered similar losses, all due to the craven, vicious acts of the three mages who sit before you." As if on cue, every mage in the chamber turned to look at Baden and his companions. "You will all remember," Sartol went on after a brief interval, drawing their gazes back in his direction, "that the eight of us—the four who died, the three accused, and myself—left here nearly five weeks ago on a mission that would carry us to Theron's Grove. There, according to a plan first developed by Baden and Trahn, we were to confront the unsettled Owl-Master, who they claimed was responsible for the recent attacks on Tobyn-Ser.

"We reached the grove in approximately a fortnight. It was an uneventful journey, which made what happened the night of our arrival there that much more shocking." He hesitated. "I remember there was a storm just around sunset. Baden and Trahn went to check on the horses. At Jessamyn's request, Alayna and Jaryd began covering our supplies, and I walked down to the river to refill our water pouches. Jessamyn and Peredur found a small cluster of trees where they started to gather torches for our meeting with Theron."

"Torches?" Mered interjected. "What for?"

"Again, at Baden and Trahn's suggestion, we planned to leave our cerylls outside the grove, thus, by their reckoning, denying Theron's spirit access to them."

Mered began to nod slowly. "Yes," he said, "I recall some mention of that during the Gathering. Proceed."

"Well, at that point, things began to happen very quickly. While at the river, I thought I heard Jessamyn cry out. Naturally, I began running back toward the camp, but when I reached it, no one was there. I looked around for some sign of what had happened, and saw mage-fire coming from the cluster of trees. Again, I ran to investigate. And just as I reached the trees, Alayna screamed and there was another burst of ceryll-light. I entered the copse, saw that Jessamyn and Peredur were dead, and ran on, hoping that I could save Alayna and Jaryd. I saw the three of them as I emerged from the trees—Orris was chasing the young ones—and immediately I threw my mage-fire at him."

"Sartol, did you actually see Orris kill Jessamyn and Peredur?" Odinan asked, his thin, quavering voice interrupting Sartol's narrative.

"No. But I believe that Alayna and Jaryd did, and that's why Orris was pursuing them when I came upon him."

"What makes you think that?"

The Owl-Master shrugged. "I have no reason to believe that Alayna or Jaryd killed the sage and the first; Baden and Trahn were not in the area just then. Hence, it had to be Orris."

"Or you," Orris chimed in.

The others in the Great Hall turned to look at the bearded mage. Sartol stretched his face into a cold grin, knowing that the gesture would do little to mask his anger. "Yes, Orris," he returned evenly, "or me." He held the other man's glare for some time, but Orris would not look away. At length, broadening his grin, Sartol swept the room with his eyes. "But as the rest of my testimony will soon demonstrate," he went on, raising his voice to carry throughout the chamber, "far from being involved in these crimes, I was very nearly another victim of the conspiracy woven by the accused."

"What did you do when you saw Orris chasing the young ones?" Odinan asked.

"Well," Sartol answered, pitching his voice to convey what he hoped would be the right blend of grief, indignation, and animosity, "as I had started to say, I threw my mage-fire at Orris, forcing him to break off his pursuit of the Hawk-Mages, but by then it was too late. Alayna and Jaryd just kept running until they reached the grove; I was too busy fending off Orris's counterattack to stop them." He closed his eyes, taking a long, shuddering breath. He was doing, he knew, very well.

Notwithstanding Orris's intrusion, he could see, from the expressions of those arrayed around the table, that he had the rapt attention of every mage in the room, even those whom he guessed would be less inclined to trust him than they would Baden. To be sure, there were those in the chamber who would not believe him, whose allegiance to Baden, Trahn, and Orris would withstand his verbal assault. But they were the minority. A sufficient number of those present remained open to persuasion; many of them had already begun to accept his version of the events by Theron's Grove. And this was only the beginning. He had been careful not to start too vehemently, to leave room for his rhetoric and fervor to build as he catalogued the atrocities committed by Baden, Orris, and Trahn. If he had the interest of his listeners this early, he would have their hearts by the end of his account.

"I don't think that my battle with Orris lasted very long," Sartol continued after pausing briefly, ostensibly to reclaim some control over his emotions, "but it seemed to go on forever. Orris was remarkably strong, far stronger than any mage I've ever encountered. I only managed to survive because, by sheerest luck, Huvan here—" the Owl-Master gestured toward the owl, which sat wide-eyed and attentive on the chair behind where he stood "—was able to kill the mage's familiar. Even so, Orris injured me, and escaped before I could take advantage of his lost power."

"Where were Baden and Trahn while the two of you were fighting?" one of the Owl-Masters inquired.

"I'm not certain. I found them a short while later. They feigned ignorance of all that had happened, and, of course, I had no reason to doubt them at the time."

"Don't forget to mention that we healed your injuries," Trahn called out from his seat at the far end of the room.

Sartol glared at the dark mage, as the others in the room turned again to face in that direction as well. Technically, the rules governing this type of Gathering entitled the accused only to ask questions, and Sartol resented these interruptions. Baden, for his part, added nothing to Trahn's intrusion, but the hint of a grin played at the corners of his mouth.

"I would not have forgotten," Sartol snarled contemptuously. "They did indeed heal me, which, of course, supports my assertion that Orris wounded me. Why else would I have needed healing?" Again he paused, this time to allow the impact of the point he had just made to reach all in the room. "Nor will I fail to mention," he added, "that Baden and Trahn helped me build a funeral pyre for the sage and her first. Their attention to detail and decorum is part of the reason their conspiracy came so close to succeeding. They even convinced me that Trahn had agreed to remain by the grove so that he could see to the safety of Alayna and Jaryd, in case Orris went after them again. I only realized later that his true purpose was to ensure that the young mages did not escape the grove with their lives."

"You say that Orris attacked Alayna and Jaryd," Ursel challenged, rising from her seat, skepticism manifest in her tone and stance, "and that you knew from his actions that he killed the sage and first. When did you begin to suspect Baden and Trahn?"

Sartol ignored the insinuation in the Hawk-Mage's voice, instead launching directly into a matter-of-fact response to her question. "As Baden and I made our way northward, back toward Amarid, I observed that he was behaving strangely. He seemed edgy, uncommunicative; I felt that he was hiding something. I assumed that he was merely worried about Jaryd," he explained, knowing how reasonable he sounded and moving ruthlessly to quell a sudden impulse to smile. "I, of course, understood, having just lost my former Mage-Attend as well." He wandered a bit from where he had been standing, running a hand thoughtfully across his brow. "But as Baden's strange mood persisted, it began to feed my suspicions and my fears. I started piecing together the circumstances leading up to the formation of our delegation, and it occurred to me that Baden and Trahn had pushed very hard for it, that perhaps they had been motivated by something other than just their concern for the Order and their belief that Theron might be behind the attacks. Then I remembered Orris's abrupt request to be included in the company traveling to the grove, and it all seemed so clear: what better place to rid themselves of their rivals for power? They could kill off Jessamyn and Peredur, blame the deaths on Theron's spirit, cease their attacks on Tobyn-Ser, and make it seem that Baden and Trahn were right about the attacks all along, thus enhancing their stature within the Order." A murmur moved through the chamber, like a breeze rustling through a forest. I have most of them, Sartol realized, enough of them I'm sure. But still, he was not finished.

"All of this remained conjecture for a while longer, but, during this time, Baden's manner turned ever more suspicious. He practically stopped eating, he slept fitfully, calling out strange, unintelligible things from his slumber. I grew increasingly concerned about Alayna and Jaryd, realizing that, even if they escaped Theron, Trahn and Orris awaited them outside the grove.

"Even in the face of these fears, though, I continued to entertain the hope that I might be wrong about Baden and Trahn; that, perhaps, Orris had acted alone. But those hopes vanished when we reached Watersbend." Sartol closed his eyes again, shaking his head slowly. "The devastation there was . . ." He swallowed. "The dead were everywhere: men and women, adults and children. Every living creature in the northern part of the village had been murdered. And the men who did it were still moving through the village when Baden and I arrived. A battle ensued. I attempted to kill both men, but Baden assaulted me before I could. In the end, I fought him off and killed the attackers. The townspeople began to thank me for what I had done, but Baden flew into a rage, screaming at me, excoriating me for not sparing the men's lives."

"Come now, Sartol," Baden said insolently. "You make it sound as though I did nothing at all."

"You're right, Baden," Sartol replied magnanimously. "I'm sorry. I do recall that, during the course of the battle, Baden killed their birds."

Baden nodded. "Thank you," he said with sarcasm.

"But," Sartol continued, pressing the point, "that just made his response to my actions that much more bewildering. He was out of control, berating me as if I had murdered his closest friends in the world."

"I understand, Sartol," Odinan broke in, "that you have witnesses who will corroborate all of this."

"That's correct," Sartol replied. "But Baden demanded that this trial begin before they could be here. Fortunately, he has agreed to accept my synopsis of their testimony."

"Ursel," Odinan went on, turning to the young mage, "I also understand that one of your patrols reached Watersbend a day or so later, and spoke with witnesses who mentioned Baden's attempt to save the men and Orris's involvement with Baden's escape from the Watersbend jail. Is this true?"

Ursel stood again, her brown eyes shifting uncomfortably from Baden, to Orris, to the old Owl-Master who had asked the question. Again, Sartol suppressed a smirk. "Yes," the Hawk-Mage answered at last, "that is true. Neysa told me of this through the Ceryll-Var. Her patrol hasn't returned yet, so we know little else of what she learned from the survivors of the Watersbend attack."

Odinan nodded. "Thank you. You may go on, Sartol."

"There's not much more to tell," the Owl-Master stated. "I had Baden arrested and then I attended to the needs of the villagers. They gave me a room at their inn and I retired for the night. But a short time later I was awakened by the villagers, who told me that a powerfully built mage with long yellow hair had assaulted the guards at the jail and helped Baden escape. I deduced that they were speaking of Orris and, fearing for my life, I fled the town. I assumed that if Orris had caught up with us, Trahn might have as well, and I dared not risk a confrontation with all three of them."

"So that was when you started back toward Amarid," Odinan ventured.

"That night, yes."

"And you had no more contact with the accused mages until their arrival here?"

"That's correct."

"Why don't you tell everyone about the men you killed, about what they carried?" Baden demanded, and Sartol was pleased to see that the gaunt Owl-Master appeared somewhat less sure of himself than he had earlier.

"I'm afraid that I don't understand," Sartol replied with uncertainty.

"What about their weapons?" Baden persisted. "How were they able to cause so much damage? Tell us that."

Sartol nodded knowingly. "Ah, yes. That was a bit strange," he acknowledged. He turned back to Odinan as he began to explain. "The men we encountered wore cloaks like ours and carried birds and cerylls as we do, but we saw their faces: they were not mages of this Order. Apparently, those who recruited them to carry out these attacks trained them in the ways of the Mage-Craft without admitting them to the Order. In this way, they succeeded in convincing the people of Tobyn-Ser—"

"I've heard enough, Sartol!" Baden cut in savagely. "What about the mechanical birds and the fire-throwing weapons? These people were outlanders, and you know it!"

Again, excited conversations, spoken in breathless whispers, threaded their way around the table. For just an instant, Sartol gazed at Baden across the elongated wooden table. It might well have been a chasm, so great seemed the distance. Then Sartol allowed himself a smile, just as Baden had smiled at him so disconcertingly the day before. He knew that he enjoyed an advantage now—Baden's claims about outlanders and artificial birds sounded preposterous. And Baden seemed to know this as well. His face looked pale beneath the thin red and silver hair, except for two bright pink spots high on his cheeks. A moment later, Sartol turned a beseeching look toward Odinan, who responded by pounding the base of his staff on the marble floor.

"Silence!" the aged Owl-Master squawked, bringing a sudden, awkward quiet to the chamber. "Please, let us remain calm. I want no more outbursts. Baden," he added, turning toward where the accused mages sat, "I must ask you to refrain from statements of that sort. You shall have your turn shortly, but until then, you are required by the rules of the Order to remain silent, except to ask questions of the accuser." Baden cast a smoldering glance in Sartol's direction, but then nodded reluctantly. "You may continue, Sartol," Odinan said, looking once more at Sartol. "Have you more to say?"

"Only this," the Owl-Master began, coloring his tone with equal shades of regret and defiance. "You are about to hear a fanciful tale, filled with intrigue and innuendo and alarming revelations. Already, we have been given a preview of what is to come. We have heard Orris attempt to blame me for the murders of the sage and her first. We have heard Baden suggest that outlanders, with mechanical birds and strange, powerful weapons, were responsible for the destruction of Watersbend. And, no doubt, the rest of Baden's testimony will be equally dramatic. Listen to it, consider it, enjoy it as you would a finely crafted fable; but please, do not be fooled by it. Do not allow them to play on your fears; do not accept wild, frightening allegations as a substitute for tangible, albeit prosaic evidence.

"I brought you the staffs of Jessamyn and Peredur; Trahn admitted that he and Baden healed the injuries I suffered in my battle with Orris; I have witnesses who saw Baden's attempt to save the men who attacked Watersbend and who heard him berate me when I managed to kill them despite his efforts. Ursel has confirmed this for us. All of this is evidence. All of this is proof. Remember it, for Baden will offer you none. He cannot, not because none remains, not because, as he might claim, it all has been lost, but because all that does exist, all that ever existed, supports what I have told you."

Sartol paused, shaking his head. "Outlanders," he said with a soft chuckle. "Mechanical birds. It is almost amusing." His smile faded, and he let his voice dip low and grow icy with contempt. "Almost. Except that these are lies designed to vindicate men who have betrayed this Order and this land; men who murdered Jessamyn and Peredur, Alayna and Jaryd; men who coordinated assaults on Sern, Taima, Kaera, Watersbend, and at least ten other villages that left thousands dead and maimed, and countless others without homes or livelihoods." He leveled a rigid finger at the accused mages. "Those three men—Baden, Trahn, and Orris—had our trust. They were our colleagues, our friends. But even more than that, they were Amarid's Children. They promised to be guardians of the land. They took an oath, just as the rest of us did. An oath to uphold Amarid's Laws. But they have mocked that oath, and they have turned their backs on those laws. And all the lies, and fairy tales, and false accusations in the world cannot undo that."

Again he stopped, encompassing the gathered mages in a glance. He had them. He sensed it in the way they regarded him, in the absolute stillness

DAVID B. COE

shaped by his words. And so, in a tone of resolve tinged but slightly with sorrow, he concluded. "All of us would like to believe that this never happened. In a way, that is the most dangerous element of Baden's story: all of us would like nothing better than to blame outsiders for the abhorrent crimes committed throughout this land. We wish that we could absolve ourselves, and the Order, of our share of the blame." He shook his head. "But we cannot. We must face what has happened; we must acknowledge what Baden, Trahn, and Orris have done; and we must set right what they have made so terribly wrong. They have shaken the people's faith in the Mage-Craft. We must restore it. They have brought fear into our land. We must eradicate it. They have defiled Amarid's Laws." He stabbed the air with an upthrust finger. "We must uphold and enforce it. And as the first step down that long, difficult path, we must punish them." He took a breath. "The penalty for what these men have done is death. They have earned their executions."

Sartol stood a moment longer, casting his gaze around the room once more, and tasting the vindication in the still-unbroken silence that met his call for retribution.

An instant later, though, as he lowered himself into his chair, the stillness was broken by the sound of one man's derisive applause.

"What marvelous theater," Baden mocked, shattering the mood Sartol had created as if it were cheap glass. "Worthy, no doubt, of Cearbhall himself. But what shall we call it?" he asked, propelling himself out of his seat. "It's too pathetic to be a comedy, and too funny to be a tragedy. Which leaves us, it seems, with farce. Wouldn't you say, Sartol?"

Their eyes met, and Sartol felt his color rising. "I'm not sure, Baden," he returned, his voice just barely under control, "diversions of this sort were never my strength. I prefer fact to fantasy."

"Funny, I would have guessed otherwise."

"Do you have evidence to present, Baden?" Sartol demanded testily. "Or will your entire defense consist of this insulting prattle?"

Baden bared his teeth in a mirthless grin. "Have patience, Sartol. Petulance doesn't become you."

Sartol opened his mouth to fling back another retort. But then he checked the impulse, leaning back in his chair instead, and permitting himself a slight smirk. The bravado with which Baden carried himself on this day had none of the power or substance or self-assurance he had shown the day before. It seemed empty, somehow; brittle. Baden was stalling, Sartol realized, the knowledge coming to him with the power of epiphany. By goading him like this, by initiating an exchange of barbs, the Owl-Master hoped not only to provoke Sartol into giving something away, but also to put off his own testimony. It seemed likely as well that Baden's need for delay grew out of what Niall had wrought the night before. And with the thought, Sartol's mind suddenly turned in a new direction. Sonel was irrelevant; a messenger, nothing more. But the two in the clearing, the two Niall had killed: they were another matter. Why would Sonel meet them outside the city unless these two had been hiding there? And why would Baden bother to hide two allies unless . . .

Baden was saying something about the grove, going over the events of that night once again, but claiming that Sartol, not Orris, had been responsible for

Jessamyn and Peredur's murders. Sartol knew that he ought to be listening, but his mind was racing to keep up with the series of revelations crashing over him like the breakers of an incoming tide. Two days before, when Niall reported to him that Trahn had been seen with Baden and Orris, Sartol had accepted the news without question, assuming that the Hawk-Mage had left Theron's Grove after convincing himself that Alayna and Jaryd were dead. But what if Trahn had left the grove with them? What if the young ones had escaped somehow from Theron, only to be killed last night by Niall? And what if Baden knew nothing of this yet; what if he still expected Alayna and Jaryd to show up at this trial? What if he was waiting for them even now, wondering at this point why they had yet to arrive? It would explain both the swagger that the Owl-Master had shown the day before, and the false confidence with which he bore himself today. It would explain why the accused mages had been willing to chance an immediate trial. It would, in short, explain everything that had been bothering Sartol since Baden's arrival in Amarid. Sensing how near he was to success, savoring the feeling as he would a cool drink on a sweltering day, Sartol looked at Niall, only to find that the older man was already staring at him, his features still pallid and taut with concern. Ah, my friend, Sartol sent wordlessly, as though the silver-haired mage might read his thoughts, if only you understood the magnitude of what you have done for me.

"It didn't occur to me to question Sartol's version of what had happened until three nights later," Baden was explaining. A quick scan around the table told Sartol that only a handful of the mages in the room believed what they were hearing from the lean Owl-Master. "We had stopped for the night, having ridden Tobyn's Plain for much of the day, and we started talking about the recent attacks. Somehow, Sartol knew already about the attack on Kaera. I hadn't mentioned it to him, nor had Trahn, and if he had learned of it through the Ceryll-Var, from another mage, he would have told us. But he never said a thing about it, and yet he already knew. That was when I started to suspect that Sartol had allied himself with outlanders, a suspicion he confirmed the following night in Watersbend. The men we encountered there recognized Sartol; one of them even started to speak to him. That was why I tried to keep Sartol from killing them, and that was why I was so angry after he did. I wanted to interrogate them, to find out who they were and where they had come from. But thanks to Sartol, that was impossible. When Sartol went off to help the villagers, and I was taken to the jail, Orris snuck into the village square. There he found the lethal mechanical birds of which I spoke before, and the strange staffs that threw flame at the touch of a button."

"Yes, yes," Sartol said disdainfully, cutting off the Owl-Master. "We've heard all of this before, Baden. But where is your evidence?" He smiled—he could not help but smile, he was beginning to enjoy himself so. "You cannot make such ridiculous claims and expect us to believe you without presenting proof."

Baden glowered at him. Perhaps he even began to speculate that Sartol had figured out what he had planned for his defense. Sartol never got the chance to consider that possibility. For, in that moment, the great wooden doors at the far end of the hall slowly swung open, and Sonel entered the Gathering

Chamber. By itself, this signified little. Niall mentioned that she had gotten away, and Sartol had suspected that she might show up. But then he saw her catch Baden's eye, saw a slow grin spread across her face as she gave him a reassuring nod. Sartol's eyes flew to Niall. Who was grinning at him: an appalling, taunting grin, the malice of which reached the older mage's dark eyes.

"You demand proof, Sartol?" Baden crowed triumphantly. "Then you shall have it!"

And feeling abruptly as though he had been thrust to the very brink of a vast, yawning abyss, tasting in that instant his own death, Sartol watched Alayna and Jaryd step forth into the chamber, bearing their magnificent hawks and another thing that he could scarcely comprehend.

20

There had come a moment the day before, as he followed Sonel down shadow-darkened alleys and through the late-afternoon crowd in Amarid's old market area, when Niall felt a strange giddiness take hold of him, intoxicating him with the thrill and the danger of what he was doing. Beyond the satisfaction and pride of having been called upon by the interim sage for such a critical assignment, he actually enjoyed the intrigue, the challenge of keeping the Owl-Master in view while making sure that she did not see him. It seemed a bit peculiar, given the circumstances, but he was having fun.

Obviously conscious of the fact that Sartol might have her followed, Sonel took a roundabout route into Hawksfind Wood, backtracking several times, and winding unpredictably through various sections of the city. Twice, Niall almost lost her: once in the labyrinth of cobblestone passageways that ran among Amarid's white and grey buildings, and a second time in the bustle and confusion of the old town center. Both times, however, he managed to spot her again. He had expected that Baden's errand would eventually carry her out of the city and, since the Larian bordered Amarid on three sides, he guessed that she would have to cross one of the bridges. Knowing where she would end up made tracking her that much easier.

His task grew somewhat more complicated when Sonel first entered the wood. Aware of how difficult it would be to move silently through the forest, yet wary of allowing Sonel to get so far ahead of him that she might veer off the path unseen, Niall moved with excruciating care. It paid off. By the time night fell, Sonel had apparently convinced herself that no one was following her. Why else would she have lit the trail with her vivid green ceryll, not bothering to shield its glow from view, and giving Niall the opportunity to follow at a safer distance? For his part, Niall muted his crystal, providing himself with just enough light to keep from stumbling on the rocks and roots that lay in the path.

At length, Sonel did leave the trail, turning onto a narrow offshoot that meandered through dense woodland and tangled brush. Niall followed, and, a short while later, he heard a voice call out to her, one that sounded puzzlingly familiar, and he saw a blue light blaze in the night. From the conversation that ensued, Niall determined that he had, indeed, found another who sympathized with Baden's cause. When the mage with the sapphire ceryll invited Sonel to join him, Niall began to creep closer so that he might hear what they said. It took him a while, concerned as he was with not making any sound that might alert Sonel and her companion to his presence. Long before he actually heard anything of their discussion, Niall realized that a second mage had also been waiting for the Owl-Master in the large clearing. This other person carried a purple crystal, and, unlike the blue, it seemed to Niall that this was a color he had seen before. He knew, though, that this could not be, that the mage who had wielded that ceryll was dead.

He would learn their identities soon enough, he decided, moving noiselessly among the trees, but first he had to glean what they planned to do. So he drew close enough to listen as they spoke of treason, and of other allies, and of turning the people of Tobyn-Ser against Sartol, all the while gathering his courage to do what he now understood was necessary. Any lingering doubts that he might have harbored as to Baden's guilt, and the validity of Sartol's concerns, evaporated in those few minutes. And with those doubts went his reluctance to take matters into his own hands. So certain was he that the conspiracy existed as Sartol had described it, that he felt capable of killing the mages before him—something he would never have dreamed possible just a few days earlier.

After several more moments, having heard enough, he stepped into the clearing, raising his maroon ceryll over his head and making it flare like mid-summer lightning to shine with the light of justice on the faces of the rene-gades.

A great deal had changed for him in the last few days; much had happened to make him feel alive again, to give him back his passion and purpose, to restore his self-respect. But none of it could have prepared him for the shock of what he saw in the wine-colored radiance of his mage-glow. He thought them apparitions at first, unsettled spirits of the young mages lost in Theron's Grove. But while one had, in fact, bound to his first familiar in this forest just a few weeks ago, the other's binding place was a hundred leagues from here. Besides, Niall had seen an unsettled spirit once—that of his own father, who died only four weeks after losing his last familiar. These two were not ghosts; they were as human as Niall himself, though how and why this should be, Niall did not understand.

For a long time, Niall said nothing, his mind reeling with the implications of Jaryd and Alayna's impossible appearance in Hawksfind Wood. For their part, notwithstanding what he would later tell Sartol, the young mages did not run, although fear and despair shone in their eyes as they regarded him silently. Sonel stared at him as well, but her expression revealed little.

Finally, Niall lowered his ceryll and muted the dazzling light he had sum-moned from it upon entering the clearing. "I hope you'll forgive me," he said into the stillness, looking at the young mages, "but I don't know whether to rejoice in your safe return or to demand that you surrender yourselves, along with your friend here, so that you can face charges of treason."

"We aren't traitors!" Jaryd fired back, his wiry frame coiled with tension, his pale eyes glimmering with mage-light and flame. "Any more than Sonel is! Nor, for that matter, are Baden, Trahn, and Orris!"

"I would expect you to say that," Niall replied coldly, "given that Baden is your uncle."

"Given what you know of me, Niall," Alayna broke in, her tone calmer than Jaryd's, "would you expect me to say that it was Sartol who murdered Jessamyn and Peredur? That it was he who chased Jaryd and me into Theron's Grove?"

Niall's mouth went dry, and he could not think of any response. Alayna had been Sartol's Mage-Attend. They had been close friends. Just within the last few days, the Owl-Master had spoken tearfully of his grief at losing her. But now she stood in this clearing, alive, claiming that Sartol had tried to kill her. It made no sense, but it made no more sense for Alayna to lie about such a thing.

"The two of you were actually in Theron's Grove?" he managed.

Alayna nodded. "We were."

"And you escaped?"

"Yes."

"Did you speak with him? Did you complete the delegation's mission?"

"In a sense, yes," Jaryd told him, his tone wary, but without the belligerence he had shown a moment before. "Theron had nothing to do with the attacks, but he has offered to help us find those who did."

Niall shook his head. "The two men who died in Watersbend—are they . . ." He trailed off, uncertain of how to proceed.

"We arrived in Watersbend after they were dead," Alayna told him. "Trahn was with us. But, from what Baden and Orris told us of the battle there, and given what we learned from Theron, we believe that they were but two of many who have come to Tobyn-Ser to commit the crimes for which Baden and the others are to stand trial."

Niall's blood turned cold. "*Come to Tobyn-Ser?* Outlanders?"

Again, Alayna nodded.

"What do they want?"

"We don't know for sure. But they seem intent upon so weakening the Order that we'll be unable to guard Tobyn-Ser from an invasion."

"You believe that Sartol is connected with these people in some way, that he has allied himself with them?"

"That's what Theron told us," Jaryd answered, "and Baden and Orris both believe that the men in Watersbend recognized Sartol and would have spoken to him had he not killed them first."

The Owl-Master took a steadying breath, attempting to grasp all that the young mages had told him. He was aware of their eyes on his face, of Sonel, taciturn and watchful, gauging his reactions. An eerie stillness blanketed the clearing, broken only by the occasional popping of the fire and the distant, repetitive call of a whippoorwill. A few minutes ago he had been prepared to kill these three mages as traitors. Now . . . now he didn't know what to think. Their accusations against Sartol were no more convincing than the charges Sartol had made against Baden and the others. Indeed, they were probably less so. Sartol, after all, had carried the staffs of Jessamyn and Peredur back to

Amarid as physical evidence of what he claimed had happened. He had witnesses.

Yet, here were Jaryd and Alayna, claiming that Sartol, not Orris, had killed the Owl-Sage and her first; claiming that they had survived a confrontation with Theron, and that Sartol, not Orris, had forced them into the grove. It was absurd. Except, listening to them speak, Niall found himself, almost against his will, acknowledging that their story had the ring of truth to it. Their mere presence in this clearing cast doubt on Sartol's story, but, more than that, Niall perceived something in their manner that gave him pause. Terrifying as it was, Niall forced himself to consider the possibility that Sartol might have lied to them all.

"You have evidence, I take it," he said at last. "You can prove all of this."

"We have physical evidence that will prove some of it," Jaryd replied cautiously. "The rest you'll have to take on faith."

Alayna passed a rigid hand through her long hair. "We would have more— at one point Orris had the weapons used by the outlanders—but Sartol destroyed it all."

"You saw him do this?"

She shook her head. "We can only assume that this is what he did."

Niall took another deep breath. "Perhaps you should show me what you do have. We'll see if it's enough."

It very nearly was. While not convinced entirely, Niall did find his faith in Sartol badly shaken by what the young mages showed him. Clearly, Jaryd and Alayna had been to Theron's Grove as they said. But, while the objects they claimed to have gathered in Watersbend looked peculiar, even alien, they did not prove conclusively that the attacks had been committed by outlanders.

"You'll have to tell this story to the rest of the Order," he told the young mages, breaking the lengthy silence that followed their description of the events at Theron's Grove and the ravaged village. "You'll come with me, so that you can attend tomorrow's trial."

"No!" Sonel insisted, speaking for the first time since Niall's arrival.

"You're in no position to disagree, Sonel. I've been given the authority—"

"I know that you aren't a foolish man, Niall," the Owl-Master cut in, her voice level. "I know as well that you wouldn't knowingly harm the Order or any of its members." She stepped forward, straight-backed and tall, until she stood directly in front of him, her eyes, green as the grass on which they stood, even with his. "But it sounds to me as if you haven't listened to anything these two have told you. They are the only witnesses to Sartol's crimes. He's already tried to kill them once. If you take them back to Amarid, he'll undoubtedly try again."

"I have a responsibility to the Order, Sonel!" Niall countered. "You accuse Sartol of treason and murder, but he contends that these are Baden's crimes and Orris's, not his. I can't judge by myself who is lying and who is telling the truth. That's for the entire Order to decide."

"Very well," she returned mildly, "but no one has accused these two of anything except being dead. Surely your duty to the Order doesn't include endangering their lives."

"I can't know for certain that their lives are in danger. I have only your word and theirs to tell me that this is so."

"Just the possibility ought to be enough!" Sonel snapped, her patience abruptly gone. "Think about what you've just heard from them! Look at the tokens they carry! It ought to be enough! Unless your loyalties lie with Sartol rather than with Tobyn-Ser."

Niall recoiled as if he had been struck. "How dare you imply such a thing!" he rasped.

Sonel met his glare, her expression undisturbed. "I have said nothing about you that you haven't already thought with regard to me."

Niall opened his mouth, a retort springing to his lips. Then he bit it back, closing his mouth again. She was right, of course. He had, in his mind, accused her of betrayal as well. Sartol had warned him of the dangers inherent in uncovering a conspiracy, of the need to avoid paranoia. But, Niall realized with sudden insight, the Owl-Master had also done all that he could to feed Niall's fears, to encourage him to see conspirators at every turn. Which fit perfectly with Jaryd and Alayna's story: if Sartol could get the Owl-Masters to suspect each other, they might not think to suspect him.

"I don't know which of us is stronger with the Mage-Craft, Niall," Sonel was saying, "but I'd guess that the difference is insubstantial. If you wish to take Jaryd and Alayna back to the city, you'll have to fight me first. And with these two on my side, you can't hope to prevail. Let's not resort to that. Go back to Amarid, Niall. Go in peace."

Niall stared at her for some time until, finally, he gave a wan smile. "It need not come to that, Sonel; you won't have to kill me. I'll leave you." He looked at the young mages. "Whatever you might think of me," he told them quietly, "please know that I'm glad you're safe. Sonel was right: I wouldn't harm you knowingly."

"Thank you, Niall," Jaryd said. The anger had vanished from his face, leaving him looking young, although not as young as Niall remembered. "You wanted us to tell our story at Baden's trial, and though we won't be leaving here with you, that has been our intention all along. Look for us tomorrow; we'll be there."

"It would be better, however," Alayna added, "if no one was expecting us."

Niall hesitated, wondering how all of this had become so complicated. "In that case," he said after a moment, "I would suggest that all of you—including you, Sonel—remain outside the city until the trial begins. I followed you at Sartol's orders, but I wasn't the only one who saw you visit Baden. Some of them may assume that there are others involved in your . . . conspiracy, and if Sartol finds out that you're allied with the accused mages, your life may be in danger as well."

Sonel nodded gravely. "Thank you, Niall. I appreciate your concern."

Without responding, Niall turned and started to leave the clearing, unsure of how he could reconcile Alayna's request to keep their secret with the faith Sartol had placed in him. Thoughts and impulses swarmed around his head like gnats on a warm afternoon, leaving him confused and disoriented.

Sonel seemed to notice this. "Niall!" she called.

He stopped without turning, waiting, but maintaining his silence.

"If you still doubt what we've told you, there is one other bit of evidence I can offer you. Baden believes that Sartol is altering the Summoning Stone, linking himself to it in some way. He has seen Sartol's ceryll-hue echoed in the stone as Sartol walks by it. Look for this; perhaps your own eyes can convince you of what we could not."

Niall held himself still for a moment after she finished. Then he began walking again, reentering the wood and allowing the narrow path to lead him back to the main trail, before following that to the city. And, as he walked, the silver-haired Owl-Master replayed in his mind his encounter with Sonel, Jaryd, and Alayna, particularly the Owl-Master's words to him as he turned to leave the clearing. If Sartol really was attempting to link himself to the stone as Sonel alleged, it would go a long way toward proving what the young mages had told him. A mage seeking only to lead the Order through legitimate means would have no need of such power, and would harbor no desire to bend the natural laws governing the Mage-Craft to that degree. In truth, Niall could not even begin to fathom the effort it would require to exert one's control over a ceryll the size of the Summoning Stone, nor could he imagine the immense power that the stone might give.

Still grappling with the magnitude of what the Order might face if Sonel was right, if, indeed, Sartol had nearly succeeded in linking himself to the stone, the mage turned his mind to his most immediate problem: Sartol expected a report from him first thing in the morning, and Niall had no idea what he would tell the dark-haired Owl-Master. He could not, in good conscience, tell Sartol that he had spoken with Jaryd and Alayna; not as long as he acknowledged even the slightest chance that they had told him the truth. And, he had to concede, he placed more faith in their story than that. Vardis had informed him on more than one occasion, usually after figuring out what he had gotten her for a birthday or anniversary, that he had no skill as a liar. His face gave him away, she had once told him. That was why he never won at ren-drah. He had not mastered the art of duplicity over the last decade, having had little occasion for practice, and the stakes now were much higher than they had ever been before. Clever as Sartol was, he would know immediately that something had happened; he would expect details, names, places. And Niall simply did not know what he would say.

The journey back to Amarid did not take him very long, and the problem still occupied his thoughts as he crossed over the Larian and back into the old town commons. Unwilling to return to the confines of his room, the Owl-Master roamed the streets and lanes of Amarid for the rest of the night, enjoying the solitude of the sleeping city even as he remained preoccupied.

So it was that his wanderings brought him, well before dawn, to the domed roof and glittering statues of the Great Hall. Realizing where he was, Niall decided to continue in the direction he had most recently taken, until he reached the wooded grounds of the First Mage's home, a short distance west of the hall.

But, in that instant, something caught his eye, something that caused his world to shift far more than anything Jaryd and Alayna had told him earlier in the night. Through the translucent white glass of the Gathering Chamber, faint and erratic, flickering like a wind-blown candle, but absolutely unmistakable, Niall saw the pale yellow light of Sartol's ceryll. It filled the inside of the building, bringing an ethereal, yellow incandescence to all the hall's windows, but clearly it was concentrated at the chamber's western end: where the Summoning Stone rested in its massive wooden stand.

Briefly, Niall considered stealing into the hall to see more clearly just what Sartol was doing. But, if Sonel had been right—which suddenly seemed likely—Sartol would have little to lose by killing him, and even less trouble doing so. The Owl-Master also contemplated returning to the clearing where he had found Alayna and Jaryd. But he could think of no compelling reason for doing this, beyond apologizing for his doubts and acknowledging, belatedly, that he believed their story. No doubt, they already had plans of their own that took into account what he had just now learned of Sartol's plot. They needed neither his aid nor his faith; only his silence. Moreover, given that he still had to meet with Sartol in the morning, the less he knew of their strategy, the better.

So, in the end, after watching the yellow light glimmer and dance within the hall for a short while longer, Niall simply walked on, following the path on which he had already decided. His thoughts, however, had begun to drift in a new direction. He no longer had any choice: he would have to lie when he met with Sartol in the morning. The question was, how?

He passed what remained of the night and the first few hours of daylight wandering the grounds of Amarid's home. Soon after dawn, the site's caretakers emerged from their modest quarters to begin working the land and tidying the house for the steady stream of visitors who came each day to see the place where the First Mage had spent his earliest years. The stewards regarded Niall with unconcealed curiosity, but, thankfully, they kept their distance, allowing him his solitude. Even so, when he finally started back toward the Great Hall, he still did not know what he would tell Sartol. He had come up with a few options, but none of them sounded convincing to his own ears; he held out little hope that they would mislead Sartol.

His pulse was racing by the time he reached the marble staircase at the Great Hall's entrance. He knew that his features had gone pale. Glancing at the hand that gripped his staff—he had already thrust his other trembling hand into a pocket of his cloak—he saw that his knuckles had whitened. He paused at the top of the steps, taking a long breath that did little to calm his nerves, before stepping into the Great Hall. Immediately upon entering the building, driven by instinct and fear, his eyes flew to the Summoning Stone, which sat at the far end of the room. Even knowing what to look for, he saw nothing unusual at first. Only as he drew closer to the stone, stepping lightly so as not to alert Sartol to his presence, did he detect the faint luminescence emanating from the giant crystal. It was fairer than Sartol's ceryll, exhibiting barely more color than the pale sands of the Lower Horn. Still, there could be no denying that the stone had begun to glow, nor that its color, as it intensified, would mirror exactly that of the Owl-Master's ceryll.

Niall halted before the stone, noting the terrible but subtle change that Sartol had effected overnight. And as he did, at long last, an idea came to him. A story to tell, one that would offer Sartol a plausible explanation for Niall's disquiet; one that would please the Owl-Master so much that he would not bother to question its veracity. For just a moment, standing in front of the crystal, only a few strides from the door to Sartol's chambers, Niall grinned. I can play this game after all, he told himself. Vardis would be amused. Then, his expression turning sober, he knocked on the door.

Had Niall been as stricken with guilt and grief as he led Sartol to believe, he probably would not have noticed the Owl-Master's dissembling. But in the wake of what really had happened last night, Niall saw it all: the manipulation, the cajolery, the false sympathy. He had been duped; they all had. Belatedly, his mind turned, with a twisting in his heart, to the stoicism with which Alayna had spoken of Sartol's treachery. He hoped that he would have the opportunity to apologize to her for his doubts.

After he left Sartol, as he made his way across the Gathering Chamber and out into the sunlit street, Niall finally felt his sleepless night begin to catch up with him. Weary and anxious, startled by the sudden tolling of the bells atop the Great Hall, and longing for his bed, the Owl-Master chastised himself for roving the city's streets when he should have been resting. Still, he hurried to the Crystal Inn, knowing that Sartol expected him to escort the accused mages to their trial. He wondered briefly, as he led Baden, Orris, and Trahn out of the tavern and back toward the hall, whether he should use this opportunity to inform Baden that he knew Jaryd and Alayna were alive, that he had allied himself with their cause. But he was not fully certain that he had. Considering the question as the four of them walked along the thoroughfare, sounding the depths of his heart, he moved in a sort of trance induced by both weariness and uncertainty. Only Baden's startling outburst, and his astonishingly accurate guess that Niall knew of Sonel's whereabouts, pulled him from his thoughts. Niall might have told Baden then of his conversation with the young mages. Indeed, he considered it. But something stopped him. It could have been the sting of Baden's tone, or perhaps his fear that Baden's emotional response would give too much away to Sartol. In truth, Niall found it hard to separate the two just then. And, in the next moment, Orris sundered the tenuous bonds that had begun to link Niall to their cause. Baden's harsh words, born of fear for Jaryd, Alayna, and Sonel, he could endure. But he would not abide Orris's self-righteous accusations.

Enraged and insulted, Niall led them the rest of the way in silence, his wrath propelling him forward as they completed the journey from the inn to the Great Hall, and he directed the accused mages to their places before the great oval table at which their fate would be determined. An instant later, though, as Sartol emerged from his quarters, drawing Niall's glance once more to the altered Summoning Stone that sat by the opening door, the Owl-Master's anger evaporated with bewildering swiftness. His indignity at Baden's insinuations and Orris's presumption was of little consequence next to the threat that this dashing, charismatic man posed to all of Tobyn-Ser. Too late, moving to his place at the table, Niall recognized that Baden and Orris, along with Trahn and the three mages he had left in the clearing the night before, embodied all the hope that remained for the Order and the land.

And half a minute into Sartol's oration, Niall lamented that they would not be enough. The Owl-Master had always been a captivating speaker, possessing a deep voice and, as Niall had recently learned all too well, an uncanny ability to make nearly any assertion sound reasonable. Those talents, combined with his poise and commanding presence, had long ago marked the dark-haired mage as one of the Order's most influential members. Now, listening as Sartol spun his tale of deception and treachery, seeing how so many of the Owl-Masters hung on the man's every word, their eyes riveted on his handsome, expressive face, Niall wondered how Baden and his allies could ever expect to prevail. He was not even immune himself. All that he had learned the previous night seemed to fade to a distant memory, replaced by dark, frightening images of conspiracy and betrayal. He knew that Sartol was lying, and yet, he found his own emotions mirrored so precisely in the nuances and shadings of the mage's voice that he felt compelled to listen, opening his mind to the reason of what Sartol said. Baden and Trahn had pushed very hard for the delegation, and Orris's request to join it had seemed oddly abrupt. Certainly, Niall had to concede, there was something strange about Baden's attempt to protect the men who destroyed Watersbend. And all the while, beneath the harsh accusations and the calls for punishment, Sartol's tone conveyed a different sentiment. *I wish I didn't have to do this,* it seemed to say, *I wish that Baden and the others had not brought us to this. But now that we are here, we must do what is right.* And Niall had begun to agree.

Baden's scornful clapping succeeded in breaking the spell Sartol had cast with his eloquence, pulling the mages back to the hard realities of the trial. But Baden could not match Sartol's rhetoric or style, and he could offer little evidence. Until Sonel arrived. Even more than Baden's caustic applause, and the bitter exchange with Sartol that followed, Sonel's arrival struck Niall like ice water thrown in his face. Suddenly, Alayna and Jaryd were with him again, in the clearing in Hawksfind Wood, offering their account of what happened by Theron's Grove. Looking past Sartol to the far end of the chamber, he saw the Summoning Stone brooding in its stand, and he thought again of what Sartol had done to it. And like the churning floodwaters of the Dhaalismin, his fury at having been deceived surged back into him, stronger even than before.

Grinning with grim satisfaction, Niall watched the scene unfold before him, relishing the sudden disintegration of Sartol's polish and confidence. He saw Sartol recognize Sonel as she stood in the Great Hall's entrance, and his smile deepened as the Owl-Master looked desperately in his direction, still not comprehending what—or rather who—had come. He watched the mage's face go rigid and white as Baden taunted him with the news that his proof had just arrived, and he saw Sartol's eyes widen, heard an enraged, disbelieving snarl ripped from the Owl-Master's throat as Alayna and Jaryd stepped into the Gathering Chamber. The arrival of the young mages plunged the room into pandemonium, as mages from both sides of the table, their relief and joy overmastering their confusion, rushed to welcome them. Niall kept himself apart from the crush, as did Sartol, who was on his feet now, standing utterly still, his eyes fixed on the table and both hands clenched tightly around his staff.

"I had hoped that you'd be pleased to see me, Sartol," Alayna called to him, as she and Jaryd moved to stand before the oval table. A strange quiet descended on the chamber, and the rest of the mages filed slowly back to their chairs. "I had hoped that you'd greet me as the others did. But I knew that you wouldn't."

"Forgive me, child," Sartol returned, looking up from the table to meet her glare. "But given the company you're keeping these days, I can't imagine that you've returned to me in friendship."

She gave a thin, mirthless smile. "It seems you can recognize the truth when you encounter it, after all." Then she raised her voice, pitching it to carry throughout the hall. "I don't know what Sartol has related to you this morning, but I can tell you this: Jaryd and I found him standing over the bodies of Jessamyn and Peredur, and it was he who chased us into Theron's Grove. He would have killed us had Orris not intervened on our behalf."

"Lies!" Sartol growled over the startled murmurs that met Alayna's declaration. "She has been corrupted by the traitors, as has Jaryd!"

"You're the only traitor in this room, Sartol," Jaryd spat back.

"Quiet!" Odinan hissed, pounding his staff on the floor. "This is a trial, not a carnival! We have procedures! We have rules! And I expect them to be observed!"

"Owl-Master Odinan," Baden broke in, his tone courteous despite its urgency. "According to the rules established by Terrall, I ask that Jaryd and Alayna be permitted, as part of our defense, to relate their version of what happened by Theron's Grove."

"I must protest!" Sartol stormed. "He's supposed to name all his witnesses in advance."

Odinan nodded. "He's right, Baden. We had no prior notice of these two."

"There's a reason for that," Baden persisted. "I had cause to believe that their lives were in danger, that if it had been known that they were here, they might have been murdered. I'm allowed to bring witnesses without notice if there are extenuating circumstances. I felt that this threat qualified."

Sartol gave a short, incredulous laugh. "There was no threat! He's fabricating one now to justify his request."

Odinan shrugged. "It's not for me to decide. As with all other disputes of this sort, this will be resolved by the gathered mages." He glanced around the room. "All those in favor of allowing Alayna and Jaryd's testimony?" Every mage in the chamber except Sartol lifted a hand.

"You may proceed, Baden."

"Thank you." The Owl-Master turned to his nephew. "Jaryd, Sartol has said that after we reached the grove, just as the storm began, he was down at the river filling our water pouches, while Jessamyn and Peredur were gathering torches. Does that match your recollection of what happened?"

Jaryd looked at Sartol and shook his head. "No, it doesn't. Sartol, Alayna, and I were having a conversation when Jessamyn approached us to say that she needed someone to cover the food and gear, and someone else to gather torches. Sartol volunteered to do the latter, leaving Alayna and me to tend to the supplies. A short while later, we saw Jessamyn making her way toward the cluster of trees where Sartol had gone. Soon after that, Peredur came by looking for Jessamyn, and we told him where he could find her. A minute or two later, we heard Jessamyn cry out. We ran to see what had happened, and, when we got there, we found Sartol standing over the bodies. I saw his owl holding the carcass of Peredur's familiar, and I accused him of murdering the sage and the first. That's when he tried to kill me. Alayna stopped him and we started to run. I thought for sure that he would kill us before we got away, but Orris intervened. We kept running, and ended up in Theron's Grove."

"Do you have any idea why he would kill Jessamyn?" Baden prompted.

The young mage held up an arm-length tree limb, within which lay his glowing blue ceryll. "This is a torch that Sartol was preparing when Jessamyn interrupted him. He placed this ceryll in it so that Theron's spirit would be able to use it to draw upon his power. He hoped that the Owl-Master would kill us all."

"Nonsense!" Sartol scoffed. "Why would I risk my own life with a stunt like that?"

"Sartol had been sick," Jaryd went on coolly, ignoring the mage's comment. "Most likely he had been pretending to be sick—and Jessamyn decided that Orris, Trahn, and he would wait for the rest of us outside the grove. He never intended to enter the grove, and he never intended for us to return. But Jessamyn uncovered his plot, and he killed her."

"This is ridiculous!" Sartol snapped. "Obviously these two are in league with Baden, and obviously, given that they're here with us, they never set foot in Theron's Grove—that was merely a ruse, intended to confuse our emotions and create just this type of contrived melodrama." The rhetoric was bold, but Niall could see in the Owl-Master's eyes that this was just another gambit. Sartol had already seen the other object that Jaryd carried, the token that Niall had looked upon the night before, scarcely trusting his own eyes. The Owl-Master was merely gambling that the rest of the mages would not believe it. Niall could also see that it was a gamble Sartol expected to lose.

"You know better, Sartol," Jaryd countered, his pale eyes blazing beneath the shock of light brown hair. "You see what I carry. Behold the staff of Theron!" he cried out, raising the charred, splintered stave over his head, and bringing a collective gasp from the gathered mages. "It was given to Alayna and me by the Owl-Master's spirit after our second night in the grove. With it, he offered his aid in combatting the outlanders responsible for the attacks on Tobyn-Ser!"

"Ridiculous!" Sartol repeated, the denial sounding hollow following Jaryd's ringing declaration. "I still have seen no proof of these outlanders, and I refuse to accept that the worthless stick he holds is Theron's staff!"

"It matches the description in the old legends," Radomil argued, drawing nods of agreement from the other mages. "As for the outlanders," he went on, turning to Baden, "I, too, would like to see some evidence."

Baden nodded. "Fair enough. Jaryd?"

The Hawk-Mage reached into his cloak and tossed onto the table the glittering glass and gold disk, and the strange scrap of dark, flexible material that Niall had seen the night before.

"Unfortunately, this is all that remains," Baden remarked, watching as the two tokens were passed around the chamber for inspection. "The golden object is the eye of one of the mechanical birds Sartol and I encountered in Watersbend. The other is a fragment of its outer covering. Orris saw more— he held the fire-throwing weapons that I have mentioned, he examined the complete remains of the two birds. But Sartol took them when he left Watersbend." He looked at the Owl-Master. "I presume they've been destroyed. Is that correct, Sartol?"

The other man began to chuckle and shake his head. "That's your proof?" he asked. "A dusty, half-burned scrap of who knows what and a shiny disk that I could balance on my little finger?"

"These objects are strange, Baden," Ursel commented, as if it were an admission, holding the two tokens in her hand. "I've not seen anything like them before." She faltered, an apology in her pale eyes. "But I find it difficult to see in these small scraps the deadly birds you've described. Don't you have anything else to offer, some other proof that outlanders are responsible for the attacks?"

"Nothing tangible," Baden conceded, "nothing I can show you." Suddenly, he grinned. "But maybe Sartol can help us with this." He turned toward the Owl-Master. "You did concede a short while ago that, during the battle in Watersbend, before you killed the outlanders, I destroyed their birds. Do you remember saying that?"

"Yes," Sartol answered, shifting uncomfortably, although his voice remained even. "Well," he hedged, "I said that you killed the birds. I never referred to the men as outlanders."

"But you admit that I destroyed the birds."

Sartol bristled. "I just said that!"

"Then why did you kill the men?"

The Owl-Master blinked. "What?"

"You told us before that these men were mages, although, you said, they didn't belong to the Order. And you just confirmed that I had already killed their birds. So why kill them?"

"They . . . they were destroying the village!" Sartol stammered, caught completely off guard by Baden's question. "They were attacking you!"

"How could they do any of those things!" Baden roared. *They had no familiars! They should have been powerless!*" He paused, allowing the import of his question to reach the other mages in the chamber. "But they weren't powerless, were they, Sartol? They were still throwing fire at me, and they were still a threat to the villagers! How's that possible, Sartol?" Every other mage in the room was staring at Baden, but the lean Owl-Master had not taken his eyes off Sartol. "Well?" he goaded. "How is this possible? You can't have it both ways: either they were mages, and you killed them for no reason, or they were outlanders, as I've been saying! Which is it!"

Sartol had not moved, but Niall could see the muscles of his jaw contorting with rage, and a single, pulsing vein standing out boldly from his neck. "No answer, Sartol?" Baden asked a moment later. "That's fine. Let's try another one: what are you doing to the Summoning Stone?"

The gaze of every person in the room swung to the giant crystal.

"What are you talking about, Baden?" Odinan asked, his voice quavering with apprehension. "What has he done?"

"He's altering it," Niall heard himself say. "He's trying to link himself to it. Look closely at the stone and you'll see that it has begun to glow with Sartol's ceryll-hue."

Odinan took a step forward. "Is this true?" he asked breathlessly.

Sartol began to laugh, drawing their attention back to him. "I've been an idiot," he said to no one in particular.

"That," Alayna observed, her voice shockingly cold, "is the first truth you've spoken today. I'm pleased to hear you say it."

Sartol looked at her, laughing no more, but still smiling thinly. "Don't be naive, child," he returned, the ice in his tone a match for hers. "I'm not repenting. This is no last-minute conversion to the side of light and virtue. I'm merely disgusted with myself. For all this time, I've had the means to achieving my purpose right here with me, and it took a useless old fool like Niall to make me realize it." He stopped, still gazing at her, the smile lingering on his lips. For her part, Niall thought, even pale with fright and heartache, Alayna looked exceedingly beautiful in that moment.

"Please believe me, my dear," Sartol went on, his voice sounding almost tender, "when I tell you that of all the things I have done, and all that I have yet to do, killing you will be the most difficult."

And as he said this last, he raised his staff as if to smite her with his mage-fire.

"Sartol, no!" Niall screamed, thrusting out his own staff and sending a rippling barrier of burgundy energy to shield Alayna from the blow. Alayna, too, had moved to guard herself, throwing up a wall of purple magic.

But the burst of power never came, had never been intended to come. At least not toward Alayna. In the last instant, even as his ceryll arced forward, Sartol spun away from his former Mage-Attend toward the one person in that magnificent hall whom he hated most. Toward Baden, who, without his ceryll, could do absolutely nothing to protect himself. Helpless to do anything but watch, his power already extended elsewhere, Niall saw a bolt of yellow fire leap from the Summoning Stone to Sartol's crystal, where it was redirected and propelled forward like a fiery comet. Hissing with energy, filling the chamber with its dazzling glow, the fireball soared over the oval table, straight at Baden's heart.

But then Niall saw something so glorious and unexpected that he actually cried outloud with wonder and hope. A shimmering curtain of blue power streamed like sunlight from Jaryd's ceryll, blocking Sartol's fireball just as it reached Baden with a concussion that rocked the hall and drove the lean Owl-Master to the floor. Drawing upon abilities as yet unfathomed, the promise of which were embodied in the fierce grey bird on his shoulder, Jaryd poured all the magic to which he had access into that shield. He held his ceryll out before him, the muscles in his arms corded and trembling, his face covered with a sheen of perspiration. Even his hawk had gone rigid, its eyes closed and its beak open, as if in a soundless cry. Together, bird and man channeled every ounce of their beings into resisting Sartol's yellow fire.

And it wasn't enough. Perhaps against Sartol alone, armed only with his ceryll, the shield would have held. Certainly it could have withstood an assault from any other mage in the room. But against the force of that blow, magnified as it was by the giant crystal that Amarid and Theron had transported back from Ceryllon a thousand years ago, the shimmering sapphire wall had to give way. How could it not? Slowly at first it bowed, sagging under that great weight like a ship's sail against a howling wind, curving, but not failing.

But the stone was so vast, and Sartol's power went so much deeper. With a malicious grin, but barely a hint of effort, Sartol escalated his assault, drawing a brighter, angrier flame from the vast crystal. Jaryd collapsed to one knee with a desperate gasp. A dreadful rending sound, emanating from the blue shield, stretched now beyond endurance, echoed through the hall. It would have failed then—indeed, the yellow had begun to seep through the blue, reaching toward Baden like a deadly hand—but, in that instant, a third light entered the fray. Sonel's green, bolstering Jaryd's blue, stopping Sartol's advance. A moment later, Radomil's ivory joined as well, and the yellow began to be pushed back. Purple from Alayna. Maroon from Niall. And soon, a myriad of colors had come to Jaryd's aid, coalescing into a white light so blinding that it seemed the sun itself burned in Amarid's Great Hall.

Yet still Sartol fought. The strain of it was visible now, in his damp, distorted features, in the sweat that darkened his cloak, and in the wild, unseeing appearance of his owl's yellow eyes. But Sartol fought. And, once again, the yellow fire began to inch forward. So strong was he, stronger, because of the stone, than any mage to have come before him, that even the combined power of all the mages in the chamber could not withstand him.

Shuddering with the effort of the battle, barely able to stand, Niall felt his power being driven back. Fighting for his life, for the memory of Vardis and the love of this land, he tried to resist. But Sartol was like the tide; he could not be stopped. Niall glanced around him, trying to gauge how much longer the rest of the mages could hold out, and, doing so, he saw one of the hall's giant, blue-clad attendants rush toward Baden. He started to cry out in warning, fearing that the man meant to do to the Owl-Master what Jaryd had kept Sartol from doing. But then Niall stopped himself, realizing with a surge of hope that the man was not threatening Baden, but rather was bringing him his staff. He also brought Trahn his ceryll, and, immediately, the two mages added their strength, orange light and brown, to the radiant white force opposing Sartol.

Once again, the balance of the battle shifted. And this time, it did not turn back. Gradually, inexorably, the pale yellow fire flowing from the Summoning Stone was halted and then repelled. His eyes widening with the realization that his power would not be enough, Sartol roared with frustration, backing toward the stone so as to concentrate all of its power toward the phalanx of mages before him. To no avail. The white light continued to advance more swiftly now, until it was Sartol who was projecting a shield against the combined power of his foes.

"You can't win, Sartol!" Baden cried, his voice taut with exertion. "Surrender or die!"

In response, Sartol gave a short, high gasp of laughter. And then he did something none of them could have foreseen. His eyes gleaming exultantly, his teeth clenched and bared in a terrible grin, he abruptly swung all of his fire, all the might he possessed, toward the source of his power, toward the great owl sitting on his own shoulder. The yellow flame engulfed the bird, killing it instantly. A split second later, with his resistance suddenly gone, the merged power of all the masters and mages in the room crashed down upon Sartol with the obliterating might of an avalanche, burying him beneath a mountain of white fire, and wiping him utterly from the face of the earth. But in that scintilla of time between the death of his owl and the impact of that fire, he rendered himself unbound, and so became one of the Unsettled, using Theron's Curse to win for himself a measure of immortality.

21

Watching the ebb and flow of the battle raging in the Gathering Chamber, seeing the two walls of light, one white, the other yellow, warring for supremacy, with Tobyn-Ser's fate poised in the balance, Orris cursed his own impotence. For at least part of the time, he knew, Baden and Trahn shared his frustration. True, they had some power that they could lend to the cause, but without their cerylls to concentrate their magic, their efforts remained superfluous. So the three of them watched, with disbelief and bitter despair, as Sartol's magic, sourced in his splendid owl, fed by his fierce ambition, and amplified by the giant crystal he had somehow managed to master proved too much even for the combined might of all the mages he faced.

Only the actions of the Great Hall attendant whom Baden had threatened the day before saved them, for it was he who brought Baden and Trahn their staffs, allowing them to tip the balance of the struggle in the very moment of Sartol's apparent victory. As it happened, the brawny attendant carried a third staff as well: Orris's staff. How could he know that this one would make no difference in what unfolded under the domed ceiling, with its magnificent likeness of Amarid and Parne? Yes, he might have noticed that Orris carried no hawk, but to most of the people in this land, the cloak and the staff were as much symbols of power as the hawk or the owl. Orris did not blame the man for bringing his staff—he was grateful beyond words for what the attendant had done in bringing Baden and Trahn theirs. When he perceived that the addition of his two friends would be enough to defeat the renegade Owl-Master, the relief he felt overwhelmed him. Still, he was not accustomed to feeling useless. Even as he observed, with grim satisfaction, the slow retreat of Sartol's yellow flame, his mind was flooded with memories of Pordath, and his heart ached once more with the pain of losing her.

Those images and emotions remained with him, albeit changed in ways he could never have anticipated, as he witnessed Sartol's final, desperate act of defiance. There had been a time, just after Pordath's death, when Orris had wished that the Owl-Master might one day experience the anguish of losing his familiar. But never had he imagined that Sartol would take the bird's life himself. He could scarcely comprehend the ruthlessness of it, the uncompromising belligerence and single-mindedness that would drive a man to choose such a violent, irrevocable solution. Orris, who had been afraid of nothing for as long as he remembered, had come, over the past few weeks, to fear Theron's Curse and the prospect of eternal unrest. And yet, Sartol had embraced these willingly, preferring them to either surrender or death. It was too much to fathom.

Glancing around the Gathering Chamber, Orris saw his own shock mirrored in the faces of his fellow mages. An appalled silence had enveloped the room. Not for a thousand years had a mage challenged the power and will of the Order; not since Theron had a mage died at a Gathering; and never before had one been killed in such a manner. Perhaps, in an odd way, a corpse would have helped to make real the incomprehensible scene that had just played itself out. But there was nothing left of the Owl-Master who, it had seemed just a short while ago, would soon lead the Order. Nothing remained even of his owl. Only the Summoning Stone, quiescent now, dark and colorless, served to remind that Sartol had attempted to rule the Order. Only a golden medallion on the Great Hall's domed roof evidenced that the Owl-Master had ever sat at the oval table. Tonight, though, in a remote corner of the Northern Plain, a figure would appear, suffused with pale yellow light, and carrying not an owl, but a large, dark hawk, the first to which he had ever bound.

Not surprisingly, Baden finally broke the stillness that had enveloped the hall. "Thank you," he said, turning to the massive, blue-robed attendant and gripping the man's shoulder. "You saved us all. Why, though? I thought you worked for Sartol."

The man shook his head. "We work for the hall, and for all of you. When Sartol hired us, he said that he needed our help in arresting traitors. He told us you had killed the Owl-Sage and that you were the ones who were behind all the attacks." The man shrugged. "When I saw that it was him and not you, I figured I'd better give you back your crystals."

Baden smiled. "I'm glad you did. What's your name?"

"I am Mansel, Owl-Master."

"Well, Mansel, this Order and all the people it serves are indebted to you."

His ears reddening with embarrassment, the man nodded, and then, without another word, he returned to his place near the hall's entrance and resumed his guard duties.

Baden watched him do this, and then he looked around the chamber at the rest of the mages. None of them had moved or made a sound. "We would do well to follow Mansel's example," Baden commented, indicating the attendant with a gesture. "Like you, I'm troubled by what has just happened here. We have a great deal to ponder and discuss in the wake of it. And we must mourn properly, not only for Jessamyn and Peredur, but also for Sartol. He was once an honored member of this Order. His fall offers lessons to all of us that we ignore at our own risk." The Owl-Master took a breath, and, when he began again, his voice conveyed a sense of urgency that it had lacked a moment before. "This, however, isn't the time for reflection or grief. Enemies of this Order and of Tobyn-Ser still walk the land, and they must be stopped before another village suffers the same fate as Kaera and Watersbend."

"The outlanders?" Radomil asked in a tight voice.

"Yes. For those of you not yet convinced, I can only give you my assurance that they are real."

"Theron told us of them as well," Jaryd added. "He had visions of them. Even with the two who died in Watersbend, there are more than a dozen of them left."

Radomil's eyes widened. "A dozen!"

"According to Theron, yes."

Several of the mages stirred, pulled from their stupor by these tidings.

"They must be stopped," Baden repeated. "But first they must be found. I'd be open to suggestions as to how we might go about locating them."

"Before I presume to suggest anything," Radomil countered, "I think I'd like to hear what Theron had to say about these people and why they're here."

Baden nodded his agreement and looked to Jaryd.

"Theron didn't tell us everything he knows," the young mage began, pushing the thick brown hair back from his forehead in a self-conscious gesture. "As you might expect, he remains hostile toward the Order, and, at first, he refused to help us at all."

"It seems to me," Odinan broke in hotly, "that we're the ones who should be hostile. He saddled this Order with the curse, not the other way around. He has no cause for such resentment."

"Not so, Odinan," Orris argued, surprising himself. "Given my current situation, I have good reason to despise Theron and to fear his curse. But hearing from Jaryd and Alayna of their encounter with the Owl-Master has convinced me that the way his life ended should not be allowed to diminish his accomplishments while alive. He, as much as Amarid, was responsible for the discovery of the Mage-Craft and the founding of this Order. It's past time we acknowledged that."

"I agree," Sonel added, as several other mages nodded as well. "And frankly, Owl-Master," she went on, turning to Odinan, "I don't think that this is the time to debate such issues."

Odinan winced slightly at the rebuke and signaled his agreement with a chagrined gesture of acquiescence.

A moment later, Jaryd began again, relating to the mages Theron's comment about the outlanders' tactics revealing their weakness. "Whatever they want," he explained, "they must first subvert the authority of the Order and eliminate the Mage-Craft as a threat. Theron also said that they have power of a sort, but not like ours, and not so strong that it can overmaster the Mage-Craft directly."

"Did he give you any sense of what this power is?" Radomil asked, his tone betraying some of the frustration that Orris had felt when he first heard of the vague hints offered by the Owl-Master's spirit.

Jaryd shook his head apologetically.

"I have some ideas on that," Baden offered, "based on my encounter with the men at Watersbend. Many of you may still be reluctant to accept my assertions about mechanical birds and weapons that throw flames as powerful as mage-fire. Again, all I can do is offer my assurance that these things exist. Orris saw them and can describe them for us." Several of the mages looked in Orris's direction, and the Hawk-Mage confirmed Baden's statement with a curt nod. "I believe," Baden continued, "that the things we saw are manifestations of the power of which Theron spoke. These people have the ability to replicate nature, and the Mage-Craft, with mechanical devices."

Niall regarded Baden anxiously. "Do you have any idea where they're from?"

"I have some thoughts on that," Orris replied. And as all the mages turned their eyes in his direction, the burly Hawk-Mage told them of his conversation with Crob of Abborij.

"I've heard similar tales about Lon-Ser," Mered admitted when Orris had finished, "from my father, who is a merchant on the Upper Horn. He said he'd heard strange stories, and I didn't get the sense that he put much stock in them." The fair-haired mage gave a rueful smile. "But he did take the time to mention them to me, which should have told me something."

"Lon-Ser," Radomil said thoughtfully, almost as if the name were new to him. "I've often been curious about life there."

Odinan scrunched his face into an expression of distaste. "Why?"

The bald Hawk-Mage shrugged and passed a hand over his bearded chin. "Tobyn-Ser and Lon-Ser began as one land. No doubt we have much in common with Lon-Ser's people." He shrugged again. "I find that intriguing."

One of the older masters snorted derisively. "I refuse to accept the idea of it. We have nothing in common with those people."

Baden turned to face the older woman. "Do you know something about them that we don't, Toinan?"

"I know what they have done," she answered haughtily. "I know that they have plotted against us and murdered our people. That, it seems to me, is quite enough."

"And what of Sartol?" Baden returned. "Didn't he do the same things?" He did not wait for her reply. "We can't assume that all the people of Lon-Ser are like these few, any more than we can allow our own people to believe that all mages are like Sartol."

Toinan inclined her head slightly, considering this. "You may be right," she conceded after a moment. "But I still don't share Radomil's curiosity. I would prefer to stay separate as we have throughout our history. It seems safer somehow."

"Safer, perhaps," Trahn remarked. "But it remains to be seen if it's still realistic after all that's happened." He turned to Baden. "For now, though, this discussion is getting us nowhere, and the longer we delay, the greater the possibility of another attack."

"I understand your impatience, Trahn," Radomil countered, "but we still don't know what they want. Surely, it's important to determine that before we act."

"We know what they want," Mered said flatly. "They want our land; they want to control Tobyn-Ser. That's what all invaders want."

Radomil let out a breath. "So then it's war we're talking about."

"They brought us to this point!" Mered pointed out fervently. "We did nothing to provoke them! But Tobyn-Ser has repelled invasions before, and we'll do so again! If they want war, then, by the gods, we'll give them a war!" The fair mage brought his fist down on the oval table, bringing cries of agreement from several other mages.

"This is premature!" Baden broke in. "Fifteen men is hardly an invasion, and we have no Bird-Sage—the gods have given no sign that we're destined for war!"

"Maybe not," Trahn said gently. "But we'd be foolish to discount the possibility, Baden. It may come to war before all of this is over. We should prepare ourselves for that." Baden said nothing, and, after a few seconds, Trahn went on. "For now, though, we should focus our efforts on the more immediate threat posed by this band of outlanders."

"Did Theron tell you anything else, Jaryd?" Radomil asked, turning to the young mage.

"He offered no more information, if that's what you mean," the young mage answered. "But, before he left us for the last time, he told us that we might have need of him again, and that he'd leave us something that would help us contact him. The next morning, we found his staff."

"But what could he have meant?" Sonel wondered aloud, her brow creased in confusion. "The staff offers no access to power. Without a ceryll, it's just wood, right?"

"Maybe if I mount my ceryll on the staff it will enable us to communicate with Theron," Jaryd suggested.

Baden shook his head. "I don't think so. As Sonel said, it's just a piece of wood."

"That may be true," Trahn argued, "but it convinced nearly everyone in this room that Jaryd and Alayna had told the truth about their encounter with the Owl-Master's spirit. Maybe that's how he intended it to be used: as a credential of some sort."

"But to what end?" Baden pressed. "A credential for whom?"

"For the Unsettled," Alayna said flatly, speaking for the first time since Sartol's death.

Slowly, Trahn began to nod, his vivid green eyes gleaming with understanding. "Of course," he breathed. "Who else would recognize it? And who else would be capable of helping us to contact Theron?"

Baden was nodding as well. "It's also possible that the Unsettled—all of them, working together—can give us the locations of the outlanders."

"Sartol is one of them now," Orris pointed out. "They may not help us."

Baden shrugged slightly. "That's a chance we have to take."

Odinan regarded him warily. "What are you suggesting?"

"I'm suggesting," Baden replied bluntly, "that we act now to eliminate this threat. We may have an opportunity to find and overpower all of these people before they do more damage. We'd be fools to let this chance slip by."

"This is not your decision to make, Baden!" the older man said pointedly. "Not alone, at any rate. We have procedures that must be followed, rules that must be observed. We don't even have a sage or a first right now. This is no time for rash actions."

"*Rash actions!*" Orris exploded, not believing what he was hearing. "What does it take to make you act, Odinan? Do the outlanders have to destroy the Great Hall before you'll notice? Do they have to kill every person in this city before you'll care enough to stop them? Or does your cowardice go beyond even that!"

"That's enough, Orris!" Niall snapped, silencing the Hawk-Mage.

For a long time, no one in the chamber spoke. Orris could still feel his ire raging inside of him, threatening to break through once again, but he knew that Niall had been right to quell him. He had gone too far. Odinan stood leaning on his staff, breathing heavily, his pale, rheumy eyes blazing at Orris from beneath wisps of white hair. Niall, too, was glaring in Orris's direction. Baden stared thoughtfully at the dark oval table, his blue eyes seeming to search the swirls of the wood grain for something to say. Surprisingly, though, it was Niall who spoke first.

"I can't condone the tone or implication of Orris's words," he said coldly, his gaze never leaving the Hawk-Mage's face. "But I must admit, Odinan, that I share his sentiment."

"What!" the old mage rasped. "You, Niall? Of all people?"

Niall allowed himself a slight grin, his eyes holding Orris's for a moment longer before they swung to meet the stunned gaze of the Owl-Master. "Yes, my friend," he returned gently. "Me. We must act now to protect Tobyn-Ser. This isn't something we should have to debate."

"But we have rules—"

"And we'll still have them when all of this is over," Niall said reassuringly. "Right now, though, we must find these people and stop them."

"But without a sage?" Odinan demanded. "Without even the rest of the Order present to share in this decision?"

"We don't need a sage to tell us what has to be done," Niall told him, "and our fellow mages would not want their absence to keep us from guarding the people of this land." He stepped forward, placing a hand on Odinan's shoulder. "There's too much at stake, my friend. Don't you see? We can't delay any longer."

Odinan passed an unsteady hand across his wrinkled forehead and let out a deep sigh. "Very well," he muttered, abruptly sounding drained. "Very well."

Orris felt his own anger sluicing away, leaving him with the recognition of what Odinan's concession had cost the old man, and with a feeling of profound gratitude for Niall's tactful intervention. He had much to learn about people, he knew, and Niall had just offered a first lesson. He glanced at the silver-haired mage, only to find that the Owl-Master was already looking in his direction. Orris smiled, hoping that Niall would understand all that the gesture was meant to convey.

"I take it," Baden said into another lengthy silence, "that we're all in agreement as to the need to act now?" The ensuing stillness served to answer his question. "Good," he went on with a roguish grin. "Then, does anyone have any recommendations as to what we should do?"

"I was under the impression that we'd already decided," Jaryd answered. "We need to contact Theron, so I guess we need to find another unsettled mage."

"I'm afraid it's not quite that easy," Baden pointed out. "If we plan to confront and subdue the intruders, we need to choose another delegation. And we need to recognize that traveling to even the nearest of the Unsettled will give our enemies several more days in which to carry out another attack. In that interval, should we recommence Ursel's patrols?"

Trahn shook his head. "That last shouldn't be necessary, Baden. Not if we use the Summoning Stone."

Niall looked sharply at the dark mage. "The stone?" *Hasn't the stone been the cause of enough trouble?* his tone and bearing seemed to say. And Orris had to admit, he shared Niall's sentiment.

"I have heard," Trahn said, "of the stone being used in times of emergency to transport members of the Order to other parts of Tobyn-Ser."

"It has been done," Toinan confirmed, "though not for many years. Of those of us who currently serve the land, only Odinan and I were members of the Order when last this was attempted. Do you remember, Odinan?"

The aged Owl-Master had lowered himself into a chair. His face looked sunken and hollow, and he offered no response other than a slight nod.

"It was just after my second Gathering," Toinan continued after a brief pause, "the morning after the Procession of Light, as I recall it. We received word of a terrible land tremor in the southern portion of the desert, and, needing to get mages to the injured people as quickly as possible, we used the Summoning Stone."

"So you know how it's done?" Baden asked.

"I do. It's not very difficult, but there are certain constraints of which you should be aware. Naturally, our ability to transport mages is limited by the number of mages who channel their power into the stone. Given the number we have here right now, your group must be kept small, and the distance you travel cannot be great. We can send no gear, no supplies, only mages and their familiars. Also, we cannot bring you back—we can only send you to your destination. That's one of the reasons the stone is used so rarely for such a purpose. That, and the fact that such an undertaking carries certain risks."

Trahn looked at the woman intently. "What kind of risks?"

"The success of the transport depends upon the ability of one person, the conduit between the mages who remain and those who go, to maintain an accurate image of the destination in his or her mind. If that image is imprecise, or if it wavers even for an instant, all those who are sent may be lost."

Baden smiled grimly. "Then we'll have to choose our conduit carefully."

Radomil turned to face the great crystal. "Do you think the stone will still work?" he asked. "Sartol altered it somehow; his death may have robbed it of the properties given to it by Amarid."

Baden turned as well. "That's possible," he acknowledged. "There's but one way to find out."

"So where are we going?" Trahn asked brightly, the familiar, fierce smile lighting his face.

No one spoke. Orris racked his brain trying to think of where the nearest of the unsettled mages might be. In truth, however, none of them knew much about the Unsettled. Even the most benign of the restless spirits elicited fear from the people of Tobyn-Ser, and members of the Order, knowing that at one time or another they were sure to be vulnerable to Theron's Curse, rarely spoke of them. No one was sure how many of them walked the land; few had even seen an unsettled mage, and those who had usually came upon them by accident. There were only two places in this land where a person could go, knowing that he or she would find one of the wandering spirits. One, of course, was Theron's Grove, and the other—

"Phelan Spur," Sonel suggested, giving voice to Orris's thought. "I think that would be our best option. It's relatively close, we know that Phelan is there, and," she added, taking a deep breath, "I've spoken with him before. I believe he'll be willing to help us."

A stunned silence fell over the hall. Several of the mages traded looks of astonishment in response to what Sonel had said.

"You've spoken with the Wolf-Master?" Ursel asked breathlessly after a moment, as if uncertain that she had heard correctly.

"Once, yes. When I was young and newly bound to my first hawk, I sought him out," she explained. "I guess I looked upon confronting an unsettled mage as a rite of passage, something I was supposed to do now that I had joined the Order. As it turned out, though, 'confront' was the wrong word. I remember Phelan as a kind man, welcoming. I sensed in him none of the hostility or bitterness that I had expected."

"You never told me about this," Baden said quietly.

Sonel shrugged. "I never told anyone until now. It was a strange experience: frightening, as you might imagine, but more than that. Even though he was kind to me, I felt as though I was intruding in some way. So I never spoke of it, I guess out of deference to Phelan."

Baden looked at her keenly. "Despite those feelings, you think he'll be sympathetic to our need?"

"Under the circumstances, I do."

Baden gazed at her for a moment longer. Then he nodded. "It sounds like a good choice, then. Unless someone has another option," he added, raising his voice. No one responded, and the Owl-Master turned to Toinan. "How many mages do you think we can send to Phelan Spur?"

The older woman glanced around the chamber, weighing Baden's question. "Five or six," she said finally. "Any more than that would leave too few to lend their power to the stone."

"I would suggest that Sonel be included in this delegation," Baden said, looking at the other mages. "Given that she's spoken with Phelan before, she may well be our best hope of convincing him to help us."

Toinan shook her head. "I don't doubt that she'd be a valuable member of this company," the older woman argued, "but she'll be much more useful as our conduit. She's been to the spur; she knows where Phelan can be found. The safety of those we send will best be served if she remains here."

Orris saw Baden and Sonel exchange a long look. At length, Sonel nodded. "Very well," she agreed. "I'll stay. But then who should we send?"

"Jaryd and Alayna spoke with Theron and brought back the Owl-Master's staff," Trahn reminded them all. "They must go."

"I agree," Baden added. "As to the others, it makes no difference to me. I volunteer to make the journey, but if there are those who would rather go in my stead, or who feel, in light of recent events, that I shouldn't go, I understand."

The mages discussed the composition of this new delegation for a few minutes longer. Normally, Orris would have been an active participant in the making of such a decision. But, for the second time in this strange and difficult day, he found himself growing acutely conscious of his powerlessness and, thus, it seemed to him, his insignificance. Listening as the Order selected Trahn, Baden, Niall, and Ursel to join Jaryd and Alayna on their journey, Orris felt a tumult of conflicting emotions rising within him. He knew that the mission carried great dangers, and yet he felt jealous at not being able to join them. Of course he hoped that they would succeed, yet the idea that they could do so without his help disturbed him greatly. He could do nothing except watch and wait. The notion of it galled him, made him want to scream in frustration. He had expected that Sartol's death would ease some of this terrible burden, but, in the end, the way the Owl-Master died only served to intensify it. Two weeks before, under a starry sky on Tobyn's Plain, Orris had sworn that he would kill Sartol. Today Sartol had died, and Orris had nothing at all to do with it. As he had nearly every day since Pordath's death, the Hawk-Mage felt utterly alone.

Having chosen their delegation, the other mages immediately began making preparations to send them to Phelan Spur. While Sonel retired into the sage's quarters to focus her mind on an image of the terrain, Toinan began to arrange those mages who would remain in Amarid around the stone. Wary of getting in the way, and still feeling self-conscious, Orris turned and began to retreat to a far corner of the hall. He was stopped, however, by a voice calling his name. He turned, and saw Niall walking in his direction.

The older man looked ill at ease as he stopped in front of Orris. They had never been entirely comfortable with each other, and the last two days in particular had put a strain on their already tense relationship. "I just want to say that I'm sorry I snapped at you," Niall said at last. He gave a rueful smirk. "It seems even when I agree with you, I sound angry."

Orris chuckled softly. "I deserved it this time. I owe Odinan an apology."

"Perhaps. Sometimes he needs to be prodded a bit. As do I," Niall added pointedly. He hesitated. "I also want to say that I'm sorry about your hawk."

As always seemed to happen when someone mentioned Pordath, Orris sensed his color rising and felt a queer constriction in his heart. He wished he could make himself disappear, and he wondered how much longer the effects of his loss would linger. Still, he held Niall's gaze. "I'll bind again soon," he said, hoping that he sounded confident. "And, in the meantime, you can strike a blow for me against the outlanders."

The older man grinned at that. "Count on it."

They stood together for a short while longer, saying nothing. Then the Owl-Master turned and started back toward the Summoning Stone. After a moment, Orris followed. He would bear witness to as much of it as he could, he decided; he could still be a part of it, even without his power. He owed them that much.

Toinan and the other mages stood in a semicircle, facing the Summoning Stone with their cerylls held out before them. The six members of the new delegation, looking tense with anticipation, had positioned themselves a few paces away, clustered with their backs to one another, pointing their cerylls in front of them so that they appeared to create a six-pointed star. And between the two groups, those whose power would feed the stone, and those who would be transported to Phelan Spur, stood Sonel, her eyes gazing without focus toward the center of the Gathering Chamber.

"Are you ready, Baden?" she called, her voice sounding small and distant.

"Yes." The Owl-Master looked as if he might say more, but, instead, he took a breath and closed his eyes.

An expectant stillness settled over the hall. The mages gathered around the stone remained motionless, their backs turned toward Orris, but Jaryd, standing between Alayna and Baden, was looking directly at him, waiting. Orris offered a reassuring smile, but Jaryd showed no sign that he had noticed. Still, nothing happened. One of the attendants at the far end of the hall coughed nervously. Orris felt the hairs on the back of his neck rise and prickle, sending a shiver down his spine.

And in that instant, without any warning, lavender light burst from Toinan's ceryll and began to flow into the Summoning Stone. A moment later, as if they had been waiting for Toinan's mage-fire as a signal, the other mages unleashed their brilliant power as well. A myriad of colors hurtled into the great crystal, uniting in a dazzling blaze of white light, and then streaming like sunlight into Sonel's ceryll, which somehow retained its green hue, even as the white bolt of magic poured through it and on toward the stones held forth by the delegation. There, though, the beam changed radically. Meeting Baden's stone, and then flowing in a hexagon around the six mages, the light became striated with their colors. Like ribbons strung together around the God's pole at the Feast of Arick each spring, the hues spun together around the delegation. Baden's orange and Trahn's brown, Ursel's grey and Niall's maroon, Alayna's purple and Jaryd's blue. Faster and faster they turned, brighter and brighter, until the radiance grew so powerful that Orris had to avert his eyes. A sudden gust of wind—who could say where it came from?—swirled through the Great Hall, whipping around the green cloaks of the masters and mages and forcing hawks and owls to raise their wings in an effort to balance themselves on the shoulders of their mages. And then, as abruptly as it all had begun, the gale subsided and the light vanished, leaving the chamber in the relative darkness of normal daylight, and in the grip of an awed, uncertain silence. Slowly, as his eyes adjusted to the new light, Orris gazed forward once more, knowing already what he would find. Or rather, what he would not find. In the space where the delegation had stood, there was nothing. Nothing at all. His friends were gone.

At first there was darkness, as thick as swamp mud and absolute, save for the faint blue glimmer of his ceryll, to which Jaryd clung with his eyes as he would a beacon in a raging storm. It was strange, because Orris, who had been standing before him in the middle of the Gathering Chamber, seemed to shield his eyes as from a glaring light, just as the shadows began to descend. But Jaryd saw only blackness and the besieged point of sapphire crystal. Then a stillness came over him—over them all, he supposed, though he was aware of no one else except Ishalla, whose talons sank painfully into his shoulder—and a bone-numbing cold encompassed him, ripping a gasp from his chest. Which alerted him to the third thing: he could not breathe, could not replace the air that the chill had torn from his now burning lungs. He felt a tremendous pressure, as though someone were kneeling on his chest. Panic rose within him; he tried to break free, to run, to escape from the frigid void into which he had fallen. But he could not move. He felt his limbs straining to thrash about, as might a drowning man in the murky, cold waters of some nightmare sea. But the darkness held him, freezing him, suffocating him.

Releasing him. Suddenly, it was over. He stood on a windy beach in the warm sun of a summer afternoon. The others were there with him, looking disoriented but unharmed. The strand on which they stood stretched for miles in each direction, its white sands littered with the worn, bone-white trunks of ancient, gnarled trees. Huge breakers, their crests swept into a fine mist by the wind, pounded ceaselessly at the shoreline, crashing down on the sand like the fists of some pitiless giant. And opposite the surf, on a tide-ravaged ledge that rose thirty feet above the beach, loomed a shadowy wood of towering, weather-beaten pines. Misshapen by centuries of potent, brine-laden winds, beaten back by season after season of ocean squalls, the trees appeared to shy away from the sea, as if afraid of joining their brethren, whose bleached skeletons lay on the sand below.

"This looks like the right place," Trahn commented over the rhythm of the surf. "But is there any way to be certain?"

Baden shook his head as he looked around at the coastline and surveyed the line of evergreens. "Not that I know of. At least not until nightfall."

Jaryd shuddered involuntarily. Even after facing Theron, he could not help but feel a certain foreboding at the thought of confronting another of the Unsettled. Glancing at Alayna, he saw the same disquiet written in her dark eyes. She stepped closer to him, placing a hand on his shoulder.

"I have no doubt that Sonel sent us to the correct spot," Baden assured them all after a brief pause, his thin hair tousled by the wind. "We need only wait and prepare ourselves." He gazed up at the sun. "It won't be dark for a few more hours, and we should all use that time as we'd like. We'll meet back here at dusk."

The others nodded and began to disperse. Ursel set out southward along the beach, scaring up a flock of gulls as she walked. Trahn moved off a short distance and sat down, facing the tide. Closing his eyes, he was soon lost in meditation.

"I was considering walking up the strand a ways," Baden said, approaching the young mages. "I don't get to do much beachcombing anymore. Would you care to walk with me?"

Jaryd looked at Alayna, who smiled and nodded. "Sounds like fun," he replied, drawing a grin from his uncle.

In the end, Niall joined them as well, and the four of them wandered slowly up the shoreline, saying little, stooping occasionally to pick up a sand-polished stone or a shining fragment of shell. Glancing back once over his shoulder, Jaryd saw Trahn's dark form, already small with the distance they had covered, framed against the light sand, and the pale tree trunks, and the foaming waters of the incoming tide.

"What can you tell us about Phelan?" Alayna asked Baden, after they had walked for some time. "I know that he bound to wolves rather than birds, and I know that he led the Order for several years. But, other than that, I know very little."

"I don't know too much more than that, actually," Baden answered, "although I do know that he bound only once in his lifetime, and that, when his familiar died, he chose never to bind again."

"Chose?" Jaryd asked sharply. "You mean he let himself die unbound?"

Baden nodded.

"But why?"

The Owl-Master shrugged. "I don't know."

"I do," Niall offered. The three mages looked at him. "When my sister and I were growing up, my father often told us Phelan's story," he explained. "He was a hero of my father's, I think. It's ironic, really," he added, stopping to gaze thoughtfully at the advancing surf, "since my father ended up dying unbound as well."

The others said nothing, waiting as Niall allowed the memory of his father to wash over him. A minute later he turned back toward them and smiled. "Forgive me," he said to Alayna. "You asked for Phelan's tale, not mine." They began to walk again. "Phelan was born not far from here, in the village of WoodSea, near where the River Halcya meets the ocean. His father was a woodcutter. Phelan had no siblings, and he never knew his mother, she having died while giving birth to him. His father never fully recovered from the loss of his wife, and, perhaps as a product of his grief, man and son were estranged from the very beginning of Phelan's life. As a boy, Phelan spent a great deal of time on his own, exploring the forests and shoreline near his home. During one of these excursions, early in the spring of his eighth year, he was caught in an unexpected blizzard. Ill-prepared for such severe weather, too far from his home to make it back safely, Phelan nearly died.

"He tried to bury himself beneath the fallen leaves of a dense grove, hoping that he could keep himself warm enough to survive. But, as he later told the story himself, he had actually passed out before nightfall. He awoke the following morning, in a warm, dark, foul-smelling den, surrounded by a family of wolves. Both adults were there, with several pups." Niall allowed himself a small smile. "Some of the legends that came later, after Phelan died, claimed that Kalba, the animal to which he later bound, was one of these pups—a sibling of sorts to the man." The Owl-Master shook his head, though his smirk lingered.

"You don't believe this?" Alayna asked.

"Phelan did not bind to Kalba for another dozen years, and their binding lasted longer than any binding in the history of the Order. Had he been one of those pups, Kalba could not have survived that long." They walked a few paces listening to the advance and retreat of the breakers. "At first, naturally, Phelan was afraid," Niall began again, his tone deepening once more as he returned to the cadence of his tale. "But he soon recognized that the wolves meant him no harm, and he stayed with them for several days, eating and sleeping as they did. When finally he returned to his home, he was perfectly healthy, save for the frostbite he suffered in the blizzard, which cost him two fingers on his left hand. But always after, he claimed, he felt a kinship to the

wolves of what was known then as Ellibar Spur. The animals often traveled
with him during his wanderings, and there are many other tales describing
these encounters which have little to do with what Phelan achieved later in his
life as a member of the Order.

"Soon after he left his home, however, as a young man seeking both his
path and peace from the conflicts that had consumed what remained of the
relationship he had with his father, he was joined by a young wolf, silver in
color, that followed him for several days. No one else saw them, and even
when he later shared so many of the stories of his life with curious admirers,
he never described what happened during those days they spent in the forests
of the spur. But when next Phelan walked among people, he had bound himself
to Kalba and, thus, become a mage.

"The two of them, wolf and man, sailed from the spur to Ceryllon that
winter, braving squalls and seas that would have daunted the most adept sailors
of the land. Many feared them lost. But they returned in the spring, and Phelan
bore a staff mounted with a ceryll whose silver tone was an exact match for
Kalba's fur. They journeyed to Amarid that year for the Midsummer Gathering,
and though the mages eventually admitted Phelan to the Order, they did so
only after a great debate. Many opposed opening the Order to someone who
hadn't bound to a hawk or owl, and others objected to the fact that the Wolf-
Master had never been anyone's Mage-Attend. Phelan, however, impressed
enough of the mages with his courage and his honesty to gain their support,
and in the years that followed, he more than justified their ultimate decision
to welcome him as a colleague. Within six years of his entrance into the Order
he had become Wolf-Sage, and none doubted that his was the strongest magic
to be wielded in Tobyn-Ser since the days of Amarid and Theron. His reputation even traveled beyond the borders of this land, to Abborij, where fear of
Phelan prevented an invasion for nearly twenty years, until he no longer led
the Order. These were years of peace and tremendous prosperity in Tobyn-
Ser, and Phelan became a hero of the land.

"Throughout this time, his bond with Kalba deepened. Never had a mage
and familiar been closer, people said at the time, and certainly no binding since
has rivaled it. Like brothers, they were. Though he was sage, Phelan never
lived in the Great Hall, preferring to sleep and hunt in Hawksfind Wood alongside his familiar. And while he was a wise leader, compassionate and caring, he
remained proud and a loner. He chose a first because the laws of the Order
demanded it, but he never consulted the Owl-Master he chose, preferring his
own counsel and such guidance as Kalba might offer. When Kalba finally died,
twenty-four years after their binding, Phelan was devastated by grief. So much
so that he vowed never to bind to another creature." Niall shrugged. "It was
a vow he kept.

"Phelan continued to attend Gatherings, and he retained a residue of his
power—more, it must be said, than most mages keep when they lose a bird.
But as one unbound, he had to relinquish his position as Wolf-Sage. He was
replaced by Glenyse, last of the Eagle-Sages, for, as soon as word reached
Abborij that the Wolf-Sage no longer ruled the Order, the Abborijis launched
their third and final invasion of Tobyn-Ser. Perhaps driven by loss and anguish,
Phelan fought in the war as one possessed. His heroics, carved with the blood-

stained blade of his great ax, enhanced his status throughout the land. But they could not assuage his pain." The Owl-Master shrugged a second time, a difficult emotion reflected on his features. "It is strange to view good health and long life as anything but a blessing," he concluded, "but Phelan's story is made all the more sorrowful by the fact that he lived for another four decades without Kalba. He died an old man, still unbound, of course, and very much alone. Since that time he has inhabited Phelan Spur as one of the Unsettled."

The four mages had stopped walking. Baden's blue eyes, lit by the afternoon sun, were fixed on the forest that fronted the beach. "It's a hard tale to hear," he said quietly. "But I suppose all the Unsettled carry such sorrow as a burden of the curse."

"That may be true for some," Alayna returned, "but Phelan's story seems easier somehow."

Jaryd looked at her with surprise. "How so?"

"No doubt losing his familiar was hard," she replied, turning to face him. "But by denying himself a second binding, and making himself one of the Unsettled, he ensured that he and Kalba would be together for an eternity." She hesitated. "There is a grief there, to be sure; he paid a tremendous price. But, in the end, he may have fulfilled his greatest desire."

Niall looked at the young woman for a long time. "I first heard this tale as a child," he finally told her, "and I've related it to many others over the course of my life. But I've never heard it put in that light before." He smiled at her. "I believe you may be right. Thank you."

Alayna blushed slightly. "What for?"

"For showing an old man that there may be comfort to be found for even the most ancient sorrows."

Alayna said nothing, but, stepping forward and raising herself onto the tips of her toes, she kissed Niall on the cheek. "And thank you for sharing Phelan's story with us."

This time, it was Niall's turn to blush, and Baden, seeing the Owl-Master's discomfort, quickly changed the subject, though not before sending a smile in Jaryd's direction. "We should start back," he remarked. "The sun will be setting soon, and I'd like to find some food before we meet with Phelan."

The others nodded their agreement, and the four mages began retracing their steps along the kelp line, the Owl-Masters walking in front, and Jaryd and Alayna following several paces behind them.

For some time, Jaryd could think only of the tale they had just heard from Niall. He grew increasingly conscious of Ishalla's talons on his shoulder and of her presence in his mind. He had only just bound to the hawk; Arick willing, he would not know the pain of losing her, or the fear of dying unbound, for many years. But the story of Phelan and Kalba had left him feeling vulnerable, and shockingly aware of the fragility of life, not only his own and Ishalla's, but all of theirs. All the power that the Mage-Craft had to offer could not shield them from their own mortality. It was something to consider, particularly now. They had, after all, come to Phelan Spur in order to find and defeat the outlanders, perhaps to do battle. And in that instant, a terrible foreboding came over him. There is a death in this, he thought.

Then, suddenly aware of Alayna walking wordlessly along the sand beside him, her long, dark hair twisting and dancing in the ocean breeze, Jaryd remembered that there already had been. Sartol died this morning, he reminded himself, his thoughts taking a new path. We killed him; all of us, including Alayna. He tried to imagine what she must have been feeling, how the day's events had affected her. But he found it hard to move beyond his own feelings of relief and satisfied vengeance. In truth, though he had never guessed that he would feel this way about any person, he was glad that Sartol was dead. Yet, he could not help but feel that this sentiment amounted to a betrayal of Alayna and the new love they shared. He looked at her, searching for something—anything—that he might say to ease her pain without falling into hypocrisy. And as seemed to have happened so often over the past few weeks, he found that she was already watching him, anticipating his mood and thoughts.

"It's all right," she told him, taking his hand as they walked. "I'm all right."

He continued to gaze at her. "You don't have to be, you know. No one would fault you for feeling confused and hurt and sad. I, least of all."

She smiled at that, though sadly. "I know. But not now. I'm trying not to blame myself for letting Sartol deceive me, but I won't forgive myself if I don't do what I can to limit the damage he's done. After we take care of the outlanders, I'll see to my own needs. Until then, I have to put them aside."

Jaryd wanted to say more, to warn her of the dangers of keeping too tight a lock on one's feelings. But he also knew that he had to trust her judgment in this matter; and he was not at all sure that he wouldn't have demanded the same stoicism of himself in a similar situation. So, after a moment, he nodded, and, still holding hands, they continued back down the strand in silence.

Trahn had not moved from where they left him, although he was speaking now with Ursel, who had returned from her stroll along the shore. With the sun dipping low in the sky above the forest, the shadows of the massive trees had begun to stretch across the beach, reaching almost to where the two Hawk-Mages sat. The first quarter of the new moon hung directly overhead, casting its pale light from the deepening blue of the late-afternoon sky.

"It'll be dark soon," Trahn noted, glancing over his shoulder to check the position of the sun. "We should probably prepare our meal now."

"If you were hungry," Baden remarked with a grin, "you should have gone ahead without us."

Trahn smiled in return. "I would have, but Ursel thought we should wait for the four of you."

"It's a good thing you arrived when you did," Ursel quipped. "He was starting to look at my hawk strangely—I think he was imagining her on a roasting spit with a shan garnish."

They all laughed as Trahn and Ursel climbed to their feet, and the mages began to prepare for their dinner. Trahn's large brown hawk and Ursel's slender black and grey bird were both unaccustomed to forest and beach terrain. Hence, Ishalla and Fylimar, and Baden's and Niall's owls, hunted for all of them, returning with game birds and rabbits, which the mages roasted over the fire. Ursel still carried in her cloak a large pouch of dried fruits and a skin filled with light, Tobyn's Plain wine that she had taken on her patrol, and she shared these as well. As shadows enveloped the beach and the sun disappeared behind the dense woodland, the company enjoyed a modest meal and quiet conversation, carefully avoiding any mention of what had happened in the Great Hall earlier in the day, and who they were about to meet in the forest that loomed darkly at their backs.

Stars began to emerge in the velvet-blue sky, and the moon, chasing the sun toward the western horizon, shone with growing brightness on the pines and the sand. And as the last vestiges of daylight vanished, the six mages turned from the now retreating tide to gaze watchfully at the forest. Muting their cerylls, they allowed the fire to burn away, unsure as they were of how easy or difficult it would be to spot the glow that would mark Phelan's arrival. And as the dancing yellow flames gave way to the angry red of the driftwood embers, a tense stillness fell over the beach. I have faced Theron, Jaryd reminded himself for the second time that day, and we have far less to fear from Phelan than we did from the Owl-Master. He knew this to be true; Niall's tale had confirmed it for him. Still, Phelan was one of the Unsettled, and they were about to meet him. Once more, as he had in the afternoon, walking back down the strand with Alayna, Jaryd had a sudden premonition of death. His pulse was like a surging river, roaring in his ears until the sound of it threatened to drown out the sea. Feeling his stomach clench itself into a fist, he wished that he hadn't eaten.

"I had hoped that this would get easier," Alayna murmured to him, the anxiety in her voice evident even though she had barely made herself heard.

He tried to smile, glancing at her briefly.

"There!" Trahn exclaimed, his voice sounding unnaturally loud.

Jaryd's eyes flew back to the wood, his heart suddenly pounding within his chest. Where a moment before there had been only shadow, he now saw a faint silver light, as if the moon had fallen from the sky to land among the trees. It grew brighter, shimmering just as Theron's radiance had, illuminating the forest from within.

Baden stood. "Come," he commanded tersely. "There's no sense in putting this off."

The rest of them rose, and the company made its way toward the glow, crossing the strand and ascending the sharp slope to the woodland. Jaryd reached the top of the ledge first, and breathless from the climb, he noted that the source of the light had drawn closer to the forest edge. He looked up at the quarter moon, then back toward the silver radiance. The one seemed a perfect match for the other.

The others soon joined him atop the sandy bluff, and slowly, the six mages filed through the trees, winding among the immense trunks until they came to a small hollow, where the ghostly pale figures of Phelan and his wolf awaited them.

The Wolf-Master was an enormous man. He stood a full head taller than Baden, who was the tallest of their group, and his chest looked to be twice as broad as the Owl-Master's. Jaryd wondered where they had ever found a cloak big enough to hold him. His forearms, as massive as tree limbs, were corded with muscle, and his neck was as thick as Jaryd's thigh. And yet, imposing though he was, he had a remarkably pleasant, open face. His curly black and grey hair and his thick beard framed a wide, full mouth and round cheeks that almost assuredly would have been ruddy had he not appeared before them as a luminescent spirit. Jaryd could only guess what color his eyes would have been. They glimmered bright and fair, like stars plucked from the sky on a clear winter's night.

A low growl drew Jaryd's gaze from Phelan to the wolf that stood beside him. Like the Wolf-Master, the animal was huge, with paws the size of Jaryd's hand. It glowed with a pale silver grey, the color of a hazy winter sun reflecting off the sea. Its eyes resembled Phelan's, and they carried an intelligence, an awareness that seemed almost alien. The fur on the creature's back and neck bristled aggressively, the frosted hairs rigid and upright. Again, it growled.

"Be easy, Kalba," the Wolf-Master comforted, in a voice as deep and gentle as an early morning tide. He stroked the animal's back, smoothing its fur. "Be easy. I'm certain that our guests have disturbed us for good reason."

"Greetings, Wolf-Master," Baden offered in a clear tone, bowing at the waist as he spoke. The others followed his lead. "Forgive our intrusion, but we have need of whatever counsel and aid you might be willing to give us. I am Baden. With me," he went on, indicating his companions one by one, "are Niall, Trahn, Ursel, Alayna, and Jaryd."

Phelan's expression remained reserved. "Be welcome to Ellibar Spur," he returned, his hand still resting on the wolf. "This is Kalba, and you seem to know who I am."

"Indeed we do, Wolf-Master. What you call Ellibar Spur we know as Phelan Spur," Baden told him. "You honor us by making us your guests."

The spirit dismissed the compliment with a gesture. "Phelan Spur," he repeated. "I find that hard to get used to. Why name this land after a ghost? Ellibar, at least, had meaning once, when we still used the old language." He fell silent for a time, as if he had forgotten that they were there. "But you have not come so far to discuss the name of this spur," he said finally, regarding them again. "You spoke of your need for counsel and aid. I take it this pertains to the outlanders."

"You know of this?"

Phelan nodded. "I have seen something of it, yes."

"Then you know of the traitor within the Order as well?"

The Wolf-Master's face seemed suddenly to turn to stone, and the gleaming eyes to ice. "I do. You have dealt with him?"

It was Baden's turn to nod. "He's dead. But the threat from the outlanders still remains. We need your help."

"Yes," Phelan agreed coldly, "you do." None of the mages spoke, and after a brief pause the Wolf-Master went on. "It should never have been allowed to progress this far," he chided. "Without the link, I can understand how the outlanders might have reached Tobyn-Ser, but once the attacks began . . ." He stopped, shaking his head. "The inaction of the Order is unpardonable. You have grown lax. What of Amarid's Law? What of your commitment to guard the people of this land?"

"We're here, Wolf-Master," Baden said simply. "Late though it is, we are here."

"Yes," Phelan snarled contemptuously. "First you ignore the problem, and now you come to me, hoping that I can rescue you from your failure. What of your Owl-Sage in all of this? Were I ruling the Order, the attacks would have ended long ago."

"Our sage is dead," Baden snapped, his patience waning. "The traitor killed her."

"Well, maybe new leadership will do the Order good."

"*Enough!*" the Owl-Master roared, taking a step forward and ignoring another growl from the great wolf. "Jessamyn was a wise and courageous leader, and I will not allow her memory to be maligned! Even by you, Phelan! Perhaps, in your time, a sage could impose his or her will upon the Order, but today, for good or ill, a sage leads by consensus. All of us are responsible for what has happened. *All of us!* Not just Jessamyn!"

For a long time, the Wolf-Master stared at Baden, his eyes cold and bright, his mouth set in a thin, taut line. Then, slowly, a smile crept across his face. "So there is some passion in you, after all," he observed. "Maybe all is not yet lost."

Baden's expression had not changed. "We don't have time for this. Do you intend to help us or not?"

Again, the spirit did not respond immediately. Instead, he turned his gaze from Baden to the other mages, and then back to the Owl-Master. "I will do for you what I can," he replied at last. "But, in truth, that is not much."

"Can you help us find the outlanders?"

"I can tell you where they are."

"Can you take us to them?"

Phelan shook his head. "No. As I indicated, my ability to help you is limited. I can give you their locations, but, by the time you reach these places, they will have moved on. And, by myself, I cannot interact with your world in any meaningful way."

"But I thought that the Unsettled were incarnations of the Mage-Craft," Jaryd broke in. "You exist solely as power, don't you?"

Phelan looked at the young mage with unconcealed curiosity. "That is true," he confirmed, "and, as such, I have no corporeal properties."

"But you could kill us if you wanted to," Jaryd persisted, "just as Theron killed those who ventured into the grove."

"An interesting way to pursue your point," the spirit commented with a smirk. "I remember similar stories about Theron's Grove from when I was alive. The Owl-Master was the first of us, and by far the most powerful. His ability to effect changes in your world may exceed mine and those of my brethren. I do not know." He turned back to Baden. "Your friend is right. We are the Mage-Craft incarnate. But our power is limited, at least individually."

Baden narrowed his eyes. "That's the second time you've said such a thing. Do you mean that you could act with the cooperation of the other Unsettled?"

"Yes. As I understand it, if all of us act in concert, we can affect events in your world. But," he continued, a note of sadness in his words, "that has never happened in the four hundred years since my death." He glanced at Jaryd again. "Theron's bitterness toward the Order endures to this day. He is more powerful than any of us, maybe than all of us combined. Without his cooperation, we cannot help you; he would disrupt any effort we might make to act on your behalf. And I doubt that he will cooperate."

Jaryd grinned. "He might surprise you." And, raising the wooden staff that he held at his side, the Hawk-Mage saw the spirit's eyes widen in amazement. "I see that you recognize this as the staff of Theron, Wolf-Master. The Owl-Master gave it to Alayna and me as a token of his goodwill."

"You have spoken with Theron!" Phelan breathed.

"Yes. Led by Owl-Sage Jessamyn, eight of us journeyed to the grove. We believed that Theron might have been responsible for the attacks, and we went to confront him. It was there that Sartol killed the sage and her first. He tried to kill the two of us as well, but we fled into the grove, where we encountered Theron's spirit. After we convinced him to help us, he told us of the outlanders and offered hints as to what they might want from Tobyn-Ser." Jaryd hesitated. "We have yet to learn the meaning of all the Owl-Master's clues, but we can't delay any longer. Theron has pledged his aid, Wolf-Master. Will you do the same?"

Jaryd endured the spirit's silent, appraising stare as best he could, feeling some relief when Phelan's eyes swung momentarily to Alayna, but meeting the gaze once again when it returned to him. "As a young man, newly bound to Kalba, I once found myself at the ruins of Rholde," the Wolf-Master related in a subdued voice. "I thought about entering the grove, about seeing Theron and speaking with him." He shook his head. "But I lacked the courage."

"Sartol was chasing us," Jaryd explained apologetically. "We didn't choose to go in. It just sort of happened."

Phelan laughed. "I do not doubt it. But," he added, his mirth fading, "you spoke with him, and you impressed him enough to earn his consideration. *He gave you his staff!*" the spirit said with wonder, shaking his shaggy head again. "Do not understate what the two of you have achieved; you may have saved Tobyn-Ser." He looked once more at Baden. "I will help you," he declared. "We will help you. But I need some time to establish a link with the rest of the Unsettled."

"Before you do, Wolf-Master," Baden said, stopping him, "you should know that the traitor died unbound today. He is now one of the Unsettled as well."

Phelan considered this for a moment. "It should not matter. Given time, he will be able to stop us, but he is new to our circle yet. He should not be a problem." With that, the Wolf-Master closed his eyes. A few seconds later, Kalba did the same.

The six mages waited silently for what seemed a long time, as Phelan, his massive frame rigid and his brow creased in concentration, attempted to contact the other spirits roaming Tobyn-Ser. The forest was utterly still, save for a soft, salty breeze that glided in off the water, and the sound of the waves drifting gently from the beach. Jaryd glanced at Baden, who returned the look with a slight shrug and an anxious expression.

Several moments later, Phelan opened his eyes again. "The link has been forged," he told them, his bright eyes seeming clouded, as if slow to regain their focus. He turned to the young mages, a strange smile tugging at his lips. "Theron sends his greetings to the two of you. And he congratulates you all on the slaying of the traitor."

Jaryd looked quickly at Alayna, but she offered no reaction.

"Thirteen of the outlanders remain," the Wolf-Master continued, "spread throughout the land in small groups." He paused.

"Where, exactly?" Baden asked. "Can you tell?"

"Of course." The spirit closed his eyes again. "There are two groups of three, one in the east-central portion of the Great Desert and the other on the Northern Plain. Six are traveling in pairs. They can be found in the southern corner of Tobyn's Plain, the Emerald Hills, and in Tobyn's Wood, not terribly far from here. And there is one traveling alone in Leora's Forest." Once more, he opened his eyes.

"So what do we do now?" Baden asked. "What are our options?"

Phelan opened his arms in a gesture of invitation. "The choice is yours. The possibilities are as boundless now as they were limited a moment ago. You must decide what you want us to do with the intruders. If you want them dead, we can kill them for you with little—"

"No," Baden broke in, shaking his head. "We want them alive. When this group is defeated, another may be sent, and we'll be no better off than we are now. We need answers that only these people can give us."

The Wolf-Master nodded slowly. "Very well. Then we will bring them to you."

"We cannot fight them all at once."

Again the spirit grinned. "You will not have to fight them at all," he returned. "We are able to track the outlanders by their strange birds and weapons. They are alien to this land—far more so than the people themselves—and so we are tuned to them in a way. We can sense them. And, when we bring the intruders to you, we can take these objects from them."

Baden cocked his head slightly. "Can you bring the weapons to us as well, perhaps later, after we've subdued the outlanders? They shouldn't be left scattered throughout the land."

"I believe we can, yes."

"That would be satisfactory," the Owl-Master replied. "Although," he added with a sheepish grin, "we may also need you to transport all of us, including the outlanders, back to the Great Hall."

"You ask a great deal, Owl-Master," the spirit observed with a grin. "We can do that as well, once the intruders are here. We will need your aid, however," Phelan went on. "How did you come here?"

Baden regarded the luminescent figure with uncertainty. "We used the Summoning Stone," he said after a moment. "Why?"

"I thought as much," the Wolf-Master remarked. "Then you are familiar with the concept of the conduit."

"Yes."

"Well," Phelan explained, "just as you needed someone to envision this place, we need one of you to visualize the outlanders for us."

"But I thought you could see them," Jaryd said. "Theron told us that he saw them."

"We do see them. But as with all things that we see, including those, like yourselves, that stand directly before us, we see them . . . differently."

"What do you mean?"

The spirit gave a small, self-conscious laugh. "I am not certain that I can explain. It has been so long since I observed anything in any other way." He made a small, helpless gesture, which looked strange coming from such a formidable figure. "It is just different." He faltered again. "It is as if I see you from very far away, but not so far that I cannot make out details, like the color of your eyes, or the plumage of your bird." He shook his head in frustration. "I cannot explain it," he said again, impatience creeping into his tone. "What is important is that we need one of you to act as our conduit, so that the image we use resembles those we transport. Without your help, the outlanders will be lost, just as you would have been had you been sent here without a proper image of the spur to guide you."

"I saw the two who died at Watersbend," Baden volunteered. "You can use that image."

"No," Phelan replied flatly, after conveying Baden's offer to the other Unsettled. He leveled a meaty finger at Jaryd. "Theron wants him, for the vision he had. The Owl-Master believes it will be stronger than any memory."

Jaryd shrugged. "All right," he agreed. "What do you need me to do?"

"In a few moments," Phelan told him with sudden kindness, "when I tell you we are ready, you must stand with your ceryll held out before you and empty your mind of all, save the image of the outlander you have envisioned."

Jaryd waited for more. "That's all?" he asked finally.

"That is all. We will do the rest." The spirit turned to Baden. "The rest of your company need only wait, although you should remain alert. The outlanders will have no weapons, but once they have arrived, I cannot control what they do. It will be up to you to keep them from escaping."

"We'll be ready," the Owl-Master replied. He glanced at Jaryd and started to say something. Then he stopped himself, and placed a hand on Jaryd's arm. "You'll do fine," he said. "I know you'll do fine."

Alayna held Jaryd close for a moment and then, with the others, stepped a short distance away. Jaryd struggled to calm himself, but the sense of foreboding had returned. It all seemed almost too easy.

"Ready yourself, Hawk-Mage," Phelan commanded, as the Wolf-Master and the great animal beside him closed their eyes again.

Jaryd did the same, focusing his mind as best he could on the vision that first came to him so many weeks ago, as he and Baden slept in the mountains above Taima. At first, the memory remained hazy, as if seen through a curtain or a fine mist. But, gradually, it grew clearer. As he had that night in the late spring, Jaryd saw a man in a long green cloak, carrying a baleful red ceryll in one hand and bearing a huge, alien bird on his opposite shoulder. Jaryd watched the figure approach him, saw the outlander remove a black feather from his cloak, waited as the man came nearer. Concentrating on this image, Jaryd was but dimly aware of the mounting gale that had begun to whip through the hollow. An instant later, however, he did perceive another presence in his mind. It took him a few seconds to realize that it was the Wolf-Master.

Be easy, the spirit sent. *Hold fast to your vision, but open your mind to us so that we might encompass it. The image is strong; you are doing well.*

Then Phelan was gone, replaced by a new consciousness, one Jaryd did not know. It seemed to move through him and over him, like the wind he so vaguely felt on his skin and cloak. Others followed in a seemingly endless procession. Time came to be measured by their passage. At one point, Theron was there, proud and fierce. *You have done well, Hawk-Mage,* he conveyed. *Remember me.* Some time later, another passed through him, one who was familiar somehow, though Jaryd could not name the presence. *I am the last,* this one sent. But these words rode a wave of harsh, malicious laughter that chilled Jaryd like ice water running down his spine.

And in that moment, the image in Jaryd's mind abruptly shattered into shards of blinding, cutting light, and Phelan erupted with a deafening, inarticulate roar. Jaryd felt himself toppling to the ground, and though he could see nothing, he was suddenly aware of the howling wind that raged all around the company.

"What is it!" he heard Baden cry out, somewhere behind him.

"It is impossible!" Phelan bellowed, his tone colored in equal measure by outrage and shock. "How can he already be so strong?"

Sartol, Jaryd realized, of course. That was the voice he had heard. "He is new to our circle yet," Phelan had said. "He should not be a problem." Oh, but he was so very strong. Jaryd had faced his power just this morning. All of them had nearly died at the Owl-Master's hands. They should have known that he would find a way to thwart them, even now. They should have known. There was a taste like ashes in Jaryd's mouth, and he could still hear Sartol's laughter echoing in his ears like vengeance.

"He has resisted us!" Phelan cried out. "He has betrayed us!"

Then the Wolf-Master's voice changed again, growing severe as he shouted out a warning. "Guard yourselves!" he cried out, his words crashing over the gale and the cold memory of laughter. "They are coming! And they can fight you!"

22

He made his way slowly through the dense woodland—Leora's Forest, they called it here, although the crude maps he had memorized prior to leaving Lon-Ser merely referred to it as "the Northwest Timber Stand"— and he navigated the rough, wooded path by the ghostly light of the moon, which filtered past the leaves and branches overhead, and by the deep, crimson glow of the stone mounted atop his weapon. There was a village a few miles ahead; already he could detect the faint scent of the smithies and cooking fires riding the light wind.

Tomorrow night, if all went according to plan, others approaching the settlement along this path would smell smoke of a different kind pouring into the night sky. He tried to smile, but even this notion could not clear the shadows from his mind. Normally he preferred working alone; he valued his solitude. But tonight, his mind churning with dark thoughts, and his stomach clenched with a fear that went far beyond the vague sense of disquiet that had gripped him for the past several days, Calbyr found himself hungry for companionship.

If someone had asked him yesterday, he couldn't really have explained what was bothering him or what had prompted these feelings of foreboding, other than to attribute them to superstition. And that was still not an admission that came to him easily. Over the past year, during his time in this strange land, he had grown increasingly superstitious, even allowing his beliefs to influence his decisions as leader of the crew.

Nothing important, nothing substantial, but he had altered the timing of certain actions to coincide with fortuitous dates, or to avoid full moons. Obviously, he would never have admitted this to the men working under him. None of them would have understood. Indeed, back in the Nal, he would never have tolerated such irrationality himself. Perhaps here, where the people were backward and unsophisticated, where the culture was underdeveloped and the wilderness unrefined, superstition was accepted. In Lon-Ser, though, people had moved beyond believing in signs and omens, at least the people he knew. Lon-Ser's technological advances had brought a more pragmatic sense of the workings of the world, and a deeper understanding of science. All of which left little room for cabalism and the foolishness that went along with it. But he had been away from home for too long. He had spent too many days wandering through forests and mountains, learning to hunt and to orient himself by the position of the sun and the moon and the stars. He had become so tuned to this blasted country that he had even begun to think like its people. That, of all things, did make him smile: the thought of himself as some sort of man of the land, or mountaineer, more like an Oracle than a Nal-Lord, was funny. Only for a moment, however. And then the black mood descended on him again. At times like these, he barely recognized himself as the man who had left the Nal two years ago to begin training the band of break-laws for this mission. He was the agent of Lon-Ser's expansion, Tobyn-Ser's conqueror. Those were the phrases Cedrych had used, anyway, and he liked the sound of them, particularly the second. But agents of expansion didn't fall prey to these invisible demons of the mind, and conquerors didn't spend so much time afraid.

Cedrych, of all people, might actually have understood. As much as Calbyr mistrusted his Overlord, and, yes, even feared him, he also felt a certain kinship to the man. Cedrych would appreciate the difficulties of this job and of functioning for so long in this alien culture. For all that had passed between them over the years, and despite the tense, at times even violent nature of the Lord-Overlord relationship, Cedrych had offered words of compassion and encouragement just before Calbyr's departure.

"We two are alike, Calbyr," he had said unexpectedly, passing a hand over his smoothly shaven head, the gaze of his one good eye and the empty, scar-ravaged socket both fixed on Calbyr's face. "We're visionaries. We see not only the future, but also the path, as yet unforged, that will lead us to it." He had placed a large though delicate hand on Calbyr's shoulder. The hand of an artist, Calbyr remembered thinking. The hand of a killer. "You will build that path, my friend. I can give you the tools, the resources you'll need. But it falls to you to use them well. I envy you, actually," Cedrych had gone on, surprising

Calbyr a second time. "You are to be the agent of Lon-Ser's expansion and the conqueror of all Tobyn-Ser. You will construct the future of which the rest of us can only dream. To be sure, not everyone here would approve of our tactics, were we to ask them now. They might not even share our aims. At least not yet. But they will, and they'll thank us. They'll thank you, Calbyr, for saving Lon-Ser, for giving it a future. Remember that when things aren't going so well. Remember it when you're weary of being so far from your beloved Nal," he had added with a crooked grin, before leading Calbyr to the door and dismissing him for the last time.

Yes. Cedrych would have understood. The recognition of this eased Calbyr's mind a bit, allowing him to consider more calmly the circumstances that had brought on this latest sense of dread. Certainly, it had begun as mere superstition. Things had been going very well for over a year now. Too well, he had begun to realize recently. In an operation like this one, there were always problems of some sort. Always. And the longer you waited for the first one, he believed, the worse it would be. But no, everything had been perfect. For over a year now. Sure, Sartol had stumbled across them early on, startling them all, and killing Yarit when the buffoon foolishly tried to blast the mage with his thrower. But Sartol proved to be a most valuable ally, giving them access to the inner workings of the Order, and helping them plot their strategy for the discrediting of Tobyn-Ser's mages and masters. And, while losing a man in a crew this small could have created difficulties, Calbyr had recognized almost from the start that Yarit had been a poor choice. He was too edgy and too stupid. If he hadn't messed up then, with Sartol, he would have later, probably at a much greater cost to all of them. All in all, their inadvertent encounter with Sartol had turned out quite well, far better than Calbyr had any right to expect.

So, too, had his own chance meeting with the man and boy he had killed on the island in South Shelter. Other people had spotted him from a distance just as this man had done. That in itself was not a problem. But the others had waved and watched him go on, thinking nothing of his failure to stop and speak with them. But this man, inexplicably, had turned and fled. Calbyr never learned why. Perhaps he just sensed something was wrong; perhaps he had a premonition of some sort. Calbyr smiled to himself, noting the irony. Whatever the reason, Calbyr had realized immediately that the man had to die, and the boy, too. Initially, he worried that this sudden escalation of the incidents for which he and his gang were responsible would create problems for them; that it might alert someone to the presence of what Sartol called "outlanders." But, as it happened, the time was right for an escalation of the attacks. Rather than complicating matters, the incident provided a convincing bridge between the relatively restrained mischief of the autumn and winter, and the more serious attacks that commenced late in the spring and intensified during the summer.

Even their mistakes, it seemed, worked out for the best. Certainly those two had. Moreover, the attacks had come off without a hitch. From all that Sartol had told him, the vandalism and the killings were having the desired effect. The people's faith in the Order was deteriorating; mages were accusing mages of treason; and the Order's chief suspect in all of these crimes had been dead for a thousand years. All of it was going according to plan. Exactly. Perfectly.

And Calbyr was terrified. Sooner or later, things were bound to fall apart. That's what he had been thinking yesterday, even as he lamented his superstitious nature.

Today, though, all that had changed. Vague forebodings had given way suddenly to a deeper, more urgent dread. It had come at last, it seemed, this collapse of the good fortune they had enjoyed. Abruptly, finally, things did not appear nearly so perfect.

First, he had not heard from Glyn and Kedar for well over a week. All the others had checked in as usual, using the communicating devices installed in their weapons to punch in their coded sequence of beeps and buzzes. But not Glyn and Kedar, not since a few days before their planned assault on Watersbend. And Calbyr was worried. All of his men knew that they were supposed to contact him just after a job. It was part of the routine: complete the task, retreat to a safe location, and send him a message giving their codes and two extra beeps to indicate that all had gone according to design. If it had just been Kedar, he might not have been so worried. The huge man had proven the value of his vast, deadly strength on several occasions, but he was somewhat slow-witted; in the excitement of the work, he could easily have forgotten to make contact. But not Glyn, whose savvy and reliability made him Calbyr's favorite among the men in his charge. Glyn understood the importance of such things. He would not have forgotten. Which could only mean that something had gone wrong at Watersbend. Calbyr shuddered involuntarily. Superstition was one thing, but when superstition and logic led to the same conclusion, that frightened him.

And then there was the second thing, more alarming even than Glyn and Kedar's silence. Early this afternoon, as he had been resting by a small stream eating a light lunch, he noticed that the luminescent yellow crystal given to him by Sartol had stopped glowing. Suddenly. Without explanation. It had been fine the night before, the last time Calbyr checked it. But now it just looked like a piece of glass, colorless and dim. He didn't know for certain what this meant, but he had an idea. And if he was right, it was bad. Very bad.

First Glyn and Kedar, now Sartol. Who would be next? For the first time since their arrival in Tobyn-Ser, Calbyr found himself wondering if it might be time to head back to the Nal. They had accomplished a good deal here. Quite possibly, they had already set in motion the process that would lead to the Order's downfall. Possibly. But not definitely. Calbyr shook his head and grinned ruefully. He knew himself too well: he had never in his life left a job unfinished, and he was not about to start now, not with what promised to be the biggest payoff of his career waiting for him at the end of it. Whatever might have happened to Glyn, Kedar, and the Child of Amarid, he decided, could be overcome. He had been in tighter spots before, and had always come out all right; better than all right, if truth be told. He quickened his pace slightly, suddenly anxious to reach the village. Perhaps, if he got there soon enough, he would not have to wait until tomorrow night.

It began innocently enough, with an unexpected gust of wind that swept through the forest, rustling the boughs above him. This gust, however, did not crest and then recede as a normal one would. Instead, it continued to mount, growing into a tempest that raced among the trees with a high, keening sound, like a cornered animal might make as it tasted the inevitability of its own death. Harder and harder it blew, until Calbyr thought that it would tear the trees from the soil and scatter Leora's Forest across Tobyn-Ser. But it was not the rush of air that stopped him in the middle of the path. Rather, it was the light. Faint at first, shimmering with the color of the moon and stars, but growing ever brighter as it closed in on him from all directions, tightening like a noose. Then, suddenly, the silvery light flared with blinding radiance and Calbyr felt himself being enveloped in a strange, deathly cold embrace. After the bright flash, it took him a moment to realize that the moonlight had vanished, to be replaced by an utter blackness that obscured everything, even the glow of his crimson stone. Only the feel of his weapon within the rigid grip of his fingers, and the ever-present weight of the synthetic ebony bird on his shoulder told him that he still possessed these things. He tried to breathe but could not. He felt terror begin to rise within him like a wild creature, and he moved instantly to quell it. And then, as the realization came to him that this must be sorcery, he heard a voice. Or rather, he felt a voice within his mind, a voice he knew. *I am undone!* Sartol told him somehow. *Avenge me, Calbyr! Kill Baden for me! Kill them all!* And, even as the cold clung to him, and his lungs began to burn for breath, he placed his thumb over the button on his thrower, and prepared himself for whatever he would meet.

"Guard yourselves! They are coming! And they can fight you!"

It actually took a moment for Niall to grasp the meaning of the Wolf-Master's words. It all seemed to change so quickly: at first, there was a beam of silver incandescence that flowed from Phelan's ceryll to Jaryd's, where it scattered like light through a prism, enveloping the young Hawk-Mage in a glimmering spiral, and arced up gloriously into the dark sky and away to the west. Then, for a time, there was silence, save for the wind that swirled around them. Jaryd and the Wolf-Master stood motionless, like statues carved from moonlight and ice, and, though Niall understood little of what he saw, he sensed the presence of countless others, a procession of souls moving slowly, peacefully through the hollow. Until, abruptly, the tableau was shattered by Phelan's howl of shock and rage and Jaryd's cry of anguish, as Sartol, reaching back across death's threshold, destroyed all that they had strived to accomplish here on the spur.   •

Initially, too shocked to do anything at all, none of them moved. But an instant later, Baden—of course it would be Baden—impelled them into action.

"Take cover!" he shouted, his voice barely carrying over the windstorm. "Go for the birds first; they're deadly! But beware! Even after their familiars are destroyed, the outlanders will retain their power!"

As he spoke, the Owl-Master ducked behind one of the massive firs that stood nearby. The others did the same, Niall hunkering down in a small depression behind the huge trunk of a fallen tree, and Alayna leading Jaryd to a spot in back of a boulder before positioning herself by another fir.

"Wolf-Master!" Baden called. "Can you mute your presence? Our knowledge of the terrain will be more of an advantage if—"

He had time for no more, for in that moment, a brilliant burst of light pierced the darkness, blazing briefly like lightning before giving way once more to the night. At the same time, the wind suddenly subsided, and an eerie calm settled over the hollow. Niall, who had been forced to avert his eyes when the light flared, swung his gaze back to where the company had been standing a few moments ago. At first, he saw nothing. But as his eyes readjusted to the darkness, he realized that the mages were no longer alone. The outlanders had come. There were about a dozen of them—thirteen, he remembered Phelan saying—all of them dressed as he was in green cloaks, and all of them carrying staffs mounted with blood-red stones. And, as his eyes continued to adjust, he could make out the outlines of the immense black birds that perched on their shoulders.

For a split second longer, all remained still. Then a stream of orange mage-fire flew from Baden's staff, forking at the last moment to catch two of the mechanical birds full in the chest. Blasts of purple and grey followed, as Alayna and Ursel also directed their fire at the black creatures, destroying two more of them. At the same time, Trahn hurled a bolt of power at one of the out-landers, hitting him in the head and killing him instantly. Niall leveled his staff at another of the invaders, but, this man, seeing what had happened to his companion, leapt to the side just in time. Still, Niall's blow caught the out-lander on the wrist, bringing a scream of pain from the man, and catapulting his weapon end over end into the woods.

All of this happened in a matter of a second or two, and, aside from Baden, who managed to destroy a third bird with another rush of sizzling orange flame, none of the mages had a chance to get off a second shot. One of the outlanders barked out a command in an alien tongue, and the strangers dove for cover in all directions. After that, Niall lost track of time. The night erupted with torrents of red light that crackled and writhed with deadly power. The mages answered with volleys of their own, or with shimmering curtains of power that shielded them from the crimson blasts. The air around them grew thick with the sound of wing beats, both natural and mechanical, and with the cries of the company's hawks and owls. Dense, swirling smoke filled the hollow, fed by the trees and brush set ablaze by the fighting, and seeming to glow with the myriad colors of the battle—orange and brown, grey and purple, blue and maroon, and, of course, the enemy's red. Niall found it increasingly difficult to keep track of who was who.

Only minutes into the battle, however, he did recognize that the company could not hold out indefinitely. The outlanders were well trained and well led. Though he could not interpret the shouted commands and responses that flew among the invaders, he quickly grasped their meaning. While initially the out-landers had taken cover in two tight clusters directly in front of where Niall crouched, they soon began to spread themselves out, creeping noiselessly through the undergrowth, and guarding one another with fierce salvos of red flame. Within moments, they had positioned themselves in a broad semicircle that threatened to outflank the mages. Worse, he could already sense that Nollstra was tiring; no doubt all the birds were fighting for their lives against the relentless creatures carried by the invaders. The mechanical birds were simply too numerous, too large, and too unnaturally swift. And, of course, as Nollstra grew weary, expending more and more energy on her own desperate struggle for survival, Niall's power waned; the laws governing the Mage-Craft were not about to bend to accommodate the company in their fight against this new enemy. Before long, all the mages would grow too weak to block the outlanders' fire. Or, worse still, they would be rendered unbound and, thus, completely defenseless. In either case, the mages had to do something. Soon.

Niall heard Ursel cry out and, spinning in her direction, saw one of the dark birds as little more than a misty shadow swooping up through the smoke, away from the Hawk-Mage. Blood flowed freely from two parallel gashes over Ursel's eye, but she seemed fine otherwise. Wasting no time, Niall twisted his body and threw a shaft of maroon flame at the retreating creature, hitting one of its wings. The bird veered abruptly into a tree and dropped to the ground in a fiery heap. But as it did, Niall felt a savage pain in his shoulder and, wrenching himself in the other direction, watched another of the creatures soar off, his own blood staining its knifelike talons. Beams of blue and orange light flew toward the creature but missed, passing harmlessly into the night. Niall felt blood soaking into his cloak from the throbbing wound, but he did not dare expend Nollstra's strength trying to heal himself.

A burst of red power slammed into the fallen trunk in front of him, sending a fountain of glowing embers and charred wood chips into the air. Instinctively, Niall ducked, the sharp movement tearing a gasp of pain from him. And, as he lay among the fir needles and mosses, his eyes closed as the wave of pain slowly receded, Niall did the math in his head. Again. And, again, the numbers seemed hopelessly uneven. Six of the mechanical birds destroyed now; one of the outlanders killed and another injured. Leaving seven of the giant creatures and eleven armed men against a company of six mages and their familiars.

And one spirit. For in that instant, Niall heard Phelan's voice rumble through the hollow, above the crackling of the flames and the cries of the mages' birds.

"Hold, enemies of Amarid!" the Wolf-Master cried out, as silver light suddenly brightened the forest. "I am Phelan, the Wolf-Master! And I have come to avenge the land!"

The crimson bursts from the outlanders' weapons abruptly ceased, although the birds continued their battle overhead. Cautiously, Niall peered out over the massive log and through the smoke to see Phelan and Kalba stepping forward into the hollow. It had to be a ruse. Just a short while before, Phelan had admitted to the company that he was powerless to help them. "I cannot interact with your world in any meaningful way," he had said. In which case—

The outlanders turned to face the spirit, leveling their weapons at him.

"Now!" Phelan bellowed.

And, as red flame leapt from the invaders' weapons toward the Wolf-Master and the great animal that stood beside him, twisting and hissing like serpents, and passing through them both as if they weren't there, all six mages stepped out into the open and hurled glowing spears of mage-fire at the men who had come to conquer Tobyn-Ser. Seven of them perished before the others realized that they had been deceived. Three of them then fled into the woods, followed by two of the mechanical birds. Eight of them now dead, three running away, another too injured to move or fight. Leaving one.

Niall knew before he looked; he sensed it, and he surprised himself with how calm he felt. Turning his gaze just slightly to the left, he had time to register the small glowing point of red that seemed to be approaching him. He had time to realize that this, in reality, was not a point at all, but rather a stream of flame aimed directly at his head. He even had time to make out the thin white scar that ran across the cheekbone and down into the light beard of the sandy-haired man who had launched this attack. But he understood immediately that he did not have enough time to shield himself from the blow.

Somewhere behind him Jaryd cried out, but already Niall was trying the one thing that remained. He could not avoid the flame, nor could he block it. But if he turned toward it, into it, he might be able to take it on the shoulder instead of the head. It wasn't much of a chance—even if the blast hit him in the shoulder, it would probably do enough damage to kill him—but it was something. It was all he had left.

Even as he threw his body forward and to the side, though, he knew that this would not be enough. Twenty years ago it would have worked. Maybe even ten years ago. But he was an old man now. Wiser than he had been, it was true, and newly reawakened to his own power and passion for living. But old. Too old. A decade of grief and apathy had taken its toll. He closed his eyes rather than watch. And then, his mind exploding with white light and a sound like thunder and the pounding surf, Niall felt the fire crash into his neck and jaw, felt it spin him around like a child's top and hammer him into the ground. For a moment, there was excruciating pain, and then, there was no feeling at all, which was more pleasant, but more frightening as well. He opened his eyes and saw that Jaryd was there above him, and Alayna, both of them with tears rolling down their cheeks. After a few seconds, Baden knelt down also, grim-faced and pale.

"Get them!" Niall shouted at the mages. At least that's what he attempted to say. But his jaw was gone and they hadn't understood. Baden was saying something. Niall could see his mouth moving, but he heard only a rush of impenetrable noise, as if there were boulders moving inside his head. He tried to tell them again to go after the outlanders, but it was no use. Besides, by this time they were gone, and only Vardis was there, kneeling beside him, smiling that wondrous, inscrutable smile. He didn't know how she had gotten there, but really, it didn't matter. He had been waiting for her so very long. Somehow he could hear her telling him to rest now. To close his eyes and rest. And he said her name, just once, but as clear as a ceryll. And then he closed his eyes, embracing the blackness as he would his one love.

Calbyr had not wanted it to come to this. Obviously, he would have preferred to continue with the attacks and follow through on their original plan. But that was not to be. And, if they had to face the mages eventually, this seemed as good a situation as he could have envisioned. From what he could tell, through the smoke and the confusion, there were only five or six of them against his entire crew. Or what was left of it. Yarit, of course, was dead, and Calbyr was certain now that Glyn and Kedar had either been captured or killed as well. The mages' initial volley had killed Keegan, and had taken out several birds. Auley had been hurt, badly, and he did not appear to be capable of

fighting. Overall, though, they still had the mages and their birds outnumbered. Moreover, given the terrain, he had no doubt that his men could prevail
in a firefight; this was what they had been trained to do, this was what they
were best at. Already they had established a crossfire, pinning down the mages,
who obviously had little experience with this sort of combat. The synthetic
birds were doing their job as well, engaging the mages' hawks and owls in
what had become, for the live birds, a desperate battle for survival. Sartol had
instructed him on a number of occasions to go for the birds first if he and his
crew ever did battle with members of the Order.

"Use those creatures of yours to attack the familiars," the Owl-Master had
said, "then go after the mages. As the birds weaken, so does the magic; kill
the bird, and the mage is yours." Calbyr had listened carefully, expecting that,
at some point, he would use this tactic on Sartol. It was funny how things
worked out.

For a while at least, Sartol's counsel proved sound, and the fight appeared
to be going their way. But Calbyr and his men were a long, long way from
Lon-Ser, and the Child of Amarid had never offered any suggestions for fighting ghosts. In truth, Calbyr and his men would never have heeded such advice
anyway. There was no more room in the violent, uncompromising culture of
the Nal for belief in ghosts than there was for superstition. Thus, he could
hardly fault his men for falling for the Wolf-Master's ploy. For just a moment,
he even allowed himself to be taken in. It was only when he saw the mages
step out from their hiding places, their staffs aimed at his men, that he realized
what had happened. He almost shouted a warning then. Perhaps he should
have. They were his men, after all. He had brought them here; he would be
responsible for their deaths. But, by that time, it was too late. And he probably
would have died for the effort.

Instead, like the three men who managed to avoid the mage-fire, he decided
to flee. But not before he took care of two items. First, he had time enough
to kill one of the mages: I owe Sartol that much, he thought, surprising himself
with the sentiment. And though he didn't know who any of them were, he
assumed, from the voice he had heard just before his arrival at this place, that
the one called Baden was here. Baden was an Owl-Master, he remembered,
and an older man. There were only two here who matched that description,
and so he guessed. And he fired, never pausing to find out if he had guessed
correctly. After that, he just barely had time enough to take care of the second
thing.

Turning his gaze from the fallen mage to Auley, he found the injured break-
law already watching him, his dark eyes wide but composed. Auley was a good
man: clever, discreet, careful without being squeamish. But he was helpless
now—his wrist looked terrible: blackened and bloody, a jagged piece of white
bone where his hand should have been. And while Calbyr could do nothing
about any others the mages might later capture, he could keep this man from
having to give anything away. Probably, Auley would have done what had to
be done. But strange things happened to men when they were in captivity:
their behavior changed, grew unpredictable. And Calbyr couldn't afford to take
any chances. He and Auley stared at each other for a moment, and then the
injured break-law nodded, once. A good man, Calbyr thought again, as he

360   DAVID B. COE

pressed the button on his thrower and watched the red flame spurt into Auley's chest.

Then Calbyr spun away and bounded out of the hollow, whistling sharply for his bird, and just barely avoiding a burst of grey flame from one of the mages. Once again relying on the light provided by the moon, and the stone that rested atop his weapon, he followed a narrow, overgrown path into the heart of the forest, feeling an unexpected rush of relief as he caught a glimpse of his bird gliding alongside him. He hoped that the confusion created by the death of the Owl-Master would give him a chance to escape. He and his men had made no provisions for regrouping after an incident of this type. Frankly, he had never entertained the notion that they might all be brought together in this way; he had split up the crew in order to avoid just this type of debacle. He expected, however, that if the other three managed to avoid capture, they would return to the LonTobyn Isthmus, the length of which they had traveled on foot when they first came to Tobyn-Ser nearly a year ago. That was where he planned to go. And then, from there, back to Lon-Ser and the Nal.

Provided that Cedrych would furnish him with a new set of birds, he could have another crew trained and ready within two years, maybe even sooner. Enough time for the mages to convince themselves that the threat had passed, but not so much that the memory of these attacks would fade from the people's minds. If he acted quickly enough, he would lose little of the momentum he had built up throughout the summer. Provided that Cedrych would help.

Calbyr flinched slightly at the thought. There hadn't been much that he could do to avoid this. He still wasn't certain how the mages had gotten him here in the first place—wherever "here" was—but he felt fairly sure that the ghost had been at least partially responsible. Surely Cedrych could not blame him for this. How was he supposed to fight a ghost? No one in Lon-Ser even believed that they existed. At least no one in the Nal. Still, he knew Cedrych would not be happy about this. Just as Calbyr answered to him, Cedrych would be held accountable by the Sovereign and the other Overlords. And they had little tolerance for failure. Cedrych might understand, or he might just kill Calbyr and find a new Nal-Lord to do the job. Calbyr swallowed. This, it seemed, was simply a chance he would have to take. He certainly had no future in this land, and anyone in Lon-Ser who needed a person of his . . . talents would recognize him as Cedrych's man: he had achieved a certain notoriety for his past accomplishments.

A sound from behind made him stop. Footsteps. One pair. Calbyr grinned in the darkness. Five mages and a ghost were one thing, but single combat was quite another. "Kill the bird, and the mage is yours," Sartol had said. Indeed. Glancing back, Calbyr already could see the light of the approaching mage. Quietly, he slipped into a cluster of trees and prepared his ambush.

The image had seared itself into Jaryd's brain like a brand, despite the tears that had blurred his vision. It would be with him for years, perhaps for the rest of his life. Half of Niall's neck and most of his jaw had simply been blown away. There was blood all over his cloak, and even those portions of his face and head that remained intact had been blackened and blistered by the heat of the outlander's fire. And still the Owl-Master was alive when Jaryd first reached him. He even tried to speak. Jaryd wanted desperately to try to heal the wounds, but he didn't know where to begin. It would have been in vain, though—Baden told him as much—and they needed to preserve their power for the invaders who remained.

Clenching his teeth against nausea, he forced himself to watch as Niall closed his eyes for the last time. Only then did he turn away, just in time to see the man who had killed the Owl-Master duck under Ursel's mage-fire and escape into the forest. Thrusting himself to his feet, Jaryd raced after the outlander. Ursel had started in pursuit as well, but Jaryd was closer to where the scarred man had entered the woods.

"I've got this one!" he called over his shoulder to the Hawk-Mage.

And then he heard Trahn's voice. "Ursel! This way, after the others!"

A moment later, Jaryd plunged into the forest, noting with gratitude that Ishalla was with him, gliding above his shoulder. Briefly, he worried about Alayna and Baden, who were doing battle with the mechanical birds that still circled over the hollow. But then he caught a momentary glimpse of the out-lander's red stone, and all other thoughts vanished from his mind.

Baden watched as Jaryd disappeared into one portion of the forest, and Trahn and Ursel into another, and then he turned his attention to the birds—four of them mechanical, three of them real—that darted and swooped among the trees and branches overhead. He could feel Anla's fatigue as if it were his own, and in a sense, it was. His power was fading; no doubt, given the increasingly labored flight of Alayna's grey hawk, so too was hers. Amazingly, Niall's bird, though released from her binding by the Owl-Master's death, continued to fight with as much fervor as the other two, perhaps more. But at this stage, against these creatures, that meant only that her cries were more strident and her escapes less narrow. They hadn't much time left.

"I can't get an angle on any of them," Alayna said a little desperately, her dark eyes fixed on the birds and her cheeks still damp with the tears she had shed for Niall. "They're all moving so fast, I'm afraid I'll hit Fylimar or one of the owls."

"I know," Baden told her, trying to keep the tension from his voice. "Take your time; impatience will only make us careless. And watch yourself," he added a few seconds later, "they may come after us, as well."

Alayna nodded, and for several moments they stood looking upward, grip-ping their staffs tightly. Then, without warning, a beam of purple light shot from Alayna's ceryll, just barely missing one of the black creatures.

"Fist of the God!" she spat.

Baden readied himself for an assault from one or more of the outlanders' birds, but it never came.

"That's peculiar," he remarked, his eyes still trained on the sky. "In Wa-tersbend, once they were alerted to my presence, they attacked at the first opportunity."

"Maybe they can't do that now," she commented.

Baden glanced at her. "What do you mean?"

"What if they need human guidance? The other birds left when the four outlanders ran away. So these must belong to the ones we killed."

"I still don't follow."

Alayna looked at him. "They're probably not bound to people the way our hawks are," she explained, "but, if they're not alive, they must receive commands in some way." She pointed a thin finger at Niall's bird. "She's still fighting because she chooses to—she doesn't need Niall to tell her. But what if the mechanical hawks do? What if the last command they were given was to fight our birds? Even if we try to kill them, they won't come after us."

"But that one just avoided your fire."

She nodded. "True, but maybe they've been given some kind of basic instinct for survival. Other than that, though, their last command might be all they're capable of doing at this point. In which case, they won't give up until they're all dead. We can't scare off one by destroying another."

Baden said nothing, for in that instant one of the huge, fell creatures wheeled directly over where they stood. The Owl-Master thrust his staff upward, summoning just enough power from Anla for a single pulse of orange fire, which crashed violently into the black bird, sending it careening off a branch and onto the ground. It twitched once, and then lay completely still.

"Well done!" Alayna called, even as she unleashed another barrage of her own, this time striking one of the birds near the edge of its wing. It veered sharply down and to the side, and managed to land safely on a nearby boulder. But Alayna wasted no time, hurling a second bolt that shattered the beast into hundreds of pieces.

Baden started to return the compliment, but, even as he did, he felt pain stab through his mind like a dagger. And looking up again, he saw with horror that Anla had been seized by one of the creatures that remained. Her feet kicking spasmodically, her wings, one of them broken, beating awkwardly, desperately against the chest of the enormous black hawk, Baden's bird struggled to break free. But the alien creature was too powerful. It hovered above them, clenching Anla in its talons, its golden eyes glimmering like gems, and its beak opened in what looked like a triumphant grin. Baden heard Alayna gasp, felt himself growing dizzy with the agony conveyed to him by his familiar. And, as he watched the black bird tighten its razor grip on Anla's neck and chest, digging its claws through the feathers and into her flesh, he understood what he had to do. Using what was left of the power he channeled from her, hoping the owl would know that he acted out of love and pride and grief, he sent one last blazing torrent of orange light at the two birds, consuming them both in a maelstrom of flame that annihilated the mechanical bird, but also killed Anla.

Baden had been unbound before, twice. But never so abruptly, and certainly never as a result of his own actions. The other birds had grown old and weak; his link to their minds and his access to their power had slackened gradually, over a period of several months. It had not been like this. He felt Anla's sudden absence from his mind as a terrible void, a vortex of loneliness that overwhelmed him. He knew without confirming it that his power was gone, but that was the least of it. He was alone again, unbound. And he had been forced to do this to himself. Forced by Sartol, who had been driven to do a similar thing just hours before. It was too much: the irony, the grief, the shock. All of it was too much. His vision was a blur and there was a rushing sound in his ears, like wind or coursing water.

He barely registered the flash of purple light that flew from Alayna's ceryll, and understood only when the Hawk-Mage came and put her arms around him that it had signified the destruction of the last alien bird.

"I'm sorry, Baden," she murmured. "I wish there was something I could have done to save her."

"There wasn't anything," he managed, "for either of us."

He stepped away from her and shook his head, feeling tears fly from the corners of his eyes. This was not the time. There were still outlanders on the spur. Trahn and Ursel were chasing them, and Jaryd. Jaryd. This was not the time. Later, he thought, I'll mourn later. He looked at Alayna, willing his eyes to focus and forcing his sorrow to the back of his mind. Already, he saw, she was gazing anxiously in the direction his nephew had gone in pursuit of the light-haired invader.

"We should go after them," she said, her eyes never leaving the forest.

"I know," he agreed, his voice thick, "but you have to let me go after Jaryd."

She whirled to face him, an argument springing to her lips.

"Hear me!" he commanded, silencing her. "He's gone after one man; Trahn and Ursel have gone after three. They need help more than he does. And," he added, opening his arms in a helpless gesture, "I can't help them anymore." He swallowed. "They need you, Alayna, and I'll do everything I can for Jaryd."

She hesitated for what seemed a long time. Then, finally, she nodded once and turned to leave the hollow.

Baden watched her go, doubts crowding his mind. Certainly he had been right in saying that Trahn and Ursel needed her more than Jaryd did. That was obvious. But, as he hurried into the woods in pursuit of his nephew and the outlander, he was far less sure that he could do anything at all to help the young Hawk-Mage.

Beginning almost as soon as he dashed out of the hollow, Jaryd caught occasional glimpses of the outlander's glowing red stone through gaps in the trees. It would come into view abruptly, swinging back and forth as the man sprinted across open patches in the wood, and then vanishing suddenly as he passed through a thicket or dense stand of trees. With Ishalla flying beside him, Jaryd pursued the blood-colored light as swiftly as the terrain would allow, leaping over the stones and downed branches that cluttered the forest floor. And though he did not feel that he was gaining any ground on Niall's killer, he knew that he wasn't losing any either. At least that's how it had seemed the last time he saw the crimson light. But that, he realized abruptly, had been some distance back, as they crested a small hill and began to descend into another hollow. Since then, the Hawk-Mage had seen no sign of the invader or his glowing weapon. The recognition of this slowed him.

He was still moving forward, though not at a full run, when he saw the red stone uncovered just a few yards ahead. Only a sharp, wickedly contorting motion downward and to the side enabled him to avoid the hot beam of scarlet fire that surged just past his head and slammed viciously into a small tree, splintering its trunk. At the same time, he heard Ishalla cry out, and, glancing upward, saw his hawk dart under the outstretched claws of the outlander's lethal, golden-eyed creature. He flung a bolt of mage-fire at the black bird as it swung around in pursuit of his familiar. But he missed, and before he could try again, he was forced to parry a second blast with a shield of sapphire magic that shuddered with the might of the invader's blow. His hawk continued to scream as her battle with the mechanical bird carried her above the trees, but Jaryd could do little to help her. The outlander was sending volley after volley of crimson fire in Jaryd's direction, forcing the Hawk-Mage to expend all his energy blocking them. And all of Ishalla's energy as well. Every shield Jaryd raised seemed to take more effort than the last. Each one seemed to sag more under the force of the outlander's blasts. And Ishalla's cries sounded more desperate with each passing moment.

And so, when the next barrage came, as Jaryd knew it would, rather than merely blocking it, Jaryd exerted his power against it. At first nothing happened, but then the glimmering blue wall he had created began to move, slowly at first, but gaining momentum gradually as it forced the blood-red beam back toward its source. The meeting point of the two flames gleamed brightly, like a purple star illuminating the forest, and allowing Jaryd to make out the outlander's features: the straight, aristocratic nose; the grim, taut mouth; the thin, pale scar that carved across the left side of his face; and the dark eyes, so filled with intellect and malice that Jaryd's blood froze just looking at them. And, as the wall of light and fire continued to advance toward Niall's killer, Jaryd saw another emotion creep across the bearded face and into the cruel eyes, and he heard the man shout out something in a language he did not understand, but in a tone that conveyed frustration and terror.

Jaryd could feel perspiration dampening his cloak, and he knew that he was taxing Ishalla to the limits of her endurance, but his mage-fire had almost reached the invader, and the man's stone had begun to glow hotly, as if it too had reached some sort of critical point. Just a minute more and—

The sudden, raking pain that spread across his back and shoulders caught Jaryd completely off guard, tearing a cry of anguish from his throat and forcing him to break off his assault on the invader. At the same time, the heavy buffeting of rough wings on his head and neck told him what had happened. Twisting his body away from the slashing of the mechanical bird's talons, the young Hawk-Mage rolled awkwardly onto his back, gasping in agony once more, and looking up to see the dark shadow descending on him again, its golden eyes and razor-sharp claws shining with the light of Jaryd's ceryll. The Hawk-Mage threw an arm in front of his face to guard himself; he tried to ward off the attack with his staff, but he had no time to use his mage-fire. He had no way of stopping the creature. He heard the outlander laugh.

And then, incredibly, at the last moment, he saw an arc of orange light swing into view with blurring speed, smashing powerfully into the head of the descending bird, and sending it sprawling heavily to the ground. He heard the outlander roar in fury, saw the man level his weapon at Baden, whose staff had smashed into the alien hawk.

But this time, Jaryd was ready. Even as the stranger loosed his red flame, forcing the Owl-Master to dive out of the way, Jaryd unleashed a killing sapphire blast of his own that engulfed the outlander in a torrent of fire and ripped one last cry from the man's seared lungs. For a moment, the burning figure stood writhing amid the flames, and then he toppled to the ground and lay still, his back arched and his fingers splayed rigidly at his sides.

Jaryd closed his eyes and took a long, steadying breath. Then he glanced up at his uncle. "Thank you," he said hoarsely. "You saved my life."

Baden offered him a hand and gently helped the Hawk-Mage to his feet. "I believe I owed you that," he said. "From this morning, in the Great Hall," he added in response to Jaryd's puzzled expression.

The young man nodded and gave a small, mirthless laugh. "That was today?" he asked wearily.

Ignoring the question, Baden looked at him with concern. "How's your back?"

"It hurts," Jaryd replied honestly.

Baden turned him around to examine the wounds. "You're bleeding pretty heavily. We should find the others and get that healed right away." He hesitated. "I'd do it myself, if I could."

Jaryd turned to face him again. "What do you—" He stopped, finally noticing what he should have seen right away. "Anla. Oh, Baden, I'm sorry. I'm so sorry."

The Owl-Master tried a small smile. Failed. "I've been unbound before," he commented soberly. "It just takes a little time."

Jaryd tried to think of something to say, but in the end, saying nothing seemed most appropriate. For a minute more, the two mages stared wordlessly at the still-burning figure that lay prone before them. Then Baden retrieved the outlander's weapon and the remains of the alien bird, and the two mages slowly made their way back, guided by the rhythmic pounding of the surf.

As he followed Baden into the hollow, walking gingerly and feeling a bit lightheaded from fatigue, Jaryd saw that the others were waiting for them. The fires left over from the battle had been extinguished. Niall's body still lay where the Owl-Master had fallen. Much to Jaryd's relief, Alayna appeared unharmed. So, too, did Trahn, and the two of them had already mended the gashes on Ursel's brow. Alayna ran to him when she saw that he had returned, but Baden stopped her.

"I'd suggest that you treat his old injuries before tackling him and giving him new ones," the Owl-Master said dryly. "He's young, but he's not that young."

Trahn hurried over when he heard this. Ursel, Jaryd realized, was standing guard over two of the outlanders.

"You're hurt?" Trahn asked sharply.

Jaryd nodded, indicating his back with a gesture. "One of the black birds got me. It would have killed me if Baden hadn't arrived when he did." This last he had intended for the Owl-Master, but Baden's attention was focused on the prisoners.

"Have they said anything?" Baden demanded of Trahn as the dark mage and Alayna tended to Jaryd's wounds.

Trahn shook his head. "Nothing yet, no." He stole a glance at them over his shoulder, a grin creeping across his features. "Both of them were hurt when we destroyed their weapons. You should have seen the looks in their eyes when we healed them."

"What happened to the third?"

Trahn's grin vanished. "I couldn't get a clear enough angle to disable him." He shrugged. "I had to kill him."

"And their birds?"

"Destroyed and retrieved."

Baden smiled, just for a moment, and he nodded. "Well done." Then he walked over to where Ursel stood with the outlanders.

For several minutes, Alayna and Trahn worked in silence, laying their hands deftly on Jaryd's back and shoulder until the pain had subsided to a dull throb that Jaryd knew would linger for several days. He flexed his shoulder, noting that most of its mobility had returned.

"You lost a good deal of blood," Trahn told him, placing a hand on his good shoulder. "Take it easy for a day or two." The Hawk-Mage smiled broadly. "I'm glad you're all right, Jaryd."

Jaryd returned the grin. "Thank you, Trahn. For everything."

Trahn gave his shoulder a squeeze and then joined Baden and Ursel, leaving Jaryd and Alayna to themselves.

"I'm glad you're safe, too," Alayna said softly, kissing his cheek. "I was worried."

Jaryd smiled. "Good." He tried to kiss her, but she bit his lip instead.

"I think you're supposed to say that you were worried, too!" she growled with mock anger.

He tried to kiss her again, and this time she let him. "I was," he told her, his tone suddenly earnest. "More than you could ever know." He put his arms around her and held her tight for several moments, saying nothing, and only letting her go when he saw that Phelan and Kalba had returned to the hollow.

For a long time, the Wolf-Master did not speak. He and the great wolf walked among the living, pausing to regard the two outlanders, one of whom tried unsuccessfully to hold the spirit's icy stare. Phelan smiled coldly when the man looked away, and then continued through the hollow, stopping finally when he reached Niall's body, and the pale owl that sat silently just above where the Owl-Master lay. "I am sorry for your friend," the spirit offered in his deep voice. He turned to Baden. "And for the death of your familiar, Owl-Master. I am familiar with that pain." Jaryd saw a difficult emotion working across the spirit's features. A few seconds later, however, he spoke again. "The one you call Sartol was more powerful than we had anticipated: your losses were a result of this miscalculation."

Phelan seemed to offer the explanation as an apology, and Baden took it as such. "You weren't the first to underestimate him, Wolf-Master," the mage answered, "and our error was far costlier than yours."

Phelan nodded. "That may be so. But you have redeemed yourselves tonight, I think." He glanced at the prisoners again. "The others are dead?"

"They are."

The spirit nodded his shaggy head. "It is well. But," he went on in a hard tone, his bright, wintry eyes encompassing all of them, "be wary, lest your vigilance slacken again! This threat may have passed, but others await you. You were right when you said that those who sent these men will send others. I am certain of it!"

Baden signaled his agreement with a curt nod. "We won't be caught off guard a second time, Wolf-Master. Not while the five of us serve Tobyn-Ser."

Once more, the Wolf-Master smiled. "I am glad to hear it," he said. "Would you return to Amarid?"

Baden cocked his head to one side. "Is that possible, given Sartol's presence in your circle?"

"He is a difficult matter," Phelan admitted. "He will keep us from acting on your behalf for a long time into the future. But we are aware of him now. Strong as he is, he is still new to the circle of the Unsettled. Theron believes that we can control him for a while. At least for tonight, if you still wish us to transport you back to the Great Hall."

Baden nodded. "We do. And our prisoners. But first we wish to build a pyre for Niall."

"Very well," the spirit agreed. "But make haste. Daylight approaches."

With Jaryd moving to watch over the prisoners, the other mages started constructing a funeral pyre of driftwood and fallen tree limbs. The outlanders remained silent, and Jaryd said nothing to them, although he watched them with unconcealed curiosity. They were both of medium build, one with black hair and a close-cropped beard, and the other clean-shaven and blond. The bearded man sat motionless, seemingly absorbed in his own thoughts, his eyes focused inward. But the other one, whom Jaryd guessed was but a few years beyond his own age, watched the mages with a mix of fear and interest. Occasionally, Jaryd found the man staring at him, or at grey Ishalla on his shoulder. But always the outlander would quickly avert his eyes.

When finally the pyre was ready, Baden and Trahn placed Niall's body on top of it, and all five mages moved to stand before it. "With wood and fire, gifts from Tobyn and Leora," Baden proclaimed to the night, "we release the spirit of Niall, Son of Amarid. Open your arms to him, Arick and Duclea, and grant him rest."

The outlanders had been led over as well, so that they could be watched, and now the bearded one laughed. "Yes, open your arms," he repeated in a strangely accented voice. "Open them wide, so that the Children of Lon can send—" A sudden blow to the stomach from Trahn's staff doubled the man over, silencing him.

"The next time you speak, it will be to answer our questions!" the Hawk-Mage hissed. "Until then, you will be still!"

In response, the man spat at the ground in front of Trahn's feet. He was rewarded with a blow to the small of the back that sent him to his knees.

An instant later, the mages lit the pyre with their mage-fire, and for several minutes they watched the flames rise to consume Niall's body. Then Baden turned to face Phelan, who was standing behind them.

"We're ready." He gestured toward the prisoners and the pile of weapons and destroyed birds that sat nearby. "You can send these things as well?"

Phelan nodded. "We can."

Baden bowed at the waist, as did the other mages. "Thank you, Wolf-Master. The people of Tobyn-Ser owe a debt to you, and to all of the Unsettled."

Phelan inclined his head in acknowledgment. "We still serve the land," he replied. "Tell this to the people."

"We will."

Phelan closed his eyes and began to ready himself for the transport. Then he stopped. "Tell me," he said, looking at Baden once more, "who was your conduit for this journey?"

"Owl-Master Sonel," Baden replied. "She told us of her encounter with you. She was the only one of us who knew the terrain."

Phelan nodded. "I remember her. She was kind and strong, even as a young woman." He paused. "Owl-Master, you say?"

"Yes."

"I am glad for her. Tell her that I still recall our conversation," the Wolf-Master requested, "and that she is welcome to return."

"I'll do that."

Once again, the silver spirit closed his eyes, and so, too, did the luminescent wolf beside him. Jaryd took Alayna's hand in his, and, a moment later, he felt the familiar rush of cold air envelop him as the Unsettled sent them back to the Great Hall.

23

Jaryd had expected that things would calm down a bit once those responsible for the land's recent troubles had been captured. Certainly, he thought, the few days following the company's return from Phelan Spur would be marked by mourning for Niall, Jessamyn, and Peredur, but also by quiet celebration for the passing of this most immediate threat to Tobyn-Ser's safety. And he had been confident that when news spread of the Order's innocence in the attacks of the past year, and of its role in apprehending those who had been culpable, the people of Amarid and Tobyn-Ser would be overjoyed. Nothing could have been farther from the reality of what occurred.

News of what had happened at Phelan Spur seemed to ride the wind like smoke from a fire, reaching every corner of the great city and filling people's heads with panic-inspiring visions of outlanders inundating both town and countryside by the thousands. Within hours of the company's return from its battle with the invaders, word of the two prisoners being held in small cells beneath the main floor of the Great Hall had lured a tremendous crowd to the streets surrounding the structure. Most were merely curious. But a sizable minority, driven, no doubt, by fear as well as anger, demanded that the two outlanders be given over to them so that justice might be done quickly and correctly. It was, Radomil later told Jaryd, a scene reminiscent of the one that greeted Baden, Trahn, and Orris when they surrendered themselves to the Order to face Sartol's accusations. Except that, in the mages' case, other members of the crowd had been reluctant to condone such violence. These onlookers, in contrast, had no such misgivings; they were more than happy to allow the outlanders to be slaughtered in the street. It took little time for the instigators to stir the throng into a vengeful frenzy, and even the pleas and threats of mages and constables could not disperse them or curb their zeal. Throughout the day and into the night, the assembly continued to grow, and while those inciting the multitude did not succeed in pushing the people to violent acts, they did keep the mood in the streets at a fever pitch.

So much so that, late that afternoon, while the members of the company still were sleeping off the effects of their long and harrowing night on the spur, Toinan, Sonel, and a majority of the other mages decided to double the number of guards assigned to the prisoners, leading others to question whether the attendants were there to prevent the outlanders' escape, or to keep them from harm. As it turned out, however, they failed at both.

One of the strangers—the bearded one whom Trahn had struck in front of Niall's pyre, Jaryd later learned—succeeded in escaping from his room that first evening. Somehow, he managed to master the lock on his door, beat into unconsciousness two of the massive attendants originally hired by Sartol, despite being barely half the men's size, and find his way to a rear door of the hall. There, however, on the verge of getting away, he stopped. Perhaps he was daunted by the sight of the angry mob outside, or maybe he was driven by his conscience to go back for his comrade. Whatever the reason, he returned to the Gathering Chamber, only to find himself confronted by five members of the Order, their cerylls ready. He quickly surrendered, and the mages escorted him back to his cell, but, after that, the attendants standing guard were replaced by mages, and their number was doubled once again. Even these steps, though, proved ineffective. Less than an hour after he was placed back in his chamber, the outlander was dead, apparently having taken some sort of poison that he had carried with him. The mages had never even learned his name.

When news of the stranger's death reached the Owl-Masters, they immediately ordered that the other outlander, the younger, fair-haired man whom Jaryd remembered looking so frightened on the spur, be stripped of his clothing, given fresh things to wear, and placed under constant watch, lest he attempt to follow in his friend's footsteps. A search of this second man's cloak revealed a small tablet that had been sewn into the lining of the garment. A local apothecary determined that it was poison, although not of a type she had ever encountered before.

All of this Jaryd, Alayna, and the rest of the company learned the following morning, a full day after their return from Phelan Spur. The battle, and the emotions of Niall's death, had left the five of them exhausted, and, after presenting the prisoners and offering a brief description of what transpired on the spur, they had gone off to get some sleep. Jaryd and Alayna took a room together at an inn near the Great Hall, and, their need of each other outweighing their fatigue, they made love in the bright morning light that streamed through the window. Tenderly, longingly, they moved together on the small bed, desperate to feel alive again after a night of killing and grief. Afterward, they drifted into a deeper sleep than either had known for several weeks, their bodies intertwined in the tangle of sheets. All through the day they slept, rising near dusk to eat a small meal and, finally, to mount Jaryd's ceryll on the staff given to them by Theron. Then they returned to the small room and slept through the rest of the night.

They were awakened early the next morning by the tolling of the Great Hall's bells. When they reached the structure a short while later, they found nearly three quarters of the Order already assembled around the table and conferring on the near escape and subsequent suicide of the outlander. Gathering what details he could from the discussion, Jaryd soon pieced together what had occurred.

"We should interrogate the prisoner who remains as soon as possible," Baden observed. The Owl-Master appeared wan and fatigued, as if he had slept poorly the previous night and day. Jaryd found himself glancing repeatedly at his uncle's shoulder or at the empty, curved perch on the Owl-Master's chair, as if he couldn't get used to the idea that Anla was dead. He couldn't even imagine what Baden must have been feeling and he repeatedly reached for Ishalla with his mind, as if to reassure himself that she was still there. "He may no longer have the poison," the lean mage went on, still referring to the second outlander, "but he might find some other way to harm himself."

"Or he might try to escape," Trahn added. "I agree with Baden. We should begin immediately."

For once, the mages arrayed around the table seemed to be in accord, as they signaled their agreement with nods. At least most of them did. "He is a dangerous man," Odinan wheezed from the far end of the council table, looking even more burdened and weary than he had a few days before, "just as his companion was. I believe we should wait until the rest of the Order arrives before deciding on any course of action."

Even this, Jaryd thought, shaking his head in disbelief. He saw Orris's jaw clench, but, surprisingly, the Hawk-Mage said nothing, leaving it instead to Baden to counter the old man's argument.

"We can't afford to wait, Odinan," Baden reasoned. "If this man escapes, or kills himself, we'll be right back where we were before we went to Phelan Spur. We need information that only he can provide."

"Perhaps, but do we need it right now?"

"I think we do."

"Such rashness cost Niall his life!" the aged mage said hotly, the color in his hollowed cheeks rising.

"If you wish to look at it in that light, fine!" Baden shot back. "It also cost me my familiar! Does that mean that we should do nothing!" The Owl-Master paused, trying to regain his composure. "If we delay, Odinan," he continued a moment later, his tone softer, "and this man escapes or dies, Niall's death, and my Anla's death, will have no meaning. You don't want that, do you?"

"Of course not!" Odinan snapped. He glanced around the chamber, the look in his eyes hostile and defensive. "You have the votes to overrule me, Baden. I'd suggest you use them. I'm not going to give in again. I did when you wanted to go to the grove, and Jessamyn and Peredur died. I did a second time when you wanted to speak with Phelan; now Niall is dead. There will be no third time. I'll not be party to another tragedy." He crossed his arms and glared at the other mages a second time. "You have heard what I have to say; now act! But don't bother me anymore with your coaxing and logic. I'm not interested."

Baden continued to gaze at the older man for some time, sadness in his pale eyes. When finally he spoke again, his tone was flat. "I propose that we begin interrogation of the remaining prisoner as soon as possible," he said formally.

Sonel, who had apparently been chosen to serve as interim sage, took a deep breath, glancing sidelong at Odinan. Then, her back straightening, she scanned the chamber, her green eyes coming to rest at last on Baden. "The proposal is heard," she replied in a strong voice. "Let us vote."

In the end, eight or ten of the older Owl-Masters sided with Odinan, but the vast majority of those present supported Baden's motion.

"So how do we do this?" Radomil asked, after the vote had been tallied. "Do we bring him before the entire Order—at least those of us who are here— or do we select a few people to do it?"

Orris shrugged. "It shouldn't matter. If we use the probing it won't matter where we do it or how many of us are present."

"The probing?" Jaryd asked.

Baden turned to face him. "Remember that night at Cullen and Gayna's house, how I got you to describe your dream?"

Jaryd nodded.

"That's a probing." The Owl-Master looked back at Orris. "You're right: if we use the probing, it doesn't matter. And it may come to that. But I'd like to try this first without using magic. I'd like to see if we can do this just by asking him questions."

Jaryd expected Orris to argue, but, again, the burly Hawk-Mage surprised him with his forbearance. "Why?" he asked.

Baden grinned. "I know it sounds far-fetched, but I'm hoping to win this man's trust. Right now we just need what information he carries, but at some point we may need his insights, his understanding of Lon-Ser. Perhaps even more than that. The probing is only as effective as the questions we ask: at a certain point we may not know the right questions."

Trahn regarded Baden keenly. "So what do you suggest?"

"You said yourself that the outlanders seemed awed by the fact that you healed their wounds on the spur," Baden reminded the dark mage. "And this second man didn't attempt escape or suicide even when he had the chance. The process may already have begun." He paused. "I'd like to speak with him in his chamber, with just one other mage present—"

"Out of the question!" Sonel broke in. "The risks are too great! Forgive me, Baden," she added, in a quieter voice, "but there must be at least two bound mages there. Odinan is correct: this man is dangerous, and we must take reasonable precautions."

Baden flushed slightly, and his mouth was set in a tight line, but after a moment he nodded. "Two is acceptable," he agreed, his tone revealing nothing.

Sonel cleared her throat uncomfortably. The air between the two Owl-Masters seemed suddenly to have been charged, as by a midsummer thunderstorm. "Would Trahn and Ursel be acceptable?" she asked hesitantly. "The outlander is familiar with them."

Baden shook his head. "They were his captors. I'd prefer two others."

"Who, then?"

The lean mage surveyed the Gathering Chamber pensively. "Radomil," he said after some time, drawing a nod of agreement from the bald mage. He looked back at Sonel. "And you."

This time Sonel's face reddened. "I'd be pleased to," she replied, assaying a smile, which Baden returned.

"Baden," Jaryd ventured, "if you don't use the probing, how can you know that the outlander won't lie to you?"

The Owl-Master raised his eyebrows speculatively and gave a small shrug. "I don't know, really. I'm hoping that, among the three of us, we'll be able to get some sense of that from listening to him and watching him. If any one of us is suspicious, we can always use the Mage-Craft to confirm what he's saying. But I'd like to at least start without it."

He looked at Sonel, who rose from her seat decisively. "We will convene again tomorrow, at mid-morning," she announced, "and the three of us will share with you what we've learned from the prisoner. I hope that, by then, the rest of the Order will have arrived in Amarid." She inclined her head slightly. "Until then," she added, dismissing them all.

The mages arrayed around the table rose and began speaking among themselves, their voices filling the Great Hall. Baden and Trahn walked over to where Alayna and Jaryd stood, their expressions serious. "I'm not certain how long this will take," Baden told them, "but Trahn and I made plans with Orris to have dinner at the Aerie tonight. I hope you two will join us."

Alayna nodded. "We'll be there. Good luck with the interrogation."

"Thanks," the Owl-Master replied, grinning reflexively as he moved off.

Trahn lingered beside the young mages and the three of them watched as Baden walked away. Then the dark mage turned to Jaryd and Alayna, the look in his vivid green eyes somber and pained. "Come with me," he said, a request in his tone. "There's someone I think we all should meet."

Trahn led them to a room in the back section of the Great Hall where they found a young girl who looked to be no more than seven or eight years old. She had straight, shoulder-length brown hair and a beautiful, open face. But Jaryd could not stop staring at her eyes. They were blue like an autumn sky and, even as she played with a set of dolls and an elaborate toy house, they seemed to be focused inward on something dark and frightening that only she could see. As the three of them watched her play, one of the hall's attendants, an older woman with kind, brown eyes and steel-grey hair, approached them.

"That's Cailin," she told them quietly. "The little girl they brought back from Kaera."

"Yes, I know," Trahn said, his attention focused on the child. "How's she doing?"

The woman shrugged. "She still doesn't say much, although she's finally eating again, which is a blessing." She shrugged again. "Considering what she's been through, I suppose she's doing as well as we've any right to expect."

Trahn nodded.

At the same time, Alayna stepped forward and knelt down beside the girl. "I'm Alayna," she told her.

The girl glanced at her briefly, and then she went back to playing with her dolls. "I'm Cailin," she answered a few moments later.

"Do you mind if I play with you?" Alayna asked. "I've always loved dolls."

Cailin shrugged ambivalently. "Sure, if you want to." Alayna picked up one of the dolls and placed it in a bedroom in the toy house, while Cailin rearranged some of the miniature furniture in the downstairs parlor. They sat in silence for a short while, playing, and then Cailin looked at the Hawk-Mage again. "You're pretty," she said.

Alayna smiled warmly. "Thank you. You're pretty, too."

"You remind me of Zanna," the little girl went on, as if she hadn't heard.

Alayna glanced up at Jaryd, the expression in her dark eyes troubled. "Is Zanna a friend of yours?" she asked, although Jaryd could tell that she already knew what Cailin would say.

"She was. She's dead now. The Children of Amarid killed her. They killed Mama and Papa, too." She looked at the grey hawk that sat on Alayna's shoulder.

"We've tried to explain to her that it wasn't the Children of Amarid," the attendant whispered to Trahn and Jaryd. "But she doesn't seem to understand." The woman shook her head sadly.

"You're a Child of Amarid, aren't you?" Cailin asked evenly, her eyes placid as they regarded Alayna.

Alayna nodded. "Yes, I am. But I promise you, we didn't kill your friend, or your mother and father."

"I know you didn't," Cailin told her. "I saw the men who did it." She looked at Jaryd and Trahn. "They weren't there either."

"The men who did it are gone now," Alayna assured her. "They won't hurt you anymore. And I promise you, they weren't Amarid's Children."

Cailin looked at her with the same calm expression, but she said nothing. A moment later, she started playing again, and she paid no more attention to Alayna. Finally, after several minutes, the young Hawk-Mage climbed to her feet and walked back to where Jaryd and Trahn stood with the attendant.

"Some people came to see her early this morning," the woman told Trahn, the apprehension in her voice mirrored by the look in her eyes. "They were from Arick's Temple. They said that, given what Cailin had been through, she should be with the Sons and Daughters of the Gods, not with the Order."

Trahn exhaled slowly through his teeth. "Does Sonel know?"

The woman nodded. "Yes. She said it would be Cailin's choice."

She looked at Trahn beseechingly, as if seeking reassurance that Cailin would not be taken away, but the mage merely shrugged. "Sonel is right. We can't keep the girl against her will."

The woman started to say something else, but then she stopped herself and, a few moments later, she walked away.

The three mages lingered for a short while longer, watching Cailin, who seemed oblivious to their presence. Then they left. Trahn returned to his room at the Aerie, but Jaryd and Alayna wandered over to the old town commons, where they spent the rest of the morning and the entire afternoon walking through the winding, cobblestone streets, drifting in and out of shops or speaking with the street merchants, who sold their wares out of wagons rather than storefronts. Their encounter with the little girl, however, continued to haunt them. So, too, did what they found in the streets of Amarid. Some of the people they saw called out greetings and asked blessings of the gods for the young mages, and a few of the vendors offered them gifts of food and merchandise, all, Jaryd realized after some time, in appreciation for the capture of the outlanders. Many others, however, too many others, regarded them with distrust or apprehension, and one man even accused the mages of protecting the prisoners out of fear that their alliance with them might otherwise be revealed. Jaryd stopped to argue with the man, but Alayna wisely pulled him away, telling him to ignore the comments. Still, this confrontation, combined with the fresh memory of Cailin and the dark mood of others they met, cast a shadow over this cloudless day. By early evening, as darkness settled over Amarid and the two young mages crossed the city on their way to the Aerie, they had both retreated into pensiveness and silence. They skirted the streets surrounding the Great Hall in order to avoid the large crowd that still lingered there, many of them now carrying torches and yelling once more for those inside to hand the prisoner over to them. Seeing the crowd from a distance, hearing their cries for vengeance and their impatience with the Order, Jaryd found himself wondering if the company's victory over the outlanders had come too late.

They reached the dingy courtyard of the Aerie a short while later. Opening the door and stepping into the noisy tavern, they immediately spotted Baden, Trahn, and Orris sitting in the far back corner. The tavern was just as Jaryd remembered it: poorly lit, smelly, and very comfortable. Looking at the dark, scarred wood of its tables, the massive chandelier, and the scuffed wooden floor, inhaling the heavy air, laden as it was with the smells of musty wine, pipe smoke, and roasting meat, he finally understood why Baden returned to this place year after year. In spite of the black mood fostered by this difficult day, he felt as though he had come home.

As he and Alayna walked toward Baden's table, he heard a woman's voice call to him from the bar. And turning to look in that direction, he saw Kayle walking toward him, the familiar crooked smile lighting her face as she brushed away an untied wisp of light hair. "Hawk-Mage!" she said warmly. "I was wondering when you were going to come see me." She gave him a hug when she reached him, and then kissed his cheek.

He smiled self-consciously. "Hello, Kayle," he said quietly, looking sidelong at Alayna. "How are you?"

"Good. You look great! I guess Theron's Grove agreed with you, eh?" She eyed Alayna appraisingly, as if noticing the Hawk-Mage for the first time.

"Kayle," Jaryd said, feeling awkward. "This is Hawk-Mage Alayna. Alayna, this is Kayle."

The barmaid stuck out her hand. "Nice to meet you, Alayna," she said evenly.

Alayna smiled sweetly. "And you."

"Go join your friends," Kayle went on, looking at Jaryd again. "I'll be over in a minute with some ale."

"Actually," Alayna said, stopping her, "I'll have some honey wine, if that's all right."

"Sure," Kayle responded over her shoulder, already walking back toward the bar.

Alayna arched an eyebrow. "Just a friend, eh?" she said, once Kayle was out of earshot.

"Yes," he replied, grinning at her

"Well, she seems nice. Pretty, too."

Jaryd nodded. "She is. Nice, I mean."

"That better be what you mean," Alayna remarked, taking his hand and leading him the rest of the way to the table.

"It's about time," Orris growled as the young mages took their seats.

A month ago, Jaryd would have bristled at such a comment, taking it as further evidence of Orris's abrasive manner. But he understood the burly mage now, and he had learned to recognize when Orris was joking and when he was not. "It's nice to know that you missed me," Jaryd quipped.

The Hawk-Mage snorted disdainfully.

"If we missed anyone," Trahn corrected, "it was your lovely companion."

Alayna smiled dazzlingly. "Thank you, Trahn."

"Actually," Baden explained, "these two are just mad because I haven't told them anything about the interrogation yet. I wanted to wait for the two of you."

Instantly, the mood around the table changed. The mirth vanished, and the four Hawk-Mages fixed their eyes on the Owl-Master.

"We learned a good deal," Baden began, his voice low and his pale eyes flicking from one mage to the next. "And, frankly, much of what Baram told us—that's his name: Baram—much of what he told us is really quite alarming."

"Did he answer your questions freely," Orris interrupted, "or did you end up using the probing?"

"Both, actually." Baden paused as Kayle brought four pints of amber ale, as well as a carafe of light wine for Alayna. He waited until she had served them and gone back to the bar before continuing. "Both," he said again. "He refused to answer our questions at first, so we used the probing. Then we gave him a second chance, and he cooperated. We returned to the probing at the very end to make certain that he hadn't withheld anything or misled us."

He stopped once again as Kayle came back with their dinners. "We were right," Baden went on after she had served them and withdrawn, "they did come here from Lon-Ser, specifically from a place called Bragor-Nal."

Trahn looked at him sharply. "Bragor-*Nal*?" he repeated.

Baden was already staring at the mage, as if he had anticipated this reaction. "I thought you'd find that interesting."

Jaryd shook his head. "I'm confused."

"*Nal* is a word from the ancient language—from our ancient language,"

Trahn told him, never taking his eyes from Baden's face. "It means 'community.' At least it does here."

Baden nodded. "Given the way Baram used it, I'd say it means the same thing there."

Trahn considered this, taking a spoonful of the rich stew Kayle had brought them. "I suppose I shouldn't be too surprised," he commented after some time. "We've always known that Tobyn-Ser and Lon-Ser share a common history."

"A common ancient history," Orris corrected, somewhat defensively.

Trahn shrugged. "Nevertheless."

Alayna turned back to Baden. "Did you get a sense of what this Bragor-Nal is like?"

"It's huge," the Owl-Master answered. "We certainly know that much. There are only two other Nals in all of Lon-Ser, and, according to our friend, this one is the largest. Each one of them is a giant city, self-contained like Amarid, but far more vast and containing thousands of times as many people. And," he added, taking a breath, "entirely dependent on the type of mechanical devices that they carried with them when they came to Tobyn-Ser."

Orris narrowed his eyes. "What do you mean?"

"It's difficult to explain," Baden said. "Many of the words he used came from his language and couldn't be translated. And much of what he talked about was alien." He glanced at Trahn. "Even with our common linguistic roots, our two lands have diverged significantly over the centuries." He turned his gaze back to Orris. "But, from what I gathered, and Sonel and Radomil agreed, it seems that this . . . skill of theirs is more than a weapon. It's a way of life. They use it to communicate, to travel, to make goods and food, as well as to make war."

Trahn ran a hand over his face. "So you're saying that the people in Bragor-Nal can make everything they need artificially, using tools?"

"Not *can*," Baden countered. "*Must*. When I say that Lon-Ser has only two other Nals, I mean that's basically all it has. From what Baram said, Lon-Ser has the Nals and mountains. And that's it. There's almost no farmland, only a few small patches of forest or desert or plain. It's just city and mountains. And very few people live in the mountains. Everything they need, they make. Just like those big black birds."

"Just three cities," Trahn commented, the awe in his voice echoing Jaryd's thoughts. "Covering a land as large as Tobyn-Ser. That's difficult to fathom."

For several moments no one at the table spoke. Jaryd sat listening to the noises of the tavern, absently taking a few mouthfuls of food and trying to imagine a society built wholly on mechanical goods, one in which nothing came directly from the land, one in which everyone lived in cities far greater than the one they were in tonight. And he couldn't do it. Each time he tried to picture it, he only saw his mother working the fields back in Accalia, or his father chopping firewood outside the house.

After what seemed a long time, Alayna stirred in her chair, as if emerging from a dream. She looked at Baden. "Did you get a sense of why they came here, of what they want from us?"

"Yes," Baden said with a thin, mirthless smile. "Not surprisingly, they seek from us what they can no longer provide for themselves."

Orris cocked his head to the side. "But you just told us that they can make everything they need."

"They can. But they can't escape the laws of nature: they've run out of room, and they've run out of the resources they used to fuel their development." He hesitated. "In truth, I didn't understand all that he said, but it seems that while they can create what they need, they can't do so without what he called basic goods, which seemed to include all the things we normally use to make things: wood, metals and minerals, and other gifts from the land that we take for granted."

"So they want our land," Jaryd interjected.

Baden nodded. "Our land, all that grows on it, all that comes from it. But it's even more than that. Not only do they need these materials, they also need room for expansion. Their cities—the Nals—are overcrowded; they've befouled the air they breathe and the water they drink. In short, they seek a new home, or at least an additional home. And we have exactly what they need." He looked at Jaryd, and then at Alayna. "What Theron told you about their tactics revealing their weakness was even more significant than we realized."

"Their needs sound no different from those that drove the Abboriji invasions," Trahn pointed out. "So why would they go about it in such a strange way?"

"That, it seems, is more a product of Lon-Ser's internal politics than anything else. The one somewhat promising bit of information that Baram offered today was that he and his comrades were acting on behalf of a small, albeit growing movement in Lon-Ser. Most of Lon-Ser's people, it seems, are as hostile toward outsiders as our people. They've gone out of their way to keep their borders closed to foreigners, and they've demanded that their advanced goods be kept confined to their land, although, as your Abboriji friend indicated to you, Orris," Baden went on, glancing at the Hawk-Mage, "their attentiveness to this last point has slackened recently." He turned back to Trahn. "Most of Lon-Ser's people wish to solve the problems I mentioned on their own, but an increasing number have begun to look beyond their borders for an answer. And at least one faction, Baram's faction, has focused its efforts on Tobyn-Ser.

"According to Baram, they had hoped to render Tobyn-Ser defenseless by undercutting the people's faith in the Order, and, eventually, destroying the Order itself. As we saw in Kaera and Watersbend, without the Mage-Craft protecting Tobyn-Ser from invasion, our people would have little chance against Lon-Ser's weapons."

Jaryd shook his head in confusion. "But if their own people didn't support the idea, how could they have hoped to succeed?"

"Baram had nothing to say about that," Baden replied, "but I have an idea or two. It sounded to me as if Lon-Ser is in the midst of a prolonged struggle for political power involving many groups. Perhaps the leaders of this one, of Baram's group, were gambling that, if they could conquer Tobyn-Ser and deliver it to the people of Lon-Ser, they could overcome any opposition they might encounter and strengthen their own position in the process. It's one thing to consider an invasion against an enemy of unknown strength, and quite another to accept the fruits of such an invasion without paying any of the costs."

"So their very success, if they had succeeded, would have overcome any opposition."

"Quite possibly, yes."

"Whatever the thinking behind their actions," Trahn commented, taking the discussion in a new direction, "it seems from what you're telling us that the threat to Tobyn-Ser remains."

Baden looked at his friend and nodded. "Of all the things I can tell you, that's the one about which I have the least doubt. Lon-Ser's problems haven't gone away, and, as a result of what the outlanders did before we stopped them, the Order is weaker now than it's been in nearly a thousand years. If anything, the threat is greater today than it was a year ago."

Jaryd signaled his agreement with a nod. "Certainly the people Alayna and I encountered today have little faith in the Order. One man accused us of conspiring with the outlanders."

"That crowd outside the Great Hall hasn't gone away either," Orris added. "I'm not sure what they want, but they haven't exactly opened their arms to me as I've passed through."

"So what do we do?" Alayna asked.

Baden glanced at Orris. "As I mentioned that night on Tobyn's Plain, as the five of us rode in pursuit of Sartol, I believe the time has come to follow through on a suggestion Orris made at the Midsummer Gathering. We need to reestablish the psychic link."

Orris regarded the Owl-Master with undisguised curiosity. "I remember you saying that. What made you change your mind about it?"

"I never really thought it was a bad idea," Baden conceded. "I just knew that the Owl-Masters would oppose it, and I thought that the journey to Theron's Grove was more likely to stop the attacks. I was wrong," he added, "and, frankly, I regret speaking out against your proposal. In doing so, I may have hurt our chances of convincing the Order to act on it now."

"You believe they'll still resist the idea," Jaryd asked, "even given what you've learned from the outlander?"

"I'm afraid I do," the Owl-Master answered, staring at his half-empty tankard of ale. "What Theron and Phelan said about the Order is true: it has grown complacent. The outlanders' campaign should never have been allowed to progress as far as it did. The Wolf-Master blamed Jessamyn, but I'm not certain that she could have compelled the Order to act even had she tried harder. During Amarid's time, and as recently as just a few hundred years ago, the Order saw itself as the protector of the land, not only from plague or internal troubles, but also from outside threats. Yet, our own early success, our ability to resist the Abboriji invaders, for instance, convinced many mages that there were no longer any threats that merited our attention. In effect, we guarded the land so well that we made ourselves lazy. Our watch on the land's borders slackened, the psychic link that Amarid first established was permitted to collapse, and still no one attacked us. I guess, up until now, we've been defended by our history, and the reputation it gave us." He looked up, his gaze falling on each of the Hawk-Mages. "Apparently, that's no longer enough."

"Although I agree that it won't be easy," Trahn said, "we must push for the link. That's our best hope."

"I agree," Orris chimed in, "but I'm not confident. Odinan seems to be digging in his heels, and he still has some support among the Owl-Masters. We should have other alternatives to offer." He grinned ruefully. "Unfortunately, I can't think of any."

The other mages chuckled, and Baden, draining what remained of his ale, signaled to Kayle for another round.

Jaryd turned to his uncle. "Won't the success or failure of our effort to reestablish the link depend in part on whom the Owl-Masters choose as the next Owl-Sage?"

Baden raised his eyebrows slightly, indicating that he hadn't considered this. "I suppose it will," he confirmed.

"Who do you expect they'll choose?" Alayna asked him.

Kayle brought their drinks before the Owl-Master could respond, and, after she departed, Baden, Trahn, and Orris embarked on a lengthy, speculative discussion of the various possible contenders for the position. At one point, without actually mentioning Anla's death, Jaryd expressed his regret that Baden could not be selected, a sentiment Trahn echoed. Baden just laughed, however, assuring them all that it was not a job he coveted.

Their conversation stretched on into the night, ending only after much of the tavern's other clientele had left. Given how late it had grown, Jaryd and Alayna decided to take a room at the Aerie for the night. Wearily, they rose from their seats to follow Trahn and Orris toward the wooden stairs that led to the Aerie's guest rooms.

"Jaryd," Baden called from the table, where he still sat, sipping the last of his ale, "may I have a word with you before you go to sleep?" The Owl-Master turned his gaze to Alayna and smiled. "I'll return him to you shortly, I promise."

She nodded and continued up the stairs, as Jaryd returned to the table.

"I know you're tired," Baden began as Jaryd sat back down, "so I won't keep you very long. But I'm wondering if you and Alayna have decided on where you're going to settle once you leave Amarid."

The inquiry took the Hawk-Mage by surprise, and for several moments he did not respond.

"You have thought about this, haven't you?" Baden persisted.

"Of course, although we haven't talked about it very much." Jaryd faltered, staring thoughtfully at the table. "Before I met Alayna, I assumed that I'd go back to Accalia, and she assumed the same thing about Brisalli. Falling in love kind of complicated things." He paused. "Each of us is willing to follow the other, and now that Sartol is dead, northern Tobyn-Ser needs a new mage or two. Of course, Radomil has been the only mage in the northwest for a few years now, and he could use the help as well." He looked his uncle in the eye. "The short answer is, we haven't decided yet. We could, conceivably, end up in either place. Why do you ask?"

Baden grinned enigmatically. "Curiosity."

Jaryd responded with a skeptical look, drawing a laugh from the Owl-Master. "All right," Baden admitted, "it's more than just curiosity. But for now, I'd ask you to leave me this secret, Jaryd. I'll explain soon enough." He paused. "I'd also like you and Alayna to keep an open mind for the time being."

Jaryd looked at his uncle searchingly, but after a few seconds he nodded.

"That's all," Baden told him. "You go join Alayna; I think I might have another ale."

Jaryd rose, but his gaze lingered on the Owl-Master's lean features. Baden seemed uncharacteristically subdued, and, once again, Jaryd had to remind himself that Anla was gone. "Are you all right, Baden?" he asked. "Do you want me to stay?"

The mage smiled sadly. "That's kind of you, but I think I'm better off alone." He looked up, meeting Jaryd's eyes. "As to whether I'm all right, I suppose I'm about as well as I could have expected myself to be under the circumstances." He averted his eyes again. "I know that's not the answer you'd like to hear, but it's the best I can do."

"I'm sorry, Baden."

"I know. And I appreciate that."

Jaryd placed a hand on the Owl-Master's shoulder and allowed it to linger there a moment before he stepped away and climbed the stairs to his room.

Alayna had left a single candle burning, but she was already in bed, breathing in a slow, regular rhythm. Jaryd tried to make as little noise as possible as he undressed and slipped under the covers, but she stirred and rolled over to face him.

"What did Baden want?" she asked sleepily, her eyes still closed.

"He wanted to know if we had decided where we're going to settle."

"What did you tell him?" she asked in the same tired voice.

"That we hadn't decided yet."

She made a small sound that may have signaled agreement. Jaryd wasn't certain. And, after a short time, her breathing slowed again, telling him that she was asleep.

Jaryd closed his eyes and tried to sleep as well, but Baden's question had started his mind working. For some time now, since Theron's Grove, really, Jaryd had taken for granted that he and Alayna would spend the rest of their lives together. And he had assumed that she shared this view. So, too, it seemed, had Baden. But his own inability to answer the Owl-Master's question made him realize that he and Alayna had made no firm plans. Indeed, they had hardly even discussed in general terms their future life together. Mostly, they had talked about their respective homes, as if they were trying to convince each other that one or the other would be the best place to live. He knew, listening to Alayna's gentle breathing beside him, that above all else, he wanted to be with this woman; to build a life with her, perhaps to have a family. And yet, he found it very difficult to let go of his dream of serving Accalia as a Hawk-Mage. Lying in the dark, wrestling with these thoughts, it was inevitable that his mind should wander back to the conversation he had had with Baden and Trahn so long ago, about the difficulties inherent in carrying on romances within the Order. Now, as then, he refused to accept that the problems could not be overcome, but, he had to admit, they did seem more daunting than he had anticipated. And, once more, he wondered why Baden had raised the issue. These questions kept him awake for some time, and even when his eyes finally did close, and his breathing slowed as Alayna's had done, they continued to trouble his sleep.

Several days passed before Baden finally revealed why he had been so interested in Jaryd and Alayna's plans. In the meantime, the Order held an open service honoring Jessamyn, Peredur, and Niall, and the Owl-Masters, after a full day of rancorous debate and secret balloting, selected Sonel as the new sage. She then chose Toinan as her first, seeking to mollify Odinan and the older masters, who had opposed her in favor of one of their own. Emerging from the Gathering Chamber late in the day, the Owl-Masters declared that the Sage-Naming would take place two days hence. Normally, such an announcement would have brought rejoicing and great anticipation to the people of Amarid. The next day, however, a small group from the horde that still lingered outside the Great Hall attempted to storm the building, apparently in an effort to find and kill the outlander, whom they now believed the Order was more interested in guarding than punishing. The men and women involved in this assault on the Great Hall were arrested by the city constable before they could do any harm, but the incident cast a pall over the preparations for the Sage-Naming. For the first time in the history of the Order, the mages were forced to ask the city constable to place guards along the route to be taken by the procession that would open the ritual.

The morning of the ceremony dawned grey and misty. And, while spectators had begun with first light to line the city streets, the conspicuous presence of the constable's officers dampened the spirit of the occasion. As the mages and masters converged on Amarid's home to line up in the procession, Baden approached Jaryd and Alayna, who had arrived early and taken their places at the end of the column. Jaryd had hardly seen his uncle since their conversation in the Aerie; Baden had spent the intervening days in deliberation with the Owl-Masters and conducting further interrogations of the outlander.

The Owl-Master looked tired and thin as he greeted the young mages, but the smile he wore seemed genuine. "Ready for your first Sage-Naming?" he asked them, nodding and waving to some of the other mages as he did.

"I guess so," Alayna replied, "although, given what happened yesterday, it doesn't feel like much of a celebration."

"I agree," Baden said sourly. "I told Sonel that I thought the guards were a bad idea, but, in truth, I understand her reasoning." He shook his head. "These are dark times," he concluded, more to himself than to the young mages.

"I'm not really certain what's going to happen today," Jaryd commented in an effort to change the subject. "What are we supposed to do?"

"You don't have to worry about doing anything," Baden told him. "Just follow the lead of the older mages and you'll be fine. As to what's going to happen," he went on, "that's changed over the years. Once, long before I joined the Order, the Owl-Sage was actually named at this ceremony—the

Owl-Masters discussed the merits and shortcomings of the various candidates in public view, casting their ballots in secret, but with an audience. As my grandmother told it to me, however, one particularly nasty debate ended that practice for good. Now, this is little more than a formality; an open validation of the decision the Owl-Masters made in closed session two days ago."

"That sounds like a much better idea," Jaryd observed. "Less chance for hurt feelings."

Baden nodded. "I guess so, although I've witnessed three Sage-Namings now, and all the deliberations have been quite civil." Baden paused to wave again as several Owl-Masters made their way past where the three mages were standing. A moment later, though, he turned his attention back to the young mages, looking intently at Alayna, and then at Jaryd. "So," the Owl-Master began, his tone changing and the expression in his pale eyes growing more serious, even as the smile lingered on his lips, "have you two decided anything yet?"

"No," Jaryd admitted. "But it might help us make up our minds if you explained why you're so interested."

The Owl-Master considered this briefly. "All right," he agreed. "The concerns I expressed to the four of you the other night about Tobyn-Ser's safety, and the role of the Order in preserving it, started me thinking that even if the entire Order won't act, a few of us might. I've already spoken with Sonel about the possibility of forging the psychic link again. She's sympathetic, but she's not convinced that the Owl-Masters will go along with it, at least not yet. And she's not willing to force them to comply, not with something this draining and difficult." He hesitated, glancing around to see if anyone else could hear.

"That being the case, I'm trying to put together a small group of mages—five or ten, more if possible—who would be willing to join me in creating our own link, one that would cast a protective net of sorts over the western edge of Tobyn-Ser, from the northern extreme of Leora's Forest to the top of the Sawblade."

"Does Sonel know about this?" Jaryd asked, eyeing his uncle closely.

Baden shook his head. "I don't think she'd object, but others would—Odinan and his allies—and they could make things very difficult for her if they learned that she knew about this. I'd rather take the blame myself if we're discovered."

Alayna passed a hand through her dark hair. "Who have you got so far?"

"Trahn, of course; Radomil; Ursel; Orris and me, once we've bound again. And Orris thinks that he can get a few of the other younger mages to join us." Baden faltered. "I would have asked the two of you sooner," he explained. "But I didn't want to disrupt your plans, if you had any. This is an important time for the two of you, and I don't want anything to get in the way." He allowed himself a slight smile. "But, with Niall gone, the Lower Horn currently has no mage serving it. And I think, if I was looking for a place to settle down, I'd find that part of Tobyn-Ser quite attractive. But that's just me." He stopped, his eyes meeting Jaryd's for just an instant before he glanced back over his shoulder. "The procession will be starting soon," he said, despite the fact that most of the mages were still milling about, speaking to one another.

"We can discuss this again later if you'd like." He started to move off. "Enjoy the ceremony," he called to them over his shoulder.

Jaryd and Alayna stood in silence watching the Owl-Master walk away. They had discussed their future together a number of times over the past three days, most recently the night before as they lay together in the candlelight in their room at the Aerie. But, while they had professed their desire to be together, they had reached no conclusions regarding where they wished to go. Baden's suggestion changed things.

"I've assumed for so long that I'd end up in Brisalli," Alayna murmured, echoing his thoughts as she broke their silence, "that I never even considered other places. And I know you've felt the same way about Accalia." She turned to him, her eyes large and dark, and so deep that he thought he might lose himself in them. "But I don't care where we go, as long as we're together, Jaryd. That's all I want."

So deep that he wondered sometimes what they saw in him. She was so strong, and intelligent, and beautiful; and she loved him. Somehow, she loved him. Suddenly, Jaryd felt himself overwhelmed by the fullness of his life. "Do you mean that?" he managed. "You'd give up Brisalli?"

She nodded, the dazzling smile spreading across her face. "Let's go to the Lower Horn," she said. "I bet it's beautiful there, and besides, Baden needs us."

He grinned, and then shrugged. "All right." It felt strange in a way to come to a decision so suddenly, after so much deliberation. "So, we're really going to do this?"

"So it seems," she answered. And then, as if to validate their choice, she stepped forward and kissed him. He, in turn, put his arms around her, and they stood holding each other for several moments, allowing the decision they had reached to sink in.

"Should we tell Baden that we've decided?" Alayna asked after some time.

Jaryd nodded, smiling; unable suddenly to stop smiling.

They hurried across the First Mage's yard to where Baden stood, and by the time they reached him, both of them were grinning broadly. "We've decided," Jaryd announced as they stopped in front of the Owl-Master. "We'll go to the Lower Horn."

The relief on his uncle's face was palpable. "Good," he breathed. "I'm very glad to hear that."

"We'd like to go to Brisalli first," Jaryd added, "and Accalia, to see our families."

Baden nodded. "Of course," he said. But even as he did, he glanced back over his shoulder to the west, as if he could see past the city and the forests and the mountains to the alien land that lay beyond Arick's Sea. And the smile on his face faded, leaving lines of concern and a look in his pale eyes that was a match for the dark clouds overhead. "Of course," he said again. "Just don't take too long."

About the Author

David B. Coe grew up just outside of New York City, the youngest of four children. He attended Brown University as an undergraduate and later received a Ph.D. in history from Stanford. He briefly considered a career as an academic, but wisely thought better of it.

He is now a freelance writer. He lives in Tennessee with his wife, Nancy J. Berner, their daughter, Alex, two lazy fat cats, and Buddy, the wonder-dog. *Children of Amarid* is his first novel. He is currently working on the next volume of the *LonTobyn Chronicle*.